ALL OUR SECRETS
ARE THE SAME

ALL OUR SECRETS ARE THE SAME

New Fiction from Esquire

Edited and with a foreword by Gordon Lish

W · W · NORTON & COMPANY · INC · New York

FIRST EDITION

Library of Congress Cataloging in Publication Data
Main entry under title:

All our secrets are the same.

   1. Short stories, American.   I. Lish, Gordon.
II. Esquire.
PZ1.A4136 [PS648.S5]   813'.01   76–40486
ISBN 0–393–08748–4

   3 4 5 6 7 8 9 0

Contents

Foreword

The call came to invite attention to the present stories, and what I wrote in service of that gesture proved more squawk than seduction. It was like a cartoon I once laughed like a loon at, the lone box displaying pedestrian confronted by petitioner, the latter suited up in sandwich boards declaring SUPPORT MENTAL HEALTH OR I'LL KILL YOU. Funny, but I do not think that's so funny any more.

The humor's running out of me. Somehow the sack that held it in dried and fissured, and the counterweight to a dark disposition has been spilling away ever since.

Still, I got rid of that original message to you—after months of admiring its rage. There must be a little laughter left in me.

I do not know what is wrong with me, why my metabolism yields anger. Certainly it seems odd that a middleman should want to hit instead of mediate. That is no way to sell a thing—with a club. And if now and then rage rightly belongs along the line of motion from writer to reader and in reverse, is not the station of editor correctly occupied by a fellow hunched over in silence? So that the harsh (or happy) feeling might safely leapfrog his back?

I think so. But thinking, Mother told me, will not make it so. Moreover, I never gave it much of a try.

Meanwhile, Father was busy mounting lessons too, instruction that rendered a zealot's regard for mixing in.

Since founding *Genesis West,* a literary magazine that served a term in the vicinity of 1962, mixing in is mainly what I have been up to, practicing an irritable partisanship on behalf of writers I believe matter most.

I wanted a war-hammer out of *Genesis West.* But where was the quarrel I was marching off to fall lustily into? Who were these belligerents I was spoiling to fight?

There was no quarrel anywhere. What is there to quarrel about?

Nor were there lying in wait hostile parties of any temper. As zero events not long after taught, people of every persuasion had other places to go.

Then I attached my combative ambitions to *Esquire.* Here was ordnance of size, a wider stance on the field of battle, a chance to do damage in bulk. That was 1970. Three years later I maneuvered to assault. Feelings unfurled for what would seize my vitals a second time, I reconnoitered the stories I'd once picked for *Esquire,* and of twice-picked stories I made the book *The Secret Life of Our Times.*

This, I thought, is something to hit them in the heart with.

I couldn't wait four minutes for the publisher to get out there with what my industry had done. *Hurry up with that weapon* is what was on my mind. In the lunatic semaphore that beckons to my strange nature, stories are rocks, and I wanted all my best ones arrayed. There was a hurling of things I ached to get recorded. I even said it out loud, even wrote for the jacket: *this book is thus an argument.*

I meant to taunt: come on out, all you wrongly counseled customers sold the bill of goods that fiction cannot stop the heart, an interval's death means stored beats to live on!

I wanted to bruise hearts into healthy paralysis—the more hunkered down into a stout indifference, the better.

But of course you have to hit that organ to hurt it. Whereas I came loaded with rocks onto a vacant landscape, a certain hollering in the distance my first sorry notice that the likeliest columns to stand against an invader were long gone, were off cutting up in some other countryside immeasurably remote from mine.

That was 1973, say—and my ground is doubtlessly no less empty now that it is 1976. It's just been three more years of more signing up, wholesale enlisting, the eager sons of those who earlier retired the honorable field now off making their own simple marks in the recruitment rolls set out by Barthes and Handke and Robbe-Grillet.

As in *those who cannot write will make their marks.*

My mother, a humanist if there ever was one, swore me to the faith that art breaks a trail for science. My father, a visionary if I ever knew one, said I'd never get rich backing a proposition like that.

But science *did*—the richer for often finding its theory in the imagination's intransitive play. I think we will agree on that.

But will we agree that my mother's gospel is losing its prophets? Your don't have to look very hard. Me, I can look any day on my desk at *Esquire.* And you can look in *TriQuarterly* or, more productively, in *The Chicago Review*—where last week I think I saw a story (?) whose composition I thought intended (?) to unfold a sequence parallel (?) or perpendicular (?) to the organization of the elements that constitute DNA, I think.

Yes.

Yet it was not all that long ago that mathematician Stanislaw Ulam could suggest that he sometimes fed his inventive thought on nutrients snatched up from topsoil novelist Vladimir Nabokov had newly laid. On the other hand, James Dewey Watson and Saul Bellow are younger men—and it was also not so very long ago the scientist among them sought to advise the artist among them that no, no, you have it backwards, it must be *we* who look to *you* to solve the world—because we know we can't, whereas you can still get away with thinking you can.

But they are old or older men, these four—and Professor Ulam is a munificent man. As for the deferential Dr. Watson, he must know something to make him worry.

Barth, Barthelme & Co. is neither very old nor very philanthropic. And: what, *it* worry?

It is rigorous and vigorous and franchising like crazy. With the result that we now have outlets called Sukenick or Klinkowitz or Bellamy doing fire-sale business on every campus. What they sell so well is a selling-out—to *technology*—now that science has targeted the liveliest marketplace. Of course there is no crisis in the hygiene of the national literature, but this will do until we get a real one.

I am wondering if we are coming up on a time when the anti-trust laws will press to be invoked. After all, the student is a kind of consumer, my father would be the first to point out.

Yet I confess to no large complaint with this threat to open competition. On the contrary, it satisfies me to have it.

Because now I know why there is a rough feeling in me.

Because now I know where to go for a squabble.

Because now my rocks are aimed on range.

Here are thirty-eight of them in a row, what I've culled from three more years of *Esquire.* In my passion, they expand to the amplitude and harden to the character of boulders. In my passion, I wish they could be twice their tumultuous number, at least increased by the durable extrusions of Ann Beattie, Howard Nemerov, Rosellen Brown, Kathryn Ungerer. In my passion, I claim continuing belief in the huge utility of literature, a human enterprise that can count for more than the living creatures its use not only exists for.

Now I am at the start of what I expect will be a long silence. I am also willing at last to hunch over.

Go ahead. Do something. Jump.

GL

ALL OUR SECRETS
ARE THE SAME

Saying Good-bye to the President

ROBLEY WILSON, JR.

We are strolling in the Rose Garden at dusk. The sky is clouded, taking on the first glow of lights from the Washington night, the traffic sounds muted by the rustling of a warm wind in the White House trees. The President walks with his hands clasped behind his back, his head bent slightly, scuffing at bits of gravel with the toes of his shoes. Behind us, at a little distance, two Secret Service men follow, talking discreetly, keeping their eyes on us.

I am the one who finally speaks, breaking a silence that has surrounded us like smoke since dinner.

"I never thought it would end this way," I say.

"No," he says. "Neither did I."

"I'll miss you."

He grins—a flicker of his mouth so slight as to be almost an inward grin. "We had good times," he says.

We turn off the path and move across a damp lawn. The agents trail us at their interval, seeming careful not to step where we have stepped, avoiding the dark places in the grass that mark where we have pressed the dew against the earth.

"I suppose you're all packed," I say.

"Almost," he says. "A few pictures. . . ." His voice falls; he finishes the sentence with a movement of his shoulders.

"I guess we'll both get over it."

"Things have a way of settling themselves."

"Will you think of me?"

"Can you imagine me forgetting?"

"Then I can live with this," I tell him.

He puts his right hand on my shoulder. "Try not to dwell on it," he says.

"All right," I tell him.

He signals to the agents. I turn away and begin walking rapidly in the direction of the traffic noise. I have given my oath I will not show tears.

We are at Key Biscayne, in a room whose two windows look across a deserted beach to the ocean. The President is standing, shoeless and shirtless, at one of the windows. It is daybreak; the sun streams around him and turns the room gold. He waves absently to a Secret Service man seated at the base of a palm tree, and with his other hand rubs at the grey hairs on his chest.

"They'll miss you," I say to him.

He sighs. "I suppose they will."

"They loved you the way a family would."

"They did—for a while, at least. I'll always have that."

"You've settled everything?"

"Oh, yes," he says. "All packed, ready to go."

He moves from the window and picks up a white shirt from the chair beside the bed. He draws it on carefully, the motions of his dressing like those of an old man.

"Can I help with the cuff links?" I ask him.

"No, no," he says. "I can manage."

I stub out my cigarette in the glass ashtray. "Then I think we'd better get on with it." I stand up.

"Just let me put on my shoes," he says.

While he sits on the edge of the bed, slipping on the shoes, I button and adjust my jacket. I say: "It's going to be a scorcher"—not because I care, but because I am embarrassed and wish to say something.

The President nods, stands, scoops up his coat. At the door of the room I put my hand out to him. His mouth hardens.

"I think we can do without those, can't we?" he says.

"Yes, sir," I say, and follow him out through the bedlam of photographers to the waiting van.

We are aboard the *Sequoia*. It is a starless night; a light breeze is blowing over the mouth of the Potomac and there is no sound save the low murmur of a foghorn. The President is kneeling at the rail of the yacht. He wears a wet suit, goggles pushed up from his brow. He is checking the pressure of his air tanks. When he talks, it is in a voice scarcely louder than a whisper, and the words come fast upon one another. The *Sequoia* rocks gently in the rising tide.

"You've got it all straight?" the President says.

"Yes, sir. Trust me, sir."

"All right." He hoists the tanks onto his back. I help him adjust the fastenings. He takes the air piece into his mouth, checks the tanks one last time.

"Good luck," I tell him.

"Thanks. Remember—not a word to anyone."

"Right."

"You won't hear from me for two weeks, but don't worry. Everything's arranged. In thirteen days, mail the package to Cuernavaca; in twenty-seven days, mail the large envelope to Caracas." He pulls down the goggles. "After that, you'll get instructions every two weeks."

"Yes, sir."

He shakes my hand. "I'm counting on you," he says. The next moment he has slipped over the side of the yacht—a dim wake phosphorescent from the ship's lights. Then a crewman appears at the rail beside me.

"What's up?" says the crewman. "I thought I heard a splash."

"You did," I tell him. "The President just fell overboard."

The crewman lights a cigarette. "No kidding?" he says. He offers me a Kool. We smoke in silence.

We are at Camp David, in a large clearing not far from the main compound. The balloon is not yet inflated; it is laid flat on the grass, nearly a hundred feet long, striped blue and white. The staff is milling about. The President is in earnest conversation with the Secretary of State. Two men in overalls are fussing with the burners, while a third man is loading the gondola.

I am standing just close enough to overhear the President.

"You've booked passage?" the President is saying.

"I have," the Secretary answers.

"Capital," says the President. "Now you'll probably lose sight of me somewhere along the north shore. You know what to do."

The Secretary nods.

I drift to the edge of the field. The balloon is being filled, the great bag beginning to tug at its shrouds, men arranged in an oval seeing to it that the balloon expands evenly. In another twenty minutes the balloon is full, bulging in the afternoon sunlight like a spinnaker, its ground crew ranged around the gondola. The President climbs in, listens to instructions from a thin man in overalls who points to the burner controls. The man backs away. The balloon begins to rise.

The President waves to the onlookers, blows kisses to his family, leans out over the ballast bags and calls out to the crowd.

"Don't worry," he says. "Keep your ears open. Keep your eyes peeled. Keep your nose clean."

He is looking directly at me as these instructions trail off and are no longer audible. I watch until the balloon is only a speck in the northeast sky. Then I return to my car. I am not certain if the President was talking to the Secretary or to me—nor am I at all clear about the meaning of the words.

We are outside the city of P., racing down a narrow road lined with scrawny trees. I am driving a black Mercedes to a secret rendezvous, the radio blaring curious music, the tires kicking up stones that bang against the car's underpan. I am driving very fast, smoking a Turkish cigarette. It is close to noon. The President, a gag over his mouth, his arms and legs trussed with clothesline, is in the trunk of the car.

Once inside the city, I drive slowly over cobbled streets, streets teeming with men and women in native dress. I reach a market-place. In the square some people are shooting a film; I count three cameras. Several men, wearing foreign garments but looking like Americans, are sitting at the edge of the market with beer bottles in their hands. I stop at a curb, not far from an alley too narrow to enter except on foot, and step out of the car. A real foreigner approaches me; he is tall, bearded, has a battered black cap pulled down to his eyes. He bows. I return the bow.

I say: *The moon is new.*

He smiles. *But the stars know the cares of eternity,* he says.

I say: *All light weakens with time.*

He says: *Try to stay out of camera range.* He enters the alley and waits for me. I follow.

"I have the order," I say.

"I have the money," he tells me, and holds up a cloth pouch. "It is in Deutschemarks."

"That's thoughtful."

"He is alive?"

"Yes," I say.

"He is strong?"

"The ordeal of travel may have weakened him."

"Where is he?"

"In the trunk, the boot of the car."

He gives me the pouch of money. "Wait five minutes," says the foreigner. "Then return to your auto, drive out of the city, and do not look back." He leaves the alley.

I wait. After five minutes have passed, I go back to the car. I look into the trunk; it is empty. I get into the car, start the engine, drive off. The cameras are grinding.

We are on the San Clemente shore at sunset.

"There never *were* such sunsets," the President says. "I'll miss them terribly."

"And they'll miss you," I say.

"I wonder," he says after a moment's musing. "Things have a way of settling themselves."

"They do, sir."

"Of course I've packed up all my belongings."

"Yes, sir."

"And sent postcards to everyone I could think of."

"Yes. I remember mailing them, sir."

The President rubs his eyes. When he turns his back on the sun, two Secret Service men duck down behind the shrubbery. The President looks natty; he is wearing a Park Service uniform, the Sam Browne belt freshly saddle-soaped, the wide-brimmed hat tipped jauntily forward. Down at the main gate a car horn sounds.

"Well," the President says, "that's my ride."

He salutes briskly and jogs down the graveled drive toward the gate. I will never see him again. A year from now I will hear that he is transferred to Yellowstone. Two years from now I will find a postcard pushed through my mail slot. It reads:

I am the world's happiest man.

We are at an airport in the Midwest. It is a crisp morning in October, a smell of snow in the air, a panorama of flat brown fields sprawling as far as the eye can see. The President's plane has just come to a stop in the terminal apron; the Secret Service is filing down from the rear exit. The forward door of Air Force One pops out and slides open. The President appears. He acknowledges us from the top of the stairway.

The terminal area is mobbed. Counts range as high as thirty thousand, and the people are—as they say—from all walks of life. The press are waving cameras, housewives wave handkerchiefs, political factionists wave signs. When the President descends, he is met by local dignitaries who take his hand and must be per-suaded—a protocol officer whispering in their ears—to let go. A military band is playing astonishing melodies. Cheers erupt on every side. Black limousines are nearly submerged under the winter coats of the crowd.

I am at his right hand as the President begins his movement from the aircraft to the limousine waiting to whisk him into the city. "Hello," the President is saying as he struggles forward. "Good morning. You're very kind. I'm delighted to be here."

To me he says: "Help me. Get me into the car, for God's sake."

I step ahead. With my elbows wide I break a path for him. The crush is incredible; every now and again I am stopped, almost thrown back.

"Excuse us," I say. Then: "Make way here. Look out. Get the hell back, will you? Move aside. *Move.*"

The crowd thickens. It is like a coagulation; our pace is excruciatingly slow. Finally, yards short of the car, I am stopped in my tracks.

"What is it?" says the President.

Before I can answer, the crowd has separated me from the President. They are upon him. When I squirm around, he is hidden from me by the swarm of men and women. The agents assigned to him are helpless; like me, they have been forced to the outside of the circle. All of us are fighting to get back in. Now I see the crowd's hands lifting items aloft—the President's coat, his necktie, his shirt; then one shoe and the other, socks, cotton underwear.

Save me! It is the voice of the President.

"Make way," I scream. "Make way!"

I can hear the President crying out for help, and once, just for an instant, I catch sight of his face, eyes wild, mouth twisted on some new word he cannot utter.

False Lights

GAIL GODWIN

Mrs. Karl Bandema
Box 59
Ocracoke, N.C. 27960   June 16

Dear Violet,

Please forgive the familiar address when I don't even know you, but the more formal would still feel strange. I hope you'll understand. Along with this note, there should arrive a small parcel containing Karl's pills. I don't know if you have a doctor on the island, so I took the liberty of having Karl's old prescription refilled. The moment his weight goes over 185, he should take one of these every morning *after breakfast*. Also, no fat or salt in food preparation, less beef, more chicken and fish, more vegetables and salads, but no dressing on the salad, unless a little lemon. (Starting the meal with the salad helps cut the appetite.) And no cheese, except cottage cheese, and no alcohol.

I trust you will accept this in the spirit in which it is sent. If at a later time you should need another refill, please don't hesitate to let me know.

Sincerely,
Annette Bandema

Mrs. Karl Bandema
231 E. 48th St.
New York, N.Y. 10017   June 18

Dear Annette,

The parcel arrived today, with your note. I will do as you say. K. is in pretty good shape at the moment. He goes for a long swim before breakfast, takes several walks by himself during the course of his working day, and then we swim and walk in the evenings. The vegetables are easy because I planted a garden. (Peas, beans, squash, cucumber, spinach, tomatoes, carrots, radishes, and three kinds of lettuce.) As for fish, no shortage of that here. I do bluefish stuffed with spinach sometimes three nights a week. There is a local doctor, but so far only I have had to go to him. I tend to get ear infections. There is no liquor store on the island. I appreciated your note and wish you all the best.

Violet

June 18—maybe June 19 by now

Dear Annette, dear Annette Bandema,

The most natural way for me to think of you is dear Mrs. Bandema, but how can there be two of us? And yet here we both are. I feel I cheated myself by mailing that letter off so quickly. I couldn't wait to write it, to hurry back to the post office and mail it, even though the mail had already gone out for the day. It said nothing, absolutely nothing. Spinach and beans, walks and swims, all wrapped up in a cautious parcel of triumphant politeness. "I will do as you say," etc. And yet I told you more about me than you told about yourself. You know, or will know when you get my letter, that I get ear infections and that I have a garden, and—if you read between the lines—that I am alone a good deal of the day. I have no knowledge about you, except what I manage to compile from my husband's novels, steering uncertainly between fiction and fact. I shouldn't probably say *my husband*. It hurts and bewilders you. It would me. It's all so strange. I think it would feel less so to me if we could meet, just the two of us, in some neutral place, the way generals of opposing sides meet to sign a truce. Not that we need sign a truce, exactly. We are not on opposite sides.

I'm going to tell you something very peculiar: I feel close to you. I think about you all the time. When I am walking around the island, or sitting on the beach by myself, or even—I hope you won't think this perverse—when I am lying in his arms. I hold imaginary dialogues with you (somewhat similar to the tone of our brief exchange, all about food and recipes and such), and sometimes I ask your advice about things I'm sure you know better than I. I often imagine you watching me, us, as I used to imagine God watching me when I was a child, and sometimes when I am swiming I find myself showing off to you in the sea, taking extra care with my strokes, or persisting a little longer than I ordinarily would if nobody were watching. And often I see little things I'd like to send to you. A tiny painting in oil, done by a local artist, of fishing boats or the lighthouse. I watch this artist work down on the beach. He is a strange, bitter sort of fellow who has lived here many years. He told me about the land pirates who used to work this stretch of shore. At night, they hung lanterns around the necks of mules and walked the animals back and forth across the sand, until some unfortunate ship captain, mistaking the swaying lanterns for lights at sea, would crash upon the shoals and spill his cargo right into their hands.

This artist has his easel rigged so he can paint six small pictures at once. He does all six seas, then all six lighthouses, or all six boats. He says there will always be pirates wherever there are fools. He sells his work to a gallery in Nags Head which hangs one at a time till that one is sold, then puts up another in its place, and so on. . . . I have often had the urge to send you one, just as I had to restrain myself the other day from buying you a shipwreck map from the Visitor's Center, when I bought myself one, a map of the Ghost Fleet, all the ships that have gone down on the Outer Banks (more than five hundred ships, all along this treacherous coast): they call this "The Graveyard of the Atlantic," and I thought you would be touched and haunted, as I was, for the whole thing is rather mysterious and puts one in the frame of mind where individual lives and who is whose wife in a particular segment of time seem suddenly so fleeting and insignificant, mere events in an infinite process of events that will all be washed away, as the sea has washed away the faces of all those drowned men. I don't understand time. The more I think about it, the less I understand it. Sometimes I am quite certain it is only a way to console ourselves about the inevitability of change, merely a word containing no real thing, no more than the shipwreck map can contain bodies or salt water—or "Mrs. Bandema" can be anything more than a legal and social convenience. There is no real Mrs. Bandema.

On such a level, I think we could meet.

On such a level, I think you could be with us now, on this island. I have so much time to myself. I would enjoy your company.

It occurs to me that as recently as a hundred years ago this letter would have been considered highly irregular, perhaps impossible. And what of a hundred years from now? Karl says the novel of 2075 would be unrecognizable to us today, that it will be a pure and better thing, tuned in to more important signals, no longer obsessed with gossip and personal petty detail. If we had lived in 2075, would marriage also be a new thing, where we could all survive together, nobody's happiness depleting anybody else's, all of us sailing through change as effortlessly as gulls through air, time no more enemy than water as seen from above? Will there be marriage, will there be wives, in 2075?

That young woman crawling through the mud, carrying medical supplies in her teeth, through two miles of mud in enemy territory: I don't know how many times I have reread that passage in Karl's book. That was you. What love, what danger, what a love story! I am sure there will be nothing in my life to compare to that. No such challenge, no such heroism. I did not have to crawl, or even walk outside my father's house, to get Karl. Karl entered my father's house, and I went straight from my father's love to Karl's, no alien land, no great test, between. I earned nothing. Heroics are not easily had for the young in our times. Perhaps that is why they go to such extremes to create their own dangers. Karl says he will never put me in a book; he says he wants me to stay where I am, on this island with him. He says that you only put people into books to improve their lives, or when they are gone, or when you are no longer able to see them. It is a kind of memorial, he says—as the shipwreck map is a memorial, I guess, and a keepsake for tourists who can never know what it is like to feel oneself dashed to pieces on rocks. And yet, though he has put you away so memorably in his books (I weep every time I read of your death, so young, at only nineteen, completed as a heroine at nineteen, before you ever had a chance to live, to marry, to have that little boy who died, but who in Karl's books has been allowed to grow up and live), you are very present to me. The real you, a woman in her fifties, goes on existing for me.

I imagine your days, tracking them alongside my own. I sometimes feel we are interchangeable, except for the accident of time. It might have been the other way around, me first, then you, a woman's face that changes through one long event of a man's, an artist's, life. It could have been me on all fours with the medicine that saved his life, and you, young and untried, years later, placing a pink tablet beside his breakfast plate with no danger to yourself, completing the journey, all danger over, all the interesting wars and legendary shipwrecks over. (". . . *With swift communications, advances in safety-at-sea techniques, and sophistication of tools for rescue, tragic incidents along the coast occur only rarely now*.") Perhaps I will send you one of these maps, after all.

I hear the ocean pounding. What are you hearing now? This is the time of night, or morning, when everything rushes through my brain. I can't stop or even control its course, so I just ride the torrent. Sometimes I don't fall asleep until I hear the birds singing. Not that I mind, it's just that insomnia seems such a waste on me. He would make so much better use of it. He salvages from everything, his anger, his disappointments, his mistakes, his boredom. He makes it all reappear in meaningful, lasting shapes. At the moment I am seeing my garden, the sea breeze ruffling the Bibb lettuces that glow faintly in the dark, delicate and phosphorescent-looking, and the weighted curves of the tomato plants, their first fruit emerging through the bluish, fringy foliage, and the straight dirt-spaces between, glinting with diamond-flakes of sand.

It appalled me at first when I had to "thin out." I knelt above those inch-high plants, thinking, "Who am I to do this, what right have I to choose?" But the book said you had to be ruthless, you weren't doing any of them a favor if you allowed them to steal from and stunt one another. So I taught myself to pull things up by the roots. Choosing between the weak and the strong, and sometimes between the strong and the stronger, is supposed to make you philosophical.

I remember a famous philosopher who once came to my father's house for dinner. He told us how, after the war, he had been taken on a tour of a concentration camp, and how he went back to his hotel seething with such impotent anger that he got a violent headache and could not eat or sleep. While still in this state, he picked up a book on Einstein and suddenly understood for the first time the world-shaking boldness of "Energy equals Mass multiplied by the square of the Velocity of Light," and was filled with a great tranquillity and acceptance, could now view the thousands of charred and tortured bodies with the same meditative, detached eye one would view the death of stars or the decay of huge primeval forests into coal. As a small girl, I thought him a very cold, strange man, for whom $E = MC^2$ could balance the shredding and burning of people. Yet, in my garden, my fingers hover, choose, pluck. I hear the old killer sea behind me murmuring in my ear, and I accept the history of doomed sailors, the inexorability of evolution, and you, crawling through enemy mud, risking your life, in a Europe of thirty-three years ago, so that I could have a husband on Ocracoke today.

Something is always plucking, thinning out. The philosopher lost his headache and went down and had a huge meal. And I, in my garden, feel less guilty about you.

Yesterday I was walking on the beach, looking for unusual shells, along that particular stretch where the *Charmer*, the *Lizzie James*, the *Lydia Willis* went down. I was thinking about the women after whom these ships were named, wondering what kind of women they had been, and what they had meant to the men who honored their names—and of course I thought then of Karl's novel, the one he calls *Yolande* (which is you) and, though he has assured me I'll never be in any book, I couldn't help wondering what he would call me, the name he would think fittest to memorialize me.

I was walking along with my head down, not paying much attention to where I was going, and walked right into the fishing line of an elderly woman standing near the surf, wearing a pair of men's trousers cut off at the knees, her skin burnt crisp as a potato chip. She said not to worry, she had caught nothing but two crabs all morning and was getting ready to quit anyway. She had sharp eyes and kept staring at my face, my legs, my wedding ring, and before I knew what was happening, I had told her all about myself. She hadn't heard of Karl, but she said she didn't read much since her husband died, she was too busy traveling, making up for lost time. She and another widow had bought a camper together and had so far camped, she said, in thirty-nine states, not counting Canada and Mexico. She asked me Karl's age, and my age, and then laughed dryly and said, "Well, dear, you'd better start making your list." I asked what list and she said, "The list of all the things you want to do, only he won't let you do, but you can do after he's gone." When I said there was nothing I wanted to do without Karl, she narrowed her old eyes and asked how long we had been married. "Oh, no wonder," she said when I told her. "You wait a couple of years."

I went back to the cottage and made lunch. Gazpacho, tuna-fish salad with only enough mayonnaise to hold it together, even though your letter had not yet arrived. I watch his calories where they provide the least enjoyment, but I doubt I will ever interfere with his lunchtime wine and soda, which he refills frequently if his morning has been especially good or bad. Yesterday it was bad. Over his second glass, he told me that he had been tricked by the dream of Art into throwing away his life, as my pirates had tricked all those captains. Nothing he had written was of any value to the future, he said; he had wasted his past producing quaint relics, and he was missing his present, imprisoning himself in a roomful of ghosts, while Life, and me in it, flowed by outside. He refilled his glass again, saying he hadn't even looked at the garden this week, and appeared to be on the verge of tears. I cleared the table and came and stood behind him and folded my hands upon his breast. I suggested we take a nap. He said I was the first person in many years to cause him to suspect real life was as interesting as fiction, but it was too late for him to change. I did something selfish: poured him more wine and we had the nap.

Was it you, many years ago, who also interested him in real life?

Today his work went so splendidly that at lunch he announced if the wind stayed behind him like this, he'd have "all those ghosts" out of his head by summer's end. He ate too fast and sloshed innumerable refills of Chablis to the brim of his glass. His eyes looked through me toward, I suppose, ecstatic horizons.

"But what will you do then?" I asked.

"I will write about whatever lies on the other side of deaths and births and ego, whatever lies on the other side of settling scores and erecting monuments." His face was angrily spiritual as he explained how the artists of the future would be impersonal receivers and transmitters of the messages of the universe. It was neither the time for mentioning your letter nor for uttering dietetic precautions. He had abandoned us for 2075.

I sat across from him, nostalgic for yesterday's nap, and imagining you and me, years from now, traveling together in our camper, both of us burned a deep earthly brown, each of us wearing an old pair of his trousers, cut off at the knees, bumping sagely up and down the roads of America's scenic landscapes, taking equal turns at the wheel, comparing our experiences as the wives of Karl Bandema.

Last Saturday Karl and I went to a party in Nags Head. We had gone over on the ferry to buy supplies, and Karl ran into a newspaper columnist he knew while we were (I'm sorry to report) in the liquor store.

"You have got to come to this party, Karl. They'll be flattered to have you, and you wouldn't believe these people. They'll furnish you with material enough to last the winter," the columnist said.

Karl frowned. "Poor old Violet here would probably like it," he said at last. "She's stuck on the island with only my boring company all week."

And I said it might be fun—because I saw that he wanted to go.

The house, large and rambling in a Victorian style of architecture, was set high on stilts, and two cabin cruisers were docked underneath. A freshly painted sign over the garage said: HAPPY SHACK. The Hon. Terence Mulvaney, Dunn, N.C.

The columnist introduced us to the host, Judge Mulvaney, a fastidious man in his sixties, with a birdlike profile and elegant manners.

"I have the greatest respect for literature," he said, shaking Karl's hand warmly. "It ranks second only to my admiration of youth and beauty," he said, shaking my hand.

"The judge is also a new bridegroom," the columnist told Karl, sending him a secret look that said, "See? I told you!"

"I don't normally wear shirts full of white ruffles," explained Mulvaney to me, "but my bride made me buy this on our honeymoon in Mexico, and her wish is my law."

Everyone around him laughed. Mulvaney looked delighted with himself. Karl took a long, deep sip of his julep, and I made my first public debut as "Mrs. Karl Bandema."

I looked around at the gracious stretches of the room, with its comfortable faded furniture, its nautical touches. "I love your house," I said.

"Thank you, it's been in the family for a long time," the judge said. "Nancy Jean will show you the rest of it." He reached an arm sideways and fluttered his suntanned fingers, and within seconds a very pretty dark-haired girl ducked up at us from under his armpit. "Nancy, honey, show Mrs. Bandema the cottage. You girls run along and have a good time," he said.

Nancy put her arm around my waist. "I think you and I have got a lot in common," she whispered. Off we went, children, Karl and the judge watching us benevolently.

She led me upstairs to an enormous old bedroom. "All in white, that's me, the all-in-white girl!" She laughed and flung herself down in a swoosh of white silk trousers on a king-size bed covered in white organdy, with at least a dozen white lace and organdy pillows. The old casement windows were open, and you could see the sound, peaceful and pink with sunset.

Nancy patted the collection of pillows. "Come lie down and let's talk! You don't want to be dragged around somebody else's old house. I'll tell you the interesting things about it later. I haven't talked to a soul my age in months. Did he divorce his old wife for you? So did mine! Does she bother you-all constantly? No? You're lucky, let me tell you! It's gotten to where I simply will not put a soufflé in the oven anymore because as sure as I do the phone rings just as I'm taking it out and it's her, with one of her ladylike suicide threats. And then at the most *inopportune* times—I'm sure you know what I mean—she calls to say she's sure a burglar has broken into their old house, or the water pipes have frozen and she can't do a thing by herself, so I have to call up the plumber or the police —the whole thing upsets Terence so—and then I have to deal with his bad mood and his guilt . . . oh, the *guilt,* I get so sick of the guilt—they hadn't slept in the same room for centuries and she was the one who wanted out first . . . listen, make yourself comfortable, let me pour you a little more. I keep a pitcher up here for myself when I get bored with the company downstairs. Don't you love this room! It was *meant* to be all in white. When his daughter—she's just a year older than me—saw the wallpaper samples and swatches of fabric I had when we were still engaged, she said, 'But Nancy Jean, you can't be meaning to put that in my father's bedroom; that's the kind of thing that's more suitable for a virgin's bower.' 'But that's just what I am, honey,' I told her. And I was, you know. The judge is a nut on chastity. You wait, when he gets into high gear tonight, he'll tell you how chastity and ambition are the lost virtues of today's young. What does your husband start preaching when he gets high?"

"How artists won't be obsessed with personal things in the future, how they will have left their egos behind in order to be transmitters for the universe."

"Honey, men will always have egos. You take my word for it."

It was dark when we went downstairs, laughing. I was tipsy.

"You have got to come visit me this winter in Dunn," Nancy said. Then she got serious and muttered off a grave recitation. "The Mulvaneys were the third family to build . . . house built over the water so sailing boats could unload luggage and parties on the porch . . ." etc., etc.

Downstairs, Judge Mulvaney was saying, "The girls have lost their maidenhood and the boys their desire to succeed. That's why this country has gone to hell. I had a reputable gynecologist sign an affidavit that Nancy Jean was chaste before I married her. . . ."

"See," whispered Nancy happily, pinching me.

Later, sitting in the circle of Karl's arm, I listened to him tell his audience how, for the artist, personal concerns will be obsolete in 2075, no more hunger for fame or recognition, no preoccupation with pettiness. "We will only be interested in our anonymous role as messengers for the universe."

I caught Nancy's eye and winked.

On the last ferry back to Ocracoke, Karl put his head down into my hair. He stood behind me at the rail. The wind was cold, but he said it cleared his head. "God, what terrible people, what a wasted evening," he moaned. He had to hold onto me to keep his balance. "Why did we go? I wish we had just gone back to our own little island and had a quiet evening. I'm going to give up drinking. I'm going to give up people—all except you. I feel set back a hundred years! As if I didn't have enough people swarming around in my head, waiting to be disposed of, waiting to be explained! Why were you gone so long? What could you have possibly found to talk about with a girl like that? An *affidavit* for chastity, for Christ's sake! What on earth could have happened in that man's life to make him do a ridiculous thing like that? Listen, do you know what I'm thinking? We could stay on the island all winter. The hell with hurricanes! Are you afraid of hurricanes? Will you stay with me, Violet? Will you stay on with me while I endure my everlasting penance? What are you thinking? Tell me the exact flow of your thoughts, everything, leaving nothing out."

I was thinking of you, Annette, wondering if you were lying in the dark imagining burglars. I did not think so. When the thing you dreaded most has already come true, what further dangers are there to imagine? I was also thinking of pirates, and ripening tomato plants, and whether Karl would mind if I visited Nancy on the mainland if we stayed for the winter in Ocracoke. And whether I should even want such a thing in the first months of married life. And I was thinking about that night at my father's. Everybody was dancing, people of all ages, my father with the student who later became his wife—all these young brides—everybody was dancing except the famous novelist who had come to speak at our college's spring symposium ("What Are Our Next Frontiers?"). Earlier that evening, he and a famous biologist had agreed onstage that a new dawn was on its way, and our next evolutionary assignment would be to carry information around the universe. "All the old concerns will be sloughed off like dead cells," the novelist had exclaimed excitedly, "all those personal, selfish concerns we believe have to be the stuff of novels." He kept wiping the perspiration from his forehead, nervous and elated; he looked like an ill man inspired by a vision of perfect health. "Then will you stop writing novels?" demanded a student in the audience. "I would hope . . . yes . . . I would hope to have the courage and intelligence to do just that," the novelist replied quickly, his voice harsh. "I mean, if I could not get a clear reception, if I couldn't hear my assignment, yes, I would certainly stop writing novels." Then Karl laughed. "Luckily, I probably won't be around long enough to greet the new world. I can indulge myself in the fancies of the old one a while longer."

Then he was watching the dancers and I was watching him. He gulped his drink in compulsive sips, his tired, slightly wild eyes skimming us from beneath bristling eyebrows. I believed I could see him rapidly picking up, sometimes putting down in the same instant, our potential mysteries. Then his gaze came to rest on me, and I asked him if he would like to dance. "I have a piece of metal in my leg," he said, "but please stay and talk to me. I am lucky to be alive." Touching his damp forehead to mine, he shouted over the music. "A very courageous French girl saved my life—just about your age."

"I wish you wouldn't abandon the old world just yet," I said to him later that night. I was then beginning to discover that world, and so far he had been the best thing in it, the most compelling figure.

And you were part of it.

"What are you thinking?" this man asked now, my husband now, in a world fast growing extinct but not yet dead. Oh no, not quite. For weren't we on a ferry crossing to an island that was ours alone?

"Perhaps we'll see a shipwreck if we stay the winter. They are rare these days, but not entirely impossible," I replied.

Now he is asleep, dreaming onward the mysteries of all those people who keep him from becoming a perfect messenger, who keep him here with me. You, in an infinite number of forms, but never older than nineteen, and that little boy who has led so many interesting lives, and maybe now the judge and Nancy Jean. I wonder what this man will make of them? Perhaps one night, in spite of himself, he'll experiment with a better form of me, and then I will join you. We will meet at last. That is a chance I made up my mind I would take. Do you think, for yourself, it's been worth it?

I am here for the time being near the dark cool of my garden, helplessly thinking of so many things, drowned captains in their watery slumbers, Nancy deep in white organdy with her judge, a million other things, all in the space of a single wink. I could no more transfer it to paper than I could have told him everything I was thinking. I do not understand time. I do not understand marriage. If they prove, like the sentimental demands of the ego, to be outdated fancies, is it that you, Annette, drowned in the same archaic sea in whose dangers I furtively rejoice?

Affectionately,
Violet

Mrs. Karl Bandema
Box 59
Ocracoke, N.C. 27960   June 25

Dear Violet,

Since there is a doctor on your island, he should be able to prescribe Karl's pills when needed from now on.

I am afraid I cannot abet you in your extensive fancies concerning other centuries. The future I leave to those who must live in it; the past, insofar as it involves my own life, is my own affair. It is very much this year and this century for me. I assure you, time is more than just a word for me.

Nor can I encourage you in your hopes for a meeting. Outside your imagination, we have nothing to offer each other. I prefer to remain

Sincerely,
Annette Bandema

(or Mrs. Bandema, if you like, but not a defeated general, not a shipwrecked or drowned swimmer, and certainly not a potential camping companion).

Horse Badorties Goes Out

WILLIAM KOTZWINKLE

I am all alone in my pad, man, my piled-up-to-the-ceiling-with-junk pad. Piled with sheet music, piled with garbage bags bursting with rubbish, piled with unnameable flecks of putrified wretchedness in grease. My pad, my own little Lower East Side Horse Badorties pad.

I just woke up, man. Horse Badorties just woke up and is crawling around in the sea of abominated filth, man, which he calls home. Walking through the rooms of my pad, man, from which I shall select my wardrobe for the day. Here, stuffed in a trash basket, is a pair of incredibly wrinkled-up muck-pants. And here, man,

beneath a pile of wet newspapers is a shirt, man, with one sleeve. All I need now, man, is a tie, and here is a perfectly good rubber Japanese toy snake, man, which I can easily form into an acceptable knot.

SPAGHETTI! MAN! Now I remember. That is why I have arisen from my cesspool bed, man, because of the growlings of my stomach. It is time for breakfast, man. But first I must make a telephone call to Alaska.

Must find telephone. Important deal in the making. Looking around for telephone, man. And here is an electric extension cord, man, which will serve perfectly as a belt to hold up my falling-downing Horse Badorties pants, simply by running the cord through the belt loops and plugging it together.

Looking through the shambles wreckage busted chair old sardine can with a roach in it, empty piña-colada bottle, gummy something on the wall, broken egg on the floor, some kind of coffee grounds sprinkled around. What's this under here, man?

It's the sink, man. I have found the sink. Wait a second, man . . . it is not the sink but my Horse Badorties easy chair piled with dirty dishes. I must sit down here and rest, man, I'm so tired from getting out of bed. Throw dishes onto the floor, crash break shatter. Sink down into the damp cushions, some kind of fungus on the armrest, possibility of smoking it.

I'm in my little Horse Badorties pad, man, looking around. It's the nicest pad I ever had, man, and I'm getting another one just like it down the hall. Two pads, man. The rent will be high but it's not so bad if you don't pay it. And with two pads, man, I will have room to rehearse the Love Chorus, man, and we will sing our holy music and record it on my battery-powered portable falling-apart Japanese tape recorder with the corroded worn-out batteries, man. How wonderful, man.

Sitting in chair, staring at wall, where paint is peeling off and jelly is dripping and hundreds of telephone numbers are written. I must make a telephone call immediately, man, that is a MUST.

Sitting in a chair, staring at wall. Unable to move, man, feeling the dark heavy curtain of impassable numbness settling on me, man.

Falling back to sleep, head nodding down to chest, arm falling off side of chair. I've found the phone, man. It was right beside me all the time, man, and I am holding it up, man, and there is margarine in the dial holes. This, man, is definitely my telephone.

". . . hello? . . . hello, man, this is Horse Badorties . . . right, man, I'm putting together a little deal, man. Acapulco artichoke hearts, man, lovely stuff . . . came across the Colorado River on a raft, man, it's a little damp, but other than that . . . can you hold on a second, man, I think I hear somebody trying to break through the window. . . .''

I cannot speak a moment longer, man, without something to eat. I am weak from hunger, man, and must hunt for my refrigerator through sucked oranges, dead wood, old iron, scum-peel. Here it is, man, with the garbage table wedged against it. Tip the table, man, Horse Badorties is starving.

Some kind of mysterious vegetable, man, is sitting in the refrigerator, shriveled, filthy, covered with fungus, a rotten something, man, and it is my breakfast.

Rather than eat it, man, I will return to my bed of pain. I will go back to my bed, man, if I can locate my bed. It's through this door and back in here somewhere, man. I must get some more sleep, I realize that now. I cannot function, cannot move forward, man, until I have retreated into sleep.

Crawling, man, over the bureau drawers which are bursting with old rags and my used-sock collection, and slipping down, man, catching a piece of the bed, man, where I can relax upon a pile of books old pail some rocks floating around. Slipping onto my yellow smeared stiff mortified ripped wax-paper scummy sheets, man. And the last thing I do, man, before I sleep, is turn on my battery-powered hand-held Japanese fan. The humming note it makes, man, the sweet and constant melodic droning lulls me to sleep, man, where I will dream symphonies, man, and wake up with a stiff neck.

Horse Badorties waking up again, man. Man, what planet am I on? I seem to be contained in some weird primeval hideous grease. Wait a second, man, this is my Horse Badorties pillowcase. I am alive and well in my own Horse Badorties abominable life.

Time to get up, to get up. Get up, man, you've got to get up and go out into the day and bring fifteen-year-old chicks into your life.

I'm moving my Horse Badorties feet, man, getting my stuff together, collecting the various precious contents of my pad, man, which I MUST take along with me. I have the Japanese fan in my hand, man, and I am marching forward through my rubbish heap.

Cooling myself, man, on a hot summer morning or afternoon, one of the two.

Over to the window, man, which looks far out over the rooftops to a distant tower, where the time is showing four o'clock in the afternoon. Late, man. I've got to get out of the pad or I will circle around in it again, uncovering lost treasures and I will get hung up and stuck here all day.

Here is my satchel, man. Now I must stuff it with essential items for survival on the street: sheet music, fan, alarm clock, tape recorder. The only final and further object which must be packed in my survival satchel is the Korean ear-flap cap in case I happen to hear Puerto Rican music along the way.

There are countless thousands of other things in these rooms, man, I should take along with me, in case of emergency, and since it is summertime, I MUST take my overcoat. I have a powerful intuition it will come in handy.

Many other things, man, would I like to jam in my satchel. All of it, man, I want to take it all with me, and that is why I must, after getting a last drink of water, get out of here.

Roaches scurrying over the gigantic pile of caked and stuck-together greasy dishes in my Horse Badorties sink. The water is not yet cold enough. I'm going to let the water run here, man, for a second, while it gets cold. Don't let me forget to turn it off.

I've got everything I need, man. Everything I could possibly want for a few hours on the street is already in my satchel. If it gets much heavier, man, I won't be able to carry it.

"I'm turning on the tape recorder, man, to record the sound of the door closing as I go out of my pad. It is the sound of liberation, man, from my compulsion to delay over and over again my departure . . . wait just a second, man, I forgot to make sure if there's one last thing I wanted to take."

Back into pad once more, man. Did I forget to do anything, take anything? There is just one thing and that is to change my shoes, man, removing these plastic Japanese shoes which kill my feet, because here, man, is a Chinese gum rubber canvas shoe for easy Horse Badorties walking. Where is the other one, man? Here it is, man, with some kind of soggy wet beans, man, sprouting inside it. I can't disturb nature's harmony, man, I'll have to wear two different shoes, man, one yellow plastic Japanese, the other red canvas Chinese, and my walking, man, will be hopelessly unbalanced. I'd better not go out at all, man.

Look, man, you have to go out. Once you go outside, man, you can always buy a fresh pair of Lower East Side Ukrainian cardboard bedroom slippers. Let's go, man, out the door, everything is cool.

Out the door again, man, and down the steps, down the steps, down . . . one . . . two . . . three flights of stairs. . . .

Jesus, man, I forgot my walkie-talkies. I've gone down three flights of stairs, man. And I am turning around and going back up them again.

I am climbing back up the stairs because, though I am tired and falling apart, I cannot be without my walkie-talkies, man. Common sense, man.

"It is miraculous, man. I am making a special tape-recorded announcement of this miracle, man, so that I will never forget this moment of superb unconscious intuition. Ostensibly, man, I returned for my walkie-talkies, but actually it was my unconscious mind luring me back, man, because I left the door to my pad wide open. Anyone might have stepped in and carried away the valuable precious contents of my pad, man. And so I am back in the scrap heap, man, the wretched tumbled-down strewn-about everything of my pad, man, and I am seeing a further miracle, man. It is the miracle of the water in the sink, man, which I left running. Man, do you realize that if I had not returned here for my walkie-talkies, I would have flooded the pad, creating tidal waves among my roaches, and also on the roaches who live downstairs with the twenty-six Puerto Rican chickens? A catastrophe has been averted, man. And what is more, now the water is almost cold, man. It just needs to run a few more minutes, man, and I can have my drink of water."

But first, man, I see that I forgot to take my moonlute, man, hanging here inside the stove. The moonlute, man, the weirdest instrument on earth, man. Looks like a Chinese frying pan, man, and I am the only one in the Occidental world who would dare to play it, man, as it sounds like a Chinaman falling down a flight of stairs. Which reminds me, man, I'd better get out of this pad, man, and down the stairs. I'm going, man, I'm on the way, out the door. I am closing up the pad, man, without further notice.

No, man, on second thought, I am not closing up my pad, man, I am returning to it once again for the last time, man, to make a single telephone call to my junkman, man, who is going to sell me a perfectly good used diving bell with a crack in it, man. It will only take the smallest part of a moment, man, for me to handle this important piece of business.

My telephone, man, how wonderful to get back to my telephone again, linking myself once more to the outer world.

"Hello, man . . . there's a shipment of organic carrots on the way, man, are you interested in a few bunches. . . ."

"Hello, man, will you get out your *I Ching*, man, and look up this hexagram I just threw, number 51, nine in the fourth place, what is it . . . *shock is mired?* Right, man, I'm hip, I lost my school bus in a swamp. . . ."

"Hello, baby, this is Horse Badorties . . . sing this note for me will you, baby, I need to have my tympanic cavity blown out: *Booooooooooooooooooooooop!*"

"Hello, Mother, this is Horse. Did I, by any chance, on my last visit, leave a small container of vitamin C tablets, little white tablets in an unmarked bottle . . . yes, I did? Good, I'll be up to get them soon, man, but don't under any circumstances take one of them."

"Hello, man, Horse Badorties here . . . listen, man, I'm sorry I didn't get over to your pad with the Swiss chard, man, but I was unavoidably derailed for three days, man. I was walking along, man, and I saw these kids, man, in the street, playing with a *dead rat*, man. I had to go back to my pad to get a shovel and bury it, man. You understand, man, kids must not be imprinted with such things. Look, man, I'll be over soon, I'll be there at . . . hold on a second, man, just a second. . . ."

"Hello, man . . . this is Horse Badorties, I've got a deal cooking, man . . . stop shouting, man . . . right, man, now I remember—I already have your bread, that is, man, I had your bread until today, man, when a strange thing happened, man, which you will find hard to believe . . . don't go away, man, I'll call you back in five minutes."

". . . hello? . . . hello, man, Horse Badorties here, man. Man, I'm sorry I didn't get over to you with the tomato surprise, man, but dig, a very strange thing happened, man. I was walking in Van Cortlandt Park, man, and suddenly I saw this airplane overhead, man, running out of gas. The cat was circling low, man, looking for a place to land. I had to guide him in, man, for a forced landing, man, and it took quite a long time, which is why I'll be late getting to your pad, man. . . ."

". . . hello, man, listen, man, I've been having fantastically precognitive dreams lately, man, I am digging the future every night, and last night I had a definite signal, man, that the flying saucers are about to land. That's right, man, I wouldn't kid you, and dig, man, I am getting everyone I know to come up to the roof of my pad, man, to watch the saucers land, as there is a possibility I'll be carried away, man, into the sky and taken to another planet. . . ."

Tired, man, I am getting so tired telephoning. I will just close my eyes for a brief nap, man. I have trained myself through the years, man, to close my eyes and sleep for exactly ten minutes, man, no more no less, and wake up perfectly refreshed.

It is morning, Horse Badorties, what a wonderful sunshining morning. Wait a second, man, it is afternoon. I overslept. I must hurry, man, *Horse Badorties must go out!*

No, no, it's dorky day again!

"Dorky dorky dorky dorky dorky dorky dorky dorky dorky

dorky . . ."

(Dorky day again, man, and I am stumbling around my pad, repeating over and over):

". . . dorky dorky dorky dorky dorky dorky dorky dorky . . ."

(Constant repetition of the word *dorky* cleans out my consciousness, man, gets rid of all the rubble and cobwebs piled up there. It is absolutely necessary for me to do this once a month and today is dorky day):

". . . dorky dorky dorky dorky dorky dorky dorky dorky . . ."

(There is a knock at the door, man, go answer it.)

". . . dorky dorky dorky dorky dorky dorky dorky . . ."

(It is a knapsack blonde chick, man! I wave her in, but I cannot stop my dorky now.)

". . . dorky dorky dorky dorky dorky dorky dorky dorky . . ."

"I got a VD shot."

". . . dorky dorky dorky dorky dorky dorky dorky dorky . . ."

"I tried hitchhiking out through the Lincoln Tunnel and the cops stopped me."

". . . dorky dorky dorky dorky dorky dorky dorky dorky . . ."

"I figured maybe I should stay in the city a while longer. I thought it must be a sign."

". . . dorky dorky dorky dorky dorky dorky dorky . . ."

"What's going on, man, what's all this dorky?"

". . . dorky dorky dorky dorky dorky dorky dorky dorky . . ."

"I brought some breakfast . . . some bread and jelly."

". . . dorky dorky dorky dorky dorky dorky dorky dorky dorky dorky dorky dorky dorky dorky dorky dorky . . ."

"Christ, man, knock if off, will you?"

". . . dorky dorky dorky dorky dorky dorky dorky dorky dorky dorky dorky dorky dorky dorky dorky dorky dorky . . ."

"You're driving me up the wall, man."

". . . dorky dorky dorky dorky dorky dorky dorky dorky . . ."

(Another knock at the door, man. It always happens on dorky day. It is a saxophone player, man.)

". . . dorky dorky dorky dorky dorky dorky dorky dorky . . ."

"How's it going, Horse?"

". . . dorky dorky dorky dorky dorky dorky dorky dorky dorky . . ."

"What's up with Horse, baby?"

". . . dorky dorky dorky dorky dorky dorky dorky dorky . . ."

"I don't know. He was like this when I got here."

". . . dorky dorky dorky dorky dorky dorky dorky dorky dorky dorky dorky dorky dorky dorky dorky . . ."

"Hey, Horse, what's all this dorky, man?"

". . . dorky dorky dorky dorky dorky dorky dorky dorky . . ."

"I have some bread and jelly in my knapsack. Do you want some?"

". . . dorky dorky dorky dorky dorky dorky dorky dorky dorky dorky dorky dorky dorky dorky dorky dorky dorky . . ."

"What is it, raspberry?"

". . . dorky dorky dorky dorky dorky dorky dorky . . ."

"Strawberry."

". . . dorky dorky dorky dorky dorky dorky dorky dorky . . ."

"Hey, Horse, man, knock it off, man, and we'll play some music."

". . . dorky dorky dorky dorky dorky dorky dorky dorky dorky dorky dorky dorky dorky dorky dorky . . ."

"He won't answer you. I know he won't answer you."

". . . dorky dorky dorky dorky dorky dorky dorky dorky . . ."

"I think maybe he's composin' some kind of song, baby."

". . . dorky dorky dorky dorky dorky dorky dorky dorky . . ."

"I thought I might stay here for a while, but I can't stay here, not with all this dorky."

". . . dorky dorky dorky dorky dorky dorky dorky dorky dorky dorky dorky dorky dorky dorky dorky dorky dorky . . ."

"Dig, baby, you can stay with me if you want. My pad's just around the corner."

". . . dorky dorky dorky dorky dorky dorky dorky dorky . . ."

"Can we go there right now? I can't take any more of this dorky."

". . . dorky dorky dorky dorky dorky dorky dorky dorky dorky . . ."

"Sure, baby, let's go."

". . . dorky dorky dorky dorky dorky dorky dorky dorky dorky dorky dorky dorky . . ."

"Do you think . . . he'll be all right?"

". . . dorky dorky dorky dorky . . ."

"Yeah, he just has to work it on out. Come on, baby, let's go. So long, man, take it easy with your dorky."

". . . dorky . . ."

Dorky day, man, has changed my life, I see that now. Because now that it is the day after dorky day, I have a clear picture of what I must do with my life. I must, man, and this is absolute necessity, *Horse Badorties must go out!* The time, man, has come to get out of the pad NOW, man, right now!

Okay, man, I am going straight out the door, without breakfast, without looking around, without further ado. I will be in actual sunlight, man, walking along. Man, I must be straightening out my life, I must be shaping up, man.

Have I forgotten anything?

Sunglasses, tape recorder, fan, umbrella, satchel, used tea bag, disgusting blobular something, my tire pump, man, and this medicinal herb from the Himalayas, the leaves of which bloom only once in a thousand years and I have a shipment of it waiting for me in a subway tunnel—go Horse, go man, out into the real world.

Wait a second, man, I've got to smoke a few of these dandelion stalks to accelerate my brain waves. However, before I make that important step, I must use the stopped-up toilet, man, down which someone flushed a Turkish bath mat by mistake. How wonderful, man, to attend to vital bodily needs before anything else. I should be out buying a dogsled, man, but first I must rearrange my piles of completely disordered everything imaginable, so I can find the toilet. That is a *must*, man.

And then I'll go out.

Summer Tidings

JAMES PURDY

There was a children's party on the sloping wide lawn facing the estate of Mr. Teyte and easily visible therefrom despite the high hedge. A dozen school-age children, some barely out of the care and reach of their nursemaids, attended Mrs. Aveline's birthday party for her son Rupert. The banquet was held on the site of the croquet grounds, and the croquet set had only partially been taken down. A few wickets were left standing, a mallet or two lay about, and a red and white wood ball rested in the nasturtium bed. Mr. Teyte's Jamaican gardener, bronzed as an idol, watched the children as he watered the millionaire's grass with a great shiny black hose. The peonies had just come into full bloom. Over the greensward, where the banquet was in progress, there was the sharp odor of nasturtiums and marigolds, the soft perfume of June roses; the trees have their finest green in this season, and small gilt-brown toads move on the earth.

The Jamaican servant hardly took his eyes off the children. Their gold heads and white summer clothing rose above the June verdure in remarkable contrast, and the brightness of so many colors made his eyes smart and caused him to pause frequently in his watering. Miss Gruber, Mrs. Aveline's secretary and companion, had promised the Jamaican a piece of the "second" birthday cake, and had told him the kind thought came from Mrs. Aveline herself. He had nodded, yet it was not the anticipation of the cake that made him so broody as it was the unaccustomed sight of so many children all at once. Miss Gruber could see that the party had stirred something in the man, for he spoke even less than usual as she tossed one remark after another across the boundary of the privet hedge separating the two large properties.

More absentminded than ever, the Jamaican went on hosing the peony bed until a slight flood filled the earth about the blooms and splashed onto his open sandals. He moved off then and began sprinkling with tempered nozzle the quince trees.

Mr. Teyte, owner of all the property that stretched far before the eye, with the exception of Mrs. Aveline's much smaller estate, had gone to a golf tournament this day. Only the white maids were inside the big house. In Mr. Teyte's absence, they were sleeping most of the day, or indifferently checking the Jamaican's progress across the lawn, the man deeply adream despite the infernal noise of those young throats.

Mr. Teyte, if not attentive or kind to the man, was in any case his benefactor, or at least this word had come to be used by people who knew both the gardener and the employer, and was even used by Galway, the Jamaican, himself. But Mr. Teyte was undemonstrative if not indifferent, paid low wages, and almost never spoke to Galway, issuing commands, which were legion, through the kitchen maids and parlor maids. But when the servant had caught pneumonia, Mr. Teyte had come unannounced to the hospital in the morning, ignoring the rule that visits were allowed only in early evening, and though he did not speak to Galway, he stood by the bed a few moments, gazing at the ailing man as if inspecting a fine riding horse that had behaved poorly on a hunt.

But Mrs. Aveline and Miss Gruber talked to Galway, and were kind to him. Mrs. Aveline even "made" over Galway. She spoke to him over the hedge every morning, and was not offended or surprised when he said almost nothing to her in exchange. She seemed to know something about him from his beginnings—at any rate, she knew Jamaica, having visited there three or four times. And so the women—Miss Gruber and Mrs. Aveline—went on speaking to him over the years, inquiring after his health, and of his tasks in the yard, and every so often bestowing on him delicacies from their liberal table.

Galway could see the children's golden heads long after they had all left the banquet and gone to the interior of the house, and even after the limousines had come and taken them to their own great houses. The blond heads of hair moved before Galway's eyes like the wild buttercups outside the great estate, strays of which occasionally appeared in the immaculate greensward, each golden corolla a sun. And then came the vision of the glimpsed birthday cake with the golden yellow center. Galway's mouth watered with anticipation, and his eyes filled with tears.

The sun was setting as he turned off the hose and wiped his fingers of the water and some rust stains, and of a kind of slime that came from the nozzle. He went into a little brick shed, and removed his wet shirt, and put on a shirt of faded pink cotton decorated with a flower design. Ah, the excitement of all those happy golden heads at the banquet—it made one too jumpy for cake!

But obedient to the invitation, Galway waited outside Mrs. Aveline's buttery for the signal to come inside and taste the birthday treat. A heavy nostalgia came over him as he waited, a recollection that weighed him down like a fever. How long he had stood on the back steps he could not say, until Miss Gruber, suddenly laughing as she opened the door to him, her face flushed, said: "Why, Galway, you know you should not have stood on ceremony! Of all people, you are the last who is expected to hang back! Your cake is waiting for you!"

Galway sat in his accustomed place, the place where so many times past he was treated to dainties.

"You may wonder about the delay." Miss Gruber spoke to him more formally than usual. "Galway, we have, I fear, bad news. A telegram has arrived. Mrs. Aveline is afraid to open it."

Having said this, Miss Gruber left the room through the swinging door that separated the kitchen from the rest of the house. Galway turned his eyes to the big white cake with the yellow center. Miss Gruber had cut into it expressly for him. The heavy silver fork in his hand was about to press down on the thick frosted slice resting on excellent china when he heard a terrible cry. He looked up, like a forest creature alarmed. The fork fell from his strong hand. The cry came again, more loudly, and then there was a cavernous silence, and then the sound of piteous weeping. The gardener knew it was Mrs. Aveline. The telegram must have carried bad news. Galway sat looking at the untasted cake, the rich yellow of its center gleaming.

Miss Gruber came through the swinging door, her eyes red, a pocket handkerchief gripped tightly in her hand, her opal necklace askew. "It was Mrs. Aveline's mother, Galway. She is dead. And such a short time since Mrs. Aveline's husband died too, you know."

Galway uttered some words of regret, sympathy.

At last Miss Gruber said: "Why, you haven't so much as touched your cake." She looked at Galway accusingly.

"She has . . . lost . . . her mother . . ." he said, after some struggle with the words.

But Miss Gruber was studying the cake.

"We can wrap it all up, the rest of it, Galway, and you can have it to sample at home, when you will have more appetite." She spoke comfortingly to him. "These things come out of the blue," she said. "There is no warning very often. The sky itself might as well have fallen on us."

Miss Gruber had worked for Mrs. Aveline for many years. She always wore little tea aprons. She seemed to do nothing but go from the kitchen to the front parlor or drawing room, and then return almost immediately to where she had been in the first place. It was she who had supervised the children's party today, ceaselessly walking around, looking down on each young head. Without her, Mrs. Aveline might not have been able to run the big house, so people said. And it was also Miss Gruber who had first told Mrs. Aveline of Galway's sterling dependability. And it was she who always insisted on summoning him when nobody else could be found to do some difficult or unpleasant task.

"So, Galway," Miss Gruber said, "I will have the whole 'second' cake sent over to you—just as soon as I find the right box to put it in."

The man rose at this, not having eaten so much as a crumb. He said several words, and what he said startled him.

"I am sorry . . . and grieve for her grief. A mother's death . . . it is the hardest loss."

Then he heard the screen door closing behind him. The birds were still, and purple clouds rested in the west, with the evening star sailing above the darkest bank of color, as yellow as the heads of the birthday children.

Galway crossed himself.

Afterward, he stood for some time in Mr. Teyte's great green backyard, and admired the way his hands had kept the grass beautiful, endowed it with life and order. The wind stirred as the light failed, and flowers that opened at evening gave out their first perfume.

On the ground near the umbrella tree, something glistened. Galway stooped down. It was the sheep shears that he used in trimming the grass near trees and bushes. Suddenly, stumbling in the twilight, he gashed his thumb on the point of the blades. He walked dragging one leg now as if it were his foot that he had slashed. The awful gush of blood somehow calmed him. He put the sheep shears away in the shed, and then went through the kitchen door and sat down at the long pine table. He got some old linen napkins from the drawer, and began making himself a bandage. Then he remembered he should have cleaned the wound. He looked about for some iodine, but there was none in the servants' quarters. So he washed the loose flesh of the wound in thick yellow soap. Then he bandaged his thumb, and sat in still communion with his thoughts.

It was night now. Outside the katydids and crickets had begun a dizzying chorus, and in the distant darkness tree frogs and some bird with a single note called together in a fury of sound.

Galway knew who would bring the cake. It would be the birthday boy himself. The gardener would be expected to eat a slice while Rupert stood looking on.

Galway's mouth went dry as sand.

The bearer of the cake and of Mrs. Aveline's goodness was coming up the path now, the gravel crunching softly with his footsteps.

Rupert liked to be near Galway, liked to give the gardener gifts from Mrs. Aveline—sometimes coins, sometimes shirts, and now, tonight, food. Rupert liked to touch Galway as he would perhaps a horse. The boy would stare at the Jamaican's brown arms, the heavy muscles, with a look of disbelief.

Then came the quickened step on the back porch, the decisive knock, and there stood Rupert Aveline, with outstretched hands, presenting the cake!

The gardener accepted the gift immediately, his head slightly bowed. He lifted the cake from the box to expose it all entire except for the one section Miss Gruber had earlier cut for him, and this piece rested neatly in wax paper alongside the otherwise intact birthday cake. Galway fell heavily into his chair, his head still bent over the offering. He felt the boy's speechless wonder, the eyes fixed on him rather than on the cake.

Galway lit the lamp, and heard the boy's cry of surprise.

"Oh, yes, my hand," the gardener said gently, and looked down with Rupert at the bandage—the blood having wetted the linen crimson.

"Shouldn't it be shown to the doctor, Galway?" the boy said, and suddenly faint, he rested his hand on the servant's good arm. The boy had gone very white. Galway quickly rose and helped him to a chair. He hurried to the sink and fetched Rubert a glass of cold water, but the birthday boy refused this, and would not release the gardener's arm.

"It is your grandmother's death, Rupert, which has made you upset. . . ."

The boy looked away, out the window, through which he could see his own house in the shimmery distance. A few lamps had been lighted over there, and the white exterior of his home looked like a ship in the shadows, a vessel moving languidly in the summer night.

Because he knew Rupert wished to see him taste the cake, the gardener set about preparing to eat.

"You are . . . a kind . . . good boy," Galway began, in the musical accent the boy delighted in hearing. "And now you are on your way to being a man," he finished.

Rupert's face clouded at this, but the music of the gardener's voice finally made him smile and nod, and then his eyes narrowed as they fixed on the bloodstained bandage.

"Miss Gruber said you had not tasted one single bite, Galway," the boy said, trying to make his voice manly and firm.

The gardener studied the cake, the frosting in the shape of flowers and leaves and images of little men and words concerning love, a birthday, the year, 1902.

Galway got two plates, his large body leaden.

"You must share a piece of your own birthday cake, Rupert. . . . I must not eat alone."

The boy nodded brightly.

The Jamaican cut two pieces of cake, placed them on large heavy dinner plates, and produced forks of solid silver. As he reached a plate to Rupert—in the movement of his heavy arm—a path of blood fell in drops upon the pine.

It was shortly afterward that the whole backyard was illuminated by flashing lights and flares. Rupert and Galway rushed to the window and stared into the night. What they saw was a torchlight parade coming up the far greensward, in the midst of this procession. Mr. Teyte himself, a bullnecked short man of middle years. Then the other men raised Mr. Teyte to their shoulders, proclaiming his victory in drunken cries.

The cries grew louder as the men approached. Their march seemed menacing somehow, and the gardener and the boy, who stood like persons besieged, listened cautiously, and then the boy put his hand in the gardener's hand.

Presently, however, they heard the procession moving off to the front of the great house, and the torchlights dimmed, and then disappeared from outside the windows as the celebration advanced toward the stately entrance of the mansion.

As if at some signal from the procession, there was a deafening peal of thunder, followed by forks of cerise lightning, and the air, so still before, rushed and rose in furious wind. The boy and the gardener heard the angry whipping of the rain against what seemed all the countless windows of the great house.

"Come, come, Rupert," Galway urged, "your mother will be sick with worry." He pulled from a hook an enormous mackintosh, and threw it about the boy.

"Quick now, Rupert, your birthday is over. . . ."

They fled across the flooded lawns where moments before the victory procession had walked with torches in dry clear evening air. Galway wore no covering, and the pink shirt was soaked through to his skin.

Miss Gruber was waiting at the door to receive the birthday boy from the gardener. In one quick movement, like a magician, she stripped from Rupert and surrendered back to Galway the mackintosh, and then she closed the door against the gardener and the storm.

The Jamaican waited for a time under a great elm tree, its leaves and branches almost protecting him from the violence of the thundershower, which now was abating.

From the mackintosh, the man fancied there came the perfume of the boy's blond hair, shampooed hours earlier for the party. The fragrance came now in great waves to the gardener's nostrils, an odor very like honeysuckle. He drew the garment to his mouth and kissed it once. He kissed it fervently, the vision visiting him again in such vivid detail: the golden heads of the birthday-party children resplendent at the banquet table.

Usurpation: Other People's Stories

CYNTHIA OZICK

Occasionally a writer will encounter a story that is his, yet is not his. I mean, by the way, a writer of *stories*, not one of these intelligences that analyze society and culture, but the sort of ignorant and acquisitive being who moons after magical tales. Such a creature knows very little: how to tie a shoelace, when to go the store for bread, and the exact stab of a story that belongs to him, and to him only. But sometimes it happens that somebody else has written the story first. It is like being robbed of clothes you do not yet own. There you sit, in the rapt hall, seeing the usurper on the stage caressing the manuscript that, in its deepest turning, was meant to be yours. He is a transvestite, he is wearing your own hat and underwear. It seems unjust. There is no way to prevent him.

You may wonder that I speak of a hall rather than a book. The story I refer to has not yet been published, and the fact is I heard it read aloud. It was read by the author himself. I had a seat in the back of the hall, with a much younger person pressing the chair arm on either side of me, but by the third paragraph I was blind and saw nothing. By the fifth paragraph I recognized my story—knew it to be mine, that is, with the same indispensable familiarity I have for this round-flanked left-side molar my tongue admires. I think of it, in all that waste and rubble amid gold dental crowns, as my pearl.

The story was about a crown—a mythical one, made of silver. I do not remember its title. Perhaps it was simply called *The Magic Crown*. In any event, you will soon read it in its famous author's new collection. He is, you may be sure, very famous, so famous that it was startling to see he was a real man. He wore a conventional suit and tie, a conventional haircut and conventional eyeglasses. His whitening moustache made him look conventionally distinguished. He was not at all as I had expected him to be—small and astonished, like his heroes.

This time the hero was a teacher. In the story he was always called "the teacher," as if how one lives is what one is.

The teacher's father is in the hospital, a terminal case. There is no hope. In an advertisement the teacher reads about a wonder-curer, a rabbi who can work miracles. Though a rational fellow and a devout skeptic, in desperation he visits the rabbi and learns that a cure can be effected by the construction of a magical silver crown, which costs nearly five hundred dollars. After it is made, the rabbi will give it a special blessing and the sick man will recover. The teacher pays and in a vision sees a glowing replica of the marvelous crown. But afterward he realizes that he has been mesmerized. Furiously he returns to the rabbi's worn-out flat to demand his money. Now the rabbi is dressed like a rich dandy. "I telephoned the hospital and my father is still sick." The rabbi chides him—he must give the crown time to work. The teacher insists that the crown he paid for be produced. "It cannot be seen," says the rabbi, "it must be believed in, or the blessing will not work." The teacher and the rabbi argue bitterly. The rabbi calls for faith, the teacher for his stolen money. In the heart of the struggle, the teacher confesses with a terrible cry that he has really always hated his father anyway. The next day the father dies.

With a single half-archaic word the famous writer pressed out the last of the sick man's breath: he "expired."

Forgive me for boring you with plot summary. I know there is nothing more tedious, and despise it myself. A rabbi whose face I have not made you see, a teacher whose voice remains a shadowy moan: how can I burn the inside of your eyes with these? But it is not my story, and therefore not my responsibility. I did not invent any of it.

From the platform the famous writer explained that the story was a gift, he too had not invented it. He took it from an account in a newspaper—which one he would not tell: he sweated over fear of libel. Cheats and fakes always hunt themselves up in stories, sniffing out twists, insults, distortions, transfigurations, all the drek of the imagination. Whatever's made up they grab, thick as lawyers against the silky figurative. Still, he swore it really happened, just like that—a crook with his crooked wife, calling himself rabbi, preying on gullible people, among them educated men, graduate students even; finally they arrested the fraud and put him in jail.

Instantly, the famous writer said, at the smell of the word *jail,* he knew the story to be his.

This news came to me with a pang. The silver crown given away free, and where was I?—I who am pocked with newspaper sickness, and hunch night after night (it pleases me to read the morning papers after midnight) catatonically fixed on shipping lists, death columns, lost wallets, maimings, muggings, explosions, hijackings, bombs, while the unwashed dishes sough thinly all around.

It has never occurred to me to write about a teacher; and as for rabbis, I can make up my own craftily enough. You may ask, then, what precisely in this story attracted me. And not simply attracted: seized me by the lung and declared itself my offspring—a changeling in search of its natural mother. Do not mistake me: had I only had access to a newspaper that crucial night (The *Post,* The *News, The Manchester Guardian, St. Louis Post-Dispatch, Boston Herald Traveler,* ah, which? which? and where was I? in a bar? never; buying birth-control pills in the drugstore? I am a believer in fertility; reading, God forbid, a *book*?), my own story would have been less logically decisive. Perhaps the sick father would have recovered. Perhaps the teacher would not have confessed to hating his father. I might have caused the silver crown to astonish even the rabbi himself. Who knows what I might have sucked out of those swindlers! The point is, I would have fingered out the magical parts.

Magic—I admit it—is what I lust after. And not ordinary magic, which is what one expects of pagan peoples; their religions declare it. After all, half the world asserts that once upon a time God became a man, and moreover that whenever a priest in sacral ceremony wills it, that same God-man can climb into a little flat piece of unleavened bread. For most people nowadays it is only the *idea* of a piece of bread turning into God—but is that any better? As for me, I am drawn not to the symbol, but to the absolute magic act. I am drawn to what is forbidden.

Forbidden. The terrible Hebrew word for it freezes the tongue—*asur:* Jewish magic. Trembling, we have heard in Deuteronomy the *No* that applies to any slightest sniff of occult disclosure: how mighty is Moses, peering down the centuries into the endlessness of this allure! Astrologists, wizards and witches: *asur.* The Jews have no magic. For us bread may not tumble into body. Wine is wine, death is death.

And yet with what prowess we have crept down the centuries after amulets, and hidden countings of letters, and the silver crown

that heals: so it is after all nothing to marvel at that my own, my beloved, subject should be the preternatural—everything anti-Moses, all things blazing with their own wonder. I long to be one of the ordinary peoples, to give up our agnostic God whom even the word *faith* insults, who cannot be imagined in any form, whom the very hope of imagining offends, who is without body and cannot enter body . . . oh, why can we not have a magic God like other peoples?

Someday I will take courage and throw over being a Jew, and then I will make a little god, a silver godlet, in the shape of a crown, which will stop death, resurrect fathers and uncles; out of its royal points gardens will burst.—That story! Mine! Stolen! I considered: was it possible to leap up on the stage with a living match and burn the manuscript on the spot, freeing the crown out of the finished tale, restoring it once more to a public account in the press? But no. Fire, even the little humble wobble of a match, is too powerful a magic in such a place, among such gleaming herds. A conflagration of souls out of lust for a story! I feared so terrible a spell. All the same, he would own a carbon copy, or a photographic copy: such a man is meticulous about the storage matter of his brain. A typewriter is a volcano. Who can stop print?

If I owned a silver godlet right now, I would say: Almighty small Crown, annihilate that story; return, return the stuff of it to me.

A peculiar incident. Just as the famous writer came to the last word—*expired*— I saw the face of a goat. It was thin, white, blurry-eyed; a scraggly fur beard hung from its chin. Attached to the beard was a transparent voice, a voice like a whiteness—but I ought to explain how I came just then to be exposed to it. I was leaning against the wall of that place. The fading hiss of *expired* had all at once fevered me; I jumped from my seat between the two young people. Their perspiration had dampened the chair arms, and the chill of their sweat, combined with the hotness of my greed for this magic story that could not be mine, turned my flesh to a sort of vapor. I rose like a heated gas, feeling insubstantial, and went to press my head against the cold side wall along the aisle. My brain was all gas, it shuddered with envy. Expired! How I wished to write a story containing that unholy sound! How I wished it was I who had come upon the silver crown. . . . I must have looked like an usher, or in some fashion a factotum of the theatre, with my skull drilled into the wall that way.

In any case, I was taken for an official: as someone in authority who lolls on the job.

The goat-face blew a breath deep into my throat.

"I have stories. I want to give him stories."

"*What* do you want?" I said.

"Him. Arrange it, can't you? In the intermission, what do you say?"

I pulled away; the goat hopped after me.

"How? When?" said the goat. "Where?" His little beard had a tremor. "If he isn't available here and now, tell me his mailing address. I need criticism, advice. I need help—"

We become what we are thought to be. I became a factotum.

I said pompously, "You should be ashamed to pursue the famous. Does he know you?"

"Not exactly. I'm a cousin—"

"*His* cousin?"

"No. That rabbi's wife. She's an old lady, my mother's uncle was her father. We live in the same neighborhood."

"What rabbi?"

"The one in the papers. The one he swiped the story from."

"That doesn't oblige him to read you. You expect too much," I said. "The public has no right to a writer's private mind. Help from high places doesn't come like manna. His time is precious, he has better things to do." All this, by the way, was quotation. A famous writer—not this one—to whom I myself once sent a story had stung me with these words; so I knew how to use them.

"Did he say you could speak for him?" sneered the goat. "Fame doesn't cow me. Even the famous bleed."

"Only when pricked by the likes of you," I retorted. "Have you been published?"

"I'm still young."

"Poets before you died first and published afterward. Keats was twenty-six, Shelley twenty-nine, Rimbaud—"

"I'm like these, I'll live forever."

"Arrogant!"

"Let the famous call me that, not you."

"At least I'm published," I protested; so my disguise fell. He saw I was nothing so important as an usher, only another unknown writer in the audience.

"Do *you* know him?" he asked.

"He spoke to me once at a cocktail party."

"Would he remember your name?"

"Certainly," I lied. The goat had speared my dignity.

"Then take only one story."

"Leave the poor man alone."

"*You* take it. Read it. If you like it—look, only if you like it!—give it to him for me."

"He won't help you."

"Why do you think everyone is like you?" he accused—but he seemed all at once submerged, as if I had hurt him. He shook out a vast envelope, pulled out his manuscript, and spitefully began erasing something. Opaque little tears clustered on his eyelashes. Either he was weeping or he was afflicted with pus. "Why do you think I don't deserve a little bit of attention?"

"Not of the great."

"Then let me at least have yours," he said.

The real usher just then came like a broom. Back! Back! Quiet! Don't disturb the reading! Before I knew it, I had been swept into my seat. The goat was gone, and I was clutching the manuscript.

The fool had erased his name.

That night I read the thing. You will ask why. The newspaper was thin, the manuscript fat. It smelled of stable: a sort of fecal stink. But I soon discovered it was only the glue he had used to piece together parts of corrected pages. An amateur job.

If you are looking for magic now, do not. This was no work to marvel at. The prose was not bad, but not good either. There are young men who write as if the language were an endless bolt of yard goods—you snip off as much as you need for the length of fiction you require: one turn of the loom after another, everything of the same smoothness, the texture catches you up nowhere.

I have said "fiction." It was not clear to me whether this was fiction or not. The title suggested it was: *A Story of Youth and Homage.* But the narrative was purposefully inconclusive. Moreover, the episodes could be interpreted on several "levels." Plainly it was not just a story, but meant something much more, and even that "much more" itself meant much more. This alone soured me; such techniques are learned in those hollowed-out tombstones called Classes in Writing. In my notion of these things, if you want to tell a story you tell it. I am against all these masks and tricks of metaphor and fable. That is why I am attracted to magical tales: they mean what they say: in them miracles are not symbols, they are conditional probabilities.

The goat's story was realistic enough, though self-conscious. In perfectly ordinary, mainly trite, English, it pretended to be incoherent. That, as you know, is the fashion.

I see you are about to put these pages down, in fear of another plot summary. I beg you to wait. Trust me a little. I will get through it as painlessly as possible—I promise to abbreviate everything. Or, if I turn out to be long-winded, at least to be interesting. Besides, you can see what risks I am taking. I am unfamiliar with the laws governing plagiarism, and here I am, brazenly giving away stories that are not rightfully mine. Perhaps one day the goat's story will be published and acclaimed. Or perhaps not: in either case, he will recognize his plot as I am about to tell it to you, and what furies will

beat in him! What if, by the time *this* story is published, at this very moment while you are reading it, I am on my back in some filthy municipal dungeon? Surely so deep a sacrifice should engage your forgiveness.

Then let us proceed to the goat's plot.

An American student at a yeshiva in Jerusalem is unable to concentrate. He is haunted by worldly desires; in reality he has come to Jerusalem not for Torah but out of ambition. Though young and unpublished, he already fancies himself to be a writer worthy of attention. Then why not the attention of the very greatest?

It happens that there lives in Jerusalem a writer who one day will win the most immense literary prize on the planet. At the time of the story the writer is already an old man heavy with fame, though of a rather parochial nature; he has not yet been to Stockholm—it is perhaps two years before the Nobel Prize turns him into a mythical figure. ["Turns him into a mythical figure" is an excellent example of the goat's prose, by the way.] *But the student is prescient, and fame is fame. He composes a postcard:*

> *There are only two religious*
> *writers in the world. You are*
> *one and I am the other. I will*
> *come to visit you.*

It is true that the old man is religious. He wears a skullcap, he threads his tales with strands of the holy phrases. And he cannot send anyone away from his door. So when the student appears, the old writer invites him in for a glass of tea, though homage fatigues him; he would rather nap.

The student confesses that his own ambitiousness has brought him to the writer's feet: he too would wish one day to be revered as the writer himself is revered.

—I wish, says the old writer, I had been like you in my youth. I never had the courage to look into the face of anyone I admired, and I admired so many! But they were all too remote; I was very shy. I wish now I had gone to see them, as you have come to see me.

—Whom did you admire most? asks the student. In reality he has no curiosity about this or anything else of the kind, but he recognizes that such a question is vital to the machinery of praise. And though he has never read a word the old man has written, he can smell all around him, even in the old man's trousers, the smell of fame.

—The Rambam, answers the old man.—Him I admired more than anyone.

—Maimonides? exclaims the student.—But how could you visit Maimonides?

—Even in my youth, the old man assents, the Rambam had already been dead for several hundred years. But even if he had not been dead, I would have been too shy to go and see him. For a shy young man it is relieving to admire someone who is dead.

—Then to become like you, the student says meditatively, it is necessary to be shy?

—Oh yes, says the old man.—It is necessary to be shy. The truest ambition is hidden. All ambitiousness is hidden. If you want to usurp my place, you must not show it, or I will only hang on to it all the more tightly. You must always walk with your head down. You must be a true ba'al ga'avah.

—A ba'al ga'avah? cries the student.—But you contradict yourself! Aren't we told that the ba'al ga'avah *is the man whom God most despises? The self-righteous self-idolator? It's written that him alone God will cause to perish. Sooner than a murderer!*

It is plain that the young man is in good command of the sources; not for nothing is he a student at the yeshiva. But he is perplexed, rattled.—How can I be like you if you tell me to be a ba'al ga'avah? *And why would you tell me to be such a thing?*

—The ba'al ga'avah, *explains the writer, is a supplanter: the man whose arrogance is godlike, whose pride is like a tower. He is the one who most subtly turns his gaze downward to the ground, never looking at what he covets. I myself was never cunning enough*

to be a genuine ba'al ga'avah; *I was always too timid for it. It was never necessary for me to feign shyness, I was naturally like that. But you are not. So you must invent a way to become a genuine* ba'al ga'avah, *so audacious and yet so ingenious that you will fool God and will live.*

The student is impatient.—How does God come into this? We're talking only of ambition.

—Of course. Of serious *ambition, however. You recall: "All that is not Torah is levity." This is the truth to be found at the end of every incident, even this one.—You see, the old man continues, my place can easily be taken. A blink, and it's yours. I will not watch over it if I forget that someone is after it. But you must make me forget.*

—How? asks the student, growing cold with greed.

—By never coming here again.

—It's a joke!

—And then I will forget you. I will forget to watch over my place. And then, when I least look for it to happen, you will come and steal it. You will be so quiet, so shy, so ingenious, so audacious. I will never suspect you.

—A nasty joke! You want to get rid of me! It's mockery, you forget what it is to be young. In old age everything is easier, nothing burns inside you.

But meanwhile, inside the student's lungs, and within the veins of his wrists, a cold fog shivers.

—Nothing burns? Yes; true. At the moment, for instance, I covet nothing more lusty than my little twilight nap. I always have it right now.

—They say (the student is as cold now as a frozen path, all his veins are paths of ice), they say you're going to win the Nobel Prize! For literature!

—When I nap, I sleep dreamlessly. I don't dream of such things. Come, let me help you cease to covet.

—It's hard for me to keep my head down! I'm young, I want what you have, I want to be like you!

Here I will interrupt the goat's story to apologize. I would not be candid if I did not confess that I am rewriting it; I am almost making it my own, and that will never do for an act of plagiarism. I don't mean only that I have set it more or less in order, and taken out the murk. That is only by the way. But, by sticking to what one said and what the other answered, I have broken my promise; already I have begun to bore you. Boring! Oh, the goat's story was boring! Philosophic stories make excellent lullabies.

So, going on with my own version (I hate stories with ideas hidden in them), I will spring out of paraphrase and invent what the old man does.

Right after saying "Let me help you cease to covet," the writer gets up and, with fuzzy sleepy steps, half limps to a table covered by a cloth that falls to the floor. He separates the parts of the cloth, and now the darkness underneath the table takes him like a tent. In he crawls, the flaps cling, his rump makes a bulge. He calls out two words in Hebrew: *ohel shalom!* and backs out, carrying with him a large black box. It looks like a lady's hatbox.

"An admirer gave me this. Only not an admirer of our own time. A predecessor. I had it from Tchernikhovsky. The poet. I presume you know his work?"

"A little," says the student. He begins to wish he had boned up before coming.

"Tchernikhovsky was already dead when he brought me this," the old man explains. "One night I was alone, sitting right there —where you are now. I was reading Tchernikhovsky's most famous poem, the one to the god Apollo. And quite suddenly there was Tchernikhovsky. He disappointed me. He was a completely traditional ghost, you could see right through him to the wall behind. This of course made it difficult to study his features. The wall behind—you can observe for yourself—held a bookcase, so where his nose appeared to be I could read only the title of a tractate of the Mishnah. A ghost can be seen mainly in outline, unfortunately,

something like an artist's charcoal sketch, only instead of the blackness of charcoal, it is the narrow brilliance of a very fine white light. But what he carried was palpable, even heavy—this box. I was not at all terror-stricken, I can't tell you why. Instead, I was bemused by the kind of picture he made against the wall—'modern,' I would have called it then, but probably there are new words for that sort of thing now. It reminded me a little of a collage: one kind of material superimposed on another kind which is utterly different. One order of creation laid upon another. Metal on tissue. Wood on hide. In this case it was a three-dimensional weight superimposed on a line—the line, or luminous congeries of lines, being Tchernikhovsky's hands, ghost hands holding a real box."

The student stares at the box. He waits like a coat eager to be shrunk.

"The fact is," continues the old writer, "I have never opened it. Not that I'm not as inquisitive as the next mortal. Perhaps more so. But it wasn't necessary. There is something about the presence of an apparition that satisfies all curiosity forever—the deeper as well as the more superficial sort. For one thing, a ghost will tell you everything, and all at once. A ghost may *look* artistic, but there is no finesse to it, nothing indirect or calculated, nothing suggesting *raffinement*. It is as if everything gossamer had gone simply into the stuff of it. The rest is all grossness. Or else Tchernikhovsky himself, even when alive and writing, had a certain clumsiness. This is what I myself believe. All that pantheism and earth-worship! That pursuit of the old gods of Canaan! He thickened his tongue with clay. All pantheists are fools. Likewise Trinitarians and Gnostics of every kind. How can a piece of creation be its own Creator?

"Still, his voice had rather a pretty sound. To describe it is to be obliged to ask you to recall the sound of prattle: a baby's purr, only shaped into nearly normal cognitive speech. A most pleasing combination. He told me that he was reading me closely in Eden and approved of my stories. He had, he assured me, a number of favorites, but best of all he liked a quite short tale—no more than a notebook sketch, really—about why the Messiah will not come.

"In this story the Messiah is ready to come. He enters a synagogue and prepares to appear at the very moment he hears the congregation recite the 'I believe.' He stands there and listens, waiting to make himself visible on the last syllable of the verse *I believe in the coming of the Messiah, and even if he tarry I will await his coming every day.* He leans against the ark and listens, listens and leans—all the time he is straining his ears. The fact is, he can hear nothing: the congregation buzzes with its own talk—hats, mufflers, business, wives, appointments, rain, lessons, the past, next week. . . . The prayer is obscured, it is drowned in dailiness, and the Messiah retreats: he has not heard himself summoned.

"This, Tchernikhovsky's ghost told me, was my best story. I was at once suspicious. His baby-voice hinted at ironies, I caught a tendril of sarcasm. It was clear to me that what he liked about this story was mainly its climactic stroke: that the Messiah is prevented from coming. I had written to lament the tarrying of the Messiah; Tchernikhovsky, it seemed, took satisfaction exactly in what I mourned. 'Look here,' he tinkled at me—imagine a crow linked to a delicious little gurgle, and the whole sense of it belligerent as a prizefighter and coarse as an old waiter—'now that I'm dead, a good quarter-century of deadness under my dust, I've concluded that I'm entirely willing to have you assume my eminence. For one thing, I've been to Sweden, pulled strings with some deceased but still influential Academicians, and arranged for you to get the Nobel Prize in a year or two. Which is beyond what I ever got for myself. But I'm aware this won't interest you as much as a piece of eternity right here in Jerusalem, so I'm here to tell you you can have it. You can'—he had a babyish way of repeating things—'assume my eminence.'

"You see what I mean about grossness. I admit I was equally coarse. I answered speedily and to the point. I refused.

"'I understand you,' he said. 'You don't suppose I'm pious enough, or not pious in the right way. I don't meet your yeshiva standards. Naturally not. You know I used to be a doctor. I was attracted to biology, which is to say to dust. Not spiritual enough for you! My Zionism wasn't of the soul, it was made of real dirt. What I'm offering you is something tangible. Have some common sense and take the box. It will do for you what the Nobel Prize can't. Open the box and put on whatever's inside. Wear it for one full minute and the thing will be accomplished.' "

"For God's sake, what *was* it?" shrieks the student, shriveling into his blue city-boy shirt. With a tie: and in Jerusalem! [The student is an absurdity, a crudity. But of course I've got to have him; he's left over from the goat's story, what else am I to do?]

"Inside the box," replies the old writer, "was the most literal-minded thing in the world. From a ghost I expected as much. The whole idea of a ghost is a literal-minded conception. I've used ghosts in my own stories, naturally, but they've always had a real possibility, by which I mean an ideal possibility: Elijah, the True Messiah. . . ."

"For God's sake, the box!"

"The box. Take it. I give it to you."

"What's in it?"

"See for yourself."

"Tell me first. Tchernikhovsky told *you*."

"That's a fair remark. It contains a crown."

"What kind of crown?"

"Made of silver, I believe."

"*Real* silver?"

"I've never looked on it, I've explained this. I *refused* it."

"Then why give it to me?"

"Because it's meant for that. When a writer wishes to usurp the place and power of another writer, he simply puts it on. I've explained this already."

"But if I wear it I'll become like Tchernikhovsky—"

"No, no, like me. Like me. It confers the place and power of the giver. And it's what you want, true? To be like me?"

"But this isn't what you advised a moment ago. *Then* you said to become arrogant, a *ba'al ga'avah,* and to conceal it with shyness—"

[Quite so. A muddle in the plot. That was the goat's story, and it had no silver crown in it. I am still stuck with these leftovers that cause seams and cracks in my own version. I will have to mend all this somehow. Be patient. I will manage it. Pray that I don't bungle it.]

"Exactly," says the old writer. "That's the usual way. But if you aren't able to feign shyness, what is necessary is a shortcut. I warned you it would demand audacity and ingenuity. What I did not dare to do, you must have the courage for. What I turned down you can raise up. I offer you the crown. You will see what a shortcut it is. Wear it and immediately you become a *ba'al ga'avah.* Still, I haven't yet told you how I managed to get rid of Tchernikhovsky's ghost. Open the box, put on what's inside, and I'll tell you."

The student obeys. He lifts the box onto the table. It seems light enough, then he opens it, and at the first thrust of his hand into its interior the box disintegrates, flakes off into dust, is blown off at a breath, consumed by the first alien molecule of air, like something very ancient removed from the deepest clay tomb and unable to withstand the corrosive stroke of light.

But there, in the revealed belly of the vanished box, is the crown.

It appears to be made of silver, but it is heavier than any earthly silver—it is heavy, heavy, heavy, dense as a meteorite. Puffing and struggling, the student tries to raise it up to his head. He cannot. He cannot lift even a corner of it. It is weighty as a pyramid.

"It won't budge."

"It will after you pay for it."

"You didn't say anything about payment!"

"You're right. I forgot. But you don't pay in money. You pay in a promise. You have to promise that if you decide you don't want the crown you'll take it off immediately. Otherwise, it's yours forever."

"I promise."

"Good. Then put it on."

And now lightly, lightly, oh so easily as if he lifted a straw hat, the student elevates the crown and sets it on his head.

"There. You are like me. Now go away."

And oh so lightly, lightly, as easily as if the crown were a cargo of helium, the student skips through Jerusalem. He runs! He runs into a bus, a joggling mob crushed together, everyone recognizes him, even the driver: he is praised, honored, young women put out their hands to touch his collar, they pluck at his pants, his fly unzips and he zips it up again, oh fame! He gets off the bus and runs to his yeshiva. Crowds on the sidewalk, clapping. So this is what it feels like! He flies into the yeshiva like a king. Formerly, no one blinked at him, the born Jerusalemites scarcely spoke to him, but now! It is plain they have all read him. He hears a babble of titles, plots, characters, remote yet familiar—look, he thinks, the crown has supplied me with a ready-made bibliography. He reaches up to his head to touch it: a flash of cold. Cold, cold, it is the coldest silver on the planet, a coldness that stabs through into his brain. Frost encases his brain. Inside his steaming skull he hears more titles, more plots, names of characters, scholars, wives, lovers, ghosts, children, beggars, villages, candlesticks—what a load he carries, what inventions, what a teeming and a boiling, stories, stories, stories! His own; yet not his own. The Rosh Yeshiva comes down the stairs from his study: the Rosh Yeshiva, the Head, a bony miniaturized man grown almost entirely inward and upward into a spectacular dome, a brow shaped like the front of an academy, hollowed-out temples for porticoes, a resplendent head with round dead-end eyeglasses as denying as bottle bottoms, and curl-scribbled beard and small attachments of arms and little antlike legs thin as hairs; and the Rosh Yeshiva, who has never before let fall a syllable to this obscure tourist-pupil from America, suddenly cries out the glorious blessing reserved for finding oneself in the presence of a sage: Blessed are You, O God, Imparter of wisdom to those who fear Him! And the student in his crown understands that there now cleave to his name sublime parables interpreting the divine purpose, and he despairs, he is afraid, because suppose he were obliged to write one this minute? Suppose these titles clamoring all around him are only empty pots, and he must fill them up with stories? He runs from the yeshiva, elbows out, scattering admirers and celebrants, and makes for the alley behind the kitchen—no one ever goes there, only the old cats who scavenge in the trash barrels. But behind him—crudely sepulchral footsteps, like thumps inside a bucket: he runs, he looks back, he runs, he stops—Tchernikhovsky's ghost! From the old writer's description the student can identify it easily. "A mistake," chimes the ghost, a pack of bells, "it wasn't for you."

"What!" screams the student.

"Give it back."

"What!"

"The crown," pursues the baby-purr voice of Tchernikhovsky's ghost. "I never meant for that old fellow to give it away."

"He said it was all right."

"He tricked you."

"No he didn't."

"He's sly sly sly."

"He said it would make me just like him. And I am."

"No," says the ghost.

"Yes!" screams the student.

"Then predict the future."

"In two years, the Nobel Prize for Literature!"

"For him, not for you."

"But I'm *like* him."

"Like is not the same as the same. You want to be the same? Look in the window."

The student looks into the kitchen window. Inside, among cauldrons, he can see the roil of the students in their caps, spinning here and there, in the pantry, in the Passover dish closet even, past a pair of smoky vats, in search of the fled visitor who now stares and stares until his concentration alters seeing; and instead of looking behind the pane, he follows the light on its surface and beholds a reflection. An old man is also looking into the window; the student is struck by such a torn rag of a face. Strange, it cannot be Tchernikhovsky: he is all web and wraith; and anyhow a ghost has no reflection. The old man in the looking-glass window is wearing a crown. A silver crown!

"You see?" tinkles the ghost. "A trick!"

"I'm old!" howls the student.

"Feel in your pocket."

The student feels. A vial.

"See? Nitroglycerin."

"What is this, are you trying to blow me up?"

Again the small happy soaring of the infant's grunt. "I remind you that I am a physician. When you are seized by a pulling, a knocking, a burning in the chest, a throb in the elbow-crook, swallow one of these tablets. In coronary insufficiency it relaxes the artery."

"Heart failure! Will I die? Stop! I'm young!"

"With those teeth? All gums gone? That wattle? Dotard! Bag!"

The student runs; he remembers his perilous heart; he slows. The ghost thumps and chimes behind. So they walk, a procession of two, a very old man wearing a silver crown infinitely cold, in his shadow a ghost made all of lit spider thread, giving out now and then with baby's laughter and odd coarse curses patched together from Bible phrases; together they scrape out of the alley onto the boulevard—an oblivious population there.

"My God! No one knows me. Why don't they know me here?"

"Who should know you?" says Tchernikhovsky.

"In the bus they yelled out dozens of book titles. In the streets! The Rosh Yeshiva said the blessing for seeing a sage!"

But now in the bus the passengers are indifferent; they leap for seats; they snore in cozy spots standing up, near poles; and not a word. Not a gasp, not a squeal. Not even a pull on the collar. It's all over! A crown but no king.

"It's stopped working," says the student, mournful.

"The crown? Not on your life."

"Then you're interfering with it. You're jamming it up."

"That's more like the truth."

"Why are you following me?"

"I don't like misrepresentation."

"You mean you don't like magic."

"They're the same thing."

"Go away!"

"I never do that."

"*He* got rid of you."

"Sly sly sly. He did it with a ruse. You know how? He refused the crown. He took it but he hid it away. No one ever refused it before. Usurper! Coveter! *Ba'al ga'avah!* That's what he is."

The student protests. "But he *gave* me the crown. 'Let me help you cease to covet,' that's exactly what he said. Why do you call him *ba'al ga'avah?*"

"And himself? *He's* ceased to covet, is that it? That's what you think? You think he doesn't churn saliva over the Nobel Prize? Ever since I told him they were speculating about the possibility over at the Swedish Academicians' graveyard? Day and night that's all he dreams of. He loves his little naps, you know why? To sleep, perchance to dream. He imagines himself in a brand-new splendiferous bow tie, rear end trailing tails, wearing his skullcap out of public arrogance, his old wife up there with him dressed to the hobbledorfs—in Stockholm, with the King of Sweden! That's what he sees, that's what he dreams, he can't work, he's in a fever of coveting. You think it's different when you're old?"

"I'm not old!" the student shouts. A willful splinter, he peels himself from the bus. Oh, frail, his legs are straw, the dry knees wrap close like sheaves, he feels himself pouring out, sand from a sack. Old!

Now they are in front of the writer's house. "Age makes no matter," says the ghost, "the same, the same. Ambition levels, lust

is unitary. Lust you can always count on. I'm not speaking of the carnal sort. Carnality's a brevity—don't compare wind with mountains! But lust! Teetering on the edge of the coffin there's lust. After mortality there's lust, I guarantee you. In Eden there's nothing but lust." The ghost raps on the door—with all his strength, and his strength is equal to a snowflake. Silence, softness. "Bang on the thing!" he commands; sometimes he forgets he is incorporeal.

The student obeys, shivering; he is so cold now his three or six teeth clatter like chinaware against a waggling plastic bridge, his ribs shake in his chest, his spine vibrates without surcease. And what of his heart? Inside his pocket he clutches the vial.

The old writer opens up. His fists are in his eyes.

"We woke you, did we?" gurgles Tchernikhovsky's ghost.

"You!"

"Me," says the ghost, satisfied. "*Ba'al ga'avah!* Spiteful! You foisted the crown on a kid."

The old writer peers. "Where?"

The ghost sweeps the student forward. "I did him the service of giving him long life. Instantly. Why wait for a good thing?"

"I don't want it! Take it back!" the student cries, snatching at the crown on his head; but it stays on. "You said I could give it back if I don't want it anymore!"

Again the old writer peers. "Ah. You keep your promise. So does the crown."

"What do you mean?"

"It promised you acclaim. But it generates this pest. Everything has its price," the writer says.

"Get rid of it!" the student shrieks.

"To get rid of the ghost, you have to get rid of the crown."

"All right! Here it is! Take it back! It's yours!"

The ghost laughs like a baby at the sight of a teat. "Try and take it off, then."

The student tries. He tears at the crown, he flings his head upward, backward, sideways, pulls and pulls. His fingertips flame with the ferocious cold.

"How did *you* get rid of it?"

"I never put it on," replies the old writer.

"No, no, I mean the ghost, how did you get rid of the ghost!"

"I was going to tell you that, remember? But you ran off."

"You sent me away. It was a trick, you never meant to tell."

The ghost scolds: "No disputes!" And orders, "Tell now."

The student writhes; twists his neck; pulls and pulls. The crown stays on.

"The crown loosens," the old writer begins, "when the ghost goes. Everything dissolves together—"

"But *how?*"

"You find someone to give the crown to. That's all. You simply pass it on. All you do is agree to give away its powers to someone who wants it. Consider it a test of your own generosity."

"Who'll want it? Nobody wants such a thing!" the student yells. "It's stuck! Get it off! Off!"

"*You* wanted it."

"Prig! Moralist! *Ba'al ga'avah!* Didn't I come to you for advice? Literary advice, and instead you gave me this! I wanted help! You gave me metal junk! Sneak!"

"Interesting," observes the ghost, "that I myself acquired the crown in exactly the same way. I received it from Ibn Gabirol. I consulted him about some of his verse forms. To be specific, the problem of enjambment, which is more difficult in Hebrew than in some other languages. By way of reply he gave me the crown. Out of the blue it appeared—naked, so to speak, and shining, like a fish without scales. Of course there wasn't any ghost attached to the crown then. I'm the first, and you think I *like* having to materialize thirty minutes after someone's put it on? What I need is to be left in peace in Paradise, not this business of being on call the moment someone—"

"Ibn Gabriol?" the old writer breaks in, panting, all attention. Ibn Gabirol! Sublime poet, envied beyond envy, sublimeness without heir, who would not covet the crown of Ibn Gabriol?

"He said *he* got it from Isaiah. The quality of ownership keeps declining apparently. That's why they have me on patrol. If someone unworthy acquires it—well, that's where I put on my emanations and dig in. Come on," says the ghost, "let's go." He gives the student one of his snowflake shoves. "Where you go, I go. Where I go, you go. Now that you know the ropes, let's get out of here and find somebody who deserves it. Give it to some goy for a change. 'The righteous among the Gentiles are as judges in Israel.' My own suggestion is Oxford, Mississippi; Faulkner, William."

"Faulkner's dead."

"He is? I ought to look him up. All right, then. Someone not so fancy. Norman Mailer."

"A Jew," sneers the student.

"Can you beat that. Never mind, we'll find someone. Keep away from the rot of Europe—Kafka had it once. Maybe a black. An Indian. Spic maybe. We'll go to America and look."

Moistly the old writer plucks at the ghost. "Listen, this doesn't cancel the Prize? I still get it?"

"In two years you're in Stockholm."

"And me?" cries the student. "What about me? What happens to me?"

"You wear the crown until you get someone to take it from you. Blockhead! Dotard! Don't you *listen?*" says the ghost.

"No one wants it! I told you!" the student screams. "Anyone who really needs it you'll say doesn't deserve it. If he's already famous he doesn't need it, and if he's unknown you'll think he degrades it. Like me. Not fair! There's no *way* to pass it on."

"You've got a point." The ghost considers this. "That makes sense. Logic."

"So get it off me!"

"However, again you forget lust. Lust overcomes logic."

"Stop! Off!"

"The King of Sweden," muses the old writer, "speaks no Hebrew. That will be a difficulty. I suppose I ought to begin to study Swedish."

"Off! Off!" yells the student. And tugs at his head, yanks at the crown, pulling, pulling, seizing it by the cold points. He throws himself down, wedges his legs against the writer's desk, tumbling after leverage; nothing works. Then he kneels, lays his head on the floor, and methodically begins to beat the crown against the wooden floor. He jerks, tosses, taps, his white head in the brilliant crown is a wild flashing hammer; then he catches at his chest; his knuckles explode; then again he beats, beats, beats the crown down. But it stays stuck, no blow can knock it free. He beats. He heaves his head. Sparks spring from the crown, small lightnings leap. Oh, his chest, his ribs, his heart! The vial, where is the vial? His hands squirm toward his throat, his chest, his pocket. And his head beats the crown down against the floor. The old head halts, the head falls, the crown stays stuck, the heart is dead.

"Expired," says the ghost of Tchernikhovsky.

Well, that should be enough. No use making up any more of it. Why should I? It is not my story. It is not the goat's story. It is no one's story. It is a story nobody wrote, nobody wants, it has no existence. What does the notion of a *ba'al ga'avah* have to do with a silver crown? One belongs to morals, the other to magic. Stealing from two disparate tales, I smashed their elements one into the other. Things must be brought together. In magic all divergences are linked and locked. The fact is, I forced the crown onto the ambitious student in order to punish.

To punish? Yes. In life I am, though obscure, as generous and reasonable as those whom wide glory has sweetened; earlier you saw how generously and reasonably I dealt with the goat. So I am used to being taken for everyone's support, confidante, and consolation—it did not surprise me, propped there against that wall in the dark, when the goat begged me to read his story. Why should he not? My triumph is that, in my unrenown, everyone trusts me not to lie. But I always lie. Only on paper I do not lie. On paper I punish, I am malignant.

For instance: I killed off the student to punish him for arrogance. But it is really the goat I am punishing. It is an excellent thing to punish him. Did he not make his hero a student at the yeshiva, did he not make him call himself "religious"? But what is that? What is it to be "religious"? Is religion any differnt from magic? Whoever intends to separate them ends in proving them to be the same.

The goat was a *ba'al ga'avah!* I understood that only a *ba'al ga'avah* would dare to write about "religion."

So I punished him for it. How? By transmuting piety into magic.

Then—and I require you to accept this with the suddenness I myself experienced it: *as if by magic*—again I was drawn to look into the goat's story; and I found, on the next-to-last page, an address. He had scrubbed out (I have already mentioned this) his name; but here was a street and a number:

18 Herzl Street
Brooklyn, N.Y.

A street fashioned—so to speak—after the Messiah. Here I will halt you once more to ask you to take no notice of the implications of the goat's address. It is an aside worthy of the goat himself. It is he, not I, who would grab you by the sleeve here and now in order to explain exactly who Theodor Herzl was—oh, how I despise writers who will stop a story dead for the sake of showing off! Do you care whether or not Maimonides (supposing you had ever heard of that lofty saint) tells us that the Messianic age will be recognizable simply by the resumption of Jewish political independence? Does it count if, by that definition, the Messiah turns out to be none other than a Viennese journalist of the last century? Doubtless Herzl was regarded by his contemporaries as a *ba'al ga'avah* for brazening out, in a modern moment, a Hebrew principality. And who is more of a *ba'al ga'avah* than the one who usurps the Messiah's own job? But thank God I have no taste for these notions. Already you have seen how earnestly my mind is turned toward hatred of metaphysical speculation. Practical action is my whole concern, and I have nothing but contempt for significant allusions, nuances, buried effects.

Therefore you will not be astonished at what I next undertook to do. I went—ha!—to the street of the Messiah to find the goat.

It was a place where there had been conflagrations. Rubble tentatively stood: brick on brick, about to fall. One remaining configuration of wall, complete with windows but no panes. The sidewalk underfoot stirred with crumbs, as of sugar grinding: mortar reduced to sand. A desert flushed over tumbled yards. Lintels and doors burned out, foundations squared like patterns on a beach: in this spot once there had been cellars, stoops, houses. The smell of burned wood wandered. A civilization of mounds—who had lived here? Jews. There were no buildings left. A rectangular stucco fragment—of what? synagogue maybe—squatted in a space. There was no Number 18—only bad air, light flying in the gape and gash where the fires had driven down brick, mortar, wood, mothers, fathers, children pressing library cards inside their pockets—gone, finished.

And immediately—as if by magic—the goat!

"You!" I hooted, exactly as, in the story that never was, the old writer had cried it to Tchernikhovsky's shade.

"You've read my stuff," he said, gratified. "I knew you could find me easy if you wanted to. All you had to do was want to."

"Where do you live?"

"Number eighteen. I knew you'd want to."

"There isn't any eighteen."

He pointed. "It's what's left of the shul. No plumbing, but it still has a good kitchen in the back. I'm what you call a squatter, you don't mind?"

"Why should I mind?"

"Because I stole the idea from a book. It's this story about a writer who lives in an old tenement with his typewriter and the tenement's about to be torn down—"

The famous author who had written about the magic crown had written that story too; I reflected how some filch their fiction from life, others filch their lives from fiction. What people call inspiration is only pilferage. ''You're not living in a tenement,'' I corrected, ''you're living in a synagogue.''

''What used to be. It's a hole now, a sort of cave. The ark is left, though. You want to see the ark?''

I followed him through shards. There was no front door.

''What happened to this neighborhood?'' I said.

''The Jews went away.''

''Who came instead?''

''Fire.''

The curtain of the ark dangled in charred shreds. I peered inside the orifice which had once closeted the scrolls: all blackness there, and the clear sacrificial smell of things that have been burned.

''See?'' he said. ''The stove works. It's the old wood-burning kind. For years they didn't use it here, it just sat. And now —resurrection.'' Ah: the clear sacrificial smell was potatoes baking.

''Don't you have a job?''

''I write. I'm a writer. And no rent to pay, anyhow.''

''How do you drink?''

''You mean *what*.'' He held up a full bottle of Schapiro's kosher wine. ''They left a whole case intact.''

''But you can't wash, you can't even use the toilet.''

''I pee and do my duty in the yard. Nobody cares. This is freedom, lady.''

''Dirt,'' I said.

''What's dirt to Peter is freedom to Paul. Did you like my story? Sit.''

There was actually a chair, but it had a typewriter on it. The goat did not remove it.

''How do you take a bath?'' I persisted.

''Sometimes I go to my cousin's. I told you. The rabbi's wife.''

''The rabbi from this synagogue?''

''No, he's moved to Woodhaven Boulevard. That's Queens. All the Jews from here went to Queens, did you know that?''

''*What* rabbi's wife?'' I blew out, exasperated.

''I *told* you. The one with the crown. The one they wrote about in the papers. The one *he* lifted the idea of that story from. A rip-off that was. My cousin ought to sue.''

''All stories are rip-offs,'' I said. ''Shakespeare stole his plots. Dostoevski dug them out of the newspaper. Everybody steals. The *Decameron*'s stolen. Whatever looks like invention is theft.''

''Great,'' he said, ''that's what I need. Literary talk.''

''What did you mean, you knew I would want to come? Believe me, I didn't come for literary talk.''

''You bet. You came because of my cousin. You came because of the crown.''

I was amazed: instantly it coursed in on me that this was true. I had come because of the crown; I was in pursuit of the crown.

I said: ''I don't care about the crown. I'm interested in the rabbi himself. The crown-blesser. What I care about is the psychology of the thing.''

This word—''psychology''—made him cackle. ''He's in jail, I thought you knew that. They got him for fraud.''

''Does his wife still have any crowns around?''

''One.''

''Here's your story,'' I said, handing it over. ''Next time leave your name in. You don't have to obliterate it, rely on the world for that.''

The pus on his eyelids glittered. ''Alex will obliterate the world, not vice versa.''

''How? By bombing it with stories? The first anonymous obliteration. The Flood without a by-line,'' I said. ''At least everything God wrote was publishable. Alex what?''

''Goldflusser.''

''You're a liar.''

''Silbertsig.''

''Cut it out.''

''Kupferman. Bleifischer. Bettler. Kenigman.''

''All that's mockery. If your name's a secret—''

''I'm lying low, hiding out, they're after me because I helped with the crowns.''

I speculated, ''You're the one who made them.''

''No. She did that.''

''Who?''

''My cousin. The rabbi's wife. She crocheted them. What he did was go buy the form—you get it from a costume loft, stainless steel. She used to make these little pointed sort of *gloves* for it, to protect it, see, and the shine would glimmer through, and then the customer would get to keep the crown cover, as a sort of guarantee—''

''My God,'' I said, ''what's all that about, why didn't *she* go to jail?''

''Crocheting isn't a crime.''

''And you?'' I said. ''What did you do in all that?''

''Get customers. Fraudulent solicitation, that's a crime.''

He took the typewriter off the chair and sat down. The wisp of beard wavered. ''Didn't you like my story?'' he accused. The pages were pressed with an urgency between his legs.

''No. It's all fake. It doesn't matter if you've been to Jerusalem. You've got the slant of the place all wrong. It doesn't matter about the yeshiva either. It doesn't matter if you really went to see some old geezer over there, you didn't get anything right. It's a terrible story.''

''Where do you come off with that stuff?'' he burst out. ''Have *you* been to Jerusalem? Have *you* seen the inside of a yeshiva?''

''No,'' I said.

''So!''

''I can tell when everything's fake,'' I said. ''What I mean by fake is raw. When no one's ever used it before, it's something new under the sun, a whole new combination, that's bad. A real story is whatever you can predict, it has to be familiar, anyhow you have to know how it's going to come out, no exotic new material, no unexpected flights—''

He pushed out at me: ''What you want is to bore people!''

''I'm a very boring writer,'' I admitted; out of politeness I kept from him how much his story, and even my own paraphrase of it, had already bored me. ''But in *principle* I'm right. The only good part in the whole thing was explaining about the *ba'al ga'avah*. People hate to read foreign words, but at least it's ancient wisdom. Old, old stuff.''

Then I told him how I had redesigned his story to include a ghost.

He opened the door of the stove and threw his manuscript in among the black-skinned potatoes.

''Why did you do that?''

''To show you I'm no *ba'al ga'avah*. I'm humble enough to burn up what somebody doesn't like.''

I said suspiciously, ''You've got other copies.''

''Sure. Other potatoes too.''

''Look,'' I said, riding malice, ''it took me two hours to find this place, I have to go to the yard.''

''You want to take a leak? Come over to my cousin's. It's not far. My cousin's lived in this neighborhood for sixty years.''

Furiously I went after him. He was a crook leading me to the house of crooks. We walked through barrenness and canker, a ruined city, store windows painted black, one or two curtained by gypsies, some boarded, barred, barbed, old newspapers rolling in the gutter, the sidewalks speckled with viscous blotch. Overhead a smell like kerosene, the breath of tenements. The cousin's toilet stank as if no one had flushed it in half a century; it had one of those tanks high up, attached to the ceiling, a perpetual drip running down the pull chain. The sink was in the kitchen. There was no soap; I washed my hands with Ajax powder while the goat explained me to his cousin.

''She's interested in the crown,'' he said.

''Out of business,'' said the cousin.

''Maybe for her,'' the goat said.

''Not doing business, that's all. For nobody whatsoever.''

"I'm not interested in buying one," I said. "Just in finding out."

"Crowns is against the law," the cousin said.

"For healing," the goat argued, "not for showing. She knows the man who wrote that story. You remember about that guy, I told you, this famous writer who took—"

"Who took! Too much fame," said the cousin, "is why Saul sits in jail. Before newspapers and stories we were left in peace, we helped people peacefully." She condemned me with an oil-surfaced eye, the colorless slick of the ripening cataract. "My husband, a holy man, him they put in jail. Him! A whole year, twelve months! A man like that! Brains, a saint—"

"But he fooled people," I said.

"In helping is no fooling. Out, lady. You had to pee, you peed. You needed a public facility, very good, now out. I don't look for extra customers for my toilet bowl."

"Good-bye," I said to the goat.

"You think there's hope for me?" he said.

"Quit writing about ideas. Stay out of the yeshiva, watch out for religion. Don't make up stories about famous writers."

"Listen," he said—his nose was splotched with pustules of lust, his nostrils gaped—"you didn't like that one, I'll give you another. I've got plenty more, I've got a grateful."

"What are you talking," said the cousin.

"She knows writers," he said, "in person. She knows how to get things published."

I protested, "I can hardly get published myself—"

"You published something?" said the cousin.

"A few things, not much."

"Alex, bring Saul's box."

"That's not the kind of stuff," the goat said.

The cousin said, "Definitely. About expression I'm not so concerned like you. What isn't so regular, anyone with a desire and a pencil can fix it."

The goat remonstrated, "What Saul has is something else, it's not *writing*—"

"With connections," said the cousin, "nothing is something else, everything is writing. Lady, in one box I got my husband's entire holy lifework. The entire theory of healing and making the dead ones come back for a personal appearance. We sent maybe to twenty printing houses, nothing doing. You got connections, I'll show you something."

"Print," I reminded her, "is what you said got the rabbi in trouble."

"Newspapers. Lies. False fame. Everything with a twist. You call him rabbi, who made from him a rabbi? The entire world says rabbi, so let it be rabbi. There he sits in jail, a holy man what did nothing his whole life to harm. Whatever a person asked for, this was what he gave. Whatever you wanted to call him, this was what he became. Alex! Take out Saul's box, it's in the bottom of the dresser with the crown."

"The crown?" I said.

"The crown is nothing. What's something is Saul's brain. Alex!" the cousin commanded.

The goat shut his nostrils. He gave a snicker and disappeared. Through the kitchen doorway I glimpsed a sagging bed and heard a drawer grind open.

He came back lugging a carton with a picture of tomato cans on it. On top of it lay the crown. It was gloved in a green pattern of peephole diamonds.

"Here," said the cousin, "is Saul's ideas. Listen, that famous writer what went to steal from the papers—a fool. If he could steal what's in Saul's brain, what would he need a newspaper? Read!" She dipped a fist into a hiss of sheets and foamed up a sheaf of them. "You'll see, the world will rush to put in print. The judge at the trial—I said to him, look in Saul's box, you'll see the truth, no fraud. If they would read Saul's papers, not only would he not sit in jail, the judge with hair growing from his ears they would throw out!"

I looked at the goat; he was not laughing. He reached out and put the crown on my head.

It felt lighter than I imagined. It was easy to forget you were wearing it.

I read:

Why does menkind not get what they wish for? This is an easy solution. He is used to no. Always no. So it comes he is afraid to ask.

"The power of positive thinking," I said. "A philosopher."

"No, no," the cousin intervened, "not a philosopher, what do philosophers know to heal, to make real shadows from the dead?"

Through thinning threads of beard, the goat said, "Not a philosopher."

I read:

Everything depends what you ask. Even you're not afraid to ask, plain asking is not sufficient. If you ask in a voice, there got to be an ear to listen in. The ear of Ha-shem, King of the Universe. (His Name we don't use it every minute like a shoelace.) A Jew don't go asking Ha-shem for inside information, for what reason He did this, what ideas He got on that, how come He let happen such-and-such a pogrom, why a good person loved by one and all dies with cancer, and a lousy bastard he's rotten to his partner and cheats and plays the numbers, this fellow lives to 120. With questions like this don't expect no replies, Ha-shem don't waste breath on trash from fleas. Ha-shem says, My secrets are My secrets, I command you what you got to do, the rest you leave to Me. This is no news that He don't reveal His deepest business. From that territory you get what you deserve, silence.

"What are you up to?" said the goat.

"Silence." I said.

"Ssh!" said the cousin. "Alex, so let her read in peace!"

For us, not one word. He shuts up, His mouth is locked. So how come G-d conversed in history with Adam, with Abraham, with Moses? All right, you can argue that Moses and Abraham was worth it to G-d to listen to, what they said Ha-shem wanted to hear. After all they fed Him back His own ideas. An examination, and already they knew the answers. Smart guys, in the whole history of menkind no one else like these couple of guys. But with Adam, new and naked with no clothes on, just when the whole world was born, was Adam different from me and you? What did Adam know? Even right from wrong he didn't know yet. And still G-d thought, to Adam it's worthwhile to say a few words. I'm not wasting my breath. So what was so particular about Adam that he got Ha-shem's attention, and as regards me and you He don't blink an eye? Adam is better than me and you? We don't go around like a nudist colony, between good and lousy we already know what's what, with or without apples. To me and you G-d should also talk!

"You're following?" the cousin urged. "You see what's in Saul's brain? A whole box full like this, and sits in jail!"

But when it comes wishes, when it comes dreams, who says no? Who says Ha-shem stops talking? Wishes, dreams, imaginations—like fishes in the head. Ha-shem put in Joseph's head two good dreams, were they lies? The truth and nothing but the truth! Q.E.D. To Adam Ha-shem spoke one way, and when He finishes with Moses He talks another way. In a dream, in a wish. That apikoros Sigmund Freud, he also figured this out. Whomever says Sigmund Freud stinks from sex, they're mistaken. A wish is the voice, a dream is the voice, an imagination is the voice, all is the voice of Ha-shem the Creator. Naturally a voice is a biological thing, who says no? Whatsoever happens inside the human is a biological thing.

"What are you up to?" the goat asked again.

"Biology," I said.

"Don't laugh. A man walked in here shaking all over, he walked out okay, I saw it myself."

The cousin said mournfully, "A healer."

The goat said, "I wrote a terrific story about that guy, I figured what he had was cystic fibrosis, I can show you—"

"There isn't any market for medical stories," I said.

"This was a miracle story."

"There are no miracles."

"That's right!" said the cousin. She dug down again into the box. "One time only, instead of plain writing down, Saul made up a story on this subject exactly. On a yellow piece of paper. Aha, here. Alex, read aloud."

The goat read:

One night in the middle of dim stars Ha-shem said, No more miracles! An end with miracles, I already did enough, from now on nothing.

So a king makes an altar and bows down. "O Ha-shem, King of the Universe, I got a bad war on my hands and I'm taking a beating. Make a miracle and save the whole country." Nothing doing, no miracle.

Good, says Ha-shem, this is how it's going to be from now on.

So along comes the Germans, in the camp they got a father and a little son maybe twelve years old. And the son is on the list to be gassed tomorrow. So the father runs around to find a German to bribe, G-d knows what he's got to bribe him with, maybe his wife's diamond ring that he hid somewhere and they didn't take it away yet. And he fixes up the whole thing, tomorrow he'll bring the diamond to the German and they'll take the boy off the list and they won't kill him. They'll slip in some other boy instead and who will know the difference?

Well, so that could be the end, but it isn't. All day after everything's fixed up, the father is thinking and thinking, and in the middle of the night he goes to an old rabbi that's in the camp also, and he tells the rabbi he's going to save his little son.

And the rabbi says, "So why come to me? You made your decision already." The father says, "Yes, but they'll put another boy in his place." The rabbi says, "Instead of Isaac, Abraham put a ram. And that was for G-d. You put another child, and for what? To feed Moloch."

The father asks, "What is the law on this?"

"The law is, Don't kill."

The next day the father don't bring the bribe. And his eyes don't never see his beloved little child again. Well, so that could be the end, but it isn't. Ha-shem looks at what's happening, here is a man what didn't save his own boy so he wouldn't be responsible with killing someone else. Ha-shem says to Himself, I made a miracle anyhow. I blew in one man so much power of My commandments that his own flesh and blood he lets go to Moloch, so long he shouldn't kill. That I created even one such person like this is a very great miracle, and I didn't even notice I was doing it. So now positively no more.

And after this the destruction continues, no interruptions. Not only the son is gassed, but also the father, and also the boy what they would have put in his place. And also and also and also, until millions of bones of alsos goes up in smoke. About miracles Ha-shem don't change His mind except by accident. So the question menkind has to ask their conscience is this: If the father wasn't such a good commandment-keeper that it's actually a miracle to find a man like this left in the world, what could happen instead? And if only one single miracle could slip through before G-d notices it, which one? Suppose this father didn't use up the one miracle, suppose the miracle is that G-d will stop the murderers altogether, suppose! Instead: nothing doing, the father on account of one kid eats up the one miracle that's lying around loose. For the sake of one life, the whole world is lost.

But on this subject, what's written in our holy books? What the sages got to say? The sages say different: If you save one life only, it's like the whole world is saved. So which is true? Naturally, whatever's written is what's true. What does this prove? It proves that if you talk miracle, that's when everything becomes false. Men and women! Remember! No stories from miracles! No stories and no belief!

"You see?" said the cousin. "Here you have Saul's theories exactly. Whoever says miracles, whoever says magic, tells a lie. On account of a lie a holy man sits in a cage."

"And the crown?" I asked.

She ignored this. "You'll help to publish. You'll give to the right people, you'll give to connections—"

"But why? Why do you need this?"

"What's valuable you give away, you don't keep it for yourself," the cousin said. "Listen, is the Bible a secret? The whole world takes from it. Is Talmud a secret? Whatever's a lie should be a secret, not what's holy and true!"

I appealed to the goat. He was licking his fingertips. "I can't digest any of this—"

"You haven't had a look at Saul," he said, "that's why."

The cousin said meanly, "I saw you put on her the crown."

"She wants it."

"The crown is nothing."

"She wants it."

"Then show her Saul."

"You mean in prison?" I said.

"In the bedroom on the night table."

The goat fled. This time he returned carrying a small gilded tin frame. In it was a snapshot of another bearded man.

"Look closely."

But instead of examining the photograph, I all at once wanted to study the goat's cousin. She was one of those tiny twig-thin old women who seem to enlarge the more you get used to their voices. She was wearing a checked nylon housedress and white socks in slippers, above which bulged purplish varicose nodules. Her eyes were terribly magnified by metal-rimmed lenses, and looked out at me with the vengefulness of a pair of greased platters. I was astonished to see that a chromium crown had buried itself among the strings of her wandering hairs: having been too often dyed ebony, they were slipping out of their follicles and onto her collarbone. She had an exaggerated widow's peak and was elsewhere a little bit bald.

The goat too wore a crown.

"I thought there was only one left," I objected.

"Look at Saul, you'll see the only one," the cousin said.

The man in the picture wore a silver crown. I recognized him though the light was shut off in him and the space of his flesh was clearly filled.

"Who is this?" I said.

"Saul."

"But I've seen him!"

"That's right," the cousin said.

"Because you wanted to," said the goat.

"The ghost I put in your story," I reminded him, "this is what it looked like."

The cousin breathed. "You published that story?"

"It's not even written down."

"Whose ghost was it?" asked the goat.

"Tchernikhovsky's. The Hebrew poet. A *ba'al ga'avah*. He wrote a poem called *Before the Statue of Apollo*. In the last line God is bound with leather thongs."

"Who binds him?"

"The Jews. With their phylacteries. I want to read more," I said.

The two of them gave me the box. The little picture they set on the kitchen table, and they stood over me in their twinkling crowns while I splashed my hands through the false rabbi's stories. Some were already browning at the margins, in ink turned violet; some were on lined school paper, written with a ball-point pen. About a third were in Yiddish; there was even a thin notebook all in Russian; but most were pressed out in pencil in an immigrant's English on all kinds of odd loose sheets, on the insides of old New Year greeting cards, the backs of cashiers' tapes from the supermarket, in one instance on the ripped-out leather insides of an old wallet.

Saul's ideas were: sorcery, which he denied—levitation, which he doubted—magic, which he sneered at—miracles, which he denounced—healing, which he said belonged in hospitals—instant cures, which he said were fancies and delusions—the return of deceased loved ones, which he said were wishful hallucinations —the return of dead enemies, which ditto—plural gods, which he disputed—demons, which he derided—amulets, which he disparaged and repudiated—Satan, from which hypothesis he scathingly dissented.

He ridiculed everything. He was a rationalist.

"It's amazing," I said, "that he looks just like Tchernikhovsky."

"What does Tchernikhovsky look like?" one of the two crowned ones asked me, and I was no longer sure which.

"I don't know, how should I know? Once I saw his picture in an anthology of translations, but I don't remember it. Why are there so many crowns in this room? What's the point of these crowns?"

Then I found the paper on crowns:

You take a real piece mineral, what kings wear. You put it on, you become like a king. What you wish, you get. But what you get you shouldn't believe in unless it's real. How do you know when something's real? If it lasts. How long? This depends. If you wish for a Pyramid, it should last as long like a regular Pyramid lasts. If you wish for long life, it should last as long like your own grandfather. If you wish for a Magic Crown, it should last as long like the brain what it rests on.

I interrupted myself: "Why doesn't he wish himself out of prison? Why didn't he wish himself out of getting sentenced?"

"He lets things take their course," said one of the two in crowns.

Then I found the paper on things taking their course:

From my own knowledge I knew a fellow what loved a woman, Beylinke, and she died. So he looked and looked for a twin to this Beylinke, and it's no use, such a woman don't exist. Instead he married a different type altogether, and he made her change her name to Beylinke and make love on the left side, like the real Beylinke. And if he called Beylinke! and she forgot to answer (her name was Ethel) he gave her a good knock on the back, and one day he knocked hard into the kidney and she got a growth and she died. And all he got from his forcing was a lonesome life.

Everything is according to destiny, you can't change nothing. Not that anybody can know what happens before it happens, not even Ha-shem knows which dog will bite which cat next week in Persia.

"Enough," said one of the two in the crowns. "You read and you took enough. You ate enough and you drank enough from this juice. Now you got to pay."

"To pay?"

"The payment is, to say thank you what we showed you everything, you take and you publish."

"Publishing isn't the same as Paradise."

"For some of us it is," said one.

"She knows from Paradise!" scoffed the other.

They thrust the false rabbi's face into my face.

"It isn't English, it isn't even coherent, it's inconsistent, it's crazy, nothing hangs together, nobody in his right mind would—"

"Connections you got."

"No."

"That famous writer."

"A stranger."

"Then somebody else."

"There's no one. I can't make magic—"

"*Ba'al ga'avah!* You're better than Saul? Smarter? Cleverer? You got better ideas? You, a nothing, they print, and he sits in a box?"

"I looked up one of your stories. It stank, lady. The one called *Usurpation*. Half of it's swiped; you ought to get sued. You don't know when to stop. You swipe other people's stories and you go on and on, on and on. I fell asleep over it. Boring! Long-winded!"

The mass of sheets pitched into my lap. My fingers flashed upward; there was the crown, with its crocheted cover, its blunted points. Little threads had gotten tangled in my hair. If I tugged, the roots would shriek. Tchernikhovsky's paper eyes looked frightened. Crevices opened on either side of his nose and from the left nostril the grey bone of his skull poked out, a cheekbone like a pointer.

"I don't have better ideas," I said. "I'm not interested in ideas, I don't care about ideas. I hate ideas. I only care about stories."

"Then take Saul's stories!"

"Trash. Justice and mercy. He tells you how to live, what to do, the way to think. Righteousness fables, morality tales. Didactic stuff. Rabbinical trash," I said. "What I mean is *stories*. Even you," I said to the goat, "wanting to write about writers! Morality, mortality! You people eat yourself up with morality and mortality!"

"What else should a person eat?"

Just then I began to feel the weight of the crown. It pressed into the secret tunnels of my brain. A pain like a grief leaped up behind my eyes. Every point of it was a spear, a nail. The crown was no different from the bone of my head. The false rabbi Tchernikhovsky tore himself from the tin prison of his frame and sped to the ceiling as if gassed. He had bluish teeth and goblin's wings. Except for the collar and cravat that showed in the photograph, below his beard he was naked. His eyeballs were glass, like a doll's. He was solid as a doll; I was not so light-headed as to mistake him for an apparition. His voice was as spindly as a harpsichord:

"Choose!"

"Between what and what?"

"The Creator or the creature. God or god. The Name of Names or Apollo."

"Apollo," I said on the instant.

"Good," he tinkled, "blessings," he praised me, "flowings and flowings, streams, brooks, lakes, waters out of waters."

Stories came from me then, births and births of tellings, narratives and suspenses, turning points and palaces, foam of the sea, mermen sewing, dragons pullulating out of quicksilver, my mouth was a box, my ears flowed, they gushed legends and tales, none of them of my own making, all of them acquired, borrowed, given, taken, inherited, stolen, plagiarized, usurped, chronicles and sagas invented at the beginning of the world by the offspring of giants copulating with the daughters of men. A king broke out of the shell of my left eye and a queen from the right one, the box of my belly lifted its scarred lid to let out frogs and swans, my womb was cleft and stories burst free of their balls of blood. Stories choked the kitchen, crept up the toilet tank, replenished the bedroom, knocked off the goat's crown, knocked off the cousin's crown, my own crown in its coat contended with the vines and tangles of my hair, the false rabbi's beard had turned into strips of leather, into whips, the whips struck at my crown, it slid to my forehead, the whips curled round my arm, the crown sliced the flesh of my forehead.

At last it fell off.

The cousin cried out her husband's name.

"Alex," I called to the goat: the name of a conqueror, Aristotle's pupil, the arrogant god-man.

In the hollow streets which the Jews had left behind there were scorched absences, apparitions, usurpers. Someone had broken the glass of the kosher butcher's abandoned window and thrown in a pig's head, with anatomical tubes still dripping from the neck.

When we enter Paradise there will be a cage of storywriters, who will be taught as follows:

All that is not Law is levity.

But we have not yet ascended. The famous writer has not. The goat has not. The false rabbi has not; he sits out his year. A vanity press is going to bring out his papers. The bill for editing, printing, and binding will be $1,847.45. The goat's cousin will pay for it from a purse in the bottom bowel of the night table.

The goat inhabits the deserted synagogue, drinking wine, littering the yard with his turds. Occasionally he attends a public reading. Many lusts live in his chin hairs, like lice.

Only Tchernikhovsky and the shy old writer of Jerusalem have ascended. The old writer of Jerusalem is a fiction; murmuring psalms, he snacks on leviathan and polishes his Prize with the cuff of his sleeve. Tchernikhovsky eats nude at the table of the nude gods, clean-shaven now, his limbs radiant, his youth restored, his sex splendidly erect, the discs of his white ears sparkling, a convivial fellow; he eats without self-restraint from the celestial menu, and when the Sabbath comes (the Sabbath of Sabbaths, which flowers every seven centuries in the perpetual Sabbath of Eden), as usual he avoids the congregation of the faithful before the Footstool and the Throne. Then the taciturn little Canaanite idols call him, in the language of the spheres, kike.

Do Not Worry About the Bear

MICHAEL ROGERS

They were sitting on a flat grey boulder of granite, still warm from the noon sun, eating bread and cheese before making camp, when they saw the grizzly come out of the dark fir trees on the other side of the shallow river. She saw the grizzly first, perhaps thirty yards distant, and froze and touched his arm very gently.

He stopped, a piece of pale cheese in one hand, and stared out across the valley. The bear was a very dark brown, a bit lighter toward the belly, and he stood on all fours, unmoving, on the scrubby ground between the river and the trees, facing east, up the valley. From this distance he appeared to be the size of an automobile.

"Jesus," she said, very quietly, "Jesus Christ."

"Just don't move," he said, not taking his eyes from the opposite shore. "Just stay still." There was some breeze, quite cool in the late afternoon sun, but the grizzly was almost directly upwind.

The bear took about five minutes to move twenty yards up the valley, staying at the ragged edge of the trees, not approaching the water. He appeared to be there simply for the last yellowing rays of the sun. Even from thirty yards, when the bear walked, they could see the muscled flesh behind his shoulders move beneath the dark fur. He was very large. After several minutes he turned abruptly away from the stream and headed back into the darkness of the low trees.

"My God," she said, after the animal had been gone for a few moments. She rubbed her small hands up and down the sleeves of her thin red hiking shirt. "I never knew they were so big."

"I don't know," he said slowly. He had returned to eating his cheese, but his gaze was still directed across the river. "I think that was a pretty big one."

She went over to her pack and pulled out her wool shirt. "Should we stay here tonight?"

"Sure," he said. In less than an hour it would be dark. "Why not?"

Although they had planned to reach this valley one day earlier, the rides out of Banff had been slow and by the time they reached the trail-head off the highway, it was so late that they slept behind a boarded-up tourist lodge for the night. In the morning, an hour or so past dawn, they started up the trail that followed for most of fifteen miles along the rocky and turbulent lower cascades of the stream. Now, in the glaciated flat of the high valley, the frigid water flowed calm and shallow. It had been an unusual autumn—one of several in a row—and even though it was not yet October, icicles and delicate accretions of frozen spray already decorated the most deeply shaded falls and pools.

"It's going to be colder than hell tonight," she said, buttoning her wool shirt, then tugging the waffled sleeves of her thermal undershirt down where the outer shirt had pulled them up. The shade had already overtaken them, the other side of the river was just losing the sunlight, and now only the snowfields and glaciers high on the peaks surrounding the valley still reflected the deep orange of the sunset they could not see. "It's those glaciers," she said. "The wind comes down those glaciers and picks up the cold and dumps it right in the valleys. I can smell the snow in the air."

He nodded as he finished his cheese, then stood up, feeling his ears. "Colder than hell," he agreed, and looked through his pack for his cap. As he located it, he looked up and caught her staring across the river. "You worried about the bear?"

"No." She shook her head briefly and pushed her hands into the pockets of her faded jeans. They had taken hot showers in Banff and now, in this light, her short brown hair was clean and golden. "I never saw a grizzly before," she said, "not close up. In real life."

"They don't bother you if you don't bother them." He put his hair under the bright yellow wool stocking cap and pulled it over the top of his ears. "That's what you told me."

"I know," she said. "If I'm worried, I'll tell you." She rubbed her arms. "It's getting cold fast."

"Put your jacket on."

They had talked about the grizzlies before. They had even talked about them those first nights, sprawled on the living-room floor of their small Los Angeles apartment, awash in a sea of maps and travel books and hiking guides, preparing the itinerary for their assault on the Canadian Rockies. He had been eager for the long-planned trip; she, less so. It had already been agreed, at her suggestion, that at the end of the fall they would separate and live apart. He had hoped then that the trip might pull them back together; he would soon turn thirty-one, she had just passed twenty-two, and to lose her now, after almost two years together, seemed a collapse so serious that he had simply decided to refuse it. Thus far he was uncertain of his success. They had been on the road now for three weeks, up through Oregon and Washington and along the Trans-Canada to Banff, and in that time, depending on circumstance, she had been alternately tense and loving. Now, however, in the midst of this exalted landscape, the quarrel seemed distant, suspended.

As sunlight drained from the sides of the peaks to the east, they lifted their packs and walked a few hundred feet up the dry bed of the stream. They left their packs at a flat space of pine-sheltered ground and continued up the stream bed to gather wood, bringing back long dry boughs of birch and pine from a clump undercut and toppled by the stream a few springs before. He broke the limbs into firewood while she went down the bank to draw water. By the time she returned, he had started the fire and laid their thin grill over a triangle of rocks.

"I sure hope I still have that cornmeal," she said. "I thought about it today and I couldn't remember where I put it." She started to dig through her pack, uprooting clothes and carrots and onions and bags of cereal, and then suddenly there was the soft clatter of plastic on hard dirt.

"You dropped the flashlight," he said quietly, sliding a birch branch into the fire.

"I know I dropped the flashlight." She picked it up and he could hear her snapping the switch back and forth. "Goddamnit."

"Those bulbs break easily," he said. "I think they make them to break."

"Shit."

"You have a spare?"

She shook her head, biting gently at her upper lip.

"Let me try."

She handed it to him across the fire circle. He snapped the switch on and then smacked the side of the flashlight against his palm, hard and rhythmically. Once or twice the light flickered.

"Hey," she said. "Hey."

The bulb refused to remain lit and finally he handed the flashlight back to her. "Sometimes you can fix them that way. You make the broken filament touch and it fuses itself."

She paused, flashlight in hand. "Forget it," she said finally, turning back to her pack and throwing the flashlight in carelessly. "Goddamn lousy thing."

Earlier in the day they had stopped at a nice pool down the trail, already dotted by chunks of floating ice, and she sat in the sun while he fished with some fresh salmon eggs purchased in Banff. In twenty minutes or so he had two big rainbows, each about fourteen inches, and he had cleaned the fish and wrapped them and placed them in his pack.

Now, while she set out the sleeping bags, he unwrapped the trout and cut off the heads and tails so they would fit the pan. If they were small fish, she would always insist on frying them intact. "It gives you handles," she would tell him. The first time they had eaten fish together, beside a river in Washington, she had cracked the cooked skulls with her teeth and sucked out the brains. He had no idea where she had thought of such a thing. She had noticed him watching with clear revulsion, and grinned at him, the greasy fish head still in front of her delicate mouth. "You don't like that?" she asked him. He had shrugged, looked down at his own fish, and since then she had never missed an opportunity to suck brains in his presence.

Tonight they ate quickly, rice and fish and fried onions, before the food cooled in the chill air. She finished first and used hot water from the pot to clean the frying pan. He gathered up all of their food into one of the stuff bags. "We might as well keep the food away from us tonight," he said. He closed the stuff bag tightly and tied it with a nylon line. He tied the other end to a small rock and went out about twenty feet from the campsite and tossed the rock over a fir limb, pulling the bag up until it hung like an effigy high in the branches.

When he returned to the campsite, she was down by the stream rinsing dishes. In the half-light he could just make out her silhouette, bulky in the down jacket, kneeling against the final luminous glow of the fast water.

"So cold," she said when she returned, carrying the clean dishes, the collar of her jacket turned up. "That water is so cold." She held her hands, blue at the nails, stretched flat above the low flames. "Goddamn," she said. "I hate that so much."

"Wasn't so long ago," he said, "that water was ice."

"I know," she said, turning her hands above the flames.

Soon she reached down and put another short stick on the fire. "I wasn't sure," she said finally, "down by the water, if I was hearing something in the trees on the other side."

"I guarantee you," he said, "that there's something in the trees. That's how the world works. Niches, they call it."

"I know," she said. "I mean something bigger."

"There's a lot of noises," he said. "That bear is ten miles away by now. He doesn't like neighbors anymore than we do."

"Uh huh," she said shortly. "I know."

When at last the darkness surrounded them totally, she went to her pack and rummaged around for a few moments and then walked out of the circle of firelight, behind his back. With a stick, he lifted their little grill off the fire and laid it aside and placed another of the dry birch logs on. In a minute or so she returned. She had something wrapped in a Kleenex and she leaned over the fire and tossed it in, burying it in the embers with a branch. In the instant before the flames took it, he thought he could see a tiny spot of blood on the white tissue.

He took a quick breath. "I didn't know you'd started," he said quietly.

She sat down on her rock, shoulders hunched, hands deep in her jacket pockets. "I did," she said, "this morning."

He stared at the blazing tissue buried in the coals. "You should have told me."

"I told you when I took my last pill, in Kamloops, remember?"

"How was I supposed to know?"

"You count on your fingers," she said, counting on her fingers. "Just like I do."

He shook his head and did not look at her. "Jesus," he repeated, almost to himself. "You could have told me."

"What's so important?" she said. "Now you know."

"Yeah," he said, and looked up, staring out past the circle of firelight. By now it was impossible to see anything beyond the radius of the blaze. Although he tried not to, he could not help looking across the river.

"Hey," she said, seeing the direction of his gaze. "Hey, wait a minute."

He looked back at her, saying nothing. Her tan face was dark in the firelight.

"Hey," she said, "there's something you're not saying."

He directed his eyes at the fire. "It's nothing," he said.

"It's about my period."

He shrugged, shook his head.

She stared at him intently. "They can smell it," she said slowly. "That's what you think. You think they can smell the blood."

"I don't know," he said softly, staring into the fire, trying to recall where he had heard the warning. "I really don't know. There's a lot of crazy stories."

She buried her hands deeper in the pockets of her jacket, gazing straight ahead. "Like sharks," she said.

"I don't know," he repeated, shaking his head, thinking hard. "I really don't know."

"Well, then maybe we should go down," she said with elaborate calm, not looking at him. "Maybe we should go down right now."

He stood and started to fasten the snaps on his jacket. "That's not a good idea," he said. "It's a little dark."

"Where are you going?" she asked.

"It's going to be fine," he said. "It's nothing to worry about." He finished the snaps. "I'm going to get some more wood."

She looked up at him. In the yellow light her eyes were very brown. "We've got a lot of wood."

"I think we might let the fire go all night."

She picked up a short branch, put it down again, brushed one hand across her forehead. "I was stupid," she said, but he was already gone, out past the edge of the firelight, to gather more wood.

"I think it's probably true," she said when he came back, dragging two long fir branches. "I've been thinking about it."

"Who knows?" he said. "We'll just keep a good fire going. Don't think about it."

He started to break the branches over a rock several feet from the fire. He raised his boot and brought the heel down sharply on the dry fir and the first crack in the night silence made him jump. "Maybe you could make up some of that tea," he said.

"Sure." She put two more branches on the fire and went to the packs.

He arranged another limb on the rock. "Any coffee left?"

"It's tied up in the tree," she said. "You just left the tea out."

"Tea's fine," he said, and broke the second limb, and this time, out of the corner of his eye, he saw her jump also.

Soon the fire had a thick bed of coals and was burning high and steady. They had pulled their flat rocks closer and now sat a few feet apart, he with his legs crossed, she with knees drawn up nearly to her chin. A sliver of moon had risen in the east, almost directly above the point on the bank where the bear had appeared.

"Some girls like periods," she said after a long silence. "Some girls say they like it because it makes them feel feminine."

"I guess that makes sense," he said, swallowing the last of his tea.

"I hate it," she said. "I think I always hated it."

He said nothing and stood up, walking around behind her to where the packs rested. When he returned with the bottle, she saw it glint in the firelight.

"None for me," she said.

He nodded, unscrewed the top of the pint, and poured the brandy carefully into the plastic cap. After he swallowed, he opened his mouth and inhaled the alcohol-filled air, rocking back and coughing as it stung his lungs. "All right," he said at last, "all right."

"But there's nothing you can do about it," she said. "You know?"

He raised the bottle and watched the firelight through the dark brown glass. "It's not your fault," he said finally.

She shook her head, very slightly and so quickly that he could not tell if it was gesture or shiver.

He drank again and this time when he set the bottle down, on the ground between them, she picked it up.

"I knew a girl once," she said, after they had half emptied the pint bottle, "who worked in this lodge in Yosemite Valley. I don't think you ever met this girl."

He nodded, said nothing, centering the bottle precisely between his boots.

"Anyway, this girl went camping with her boyfriend up near this waterfall and they woke up in the middle of the night and there was a big black bear walking around their camp looking for food. They just laid still because the bear was so close they didn't want to try to scare it away. Pretty soon the bear came over to her sleeping bag, maybe she spilled food on it or something, I don't know, and it started to roll her over. It was just a black bear, but it stuck its snout under her and rolled her over and over until it rolled her against this tree and she wouldn't roll any more. Then the bear went away. She stuck her head out of her sleeping bag and her boyfriend was gone. She went back to sleep and he came back two hours later with two rangers on horses. Everyone was really pissed at him."

He considered this, broke a stick for the fire. "What was he supposed to do?"

She shrugged. "I don't know," she said. "How should I know?"

He nodded and then there was a short stretch of silence. "Why don't you put your arm around me?" she said finally. "It's pretty cold."

He pulled his rock closer and put his arm around her waist, resting his hand on the rough denim over her thigh. "How's that?"

"All right."

"You thinking about the grizzly?"

She glanced at him briefly, half smiling. "What grizzly?"

"That's good," he said, and he sat with his arm around her until his knuckles were nearly frozen, and then he returned the hand to his jacket pocket.

After an hour or so there was a loud noise a distance up the slope above them, in the direction of the hanging stuff bag. He jerked his head around and stared out into the blackness for a long time. "Branches," he said finally. "Something small."

She continued to look into the fire, saying nothing.

"This is going to be a long night," he said.

"Let's talk some more."

"Okay."

"Your turn."

He leaned back and crossed his legs again in front of his rock. "That farm in Washington was nice." A young long-haired couple had given them a ride, then a place to sleep, on a small farm far from the highway, surrounded by apple trees. "I'd like a place like that sometime," he said. "It could be a nice life."

"The guy kept staring at my crotch," she said.

"Huh?"

"Yeah."

"I'll be damned," he said. "I didn't notice that."

She shrugged and held the brandy bottle up to determine its contents. "I think they wanted to swap around with us."

He frowned. "Why didn't they say something?"

"Oh, they said a lot of things, I think," she told him. "I don't know. Maybe I just imagined it."

He shook his head and stared at the fire. "Did you want to?"

"No," she said. "Of course not."

His back had started to ache, so he slid his rock farther from the fire, lowered himself to the ground, and used the piece of granite as a backrest.

"That can't be very comfortable," she said, watching him. "You can put your head in my lap if you want."

"No," he said. "This is fine."

Although he did not doze, his mind passed through moments of inattention, and it was some time before he noticed that she was growing agitated. She started by peeling the bark from branches with her fingers and then snapping the naked twigs into fragments; soon she had started to work on her fingernails.

"Hey," he said, "what you gonna have left to scratch my back with?"

She looked down at her nails and then up at him. "I'll use my teeth," she said.

"Well," he said, "okay," and looked back at the fire.

"Hey," she said, after a few more seconds had passed. "Fear of the dark. What's the fancy name for that?"

He had begun to use his pocketknife to whittle a stick of birch, and took a few more cuts in silence as he tried various names. "I don't know," he said finally. "Something-phobia, I guess."

"Because everybody's got it," she said.

"I'm not afraid of the dark," he said. "I may be afraid of what's in the dark, but not the dark itself."

"But if it's really dark, how do you know what's in it?"

He sawed off the point of the stick and started over again. "Because," he said, and then he said nothing more.

"Because you've never even thought about it," she said.

After hours had passed, the thin moon had climbed entirely through the archer and now hung high above the scorpion. Neither of them had said more than a few words for a long time, and then only to comment on some new noise. Once, a small rockfall, somewhere up the stream bed, had brought him clear to his feet.

Finally he walked out of the firelight to make a long steaming arc beneath the bright spill of the Milky Way, feeling the chill air and hearing the rush of the shallow water. Soon he was able to see the opposite bank of the river. The trees were blackness; the boulders and rocks of the bank a luminescent grey; the water a barely visible ribbon of light-flecked movement. In the other direction, the campfire was a bright orange flare in the center of a diminishing aura, capped with a colorless plume of smoke ascending on the light, disappearing without a trace into the night sky. He was surprised to see how close they had been sitting to the fire; the girl leaned forward on her rock, elbows on her knees, chin in hands, staring into the center of the fire. After a few moments she looked out into the darkness and called his name.

"Are you all right?"

"Fine."

When he returned to the fire, he suggested that she bring her sleeping bag over closer and try to get some sleep.

"I'm all right," she told him.

"You'll feel better if you sleep."

"You sleep," she said. "It's your idea. I'm okay."

"You sleep first, and I'll wake you up in a few hours and we'll trade."

"No thanks."

She appeared to concentrate on moving her boots to a position more distant from the fire. He picked up a stick of fir and snapped it in half over his leg and fed one portion to the fire.

"Don't you just hate this?" she said softly as he placed the stick.

He looked over at her quickly. She had sat up straight and was looking over the fire, into the darkness on the other side.

"What?"

"You heard me," she said. "I said don't you just hate this."

He started to examine the palm of one hand for new cuts and abrasions. "Ah," he said slowly, "you mean the whole trip, or up here, or just tonight, or the—"

"This whole thing," she said. "Being weak and scared."

"Who's weak and scared?"

She made a face. "Both of us. You and me. Tiny and blind, all huddled around a fire."

"Compared to the bear, you mean."

"Yeah," she said, after a moment. "Compared to the bear."

"Don't worry about the bear."

She had started to grow restless again, he noticed, standing up and sitting down and playing with twigs in the dirt. There was perhaps a quarter inch left in the brandy bottle and he handed it to her.

She finished it with one swallow.

"Now go lie down."

"No, damn it," she said quietly, "I already said I didn't want to lie down."

He shrugged and started to loosen the laces on his boots. "Long walk tomorrow."

"When I feel like lying down, I'll lie down," she said, her voice rising. "You're the one who's talking about it all the time, why don't you lie down?"

"Okay," he said. "Forget it."

She began to make a small pile of pebbles between her feet, stacking and unstacking, making patterns, shaking them in her hands like dice. Occasionally she would look up, glance from side to side out into the night. Finally she stood up.

"I have to go take a piss," she said.

He nodded, not looking up. "Don't get lost."

She zipped up her jacket and jammed her hands into her pockets and started out of the firelight circle, heading up the dry stream bed.

"It's easier to go the other direction," he called after her.

She gave no indication of hearing and in a moment he could see no more of her.

The fire had grown lower but now he was certain there would be wood enough to last the night. He broke a stick in two and built the blaze higher, leaning back to avoid the smoke of the new wood. He was not sleepy, and in fact the night had infused him with new energy. It was not a dangerous situation: he understood the danger was almost entirely in their minds, yet it was real enough to have an edge. It would be something they could talk about for a long time; at some point, it might even become humorous.

Soon the new wood was charred and blackened end to end and the girl had not returned. Once he heard a noise, at some distance, but now there was silence, and when he stood to look around, he could see nothing in any direction. It was odd because he had expected her to return in a matter of moments. He sat again, kicking the empty brandy bottle aside.

After ten minutes had passed, and he had heard no more sound, he stepped out of the circle of light and allowed his eyes to adjust. The narrow moon and the brightness of the Milky Way still gave enough light to make out some detail: the shape of boulders, the movement of water in the stream. There was no sign of her in the faintly luminous landscape that surrounded him.

Oh Christ, he thought. He reached for his sheath knife, hung on the right side of his belt, and tried the shiny leather cover, unsnap-ping and snapping it twice. There was no way she could have gotten into trouble. All she had to do was walk out ten feet and drop her pants and walk back. She was always quick; it should have taken her two minutes at most. Now it had been fifteen.

He took one more step away from the firelight and cupped his hands to his mouth and called her name.

The thin quality of his voice startled him in the night silence. He cleared his throat and tried again, more loudly, and heard a faint echo from some surface upstream. And then silence, except for the sound of the stream.

He called again.

He turned and faced the stream and yelled once, twice more, and this time his voice vanished without echo.

He would have to go out and look for her. He returned to the fire, his stomach feeling light, and sat to relace his boots more tightly. The rocky moraine made for treacherous walking, and he suddenly suspected that she had slipped and struck her head. It could have happened very quickly. He fastened his jacket while still sitting, and loaded four more pieces of birch onto the fire, stacked to burn slowly.

He sat a bit longer and tried twice to draw his hunting knife. It was difficult with the long parka closed and he considered moving his belt on top. Oh Christ, he thought again, and stood and started out into the darkness. He waited just outside the firelight until his eyes adjusted and then he began to move. He could barely see his footing in the blue night and so planted his feet carefully, testing for loose rock with each short step. Soon the campfire was a dot of orange behind him.

His vision improved quickly as he moved up the stream, and soon he could scan most of the distance back to the campfire and see that there was nothing but ground and rock. The girl was nowhere within sight. By now he was some distance from the campsite, and he paused and squatted down on the rocks to think. On one side the stream ran quietly, a soft constant rushing. On the other, scattered stands of trees—tall, black outlines—ran across the base of the mild slope that was itself invisible in the night.

Perhaps she had gone into the trees, although there was really no reason for her to do so. He decided that it would be worth a look: he would walk up to the trees and follow them back to the campsite, and then, if he had no luck, feed the fire again and think what next to do. Possibly he could fashion some sort of torch.

He crossed the thirty feet of rock and was into the trees quickly, and immediately the texture of the darkness changed. Even though this first stand of fir was sparse, the blackness was nearly total, and he had to step carefully, one hand in front of his face to ward off the thin branches he would not see until they stuck him. He had not even been thinking of the bear, but now, with his vision so foreshortened, he regretted sharply the loss of the flashlight. He tried to move through the trees as quickly as possible, watching closely for the girl, but still keeping a direct course.

It was in the third stand of trees, the most dense, at least thirty feet in length, that he was suddenly aware something large was nearby. At the sound of the cracking branch from the dark slope above him, he froze and dropped to one knee, a hand on his knife, unmoving for a long moment. Should he call her name? In that space of absolute concentration he felt as if every surface of his body had become sensitive to the night: a single elongated nerve. Silence met his concentration: the noise of the stream, now muted, and the beginnings of a quiet breeze. Nothing else.

After a few moments he rose to his feet and continued. The first priority was to get back to the campsite, to the fire that was already just a glow through the fir boughs. He stepped a few yards toward the stream, so that he moved just at the end of the stand. Cornered among the trees, he would have little chance, but on the rocks he could try to break for the campfire.

He moved another twenty feet with knife now in hand, hearing nothing more, peering between the dark trees, hoping that at least the pale face of the girl could be seen—the rest of her cloth-ing blue and invisible—but he saw nothing unusual. Nothing, in fact, at all.

He was still some distance from the glowing bed of the campfire when, abruptly, he felt a panic fill his lungs like water, a sense of being surrounded, an urgency that caused him to spin around and stare into the darkness, to the right, to the left, seeing nothing, hearing nothing, aware of nothing but the total alarm that electrified his blood, tightened his grip on the bone-handled knife, flogged his senses, and spun him around once more and started him, in long strides, for the orange smear of embers—and then, before even three steps were complete, a gentle touch landed on his right shoulder, the suddenness of shock multiplying its force a thousand-fold into a massive blow, and he turned once again, pulling back convulsively, crying out with wordless fear, but as he turned, the edge of his boot caught and he fell backward, onto the rocks, the knife flying from his hand and clattering back into the darkness as he barely caught himself, one hand thrown back to cushion his fall, one arm kept forward to guard his face, and graceless and hopeless and sprawling, he landed on the stream bed, staring up at the sky with eyes opened wide.

"Jesus!" a voice gasped from somewhere above him. "I'm sorry."

He gazed up, uncomprehending, unmoving, senses still screaming.

"I'm sorry," she said again, and then a vague black shape moved to help him up. "I thought you saw me. I was sitting on a rock up there."

He brushed away her arms and raised himself slowly from the ground. In the fall a rock had struck hard just above his left kidney and it was the pain, first of all, that cleared his head. When at last he stood, he stared into the faint circle of her face. "What the *hell*," he said finally, voice barely under control, "are you doing sitting out here in the goddamn *dark*?"

She took a half step backward and balanced herself with a touch against a tree trunk. "I was watching the stars," she said slowly. "I mean, I wanted to see the stars, and I wanted to be alone for a while."

His breath was still quick and short, and briefly he reached down to rub a new pain in his calf. "Fine," he said, "now let's go back to the fire."

He began to turn, and she reached out and touched the sleeve of his jacket. "I mean," she said, "don't be angry, just listen. As soon as I walked away from the fire and was alone, I wasn't afraid any more. Can you just try to understand that? That's what I wanted."

He gazed at the disk of face surrounded by dark parka. "Okay," he said, "I'm going back to the fire," and he turned and started out of the trees.

"Wait," she said.

He turned once more and saw, in the faint light, that she was holding her hand out. "I'm sorry," she said. "I'll come too."

He paused briefly, at the edge of the dark trees, and then walked back. He took her hand and then, before taking even a single step, they both heard the sound of an extremely large animal crossing the shallow stream very close to where they stood.

"Christ," he said, softly, urgently, and tugged once at her hand.

For a moment she hesitated, and he dropped her hand to run out of the trees onto the dry stream bed, and then stopped, the girl close behind him, his stomach, lungs, throat clenched and frozen, to stare blankly at their campfire, now smokeless and dead in the dim blue starlight that seemed suddenly to surround him with arms as long, as wide, as cold as the highest glacier above the valley.

Preparation for a Collie

JOY WILLIAMS

There is Jane and there is Jackson and there is David. There is the dog.

David is burying a bird. He has a carton in which cans of garbanzos were once packed. It is a large carton, much too large for the baby bird. David is digging a hole beneath the bedroom window. He mutters and cries a little. He is spending Sunday morning doing this. He is five.

Jackson comes outside and says, "It's too bad you didn't find a dead swan. It would have fit better in that hole."

Jackson is going to be an architect. He goes to school all day and he works as a bartender at night. He sees Jane and David on weekends. He is too tired in the morning to have breakfast with them. Jane leaves before nine. She sells imported ornaments in a Christmas shop, and Jackson is gone by the time Jane returns in the afternoon. David is in kindergarten all day. Jackson tends bar until long after midnight. Sometimes he steals a bottle of blended whiskey and brings it home with him. He has no taste in whiskeys. He acknowledges this to himself angrily. He wants to know what he is doing. He wears saddle shoes and a wedding ring. His clothes are poor but he has well-shaped hands and nails. Jane is usually asleep when Jackson gets in bed beside her. He goes at her without turning on the light.

"I don't want to wake you up," he says.

Jackson is from Virginia. Once, for some reason Jane forgets, a photograph of him in period dress appeared in *The New Yorker* for a VISIT WILLIAMSBURG· advertisement. They have saved the magazine. It is in their bookcase with their books.

Jackson packs his hair down hard with water when he leaves the house. The house is always a mess. It is not swept. There are crumbs and broken toys beneath all the furniture. There are cereal bowls everywhere, crusty with soured milk. There is hair everywhere. The dog sheds. It is a collie, three years older than David. It is Jane's dog. She brought it with her into this marriage, along with her Mexican bowls and something blue.

Jane could be pretty but she doesn't know how to arrange her hair. She has violet eyes. And she prefers that color. She has three pots of violets in the living room on Jackson's old chess table. They flourish. This is sometimes mentioned by Jackson. Nothing else flourishes as well here.

Whenever Jackson becomes really angry with Jane, he takes off his glasses and breaks them in front of her. They seem always to be the most valuable thing at hand. And they are replaceable, although the act causes considerable inconvenience.

Jane and David eat supper together every night. Jane eats like a child. Jane is closest to David in this. They are children together, eating junk. Jane has never prepared a meal in this house. She is as though in a seasonal hotel. This is not her life; she does not have to be this. She refuses to become familiar with this house, with this town. She is a guest here. She has no memories. She is waiting. She does not have to make anything of these moments. She is a stranger here.

She is waiting for Jackson to become an architect. His theories of building are realistic but his quest is oneiric, he tells her. He sometimes talks about "sites."

They are getting rid of the dog. Jackson has been putting ads in the paper. He is enjoying this. He has been advertising for weeks. The dog is free and many people call. Jackson refuses all callers. For three weekends now, he and Jane have talked about nothing except the dog. They realize that the absence of the dog will not alter their life, yet they cannot stop thinking about it, this dog, this act, this choice that lies before them.

The dog has crammed itself behind the pipes beneath the kitchen sink. David squats before him, blowing gently on his nose. The dog thumps its tail on the linoleum.

"We're getting rid of you, you know," David says.

Someone has stopped at the house to see the dog. It is Saturday evening.

"Is he a full-blooded collie?" the person asks. "Does he have papers?"

"He does not say," Jackson smiles.

After all these years, six, Jane is a little confused by Jackson. She sees this as her love for him. What would her love for him be if it were not this? In turn, she worries about her love for David. Jane does not think David is nice-looking. He has many worries, it seems. He weeps, he wets the bed, he throws up. He has pale hair, pale flesh. She does not know how she can go through all these days, each day, embarrassed for her son.

Jane and Jackson lie in bed.

"I love Sundays," Jane says.

Jackson wears a T-shirt. Jane slips her hand beneath it and strokes his chest. She is waiting. She sometimes fears that she is waiting for the waiting to end, fears that she seeks and requires only that recognition and none other. Jackson holds her without opening his eyes.

It is Sunday. Jane pours milk into a pancake mix.

Something gummy is stuck in David's hair. Jane gets a scissors and cuts it out.

Jackson says, "David, I want you to stop crying so much and I want you to stop pretending to bake in Mommy's cupcake tins." Jackson is angry, but then he laughs. After a moment, David laughs too.

That afternoon, a woman and a little girl come to the house about the dog.

"I told you on the phone, I'd give you some fresh eggs for him," the woman says, thrusting a child's sand bucket at Jane. "Even if you decide not to give the dog to us, the eggs, of course, are still yours." She pauses at Jane's hesitation. "Adams," the woman says.

Jackson waves her to a chair and says, "Mrs. Adams, we seek no personal aggrandizement from our pet. Our only desire is that he be given a good home. A great many people have contacted us and now we must make a difficult decision. Where will he inspire the most contentment and where will he be most contented?"

Jane brings the dog into the room.

"There he is, Dorothy!" Mrs. Adams exclaims to the little girl. "Go over and pet him or something."

"It's a nice dog," Dorothy says. "I like him fine."

"She needs a dog," Mrs. Adams says. "Coming over here, she said, 'Mother, we could bring him home today in the back of the car. I could play with him tonight.' Oh, she sure would like to have this dog. She lost her dog last week. A tragedy. Kicked to death by one of the horses. Must have broken every bone in his fluffy little body."

"That's a pity," Jackson says.

"And then there was the accident," Mrs. Adams goes on. "Show them your arm, Dorothy. Why, I tell you, it almost came right off. Didn't it, darling?"

The girl rolls up the sleeve of her shirt. Her arm is a mess, complexly rearranged, a yellow matted wrinkle of scar tissue.

"Actually," Jackson says, "I'm afraid my wife has promised the dog to someone else."

After they leave, Jackson says, "My God, weren't they brutish.

Like trained bears."

The dog walks slowly back to the kitchen, swinging its high foolish hips. David wanders back to the breakfast table and picks up something, some piece of food. He chews it for a moment and then spits it out. He kneels down and spits it into the hot-air register.

"David," Jane says. She looks at his face. It is calm and round, a child's face.

It is evening. On television, a man dressed as a chef, holding six pies, falls down a flight of stairs. The incident is teaching numbers.

SIX, the screen screams.

"Six," David says.

Jane and Jackson are drinking whiskey and apple juice. Jane is wondering what they did for David's last birthday, when he was five. Did they have a little party?

"What did we do on your last birthday, David?" Jane asks.

"We gave him pudding and tea," Jackson says.

"That's not true," Jane says, worried. She looks at David's face.

SIX TOCKING CLOCKS, the television sings.

"Six," David says.

Jane's drink is gone. "May I have another drink?" she asks politely, and then gets up to make it for herself. She knocks the ice cubes out of the tray and smashes them up with a wooden spoon. On the side of the icebox, held in place by magnets, is a fragment from a poem, torn from a book. It says, *The dead must fall silent when one sits down to a meal.*

Jane returns to the couch and David sits beside her. He says, "You say 'no' and I say 'yes.' "

"No," Jane says.

"Yes," David yells, delighted.

"No."

"Yes."

"No."

"Yes."

"Yes."

David stops, confused. Then he giggles. They play this game all the time. Jane is willing to play it with him. It is easy enough to play. Jackson and Jane send David to a fine kindergarten and are always buying him chalk and crayons. Nevertheless, Jane feels unsure with David. It is hard to know how to act when one is with the child, alone.

The dog sits by a dented aluminum dish in the bright kitchen. Jackson is opening a can of dog food.

"Jesus," he says, "what a sad, stupid dog."

The dog eats its food stolidly, gagging a little. The fur beneath its tail hangs in dirty beards.

"Jesus," Jackson says.

Jane goes to the cupboard, wobbling slightly. "I'm going to kill that dog," she says. "I'm sick of this." She puts down her drink and takes a can of Drano out of the cupboard. She takes a pound of hamburger which is thawing in a bowl and rubs off the soft pieces onto a plate. She pours Drano over it and mixes it in.

"It is my dog," Jane says, "and I'm going to get rid of him for you."

David starts to cry.

"Why don't you have another drink?" Jackson says to Jane. "You're so vivacious when you drink."

David is sobbing. His hands flap in the air. Jackson picks him up. "Stop it," he says. David wraps his legs around his father's chest and pees all over him. Their clothing turns dark as though, together, they'd been shot. "Goddamn it," Jackson shouts. He throws his arms out. He stops holding the child but his son clings to him, then drops to the floor.

Jane grabs Jackson's shoulder. She whispers in his ear, something so crude, in a tone so unfamiliar, that it can only belong to all the time before them. Jackson does not react to it. He says nothing. He unbuttons his shirt. He takes it off and throws it in the sink. Jane has thrown the dog food there. The shirt floats down to it from his open fist.

Jane kneels and kisses her soiled son. David does not look at her. It is as though, however, he is dreaming of looking at her.

Let the Old Dead Make Room for the Young Dead

MILAN KUNDERA

1

He was returning home along the street of a small Czech town where he had been living for several years. He was reconciled to his unexciting life, his backbiting neighbors, and the monotonous rowdiness that surrounded him at work, and he was walking so totally without seeing (as one walks along a path traversed every day) that he almost passed her by. But she had already recognized him from a distance, and, coming toward him, she gave him that gentle smile of hers. Only at the last moment, when they had almost passed each other, did that smile ring a bell in his memory and wake him from his dream.

"I wouldn't have recognized you!" he apologized, but it was a stupid apology, because it brought them precipitately to a painful subject, about which it would have been advisable to keep silent; they had not seen each other for fifteen years and during this time they had both aged. "Have I changed so much?" she asked, and he replied that she hadn't, and even if this were a lie it wasn't an out-and-out lie, because that gentle smile (expressing demurely a capacity for some sort of eternal enthusiasm) emerged from the distance of many years quite unchanged, and it confused him. It evoked for him so distinctly the former appearance of this woman that he had to make a definite effort to disregard it and to see her as she was now: she was almost an old woman.

He asked her where she was going and what was on her agenda, and she replied that she had nothing else to do but wait for the train which would take her back to Prague that evening. He felt pleasure at their unexpected meeting, and because they agreed (with good reason) that the two local cafés were overcrowded and dirty, he invited her to his bachelor apartment, which wasn't very far away. He had both coffee and tea there, and, more important, it was clean and peaceful.

2

Right from the start it had been a bad day. Twenty-five years before she had lived here with her husband for a short time as a new bride; then they had moved to Prague, where he'd died ten years back. He was buried, thanks to an eccentric wish in his last will and testament, in the local cemetery. At that time she had paid in advance for a ten-year lease on the grave, but a few days ago she had become afraid that the time limit had expired and that she had forgotten to renew the lease. Her first impulse had been to write to the cemetery administration. But then she had realized how futile it was to correspond with the authorities, and so she had come out here.

She knew the path to her husband's grave from memory, and yet today she felt all at once as if she were in this cemetery for the first time. She couldn't find the grave and it seemed to her that she had gone astray. It took her a while to understand. There, where the grey sandstone monument with the name of her husband in gold lettering used to be, precisely on that spot (she confidently recognized the two neighboring graves), now stood a black marble headstone with a quite different name in gilt.

Upset, she went to the cemetery administration. They told her that upon expiration of leases graves were canceled. She reproached them for not having advised her that she should renew the lease, and they replied that there was little room in the cemetery and that the old dead ought to make room for the young dead. This exasperated her and she told them, holding back her tears, that they knew absolutely nothing of humaneness or respect for man. But she soon understood that the conversation was useless. Just as she could not have prevented her husband's death, so also was she defenseless against his second death, this death of an old dead man, which no longer permitted him to exist even as a dead man.

She went off into town and anxiety began to mix in with her sorrow. She tried to imagine how she would explain to her son the disappearance of his father's grave and how she would justify her neglect. At last fatigue overtook her. She didn't know how to pass the long hours until time for the departure of her train. She no longer knew anyone here, and nothing encouraged her even to take a sentimental stroll, because over the years the town had changed too much and once-familiar places looked quite strange to her now. That is why she gratefully accepted the invitation of the (half-forgotten) old acquaintance whom she'd met by chance. She could wash her hands in his bathroom and then sit in his soft armchair (her legs ached), look around his room, and listen to the boiling water bubbling away behind the screen that separated the kitchen nook from the room.

3

Not long ago he had turned thirty-five and exactly at that time, he had noticed that his hair was thinning visibly. Certainly it was ridiculous to make thinning hair a matter of life or death, but he realized that baldness would change his face and that his hitherto youthful appearance was on its way out.

And now these considerations made him think about how the balance sheet of this person (with hair), who was just about to take his leave, actually stood, what he had actually experienced and enjoyed. What astounded him was the knowledge that he had experienced rather little. When he thought about this he felt embarrassed, ashamed, because to live here on earth so long and to experience so little—that was ignominious.

What did he actually mean when he said to himself that he had not experienced much? Did he mean by this travel, work, public service, sports, women? Of course he meant all of these things—yet, above all, he meant women. Because if his life were deficient in other spheres, this certainly upset him; but he didn't have to lay the blame for it on himself: not for work that was uninteresting and without prospect; not for curtailing his travels because he didn't have money; not even for the fact that when he was twenty he had injured his knee and had had to give up sports. But women was a sphere of relative freedom, and that being so, he couldn't make any excuses about it. Women, he decided, was the one legitimate criterion of life's density.

But as ill luck would have it, things had gone somewhat badly for him with women. Until he was twenty-five (though he was a good-looking fellow), shyness would tie him up in knots; then he fell in love, got married, and for seven years had persuaded himself that it was possible to find infinite erotic possibilities in one woman. Then he got divorced and the one-woman apologetics, this illusion of infinity, dissolved, and in its place came an agreeable taste for and boldness in the pursuit of women, a pursuit of their varied finiteness. Unfortunately, his bad financial situation frustrated his new-found desire (he had to pay his former wife alimony for their child, whom he was allowed to see once or twice a year), and the conditions in the small town were such that the curiosity of neighbors was as great as the choice of women was scant.

And time was already passing very quickly and all at once he was standing in the bathroom in front of the oval mirror located above the washbasin. He held a hand mirror and was transfixed examining the bald spot that had begun to appear, realizing, in the moment, that what he'd missed couldn't be made good. He found himself in chronic ill humor, and was even assailed by thoughts of suicide. Naturally (and it is necessary to emphasize this in order that we should not see him as an hysterical or stupid person), he appreciated the comic aspect of these thoughts, and he knew that he would never carry them out (he laughed at his suicide note: *I couldn't put up with my bald spot. Farewell!*), but it is enough that these thoughts, however theoretical they may have been, assailed him at all. Let us try to understand: the thoughts made themselves felt like the overwhelming desire to give up the race makes itself felt within a marathon runner, when in the middle of the distance he discovers that shamefully (and moreover through his own fault, his own blunders) he is losing.

He bent down over the small table and placed one cup of coffee on it in front of the couch (where he later sat down), the other in front of the armchair, in which his visitor was sitting. He said to himself that there was a curious malice in the fact that he had met this woman—with whom he'd once been head over heels in love and whom, in those days, he'd let escape (through his own fault, his own blunders)—precisely when he found himself in this state of mind and at a time when it was no longer possible to rectify anything.

4

She would hardly have guessed that she appeared to him as that woman who had escaped him; still, she was aware of the night they'd spent together. She remembered how he had looked then. (He had been twenty, hadn't known how to dress, and used to blush, and his boyishness had amused her.) And she remembered herself. (She had been thirty-five, and a certain desire for beauty had driven her into the arms of other men, but at the same time away from them. She always imagined that her life should resemble an elegant ball, and she feared that her unfaithfulness to her husband might turn into an ugly habit.)

She had decreed beauty for herself, as people decree moral injunctions for themselves. If she had noticed any ugliness in her life, she would perhaps have fallen into despair. And because she was now aware that after fifteen years she must seem old to her host (with all the ugliness that age brings with it), she wanted quickly to unfold an imaginary fan in front of her own face, and to this end she deluged her host with hasty questions: she asked him how he had come to this town; she asked him about his job. She complimented him on the coziness of his apartment, and praised the view from the window over the rooftops of the town (she said that it was in no way a special view, but that there was a certain airiness and freedom about it). She named the painters of several framed reproductions. Then she got up from the table with her unfinished cup of coffee in her hand and bent over a small writing desk, upon which there were a few photographs in a stand (it didn't escape her that among them there was no photo of a young woman), and she asked whether the face of the old woman in one of them belonged to his mother. He confirmed this.

Then he asked her what she'd meant when she'd told him earlier that she had come here to settle "some affairs." She really dreaded speaking about the cemetery. When he insisted, she finally confessed (but very briefly, because the immodesty of hasty frankness had always been foreign to her) that she had lived here many years before, that her husband was buried here (she was silent about the cancellation of the grave), and that she and her son had been coming here for the last ten years, without fail, on All Souls' Day.

5

"Every year?" This statement saddened him and once again he thought that a spiteful trick was being played on him. If only he'd met her six years ago when he'd moved here, perhaps it would have been possible to save everything. She wouldn't have been so marked by age, her appearance wouldn't have been so different from the image he had of the woman he had loved fifteen years before. It would have been within his power to surmount the difference and perceive both images (the past and the present) as one. But now they stood hopelessly apart.

She drank her coffee and talked. He tried hard to determine precisely the extent of the transformation by means of which she was eluding him for the second time. Her face was wrinkled (in vain did the layer of powder deny this). Her neck was withered (in vain did the high collar hide this). Her cheeks sagged. Her hair (but it was almost beautiful!) had grown grey. Her hands drew his attention most of all (it was not possible to touch them up with powder and paint): blue bunches of veins stood out on them, so that all at once they were the hands of a man.

Pity and anger inspired him to want to drown the occasion in alcohol; he asked her if she fancied some cognac (he had an open bottle in the cabinet behind the screen). She replied that she didn't, and he remembered that years before she had drunk almost not at all, perhaps so that alcohol wouldn't make her behave contrary to the demands of decorum. And when he saw the delicate movement of the hand with which she refused the offer of cognac, he realized this charm, this magic, this grace that had enraptured him, was still the same in her, though hidden beneath age.

When it crossed his mind that she was cut off from him by old age, he felt immense pity for her, and this pity brought her nearer to him (this woman who had once been so dazzling, before whom he used to be tongue-tied), and he wanted to have a long conversation with her and talk to her the way a man would talk with his girlfriend when he felt depressed. He started to talk (and it did indeed turn into a long talk), and eventually he got to the pessimistic thoughts that had visited him of late. Naturally he was silent about the bald spot that was beginning to appear (it was just like her silence about the canceled grave). But his vision of the bald spot encouraged him to say that time passes more quickly than man is able to live, and that life is terrible because everything in it is necessarily doomed to extinction. He voiced these and similar maxims, to which he awaited a sympathetic response; but he didn't get it.

"I don't like that kind of talk," she said, almost vehemently. "All that you've been saying is awfully superficial."

6

She didn't like conversations about growing old or dying because they contained images of physical ugliness. Often she repeated to her host that his opinion was superficial. After all, she said, man is more than just a body that wastes away: a man's work is substantial and that is what he leaves behind for others. Her advocacy of this opinion wasn't new; it had first come to her aid when, twenty-five years earlier, she had fallen in love with her husband, who was nineteen years older than she. She had never ceased to respect him wholeheartedly (in spite of all her infidelities, about which he either didn't know or didn't want to know), and she took pains to convince herself that her husband's intellect and importance would outweigh the heavy load of his years.

"What kind of work, I ask you! What kind of work do we leave behind!" protested her host with a bitter smile.

She didn't want to refer to her dead husband, though she firmly believed in the lasting value of everything he had accomplished. She therefore only said that every man accomplishes something, which in itself may be most modest, but that in this and only in this is his value. Then she went on to talk about herself, how she worked in a house of culture in a suburb of Prague, how she organized lectures and poetry readings. She spoke (with an excitement that seemed out of proportion to him) about "the grateful faces" of the public, and straight after that she expatiated upon how beautiful it was to have a son and to see her own features (her son looked like her) changing into the face of a man, how it was beautiful to give him everything a mother can give a son and then to fade quietly into the background of his life.

It was not by chance that she had begun to talk about her son, because all day her son had been in her thoughts, a reproachful reminder of the morning's failure at the cemetery. It was strange; she had never let any man impose his will on her, but her son subjugated her, and she didn't know how. The failure at the cemetery had upset her all the more because she felt guilty before her son and feared his reproaches. Of course, she had long suspected that her son so jealously watched over the way she honored his father's memory (after all, it was he who insisted every All Souls' Day that they should visit the cemetery) not so much out of love for his dead father, as from a desire to usurp his mother, to assign her to a widow's proper confines.

She never heard him suggest it, but she guessed against her will that the idea that his mother might still have sexual emotions disgusted him. Everything in her that remained sexual disgusted him, and because the sexual implies the youthful, he was disgusted by everything still youthful in her. He was no longer a child, and this mother's youthfulness (combined with the aggressiveness of her motherly care) thwarted his relationships with girls. He wanted to have an old mother. Only from such a mother would he tolerate love and only of such a mother could he be fond. And although she realized that in this way he was pushing her toward the grave, she had finally submitted to him, succumbed to his need, and even idealized her capitulation, persuading herself that the beauty of her life consisted precisely in giving way to another life. In the name of this idealization (without which the wrinkles on her face would have made her far more uneasy), she now conducted, with unexpected heat, this dispute with her host.

But he suddenly leaned across the little table that stood between them, stroked her hand, and said, ''Forgive me for my chatter. I always was an idiot.''

7

Their dispute didn't irritate him; on the contrary, his visitor yet again confirmed her identity for him. In her protest against his pessimistic talk (wasn't this above all a protest against ugliness and bad taste?), he recognized her as the person he had once known, so her former appearance and their old story filled his thoughts all the more. Now he wished only that nothing destroy the intimate mood so favorable to their conversation (for that reason he stroked her hand and called himself and idiot), and he wanted to tell her about the thing that seemed most important to him at this moment: their adventure together. For he was convinced that he had experienced something very special with her.

He no longer remembered how they had met. Apparently, she had sometimes come in contact with his student friends, but he remembered perfectly the Prague café where they had been alone together for the first time. He had been sitting opposite her in a plush booth, depressed and silent, but at the same time thoroughly elated by her delicate hints that she was favorably disposed toward him. He had tried to visualize (without daring to hope for the fulfillment of these fancies) how she would look if he kissed her, undressed her, and made love to her. He had tried a thousand times to imagine her in bed, but in vain. Her face kept on looking at him with its calm, gentle smile, and he couldn't (even with the most dogged efforts of his imagination) distort it with the grimace of physical ecstasy. She absolutely defied his imagination.

And that was the situation, which had never since been repeated in his life. He had stood face to face with the unimaginable during that very short period, a heavenly period when fancy is not yet satiated by experience, has not become routine, knows little, and knows how to do little, a time when the unimaginable still exists, a time when, should the unimaginable become reality, a man will be seized by panic and vertigo. Such vertigo did actually overtake him, when, after several further meetings, in the course of which he

hadn't resolved anything, she began to ask him in detail and with meaningful curiosity about his room in the student dormitory, so that she soon forced him to invite her there.

He shared the little room with another student, who had promised not to return till after midnight. He tidied up the room, and at seven o'clock (it was part of her refinement that she was habitually on time) she knocked on the door. It was September and only gradually did it begin to get dark. They sat down on the edge of a cot and kissed. Then it got even darker and he didn't want to switch on the light because he was glad that he couldn't be seen, and hoped that the darkness would relieve the embarrassment in which he would find himself at having to undress in front of her. He didn't dare to undo her first button, so that in the end she stood up and, asking with a smile, ''Shouldn't I take off this armor?'' began to undress. It was dark, however, and he saw only the shadows of her movements. He hastily undressed too and they began to make love. He looked into her face, but in the dusk her expression entirely eluded him. He regretted that it was dark, but it seemed impossible for him to get up and move away from her to turn on the switch by the door, so he went on straining his eyes. But he didn't recognize her. It seemed to him that he was making love to someone else—someone quite unreal.

Then she got on top of him (he saw only her raised shadow) and, moving her hips, she said something in a muffled tone, in a whisper, and it wasn't clear whether she was talking to him or to herself. He couldn't make out the words and asked her what she had said. She went on whispering, and even when he clasped her to him again, he couldn't understand what she was saying.

8

She listened to her host and became increasingly absorbed in the details, which she had long ago forgotten: for instance, in those days she used to wear a pale blue summer suit, in which, they said, she looked like an angel (yes, she recalled that suit); she used to wear a large ivory comb stuck in her hair, which they said gave her a majestic, old-fashioned look; at the café she always used to order tea with rum (her only alcoholic vice), and all this pleasantly carried her away from the cemetery, away from her sore feet, and away from the reproachful eyes of her son. Look, it flashed across her mind, regardless of what I am like today, if a bit of my youth lives on in this man, I haven't lived in vain. This immediately struck her as a new corroboration of her conviction that the worth of a man lies in his ability to extend beyond himself, to go outside himself, to exist in and for other people.

She listened, and didn't resist him when from time to time he stroked her hand. The stroking merged with the soothing tone of the conversation and had a disarming indefiniteness about it. For whom was it intended? For the woman about whom he was speaking or for the woman to whom he was speaking? After all, she liked the man who was caressing her; she even said to herself that she liked him better than the youth of fifteen years ago, whose boyishness, if she remembered correctly, had been rather a nuisance.

When he got to the place in his account where her moving shadow had risen above him and he had endeavored to understand her whispering, he fell silent, and she (foolishly, as if he would know these words) asked softly: ''And what did I say then?''

9

''I don't know,'' he replied. He didn't know. At that time she had eluded not only his fancies but also his perceptions; she had eluded his sight and hearing. When he had switched on the light, she was already dressed. Everything about her was once again sleek, dazzling, perfect, and he vainly sought a connection between her face in the light and the face that a moment before he had been guessing at in the darkness. They hadn't parted yet, but he was already trying to remember her. He tried to imagine how her face and body had looked when they'd made love a little while before. But she still defied his imagination.

He had made up his mind that next time he must make love to her with the light on. Only there wasn't a next time. From that day on she adroitly avoided him. He had failed hopelessly, yet it wasn't clear why. They'd certainly made love beautifully, but he also knew how impossible he had been beforehand, and he was ashamed of this.

"Tell me, why did you avoid me then?"

"I beg you," she said in the gentlest of voices, "it's so long ago, that I don't know. . . ." And when he pressed her further, she protested. "You shouldn't always return to the past. It's enough that we have to devote so much time to it against our will." She said this only to ward off his insistence (and perhaps the last sentence, spoken with a light sigh, referred to her morning visit to the cemetery). But he perceived her statement differently: as an intense and purposeful clarification for him of the fact (this obvious thing) that there were not two women (one past and one present), but only one and the same woman, and that she, who had eluded him fifteen years earlier, was here now, was within reach of his hand.

"You're right, the present is more important," he said in a meaningful tone, and looked intently at her face. She was smiling with her mouth half open and he glimpsed a row of white teeth. A recollection occurred to him: that time in his room, she had put his fingers into her mouth, bitten them hard until it had hurt. But before the bite, he had felt the inside of her mouth and found that on one side the back upper teeth were missing (this had not discouraged him at the time; on the contrary, such a trivial imperfection went with her age, which attracted and excited him). But now, looking into the crack between her teeth and the corner of her mouth, he saw that her teeth were strikingly white and none were missing, and this made him shudder.

"Don't you really feel like having some cognac?" he said. When with a charming smile and a mildly raised eyebrow she shook her head, he went behind the screen, took out the bottle, put it to his lips, and drank. Then it occurred to him that she would be able to detect his secret action from his breath, and so he picked up two small glasses and the bottle and carried them into the room. Once more she shook her head. "At least symbolically," he said, and filled both glasses. He clinked her glass.

"To speaking about you only in the present tense!" He downed his drink, she moistened her lips.

He took a seat on the arm of her chair and seized her hand.

10

She hadn't suspected it could come to this sort of intimacy, and at first she felt dismay, as if it had come before she had been able to prepare herself (that perpetual preparedness, familiar to the mature woman, she had lost long ago). Then he moved her from the armchair to the couch, clasped her to him, and stroked her body. In his arms she felt amorphously soft.

The moment of dismay passed in his embrace and she, though no longer the beautiful woman she had once been, now began to rediscover her former character. She regained a feeling of herself, her knowledge, and once again found the confidence of an erotically adept woman. Because this was a confidence long unfelt, she experienced it now more intensely than ever. Her body—a short while before trapped, alarmed, passive, soft—revived and responded with its own caresses. She considered the expertise of these caresses and it gratified her. The way she put her face to this body, the delicate movements with which her body answered his embrace, she found all this not like something she was affecting, but like something essential, as if this were a homeland (ah, land of beauty!) from which she had been exiled and to which she was returning in triumph.

Her son was now infinitely far away. When her host had embraced her, in a corner of her mind she had caught sight of the boy warning her of the danger. Now there remained only she and the man who was stroking her. But when he placed his lips on her lips and wanted to open her mouth with his tongue, everything was suddenly wrong. She clenched her teeth, and she didn't give herself to him; then she gently pushed him away and said: "No. Really, please, I'd rather not."

When he kept on insisting, she held him by the wrists of both hands and repeated her refusal. Then she said (it was hard for her to speak, but she knew that she must speak if she wanted him to obey her) that it was too late for them to make love. She reminded him of her age: if they did make love, he would be disgusted with her and she would feel wretched about this, because what he had told her about the two of them was for her immensely beautiful and important. Her body was mortal and wasted, but she now knew that of it there still remained something incorporeal, something like the glow that remains after a star has burned out. What did it matter that she was growing old if her youth remained preserved—intact—within someone else? "You've erected a memorial to me within yourself. We cannot allow it to be destroyed. Please understand me." She warded him off. "Don't let it happen. No, don't let it happen!"

11

He assured her that she was still beautiful, that in fact nothing had changed, that a human being always remains the same, but he knew that he was deceiving her and that she was right. After all, he was well aware of his sensitivity to things physical, his increasing fastidiousness about the defects of a woman's body, which in recent years had driven him to ever younger and therefore, as he bitterly realized, ever emptier women. Yes, there was no doubt about it: if he got her to make love, it would end in disgust—and this disgust would then tarnish not only the present moment, but also the image of the woman of long ago, an image he cherished like a jewel in his memory.

He knew all this, but knowing was not feeling; knowing meant nothing in the face of his desire, which knew only one thing: the woman he had thought of as unattainable and elusive for fifteen years—was here. At last he could see her in daylight, could see from her body today what her body had been then, from her face today what her face had been then. At last he might see her (unimaginable!) making love—the movements, the orgasm.

He put his arms around her shoulders and looked into her eyes: "Don't fight me. It's absurd to fight me."

12

She shook her head. She knew that it wasn't absurd for her to refuse him. She knew men and their approach to the female body. She knew that in love even the most passionate idealism will not rid the body's surface of its terrible, basic importance. It is true that she still had a nice figure, that in her clothes she still looked quite youthful. But she knew that when she undressed she would expose the wrinkles in her neck, the long scar from a stomach operation years before, and her grey hair. She wasn't ashamed of the grey hair on her head, but that which she had in the center of her body she wore like a secret badge of dishonor.

And just as the consciousness of her present physical appearance, which she had forgotten a short while before, returned to her, so there arose from the street below (until now, this room had seemed to her safely high above her life) the anxieties of the morning. They were filling the room, alighting on the prints behind glass, on the armchair, on the table, on the empty coffee cup—and her son's face dominated their procession. When she caught sight of it, she blushed and fled somewhere deep inside herself. Foolishly, she had been on the point of wishing (at least for the moment) to escape, and now she must obediently return and admit that it was the only path suitable for her. Her son's face was so derisive that, in shame, she felt herself growing smaller and smaller before him until, humiliated, she turned into the scar on her stomach.

Her host held her by the shoulders and once again repeated: "It's absurd for you to fight me," and she shook her head, but quite mechanically, because what she was seeing was not her host but her own youthful features in the face of her son, whom she hated the more the smaller and the more humiliated she felt. She heard him reproaching her about the canceled grave, and now, from the chaos of her memory, there leaped the sentence: *the old dead must make room for the young dead.*

13

He didn't have the slightest doubt that this would actually end in disgust. After all, he couldn't even give her a look (a searching and penetrating look) without feeling a certain disgust. But the curious thing was that it didn't make any difference to him. On the contrary, it excited him and goaded him on, as if he were wishing for this disgust. The desire to see, finally, in her body, what he had for so long not been permitted to see was mixed with the desire to debase this vision.

Where did this come from? Whether he realized it or not, a unique opportunity was presenting itself. To him, his visitor stood for everything that he had not had, that had eluded him, that he had overlooked, that by its absence amounted to what was so intolerable to him—his age, his thinning hair, his dismally meager balance sheet. And he, whether he realized it or only vaguely suspected it, could now strip all the pleasures that had been denied him of their significance and color (for it was precisely their colorfulness that made his life so sadly dull). It would be revealed that they were worthless, only appearances doomed to destruction, only dust transforming itself. He could take revenge upon them, demean them.

"Don't fight me," he repeated, and made an effort to draw her close.

14

Before her eyes she saw her son's derisive face, and when now her host drew her to him by force, she said, "Please, leave me alone for a minute," and released herself from his embrace. She didn't want to interrupt what was racing through her head: the old dead must make room for the young dead and memorials were no good and her memorial, which this man beside her had honored for fifteen years in his thoughts, was no good, and her husband's memorial was no good—and yes, my boy, all memorials were no good, she addressed her son. And with vengeful delight she watched his contorted face and heard him cry, "You never spoke like this, Mother!" Of course she knew that she'd never spoken like this, but this moment was full of a light under which everything was different.

There was no reason why she should give preference to memorials over life. Her own memorial had a single meaning for her: that at this moment she could abuse it for the sake of her body. The man who was sitting beside her appealed to her. He was young and very likely (almost certainly) he was the last man who would appeal to her and whom, at the same time, she could have—and that alone was important. If he then became disgusted with her and destroyed her memorial in his thoughts, it made no difference, because her memorial was outside her, just as his thoughts and memory were outside her, and everything that was outside her made no difference. "You never spoke like this, Mother!" She heard her son's cry, but she paid no attention. She was smiling.

"You're right, why should I fight you?" she said quietly, and got up. Then she slowly began to unbutton her dress. Evening was still a long way off. This time the room was full of light.

In the Oasis Room

JAMES S. REINBOLD

Arlen Farner hurried through the Karlbenz station carrying a small suitcase in one hand, his ticket in the other. As Farner approached the train, a conductor walked over and took the ticket.

"Three minutes," the conductor said, glancing first at his pocket watch and then to the other end of the empty platform.

Farner nodded and boarded the train. He took a seat in a second-class compartment and looked out the window. The conductor sounded his whistle and the train moved out of the station into the night. There were scattered lights burning in Karlbenz and among these Farner traced the outline of the main street, trying to find his house. The train gathered speed and was soon moving rapidly through the countryside, leaving all light behind. It was very dark and all Farner could see was blackness flat against the window. He sat back in the seat and listened to the wheels. When the conductor walked past the compartment, Farner asked for the correct time and set his watch.

As the train sped through the night, Farner thought about seeing Delfa again. Twenty years had passed since Farner had left Delfa's school and begun a successful life as an organist. But his career was ruined months later by a series of stomach and intestinal disorders that forced him to live weeks at a time in hospitals and clinics. Neither Farner's health nor his spirit ever returned. Now he was going back to Genz to see Delfa, to celebrate the maestro's seventieth birthday.

Farner woke from a light sleep as the train reached a tiny rural station—a pavilion with benches and a small ticket office. He watched from his window for any sign of activity. There was none. Farner imagined all six coaches of this train deserted and himself the only passenger peering out a curtained window. The conductor walked under Farner's window and nodded. There was the whistle again, and the train moved forward effortlessly.

At Köln, Farner was obliged to change trains. The air in the station was warm. It smelled of oil, and Farner began to feel sick.

On the lower level, the express waited. Farner bought a newspaper and magazine at the kiosk and he boarded the train. It was one o'clock in the morning; arrival at the Genz station was scheduled for seven. Farner took two pills to settle his stomach and tried to relax. His stomach convulsed and he wiped his mouth with his handkerchief and took deep breaths. He removed his coat and put it on the rack above, beside his suitcase. Then he unlaced his shoes and tried to stretch out comfortably, propping up his feet on the seat across from him. He reached into his shirt pocket for a small cigar, but smoking it invoked a fresh attack of nausea.

Farner stood up, slipped quickly into his shoes, and opened the compartment door. The air in the aisle was cool. He breathed powerfully and walked up and down the aisle before returning to his compartment. Moments later a man appeared at Farner's compartment door, slid it open, and entered. The man nodded to Farner and then stuggled to get an enormous red suitcase up onto the overhead rack. The smell of schnapps had entered the man's clothing and now filled the entire compartment. But the man did not seem drunk. He sat quietly across from Farner, hands folded in his lap. Presently the man introduced himself.

"My name is Grepp," he said. "Heinz Grepp."

Farner nodded and shook Grepp's hand.

"Arlen Farner," Farner replied.

"Yes, very good," Grepp said. "I am going to Genz, you know. I have been visiting my aunt, and now I return to work. I am the bartender at the Hotel Excalibur."

Farner nodded, then realized that Grepp anticipated a greater response, for the man tilted his head to the side and stared.

"Well, now," Grepp said. "You have never heard of the Hotel Excalibur?"

Farner said that he had not, and wiped his forehead and lips with his handkerchief.

"It is only the largest hotel in Genz," Grepp said. "And very expensive. I have lost some good money visiting my aunt, but she was ill and it could not be helped. Of course, no one at the hotel wanted me to go. I am the head bartender in The Oasis Room, you see.''

''And how is your aunt?'' Farner asked.

''Oh, my aunt.'' Grepp laughed. ''She is better. Just a bad cold. Old people think it is something incurable, whatever it is. I had to spend a whole week convincing her it was otherwise. But my niece was there, so it was not all bad. Very nice.''

''But old people die,'' Farner replied.

Grepp laughed again. ''I am glad I did not tell her that,'' he said.

Farner turned to the window and tried to find a reflection.

''Yes, but my niece,'' Grepp went on. ''Very nice.'' He made curving lines with his hands, shaping the form of a woman.

Farner could think of no reply and soon Grepp closed his eyes, a smile on his face. When Farner was sure Grepp was asleep, he too closed his eyes.

It was nearly four-thirty when Farner awoke. The sky seemed brighter. Farner was relieved to find the night nearly over. Grepp was still sleeping. Farner swallowed two more pills, and then took down his suitcase and examined its contents. Everything was in order. Farner put the suitcase back up on the rack and looked out the window again.

The landscape was flat farmland. Cows slept in fields that were blanketed by dew. A narrow dirt road ran parallel to the railroad tracks and then wound away to meet the horizon. Farner wiped his forehead. His stomach moved. He dabbed at the corners of his mouth and lips.

Grepp looked sharply around the compartment when he awoke, as if he did not know where he was, and then he smoothed his hair and blew his nose.

''Have you seen my associate?'' Grepp asked.

''I haven't seen anyone,'' Farner said. ''What does your associate look like?''

''I don't know,'' Grepp said. ''Young. Dark hair. He is wearing a brown suit. Perhaps he walked past while I was sleeping.''

Farner shook his head.

Grepp scratched himself and opened the sliding door. He looked up and down the empty aisle and then drew his head back inside.

''My associate is probably sleeping somewhere,'' Grepp said. ''Oh, he is very drunk.''

Farner watched as Grepp reached up, took down the huge red suitcase, and unfastened the straps that held it closed. The clothing inside lay unfolded and scattered. Grepp probed beneath underwear and ties until he found a tiny bottle of liquor. He broke the seal with his fingernail and screwed off the cap.

''Medicine for the stomach,'' Grepp said. He drank the contents of the bottle in one gulp, replaced the cap, and then tossed the bottle under the seat.

''I wonder where my associate is,'' he said. ''Sleeping it off somewhere, I suppose.'' He winked at Farner and laughed.

Before closing the suitcase, Grepp took out a large portable radio. It occurred to Farner that Grepp and his friend might be thieves and that this radio had been stolen. Farner imagined Grepp's friend looting compartments, not sleeping, and thought that he too would be robbed before the train reached Genz.

Grepp adjusted the aerial to its maximum length and ran the needle up and down the bands. Static crackled through the compartment.

''I think I am getting something,'' Grepp shouted.

It was a news broadcast in a language Farner did not understand. Grepp listened for a while before he began searching through the static again. He tried another band, shortened the aerial, and turned the radio from side to side. But nothing worked. Finally, he turned the radio off.

''Later, perhaps,'' Grepp said.

Grepp put the radio on the seat and then reached into his shirt pocket for a roll of mints. Farner refused at first, but Grepp per-

sisted until Farner took one, which he pretended to put into his mouth. When Grepp was not looking, Farner slipped the mint into his pocket.

Farner began perspiring again. He pressed the handkerchief to his face and neck. He swallowed two more pills, then looked at his watch and calculated how much longer it was to Genz.

''Ah, my associate,'' Grepp suddenly announced.

Farner turned to the compartment door. He tried to calm himself, but it was useless. His hands trembled. He gagged and held the handkerchief to his mouth.

A man wearing a brown suit stopped outside the door. When the man saw Grepp, he pulled the door open.

''This is my associate,'' Grepp said. He laughed and slapped the man on the knee. ''Did you have a good sleep?''

The man took a seat and sighed. His black hair was combed straight back and his black moustache was very neatly clipped. Grepp turned his attention back to the radio, from which there came the sounds of a big band.

''Ah, Harry James,'' Grepp said. ''Very good.''

The three men sat quietly and listened to the radio. Farner waited for the men to rob him. At last Grepp turned off the radio and fell asleep, and his friend began to speak quietly to Farner.

''Have you been talking to him?'' the man asked.

Farner nodded and stared at Grepp.

''You are going to Genz? Is that right?'' the man asked.

Farner nodded. ''Yes, my music teacher,'' he said.

''I see,'' the man replied. ''Grepp told you he was the bartender at The Oasis Room, I suppose. Well, for many years he was, until he was dismissed. You see, it is a very good job.'' The man tapped his head and looked at Grepp. ''He never got over it.''

''What does he do?'' Farner asked.

''He is the caretaker for a small estate outside of Genz. It is very sad. I don't know what he is doing here. You heard from him who I am?''

Farner stared at the man.

''Yes, that is correct. My name is Franz.'' He handed Farner a card. ''I run The Oasis Room now.''

''And is that his radio?'' Farner asked, pointing.

''Well, I suppose it is,'' Franz said.

Grepp woke up and blew his nose. Franz turned again to Farner. ''Watch,'' he said, and began speaking loudly: ''*So . . . you . . . must . . . stop . . . at . . . The . . . Oasis . . . Room . . . and . . . have . . . some . . . drinks . . . with . . . us. . . . My . . . friend . . . is . . . the . . . head . . . bartender . . . there.*''

Farner wiped his brow.

''I don't know,'' he stammered.

Franz leaned closer to him and spoke intimately.

''You *must*,'' Franz said. ''We are friends.''

''Yes, we are all friends. We get along fine,'' Grepp said.

''I don't know,'' Farner said, his head swimming.

Franz looked at Farner strangely. Grepp turned on the radio again.

''Caterina Valente,'' Grepp said. ''Very nice voice.''

''I don't know,'' Farner said loudly. ''I can't. I haven't got the time.'' He touched his forehead and neck with the handkerchief.

''You have time,'' Franz said. ''The Excalibur is a good hotel. Expensive, but well worth it. My friend Grepp will provide all drinks.''

Franz put his hand on Farner's shoulder and shook him gently. Then Franz reached into his coat pocket and pulled out a small bottle of wine. Grepp looked up from the radio and smiled.

''My associate. Always drinking.'' Grepp laughed and shook his head, then pointed to the radio. ''Sammy Kaye,'' he said. ''Very good.''

''Do you like Rhine wine?'' Franz said to Farner as he peeled away the foil. Franz took a drink from the bottle and passed it to Farner. Farner shook his head.

''Oh, come,'' Franz said. ''You must have a drink.''

"No, I cannot," Farner said. "My stomach. I have not eaten."

"Nonsense," said Grepp. "Rhine wine is very good for the stomach."

Franz offered the bottle again. This time Farner took a sip.

When the train arrived at Genz, Franz rolled the empty bottle beneath his seat. Farner had drunk as little of the warm wine as possible, but still he felt dizzy and flushed.

He watched from the compartment window as Franz and Grepp made their way to the terminal, taking turns carrying the red suitcase. Only when they had disappeared into the crowd did Farner collect his newspaper, magazine and suitcase and leave the train.

He went through the terminal cautiously, watching in all directions for Franz and Grepp. In front of the building, Farner hailed a taxi.

"A good hotel," Farner said to the driver.

The driver turned around.

"There is only one good hotel," the driver said.

Norwegians

PATRICIA ZELVER

This time Mr. and Mrs. Jessup just concentrated on one country—Norway. "Norway isn't ruined by tourism, yet," Mr. Jessup said. "Let's do Norway before it turns into a Venice."

"The country of Norway is extremely picturesque and not yet ruined by tourism," Mrs. Jessup dictated into her husband's portable dictating machine as she sat in the bedroom of their inn. The tapes were mailed to Mr. Jessup's office in Evanston, typed and Xeroxed by his secretary, and distributed to relatives, friends and business associates. The letters were Mr. Jessup's idea. Mrs. Jessup had done it in the Orient, too, and everyone had commented favorably. The first time she felt shy, but now she had developed more facility. Mr. Jessup said he thought it was good for Mrs. Jessup. Since their two sons had grown up and married, he had detected a lack of purpose in her life. Recently, he had had a physical by their family doctor. The doctor had inquired after Mrs. Jessup; Mr. Jessup had mentioned that this was a difficult time in a woman's life.

Mrs. Jessup told the machine about the fjords, the curious little Lapps, the stave churches, the Viking ships, the Munch Museum, and their visit to the home of a Norwegian couple in Bergen. The man had a connection with Mr. Jessup's firm. Sometimes Mrs. Jessup used a little book for help, which Mr. Jessup had purchased for her in Oslo. It was called *Facts about Norway.*

"The predominating trees in Norwegian forests, which cover nearly one fourth of the land, are fir and pine, but birch and other deciduous trees are found even in mountainous districts," the book said.

Mrs. Jessup changed this when she talked to the machine, to make it sound more like her own style. *"Most of the trees are fir and pine,"* she told the machine, *"but there are also some birch and other deciduous trees."'*

After seeing what Mr. Jessup called the "main attractions," Mr. Jessup had gone to a "simpatico" traveling agent in their Oslo hotel and told him they wished to settle down for a week in a small country village with its own industry, unconnected with the tourist trade, a place where they could rest and "walk among the people." "This," Mr. Jessup said to Mrs. Jessup, "is the way to end a trip."

"We are now in a quaint rustic inn in a small fishing village, unconnected with the tourist trade," Mrs. Jessup said to the machine, while Mr. Jessup unpacked. *"It is not a fancy resort. Far from it! Papa, at the desk; Mama, in the kitchen; the children helping out. Here we will rest and walk among the people, which is the best way to end a trip."*

After a simple lunch in the inn's sedate dining room, they went back up to their room again. Mr. Jessup always lay down for a half hour after his noon meal; the doctor had told him this was one of the best ways for men with responsibilities, such as he had, to avoid getting into trouble. Mrs. Jessup continued with her letter.

"The room in our inn looks out upon the water," she said to the machine. She spoke in a low voice so as not to disturb her husband. *"The water is grey, dotted with grey rocks. Grey rocks, grey gulls, a grey sky. An ancient lighthouse stands on the rocky promontory across the water in all its pristine glory. Picturesque–"*

She stopped, remembered she had used that word before lunch. She erased the tape and went on. *"Fishing boats, straight out of an Impressionistic painting, bob up and down beside an empty wharf."*

Mrs. Jessup glanced at Mr. Jessup; his eyes were open. "Is the water a fjord?" she asked him.

"We've seen our fjords," said Mr. Jessup with an encouraging smile. "It's more of a bay."

"Having had our fill of fjords, the water is more of a bay," said Mrs. Jessup to the machine.

When Mr. Jessup had finished his rest period, they both put on their new Norwegian sweaters. Mr. Jessup put on his Tyrolean hat, which was decorated with a perky little brush, and slung his camera bag over his shoulder. They went downstairs again. Mr. Jessup asked Papa at the desk if there were anything especially worthwhile seeing in the village. They were particularly interested in old architecture, he said.

There was a long silence. "Well, that depends," said Papa. "What I might consider worth seeing you might not consider worth seeing. People differ, you see."

"The Norwegians are not servants," said Mr. Jessup as they went out the front door for their walk. "There's no 'yes, sir; no, sir.' No bowing and scraping. No spit and polish, like the English."

"The English do a lot of polishing," Mr. Jessup agreed, recalling the glowing silver tea sets and the shining brass hardware.

"It has to do with courage in the face of adversity," Mr. Jessup said.

"Polishing?" said Mrs. Jessup.

"Keeping up appearances, despite all," Mr. Jessup said.

"The Norwegians don't seem to polish," she said. She thought for a moment. "But Norwegians are courageous, too, aren't they?" she said.

"We know that they are," said Mr. Jessup. "Their Vikings,

their Resistance, their brave battle with the sea. It's another tradition, that's all. That's why we travel. The Norwegians are a proud and independent race.''

Mrs. Jessup made a note in her head of this last phrase for her letter. ''Though the Norwegians do not polish like the English,'' she said to herself, ''they are a proud and independent race.''

It was a cool September afternoon. ''A hint of winter in the air,'' said Mr. Jessup, buttoning up his sweater. They were walking through a small park. A young woman in a mini-skirt and boots sat on a bench beside a baby buggy. Mrs. Jessup, thinking of her new grandchild, hesitated for a moment beside the buggy, then peeped inside it. Mr. Jessup, who liked to walk briskly—the doctor had told him this was the best sort of exercise for men who spent their days at their desks—was already some paces ahead of her. When he noticed that Mrs. Jessup was not beside him, he stopped; he waited with a courtly patience as she admired the infant and congratulated the mother. Suddenly, Mrs. Jessup sensed his absence. She scurried to catch up with him, as if she had been caught daydreaming in school. Mr. Jessup took her hand in his and squeezed it tenderly.

There were two statues in the park. One statue, on a pedestal, was a bronzed, bearded gentleman in a frock coat, with a watch and chain dangling from his vest pocket; the other—made of white stone —was a slim young girl, naked, with small, high breasts and flowing, snakelike hair. The girl stood, proud, under the gentleman's sober gaze.

Mr. Jessup stopped in front of the man. He studied the inscription on the base of the pedestal. ''Henrik Ibsen,'' he said. He glanced at the girl. ''The nude was obviously done later,'' he told Mrs. Jessup. ''I must say, it's a curious juxtaposition.''

''Maybe somebody was playing a little joke,'' said Mrs. Jessup.

''Ibsen,'' said Mr. Jessup, ''is one of their national heroes.''

''That's what makes it funny,'' Mrs. Jessup said. ''It wouldn't be funny if he wasn't.''

''You don't make jokes with public money,'' Mr. Jessup said. ''I would guess it was just bad planning,'' he said.

They walked on. School was just out and the streets were alive with children. Two large boys were tussling, while a circle of their companions cheered them on. A tiny girl, with a mass of curly yellow snarled hair, stuck out her tongue at Mrs. Jessup. When Mr. Jessup wasn't looking, Mrs. Jessup stuck out her tongue at the girl. A small boy picked up a rock and pretended he was going to hurl it at Mr. Jessup. Mr. Jessup gave him a stern look. The boy laughed and made an obscene gesture with his finger. Mrs. Jessup giggled.

''Rowdy bunch,'' said Mr. Jessup, taking Mrs. Jessup's arm.

A few blocks further, they found themselves in front of a small military installation surrounded by a stone wall. Its gate was guarded by a young soldier with long hair hanging out from beneath his helmet. Mr. Jessup looked past the soldier through the open gate. ''There are some interesting old buildings in there,'' he said to Mrs. Jessup. ''I wonder if the fellow speaks English.''

He went up to the guard. ''We are Americans,'' he said.

The guard nodded solemnly.

''My wife and I would like to take a look at the old buildings in there. Would this be possible?''

''Sorry,'' said the guard, ''it's against the rules.''

At that moment, a hatless officer, wearing three stars on his epaulets, strode out of the gate; Mr. Jessup waited until he was out of earshot of the guard, and then approached the officer. ''Excuse me, sir,'' he said respectfully.

The officer stopped.

''We are Americans. We are traveling in your splendid country. I happened to notice the fine old buildings in your presidio. They appear to date from medieval times.''

''Yes, yes, very old,'' said the officer.

''I wondered if it would be possible for my wife and I to take a look at them?''

The officer pulled a billfold out of a pocket and removed a card

and handed it to Mr. Jessup. ''My card,'' he said affably. ''Just tell the guard at the gate that I said you may go in.''

''That's extremely generous of you, sir,'' Mr. Jessup said.

''My pleasure,'' said the officer, with a little bow of his head; then he hurried on.

Mr. Jessup looked at the card, then smiled at Mrs. Jessup. ''It's usually simply a matter of approaching the right person,'' he said. He went up to the guard again and presented the card. The guard gave it an indifferent glance and handed it back. ''Your General said we might see the old buildings,'' Mr. Jessup said.

''Sorry,'' said the guard, ''it's against the rules.''

Mr. Jessup's voice took on a slight edge of exasperation. ''But you saw me, just this moment, talking to him!'' he said.

The fellow grinned. ''Yes, but you see, it's like this,'' he said. ''The General isn't here now, is he? I'm the boss now.''

''It's easy to see how the Germans took over if their privates make up all the rules,'' Mr. Jessup said to Mrs. Jessup as they left.

Mrs. Jessup remembered seeing a church when they had entered town. She knew Mr. Jessup liked taking photographs of churches. She led him around another gang of loitering, noisy youths, down a narrow street of small shops and across a plaza. ''Voilà!'' she said proudly, pointing to a small yellow wooden building with a cross on its top, surrounded by a graveyard.

''It's not a stave church, is it?'' Mrs. Jessup said, a bit apologetically.

''We've seen our stave churches,'' said Mr. Jessup. ''They resemble Siamese temples. Siam. Thailand, now. Remember?''

''Oh, yes,'' said Mrs. Jessup.

''Still—it has a nice simplicity.'' Mr. Jessup walked up the steps and tried the door. It was locked. He backed up a few steps, unzipped his camera bag and began to tinker with his equipment, measuring the light with a meter, adjusting the lens. ''You stand on the porch,'' he said.

Mrs. Jessup knew how long it took Mr. Jessup to set things up properly when he took a picture; he took great pride in his photography. She would try to look bright and alert, but her mind would often wander. Standing on the steps of Nôtre Dame, she had seen a dog trot by and was reminded of a dog she had loved as a child; in front of the Taj Mahal, the warm, muggy air had taken her back to a summer evening and a boy. She had laughed out loud, remembering. Mr. Jessup had caught her laugh in the picture. After their trip, when they had presented their usual slide show for their friends, there she was—laughing—and everyone had remarked how much Mrs. Jessup seemed to be enjoying her exotic adventure.

''I haven't had my hair done for days,'' she told Mr. Jessup now. ''You take the picture and I'll go for a walk in the graveyard.''

Mrs. Jessup walked around the church on a path which led through the graves. An old woman was bent over one of them, busily pulling out weeds from around a flat stone marker. Mrs. Jessup stood quietly in back of her and tried to make out the words carved on the stone. They were in Norwegian, but she could read the name and date.

Olaf Olafson
1923-1940

Olaf Olafson had been seventeen when he died, Mrs. Jessup thought. Danny Plummer—that had been the name of her boyfriend—had been twenty when he was killed on Guadalcanal.

The woman looked up at Mrs. Jessup. Mrs. Jessup smiled at her shyly. ''Your son?'' she said, rocking an imaginary baby in her arms.

The old woman nodded. She picked up her black pocketbook, which was on the ground beside her, and stood up. She opened the bag and took out a photograph and showed it to Mrs. Jessup.

''He was very handsome,'' said Mrs. Jessup, hoping that by her tone and expression the old woman would understand.

The old woman put her pocketbook back upon the ground. She stood up. Her body stiffened in a mock military posture; she swung one hand to her forehead in a Nazi salute. Then she dropped her hand, put both hands around her thin neck and twisted them; her face grew contorted, her tongue hung out.

Mrs. Jessup gasped. Olaf Olafson had been hanged, she thought. Danny Plummer's body had been shattered by a mortar shell.

Mrs. Jessup took the old woman's hand and shook it. She walked slowly back around the church, wiping tears from her eyes.

Mr. Jessup was still tinkering with the camera. "I've been waiting for you," he said jovially. "I need some human interest."

Mrs. Jessup took out her comb and combed her hair and posed for him on the church steps.

"You look like you just lost your last friend," said Mr. Jessup. "Let's have a little smile. Come on, now. Say cheese."

Mrs. Jessup said "cheese," and Mr. Jessup snapped the shutter.

"That could be a good one," he said, putting his camera equipment away. "The light was perfect."

"The people of Norway are a proud and independent race," Mrs. Jessup said into the machine, while Mr. Jessup took his shower before dinner. She paused. She could not write about Olaf Olafson—not in this kind of letter. It was not what people would expect. Nor did she think Mr. Jessup would approve. She had not, in fact, even told Mr. Jessup about Olaf. She was not sure why she had not told him. He was a kind and thoughtful man. He would certainly have been sympathetic.

"Norwegians differ from the English, another proud and independent race, in that they do not spend their time polishing," Mrs. Jessup told the machine. *"Despite this, it is a clean country. Handsome statues adorn its plazas. Architecture of a simple design—"*

She had never told Mr. Jessup about Danny Plummer, either. She had told no one at all. When he died, nobody knew she had lost a lover. She was not the same person who had loved the dead boy, anyhow.

"Architecture of a simple design—" she repeated to the machine. She seemed to be bogging down. Perhaps it would help to look at *Facts About Norway* again. This time she talked directly from the book: *"Rich grave finds from the Viking age around 1000 A.D. show that even at that time Norwegians had a great sense of beauty, color and form, and liked to surround themselves with beautiful things."*

Mr. Jessup came out of the shower, wrapped in a towel, all pink and steamy.

"This afternoon," Mrs. Jessup was saying in her own words now, *"we went for a pleasant walk. There is a hint of winter in the air."*

Mr. Jessup smiled at her approvingly.

Mrs. Jessup showered and put on a simple black dress and the pearls Mr. Jessup had given her for their thirtieth wedding anniversary. Mr. Jessup complimented Mrs. Jessup upon her appearance. They were about to go down for an early dinner when they heard a commotion below their window. Mrs. Jessup looked out. "Something is happening on the wharf," she said. "Another boat has come in."

"I could stand more of a stroll before eating," Mr. Jessup said.

The whole town seemed to be on the wharf; it was like a carnival. They surrounded the boat, which had just arrived; its decks were filled to the gunwales with tiny silver fish.

"It's a herring catch," said Mr. Jessup.

The fishermen were shoveling up the herring and dropping them into crates. The kids had gone wild. They swarmed over the boat, balanced on the gunwales, climbed the rigging and threw themselves recklessly into the shining, slippery catch. A few older boys, mimicking the men, were trying to help out. No one seemed to mind.

"Someone should stop those kids. These are busy men," said Mr. Jessup.

Mrs. Jessup did not answer. She was looking on in amazement.

As she looked, the same little girl she had seen in the park poked her head out of the herring; her tousled hair glistened with fish scales. She saw Mrs. Jessup and stuck out her tongue again, with a grin. Mrs. Jessup stuck out her tongue in reply.

"The Northern waters being so frigid, the local custom here is to swim in herring," Mrs. Jessup said to herself, as if she were talking to the machine. *"I felt a bit timid at first, but soon I too slipped off my shoes and stockings and joined the natives. The sensation is unique, one might go as far as to say 'indescribable.' I have experienced nothing like it in all my travels throughout the world."*

Maybe I'm going cuckoo, she thought, as Mr. Jessup led her back down the wharf through the noisy crowd.

It was now very cold. Mrs. Jessup shivered and put up the collar of her coat.

"Chilly?" said Mr. Jessup with concern.

"A bit," Mrs. Jessup said.

They were passing a pub next to the inn. It was crowded with people from the wharf and soldiers from the army post. Loud voices and the clinking of beer mugs came from the open door.

"A drink would warm you up," said Mr. Jessup.

They entered the pub. The tables were all filled. Two young men, noticing their predicament, beckoned the Jessups to join them.

"Thank you very much, gentlemen," said Mr. Jessup in a hearty voice as the Jessups sat down between them.

The young men spoke English; they were from Bergen; they were in the army reserve, spending two weeks here on compulsory military duty. "We are here to save our country," one of them said. They both laughed; they seemed to be a little drunk. The General the Jessups had met that morning was at a nearby table; he greeted them with a loud, "Hello, my friends!"

Everyone seemed to be enjoying himself immensely.

The second young man—an exceptionally handsome young man, thought Mrs. Jessup—spoke to them. "You are Americans?" he said.

"Tourists," Mrs. Jessup was about to say; then she remembered that Mr. Jessup did not care for that word.

"We are Americans here to see your country," Mr. Jessup said. He signaled to a waiter. "May I offer you gentlemen two more beers?" he said.

"Thank you," said the first young man.

Mr. Jessup ordered a glass of sherry for Mrs. Jessup, and three beers.

"And what do you think of our country?" the second young man said to Mrs. Jessup.

"We think it's very beautiful. We like it very much." She looked at Mr. Jessup for confirmation, but he was busy paying the waiter for the drinks.

"Yes, we Norwegians are very fortunate," the second young man said. "I went to school in your country, by the way. I went to the University of California. Every weekend, I drove up to your Sierra to ski."

"Did you ever consider staying there?" said Mr. Jessup.

The young man laughed, as if at some secret joke. He said, "I'm a Norwegian. Perhaps if I were a Dane or a Swede I might have considered the—ah—business possibilities. But I'm a Norwegian, you see."

"It must be like belonging to a private club," Mrs. Jessup said. She felt oddly envious, as if she were standing by a window looking in at a nice party to which she had not been invited.

"Yes, yes, that's an excellent analysis," the young man said to her. His eyes, she noticed, were incredibly blue and fringed with long curly pale lashes.

"If it's so satisfactory being a Norwegian," said Mr. Jessup, "—I'm only asking out of an intellectual curiosity, you understand—how do you explain your high suicide rate?"

The young man smiled. He had a charming dimple on his left cheek; Mrs. Jessup almost had to keep herself from reaching out to touch it. The sherry, she thought, must have gone to my head.

"Perhaps you are confusing us with the Swedes," the young man was saying to Mr. Jessup. "Still, we Norwegians commit suicide now and then." He tipped his chair back, took a swallow of beer, then put the mug down. He leaned toward Mr. Jessup. "You know what they say of us Norwegians? They say, 'You only get to know a Norwegian—up to a point.' "

Mrs. Jessup wanted to ask, "At what point *don't* we get to know you?" but she was afraid that this might sound forward.

"In other words, you can't explain it," said Mr. Jessup, genially.

"Everything cannot be explained," the young man said. "Some say it's lack of sun. Others say we live, then we die, on our own, so to speak, when it suits *us*."

"I hope it suits *you* to live!" Mrs. Jessup said, with sudden feeling.

This time the young man smiled at her—a sweet, strangely compassionate smile.

"Norwegian men have incredibly blue eyes and sweet smiles," Mrs. Jessup said to herself, as if she were dictating again. *"They are also extremely compassionate and understand the secret heart of woman. How do I know this? Shall we just call it my little indiscretion?"*

Oh, dear, I really must be tipsy, she thought. She put her glass down, hurriedly.

"Ready?" said Mr. Jessup to her.

Mrs. Jessup stood up.

"It was most kind of you to ask us to join you, gentlemen," said Mr. Jessup, shaking hands with both young men.

As they left, the General rose and gave them a salute. Mr. Jessup nodded briskly at him, then guided Mrs. Jessup in a different direction toward the door.

"Norwegians," Mrs. Jessup said to the machine that evening after dinner, *"are very proud of their nation."*

Mr. Jessup was already in bed, reading, but Mrs. Jessup had not yet undressed. Her memory was not as good as it used to be, and she wanted to get her impressions down before she lost them.

"There's something all over your shoes," Mr. Jessup said.

Mrs. Jessup glanced down. Her black suede traveling shoes glittered with shining dots, like sequins. She stared at them for a moment. "I think it's the herring from the wharf," she said.

"Better get them off now," Mr. Jessup said.

She got up from her chair and went to the armoire and took out her suede brush. She slipped off her shoes and brushed them carefully. The silver scales flew off and disappeared into the rug. Again, Mrs. Jessup felt the same peculiar sadness she had felt in the pub. She returned quickly to her job.

"It could perhaps be compared to belonging to an exclusive club," she continued. She paused, considered for a moment, then went on. *"There is an old saying, 'You only get to know a Norwegian up to a point.' "* This last sentence bothered her. She decided to play it back for Mr. Jessup.

"Sounds fine to me," Mr. Jessup said.

"But you could say it about anyone, couldn't you? Not just about Norwegians?" Mrs. Jessup said.

"I would say it applies to Norwegians very well," said Mr. Jessup. "No one would say it about you, for example, would he?"

Mrs. Jessup thought for a moment. Then she decided that Mr. Jessup was, as usual, right.

The Blind Side

BRUCE JAY FRIEDMAN

"The thing I like about Harry Towns is that everything astonishes him."

A writer friend he loved very much had been overheard making that remark, and as far as Harry Towns was concerned it was the most attractive thing anyone had ever said about him. He wasn't sure it suited him exactly. Maybe it applied to the old him. But it did tickle him—the idea of a fellow past forty going around being astonished all the time. On occasion, Towns would use this description in conversations with friends. It did not slide neatly into the flow of talk. He had to shove it in, but he did it anyway because he liked it so much. *Astonished* was probably too strong a word, but in truth hardly a day passed by that some turn of events did not catch him a little off guard. In football terms, it was called getting hit from the blind side. For example, one night, a girl he thought he knew pretty intimately suddenly came up with an extra marriage; she was clearly on record as having had one under her belt, but somehow the earlier union had slipped her mind. And for good measure, there was an eight-year-old kid in the picture too, one that was stowed away somewhere in Maine with her first husband's parents. She had neglected to mention him, too. On another occasion, a longtime friend of Towns' showed up unannounced at his apartment with a twin brother, thin, pale, with a little less hair than Towns' buddy, and a vague hint of mental institutions around the eyes; but he was a twin brother, no question about it. So out of nowhere, after ten years, there were not one but two Vinny's and Harry Towns was supposed to absorb the extra one and go about his business. Which he did, except that he had to be thrown a little off stride. It was that kind of thing. Little shockers, almost on a daily basis.

If there were small daily shockers in his life, the broad lines of Harry Towns' history had been clean and predictable. He had a good strong body and a feeling that it was not going to let him down. He'd always sensed that he would have a son and they would have baseball catches in a backyard somewhere. He had the son and they had plenty of catches. About ten years' worth. After a shaky start, he realized he had the knack of making money, not the kind that got you seaside palaces, but enough to keep everyone comfortable. Which he did. Early in his marriage he saw a separation coming; he wasn't sure when, but it was coming all right, and it came. He had read somewhere that when it came to the major decisions in life, all you had to do was listen to the deep currents that ran inside yourself, and they would tell you which way to go. He listened to his and they told him to get going. His wife must have been tuned in to some currents of her own. So they split up and there wasn't much commotion to it. He gave them both a slightly above-average grade on the way they had handled it. So there had been some significant detours along the way, but you couldn't say, in the overall, there had been any wild outrageous swerves to his life.

Only when it came to his father did Towns get handed a script that was entirely different from the one he had in mind.

For forty years, Towns' mother and father had lived in a section of the city that, to use the polite phrase, had "gone down." To get impolite about it, it meant that the Spanish and black people had moved in and the aging Jews, their sons and daughters long gone, had slipped off to "safer" sections of the city. Towns didn't know whether any of this was good or bad, but he knew no matter how you sliced it, it was now a place where old people got hit over the head after dark. Young people did too, but especially old people. Harry Towns' father had plenty of bounce to his walk and had been taking the subway to work for sixty years. Towns was fond of saying that his father was "seventy-five, going on fifty," yet technically speaking, his parents were in the old department and he didn't want to get a call one day saying they'd been hit over the head. He wanted to get them out of there. It was just that he was a little slow in getting around to doing something about it. He sent them on a couple of vacations to Puerto Rico. He took them to at least one terrific restaurant a week and he phoned them all the time, partly to make sure they hadn't gotten killed. The one thing he didn't do was rent an apartment for them, get it furnished, lay out a year's rent or so, take them down to it and say, "Here. Now you have to move in. And the only possible reason to go back to the old place is to get your clothes. And you don't even have to do that." Towns was in some heavy tax trouble and he was not exactly setting the world on fire in the money category, but he could have pulled it off. Still, Towns didn't do any of this for his folks, and it was a failure he was going to have to carry around in his chest for a long time afterward.

One day, Towns' mother received a death sentence and it all became academic. She wasn't budging and *forget* about a tour of the Continent before she went under. Maybe Towns would take one when he got *his* verdict; she just wanted to sit in a chair in her own apartment and be left alone. It was going to be one of those slow, wasting jobs. She would handle it all by herself and give the signal when it was time to go to the hospital and get it over with. As she got weaker, Towns' father got more snap to him. It wasn't one of those arrangements where you could say, metaphorically, that her strength was flowing into him. And that he was stealing it from her. It's just that he had never handled things better. He had probably never handled things at all. It got into areas like holding her hand a lot even in the very late stages when she had turned into some kind of sea monster and the hands were great dried-out claws. (Towns had seen something like what she'd become at an aquarium somewhere, an ancient seal that could hardly move. It wasn't even much of an attraction for people; it just sat there, scaled and ancient, and about all you could say about it was that it was alive.) When they took her false teeth out so she wouldn't be able to swallow them, it gave her mouth a broken-fence-post look, with a tooth here and a tooth there, but Towns' father kissed her snaggled lips as though she were a fresh young girl. He just didn't see any monster lying there. Harry Towns did, but his father didn't.

When he was a boy, Towns remembered his father wearing slipovers all the time. He'd been a little chilly all his life. The radiation made his mother yearn for cold air, so Towns' dad lay there next to her all night with great blasts of bedroom air-conditioning showering out on the two of them, offering her the soothing cold while his own bones froze. Towns didn't know it at the time, but he was going to remember all of this as being quite beautiful. And it hadn't been that kind of marriage. Yet he led her gently into death, courtly, loving, never letting go of her hand, in some kind of old-fashioned way that Towns didn't recognize as going on anymore. Maybe it went on in the Gay Nineties or some early time like that.

And Towns' father kept getting bouncier. That was the only flaw in the setup. He probably should have been getting wan and grey, but he got all this extra bounce instead. He couldn't help it. That's just the way he got. The only time he ever left Towns' mother was to go down to work. He would bounce off in the morning looking nattier than ever. He was the only fellow in the world Towns

thought of as being natty. Maybe George Raft was another one. Towns remembered a time his father had been on an air-raid-warden softball team and gone after a fly ball in center field. He slipped, fell on his back, got to his feet with his ass all covered with mud—but damned if he didn't look as natty as ever. In fact, there was only one un-natty thing Towns could remember his father ever doing. It was when he took his son to swimming pools and they both got undressed in public locker rooms and his father tucked his undershirt between his legs so Towns couldn't see his pecker. It was probably designed to damp down the sexiness of the moment, but actually it worked the other way around, the tucked-in undershirt looking weirdly feminine on a hairy-chested guy.

It was a shame the old man had to leave Towns' sick mother to go down to work. There was a Spanish record shop across the street that played Latin rhythm tunes full blast all day long and into the night. There was no way to get it across to the owners that a woman was dying of cancer about fifty feet away and two stories up and could they please keep the volume down a little. In their view, they were probably livening up the neighborhood a bit, giving it a shot in the arm. On two occasions, the apartment was robbed, once when his mother had dozed off. The second time, she sat there and watched them come in through the fire-escape window. They took the television set and a radio. The way Towns got the story, she merely waved a weary sea claw at them as if to say, "Take anything you want. I've got cancer." The news of the robberies just rolled off the shoulders of Towns' dad. It didn't take a bit of the bounce out of him. He comforted Towns' mother with a hug and then zipped inside to cook up something she could get down.

A cynical interpretation of all this snap and bounciness might have been that Towns' dad was looking up ahead. Towns was fond of saying his father had never been sick a day in his life. Actually, it wasn't quite true. He had had to spend a year strapped to a bench for his back and Towns remembered a long period in which his dad was involved with diathermy treatments. They didn't sound too serious, but Towns was delighted when his father got to say good-bye to them. That was about the extent of it. He had every one of his teeth and a smile that could mow down entire crowds. Towns' dentist would stick an elbow in his ribs and say, "How come you don't have teeth like your dad's?" Tack on all that nattiness and bounce and you had a pretty attractive guy. Maybe he was just giving the old lady a handsome send-off so he could ease his conscience and clear the decks for a terrific second time around. Was it possible he had someone picked out already? For years, Towns' mother had been worried about a certain buyer who had "worked close" with Towns' dad. Except that Towns didn't swallow any of this. There were certain kinds of behavior you couldn't fake. You couldn't hold that claw for hours and kiss that broken mouth if you were looking up ahead. You could do other things, but you couldn't do those two. At least Towns didn't think so. Besides, he was doing a bit of looking up ahead on his dad's behalf. He had put himself in charge of that department. And that's about all he was in charge of. He was almost doing a great many things. He almost went down to the Spanish record shop and told them that they had better lower the music or he would break every record over their goddamn heads. After the second robbery, he almost called a homicide detective friend to say he wanted to make a thorough cruise of the neighborhood and take a shot at picking up the guys who'd come up through the fire escape. He came very close to getting his mother to switch doctors, using some friends to put him in touch with a great cancer specialist who might give her a wild shot at some extra life. Over and over, he asked his father if he needed any money, to which he would reply, "We've got plenty. You just take care of yourself." One day Towns said the hell with it and wrote out a check for two thousand dollars. Mysteriously, he never got around to mailing it. There was only one department in which he demonstrated some follow-through. It's true he hadn't rented an apartment for his parents and gotten them out of their old neighborhood, but that's a mistake he wasn't going to make again. He would wait a polite amount of time after his mother died and then he would make his move, set up the place, get his father in there if he had to use a gun to get the job done. Towns sure as hell was getting at least one of them out. He was going to put his father right there where he could bounce over to work and never have to ride a subway again. About ten blocks away from work would be perfect. Towns' father didn't want to retire. That business place of his was like a club; his cronies were down there. And the crisp ten-block walk to work would keep that snap to his walk. There was more to the script that Towns had written. His father could take broads up there with him. That buyer, if he liked, or anyone else he felt like hanging out with. Someone around forty-seven would be just right for him. Towns would scoop up a certain girl he had in mind and maybe they would all go out together. He didn't see that this showed any disrespect for his mother. What did one thing have to do with another? Once his father was located, they would live near one another and spend more time together, not every night, but maybe twice a week and Sundays for breakfast. Towns had had his father out with some friends and some of them said he fit right in with them. It was nice of them to say this. And even if Towns' dad didn't exactly fit right in, at least he didn't do any outrageous old-guy things that embarrassed everybody. They would just have to accept him once in a while whether he fit in or not. Otherwise Towns would get some new friends.

That was the general drift of the script he had written for his father. But the key to it was the apartment. Right there on lower Park where he could bounce on over to work every morning.

Right after they buried his mother, Towns called a real-estate agent and told her to start hunting around in that general lower Park vicinity. He used the same agent who'd gotten him his own apartment. He read her as being in her late thirties and not bad. Nothing there for him but maybe for his father. Towns' dad and the agent would prowl around, checking out apartments and maybe get something going. Towns didn't have the faintest idea if his father's guns were still functioning in that area, but he preferred to think they were. Maybe he would ask him. So Towns set the apartment hunt in motion after a few weeks; he took his father to dinner at a steak house and hit him with it. "Let's face it, fun is fun, but you got to get out of there, Dad."

"I know, Harry, and I will, believe me, but I just don't feel like it right now. I have to feel like it. Then I will." And then Harry Towns noticed that his father had lost a little weight, perhaps a few more pounds than he had any business losing.

"I don't have any appetite," Towns' dad said.

"But look how you're eating now," Towns told him. And, indeed, his father had cleaned up everything in front of him. Then Towns gave his father a small lecture. "Let's face it, Dad, you're a little depressed. You can't live with somebody that long and then lose them and not be. Maybe you ought to see somebody, for just an hour or two. I had that experience myself. Just one or two sessions and I got right back on the track." Towns didn't want to use the word *psychiatrist*. But that's what he had in mind. He knew just the right fellow, too. Easy on the nerves and almost the same age as his father. He had expected to hear some grumbling, but his father surprised him by saying, "Maybe you have a point there." And then Towns' dad looked at him with some kind of wateriness in his eyes. It wasn't tears, or even the start of them, but some kind of deep and ancient watery comprehension. Then he cleaned off his plate and brought up the subject of bankbooks and insurance. Towns felt he was finally getting in on some secrets. Towns' dad had about fifty grand in all and he wanted his son to know about it, "just in case anything happens."

"Nothing's going to happen," said Towns.

"Just in case. I want it split fifty-fifty, half for you and half for your brother."

"Give it all to him," said Towns.

"Half-and-half," said his father, "right down the middle. And it's nothing to sneeze at."

"I know that."

"I thought you were making fun of it."

"I wasn't," said Towns. "But will you get the goddamned apartment?"

"I will," his father said, mopping up the last of the cheesecake. "But first I have to feel like it."

The appetite thing worried Towns. He was sure it connected up to some kind of depression, because his dad ate so well when he was out with Towns. But he couldn't have breakfast with his father every morning. And no matter how much he loved him, he couldn't eat with his father every goddamned night. Towns finally teamed the old man up with the real-estate lady and on a Saturday morning they checked out a few available apartments on lower Park. That afternoon, the woman called Towns and said his father had gotten dizzy in one of the apartments and hit his head on the radiator. She said she had made him swear he was all right before she let him go home. Towns got his father to go down to the doctor—he admitted to getting dizzy once before on the subway and having to ask someone for a seat—and they ran some tests. They used the same doctor who hadn't performed any particular miracles on his mother's claws. Towns had meant to switch off to another one, but that was something else he had not gotten around to. The tests zeroed in on his dad's prostate and Towns felt better immediately. He had a little condition of his own and he knew it was no toothache, but there was no way it could turn you into a Marineland exhibition. The prostate had to go and the fellow who would take it out was named Dr. Merder. Towns and his dad had a good laugh about that one. If you were a surgeon with a name like that, you had better be good. So they didn't worry a bit about him. The book on the doctor was that he had never lost a prostate case. Towns' dad checked into the hospital. He was concerned about how the business, or "place" as he called it, would run in his absence, and he didn't relax until the boss called and told him to take it easy, they would cover for him and everything would be just fine, just relax and get better. The boss was around thirty years younger than he was, but Towns' dad couldn't get over his taking out the time to do a thing like that.

Once in the hospital, he went from natty to dignified. Maybe he had always been dignified, even though he had blown his one shot at being head of his own business, years before. Using some fancy accounting techniques, his partners had quickly cut him to ribbons and eased him out of his share of the firm. This would have left most men for dead, but Towns' dad had simply gone back to his old factory job as second-in-command, dignified as ever. In the hospital, the only thing his dad used the bed for was sleeping. He sat in a flowered New England chair, neat as a pin, reading the books Harry Towns brought him. His favorite kind of book dealt with generals and statesmen, people like Stettinius, Franklin Delano Roosevelt—and the goings-on behind the scenes during World War II.

Along with at least one volume about Secret Service shenanigans, Towns would also bring a fistful of expensive Canary Island cigars. For most of his life, his father had smoked a cheaper brand, Admiration Joys, but in recent years Towns had promoted him to these higher-priced jobs. His dad complained that Towns was spoiling him. Sixty cents was too much to spend for a cigar. And there was no way to go back to the Joys. But he got a lot of pleasure out of the new ones. Towns had gotten the cigar habit from his father; he remembered a time when his father would greet a friend by stuffing a cigar in his handkerchief pocket and the friend would do the same for Towns' dad. It seemed like a fine ritual and Towns was sorry to see it go; there was probably a book around now proving it was all very phallic and homosexual. Now, when Towns showed up with the cigars, his father would say, "What the hell am I supposed to do with them?"

"Smoke 'em," said Towns.

"What if I don't feel like it?"

"Then just take a few puffs."

"All right, leave 'em there."

And his dad would. He would take a few puffs of each one. So they wouldn't go to waste.

They kept taking more tests on Towns' dad; he didn't leave the room very often, but he did spend a little time with one other patient and he got a tremendous kick out of this fellow. He was trying to impeach the President and Towns' father couldn't get over that. If he had great admiration for people like Cordell Hull and Omar Bradley, his respect for the office of the Presidency was absolutely overpowering. The idea of a guy running around trying to get the President impeached tickled the hell out of his dad. It was so outrageous. "You got to see this guy," he told Towns. "He's got a sign this big over his door, some kind of impeachment map. He's trying to get some signatures up. And he's important, too. I don't know what the hell he does, but he gives off an important impression. He says he wants to meet you."

"What's he want to meet me for?"

"I don't know. Maybe he heard you were important, too. Why don't you go over there and give him a tumble."

Towns wasn't terribly interested in the impeachment man. He was more interested in the tests. But for his father's sake, he met the fellow in the lounge. He was a sparse-haired gentleman, a bit younger than Towns' father, and he talked a mile a minute, but he seemed to be carefully staying off the subject of impeachment. At the same time, he kept checking Towns' eyes as if he was looking for a go-ahead signal. Towns gave him a signal that said nothing doing.

"What'd you think of him?" Towns' father asked, as they walked back to the room.

"He's all right," said Towns.

"Well, I don't know what *you* think of him, but to me he's really something. Imagine a thing like that. Going around trying to impeach the President of the United States." All the way back to his room, Towns' dad kept clucking his head about the fellow. He acted as though it were the most amazing thing he had ever come across in all his seventy-five years.

"Would you like to see that map he's got on the outside of his door?"

"I don't think so, Dad."

"I think you ought to take a look at it."

"Maybe I will, on the way out."

They decided to build up Towns' dad by giving him a couple of transfusions before the surgery. While this was going on, Towns ran into a nurse who came an inch short of being one of the prettiest girls he knew in the city. He had always meant to get around to her, but she lived with a friend of his and he claimed that was one rule he would never break. Or at least he'd try not to break it. She had a private patient down the hall and said she knew about his father and that a week before he had stood just outside his door and asked her to come in and have a cookie. Towns wished his father had been much more rascally than that. Why didn't he just reach out and pinch her ass? On the other hand, the cookie invitation was something. He made her promise to go in and visit his dad and sort of kid around with him and she said of course she would, Towns didn't even have to ask. He had the feeling this was the kind of girl his father would love to fool around with in an old-guy way.

The transfusions gave Towns' father some fever, but they went ahead and operated anyway. This puzzled Towns a bit. Except that his father seemed to come out of the surgery all right. He didn't appear to be connected up to that many tubes, which struck Towns as a good sign. Towns kept bringing him books about desert warfare, the defense of Stalingrad, Operation Sea Lion, but he kept them over to the side where his father couldn't see them and have to worry about not wasting them. Before they got spoiled. On the third day after the surgery, Towns brought along a real torpedo of a cigar, long, fragrant, aromatic, the best he could find.

"What'd you bring that for?" asked his father, who was down to one tube.

"Why do you think?"

"I ain't smoking it, Harry."

"The hell you're not."

The next day, his father looked a little weaker, but the doctor said it was more or less normal to take a little dip on the way back from surgery. When they were alone, Towns' father asked his son, "What the hell are you doing here?"

"I came to see you, Dad."

His father turned his head away, waved his hand in disgust and said, "You ain't gonna do me any good." Then he turned back and chuckled and they started to talk about what was going on outside, but that cruel random slash had been there. Maybe you were allowed to be a little cruel right after surgery. Towns wasn't sure. It was only the second piece of bad behavior Towns could think of since he'd been born. The other had to do with Towns at around eight or nine, using a word about somebody; he didn't know what the word meant, but his father instantly lashed out and belted him halfway across the city. So that made two in fifty years. That word and "You ain't gonna do me any good." Not a bad score. The next morning, the doctor phoned and told Towns he had better come down, because his father's pulse had stopped. "What do you mean stopped?" Towns asked.

"The nurse stepped out for a second and when she came back he had no pulse. She called a round-the-clock resuscitation team and they were down there johnny-on-the-spot. They do quite a job."

"How come the nurse stepped out?"

"They have to go to the bathroom."

"Is he gonna live?"

"It depends on how long his pulse stopped. We'll know that later."

Towns got down there fast. He met the doctor in the intensive-care unit. The doctor asked if he would like to see the team working on his dad and he said he would. He took Towns down the hall and displayed the huge resuscitation outfits. His father was hooked up to plenty of tubes now. He was like a part in a huge industrial city. He was the part that took a jolting spasmodic leap every few seconds. Towns got as close as he could—what the hell, he'd seen everything now. He tried to spot something that wasn't covered up by gadgets. Something that looked like his father. He finally picked off a section from the wrist to the elbow that he recognized as being his father's arm. He was pretty sure of it. "There's no point in your staying around," the doctor said. "I know that," said Towns. He went up to his father's room and got the cigar. Then he walked to the end of the hall and took a look at the impeachment map. It showed how much strength the fellow had across the country. He didn't have much. A couple of pins in Los Angeles, Wisconsin, New York and out. On the way down, Towns stopped in at the commissary and had some peach yogurt. It was the first time in his life he had ever tasted yogurt and it wasn't bad. It went down easy and it didn't taste the way he imagined it would. He made a note to pick up a few cartons of it. He went back to his apartment and fell asleep. The call came early in the evening. Towns had promised himself he would fix the exact time in his mind forever, but a week later he couldn't tell you what time or even what month it had happened.

"That's it, huh?"

"I'm afraid so," said the doctor. "About five minutes ago. I'd like to get your permission to do a medical examination of Dad so that maybe we can find our something to help the next guy who comes in with the same condition."

"How come you operated on him with fever?"

"We tried to contact you on that to get your permission."

"You should've tried harder."

"See," said the doctor, "that's just it. We talk to people when they're understandably upset and they say no to medical examinations. In Sweden, it's automatic."

"Work a little harder on what you know."

"The next one could be your child. Or your children's children."

"Up yours, doctor."

So that was it. The both of them. And for the moment, all Harry Towns had out of it was a new expression. Back to back. He had lost both his parents, back to back. He leaned on that one for about six months or so; especially if someone asked him if he was low or why he was late on a deadline. "Hey," he would say, "I lost both my parents, back to back." And he would be off the hook. He told his brother from Omaha to fly in as fast as possible and take care of everything, clean out his dad's apartment, settle the accounts, the works. He was better at that kind of thing. Maybe Towns would be good at it too, but he didn't want to be. The only thing he could hardly wait to do was get in touch with the rabbi who had officiated over his mother's funeral. He was a fellow the chapel kept on tap in case you didn't have any particular rabbi of your own in mind. It was like getting an attorney from Legal Aid, except that the rabbi turned out to be a real find. He showed up in what Harry Towns liked to recall as a cloud of smoke, with a shiny black suit and one of those metaphysical tufts of hair sticking up on his head. He turned up two and a half minutes before the ceremony and asked Towns to sum up his mother. "What are you, nuts?" said Towns. "Trust me," said the rabbi, a homely fellow with an amazingly rocklike jaw that was totally out of sync with his otherwise wan talmudic features. Towns took a shot. He told him they really shouldn't have limo's taking his mother out to the grave, they ought to have New York taxis. Whenever she had a problem, she would jump in one and have the driver ride around with the meter going while she talked to him until she felt better. Then she would pay the bill, slap on a big tip and hop out. That was her kind of psychoanalysis. She couldn't cook and Towns didn't want anyone laying that word "housewife" on her. Not at the funeral. It was very important to get her right. This was almost as important to him as losing her. She was close to cabbies, bellhops and busboys, and she could brighten up a room just by walking into it. And damned if this faded little mysterious house rabbi didn't get her. In two and a half minutes. "Sparkle" was the key word. And it was his own. He kept shooting that word "sparkle" out over the mourners and it was as if he had known her all his life. Towns had never seen a performance quite like that. After they had buried her in the Jersey Flats, the rabbi asked if anyone could give him a lift back to New York City. Everyone was staying at an aunt's house in Jersey, so no one could. With that, the rabbi hopped on the hearse. And then he disappeared; once again, it might have been in a cloud of smoke. And he was only seventy-five bucks. So you can see why Towns was anxious to have him back for a repeat performance. It was enough to get Towns back to religion. Why not, if they had unsung guys around like that. Except that the minute the rabbi showed up at the chapel the second time, something was a little off. He looked barbered for one thing. And he was wearing flowing rabbinical robes. What happened to the black shiny suit that he had probably brought over from Poland. And he didn't get Towns' father at all. "Good, honest, hardworking man." "Lived only for his family." Crap like that. Right out of your basic funeral textbook. The very thing Towns wanted to head off. His diction was different, fancier. He could have been talking about anybody.

It occurred to Harry Towns that maybe there wasn't any way to get his father. Maybe that was it—honest, hardworking, etc. But for Christ's sake, the rabbi could have found *something.* "Sparkle" wasn't it—he had used that anyway—but how about that bounce in his walk? What about nattiness for a theme? The sharpness of his beard against Harry Towns' face when he was a kid? Anything. Just so they buried the right person. Out they went to the Jersey Flats again, and his father went in the ground, alongside his mother. Towns was sore as hell at the rabbi for letting him down and not getting his father right. And for not being that magical fellow with the tuft of hair who had shown up in a cloud of smoke and almost got him back to religion. After everyone had climbed back into the limo's, Towns went back to the grave and stuck that big torpedo of a cigar inside. He was aware of the crummy sentimentality involved—and he knew he would probably tell it to a friend or two before the week was over—as an anecdote—but he did it anyway. No one was going to tell him whether to be sentimental or not—not when he had just lost his mother and father. Back to back.

He hung around the city for a time while his brother cleaned things up for him. He said he didn't want anything from the apartment except an old-fashioned pocket watch he remembered. And maybe his dad's ring, with the initials rubbed over with age so

you couldn't really make them out. They got the finances straightened out in his brother's hotel room. And there was a handful of salary checks to be divided up. So Towns finally found out his father's salary. He was sorry he found out. Towns hugged his brother, saying, "Let's stay in touch. You're all I've got," and then his nephew came dancing out in one of his father's suits. Wearing a funny smile and looking very natty. Towns recalled a fellow he had once worked for who had come to the office wearing his father's best suit, one day after the old man had died. At the time he wondered, what kind of a guy does that? Now, his brother said, "It fits him like a glove, so why not?" Towns couldn't answer that one. He just felt it shouldn't be going on. About a month later he changed his mind and was glad the kid took the clothes.

Harry Towns planned on taking a long drive to some place he hadn't been so he could be alone and sort things out—but he got whisked off to California on a job he felt he couldn't turn down. He told himself the work would be good for him. Just before he left, he ran into the cookie nurse at a singles place and asked her if she had ever gone in and fooled around with his father. She said she had but Towns could see she hadn't. No wonder he hadn't moved in on her. It wasn't that she was going with his friend. The guy wasn't that close a friend. It was this kind of behavior. She would tell you that she would go in and screw around with your father and then she wouldn't.

Towns polished off the California work in about a week; whenever it sagged a little, he would say, "Hey, listen, I just lost both my parents, back to back." It burned him up when people advanced the theory that his father died because he couldn't live without his wife. Towns heard a lot of that and he didn't buy any of it. He hadn't lived with anyone for fifty years the way his father had, and it didn't look as if there was going to be time to squeeze someone in for half a century. But he just couldn't afford to think that if you loved someone very much and they died, you had to hop right into the grave with them. He preferred to think that you mourned for them and then went about your business.

He started in on an erratic crying schedule. The first burst came at the Los Angeles airport. Then he got on the plane and cried all the way to Nevada. Back East, he gave himself the job of copying over his address book. Halfway along, he came to his father's name and business number. He really went that time. For a period there, he didn't think he was ever going to stop. It was having to make that particular decision. What do you do, carry your dead father over into the new address book or drop him from the rolls? No more father, no more phone number, and you pick up that extra space for some new piece of ass.

He never did get to take that drive. The one in which he was going to go to a strange place and get things straight. The awful part is that Towns never seemed to get any huge lessons out of the things that happened to him. He was brimming over with small nuggets of information he had gathered for his work. For example, when frisking a homicide suspect in a stabbing case, the first thing detectives check for is a drycleaning ticket—on the theory that the suspect is going to ship his bloodstained clothing right off to the cleaner's. When shot at, cops are taught to jump to their left since most gunmen are right-handed and will either fire wide of the mark or, at worst, nick a shoulder. Towns kept his young son enthralled for hours with this kind of information. But he didn't own any real wisdom and this bothered him. Instead, he borrowed other people's. Never sleep with a woman who has more problems than you do. Nelson Algren. Don't look over your shoulder because someone might be gaining on you. Satchel Paige. People behave well only because they lack the character to behave poorly. La Rochefoucauld. Take short views, hope for the best and trust in God. Some British guy. Stuff like that. Wasn't it time for him to be coming up with a few of his own? Pressed to the wall, Towns would probably produce this list:

1. Be very lucky.

2. Watch your ass. Because if they could get your father's pulse to stop—considering the way he looked, the way he bounced along,

the smile, and the fifteen years, minimum, that Harry Towns had scripted up for him—if they could keep him out of that paid-for apartment on lower Park, and on top of everything, get him to die back to back with Towns' mom, the two of them stowed under-ground in the Jersey Flats, all bets were off and anything was possible. Anything you could dream up. You name it. Any fucking thing in the world.

A Game Without Children

RICK DE MARINIS

Nina Weems wakes, thinking: *spider*. The boy hangs over her, descending, the small muscles of his face rigid. In the sun, next to the pool, lying on the dry prickly grass, she has been having her appliance dream: the smooth porcelained surfaces, the mute whir of motors, the precise ratchetting of cycling mechanisms, the sense of hidden mechanical intelligences that schedule unerring processes, tne intimacy of the alternating current's hum. She has just touched the refrigerator's handle, the cold welcome of chrome, when she wakes. She shades her eyes against the bright sky. The boy is looking at her. *Spider,* she thinks, her heart believing it: *spider*! The descent of the boy is windblown and slow. He hangs on visible thread, the trajectory of his fall slow and steep, wind-guided, predatory. She reaches for her robe, succeeds only in opening herself to closer inspection, but he has already passed overhead and is now dropping behind the row of young eucalyptus trees that borders her property. His legs are heavily padded. He wears jump boots. He is helmeted and gloved. A harness connects him to bright, triangular wings. The wings are made of white fabric ribbed with aluminum struts. When he passes over her, he grins and attempts a gesture, but only his elbows move. His hands are tightly committed to the handgrips that guide his flight. His smile works against the frozen concentration of the rest of his face. She has not covered herself in time at all, and when her fear passes she throws the robe aside and curses, but not loudly, because, like the white machines, he is gone.

The game of blind euchre is particularly suitable to hot weather, as it requires no skill and little thought. The cards are held so that each player sees every hand except his own. If he wins, it is always and entirely blind luck. Nina put the game book back on the shelf and returned to the party. The men were becoming political. Her hus-band, Walt, looked bored. "We need men in high places who take corruption for granted," he said. "If you want to survive, you start from there." A man who was very drunk, an internist, said, "You turd, Weems." He was spilling his drink on himself but no one called it to his attention. The women had moved into the kitchen. Louella Sternlich was making coffee. The conversation, which had been about something else, changed abruptly. "This *house*," someone said. "Nina, you absolute creature!" Someone else said: "One hundred seventy thou." Nina took the deck of cards out of the odds-and-ends drawer, cut to the five of clubs, put them back. "Look at that *brutish* ring," said a woman she did not know. Someone held Nina's hand up. The ring had once belonged to the Duchess of Romagna. It was a large, crested, black stone. There was a hidden stem that opened a secret compartment. When the conversation shifted to hot-weather recipes, Nina turned her back on the others, pressed the hidden stem, and poured a grainy blue powder into her drink. She went to the double glass doors, slid them apart, and stepped into the arboretum. There was no wind but something was moving in the branches of the fruitless mulberry. Nina circled the tree. There was a dark shape fastened to the narrow trunk, about halfway up and obscured by the leaves and branches. The moon flared behind the row of eucalyptus. The air was sweet with night-blooming jasmine. The dark shape in the mulberry tree spoke to her.

"What is this place called?" it asked.

"Ciudad de Sobrante," she said.

"What does it mean?"

"It means City of Excess. But the developer does not encourage literal translation."

"The same word in two languages often produces independent responses. Is that what the developer says?"

Nina said: "My husband is the developer."

Nina walked to the pool. The figure in the tree came down, breaking small branches in its descent, a short, stocky man wearing horn-rimmed glasses. He followed Nina to the edge of the pool and stood next to her. He slipped his arm around her waist. "Are we old friends?" Nina asked. He took her glass and drank from it. Nina thought about the grainy powder but did not speak. The knuckle of his thumb nudged her breast.

"My name is Mel Cantini," he said. "I used to be a priest, S.J., but now I teach moral physics at the University of California."

She pushed his hand away and climbed the steps to the diving platform. Mel Cantini followed her. On the platform he turned in dangerous circles, waving his arms. "All this," he said, "This *ciudad*, is regrettable."

"Are you an ecologist or something?" Nina asked.

"No. An entropist." He sat down and unlaced his shoes. "This *ciudad* ignores entropy." He pulled off his socks and then his shirt. "It ignores the coming final equilibrium." He stood up and unbuck-led his belt. His pants fell to his feet. "It's blind to real events. It's a stone-deaf falcon." He stood on his toes and imitated the flight of a bird. "Turning and turning in the widening gyre," he recited over and over in a reckless brogue, until his clowning took him to the edge of the platform and beyond it. He struck the water at a comic angle and sank to the bottom of the pool where he sat throwing slow-motion jabs and uppercuts. He still had his glasses on. Through the water's green lens he seemed elongated—a hairy giant having spasms. He looked up, blinded by the underwater lamps, to where she had been standing, and waved. But Nina had left. She went to the garage and started the Alfa. She backed it out of the semicircular driveway. For the rest of the evening, she drove through the development, slowly, concentrating hard on the mechanics of driving, repeating the names of streets aloud. *Timar. Pinzón. Reyezuelo. Corneja. Halcón. Grulla.*

A hill studded with granite boulders forms the north wall of Ciudad de Sobrante. An eight-foot wall of white brick seals off the rest of the development from the dry rolling hills of thistle, mesquite, sage, yarrow, amaranth and nopal. Seventeen miles of two-lane highway connects the development to La Corteza, the nearest town. The highway has twenty-eight curves, four steep grades, one crossroad that leads, in one direction, to the sea, and in the other, to the desert. Motion and sound are absent. Once a day, a passenger jet chalks the sky. This happens at five minutes past noon, every day except Sunday. Nina does not like the sound of this jet. At noon, she goes into a bathroom, turns on the shower and puts cotton in her ears. When ten minutes have passed, she takes the cotton out, turns off the shower, listens. If the silence has closed in again, she goes out to the kitchen and fixes herself a sandwich and begins to think about dinner. Walt is easy to please. Salisbury steak with steamed vegetables is his favorite meal. He was not born with money. His success has come in recent years. Walter Kenneth Weems, developer. He is tall, athletic, fifty. He was an all-conference end. He flies his own Cessna to Los Angeles, San Diego, Palm Springs and Las Vegas. He has an asphalt airstrip just outside the walls of the development. Walt and Nina have been married nine years. Nina is thirty-eight. "I'm a lucky woman," she tells herself, knowing that it is true.

"There is a man here to see Mr. Weems," said the guard at the gate. "Says he represents Electro-Tell." Nina had the guard spell Electro-Tell. "What does it mean?" she asked herself. "Mr. Weems is in Phoenix," she said. She heard the guard tell this to the man. The guard was arrogant and quietly threatening. He was a professional protector of the wealthy. "Mrs. Weems," he said, "he wants to see you, if that's okay. Shall I get rid of him?" Nina hesitated. She repeated the word Electro-Tell to herself. "No," she told the guard. "Send him up." The guard didn't speak or hang up. Then he said, "Mrs. Weems, you're sure?" "I'm sure," she said. She hung up and waited. She could not sit. Finally she heard his car. She sat on the sofa and picked up a magazine. She leafed through it hurriedly, then leafed through it again, reading the number of each page aloud. The doorbell rang. She let it ring again, twice, then answered it. A tall, glistening man stood before her holding a heavy black case.

"You're a Negro," she said.

"Correct," said the man, agreeably.

"Then Virgil did right," she said.

"Virgil is the tiny Prussian at the gate?" he asked.

"Correct," said Nina.

"My name is Joseph Zimmerlee, field representative for Electro-Tell Incorporated. Home security systems."

Nina opened the door wider so that he could bring in the bulky case. She sat on the couch and Joseph Zimmerlee knelt on the floor next to the case. He released its several clasps and raised the lid. He spread his long narrow hands over it, palms up, and said, "Voilà, Mrs. Weems." He took out a wallet-size instrument. "Firstly," he said, "let us look at the Portable Interrogator. It provides instant answers to your security questions, regardless of your location relative to the intruder." He opened the instrument and touched a red button. A light began to flash. He closed it and returned it to the case. "Secondly," he said, "we have the Compression Analyzer. Any sound, within or beyond the range of human hearing, is instantly analyzed for content and purpose." He held up a narrow panel with small meters on it. "And these," he said, holding two bean-size objects in his other hand, "you place in your ears. Remote adapters." He removed a larger mechanism from his case. It had movable parts. A device telescoped out of one of the parts. An egg-shaped housing was mounted on a tripod. Joseph Zimmerlee pressed a toggle and the egg-shaped housing began to rotate. A high-pitched electrical whine filled the room. On one of the components there were dials that gave readings in terms of azimuth, range, elevation, and decibels. "Remote Intention Discriminator," he said, in explanation. Nina looked at him without understanding. "A laser penetration device," he said. "The probe will automatically seek a resonator. The window, for example, of your neighbor's house across the street. Sound produced within will

modulate, through the resonator, the beam's frequency. This modulation is translated into intelligible information by the receiver. Shall I demonstrate?" Nina felt a pleasant paralysis of the muscles in her back where they joined the spine. Her breathing increased. Joseph Zimmerlee did not look at her but he was smiling as if he had seen deeply into her heart. She took the earphones he offered her. They were enormous and heavily cushioned. Joseph Zimmerlee went to the window and opened the drapes. He read the meters on the control panel. He made an adjustment. The rotating probe stopped. In the earphones Nina heard the voice of Louella Sternlich say, "You eat that, Rajah, or Mama will restrict your toy!" Louella was talking to her Pekingese. Rajah barked and growled. Joseph Zimmerlee looked at Nina. "A melancholy science," he said. "A vile necessity. But we must yield to all the possibilities of our arts, correct?" Louella Sternlich said: "Oh, please, Rajah, I'm in such a *state*! You are making Mama suffer deliberately!"

Nina removed the earphones. For the first time she noticed that Joseph Zimmerlee's head was shaved. "You are a religious man," she said.

"Correct," he said, and, anticipating her next question, added: "Though you despise the pig, you love the bacon, no?"

"If that's your attitude, what makes you think I will buy any of your devices?"

"For the same reason I sell them, Mrs Weems. Need. Yours is metaphysical and mine is physical, but there is a touching correspondence, wouldn't you agree?" His smile was bright and final. Nina put the earphones back on her head. Louella Sternlich was still talking to her dog. "But I *do* love you, bunny lickums," she said, and began to weep, copiously, with joy, ecstasy.

In their nine years of marriage, Nina had never seen Walt angry, really angry. They had driven over to La Corteza for a late-afternoon drink. Someone in the town's only tavern had set off a string of firecrackers close to the Weemses' table. Walt turned white, his knuckles whitening on his glass, the bridge of his nose, white. The man started to light more firecrackers. It was the Fourth of July. There had been a parade. The tavern was filled with men and women in costume. A red-faced man dressed as the Patriotic Repairman had joined them at the table. He was drunk and had touched Nina several times with his metallic glove, winking moronically. Once he whispered into her ear: "I've had my eye on you for some time. I can fix it." More firecrackers went off. Walt stood up, shaking with rage. He found the man with the firecrackers and took away his matches. The man slapped Walt on the chest, weakly. Walt spun the man around and knocked him down. A heavy woman grabbed Walt by the shirt and said, "Hey." Walt knocked her down, too. Someone threw a glass of tequila into his face. A mariachi band from Mexicali began to play the national anthem. Nina pulled Walt out of the tavern. When they reached the Alfa, they found a baby wrapped in newspapers, lying on the driver's seat. It was a Mexican baby, no more than a few weeks old. It was crying. Walt picked the baby out of the seat and handed it to the first woman he saw. He gave the woman a dollar. The old woman held the baby for a long moment, then shrugged her shoulders and put the baby down on the sidewalk, next to a drainpipe. "Soon as they smell you out, they take your pants down," said Walt, as he accelerated through the town.

There is a movie on about Lord Baltimore or somebody, starring Tyrone Power or somebody. A sandstorm is trying to come over the mountains from the desert. The temperature is over one hundred and ten. The wind whistles in the eaves, archways, and casements. Nina turns up the volume. The announcer says, "Maryland is such a pretty name for a state," and Nina is thinking about the truth of this sentiment. She pictures rolling green hills, cherry blossoms, fragrant ponds, songbirds, a man on horseback. "I pay no tribute to the past," says Lord Baltimore, or whoever. A wind chime falls into a cactus. Nina goes into the bathroom and turns on the shower. There is a noise the shower does not drown out. A long scraping, a clubbing, a child's voice. She turns the shower off and goes to the kitchen. The trees of the arboretum are alive with wind. Beyond the trees, near the pool, there is a boy on his hands and knees, crawling desperately but making no progress. He is tangled in his wings. The wings are rising and falling in the gusty wind. Nina goes out to help him. "I hit your antenna," says the boy. His nose is bleeding and his arms are scraped. Nina brings the boy into the cool house and makes him some cocoa. He is fifteen or sixteen, but small, delicate. He drinks the cocoa silently at the kitchen table, looking, from time to time, out the sliding glass doors at his broken wings crabbing along in the grass. Nina says: "I ought to be very annoyed with you." The boy looks at her sheepishly. She touches his hair. She scolds him for playing in such dangerous weather. The boy winces. He tells her about his wings, revealing a technical sophistication and a dedication to powerless flight that she finds moving. He speaks rapidly of camber, lift, interface stress, glide angle, metal fatigue, and thermals. Nina changes the subject. "What are you studying in school?" she asks. He tells her that history is his favorite subject. He finds that science classes are worthless because they are geared for those of marginal ability. He speaks of Portugal.

"Portugal," he says, his small voice rapturous, "is outside normal time and space. The sky is violet and filled with powerless machines. The air is quiet. Everyone thinks to himself. Random speech is considered evil. There is no television. Each town has a huge radio that whispers instructions in the square. There is a place called the 'Cathedral of the Brain.' Lost sailors are taken there. It is not so much a nationality as it is a principle of order, a containment of energy." He looks at her then, his eyes like small, glossy buttons. He pushes his empty cup toward her. "And when the Portuguese come in," he says, slowly, "they come with both feet."

Walt sits up suddenly. Nina turns on the night-table lamp. Walt says, "Ready?" Nina nods yes. Walt throws back the covers and gets out of bed. He starts to breathe heavily, as if a powerful emotion were moving him. He begins to sweat. He unbuttons his pajama tops. He puts his fists against his temples and closes his eyes. "I'm blank," he says, "dear God, I'm blank."

Nina gets out of bed and puts on her robe. Walt is leaning against the wall, trembling. Nina takes his hand and leads him into the kitchen. She puts on a pot of coffee. Walt goes to the sink and splashes cold water on his face. They sit down together in the breakfast nook. Walt presses his fists against his temples. "Still blank?" Nina asks. He looks at her. His eyes are indecipherable.

"Something is wrong with me," he says, his voice quiet and guarded. Nina gets two cups out of the cupboard and fills them with coffee. "Look," Walt says, "This is going to sound crazy, but . . . but would you mind telling me my name?"

Nina sips from her cup. "Philip Warburton," she says, tonelessly.

"No, I mean it. I'm not kidding this time."

"Are you telling me that you don't remember it, you really don't?"

"I said I wasn't kidding this time."

"Jonathan Cardwell," Nina says.

"Please," says Walt. "*Please.*"

"William Keesler."

Walt looks at her. "You're supposed to be my *wife*," he says. "You're really not kidding this time, are you?"

"I'm blank," says Walt, turning his face away.

"You actually can't remember your name?" Walt shakes his head. "Or my name?" Walt shakes his head. "Or the names of our children?" Walt looks at her.

"We don't have any children," he says.

"Well, there you are," Nina says.

They go into the living room. Nina puts a record on the stereo. They dance a slow two-step to an old Guy Lombardo record. "Tell me your name," he whispers into her ear. "Jenny Melrose," she says. He dances her over to the couch and pushes her down into the cushions. He opens her robe. "Jenny," he says. "I'm so frightened."

"Phil," Nina says. "Oh, Phil."

They were seven thousand feet over the coast of Southern California. It was Elmo Ripley's plane, Walt's business partner's. Elmo had not sobered up from the previous night in Las Vegas. They were all going to Oakland or Santa Cruz or Monterey or someplace else. Elmo wanted to arm wrestle. He and Walt went into the passenger compartment. "Who's going to fly the plane?" Nina asked. "You are, Nina," said Elmo, and they left her alone. She had been sitting next to Elmo in the copilot's seat. Peggy Ripley came up and sat next to her. "It's easy," she said. "You just keep the nose on the horizon, and that needle by your knee on zero," "I think the next omni station is Santa Barbara," said Elmo from the rear of the plane. Nina gripped the wheel. The engines began to labor. "You've let the horizon get away from you, doll," said Peggy Ripley. Nina pushed the wheel forward. The engines began to rise in pitch. Nina did not like the sound. She let go of the wheel and clamped her hands on her ears. The horizon rose to the top of the windshield, like water filling a tank. "You're diving, doll," said Peggy.

Hold this party in the attic, if you have one. The invitations should be in the form of warrants. When the guests arrive, tell them they will be expected to "pay" for everything in "spades." Start them on a pin hunt. Prepare a little "story," using the names of as many different animals as possible. Whisper to each guest the name of some animal. Tell him his number and that when his number is "up" he must drop everything and imitate this animal in some way but not call the animal's name aloud. The penalty is "exclusion." To some give the word Angina, *to others,* Infarct, *and to others,* Polymorphonuclear. *Of course, the ladies must be in "fetching" costume. Your guests will not be bored.*

An ape and a bear carried Nina into the rumpus room. They put her on the pool table and would not let her sit up. The ape pushed the bear. "Let me handle this," said the ape. "I can fix her." The bear dragged the ape away. They rolled on the floor, laughing in their animal heads. They were good fellows, neighbors. Nina dozed. She had emptied the contents of her ring into her last drink. Her lips were numb. She felt nothing from the waist down. The pool table was like cool marble. Someone behind her head was whistling a melody from Wagner. She could feel the needle of air from the whistler's lips. It was a pleasant moment. They were all pulling for her. "Refrigerator dream," she said. *"Now."*

The hum of electric motors begins.

The lights of the Ciudad are below her. The party has moved to the hillside, among the granite boulders. Someone says, "Strap it here. No, *here.*" Someone else says, "Don't relax, Jesus, don't relax!" A masterful voice she has never heard before says, *"You must push."* Several strong men are holding her aloft. A bald man is kneeling between her legs hefting a stone. He draws the stone out of her thighs. "It's a beautiful thirty-pound stone," he says, holding it high. She is slippery with sweat and oil. A drink is raised to her lips. Someone mops her forehead with a sock. She feels a mouth on her arm, the flexing tongue. There is a woman holding a can of compressed salad oil, and she says, "The grand finale."

Canvas straps flatten Nina's breasts and someone is drawing laces together at her spine. Six men, holding her thighs and arms, begin to trot through the field of stones, their drinks spilling. They urge her to fly. Her heart is wild and erratic, like a stunned bird. The threads at her spine jerk her away from the hill. A heavy cheer bursts from below.

She sees someone, a man, looking up, shading his eyes against the glare of light. He moves quickly one way, then the other, then freezes. *Spider,* Nina thinks, scissoring the air with her padded legs. *He sees the spider.*

The man turns, loses his balance, recovers, and runs to the safety of his garage.

Quadberry

BARRY HANNAH

When I was ten, eleven, and twelve, I did a good bit of my play in the backyard of a three-story wooden house my father had bought and rented out, his first venture into real estate. We lived right across the street from it, but over here was the place to do your real play. There was an old harrowed but overgrown garden, a vine-swallowed fence at the back end, and beyond the fence a cornfield which belonged to someone else. This was not the country. This was the town, Clinton, Mississippi, between Jackson on the east and Vicksburg on the west. On this lot stood a few water oaks, a few plum bushes, and much overgrowth of honeysuckle vine. At the very back end, at the fence, stood three strong nude chinaberry trees.

In Mississippi it is difficult to achieve a vista. But my friends and I had one here at the back corner of the garden. We could see across the cornfield, see the one lone tin-roofed house this side of the railroad tracks, then on across the tracks were many other bleaker houses with rustier tin roofs, smoke coming out of the chimneys in the late fall. This was niggertown. We had binoculars and could see the colored children hustling about and perhaps a hopeless sow or two with her brood enclosed in a tiny boarded-up area. Through the binoculars one afternoon in October we watched some men corner and beat a large hog on the brain. They used an ax and the thing kept running around, head leaning toward the ground, for several minutes before it lay down. I thought I saw the men laughing when it finally did. One of them was staggering, plainly drunk to my sight from three hundred yards away. He had the long knife. Because of that scene I considered Negroes savage cowards for a good five more years of my life. Our maid brought some sausage to my mother and when it was put in the pan to fry, I made a point of running out of the house.

I went directly across the street and to the back end of the garden behind the apartment house we owned, without my breakfast. That was Saturday. Eventually, Radcleve saw me. His parents had him mowing the yard that ran alongside my dad's property. He clicked off the power mower and I went over to his fence, which was storm wire. His mother maintained handsome flowery grounds at all costs; she had a leaf-mold bin and St. Augustine grass as solid as a rug.

Radcleve himself was a violent experimental chemist. When Radcleve was eight, he threw a whole package of .22 shells against the sidewalk in front of his house until one of them went off driving lead fragments into his calf, most of them still deep in there where the surgeons never dared tamper. Radcleve knew about the sulfur, potassium nitrate and charcoal mixture for gunpowder when he was ten. He bought things through the mail when he ran out of ingredients in his chemistry sets. When he was an infant, his father, a quiet man who owned the Chevrolet agency in town, bought an entire bankrupt sporting-goods store, and in the middle of their backyard he built a house plain-painted and neat, one room and a heater, where Radcleve's redundant toys forevermore were kept —all the possible toys he would need for boyhood. There were things in there that Radcleve and I were not mature enough for and

did not know the real use of. When we were eleven, we uncrated the new Dunlop golf balls and went on up a shelf for the tennis rackets, went out in the middle of his yard, and served new golf ball after new golf ball with blasts of the rackets over into the cornfield, out of sight. When the strings busted we just went in and got another racket. We were absorbed by how a good smack would set the heavy little pills on an endless flight. Then Radcleve's father came down. He simply dismissed me. He took Radcleve into the house and covered his whole body with a belt. But within the week Radcleve had invented the mortar. It was a steel pipe into which a flashlight battery fit perfectly, like a bullet into a muzzle. He had drilled a hole for the fuse of an M-80 firecracker at the base, for the charge. It was a grand cannon, set up on a stack of bricks at the back of my dad's property, which was the free place to play. When it shot, it would back up violently with thick smoke and you could hear the flashlight battery whistling off. So that morning when I ran out of the house protesting the hog sausage, I told Radcleve to bring over the mortar. His ma and dad were in Jackson for the day, and he came right over with the pipe, the batteries, and the M-80 explosives. He had two gross of them.

Before, we'd shot off toward the woods to the right of niggertown. I turned the bricks to the left; I made us a very fine cannon carriage pointing toward niggertown. When Radcleve appeared, he had two pairs of binoculars around his neck, one pair a newly plundered German unit as big as a brace of whiskey bottles. I told him I wanted to shoot for that house where we saw them killing the pig. Radcleve loved the idea. We singled out the house with heavy use of the binoculars.

There were children out in the yard. Then they all went in. Two men came out of the back door. I thought I recognized the drunkard from the other afternoon. I helped Radcleve fix the direction of the cannon. We estimated the altitude we needed to get down there. Radcleve put the M-80 in the breech with its fuse standing out of the hole. I dropped the flashlight battery in. I lit the fuse. We backed off. The M-80 blasted off deafeningly, smoke rose, but my concentration was on that particular house over there. I brought the binoculars up. We waited six or seven seconds. I heard a great joyful wallop on tin. "We've hit him on the first try, the first try!" I yelled. Radcleve was ecstatic. "Right on his roof!" We bolstered up the brick carriage. Radcleve remembered the correct height of the cannon exactly. So we fixed it, loaded it, lit it, and backed off. The battery landed on the roof, blat, again, louder. I looked to see if there wasn't a great dent or hole in the roof. I could not understand why niggers weren't pouring out distraught from that house. We shot the mortar again and again, and always our battery hit the tin roof. Sometimes there was only a dull thud but other times there was a wild distress of tin. I was still looking through the binoculars, amazed that the niggers wouldn't even come out of their house to see what was hitting their roof. Radcleve was on to it better than me. I looked over at him and he had the huge German binocs much lower than I did. He was looking straight through the cornfield, which was all bare and open with nothing left but rotten stalks. "What we've

45

been hitting is the roof of that house just this side of the tracks. White people live in there,'' he said.

I took up my binoculars again. I looked around the yard of that white wooden house on this side of the tracks, almost next to the railroad. When I found the tin roof, I saw four significant dents in it. I saw one of our batteries lying in the middle of a sort of crater. I took the binoculars down into the yard and saw a blonde middle-aged woman looking our way.

''Somebody's coming up toward us. He's from that house and he's got, I think, some sort of fancy gun with him. It might be an automatic weapon.''

I ran my binoculars all over the cornfield. Then, in a line with the house, I saw him. He was coming our way but having some trouble with the rows and dead stalks of the cornfield.

''That is just a boy like us. All he's got is a saxophone with him,'' I told Radcleve. I had recently got in the school band, playing drums, and had seen all the weird horns that made up a band.

I watched this boy with the saxophone through the binoculars until he was ten feet from us. This was Quadberry. His name was Ard, short for Arden. His shoes were foot-square wads of mud from the cornfield. When he saw us across the fence and above him, he stuck out his arm in my direction.

''My dad says stop it!''

''We weren't doing anything,'' says Radcleve.

''Mother saw the smoke puff up from here. Dad has a hangover.''

''A what?''

''It's a headache from indiscretion. You're lucky he does. He's picked up the poker to rap on you, but he can't move further the way his head is.''

''What's your name? You're not in the band,'' I said, focusing on the saxophone.

''It's Ard Quadberry. Why do you keep looking at me through the binoculars?''

It was because he was odd, with his hair and its white ends, and his Arab nose, and, now, his name. Add to that the saxophone.

''My dad's a doctor at the college, Mother's a musician. You better quit what you're doing . . . I was out practicing in the garage. I saw one of those flashlight batteries roll off the roof. Could I see what you shoot 'em with?''

''No,'' said Radcleve. Then he said: ''If you'll play that horn.''

Quadberry stood out there ten feet below us in the field, skinny, feet and pants booted with black mud, and at his chest the slung-on, very complex, radiant horn.

Quadberry began sucking and licking the reed. I didn't care much for this act, and there was too much desperate oralness in his face when he began playing. That was why I chose the drums. One had to engage himself like suck's revenge with a horn. But what Quadberry was playing was pleasant and intricate. I was sure it was advanced, and there was no squawking as from the other eleven-year-olds on sax in the band room. He made the end with a clean upward riff, holding the final note high, pure and unwavering.

''Good!'' I called to him.

Quadberry was trying to move out of the sunken row toward us, but his heavy shoes were impeding him.

''Sounded like a duck. Sounded like a girl duck,'' said Radcleve, who was kneeling down and packing a mudball around one of the M-80s. I saw and I was an accomplice, because I did nothing. Radcleve lit the fuse and heaved the mudball over the fence. An M-80 is a very serious firecracker; it is like the charge they use to shoot up those sprays six hundred feet on July Fourth at country clubs. It went off, this one, even bigger than most M-80s.

When we looked over the fence, we saw Quadberry all muck specks and fragments of stalks. He was covering the mouthpiece of his horn with both hands. Then I saw there was blood pouring out of, it seemed, his right eye. I thought he was bleeding directly out of his eye.

''Quadberry?'' I called.

He turned around and never said a word to me until I was eighteen. He walked back holding his eye and staggering through the cornstalks. Radcleve had him in the binoculars. Radcleve was trembling . . . but intrigued.

''His mother just screamed. She's running out in the field to get him.''

I thought we'd blinded him, but we hadn't. I thought the Quadberrys would get the police or call my father, but they didn't. The upshot of this is that Quadberry had a permanent white space next to his right eye, a spot that looked like a tiny upset crown.

I went from sixth through half of twelfth grade ignoring him and that wound. I was coming on as a drummer and a lover, but if Quadberry happened to appear within fifty feet of me and my most tender, intimate sweetheart, I would duck out. Quadberry grew up just like the rest of us. His father was still a doctor—professor of history—at the town college; his mother was still blonde, and a musician. She was organist at an Episcopalian church in Jackson, the big capital city ten miles east of us.

As for Radcleve, he still had no ear for music, but he was there, my buddy. He was repentant about Quadberry, although not so much as I. He'd thrown the mud grenade over the fence only to see what would happen. He had not really wanted to maim. Quadberry had played his tune on the sax, Radcleve had played his tune on the mud grenade. It was just a shame they happened to cross talents.

Radcleve went into a long period of nearly nothing after he gave up violent explosives. Then he trained himself to copy the comic strips, *Steve Canyon* to *Major Hoople,* until he became quite a versatile cartoonist with some very provocative new faces and bodies that were gesturing intriguingly. He could never fill in the speech balloons with the smart words they needed. Sometimes he would pencil in ''ERR'' or ''WHAT?'' in the empty speech places. I saw him a great deal. Radcleve was not spooked by Quadberry. He even once asked Quadberry what his opinion was of his future as a cartoonist. Quadberry told Radcleve that if he took all his cartoons and stuffed himself with them he would make an interesting dead man. After that, Radcleve was shy of him too.

When I was a senior we had an extraordinary band. Word was we had outplayed all the big A.A.A. division bands last April in the state contest. Then came news that a new blazing saxophone player was coming into the band as first chair. This person had spent summers in Vermont in music camps, and he was coming in with us for the concert season. Our director, a lovable aesthete named Richard Prender, announced to us in a proud silent moment that the boy was joining us tomorrow night. The effect was that everybody should push over a seat or two and make room for this boy and his talent. I was annoyed. Here I'd been with the band and had kept hold of the taste among the whole percussion section. I could play rock and jazz drum and didn't even really need to be here. I could be in Vermont too, give me a piano and a bass. I looked at the kid on first sax, who was going to be supplanted tomorrow. For two years he had thought he was the star, then suddenly enters this boy who's three times better.

The new boy was Quadberry. He came in, but he was meek, and when he tuned up he put his head almost on the floor, bending over trying to be inconspicuous. The girls in the band had wanted him to be handsome, but Quadberry refused and kept himself in such hiding among the sax section that he was neither handsome, ugly, cute, or anything. What he was was pretty near invisible, except for the bell of his horn, the all-but-closed eyes, the Arabian nose, the brown hair with its halo of white ends, the desperate oralness, the giant reed punched into his face, and hazy Quadberry loving the wound in a private dignified ecstasy.

I say dignified because of what came out the end of his horn. He was more than what Prender had told us he would be. Because of Quadberry, we could take the band arrangement of Ravel's *Bolero* with us to the state contest. Quadberry would do the saxophone solo. He would switch to alto sax, he would do the sly Moorish ride.

When he played, I heard the sweetness, I heard the horn which finally brought human *talk* into the realm of music. It could sound like the mutterings of a field nigger, and then it could get up into inhumanly careless beauty, it could get among mutinous helium bursts around Saturn. I already loved *Bolero* for the constant drum part. The percussion was always there, driving along with the subtly increasing triplets, insistent, insistent, at last outraged and trying to steal the whole show from the horns and the others. I knew a large boy with dirty blond hair, name of Wyatt, who played viola in the Jackson Symphony and sousaphone in our band—one of the rare closet transmutations of my time—who was forever claiming to have discovered the central *Bolero* one Sunday afternoon over FM radio as he had seven distinct sexual moments with a certain B., girl flutist with black bangs and skin like mayonnaise, while the drums of Ravel carried them on and on in a ceremony of Spanish sex. It was agreed by all the canny in the band that *Bolero* was exactly the piece to make the band soar—now especially as we had Quadberry, who made his walk into the piece like an actual lean Spanish bandit. This boy could blow his horn. He was, as I had suspected, a genius. His solo was not quite the same as the New York Phil's saxophonist's, but it was better. It came in and was with us. It entered my spine and, I am sure, went up the skirts of the girls. I had almost deafened myself playing drums in the most famous rock and jazz band in the state, but I could hear the voice that went through and out that horn. It sounded like a very troubled forty-year-old man, a man who had had his brow in his hands a long time.

The next time I saw Quadberry up close, in fact the first time I had seen him up close since we were eleven and he was bleeding in the cornfield, was in late February. I had only three classes this last semester, and went up to the band room often, to loaf and complain and keep up my touch on the drums. Prender let me keep my set in one of the instrument rooms, with a tarpaulin thrown over it, and I would drag it out to the practice room and whale away. Sometimes a group of sophomores would come up and I would make them marvel, whaling away as if not only deaf but blind to them, although I wasn't at all. If I saw a sophomore girl with exceptional bod or face, I would do miracles of technique I never knew were in me. I would amaze myself. I would be threatening Buddy Rich and Sam Morello. But this time when I went into the instrument room, there was Quadberry on one side, and, back in a dark corner, a small ninth-grade euphonium player whose face was all red. The little boy was weeping and grinning at the same time.

"Queerberry," the boy said softly.

Quadberry flew upon him like a demon. He grabbed the boy's collar, slapped his face, and yanked his arm behind him in a merciless wrestler's grip, the one that made them bawl on TV. Then the boy broke it and slugged Quadberry in the lips and ran across to my side of the room. He said "Queerberry" softly again and jumped for the door. Quadberry plunged across the room and tackled him on the threshold. Now that the boy was under him, Quadberry pounded the top of his head with his fist made like a mallet. The boy kept calling him "Queerberry" throughout this. He had not learned his lesson. The boy seemed to be going into concussion, so I stepped over and touched Quadberry, telling him to quit. Quadberry obeyed and stood up off the boy, who crawled on out into the band room. But once more the boy looked back with a bruised grin, saying "Queerberry." Quadberry made a move toward him, but I blocked it.

"Why are you beating up on this little guy?" I said. Quadberry was sweating and his eyes were wild with hate; he was a big fellow now, though lean. He was, at six feet tall, bigger than me.

"He kept calling me Queerberry."

"What do you care?" I asked.

"I care," Quadberry said, and left me standing there.

We were to play at Millsaps College Auditorium for the concert. It was April. We got on the buses, a few took their cars, and were a big tense crowd getting over there. To Jackson was only a twenty-minute trip. The director, Prender, followed the bus in his Volkswagen. There was a thick fog. A flashing ambulance, snaking the lanes, piled into him head on. Prender, who I would imagine was thinking of *Bolero* and hearing the young horn voices in his band—perhaps he was dwelling on Quadberry's spectacular gypsy entrance, or perhaps he was meditating on the percussion section, of which I was the king—passed into the airs of band-director heaven. We were told by the student director as we set up on the stage. The student director was a senior from the town college, very much afflicted, almost to the point of drooling, by a love and respect for Dick Prender, and now afflicted by a heartbreaking esteem for his ghost. As were we all.

I loved the tough and tender director awesomely and never knew it until I found myself bawling along with all the rest of the boys of the percussion. I told them to keep setting up, keep tuning, keep screwing the stands together, keep hauling in the kettledrums. To just quit and bawl seemed a betrayal to Prender. I caught some girl clarinetists trying to flee the stage and go have their cry. I told them to get the hell back to their section. They obeyed me. Then I found the student director. I had to have my way.

"Look. I say we just play *Bolero* and junk the rest. That's our horse. We can't play *Brighton Beach* and *Neptune's Daughter*. We'll never make it through them. And they're too happy."

"We aren't going to play anything," he said. "Man, to play is filthy. Did you ever hear Prender play piano? Do you know what a cool man he was in all things?"

"We play. He got us ready, and we play."

"Man, you can't play any more than I can direct. You're bawling your face off. Look out there at the rest of them. Man, it's a herd, it's a weeping herd."

"What's wrong? Why aren't you pulling this crowd together?" This was Quadberry, who had come up urgently. "I got those little brats in my section sitting down, but we've got people abandoning the stage, tearful little finks throwing their horns on the floor."

"I'm not directing," said the moustached college man.

"Then get out of here. You're weak, weak!"

"Man, we've got teen-agers in ruin here, we got sorrowville. Nobody can—"

"Go ahead. Do your number. Weak out on us."

"Man, I—"

Quadberry was already up on the podium, shaking his arms.

"We're right here! The band is right here! Tell your friends to get back in their seats. We're doing *Bolero*. Just put *Bolero* up and start tuning. *I'm* directing. I'll be right here in front of you. You look at *me!* Don't you dare quit on Prender. Don't you dare quit on me. You've got to be heard. *I've* got to be heard. Prender wanted me to be heard. I am the star, and I say we sit down and blow."

And so we did. We all tuned and were burning low for the advent into *Bolero*, though we couldn't believe that Quadberry was going to remain with his saxophone strapped to him and conduct us as well as play his solo. The judges, who apparently hadn't heard about Prender's death, walked down to their balcony desks.

One of them called out "Ready" and Quadberry's hand was instantly up in the air, his fingers rock-hard as if around the stem of something like a torch. This was not Prender's way, but it had to do. We went into the number cleanly and Quadberry one-armed it in the conducting. He kept his face, this look of hostility, at the reeds and the trumpets. I was glad he did not look toward me and the percussion boys like that. But he must have known we would be constant and tasteful because I was the king there. As for the others, the soloists especially, he was scaring them into excellence. Prender had never got quite this from them. Boys became men and girls became women as Quadberry directed us through *Bolero*. I even became a bit better of a man myself, though Quadberry did not look my way. When he turned around toward the people in the auditorium to enter on his solo, I knew it was my baby. I and the drums were the metronome. That was no trouble. It was talent to keep the metronome ticking amidst any given chaos of sound.

But this keeps one's mind occupied and I have no idea what Quadberry sounded like on his sax ride. All I know is that he looked grief-stricken and pale, and small. Sweat had popped out on his forehead. He bent over extremely. He was wearing the red brass-button jacket and black pants, black bow tie at the throat, just like the rest of us. In this outfit he bent over his horn almost out of sight. For a moment, before I caught the glint of his horn through the music stands, I thought he had pitched forward off the stage. He went down so far to do his deep oral thing, his conducting arm had disappeared so quickly, I didn't know but what he was having a seizure.

When *Bolero* was over, the audience stood up and made meat out of their hands applauding. The judges themselves applauded. The band stood up, bawling again, for Prender and because we had done so well. The student director rushed out crying to embrace Quadberry, who eluded him with his dipping shoulders. The crowd was still clapping insanely. I wanted to see Quadberry myself. I waded through the red backs, through the bow ties, over the white bucks. Here was the first-chair clarinetist who had done his bit like an angel; he sat close to the podium and could hear Quadberry.

"Was Quadberry good?" I asked him.

"Are you kidding? These tears in my eyes, they're for how good he was. He was too good. I'll never touch my clarinet again." The clarinetist slung the pieces of his horn into their case like underwear and a toothbrush.

I found Quadberry putting the sections of his alto in the velvet holds of his case.

"Hooray," I said. "Hip damn hooray for you."

Arden was smiling too, showing a lot of teeth I had never seen. His smile was sly. He knew he had pulled off a monster unlikelihood.

"Hip hip hooray for me," he said. "Look at her. I had the bell of the horn almost smack in her face."

There was a woman of about thirty sitting in the front row of the auditorium. She wore a sundress with a drastic cleavage up front; looked like something that hung around New Orleans and kneaded your heart to death with her feet. She was still mesmerized by Quadberry. She bore on him with a stare and there was moisture in her cleavage.

"You played well."

"Well? Play well? Yes."

He was trying not to look at her directly. Look at *me*, I beckoned to her with full face: I was the *drums*. She arose and left.

"I was walking downhill in a valley, is all I was doing," said Quadberry. "Another man, a wizard, was playing my horn." He locked his sax case. "I feel nasty for not being able to cry like the rest of them. Look at them. Look at them crying."

True, the children of the band were still weeping, standing around the stage. Several moms and dads had come up among them, and they were misty-eyed too. The mixture of grief and superb music had been unbearable.

A girl in tears appeared next to Quadberry. She was a majorette in football season and played third-chair sax during the concert season. Not even her violent sorrow could take the beauty out of the face of this girl. I had watched her for a number of years—her alertness to her own beauty, the pride of her legs in the majorette outfit—and had taken out her younger sister, a second-rate version of her and a wayward overcompensating nymphomaniac whom several of us made a hobby out of pitying. Well, here was Lilian herself crying in Quadberry's face. She told him that she'd run off the stage when she heard about Prender, dropped her horn and everything, and had thrown herself into a tavern across the street and drunk two beers quickly for some kind of relief. But she had come back through the front doors of the auditorium and sat down, dizzy with beer, and heard Quadberry, the miraculous way he had gone on with *Bolero*. And now she was eaten up by feelings of guilt, weakness, cowardice.

"We didn't miss you," said Quadberry.

"Please forgive me. Tell me to do something to make up for it."

"Don't breathe my way, then. You've got beer all over your breath."

"I want to talk to you."

"Take my horn case and go out, get in my car, and wait for me. It's the ugly Plymouth in front of the school bus."

"I know," she said.

Lilian Field, this lovely teary thing, with the rather pious grace of her carriage, with the voice full of imminent swoon, picked up Quadberry's horn case and her own and walked off the stage.

I told the percussion boys to wrap up the packing. Into my suitcase I put my own gear and also managed to steal drum keys, two pairs of brushes, a twenty-inch Turkish cymbal, a Gretsch snare drum that I desired for my collection, a wood block, kettle-drum mallets, a tuning harp, and a score sheet of *Bolero* full of marginal notes I'd written down straight from the mouth of Dick Prender, thinking I might want to look at the score sheet sometime in the future when I was having a fit of nostalgia such as I am having right now as I write this. I had never done any serious stealing before, and I was stealing for my art. Prender was dead, the band had done its last thing of the year, I was a senior. Things were finished at the high school. I was just looting a sinking ship. I could hardly lift the suitcase. As I was pushing it across the stage, Qaudberry was there again.

"You can ride back with me if you want to."

"But you've got Lilian."

"Please ride back with me . . . us. Please."

"Why?"

"To help me get rid of her. Her breath is full of beer. My father always had that breath. Every time he was friendly, he had that breath. And she looks a great deal like my mother." We were interrupted by the Tupelo band director. He put his baton against Quadberry's arm.

"You were big with *Bolero*, son, but that doesn't mean you own the stage."

Quadberry caught the end of the suitcase and helped me with it out to the steps behind the auditorium. The buses were gone. There sat his ugly ocher Plymouth; it was a failed, gay, experimental shade from the Chrysler people. Lilian was sitting in the front seat wearing her shirt and bow tie, her coat off.

"Are you going to ride back with me?" Quadberry said to me.

"I think I would spoil something. You never saw her when she was a majorette. She's not stupid, either. She likes to show it off a little, but she's not stupid. She's in the History Club."

"My father has a doctorate in history. She smells of beer."

I said, "She drank two cans of beer when she heard about Prender."

"There are a lot of other things to do when you hear about death. What I did, for example. She ran away. She fell to pieces."

"She's waiting for us," I said.

"One damned thing I am never going to do is drink."

"I've never seen your mother up close, but Lilian doesn't look like your mother. She doesn't look like anybody's mother."

I rode with them silently to Clinton. Lilian made no bones about being disappointed I was in the car, though she said nothing. I knew it would be like this and I hated it. Other girls in town would not be so unhappy that I was in the car with them. I looked for flaws in Lilian's face and neck and hair, but there weren't any. Couldn't there be a mole, an enlarged pore, too much gum on a tooth, a single awkward hair around the ear? No. Memory, the whole lying opera of it, is killing me now. Lilian was faultless beauty, even sweating, even and especially in the white man's shirt and the bow tie clamping together her collar, when one knew her uncomfortable bosoms, her poor nipples. . . .

"Don't take me back to the band room. Turn off here and let me off at my house," I said to Quadberry. He didn't turn off.

"Don't tell Arden what to do. He can do what he wants to," said Lilian, ignoring me and speaking to me at the same time. I couldn't bear her hatred. I asked Quadberry to please just stop the car and let me out here, wherever he was: this front yard of the mobile home would do. I was so earnest that he stopped the car. He handed back the keys and I dragged my suitcase out of the trunk, then flung the keys back at him and kicked the car to get it going again.

My band came together in the summer. We were the Bop Fiends . . . that was our name. Two of them were from Ole Miss, our bass player was from Memphis State, but when we got together this time, I didn't call the tenor sax, who went to Mississippi Southern, because Quadberry wanted to play with us. During the school year the college boys and I fell into minor groups to pick up twenty dollars on a weekend, playing dances for the Moose Lodge, medical-student fraternities in Jackson, teen-age recreation centers in Greenwood, and such as that. But come summer we were the Bop Fiends again, and the price for us went up to $1,200 a gig. Where they wanted the best rock and bop and they had some bread, we were called. The summer after I was a senior, we played in Alabama, Louisiana, and Arkansas. Our fame was getting out there on the interstate route.

This was the summer that I made myself deaf.

Years ago Prender had invited down an old friend from a high school in Michigan. He asked me over to meet the friend, who had been a drummer with Stan Kenton at one time and was now a band director just like Prender. This fellow was almost totally deaf and he warned me very sincerely about deafing myself. He said there would come a point when you had to lean over and concentrate all your hearing on what the band was doing and that was the time to quit for a while, because if you didn't you would be irrevocably deaf like him in a month or two. I listened to him but could not take him seriously. Here was an oldish man who had his problems. My ears had ages of hearing left. Not so, I played the drums so loud the summer after I graduated from high school that I made myself, eventually, stone-deaf.

We were at, say, the National Guard Armory in Lake Village, Arkansas, Quadberry out in front of us on the stage they'd built. Down on the floor were hundreds of sweaty teen-agers. Four girls in sundresses, showing what they could, were leaning on the stage with broad ignorant lust on their minds. I'd play so loud for one particular chick, I'd get absolutely out of control. The guitar boys would have to turn the volume up full blast to compensate. Thus I went deaf. Anyhow, the dramatic idea was to release Quadberry on a very soft sweet ballad right in the middle of a long ear-piercing run of rock-and-roll tunes. I'd get out the brushes and we would astonish the crowd with our tenderness. By August, I was so deaf I had to watch Quadberry's fingers changing notes on the saxophone, had to use my eyes to keep time. The other members of the Bop Fiends told me I was hitting out of time. I pretended I was trying to do experimental things with rhythm when the truth was I simply could no longer hear. I was no longer a tasteful drummer, either. I had become deaf through lack of taste.

Which was—taste—exactly the quality that made Quadberry wicked on the saxophone. During the howling, during the churning, Quadberry had taste. The noise did not affect his personality; he was solid as a brick. He could blend. Oh, he could hoot through his horn when the right time came, but he could do supporting roles for an hour. Then, when we brought him out front for his solo on something like *Take Five,* he would play with such light blissful technique that he even eclipsed Paul Desmond, who had recorded it originally with Dave Brubeck. The girls around the stage did not cause him to enter into excessive loudness or vibrato.

Quadberry had his own girl friend now, Lilian back at Clinton, who put all the sundressed things around the stage in the shade. In my mind I had congratulated him for getting up next to this beauty, but in June and July, when I was still hearing things a little, he never said a word about her. It was one night in August, when I could hear nothing and was driving him to his house, that he asked me to turn on the inside light and spoke in a retarded deliberate way. He knew I was deaf and counted on my being able to read lips.

"Don't . . . make . . . fun . . . of her . . . or me. . . . We . . . think . . . she . . . is . . . in trouble."

I wagged my head. Never would I make fun of him or her. She detested me because I had taken out her helpless little sister for a few weeks, but I would never think there was anything funny about Lilian, for all her haughtiness. I only thought of this event as monumentally curious.

"No one except you knows," he said.

"Why did you tell me?"

"Because I'm going away and you have to take care of her. I wouldn't trust her with anybody but you."

"She hates the sight of my face. Where are you going?"

"Annapolis."

"You aren't going to any damned Annapolis."

"That was the only school that wanted me."

"You're going to play your saxophone on a boat?"

"I don't know what I'm going to do."

"How . . . how can you just leave her?"

"She wants me to. She's very excited about me at Annapolis. William [this is my name], there is no girl I could imagine who has more inner sweetness than Lilian."

I entered the town college, as did Lilian. She was in the same chemistry class I was. But she was rows away. It was difficult to learn anything, being deaf. The professor wasn't a pantomimer —but finally he went to the blackboard with the formulas and the algebra of problems, to my happiness. I hung in and made a B. At the end of the semester I was swaggering around the grade sheet he'd posted. I happened to see Lilian's grade. She'd only made a C. Beautiful Lilian got only a C while I, with my handicap, had made a B.

It had been a very difficult chemistry class. I had watched Lilian's stomach the whole way through. It was not growing. I wanted to see her look like a watermelon, make herself an amazing mother shape.

When I made the B and Lilian made the C, I got up my courage and finally went by to see her. She answered the door. Her parents weren't home. I'd never wanted this office of watching over her as Quadberry wanted me to, and this is what I told her. She asked me into the house. The rooms smelled of nail polish and pipe smoke. I was hoping her little sister wasn't in the house, and my wish came true. We were alone.

"You can quit watching over me."

"Are you pregnant?"

"No." Then she started crying. "I wanted to be. But I'm not."

"What do you hear from Quadberry?"

She said something, but she had her back to me. She looked to me for an answer, but I had nothing to say. I knew she'd said something, but I hadn't heard it.

"He doesn't play the saxophone anymore," she said.

This made me angry.

"Why not?"

"Too much math and science and navigation. He wants to fly. That's what his dream is now. He wants to get into an F-something jet."

I asked her to say this over and she did. Lilian really was full of inner sweetness, as Quadberry had said. She understood that I was deaf. Perhaps Quadberry had told her.

The rest of the time in her house I simply witnessed her beauty and her mouth moving.

I went through college. To me it is interesting that I kept a B average and did it all deaf, though I know this isn't interesting to people who aren't deaf. I loved music, and never heard it. I loved poetry, and never heard a word that came out of the mouths of the visiting poets who read at the campus. I loved my mother and dad, but never heard a sound they made. One Christmas Eve, Radcleve was back from Ole Miss and threw an M-80 out in the street for old times' sake. I saw it explode, but there was only a pressure in my ears. I was at parties when lusts were raging and I went home with two girls (I am medium handsome) who lived in apartments of the old two-story 1920 vintage, and I took my shirt off and made love to them. But I have no real idea what their reaction was. They were stunned and all smiles when I got up, but I have no idea whether I gave them the last pleasure or not. I hope I did. I've always been partial to women and have always wanted to see them satisfied till their eyes popped out.

Through Lilian I got the word that Quadberry was out of Annapolis and now flying jets off the *Bonhomme Richard,* an aircraft carrier headed for Vietnam. He telegrammed her that he would set down at the Jackson airport at ten o'clock one night. So Lilian and I were out there waiting. It was a familiar place to her. She was a stewardess and her loops were mainly in the South. She wore a beige raincoat, had red sandals on her feet; I was in a black turtleneck and corduroy jacket, feeling significant, so significant I could barely stand it. I'd already made myself the lead writer at Gordon-Marx Advertising in Jackson. I hadn't seen Lilian in a year. Her eyes were strained, no longer the bright blue things they were when she was a pious beauty. We drank coffee together. I loved her. As far as I knew, she'd been faithful to Quadberry.

He came down in an F-something Navy jet right on the dot of ten. She ran out on the airport pavement to meet him. I saw her crawl up the ladder. Quadberry never got out of the plane. I could see him in his blue helmet. Lilian backed down the ladder. Then Quadberry had the cockpit cover him again. He turned the plane around so its flaming red end was at us. He took it down the runway. We saw him leap out into the night at the middle of the runway going west, toward San Diego and the *Bonhomme Richard.* Lilian was crying.

"What did he say?" I asked.

"He said, 'I am a dragon. America the beautiful, like you will never know.' He wanted to give you a message. He was glad you were here."

"What was the message?"

"The same thing. 'I am a dragon. America the beautiful, like you will never know.' "

"Did he say anything else?"

"Not a thing."

"Did he express any love toward you?"

"He wasn't Ard. He was somebody with a sneer in a helmet."

"He's going to war, Lilian."

"I asked him to kiss me and he told me to get off the plane, he was firing up and it was dangerous."

"Arden is going to war. He's just on his way to Vietnam and he wanted us to know that. It wasn't just him he wanted us to see. It was him in the jet he wanted us to see. He is that black jet. You can't kiss an airplane."

"And what are we supposed to do?" cried sweet Lilian.

"We've just got to hang around. He didn't have to lift off and disappear straight up like that. That was to tell us how he isn't with us anymore."

Lilian asked me what she was supposed to do now. I told her she was supposed to come with me to my apartment in the old 1920 Clinton place where I was. I was supposed to take care of her. Quadberry had said so. His six-year-old directive was still working in her brain.

She slept on the fold-out bed of the sofa for a while. This was the only bed in my place. I stood in the dark of the kitchen and drank a quarter bottle of gin on ice. I would not turn on the light and spoil her sleep. The prospect of Lilian asleep in my apartment made me feel like a chaplain on a visit to the Holy Land; I stood there getting drunk, biting my tongue when dreams of lust burst on me. That black jet Quadberry wanted us to see him in, its flaming rear end, his blasting straight up into the night at mid-runway—what precisely was he wanting to say in this stunt? Was he saying remember him forever or forget him forever? But I had my own life and was neither going to mother-hen it over his memory nor his old sweetheart. What did he mean, *America the beautiful, like you will never know*? I, William Howly, knew a goddamn good bit about

America the beautiful, even as a deaf man. Being deaf had brought me up closer to people. There were only about five I knew, but I knew their mouth movements, the perspiration under their noses, their tongues moving over the crowns of their teeth, their fingers on their lips. Quadberry, I said, you don't have to get up next to the stars in your black jet to see America the beautiful.

I was deciding to lie down on the kitchen floor and sleep the night, when Lilian turned on the light and appeared in her panties and bra. Her body was perfect except for a tiny bit of fat on her upper thighs. She'd sunbathed herself so her limbs were brown, and her stomach, and the instinct was to rip off the white underwear and lick, suck, say something terrific into the flesh that you discovered.

She was moving her mouth.

"Say it again slowly."

"I'm lonely. When he took off in his jet, I think it meant he wasn't ever going to see me again. I think it meant he was laughing at both of us. He's an astronaut and he spits on us."

"You want me on the bed with you?" I asked.

"I know you're an intellectual. We could keep on the lights so you'd know what I said."

"You want to say things? This isn't going to be just sex?"

"I could never be just sex."

"I agree. Go to sleep. Let me make up my mind whether to come in there. Turn out the lights."

Again the dark, and I thought I would cheat not only Quadberry but the entire Quadberry family if I did what was natural.

I fell asleep.

Quadberry escorted B-52s on bombing missions into North Vietnam. He was catapulted off the *Bonhomme Richard* in his suit at 100 degrees temperature, often at night, and put the F-8 on all it could get—the tiny cockpit, the immense long two-million-dollar fuselage, wings, tail, and jet engine. Quadberry, the genius master of his dragon, going up to twenty thousand feet to be cool. He'd meet with the big B-52 turtle of the air and get in a position, his cockpit glowing with green and orange lights, and turn on his transistor radio. There was only one really good band, never mind the old American rock-and-roll from Cambodia, and that was Red Chinese opera. Quadberry loved it. He loved the nasal horde in the finale, when the peasants won over the old fat dilettante mayor. Then he'd turn the jet around when he saw the squatty abrupt little fires way down there after the B-52s had dropped their diet. It was a seven-hour trip. Sometimes he slept, but his body knew when to wake up. Another thirty minutes and there was his ship waiting for him out in the waves.

All his trips weren't this easy. He'd have to blast out in daytime and get with the B-52s, and a SAM missile would come up among them. Two of his mates were taken down by these missiles. But Quadberry, as on saxophone, had endless learned technique. He'd put his jet perpendicular in the air and make the SAMs look silly. He even shot down two of them. Then, one day in daylight, a MIG came floating up level with him and his squadron. Quadberry couldn't believe it. Others in the squadron were shy, but Quadberry knew where and how the MIG could shoot. He flew below the cannons and then came in behind it. He knew the MIG wanted one of the B-52s and not mainly him. The MIG was so concentrated on the fat B-52 that he forgot about Quadberry. It was really an amateur suicide pilot in the MIG. Quadberry got on top of him and let down a missile, rising out of the way of it. The missile blew off the tail of the MIG. But then Quadberry wanted to see if the man got safely out of the cockpit. He thought it would be pleasant if the fellow got out with his parachute working. Then Quadberry saw that the fellow wanted to collide his wreckage with the B-52, so Quadberry turned himself over and cannoned, evaporated the pilot and cockpit. It was the first man he'd killed.

The next trip out, Quadberry was hit by a ground missile. But his jet kept flying. He flew it a hundred miles and got to the sea. There was the *Bonhomme Richard,* so he ejected. His back was snapped but, by God, he landed right on the deck. His mates caught him in their arms and cut the parachute off him. His back hurt for weeks, but he was all right. He rested and recuperated in Hawaii for a month.

Then he went off the front of the ship. Just like that, his F-8 plopped in the ocean and sank like a rock. Quadberry saw the ship go over him. He knew he shouldn't eject just yet. If he ejected now he'd knock his head on the bottom and get chewed up in the motor blades. So Quadberry waited. His plane was sinking in the green and he could see the hull of the aircraft carrier getting smaller, but he had oxygen through his mask and it didn't seem that urgent a decision. Just let the big ship get over. Down what later proved to be sixty feet, he pushed the ejection button. It fired him away, bless it, and he woke up ten feet under the surface swimming against an almost overwhelming body of underwater parachute. But two of his mates were in the helicopter, one of them on the ladder to lift him out.

Now Quadberry's back was really hurt. He was out of this war and all wars for good.

Lilian, the stewardess, was killed in a crash. Her jet exploded with a hijacker's bomb, an inept bomb which wasn't supposed to go off, fifteen miles out of Havana; the poor pilot, the poor passengers, the poor stewardesses were all splattered like flesh sparklers over the water just out of Cuba. A fisherman found one seat of the airplane. Castro expressed regrets.

Quadberry came back to Clinton two weeks after Lilian and the others bound for Tampa were dead. He hadn't heard about her. So I told him Lilian was dead when I met him at the airport. Quadberry was thin and rather meek in his civvies—a grey suit and an out-of-style tie. The white ends of his hair were not there—the halo had disappeared—because his hair was cut short. The Arab nose seemed a pitiable defect in an ash-whiskered face that was beyond anemic now. He looked shorter, stooped. The truth was he was sick, his back was killing him. His breath was heavy-laden with airplane martinis and in his limp right hand he held a wet cigar. I told him about Lilian. He mumbled something sideways that I could not possibly make out.

"You've got to speak right at me, remember? Remember me, Quadberry?"

"Mom and Dad of course aren't here."

"No. Why aren't they?"

"He wrote me a letter after we'd bombed Hué. Said he hadn't sent me to Annapolis to bomb the architecture of Hué. He had been there once and had some important experience—French-kissed the queen of Hué or the like. Anyway, he said I'd have to do a hell of a lot of repentance for that. But he and Mom are separate people. Why isn't *she* here?"

"I don't know."

"I'm not asking you the question. The question is to God."

He shook his head. Then he sat down on the floor of the terminal. People had to walk around. I asked him to get up.

"No. How is old Clinton?"

"Horrible. Aluminum subdivisions, cigar boxes with four thin columns in front, thick as a hive. We got a turquoise water tank; got a shopping center, a monster Jitney Jungle, fifth-rate teenyboppers covering the place like ants." Why was I being so frank just now, as Quadberry sat on the floor downcast, drooped over like a long weak candle? "It's not our town anymore, Ard. It's going to hurt to drive back into it. Hurts me every day. Please get up."

"And Lilian's not even over there now."

"No. She's a cloud over the Gulf of Mexico. You flew out of Pensacola once. You know what beauty those pink and blue clouds are. That's how I think of her."

"Was there a funeral?"

"Oh yes. Her Methodist preacher and a big crowd over at Wright Ferguson funeral home. Your mother and father were there. Your father shouldn't have come. He could barely walk. Please get up."

"Why? What am I going to do, where am I going?"

"You've got your saxophone."

"Was there a coffin? Did you all go by and see the pink or blue cloud in it?" He was sneering now as he had done when he was eleven and fourteen and seventeen.

"Yes, they had a very ornate coffin."

"Lilian was the Unknown Stewardess. I'm not getting up."

"I said you still have your saxophone."

"No I don't. I tried to play it on the ship after the last time I hurt my back. No go. I can't bend my neck or spine to play it. The pain kills me."

"Well, *don't* get up, then. Why am I asking you to get up? I'm just a deaf drummer, too vain to buy a hearing aid. Can't stand to write the ad copy I do. Wasn't I a good drummer?"

"Superb."

"But we can't be in this condition forever. The police are going to come and make you get up if we do it much longer."

The police didn't come. It was Quadberry's mother who came. She looked me in the face and grabbed my shoulders before she saw Ard on the floor. When she saw him she yanked him off the floor, hugging him passionately. She was shaking with sobs. Quadberry was gathered to her as if he were a rope she was trying to wrap around herself. Her mouth was all over him. Quadberry's mother was a good-looking woman of fifty. I simply held her purse. He cried out that his back was hurting. At last she let him go.

"So now we walk," I said.

"Dad's in the car trying to quit crying," said his mother.

"This is nice," Quadberry said. "I thought everything and everybody was dead around here." He put his arms around his mother. "Let's all go off and kill some time together." His mother's hair was on his lips. "You?" he asked me.

"Murder the devil out of it," I said.

I pretended to follow their car back to their house in Clinton. But when we were going through Jackson, I took the North 55 exit and disappeared from them, exhibiting a great amount of taste, I thought. I would get in their way in this reunion. I had an unimprovable apartment on Old Canton Road in a huge plaster house, Spanish-style, with a terrace and ferns and yucca plants, and a green door where I went in. When I woke up I didn't have to make my coffee or fry my egg. The girl who slept in my bed did that. She was Lilian's little sister, Esther Field. Esther was pretty in a minor way, and I was proud how I had tamed her to clean and cook around the place. The Field family would appreciate how I lived with her. I showed her the broom and the skillet, and she loved them. She also learned to speak very slowly when she had to say something.

Esther answered the phone when Quadberry called me seven months later. She gave me his message. He wanted to know my opinion on a decision he had to make. There was this Dr. Gordon, a surgeon at Emory Hospital in Atlanta, who said he could cure Quadberry's back problem. Quadberry's back was killing him. He was in torture even holding up the phone to say this. The surgeon said there was a seventy-five/twenty-five chance. Seventy-five that it would be successful, twenty-five that it would be fatal. Esther waited for my opinion. I told her to tell Quadberry to go over to Emory. He'd got through with luck in Vietnam, and now he should ride it out in this petty back operation.

Esther delivered the message and hung up.

"He said the surgeon's just his age; he's some genius from Johns Hopkins hospital. He said this Gordon guy has published a lot of articles on spinal operations," said Esther.

"Fine and good. All is happy. Come to bed."

I felt her mouth and her voice on my ears, but I could hear only a sort of loud pulse from the girl. All I could do was move toward moisture and nipples and hair.

Quadberry lost his gamble at Emory Hospital in Atlanta. The brilliant surgeon his age lost him. Quadberry died. He died with his Arabian nose up in the air.

That is why I told this story and will never tell another.

The Baby's Second Story

JONATHAN BAUMBACH

"If everyone is an artist," it says in the book that I am reading, "then of course the distinction between artist and non-artist ceases to have any weight." At the very moment this negligible observation crosses my path, the baby comes padding into my study to announce himself. What he likes to do when I am reading—it is, I plan to tell him when he's older, the instinct of a critic—is to sit on the book, obscuring the text. He does it with good and bad books alike, fiction and nonfiction, old journalism and new, so that one can never accuse him of facile discrimination. Although young in the ways of the culture, he has no patience with competition, will not tolerate the least of it. He has a new story to tell, he says, if I am up to some undistracted listening, though it is not really a story but a dream.

I should first like to finish the chapter I am reading, I say, a nominal protest.

Then I won't tell it to you, he says, standing up briefly as if he intended to leave.

You have to learn patience, I say.

Why? says the baby. This is the way my dream was when it was a dream. First you have to close the book. First you have to put the book on the floor. First you have to say I want to hear the story and first you have to tear up the book and throw it away.

I remove the book as a compromise, sliding it out from under him not without some difficulty as he refuses to raise his behind. The dream or story follows after a moment of silence, in which he recollects or invents his narrative. His second story is less fresh than the first, though of greater technical sophistication.

The baby is in his room, playing an arcane game of his own device with his grandmother, when an uninvited robot comes in through the window.

He's a friendly robot, says the grandma, but the baby tells her that the only friendly robot is a robot that's not in the room chasing you. To get away from a robot you have to avoid stepping on the floor.

Their escape is made possible by the limited mobility of the robot, who can only go straight ahead or straight behind. The grandma stays with the robot, who has bumped his toe against a wall and needs someone to kiss him. The baby has given up kissing, except before taking a nap, which is a time in which principle might be relaxed.

The next time the baby sees his grandma she is very sad. Her father is sick. The nature of it is that he won't get out of bed and he won't talk. "Don't be sad," the baby says, but then a wind comes along and the grandma is lifted in the air. A bird flies by, followed by a monkey. It is very sad. The baby follows the wind in order to be able to catch his grandma when she falls.

The bird is the first to fall and hits the baby on the head with a loud noise. The next thing that falls on his head is a red tennis ball, then an orange, then a grape, then another red tennis ball, then a monkey's tail, then a peanut butter sandwich. Someone says, "Watch out, it's raining tennis balls." Across the street a lion, eating a red pickle, is hit on the head by seventeen tennis balls, one

after the other. The baby doesn't know whether to laugh or cry. To protect himself, he borrows an umbrella.

The robot is dressed up to look like the President and he says to the baby when he passes him on the street, "Your nose is running, young fellow." The baby notices that the robot's nose is also running, but is too discreet to mention it. "And wash your dirty hands," says the robot, "or you won't get any dinner."

Through a face that refuses to cry, the baby says, "What about you?"

"I'm perfect. I'm perfect," says the robot, bumping into a hydrant, which makes fire come from his eyes.

The baby, who knows not to play with fire, runs away, and the robot, disguised now as a lady with a shopping cart, wheels after him. The robot follows the baby into an A&P, where the baby hides, curled up like a ball, in a bin of grapefruit. By mistake, an old woman with glasses, her hair in curlers, stuffs him in her shopping basket.

The check-out girl says, "Has anyone told you, madam, that there's a baby mixed in with your grapefruit? I don't know what we're charging for babies this week. I'll have to ask the assistant manager."

The old lady shakes her head and says nothing. "Doris," the check-out girl calls to the one in the next aisle, "are babies on special this week?"

"You got me," says Doris.

The old lady with the curlers, who still hasn't said anything, picks the baby up and returns him to the fruit bin. A man with a black crayon writes twenty-five cents on his forehead and squeezes his bottom.

Someone else puts him in his cart. This time it is the robot, pretending to be a robot, and the baby knows he is in trouble. Just then his grandma comes into the store and says, "What are you doing with my baby?" She lifts the baby out of the robot's cart and gives him a kiss and a warm cookie.

The robot is sad, but everyone else (in the A&P) is happy and runs around throwing oranges and reciting the alphabet.

Later, the baby's grandma is lost again. Before the baby can look for her, he has to eat his lunch, take a short nap and go to a movie—all prior commitments. The movie he sees is called *Dog Meets Cat* and is in Spanish. The baby doesn't know any Spanish, though is reviewing the movie for a new magazine called *Puppy* (in Spanish), so does his best, despite the frailty of his comprehension, to follow the story. It is about a dog who meets a cat, loses the cat, and regains the cat at the end. The opening sentence of the baby's notice is something like: *"Dog Meets Cat* may not please everyone, but it is fast-moving, of enduring importance, true, and in a foreign language."

The robot is after him again, this time disguised as a soda-vending machine. "You can't have any Coke," the robot says, "until you wash your face."

No robot is going to make him wash his face. The baby is about to leave the movie, which is the same thing over and over again, to look for his missing grandma, when the robot offers him a cherry soda with crushed ice to stay with him.

"My grandma will give me two cherry sodas," says the baby.

"I'll give you three," says the robot, "and I'll throw in a bag of popcorn and a toy gun that can blow people's heads off if they're wearing hats or have curlers in their hair."

The baby says yes, then no, then yes, then no, then goes to sleep. In his dream, the robot gives him an empty cup, saying it is cherry soda when it is only air. When the baby wakes up from his nap, everyone is gone.

The baby, wondering if it is tomorrow yet, gets a phone call from his grandma's mysteriously sick father, saying that the grandma is still missing. She was last seen, according to the sick father, getting into either an elevator or a washing machine.

The baby gets out of his crib as quietly as he can so as not to wake the robot who sleeps standing up. The baby walks down the stairs on tiptoe, carrying a plastic baseball bat and wearing his cape and sunglasses. The robot trips him halfway down and the baby falls, bumping his knee and losing his glasses. At the first fallen tear, the baby's grandma comes in and picks him up.

"My gramma," he says.

"My baby," she says.

They say the same thing several times, then hug each other and shake hands, which is what the baby likes to do.

"When are you going to stop sucking your thumb?" the robot says in a teasing voice. "Why don't you grow up?"

"You just wish you could suck your thumb," the grandma says, and the robot sticks his tongue out and disappears.

They look for the robot—it is best to know where he is so he can't surprise you by being somewhere else—but are unable to find where he is hiding. Later, the robot is lying on the floor and banging his head and the grandma gives him some of the baby's lunch to make him stop. After lunch, the robot cries so loud—it is all a pretense —the grandma has to take him home with her so he won't disturb the neighbors.

It is then that the baby realizes that the grandma was not the real grandma and that the robot was not the real robot. When his mother and father are in the bathroom, brushing teeth and flushing the toilet, the baby leaves the house to look for the real grandma.

He asks a man at a garage if he happened to see his grandma.

"She stopped in for gas yesterday," the man says, "and that's the last I saw her. She was in such a hurry she left her car behind."

Curious, the baby thinks, since she doesn't even have a car. It strikes him that she may have been getting gas for her sick father's car, which is broken, or, the more likely alternative, that it was the robot again impersonating his grandma.

Taking the car from the garage, his grandma's father's or one that looks just like it, the baby goes to a number of places to look for his grandma—the post office, the museum, the bank, two different schools, and a restaurant which specializes in vegetables. She is not at any of the places he looks, though she has been seen earlier at each of them.

At the bank, the robot says to him, "Stand up straight, young man, or your head will fall off. Didn't anyone ever tell you not to put your hand there?"

The baby thinks his grandma must be sad being lost, which makes him cough a little, a mere clearing of the throat.

"Cover your mouth," the robot says. "Turn your face away when you cough. Why are you squirming like that? Do you have to go wee-wee or something? Sit up straight."

At the barbershop, the robot says to him, "Your hair is so long you look like a girl."

"It's all right," the baby whispers. "My grandma says it's all right."

Wherever the baby goes, the missing grandma has just left or is planning to be there some other time. The robot, on the other hand, is sometimes there and sometimes not.

At the restaurant, the robot says, "You have to finish everything on your plate or you can't come here anymore."

The baby likes to leave things over, a few things, so as not to leave the plate without protection. When the baby's head is turned—he is looking to see if his grandma is coming out of the bathroom—a fork with a piece of cold meat at the end is jabbed at his mouth.

Pfuii! Aghh! The piece of meat flies straight up and sticks to the ceiling.

"Can you do that again?" the robot asks, but the baby says he will not do another trick until he finds the missing person who is his grandma.

At the museum, the robot says, "If you touch those masks, you'll have to pay for them. Your father will have to work two hundred years to make enough money to pay for those masks." The baby walks around with his hands in his pockets.

At the post office, the baby gets a letter from his grandma in which she says that her sick father is fully recovered but now she is the sick one.

The baby writes a letter to his grandma, telling her of his adventures in her absence, but she never gets to see it. The robot, dressed up as a mailman, eats the paper.

It is one of the most disgusting and unlikable things the baby has ever witnessed.

The baby writes another letter. "I am angry," he writes in red pencil. "I am angry and also sad. No one tells me anything. How am I supposed to know what's going on? My grandma is the only one that tells the truth and I don't know how to find her."

When the sick grandma reads the letter, tears fill her eyes and she gets up and walks around. The robot comes into the room and she chases him away, saying, "I'll never talk to you again because you ate the baby's letter."

The robot is ashamed and stands in the corner and says, "I am . . . perfectly awful." When he walks forward, he bumps into the wall. The unexpected contact knocks him over and he puts his thumb in his mouth, and his thumb begins to rust. The grandma says that she will not give him a kiss no matter how much he cries.

The robot gets sick. His eyes swell up and his nose begins to melt.

"Do you know who died?" the baby asks.

"Who?"

"I read it in The New York Times. My grandma died."

Climbing down, the baby retrieves my book from the floor and returns it, shadows of distraction in his face.

"Is that the end of the story?" I ask him.

"It was a dream," he says, plugging his mouth with his thumb. "Tomorrow, I'll tell you the story that my real grandma told me. Is it tomorrow now?"

I say that when he wakes from his nap it will be tomorrow.

He closes his eyes just for a moment as if testing the integrity of the room in his absence. "That's what you always say," he says. "You know, I like you."

"I like you too."

"You know why I like you? I like you because you like me."

When he leaves, padding out in his inconspicuous way, I reread the sentence I was on when he came in, read it over many times, uncomprehendingly, before going on to the next.

Ball

SAM KOPERWAS

A flower grows for every drop of rain that falls. Don't tell me no. In the middle of the darkest night, there is still a candle that is glowing. This I believe. *Glowing.* If a lost person wanders in the street, somebody will come along to find the way for him. I would swear it on bibles. I *believe.*

It is my son who does not believe.

He stands in front of me, six-five. His arms hang down to his knees, to his ankles. You don't know how much I love him, my boy. I jump up to hug him. I press my face into his chest.

"You're a basketball player," I yell up to him. "Become a Knickerbocker, son. Listen to your father. Be a Piston, a Pacer."

I stuff vitamins into all his openings. In the house he has to wear lead weights under his socks if he wants to eat.

My son hates a basketball.

He reads books about blood circulation and heart conditions. Set shots he doesn't want to know from. I have to twist the boy's arm before he'll stand up straight.

"Floods wiped out a village in Pakistan," he cries to me. His shoulders slump like rooftops caving in. "Puerto Ricans push carts in the gutter. Beaches are polluted. Where has the buffalo gone?"

"Grow up!" I shout. "What kind of talk is this from a boy? Play basketball and make money. Practice sky hooks. Forget floods, forget buffalo—you're not even a teen-ager yet. What I want from you are slam dunks. God made you tall. Run! Dribble!"

"Pop," he sobs to me.

"My boy," I say.

The kitchen tells the story. A history book of inches and feet is here. Growth is here, all the measurements right from the start.

"This is you," I holler. I point to pencil scratches on a leg of the kitchen table. "Right from the hospital I stood you up on those fabulous legs of yours."

I touch one mark after another. Tallness, like a beautiful bean-stalk, climbs up the broom closet, up the refrigerator, a ladder of height. The inches add up, interest in the bank.

The boy stoops over. These measurements are making him sick. He takes his size like you take a ticket for speeding.

"I can't, Dad. Rapists and inflation and tumors are everywhere."

I grab the boy by the arm. I pull him to the refrigerator, push him against the door, stand him up tall. I point with a father's finger to faint key scratches on the door.

"Nursery school!" I scream. "Right here, son. What a smoothy you were, what a natural. Slop from the table you palmed with either hand. This is your father talking to you. When I cut your bites too big to finish, swish in the garbage bag you dunked them. I saw an athlete, son. I saw a millionaire."

My boy shuts his eyes. He sees stethoscopes behind them. I see basketballs.

The do-gooder, he refuses to shoot basketballs. Instead, he reaches for the encyclopedia. My son curls up to read.

Six-six, and growing every day like good stocks. This is an athlete. This is handsome, long and tall, and getting big and getting bigger.

I give him rabbit punches in the kidneys.

"Son," I explain to him.

"Dad," he mumbles.

I take my boy to the school yard. Above us is a basket. I point. "Here is a ball. Shoot it!" I shout.

My son looks at the ball in his hands. Then he looks down at me. "I can't, Pop."

Tears plip on his huge sneakers.

"I don't see little rubber bumps, Dad, I see faces of tiny orphans all over the world. Instead of black lines, I see segregation and the bald eagle that's becoming extinct. I see unhappiness and things that have to be stitched back together."

He drops the ball, klunk.

I chase after the ball. My boy runs next to me. Frazier does not run smoother, believe me. It breaks my heart.

I bounce the ball to my son and it hits his stomach. He doesn't move the hands that could squash watermelons.

"Wilt Chamberlain has a swimming pool in his house!" I scream up to the boy. "Your father is talking to you. In the *house!*"

Closer to six-eight than to six-seven and larger every day, every day shooting up like the price of gold. I need a chair to measure him.

"I won't play basketball," he cries to me. "I want to be something. A heart surgeon. I have to help people. How can I play basketball after what we've done to the Navaho and the Cherokee?"

I reach up and grab the boy's ear. I drag him to the basket. I shove the ball into his hands.

"Shoot!" I yell. "Stuff it in! Dribble like Maravich. This is your father speaking to you. Spin the ball on a finger. Make it roll down your arms and behind your neck. Score baskets, son! Make money. Bring scouts. Bring Red Holzman. I want contracts on the doorstep, I want promises."

I stand toe to toe with the boy, nose to stomach.

I slam the ball into his belly.

"Son," I whisper.

"Pop," he moans.

You should eat an apple every day. This is a proven fact. Every prayer that comes out of your mouth gets listened to. This also is proven. Nobody can tell me different. Somebody up there hears every single word. Argue and I'll slap your eyes out. We live in the land of opportunity.

My boy will be a basketball player.

I slip the ball into his bed at night. I put it on the pillow next to his big sad face.

The boy opens his eyes. They are round, like hoops.

"Dad."

"Son."

Under his bed there are electric basketball games covered with dust. Coloring books of basketball players turn yellow in his closet. Basketball pajamas the boy has outgrown I will never throw away.

"Dad."

"Son."

I am with him at the table when he eats. I love the boy. I marvel at his appetite, whole shipments he packs away. My son can shovel it in. Lamb chops I set before him with gladness. My eyes are tears when he clears the table, the hamburgers and the shakes and the fries. I make him drink milk. Inside, he is oceans of milk.

"Eat!" I scream. "Get tall and taller. Grow to the skies."

My son rips through new sneakers every two weeks. Owners, managers, franchisers would kill for him right now.

"People starve," the boy says. "There are earthquakes in Peru that don't let me sleep nights. Squirrels are catching cold in the park. Drug addicts and retarded children walk the streets."

My flesh and blood weeps before me, my oil well. Cuffs never make it past the boy's ankles. In less than a week any sleeve retreats from his wrists.

"I'm not even thirteen," he sobs. "There's so much to do. Workers without unions get laid off. Every day the earth falls a little closer into the sun. Kidneys fail. I don't know what to do, Pop. Mexicans get gassed. Puppies have to pick grapes."

I run over to the boy. He stoops to hug me.

"You're hot property," I shriek up to him. "Listen to your father. You're land in Florida, son. Scoop shots and pivots. I'm your father. Bounce passes and free throws. Listen to me."

I run to the bedroom. I drop the ball at his feet.

"Look, son. Red, white, and blue. What more could a boy ask for?"

He doesn't pick it up. I have to put the ball in his arms. He cries. He lets the ball drop to the floor. Tears pour down on me from above.

"Son," I say.

"Pop," he says.

I lead my boy to a gymnasium. I push him under a basket.

"Turn-around jumpers and tip-ins," I shout up. "That's what I want from you. I want rebounds."

"Please, Pop."

"You're just a boy," I beg. "Listen to your father."

I hold the ball out for him to take.

"Pop," he says.

"Son," I say.

He takes the ball.

A baby cries and I am moved. A leaf gets touched and I melt. A son bends to take a ball from his father's hands, and . . . I . . . know . . . why . . . I . . . believe.

My son *spins* the ball. My son *eyes* the seams. My son *pats* the ball. My son *tests* the weight.

"I don't know, Pop."

I reach up a fatherly hand. I tap my boy on the chest.

"Factories murder the air. Russians steal fish."

"It was meant for you, son. Try it."

My son drops the ball with just a hint of English and it comes right back to him. He spins the ball again. It bounces back.

My son smiles.

He performs, he does tricks, he experiments. The kid is Benjamin Franklin with a kite, Columbus with a boat. Tears run from our eyes. This is an athlete in front of me. He is happy and tall.

My son is bouncing the ball.

I point to the net. He squeezes the ball. He shakes it. He shoots. *Swish.*

My son makes baskets. Shot after shot, swish.

I love him. He sinks hook shots, jumpers from half court.

"Dad!" he shouts.

"My boy!" I scream.

He stands up tall. He tosses in baskets from everywhere. He reaches up and drops it through. He holds it with the fingertips of one hand. My six-tenner, he dunks it backward.

He runs, he jumps. He grows. His shoulders straighten, knees straighten. My son is a tree.

He zooms up taller, my seven-footer. I love him. He is enormous.

Buttons pop. The boy tears through his clothing. He grows taller. He throws it in with his eyes closed. His head grows over the rim, over the backboard. His fingers reach from one end of the court to the other.

"Son," I call up to him.

"Pop, Pop, Pop."

He grows taller still. He blasts through the ceiling. My son stands tall and naked. His head is in the sky. I love him, my monster.

He pushes himself up higher. He skyrockets above us. The boy is taller than buildings, bigger than mountains.

"Son," I call.

"Pop, Pop, Pop," he bellows from afar.

The boy is gigantic.

He pushes aside skyscrapers. He swallows clouds. He grows. He swats airplanes from the sky with either hand, crushes them between his fingers. He blots out the light.

My son keeps growing. There is thunder when he speaks, an earthquake when he moves. People die.

The boy grows and grows.

"Son," I sob.

"Pop, Pop, Pop!"

He grows in the sky. He stretches to the sun. My boy leaps past stars.

"Pop, Pop, Pop!"

But it is no longer a human voice I hear from the heavens. When my son speaks, it is the crashing of meteors, the four corners of the galaxy wheeling, wheeling, wheeling toward that outer horizon where the Titans themselves lob a furious ball in lethal play, and the score is always climbing. It is the playground where suns and moons careen in hopeless patterns. It is a void where victors hold frivolous service and cause thunder with tenpins, where old men shower the rain with unholy weeping, where solar systems are deployed in the secondary and every atom is a knuckle ball.

In this I sadly believe.

"Son," I say.

"Pop."

The boy is beside me. He is a good boy, a boy who wants to help people: he is young. This boy knows compassion, tenderness, genetics. His head is not in the clouds.

I buy microscope sets for him, medical journals. I bring home tongue depressors for the boy. We dissect frogs together. We cure diseases.

"I've seen things, Dad," he tells me. "My eyes have been opened."

"We'll make remedies, son. You'll heal the sick, comfort the needy."

"I can't explain it, Dad. It's all more than a basketball."

"You'll patch holes in the earth, son. You'll feed Biafrans, help birds fly south in winter. You'll bring peace to the Mideast, equal rights to women."

My son spins the ball in front of him. My son eyes the seams. My son pats the ball. My son tests the weight.

"You'll plug up radium leaks, son, solve busing problems. You'll put the business to venereal disease. You'll grow bananas that don't spoil. Listen to me. You'll invent cars that don't shrink, cotton goods that run on water. I am your father."

The boy does not hear. Nobody does. Babies are born every second and every one of them cries. Leaves by the millions turn brown in the street. The sky is all poisonous particles.

"Son."

"Dad?"

He shoots the ball at a basket. *Swish.* He spins them in off the backboard. *Swish.* Flips from corners. *Swish.*

I clutch at my chest.

"Here comes a lefty hook, Pop."

Swish.

I collapse at his feet. The boy looms over me. Cancers strike at my vitals. Seizures grip me. Plagues and pestilence and uncertainty flood my veins. Pandora's box breaks open in my heart.

My son looks down at me. He twirls the ball on a terrible finger. I look up at a son whose hands could cradle nations.

"Son," I beg.

"Not now, Pop."

He bounces the ball on my stomach. Once, twice, three times for luck. He dribbles between his legs, behind his back. My son flies to the basket. My son soars to his laurels over my dead body.

Trophies

HILMA WOLITZER

Howard's father died, moving Howard up one generation and canceling forever his coming attractions of life.

His father had been a gloomy man given to terrible bulletins of what it was like to be forty or fifty or sixty. Howard has untimely grey hairs and he's worried about growing old. Promises of pensions, matured insurance policies, and senior citizens' discounts don't cheer him at all.

"Distinguished one minute, extinguished the next," Howard says.

I can't argue with that.

Sometimes he does exercises in the morning. Slowly, slowly, like Lazarus, he rises into sit-ups, pulling his prospects into shape. He nibbles sunflower seeds, sowing them into furrows under the sofa cushions, and he cannot in good conscience eat eggs any more. Instead, he eats honey and wheat germ and remarks on the early deaths of famous nutritionists. They die the same ways we do, Howard says, even in car wrecks and in floods.

Now his father was dead of natural causes.

I helped Howard pack a suitcase so that he could visit his mother in Florida for a few days and prepare her for survival.

"Why are you packing *these*?" he demanded, pulling out his bathing trunks and the T-shirt with crossed tennis rackets on the pocket.

"It's hot down there," I said. "You're going to *Florida.*"

"I'm not going for fun, you know." He crammed other things into the suitcase instead: grey scratchy sweaters, dark socks for the sober business of mourning—forcing New York and winter, the gloom of subways and museums, in with his underwear.

"We'll keep in touch," he promised, and the children and I stayed in the airlines terminal until the plane lifted him away.

Back in the apartment again, things weren't so bad. I made a baked eggplant for supper, something I like that Howard hates. I slept in the middle of the bed, using both pillows. I kept all the lights on, a childhood luxury.

Still, Howard was everywhere: his fingerprints in crazy profusion on the furniture, his Gouda cheese gathering mold in the refrigerator, the memory of his sleeping hand on my hip. All night I was a sentry waiting for morning. The children breathed hopefully on the other side of the wall.

In the daytime I sat with the other mothers in the playground. The baby slept under cold sweet blankets in her carriage, and I rocked her with an aimless rhythm, like a tic. Jason was in the sandbox, among friends. They poured sand into his cupped hands, and it slid down the front of his nylon snowsuit. All around me my potential friends sat on benches. On the bench facing me there were two black women in bright winter coats and scarves. Every once in a while their voices came to me deep and resonant on currents of air, as if they were speaking all the songs from *Porgy and Bess*. I thought I could fall asleep listening to their voices, feeling as peaceful and drugged as I do when Howard combs my hair.

I looked up and found our kitchen window nineteen stories up. I marked it with an X the way vacationers mark their hotel rooms on postcards.

Having a wonderful time. Wish you were here.

In the laundry room the man from apartment 16J was waiting for his wash to be finished. There was something intimate in our sitting together like that, watching his sheets tangled and thrashing like lovers in the machine. Pajamas, nightgowns, towels mingling, drowning.

We smiled at one another but we didn't speak. His wife, I'd heard, was a forbidding woman. Wretched hair, folded arms, a masculine swagger. But he looked like a passionate man. You can tell sometimes by the urgency of gestures and by the eyes. His wife goes to work and he's home alone all day because of some on-the-job compensation case. He jammed his laundry, still damp and unfolded, into a pillowcase and he left.

What part of him was wounded or damaged?

That night Howard called from Florida. We shouted to one another over the distance of rooftops and highways.

"How is your mother?" I asked.

"It's very sad down here," he said.

His mother pulled the phone from his hand.

"Your husband is your best friend in the world!" she shouted.

Then Howard was back. "They had two of everything. Place mats. Heating pads. Barcaloungers."

"You were his favorite!" his mother cried, currying false indulgence for the dead.

Of course it wasn't true. If such things can be measured, I may well have been Howard's father's *least* favorite. He tried to buy me off once with two hundred dollars and a trip to the Virgin Islands.

Bygones.

"What can I say?" I said.

Then Howard spoke. "I'm trying to straighten things out. It could take a few extra days. It's really sad here." He kept his voice low, but it sounded sun-nourished, tropical.

Later, the phone rang again and this time it was a breather. I figured it had to be that love-locked man in 16J. The woman he was married to would never bend to ecstasy. Instead, she was the prison matron of his lust, the keys to everything hanging just out of reach below her waist.

Did 16J know Howard was away? News travels fast in these big buildings.

"Who is this?" I demanded, but he chose to remain silent, to contain his longings for other days, better times.

One day the children and I went to visit my mother and father. Everything in their apartment was covered in plastic: lampshades, sofas, chairs. Photographs ticked away in mirror frames and on tables. The specter of death was there and I embraced my father in a wrestler's hold.

"How are you!" I cried.

"Don't worry about him," my mother said. "*He's* not going anyplace"

"I'm in the pink," my father admitted.

Back home again, Howard called and I tried to keep things light. "We all miss you," I said. "We've had colds. Jason wanted to know if your plane crashed."

"The kid said that?" Howard asked. He spoke soothing words to Jason. I held the receiver to the baby's ear too.

"It snowed again," I told him.

He said it was murderously hot in Florida and there were jellyfish in the water. He had to wear his father's swim trunks.

"This business could break your heart," he said.

16J's wife came to collect money to combat a terrible disease.

"Come right in," I said. "Why don't you sit down."

I went to get my purse, leaving her stonefaced, alone with the children. Did she suspect anything? Had she come to give fair warning? What would she say, this gauleiter of dreams?

But she said nothing. After she left the apartment, I looked for messages, for words printed in furniture dust. But there was only my receipt for the donation and a pamphlet telling why I should have given more.

It's lonely here, I thought. Quiet as an aftermath. Howard's presence was fading. Only the Gouda cheese, unspeakable now. I remembered that his mother had never liked me, either. She used to send him to the store for Kotex to remind him of her powers. She bought him a meerschaum pipe and a spaniel puppy to divert his course. But I was triumphant anyway.

Now I imagined a thousand and one Floridian nights, the air-conditioner humming in orchestral collusion with her voice, her voice buying time. She had an armory of ammunition, steamer trunks stuffed with childhood. In my head I scratched the air-conditioner for the sake of authenticity. She fanned him with a palm leaf instead, a cool maternal breath on his burnished head.

"So, where was I?" she asks.

Howard's hair lifts lightly in the breeze. His eyes shut. Her voice shuffles into his sleep, into mine.

In the middle of the night I heard footsteps in the hallway outside the apartment. Then, an eloquent silence. I tiptoed to the door, pressed my ear against it.

"Who's there?" I whispered. "Is it you?"

But no one answered. Deferred passion could drive a man crazy. He would probably want klieg lights lit to match the intensity of his craving, and a million weird variations on the usual stuff. His sheets in the washing machine were green, I remembered. Small scattered flowers on a limitless green field.

I went back to bed and let my blood settle. Maybe it was my motherhood he coveted. There are men like that, childless themselves, who long for the affirmation of new life around them. Mother. Food. Ecstasy. Love. Between a woman's thighs they can either be coming or going, just delivered into the world or willing to leave it in one exquisite leap of desire.

Spring threatened, and my mother said, "He's taking his sweet time about coming home."

"Things are bad there," I said. "You know Florida."

"I know one thing," she said darkly.

I called Howard, but no one answered. I let the phone ring fifty times. They were walking together under palm trees, their faces dappled with sunlight and shadow. Later, the would go marketing, just enough for the two of them. Then they would rest on the Barcaloungers.

The man in 16J paced restlessly in his apartment, a junior four with a gloomy exposure. The incinerator door clanged. Children's voices rose from the playground. I played a hundred games of solitaire, but I never won. Later, I found the ten of hearts under the mattress in the baby's crib.

The next day I called Howard again. His mother answered the phone. They were just going to have lunch. I could hear dishes clatter, water running.

"What's up?" Howard asked. He wondered why I was calling before the rates changed.

"There's this man," I said.

"Who? What? I can't hear you, wait a minute." The background noises subsided.

"A *madman*!" I screamed at a splintering pitch. Then softly, "I'm afraid he's fallen in love."

"What!" Howard shouted. "Has he touched you? My God, did you *let* him?"

"It hasn't come to that," I said. "Not yet."

The plane circled for two hours before it came down. Howard looked like a movie star, tanned and radiant. The children wriggled to get to him. He carried a cardboard box under his arm. Souvenirs, I thought. Presents. A miniature crate of marzipan oranges. A baby alligator for Jason.

When we were in the car, Howard opened the box. There were no presents. There were just some things of his father's that his mother wanted him to have. Shoe trees. An old street map of Chinatown and the Bowery. A golf cap with a green celluloid visor. It was a grab bag of history, her final weapon.

Oh, it had seemed so easy. The car was stuck in an endless ribbon of traffic. My hand rested on Howard's knee, and the children were asleep in the back seat. I would have settled for just this, all of us stopped in time.

But Howard sighed. "A man has to live," he said.

The Consolations of Philosophy

JOHN L'HEUREUX

Mr. Kirko was taking his time dying in bed number seven. He just kept lying there week after week.

"Not even getting any worst. At least not to the naked eye," said his daughter Shelley. "Look, I've got obligations, the children," she said.

"Obligations we've all got," her brother Mervin said. "You've got obligations. Angel's got obligations. And my obligations you know. I'm the son. So forget your obligations sometime. It's Papa."

"It's too true. It's Papa," said Angel, who was unmarried and had nothing. "He's all I've got," Angel said.

"And *he's* dying," Shelley said.

The orderlies came hollering, "Beds number seven and eight," and pulled the curtains around to make tents. Then they staggered off with Mr. Kirko and bed number eight to give them baths. These were old orderlies and their backs didn't straighten much anymore, so they just put Mr. Kirko and bed number eight in the water and let them sit there. Then these orderlies broke out the old Camels and smoked while the sick people sat in hot water till their behinds shriveled.

"This is how it is when you're one of the masses," one said.

"Rome wasn't built in a day," the other said.

Then one said a lot and the other said a lot and they checked to see if Mr. Kirko's behind was shriveled, and it was, so they got their hooks under his armpits and dragged him out of the tub. He groaned and his eyes rolled up, but at least he didn't die on them. They sat him on a three-legged stool to dry him. The stool scraped on the tile floor.

"Hear that noise?" Mr. Kirko asked.

They stopped toweling him because he never spoke and now he was speaking.

"That's the springs in my behind, breaking."

He threw up then, yellows and browns, and most of it went into his slipper.

"Goddamned pigs when they get old."

"There's no fool like an old fool."

These orderlies slammed his foot into the slipper and propped him against the wall. His face was all red from his bath and his foot was yellow and brown.

They checked to see if bed number eight's behind was shriveled, and it was, so they got their hooks into him and started to drag, but he wouldn't give. They let him have a little punch in the head to show they meant business, but it didn't do any good because he only gave a moan or two and died.

"Well, naught is certain save death and taxes."

"We'll let this sleeping dog lie."

They staggered back to bed number seven with Mr. Kirko. The son, Mervin Kirko, was pacing up and down outside the room, looking at his watch. Angel Kirko, who had nothing, was standing in the corner twisting her handkerchief. Shelley Kamm was looking through her purse and sighing a lot.

"Did we have a nice bathie-poo?" Shelley said to her father as these orderlies pulled the curtains.

"It's little enough to have," Angel said.

Inside the tent the orderlies rested for a while and then they each took an arm of Mr. Kirko and counted down. "Three, two, one, GO!" And he went up onto the bed, heard first. His head went shlunk into the wall. He wailed for a minute, then tuned down to a whine.

They threw back the curtains and approached the weeping women.

"It's an ill wind that blows no good," one said.

"It's too true," Angel said.

"It's a mercy some of them go when their time has come," the other said.

"I know you're doing everything you can," Shelley said.

On the way out these orderlies nodded at good old Mervin.

"You can just pace around," they said. "Up and down, back and forth, you name it."

Angel and Shelley didn't know what to do next.

"He doesn't look any worst to me," Shelley said.

"Not to the naked eye, he doesn't," Angel said.

"Oh, nurse, nurse," Shelley said, calling Nurse Jane. "He doesn't look any worst, does he?"

"Well, he's going to be," Nurse Jane said. "They don't just go in and out of here unless they're seriously, you know. What he needs is some needles and bottles, some pickies and pokies, and a tube up his nose."

Nurse Jane returned with everything she promised.

"Bed number eight," she said to Angel. "Where is he?"

"Personally, I don't know," Angel said. "I haven't the slightest."

"She hasn't the slightest," Shelley said. "She's never had anything and now she's losing her papa."

"It's a matter of professionalism," Nurse Jane said. "There are lists to be filled out, tags, markers, numbers, identity bands, indicators, thingamabobs, you have no idea. So you can't just have bed numbers disappearing. So you've got to tell me everything you can about this case. Now you, Miss Kirko, when did you last see bed number eight?"

"Well, I'll do my best," Angel said. "He was last seen by me personally when they staggered him off for his bath."

"Bath," Nurse Jane said and stalked away, kachung, kachung. "Very good," she said a few minutes later. "Very good, Miss Kirko. We found him dead in the bath and so he's accounted for." She leaned across Shelley and put her hand gently on Angel's bosom. "It's just so we know," she said tenderly. "We have to know."

"It can't be easy," Angel said.

"It's the children I worry about," Shelley said.

"When the doctor comes, you'll see," Nurse Jane said, and wheeled the empty bed out of the room.

The doctor appeared at seven o'clock on the bonker. He had a clipboard in his hand and he kept looking from it to the place where bed eight used to be.

"I see they've dispatched bed eight," he said. "You must be the Kirkos. You belong to bed seven."

"Yes, we're the Kirkos," Mervin said. "I'm the son and these are the two daughters, Angel Kirko and Shelley Kamm. Shelley was a Kirko before she was a Kamm.''

"How do you do," they all said, shaking everything.

"I'm Doctor Robbins," Doctor Robbins said.

"Doctor Robbins," they all said, grateful as anything.

Angel and Shelley took a good long look at Doctor Robbins while he took a good long look at Mr. Kirko. In each arm old Kirko had needles that ran down from bottles full of white and bottles full of yellow, and there was a tube up his nose that went somewhere and another tube that ran from his winkler into a bottle under the bed. Mr. Kirko was getting the full treatment.

"You're very young for a doctor," Shelley said, taking in the little bulge in his white pants.

"But competent," Doctor Robbins said.

"Oh, I didn't mean," Shelley said.

"We never meant," Angel said.

"Of course, of course," Doctor Robbins said, and he bit the inside of his face so they'd know.

"I'll wait outside," Mervin said.

"You can pace up and down," Doctor Robbins said. "Or back and forth."

The doctor stood for another while looking at Mr. Kirko. He plucked at the only leg Mr. Kirko had; it looked like turkey.

"I think that leg's going to have to come off," the doctor said.

"Oh no!" Angel said, fainting.

"Oh, God in heaven!" Shelley said.

Angel kept on fainting.

"Mervin! Mervin! We've got a make a decision. This Doctor Robbins here says the leg has got to come off. It's our duty to decide," Shelley said.

Mervin came back in from his corridor.

"These are the moments one dreads, Doctor," Mervin said.

"On no!" Angel said, fainting some more.

"Before we decide," Shelley said, "I think I should have a word with the doctor in private."

"I've never had anything," Angel said as Mervin dragged her from the room.

Shelley shut the door and leaned against it, her head thrown back. Outside she could hear them pacing up and down, back and forth.

"I thought we should have a word alone," Shelley said.

"Most understandable at a time like this, Mrs. Kamm," he said, reaching for his zipper.

"Yes, it's difficult for all of us, Doctor. It's the children I worry about." She slipped off her panties and in one graceful motion scooped them up from the floor and tucked them into her purse.

They stood for a moment looking at bed number seven.

"We could put him on the floor, Doctor. He wouldn't mind."

"It's better the patient not be disturbed," he said, and gave a little tweak to a tube here and a tube there.

"Oh, dear," Shelley said.

"Now if you will please step over to the door and lean your back against it, so," the doctor said. "Very good. And now we'll lift this skirt and—yes, you'll have to bend your knees as if you were sliding down the wall, that's right—and then I'll just slip this in here. Um, we need a little wiggly, then oomph, there we are."

"Yes, that does do nicely, Doctor Robbins," Shelley said.

They stood there like a Rorschach.

"Perhaps, Mrs. Kamm, you'd prefer to put your purse on the floor."

"Oh, silly of me."

"Just drop it. That's right. And then you can put your hands right here."

"Oh," she said. "Oh."

"I think you'll find, Mrs. Kamm, that once your father's leg comes off, you'll be more than pleased you agreed to it."

"Oh, I'm sure you're right, Doctor Robbins. It's just that, you know, we've known him so long, Doctor, and always with the leg."

"Yes, yes, of course. These feelings are natural. There would be something wrong if you didn't feel them."

"Oh, yes," she said.

"Could you move that knee out a little, and away?"

"Like this?"

"Fine," he said. "Well, at least we're having marvelous weather . . . for this time of year."

"Marvelous," she said. "Doctor, I want to thank you sincerely for giving us your valuable time. We truly appreciate it."

"A doctor does his best," he said. "Comfortable?"

"Mmmm, yes, Doctor. I hope you won't think me overly personal, but I couldn't help noticing what an enormous jumjum you have."

"Oh, I don't know," he said, shrugging modestly.

"Oh, you do, you do. Truly."

He gave her a little jab to the left.

"Thuth thuth thuth," they laughed.

"You must have gone to a wonderful medical school," she said.

"Harvard," he said. "They teach you everything."

"It must be wonderful," she said.

"Philosophy," he said. " 'Every proposition is true or false.' Langer."

"That's deep," she said.

"Heidegger," he said. " 'Listen to what is not being said.' "

"That's deep too," she said.

"Bucky Fuller," he said. " 'Everything that goes up must come down.' "

"I've heard that one," she said.

"Human behavior is a language," he said.

"Yes," she said.

"If the material of thought is symbolism, then the mind must be forever furnishing symbolic versions of its experiences," he said. "Otherwise thinking could not proceed."

"Ooh," she said, moving her right hip forward and backward in a new way.

"Perhaps I'm being too technical, Mrs. Kamm?"

"Oh no, Doctor, no. Those are beautiful thoughts," she said.

"Very well," he said. "Now, Mrs. Kamm, if you would just move this foot forward and in a bit."

"Oh!"

"You see?"

There was a banging outside the door, bonka bonka bonk.

"It's Angel," Shelley said.

"If you'll concentrate, please?" he said.

"Oom, oom," she said, and her feet rose from the floor.

Their bodies began to shake like dustrags, and then she bit his neck, and then he punched her ribs to make her stop. Finally, she shook uncontrollably and he tore at her hair.

Bonka bonka bonk at the door.

"Hungh," he said, pulling her loose and dropping her in the corner. "Hungh," he said again, and stood looking down at the ruined jumjum.

Bonka bonka bonk at the door again.

"It's me," Angel's voice said. "I want to come in."

"I'm just pacing," Mervin said from down the corridor.

Shelley brushed off her dress and patted her hair into place. "It's not bad enough about Papa," she said. "They have to make a scene in the corridor."

"It's the tension," Doctor Robbins said, all zipped and polished. He opened the door. "Come in," he said. "Your sister has reached her decision."

"The leg has got to come off," Shelley said. "Doctor Robbins is right."

"What's all this?" Angel said, pointing to the chunks of Shelley's hair with blood on the ends.

"That's my hair," Shelley said. "These decisions are never easy, Angel."

"Whatever the doctor says," Mervin said.

"I'll tell Nurse Jane," Doctor Robbins said.

In a moment the two orderlies came hollering. "Bed number seven," and wheeled out the last of Mr. Kirko. It was a sad noise going.

"Man proposes, God disposes," one said.

"Every cloud has a silver lining," the other said.

Angel and Shelley and Marvin stood in the empty room looking at one another.

"Once that leg is gone, it will be different."

"That leg was the trouble."

"He never looked any worst. Not to the naked eye."

"He looked worst with tubes and needles."

"And the thing in his winkler."

"There's nothing left to do but pray."

"It's too true."

A storm broke outside the window. They all went and looked at it. Rain fell like swords.

"Well, at least he's not out in that storm."

"Oh, nature is terrible," somebody said.

"True, true," everybody agreed.

The Leaves, the Lion-Fish, and the Bear

JOHN CHEEVER

I think of an autumn afternoon in a house outside Newburyport. I had been playing football, a fact I throw in lest someone think I was housebound. I was reading Romain Rolland. It was that long ago. Had I wanted to write a narrative—a story—about the place, there was an abundance of raw material. My host was having an affair with the cook. At that hour on Sunday afternoon, he was probably in her cozy bed. My brother was having an affair with a neighbor's wife. They were probably in the woods. The mortgage payments were overdue. The bank had made a threatening call on Friday. The Myopia Hunt Club had ridden through the cornfield and had refused to pay damages. All of this could be worked into a tale, but what concerned me was the opening of a door.

My hostess, my friend, came in, carrying an armful of autumn leaves. The leaves, I suppose, were maple and beech. She put the leaves into a vase and exclaimed: "See what I've found!" One of her charms was the purity of her voice. This exclamation, much more than what was going on in the beds around me, seemed to clarify that moment, that house, my deepest feelings about love and death.

Colored leaves at that time of year were as common as dirt, and she had found nothing at all, but the exclamation was to ring through the rest of my life, fortifying my feeling that a trauma can, in spite of its definition, involve happiness and contentment.

One Sunday afternoon, many years later, driving across southwestern Russia to the mountains of the Turkish border, I saw that most of the women walking along the side of the road were carrying autumn leaves. Would the leaves be made into poultices, medicinal teas, panaceas? Or would these women, as my friend had done, put the leaves into some dusty vase and exclaim, as my friend had done: "See what I've found!"?

The scene changes to a coral island in the Lesser Antilles, an ancient volcano, I suppose. There were no natural beaches. The shores were strewn with coral fragments, so like human bones that they gave to that tropical landscape the appearance of some mass grave or battlefield. Underfoot, the coral rang like china.

A small sandy beach had been built in front of the hotel. It was protected by a coral breakwater with a narrow pass to the open sea. There were tennis courts and sailboats, but most of the customers occupied themselves either with snorkeling or getting a superb tan. This was off the coast of Venezuela—three hundred miles north of the equator—and the golden hues one could achieve here, with the right oils, made a Florida tan seem sickly.

The tanners would appear at around ten. The wife would oil her husband and then he would oil his spouse. They exchanged notes on oiling and admired one another's color. They were very thorough and used foil screens for the skin beneath their chins and the backs of the knees. Some people did nothing but this for the ten days that was the usual stay.

The snorkelers, on the other hand, wore shirts to protect them from the sun. There was a ritual in entering the water. First you cleansed the glass of your mask with a detergent. Then you put on your flippers and backed into the water of the cove. You swam past the breakwater to where there was a submarine cliff that dropped four thousand feet. Along the edge of the cliff you saw an unusual display of brilliantly colored fish. Some people occupied themselves with this for hours and days.

One of the most enthusiastic snorkelers was a single, good-looking woman—in her thirties, I guess. Her hair was a dark blond. She had a good figure. Her breasts were small but pretty and could be seen when she leaned forward. Late one afternoon—it was five or six—she came out of the waters of the cove and began to cry.

"Oh, my God," she said. "Oh, my God."

She was trembling. She kicked off her flippers.

"What's the matter, dear?" one of the tanners asked. "What did you see?"

"I don't want to talk about it," the woman cried. "I just wish I hadn't seen it. Oh, my God."

"But what was it honey? What was it you saw?"

"I need a drink," the woman said. "I just want to forget about it."

She left her gear on the sand and went up to the bar. The proprietor was mixing drinks. He was a very big man with a glass eye. He didn't ask what had frightened her. Perhaps he knew. So great was her trembling, she had to hold her glass with both hands.

"Oh, my God," she said. "Oh, my God."

"What was it that you saw?" someone asked.

She didn't answer. She finished her drink, had another, and went out of the bar.

"It was probably a lion-fish," the proprietor said. "One lives in a cave below the cliff. People are sometimes frightened."

He seemed a little frightened himself when he said this. He seemed uneasy. Was he afraid that the lion-fish would harm his business? Or had the woman seen something stranger and more mysterious?

Half an hour later she appeared in the lobby, dressed for the mainland. She paid her bill with a check. The cashier reminded her that she had left her snorkel on the beach.

"I don't want it," the woman said. She was very emotional. "I don't want it." She took a cab to the airport although there wasn't another plane out until nine.

After dinner, in the bar, we asked one another what the woman could have seen. One old lady claimed that is must have been something occult. The proprietor kept repeating that it was nothing but a lion-fish.

"She was a very nervous woman to begin with," he said. "She's stayed here before. Last year she was indicted for the murder of her husband. She was acquitted, but she's a very disturbed person. Anything would set her off."

In the morning I gave up snorkeling and joined the tanners. I did not, for the rest of my ten days there, go beyond the breakwater. I tried, but whenever I approached the gap I would become so frightened and short-winded that I was in danger of drowning. I couldn't discover what I was afraid of, but I dreamed twice that the breakwater and submarine cliff was a metaphor for something mysterious in my own nature.

Anyhow, I got a great tan.

Whenever I remember or dream about my family, I always see them from the back. They are always stamping indignantly out of concert halls, theatres, sports arenas, restaurants, and stores. "If Koussevitzky thinks I'll listen to *that*. That umpire is a crook. This play is filthy. I didn't like the way that waiter looked at me. The clerk was impudent." And so on. They saw almost nothing to its completion and that's the way I remember them, heading for the exit. It has occurred to me that they may have suffered terribly from claustrophobia and disguised this weakness as moral indignation.

They were also bountiful, especially the ladies. They were always raising money to buy skinny chickens for people who lived in tenements or organizing private schools that would presently go bankrupt. I suppose they did some good, but I always found their magnanimity painfully embarrassing. My brother Eben possesses both of these traits. He finds most waiters, barmen, and clerks impertinent, and he often makes a scene. He doesn't distribute chickens, but on Saturday morning he reads to the blind at the Twin Brooks Nursing Home.

One Saturday, I went out to the country where he lives to observe his good works.

The Twin Brooks Nursing Home is a complex of one-story buildings with such a commanding view of the river and its mountains that one wonders if this vastness will console or embitter the dying. The heat, when we stepped into the place, was suffocating, and as I followed Eben down the hall I noticed how heavily perfumed was the overheated air. One after another I smelled, with my long nose, imitations of the thrilling fragrances of spring and verdancy. Pine drifted out of the toilets. The parlors smelled of roses, wisteria, carnations and lemons. But all of this was so blatantly artificial that one could imagine the bottles and cans in which the scents were sold.

The dying—and that's what they were—were exhaustively emaciated.

"Your group is waiting in the Garden Room," a male nurse told Eben. He also gave me the eye. I suppose the place was called the Garden Room because the furniture was iron and reminiscent of gardens. There were eight patients. They were mostly in wheelchairs. One of them was not only blind but her legs had been amputated at the thigh. Another blind woman was heavily rouged. I'd seen this on old women before and wondered if it were an eccentricity of age—although she couldn't have seen what she was doing.

"Good morning, ladies and gentlemen," said Eben. "This is my brother. We will continue to read *Romola* by George Eliot. Chapter Five. *The Via de' Bardi, a street noted in the history of Florence, lies in Oltrarno, or that portion of the city which clothes the southern bank of the river. It extends from the Ponte Vecchio to the Piazza de' Mozzi at the head of the Ponte alle Grazie; its right-hand line of houses and walls being backed by the rather steep ascent which in the fifteenth century was known as the Hill of Bogoli, the famous stone-quarry whence the city got its pavement—of dangerously unstable consistence when penetrated by rains. . . ."*

The blind were inattentive. The rouged woman fell asleep, and the amputee wheeled herself out of the room after a page or two. Eben read to the end of the chapter, and as we were leaving I asked him why he had chosen *Romola*.

"It was their choice," he said.

"But she fell asleep," I said.

"They often do," he said. "One doesn't, this late in life, blame them for anything. One doesn't take offense."

We went back to his house for a drink.

He lived in an old house—so do we all. There were cobwebs on the lamps and holes in the rug. His wife sat in the kitchen, sobbing. His daughter, married and divorced four times at thirty, had her fifth possibility on the telephone. Eben's oldest son was serving a three-year term in the Cincinnati Workhouse for his part in the Peace Movement.

My brother seemed quite grouchy when he went into the pantry to mix the drinks. I could hear his wife.

"I'm leaving," she sobbed, "I'm leaving. I don't have to listen to your shit anymore."

"Oh, shut up," he said. "You've been leaving weekly or oftener for as long as I can remember. You started leaving me before you asked me to marry you. Leave. My God. Unless you rent space in a warehouse, there isn't a place in the country with enough room for your clothes. Leave. Walk out. You're about as portable as the Metropolitan Opera Company's production of *Turandot*. Just to get your crap out of here would keep the moving men busy for weeks. Your piano. Your grandfather's crappy library. That bust of Homer. . . ."

"I'm leaving," she sobbed, "I'm leaving."

"Stop saying that!" he shouted. "How can I be expected to take seriously, even in a quarrelsome way, a woman who relishes lying to herself!"

He closed the kitchen door and handed me my drink.

"Why are you so cruel?" I asked.

"I'm not always cruel," he said. "I think I've gone to extraordinary lengths to build up some understanding. She wanted a television set for the kitchen and so I bought one. She immediately began talking to it and stopped talking to me. The first thing in the morning, she would go downstairs and start talking to the television. When she sleeps, she wears a kind of hat like a shower cap and she puts a lot of rejuvenating oils on her face. So there she sits in the morning, with this hat on, talking a mile a minute to the television set. She contradicts news reports, laughs at the jokes, and keeps up a general conversation. When I go to work, she doesn't say good-bye, she's too busy talking to the television. When I come home in the evening, she sometimes says hello, but very seldom. She's usually too busy chatting with the newsmen to pay any attention to me. Then, at half past six, she says: 'I'm putting dinner on the table.' That's sometimes the only sentence I get out of her during a full day. Then she serves the food and takes her plate back to the kitchen and eats her dinner there, talking and laughing at a show called *Trial and Error*. When I go to bed, she's talking to an old movie.

"So let me tell you what I did. I have a friend named Potter. He's a TV man. We ride into town on the train together sometimes. So I asked him if it was hard to get on *Trial and Error*, and he said no, he thought he could arrange it. So he called me a few days later and he said they could use me on *Trial and Error* the next day. It's a live show and I was to get to the studio at five for makeup and so forth. It's one of those shows where you pay forfeits and what you had to do that night was walk over a water tank on a tightrope. They gave me a suit of clothes because I'd get wet and I had to sign all sorts of releases. So I got into this suit and went through the first part of the show, smiling all the time at the cameras. Then I climbed up to the tightrope and started over the pool and fell in. The audience didn't laugh too uproariously, so they taped in a lot of laughter. So then I got dressed and came home and shouted: 'Hey, hey, did you see me on television?' She was lying in the living room by the big set. She was crying. So then I thought I'd done the wrong thing, that she was crying because I looked like such a fool, falling into the tank. She went on crying and sobbing, and I said: 'What's the matter, dear?' And she said: 'They shot the mother polar bear, they shot the mother polar bear.' Wrong show! I got the wrong show, but you can't say that I didn't try. Let me fix your drink.''

''Why do you live like this?'' I said.

''Because I love it,'' he said.

Then he bent down and, so help me God, he kissed the carpet. It was one of those threadbare Orientals that seem to manufacture dust and that would have belonged to Mother or perhaps Grandmother.

I went out. I didn't say anything. I just went away.

When Muzzy and Dazzy got married, they were both working at the Tubular Rivet Factory and they didn't have any time for a honeymoon, so on their twenty-fifth wedding anniversary they drove north to the Harkness Motor Inn and rented the wedding suite. As soon as they got into the room, Dazzy called room service and ordered a beer for Muzzy, which was what she liked, and a double martini for himself, but before the waiter could get there with the drinks Dazzy had his business into her and was hitting it forty strokes to the minute. He put a towel around his middle and let the waiter in, who naturally smiled when he saw clothes thrown all over the place. Then Dazzy had a couple of sips from his drink and was back into her again and when he blew his lump, she let out a yell and he fell down on top of her as if he'd been brained.

So then they both took a bath and put on their best clothes and went to the Ye Olde Yukon Tavern, where the waiters were dressed like prospectors and where Dazzy and Muzzy each had a prospector's steak at six dollars apiece.

Then they went back to their suite and he was into her again and this time they took about an hour at it: they'd had enough practice. Well, this wore them both out and they fell asleep. But in the morning, when Muzzy was trying to call room service and order some breakfast, Dazzy was into her again, standing up, which was one of his favorite things, but when he blew this time he had a terrible headache afterward and he had to realize that he was getting old.

After breakfast they took a bath again and went for a walk in the zoo. It was a cold, dark day and there wasn't anybody in the zoo, not even any attendants. So then they heard a crying from the bear cage and they went there, and there was a bear, a black bear, and he was crying and limping around, and Dazzy called to him and the bear came right over and held up his paw, in which there was a rusty nail.

So Dazzy called for an attendant, but there wasn't anybody there at all, and what Dazzy did then was to step over the fence and reach right into the bear's cage and pull the rusty nail out of that paw, and the bear seemed to thank him. Muzzy said that she could swear the bear smiled, and Dazzy said that if he was ever thrown into a cage of bears by his enemies he hoped this bear would be one of the bears.

So then they went shopping. First they went to Woolworth's, where Muzzy couldn't find anything she liked. Then they went to J. J. Newberry, where Muzzy got a nice string of beads, and afterward she bought a picture frame at Kress.

By this time, Dazzy was anxious to get back to the bridal suite, and so they hurried back, and he tore some buttons off his shirt getting out of it.

He was beginning to feel a little worn out, so he called room service and ordered a double martini and a beer for Muzzy and the shrimp salad plate for them both, and afterward they took a nap. He slept longer than she did and in a little while she got up and took a bath because she really needed one and she looked at the pictures on the walls, pictures of flowers, and wondered who had chosen the pictures. She wondered had it been a man or a woman and she

guessed it was a woman. She thought she could see the woman. The woman was wearing gloves and a hat with a veil.

Then Muzzy wondered who had chosen the furniture and the curtains and the rug and so forth, and she guessed it was the same woman, a professional.

Then Muzzy sat on the edge of the bed and looked at Dazzy. He was snoring and his hair was grey but she thought he was a nice-looking man, that she really loved him even though they had quarreled plenty, and that loving him was a pleasure and it made her feel young and contented and more peaceable than any other experience she had ever had.

So then she kissed him on the forehead and he went on sleeping and she kissed him on the lips and he went on sleeping and then she reached down through his belly hair which was turning grey and woke him up the way he liked to be waked up.

So it was about a half hour later, when they were practically writing sexual history, that the door burst open and all the children came in with a wedding-anniversary cake and a box in which there was a silver-plated coffee set—a pot and creamer and sugar bowl—which Muzzy had always wanted.

Well, the children were very embarrassed at what was going on; being married themselves, you might think they would understand, but they never did. Such things made them think their parents frivolous, as if they'd sooner have parents who hated one another. Well, the children cooled their heels in the parlor while Muzzy and Dazzy washed and dressed, and then they all drank champagne and the children went home.

So then Muzzy and Dazzy went to The Cimarron Room, where there was music and dancing and they had the roast beef au jus A La Pony Express. The waiters were dressed like pony-express riders, and Muzzy and Dazzy danced until about eleven and drank a bottle of sparkling burgundy, but Dazzy was finally worn out and went right to sleep, and in the morning they had breakfast at the coffee shoppe and drove home, and went back to work at the Tubular Rivet Factory.

Harry French's father was an investment banker. He was a large man who had played football at college and who brought to his business methods a good deal of backfield razzle-dazzle. He was not actually dishonest, but he was at times untruthful. His father had died suddenly, leaving him outright an estate of over two million. The death tax was exorbitant and left with Mr. French an abiding detestation of the government. He referred to the low-rental housing developments in New York City as ''my housing developments.'' He was being robbed of his patrimony to support inefficient welfare agencies, degenerate ballet dancers, and to encourage the proliferation of inferior human material. He and his wife, who had also inherited a good deal of money, considered their wealth to be providential, and when they went to church, as they did once a month, they got to their knees and sincerely thanked God for trusts A/34, C/14, and L/21. It seemed to be a kind of blessedness.

The Frenches' only son, Harry, was disappointingly sensitive and introspective, but this was nothing to worry about. Fresh air and exercise would reform his nature, and the boy was given lessons in tennis, sailing, golf, etc.

The following events took place on Harry French's seventh birthday.

His birthday that year fell on a Thursday, in January, but it would be celebrated on Saturday. A dozen classmates had been asked for lunch. The house was ready for a party. Ella, the cook, was basting a turkey in the kitchen. Ethel, a part-time maid and waitress, was sitting by the kitchen window describing the symptoms of an illness that had recently incapacitated her husband. Mrs. French checked the dining room, where the table was set, checked the library and the living room, where fires were burning. Everything was polished and fragrant, and outside the long windows Mrs. French could see that the sloping lawn was covered with frozen snow.

This was important because Harry's big present was a bobsled.

''Harry,'' she called. ''Harry!''

There was no answer.

Harry was in his room. The bobsled was meant to be a surprise, but he had seen it in the garage. The beating of his heart was painful. His hands were wet. He was enduring all the symptoms of terror.

Harry French hated sledding. He didn't know why, and had, for a boy of seven, brought a good deal of intelligent scrutiny to the problem. But he had hit on no explanation. He had never been in a sledding accident, he loved his mother and his father and had no reason to think of a bobsled as a devastating sexual image, but it had over his spirit the power of some implement of torture with which his flesh was familiar. He could have been described, before he discovered this terror, as a sensitive but genuinely innocent boy, high-spirited and truthful. But his fear of sledding had corrupted him.

He had been invited to a coasting party at the Littles' a week ago. In order to get out of this, he claimed to be ill. Untruthfulness did not come naturally to Harry French—it was the first lie of any magnitude that he had ever told—and off in bed with his counterfeit illness, he felt corrupt. A day or so later, some friends came to go coasting on his lawn. He met them at the back door and, by promising to pay them twenty-five cents, he got them to change their plans and spend the afternoon playing Parcheesi. His mother was out, and in order to get the money for the bribe, he had to steal it from her room. This was the first theft Harry French had ever committed and, as did his untruthfulness, it gave him some insight into the knowledge of evil.

If Harry went to his father and said, in a frank and manly way, that for some mysterious reason coasting frightened him, he guessed—and he was right—that his father would not understand. Mr. French, at fifty, loved to speed down his lawn on a sled. If Harry told him the truth, Mr. French would try to understand, and would conclude that the boy simply lacked experience.

"But it's fun!" Mr. French would exclaim. "Just let me show you. It's really great fun and you never feel the cold."

Harry had gone so far as to be forced into a reverie where his father's firm transferred Mr. French to Jamaica or to the Bahamas—someplace where snow never fell.

Coasting seemed to be the single obstruction in Harry French's life. During the summer months he played ball, swam, and sailed. In the autumn, he accompanied his father when he went hunting. But as the last of the leaves came down, they would be followed, Harry knew, by snow, and the snow by coasting. Going into the attic to find a hammer, Harry felt his heart turn at the sight of sleds piled in a corner.

It was half past twelve. The guests were expected in a few minutes. Mr. French was in the library drinking a whiskey with Mrs. French. He would give Harry the bobsled after Harry had opened his other presents. There would be time for a run before lunch. The snow was fast and, by turning left at the big maple tree, one could go all the way down to the pond. Love moved him. He loved his son, he loved coasting, he loved the lights of a winter day, he loved the cold air, and he would share this with his only son.

Harry, upstairs in his room, was thinking seriously of suicide.

Sickness, feigned sickness, would not work. Harry could not disappoint his parents by falling ill on his birthday. He liked his classmates, he enjoyed their esteem, and the thought of being disgraced in their eyes was painful. He could go to the bathroom and cut his throat with a razor blade. He could pack some clothes, steal some more money, and run away. He could claim to be suffering from some sudden lameness that would let him get through the party but keep him off the bobsled. This seemed like a good idea.

He heard a car stop at the front of the house.

"Oh, Harry!" his mother called. "Bobby Howland is here!" Harry opened his door and limped, with twisted leg, toward the stair. But when he heard the voices of his friends in the hall, this lie seemed so disgraceful that he ran down the stairs as he was able. Mr. French's broad smile told Harry that time was running out. In another half hour or less he would be expected to drag the bobsled up the hill, feeling like some remnant of himself.

The other guests arrived, and Harry opened their presents in the hall. His father was beaming. "Could Ella put lunch back fifteen or twenty minutes?" Mr. French asked his wife.

"Why, I think so, dear," she said.

"Then let's go out," he said. "We have a surprise."

They put on coats and went out to the garage where the crimson sled, decorated with gold, was waiting.

"Isn't it a beauty!" Mr. French said. "You get the first run, Harry. I think you can make it all the way to the pond if you turn left at the maple."

Harry picked up the sled rope. He merely did what he had to do. He climbed into the seat of that hated engine, with its brake and steering wheel, and got it into motion. It picked up speed quickly. The wind burned his ears and his eyes filled with tears. He aimed the sled directly at the maple tree, and eight or so feet in front of this obstacle he rolled clumsily off the seat onto the crusty snow. The bobsled flew on into the maple tree and crashed into pieces.

"Oh, Harry," Mr. French cried. He ran past his son down the lawn to the wreckage. "Oh, why did you do it, Harry? Why did you have to do this on your birthday?"

"The steering thing wasn't working," Harry said. "I couldn't steer. It wouldn't steer."

He told the lie shamelessly, with exultation, and, watching his father bend over the broken toy, Harry French saw that his father was a fool, the inhabitant of a world of fools, a prophet of foolishness. He hated the man. There was nothing bitter in what Harry felt. He felt a strength he had never experienced before, and he walked away from that scene with something like arrogance. He had cut his face and his mother dressed the cut tenderly while Mr. French drank several more whiskeys.

The birthday lunch was gloomy—Harry remained arrogant—and everyone left early. The bobsled was burned for kindling and never mentioned again.

Larry Estabrook had read about homosexuality in the newspaper and understood that it was confined to biological degenerates and men in prison. But the following event took place.

Estabrook had gone West to consult with a distributor in Colorado. He flew to Denver, rented a car at the airport, and started north. It was a long and a lonely drive. The music on the radio annoyed him, and he was even more annoyed by a literary interview in which an author said: "Literature is our only coherent history of man's struggle to be illustrious."

Estabrook turned off the radio. An hour or so out of Denver, he picked up a hitchhiker for company. The stranger introduced himself as Roland Stark. He was neatly dressed, in his thirties, and the skin of his face was welted and scored from a severe attack of acne. He had been to the funeral of an aunt in Kansas and was going home to the little town of Strummond, where he sold automobiles. Stark said he had a wife and four children, and showed Estabrook a colored photograph of his family. The woman was young and pretty. One of the children was very fat, but they all looked comely and cheerful.

Stark explained that he was hitchhiking because it was the easiest way home. There were no planes or trains to Strummond and there was only one bus a day. There was nothing genteel or apologetic about this explanation. He had gone to the funeral with the hope of inheriting some money. He had counted on at least five thousand, but all he got was a three-hundred-dollar bequest earmarked for the education of his children.

As Estabrook drove up into the mountains, it began to snow. The storm came on swiftly, and when Estabrook turned on the radio, the weather report predicted a severe blizzard and hazardous driving. Estabrook said he thought he would spend the night in a motel. They checked into a motel called The Windmill and had some supper in the restaurant. Back in their room, Stark pulled a bottle of whiskey out of his suitcase and so did Estabrook. They got ice and settled down to some serious drinking.

The room was warm and well lighted, and outside they could hear the wind and see the snow falling against the light. After his third drink, Estabrook stripped down to his underpants and so did Stark. They talked about friends, schools, state income taxes, business practices, and they exchanged beliefs, opinions, and anecdotes.

"I think I'll have one more," Estabrook said, pouring himself a fourth drink.

Stark did the same.

Estabrook fell asleep and awaked sometime before dawn. He was waked by the loud and diverse noises of Stark's snoring. His fatty part of his palm and blood spurted out. "Oh, shit!" he said.

"What's wrong?" said Stark, coming to the door of the bathroom.

"I cut myself," said Estabrook.

"I'll fix it," said Stark. "I used to be a medic."

He cut a hand towel into strips with a razor blade, washed the wound and bandaged it expertly.

There is some inescapable tenderness in the act of binding a wound, and this seemed to overtake these strangers. Suddenly, blindly, they moved toward one another and then moved from the bathroom into one of the beds. They were both inexperienced and reverted to the makeshift sexual horseplay of adolescence.

Estabrook fell asleep and awaked sometime before dawn. He was waked by the loud and diverse noises of Stark's snoring. His companion was breathing into his face and the man's breath was poisonous.

Stark had his arms around Estabrook and was holding him with a desperate intensity, as if Estabrook were some sort of support or lifesaver that would keep him from drowning.

The ungainliness of two grown, drunken, naked men in one another's arms was manifest, but Estabrook felt that he looked onto some revelation of how lonely and unnatural man is and how bitter, deep, and well concealed are his disappointments.

Estabrook knew he had done that which he should not have done, but he felt no remorse—felt instead a kind of joy at seeing this much of himself and another. There were no concealments in that hour. These men were what they were—bewildered, naked, natural, and perhaps content—and instead of freeing himself from Stark's embrace, Estabrook put his arms around the stranger.

The snow was over by morning. The roads were cleared. It seemed to these men, as they shaved and dressed, that there was nothing shameful about what had passed between them. They joked amiably about one another's performance. They had breakfast in the restaurant, where another customer said he was driving straight through to Strummond, and so Stark and Estabrook said good-bye at the gas pumps. They would never meet again.

Estabrook was astonished to find that he could convince himself he had merely discovered something about himself and his kind. When he returned home at the end of the week, his wife looked as lovely as ever—lovelier—and lovely were the landscapes he beheld.

Walking is not a sport, of course, although in some parts of the world *to take a walk* is spoken as if it were a game with ground rules and losses.

These days I walk with my dogs late in the afternoon. I take a path through the woods that I scythed and brush-hooked for my wife, before she left me. Two or three miles from here is a small white house by a pond. It belongs to some people named Latham who have two children. The house is quaint and freshly painted. I mentioned this because there is, in our neighborhood, some confusion between architectural decorum and moral probity. When violence or tragedy happens, the local paper always points out that it happened in a two-hundred-thousand-dollar house with a beautifully landscaped swimming pool—as if there were some connection between real-estate values and serenity.

In the winter, when the pond was frozen, I used to play hockey there with the Lathams' son Charlie. Charlie was a very enthusiastic player and a clumsy skater. He kept falling down. I remember thinking, as I watched him chase the puck, that this enthusiastic pursuit would carry through his life and make it an interesting one. I was mistaken. He was last heard from in a commune in Tangier, half dead from an overdose of drugs. The whereabouts of his sister—a lovely girl— is unknown.

As I passed the house yesterday, Mrs. Latham stopped me.

"Oh, what a day," she exclaimed. "Oh, what a day I've had! You know I have an antique shop in North Weston. I've had it for eight years. With Paul out of work, it's the only thing that keeps the family together. Well, in the morning, when I open the shop, I put a few attractive attention-getters out on the sidewalk, to bring in customers. This morning I put out a number of things, including a beautiful little china chamber pot. China. Not earthenware. A few minutes later, two men came along in a blue pickup truck and one of them got out and took my chamber pot. I locked up the shop, got into my Mustang, and started to chase them. They went out onto Route Twenty, went through a red light by the church, and turned in at the cemetery. I chased them all over the cemetery—we were going about seventy miles an hour—and then they went back to Route Twenty and headed north. A truck came between us, but I passed him on Tatum's Hill and tailed them again. In Townley, they turned right on Ridgecrest Road. They turned left on Elm Road, went around the block twice, and started up Hill Street. I don't know why we didn't get arrested. We went through every traffic light. Well, we were almost to the village of Bardonville when they stopped and one of them got out and asked: Why are you chasing us, lady? So I said, I want my chamber pot, you stole my chamber pot. So he said, I just took it for a bet, you can have it back. So they gave me my chamber pot, and I got their number and went to the police. Well, the police asked which one of them stole it. You can't prefer charges unless you know which one was the thief. So I gave the police a piece of my mind and took my chamber pot back to the shop and that's been my day."

I said good-bye. It was getting dark. The first stars were coming out. I wished on them for love as I always do, and walked the dogs home.

The Immense Walk of the Late-Season Traveler

TOM COLE

A peculiarity of the ridge above Dubrovnik: it divides the Mediterranean from the Balkan world.

On the sea side, sheltered from the wind, it is all a question of tomatoes, vineyards, lemon, colored walls, a white steamer, bell towers.

But a traveler climbing up that face of the ridge, whether to see the sunset or to exert himself or to soothe his nerves, will find a completely different world when he reaches the top, if he simply turns around and faces the interior. Late one afternoon, a certain traveler did this—turned his back on the view he had clambered up to see, and found himself instead on a thin path through northern bushes beaten flat by the wind toward a horizon of grey ridges, one after another, each one stonier than the last.

His shadow was cast ahead of him as he walked, and the bushes for a while glowed with late green. By the time the first star came out he had almost crossed the next ridge, meeting along the path only one man, who smoked a Turkish pipe and turned his face away as they passed.

Our man climbed on, following the goat path, until he saw dark mountains ahead and, nearer, a village: pinpoints of light straggling up a slope.

Dogs barked as he approached. Also, there were goats. Near the first low houses, a pair of dogs showed interest in the man, and howled, pointing their muzzles up toward the stars. They followed at his heels, snapping and growling, driving him along, until the door of one of the cottages opened and an old man appeared, lamplight behind his head making a frizzy halo. The old man called, calmingly, to the dogs, and then left a space afterward in which the stranger could say something, if he chose. There was a civilized quality to the creation of this space: the stranger was free to trudge right through it, or free to try something more. Woodsmoke, or peatsmoke, drifted down.

"Nice night," the stranger said, clumsily.

"What do you mean?" said the old man.

The stranger thought a moment, about what kind of sentence he could form. "No snow," he said.

"That's so," said the old man. "No earthquakes, either." The man was nodding, in the lamplight, his face hidden. The light came out somewhat onto the stranger's face, and the dogs sat back on their haunches, panting, waiting for the man's next move.

"That's it," said the stranger. "No snow. No earthquakes."

"Yes," said the old man.

" 'Earthquakes' is a nice word, though."

"It is?"

The dogs stayed on the alert, looking from one man to the other when sounds came out, in faith, perhaps, that something exciting was about to happen.

" 'Earthquakes' is an interesting word, the first time you hear it." The stranger had been working that sentence out in his mind. The dogs seemed to like it.

"I suppose," said the old man. "But I can't remember, to tell the truth. The meaning is not nice."

"The meaning is not nice," the stranger nodded, agreeably. "That's so." What he most liked to do, for the moment, was to repeat the old man's sentences, knowing that he was thereby saying something authentic, in Croatian, with the right order of words.

"The meaning is not nice, but the word is nice."

"You mean the sounds? The way the word sounds?"

"That's it!" said the stranger. "The sounds! The way the word sounds!"

"You're a foreigner?" said the old man.

"I'm a foreigner."

"Would you like to cross the threshold?" the old man said. "I can offer you a drop to drink, and we can repeat the sounds of various words."

"Thank you. . . . 'Threshold' is a nice word."

"Indeed?" said the old man guiding him in. "I suppose so."

There was a heap of twigs and dried brush in a corner, but the actual fire, waning toward embers, seemed to feed on large earth flakes of some kind. The interior walls were plastered thickly in some parts and whitewashed over stone in others. The old man bade the stranger to sit at a rough table, and brought forth a bottle with two glasses. One of the dogs stretched out at the fire; the other took its comfort under the table, laying its nose on the stranger's feet.

"Plum brandy?" said the old man.

"Thank you, indeed."

They held their glasses up, in a tacit toast, and drank. The brandy, close to the nose, smelled autumnal, as when various unusual stubbles are being burned off the farmland.

"So . . ." said the old man, setting down his glass. "I enjoyed our conversation outside. It wasn't the usual thing. And yet I'll be the first to admit it was becoming somewhat repetitive."

"Repetitive?"

"Going around in a circle. On the other hand, the dogs liked you, which I take as a good sign."

"Yes . . . ah . . . dogs and children."

"Dogs and children what?"

"It is said they know things."

"Not a very good saying," the old man said. "I hope your people have better sayings than that. I myself should say that dogs and children know different kinds of things and might well disagree about any one particular thing."

The old man took another sip of brandy, and continued. "I'm enjoying this part of our conversation much more than the first part because I have since realized that you cannot speak the language very well while I, of course, speak it natively. This gives me an advantage. No doubt I seem quite interesting to you, at least up to a point, because you can't think of an appropriate answer to what I say. I even begin to find myself reasonably witty and original. That is one of the pleasures in talking to an asbolute stranger. My guess is that you would like to hear about my early experiences, life under the Turks and so forth, finding great vividness in the things I have to tell. Whereas just a while ago, before the dogs ran outside to start barking at you, I clearly remember finding myself not vivid in the least. The only drawback in this otherwise delightful arrangement we have tonight is that I am not sure whether or not you understand a word I say. Do you?''

"I do, yes . . . but I cannot give good answers right now."

"Ah. When do you think you'll be able to?''

"I don't know. In a year? Perhaps two?"

"Yes, well, there we have some difficulties to face. For one thing, I'm not so well as I might be and could die before you build up a decent vocabulary. Please believe, I don't say that to dramatize myself, or not only to dramatize myself, but I have seen men considerably younger die for no good reason, thereby missing all kinds of good things they could have enjoyed later on—oh, grasshoppers, figs, things like that, which you hardly think about in the off-season but which you certainly would be pleased to see again if you hadn't died in the meantime. It does happen. That is all I mean to say, and we needn't go back to this subject at all unless there was some word in there—'grasshopper,' possibly—which has particular sounds that you would enjoy repeating for a while. Also, if you have bodily needs of any kind—sleep, thirst, evacuation—please let me know. I am on no schedule of any kind myself, nor have I done any kind of useful work since the attempt to collectivize this village some time ago. I was replaced by a combination sower-harvester-thresher manufactured in a small town near Chicago, Illinois. I believe it was intended for use on the fertile plains thereabouts, or at least on a gentle hillside—I recall some talk that one could set the cutter bar, which was wider than this house, at an angle. However, the land here is rocky and very steep, and the machine broke after a few tries. Another point I should mention is that we had never tried to harvest large-scale crops here before, at least not as far as I know. This is sheep-tending country and we only grow a few garden vegetables for ourselves. We also have a rich natural supply of stones and thistles. I suggested early on that the cutter bar could be used for shearing the sheep, if we could just keep enough sheep in a straight line to make it worthwhile for the machine to have a go at them. My cousin, Khanko, one of those who will never see another grasshopper or pluck another fig, pointed out that you wouldn't get a good uniform shearing unless you had a mechanism for making the sheep revolve between passes of the machine, an attachment that neither the government nor the International Harvester Company had seen fit to send along, and in any case the harvester-thresher would take the legs off the sheep while trying to get at the underwool. I suggested that we put the sheep on spits, revolve them for the cutter bar to do its work, then keep them revolving, make a fire, drive the harvester away, and eat the sheep. Khanko said that was very fine, in its way, but then we would have no more sheep for the rest of the year—how were we supposed to eat? I suggested that we eat as much as possible on the day of the great harvest and worry about the morrow when it comes. Khanko said that worrying about the morrow when it comes could hardly be considered the essence of centralized planning for the economy. That all took place at the first meeting of our village collective, as a result of which Khanko and I, despite our advanced years, were never again welcomed into positions of authority. That was suitable for me, who had secretly been longing for a life of idle reflection, but less suitable for Khanko, who was supposed to be chairman of the collective and was subsequently put in jail. But all this is beside the point. Being a foreigner, you would probably like to hear what happened to the machine. It was dismantled. There was a change in international politics, as a result of which the United States put an embargo on all replacement parts to our village and no doubt to other villages as well. We began to take the machine apart for toys, plumb weights in fishing, weapons to use against the Serbs if they tried to collectivize us again, and humble decorations for our homes. Then there were two more changes in politics. As a result of the first change, replacement parts for the harvester-thresher did

finally arrive from the United States. Unfortunately, the machine had been distributed all over the valley by then, but the parts were quite shiny and handsome, and people often came by to admire them. By the other change, it was decided that villages did not have to collectivize after all, and Khanko was released from jail, but he no longer had his zest. Am I boring you?''

The stranger said, no, not at all. Although this was not the usual conversation, he found it all very interesting and full of zest.

The old man tended the wick of his lamp and then lit up a pipe.

"Good," the old man said. "You're supposed to find this interesting. That's what I'm here for. You're not the first foreigner to happen along this way. No," the old man said thoughtfully, "by no means the first. You people seem to feel cut off from something and the government keeps this village here to provide it. Built by the National Film Board, and you'll see in the morning how surprisingly authentic it is. First thing, we had to take down all the power lines in this area and advertise for whatever oil lamps were still stowed away in cellars or barns in the interior. Peat moss for the fireplace we import from Ireland; anybody can see we don't have any timber left around here—Venetians took it all for their ships round about the time they were losing their power, and they didn't have much of a taste for reforestation—you look through their history and find a very marked absence of any interest in putting back trees taken from other people's hillsides. Same with their pictures—all you see are crowds of young fellows in feathered hats and bright stockings parading around while the Turks were taking over and our soil was eroding away—but that can't be helped now. Anyway, oil heat wouldn't have the right feel for you foreigners wandering in. Hence, our peat-moss trade with Ireland. We have to smuggle it up overland at night so the tourists won't find us out. It makes a nice even fire, though, and I've come to like it since I was assigned here. In fact, I love it, and the dogs do, too, so I've been thinking about applying for an exit visa to Ireland after my tour of duty is over here, because in all frankness my retirement salary, despite the government's generosity and concern, will not suffice to keep me in imported peat moss to the end of my days, and I don't see how I can live without it now. In fact, I love this village just as it is and I regret sometimes that it has no economic function except the providing of restful illusions. You'll hear bells by your window tomorrow at dawn; a man will be coming by with his herd to sell goat's milk and goat's cheese for your breakfast. It's wonderful stuff, I'm not denying that—but do you know how much it costs the Tourist Board to keep those goats going? The goatherd is a character actor from Belgrade, of course—again, I'd be the last to deny the quality of what we do here, but he only does one or perhaps two performances a week, except in the peak season, and yet he draws his full salary as People's Artist. But I do feel that I've talked too much about myself and our program without giving you a chance to rest, or reflect, or unburden your heart in the clumsy phrases of a newly learned language, which always seems to make people feel better than having to tell the truth in words they've been using all their lives. Is the dog's nose getting heavy on your feet?''

The stranger shook his head and, somewhat glazed, stared at the old man.

"There are disadvantages to the life up here," the old man said. "It's not all peat moss and plum brandy, and I would be doing you a disservice if I gave you that impression. We're situated quite high here, as you can see, especially as far as western exposure is concerned. The only high point on the side toward the sea is the ridge you crossed to get here, and that's a few hundred meters lower than our slope. What that means is that we could be getting Italian television by direct beam across the Adriatic—in fact, there was quite good reception in this area before the electrical power was dismantled for the Village Validation program, as I think I mentioned before. Now, I've lived a long time, survived more than a few wars, and I'm not the kind of man to have illusions about Italian television. What they're mostly concerned with over there is selling a lot of soap and chocolates. It happens that I personally don't need a lot of soap and chocolates. I've learned to live according to a few basic, simple patterns—the dust rising and settling in the village street, the goat bells ringing at dawn when the character actor from Belgrade comes by, things like that—and if I had a functioning television set, I can assure you that I'd be the first to scorn it. The trouble is that I don't have one, and so I've begun to be tormented by a feeling that I'm missing something. I know that it's an illusion, but as the long nights go by, especially in the off-season and if there's no agreeable and interesting foreigner like yourself who happens to wander by, well, then I begin to get this terrible feeling of being cheated. It's not a feeling I respect in any way, but it's a feeling I have, and we have to deal with it as it is. I notice you're shifting in your seat. Do you have a bodily need?"

No, the stranger said. Not a bodily need. . . . But he was "tormented by a feeling."

" 'Tormented by a feeling'?" the old man said. "But what an eloquent expression!"

"You used it yourself," said the stranger. "Two minutes ago."

"All the more reason to congratulate you—on your alertness! You single out only the meatiest phrase to parrot and ignore the rest. I feel certain that you will be conversing much sooner than you think, perhaps even before I die, which gives me something clear and definite to look forward to, instead of daydreaming about getting an exit visa to Ireland. What is it exactly that torments you?"

The stranger shifted again in his seat, hesitating. He felt uneasy about declaring himself, but he feared that if he waited too long he would be asked once again about his bodily needs. The old man poured off a round of plum brandy, added a slab of peat moss to the fire, filled and lit his pipe again, and generally made it known that he had plenty to do for the moment, so that the stranger need not rush into speech without time to prepare. Finally, the stranger said, "It's the conversation."

"The *conversation*? Our conversation torments you? You no longer find it interesting? You are going to report me to the National Tourist Board?"

"Oh, no," the stranger hastened to say. "Oh, no. I find the conversation quite interesting . . . but I do not find it true."

"Let us look into this," said the old man, tamping and puffing. "Do you find that the entire conversation is composed of lies? That each separate part is untrue? Or is it something more subtle? If you would like, we can turn off the tape machine, then you may feel freer to attack me, off the record, shall we say."

"There! You see?"

"There what?" said the old man, mildly.

"You say a tape machine is recording our conversation. But you also say there is no electricity."

"Batteries," said the old man. He reached behind a pile of peat moss to lift out a black, compact recorder.

"Where do you get the batteries?"

"National Tourist Board," said the old man. "There are shipments twice a month, concealed in a peasant cart, along with our performance sheets and recommendations from the Conversation Committee."

"I'm sorry . . ." said the stranger, growing more suspicious despite the facts before his eyes.

"Oh, you mustn't be sorry. I am not stationed here to make you feel sorry. Quite the contrary. . . ."

"I'm sorry," the stranger interrupted, his speech growing bolder. "I'm sorry, but I do not believe any of this. . . ." He began to grope for words and sentence structure, with the old man smiling and nodding encouragement. "No. . . . It is, as you said, something more subtle. . . . Not that each separate part seems untrue. . . . Some separate parts seem true. . . . But if you put one separate part next to another separate part, then you see that the entire conversation itself cannot be true. . . ."

"Can you possibly give me an example?" said the old man. "Or would you rather rest from the strain?"

"I can give you an example," said the stranger, rallying himself. "First . . . there are. . . ." He stumbled for a way to launch in. The old man beamed his unfailing encouragement again. "You

spoke about . . . you first said this village was collectivized. You spoke about sheep, and your cousin Khanko in jail, and the harvester machine. . . . Next, you said this village was not a village at all, but was built by the National Film Board . . . for us foreigners. . . . You said, it was 'authentic,' but not a real village. . . . Well, if you put the first separate part next to the second separate part, you can see . . . something is not . . . right!"

The stranger slumped back, exhausted.

"Ah," the old man said. "That's just the point! That is the very problem, to whose core you have penetrated so quickly. You really must strive to enlarge your vocabulary, because I begin to sense behind your rudimentary phrasing a very active mind trying to come up for air. The problem of which you speak can best be thought of as jurisdictional, and on a national scale. The National Film Board did build this village authentically, so authentically in fact that it fooled the National Farm Board. The National Farm Board, seeing an authentic uncollectivized village, moved in to collectivize, quite reasonably, according to its own lights, I suppose. . . . For the National Film Board to announce to all the world that the village was, in essence, fake would defeat its purpose, we can assume, and I have also heard rumor that some of its technicians felt quite smug about putting one over on the National Farm Board. In any case, as I'm sure you know, it's hard enough to collectivize a real village —given the peasant mentality—let alone try to—"

"But what about your cousin, Khanko?" the stranger wailed, interrupting again.

"What do you mean, what about him?"

"You said he was chairman of the collective . . . and they put him in jail! If the village is only . . . built by the Film Board, for foreigners. . . . how can that be?"

"My cousin, Khanko, rest in peace, played his part beautifully. Utterly fooled the people from the National Farm Board, who are, to put it mildly, not the most imaginative people who have ever passed through Croatia. I thought I told you, all the performers in the village are first-rate. Have I not mentioned the character actor from Belgrade who comes around with the goats at dawn? Of course I have! Several times! Perhaps you'd better get some rest."

"No, no, no. . . ! You said, this village has tended sheep for eight hundred years. . . ! You said, you grow only a few vegetables for yourselves. . . ! That was the point of your story . . . about the harvesting machine from Chicago, Illinois!" The stranger was growing petulant, and the old man looked at him sympathetically. One of the dogs, however, was disturbed at the stranger's tone of voice, and began to growl.

The old man made a soothing syllable to the dog, and to his guest he said, "It may be the lateness of the hour, or perhaps the strangeness of finding yourself here, which I can certainly understand, but you are beginning to muddle your facts. I am, I confess, a little surprised at you, I said this was sheep-tending *country*, hereabouts, and that is the very reason why the National Film Board chose this area for the accurate fabrication of a shepherds' village. Is that impossible to grasp? I never said how many hundred years sheep have been tended here, because I do not know. I said large-scale crops have *never* been harvested in this region, at least for the last eight hundred years, as far as the record shows. *That* was the point about the harvester-thresher from Chicago, Illinois—it is not only facts that you are muddling *now*. . . . We of the staff naturally grow a few garden vegetables for our own tables because that is what people often do when they come to live in the country. Does all this really seem so hard to comprehend? I begin to feel that your problems are not necessarily restricted to newness at the language."

"Don't get so huffy," said the stranger.

"*Huffy*? Wherever did you learn that expression? Not from me, surely."

"Oh, I knew a word or two on my own," the stranger said. "I do not always have to repeat your words."

"I fail to understand your attitude," said the old man. "I have done a great deal for you. When I first met you, you could barely string three words together, whereas now you hold forth like a radio. You were a foreigner, alone, at night, on an isolated hillside, defenseless against animals and antisocial forces. I took you in, gave you warmth and a friendly bottle, opened up to you my own innermost secrets and those of our unhappy homeland, and what have you given in return? What have you provided? Do you think your mere presence here is such a reward? Who do you think you are?" The old man raised both hands, in a crescendo gesture, and both dogs began to howl menacingly.

The stranger tried to rise, in protest, but the dogs snarled and yapped so savagely, showing their long, white, dripping teeth, that he fell back into his chair despondently.

"I don't understand," the stranger finally said. "What do you want of me?"

The old man leaned closer, gave him the beginnings of an imploring look; his voice grew confidential. "I want you to get me out of here."

"Out of here? How can I. . . ? Why don't you just . . . leave?"

"The dogs won't let me. They are in the pay of the government, so to speak, and if I wander so much as fifteen steps from the doorway they set upon me savagely. I had hopes from the moment I saw your rapport with them that perhaps you would consent to occupy them with soothing attentions and various noises while I quietly go into exile."

"Where will you go?"

"Don't you have a hotel room in Dubrovnik? I shall go there first."

"But what about . . . me?"

"Oh, I'm afraid the dogs won't allow you to leave, once they realize that you're the only one here. I assume that you wandered up here for a reason, some natural affinity with thistles or a quest for monastic rigors as opposed to the soul-rending distractions and incessant hoopla of the world capitals. Whatever it is along the line of starkness or quietude that you sought, you will have it here to the full, and should your good intentions waver, you have the dogs close at hand to keep you from acting on the weaker impulses of your spirit. The National Food Board will provide you with adequate meals. Imported chick-peas and soy meal predominate. Twice a week, goat's milk. You seem a contemplative sort of person, and the National Food Board representative will wear soft boots if you like and leave the food basket on your doorstep so that your thoughts need not be disturbed. The dogs are perfectly willing to have you take a few steps outside for a food basket or a breath of air, so long as you step right back inside again. I myself will watch Italian television for a while, in Dubrovnik, until I learn once again to see through the last, grotesque spasm of commercial capitalist culture."

The stranger studied the old man. For the first time he felt detached, and in command of a situation he was only now beginning to understand.

"I see," said the stranger.

"You do? I am surprised. I expected you to put up serious, perhaps even physical, resistance to what I am proposing. After all, from your point of view there must be some disquieting concerns —such as my running up a large hotel bill in your name while you remain here imprisoned on a peat flake. But perhaps you are one of those rare persons who are above all selfish considerations. I certainly hope so, as that would make it much easier for me to ask you to take on my own conditions of privation and boredom while I go off to dip into that hysterical and picturesque egoism I hear so much about in literature and song from beyond the ridge."

"One question," the stranger said.

"Only one? I can't help feeling that in your place I would have several. Please ask."

"I shall. Are you. . . ? I don't know the word."

"Let us seek the word together. Can you approximate it? Place it within an area of meaning so that we can gradually circle and close

in upon it like dogs and beaters upon a savage animal in Africa?"

"Yes," said the stranger. "All right. . . .What is the word when the . . . things that happen inside your head are not . . . the same as things that happen outside your head?"

"Ah," the old man said. "This is enjoyable. This is a step considerably beyond my making the sound of a word and your repeating it. This is common endeavor, this is intellectual converse and a joining of energies. We need a word. You awkwardly but stubbornly define it, using the meager yet curiously effective vocabulary at your disposal. You know the meaning of the word you seek but not the word itself, whereas I undoubtedly, in the richness of my years and native experience, do know the word but must grope toward your meaning. Together we hope to fill the void where that missing word should be, so that you can ask me the one question you have about our quite remarkable, if not unprecedented, relationship."

"Let us try," said the stranger.

"Very well. Is the word you seek: 'incorrect?' "

The stranger shook his head.

"Unorthodox? Mistaken? Unsynchronzied? Wrong? Deluded? Crazy?"

" 'Crazy' is the word," the stranger said. "Are you crazy?"

"Yes," said the old man. "I am crazy."

The stranger nodded, his understanding confirmed. The old man nodded too. Agreeably. They nodded at each other. The dogs dozed. The peat fire whispered.

"So," the stranger said, finally.

"So," the old man said.

"Where does that leave us?" the stranger said.

"Where does *what* leave us?" the old man said.

"Well. . . ." The stranger hesitated, being fastidious, but then pressed on. "You say you are crazy. Then how much of what you said before should I believe?"

"I wouldn't believe, if I were you, any more than I wanted to."

"Do I really have to stay here?" said the stranger.

"Did we make an arrangement?" the old man said.

"Didn't we?"

"I'm afraid that things are too complicated for you here," the old man answered. "You never should have ventured inland. I suggest that you stay closer to the freshly painted towns along the coast. Do not stray too far from travel agencies. I should say, not more than a half hour from the nearest office. That is my advice to you."

"I did not ask your advice."

"All the great sages are to some degree crazy. They tend to chew laurel leaves or sit on tripods. Is that not so? You rarely see a wholly sane man, such as a tire manufacturer, sitting on a tripod. But do not expect anything from him beyond tires. On the other hand, there is certainly no shame in accepting oracular advice from a crazy man who lives alone on a hill. In that field, we are the specialists. Also, your grasp of the language has noticeably improved. You don't stutter or grow depressed in mid-sentence as you did earlier this evening. No doubt, this is the longest conversation you have ever had, or are likely to have, in Croatian."

"It is."

"Will you thank me, then, and wish me well?"

"I do. You have been most kind. I wish you very well."

"I wish you the same. Now I suggest that you go back, as I have another client coming in half an hour. You will probably pass him on the path as you descend. If you please, just nod tactfully to him and pass on. Sometimes people are embarrassed to be seen coming up here. And remember my advice to you: not more than half an hour from the nearest tourist office or American Express. Keep to that regimen and you'll do fine."

The stranger got up to go. "Will the dogs harm me on the way out?"

"You must get over these absurd fears."

"I shall try. . . . Good-bye, then."

"Good-bye."

"I find it hard to leave."

"I know," the old man said. "The peat fire is soothing and there are no trucks to dodge."

"No snow," said the stranger, wrenched by an unexpected nostalgia. "No snow. . . . No earthquakes, either."

Now the old man took the stranger's hand in his own leathery but kindly palm—half in a gesture of cordiality but half, unquestionably, as a way to guide him out the door.

"What you have learned here," the old man said, "you must now take with you into the outer world. It would have no meaning for you to stay here with me and it would use up too much tape on my recorder."

"Are you going to erase me?"

"Certainly not," the old man said, in a tone of professional reassurance. "I shall keep you intact and properly stored, with all the others."

"I suppose I'll not see you again, then . . ." said the stranger.

They were at the threshold. The night was starry, smoky.

"Only if you need me . . . and I rather hope that you will not."

The stranger went out into the night, along the stony road. His shadow, thrown ahead of him by the flame lamps. wavered. The dogs barked farewell from the doorway.

Passing him on the slope, behind a pencil light, was a man in a whipcord jacket from Abercrombie and Fitch or perhaps Harrod's. The stranger might have nodded, wanting to share for a moment his sense of illumination, but the other's face was cast down, and in shadow. It did not seem right to intrude.

The Trouble with Being Food

FREDERICK BUSCH

I was a very fat boy and always had to tolerate mezzanines in clothing stores called Big Guys and Muscle Builders, and in smaller shops in our neighborhood I would suffer comments from little men and women, spoken at my parents from between my legs, such as, "He needs a lot of room in the seat, huh?" Then, in college, I grew thin without trying, and loved it, and wore as little as I could to show as much of my smallness as was possible. When I left school, I ballooned again—and as I've wandered, I've swelled.

But Katherine, whom I travel to in Montpelier, Vermont, where she lives with her kids, from Cicero, New York, where I live with myself and little income, says she loves my stomach, which stays round when I lie down. She holds it sometimes between her hands. I try to cram it all inside her cold palms.

I'm not in good health. I try not to pant on the pillow after love.

On the pillow after love at night in Vermont I hear my heart knock, and it wakes me. Katherine snores. My pillow is a drum; I hear my heart. It haunts me out of sleep.

Katherine stops snoring and says, "What is it?"

I say, "Me."

She says, "Oh." Then: "I thought it was one of the kids." Then: "Or Marlon Brando." Then she snores.

I say it to myself: tomorrow morning I'm going on a diet. I'm losing seventy-five pounds. I'll become superb. Because when I have the heart attack, I don't want my nurses making jokes about me.

I fold the pillow so it hurts the back of my neck, and I lie against my rock, a holy man, impressed that I'm not afraid, but earnest about staying up all night so as not to hear my heart do what it does in the darkness: surge to the base of my throat and rap like fists, race my pulse up, cover my forehead and neck with sweat. I am no longer impressed, and I *am* afraid, and I wonder if Katherine will wake to find my body in bed in her home but no one home in the skin.

This is not a fertile pursuit. I consider her sons—slender like her, like their long-gone crazy father whom we often discuss, matter-of-factly, because Katherine and I are adults and this is her history: what can we do but discuss? (We can burn his clothing, cauterize her cervix of his trace, defile his name in the children's ears and hire assassins to hunt him into terror and death.) But we discuss—it's what she needs. And in her old farmhouse surrounded by potato fields, wind with the smell of snow lying up against our breathing, I lie against Katherine, blink against sleep and the dreams of my fat body, and consider her sons.

The question is whether Sears, Roebuck will question my lie that Rocky and Bob are my sons too. They're listed on the application I returned, which came to tell her about life insurance for less than seven cents a day, which everyone needs because in America there's death by accident every five minutes. It said, "Think what a check for $100,000 can mean to your loved ones at such a time."

All right: a fertile pursuit.

What I'm waiting for, of course, is the burst of pain up my neck, the tingling fingers. What I'm waiting for is a way to fall beneath a truck before that happens: accidental death, and an end, by the way, to nighttime snacks and the sneaking of seventh helpings—the ultimate diet.

So here I am now, insured but still breathing, though not awfully well, at Katherine's living-room window. The coffee is made, the house is in its early Saturday morning ease. Upstairs, Bob rolls against the bars of his crib and they rattle, but everyone sleeps. The light swings through the town. It squeaks over fog frozen onto cornstalks that flap, and over the telephone wires fencing in the leafless trees on either side of the road. Everything had just been blue, and then it was ashen with cold sun on houses and fields. And now it's morning, the truck is idling at the trees beside Purdy's Bridge while the hydraulic hoist lifts a workman up to prune the branches that in winter might fall under snow loads and snap the telephone cable into silence.

While one man from the telephone company uses his chain saw and hooks, another in an orange safety vest gathers fallen branches and throws them into the back of the truck. Then he waits for the hoist to come down, then gets inside and drives to the next stand of trees, gets out and places the yellow sign in its metal frame on the road in front of the truck. It says: MEN WORKING IN TREES, and he gathers more grey wood as the saw tears. I think of men in the crotches of all the trees everywhere, repairing shoes, restringing guitars, mitering wood, filing down ignition points. All of them are loved by fine women, everyone is smiling, and chamber music makes the shape of a room above the road and fills it. Yellow light from the top of the cab, in its squeaky swinging bubble, jumps through the town. And here comes Katherine, softly through the cold morning in her wooden house while children breathe upstairs and flatter us with their serenity. By keeping silent, we pretend to give them cause for calm sleep: that lie of family love.

Think what a check for $100,000 can mean to your etc.

Heart disease makes you look *in*. So as Katherine walks across her living room—tall in a fleecy blue bathrobe that ties beneath the breasts, big of foot in slippers of fleece, long-faced, shining, glad—I hear my heart rock wetly in my chest. The pulse feels fast; I want to clock it.

She watches my eyes; she feels me sliding in and hooks me out as the light of the truck creaks by: "Good morning, good morning. Are you leaving us for good?"

I shake my head and smile.

She says, "Are you leaving us for a quickie back home?"

Shake.

"Are you tired of older women? Am I scary-looking in the morning?"

Shake again. Reach for her furry front and pet it.

"So why are you sneaking around the house? You make coffee at dawn like a husband. Pad-pad-pad in your bare feet. Clank the pot like a cymbalist."

"That's me. Your community orchestra. Music to get laid by."

She pushes into my palm, we hug in until our crotches dock through cloth. We spill coffee, chunk the mugs onto the white-painted windowsill, back off and circle around the sofa, which is at right angles to the window: she goes her way around, and I go mine, and we meet at adjacent cushions. When I sit, my stomach presses up inside my body and squeezes my lungs. It feels like that. I pant, looking at the framed prints, cherry wood and clear-grained maple, textures that want to be touched. The hope, I guess, is that she'll look where I do, instead of at me. Or do I want her to watch me and say, *What's wrong?* so I can be brave and start a fight in defense of not complaining—and thus complain while chalking credits up for courage, strength, great pain?

She looks at the walls and I grunt up onto my feet—a lesser stegosaurus in glasses and corduroy trousers—and then I walk around, breathing. I bring our coffee from the windowsill and hand a cup over her shoulder. When she bends to drink, I bow to graze on her long neck. She puts her cup on the mahogany table, but I can't reach there and, bending as I am to chew on the back of her neck, I can't set down the cup. So I hang as if fastened by my teeth at great height. She feels this, then she feels the coffee droplets, then she turns—her face knocks my glasses from one ear—and when she laughs she wakes the children up.

Think what a check for etc. can mean.

So we go upstairs and get hugged by sleepy kids. Rocky is talking already: he wonders if we can find an Indian longhouse or at least a war canoe buried in the backyard field that goes to the looping river. Bob's trying to climb from his crib. Washcloths, turtleneck jerseys, miniature dungarees, small shoes, and all the time, "No, honey, put this hand through *here*," as I help to dress someone else's children in a house he signed a mortgage for, and there is a two-room apartment in Cicero, New York, where I am not listening to good opera on a bad record player while starting my survey of the week's *TV Guide* to see what films I'll watch at nine and then eleven-thirty and then one-fifteen.

Downstairs, Bob watches Katherine fill a bowl with cereal and milk. He drops his spoon on the floor, smiles a sly one at me, bends to his bowl, saying, "More?" Rocky drinks orange juice and says, "Mommy, I have dripping sinuses, I can't eat. Okay?"

Katherine says, "No."

I say, "Perhaps this isn't wise . . ."

Katherine, looking at my face, says, "No to you, too."

"I would like to marry this," I say.

Rocky says, "I'll *up*chuck if I eat."

Katherine says, "You better not, boy."

"Which one, Kath?"

"Both of you."

Which leads us to stacking the dishes, brushing our teeth—Bob chews a small brush ropy with ancient Crest—and the zipping of quilted jackets. Then, Katherine towing Bob in a wagon with wooden sides, we walk down the road toward the postal substation, Rocky speculating on what happened to the Indians: "Then, after the settlers shot their buffaloes, they got extinct? Like dinosaurs? They went into the ground?"

"No," I tell him, "there are lots of Indians left. A lot of them live near Syracuse. A lot live everywhere."

"Then where's their spears and bow and arrows?"

"No, they're like us now, hon. They wear the same kind of clothes and work in offices. . . ."

"Do you have any in your office, Harry?"

"Oh, sure. Chiefs, too. Chiefs all over the place."

"Do they got any knives?"

"*Knives*? Listen . . ."

Katherine says, "Let's be quiet for a while, Rocky, okay? Let's listen to the morning for a while."

Bob, in his wagon, is a motor pukketing to the motion of his ride. Rocky and I keep still. We hear woodpeckers and the snarl of jays, local dogs, cars on distant roads that are aimed for the Saturday errands I crave: the lumberyard drive, haul to the local dump, the station-wagon mission with kids in the back and no hurry, and then home to soup and soda and the wind blowing from the river.

At the post office, which is someone's garage, Katherine and Rocky go in for the mail while I stand with my legs apart and, holding Bob's wrists, swing him below me and back and forth. He shouts and laughs his laugh: he's a lump of heavy cloth and knitted cap and scarf, his breath, small white smoke puffs. Then I put him back in the wagon—"More?" he says, holding his hands up. "More?"—and I listen to the knock in my chest, the steamwhistle noises.

I work at my breathing. I have eaten no breakfast and promise to starve all day. I breathe.

Rocky stoops at the post-office door and plays with a cat. The cat doesn't want to play, but Rocky nails it down with his hand, crushing the soft neck to the ground, cooing, "Ah, ba-by."

Katherine comes out with some magazines and an opened letter. Her eyes are like the eyes in a drawing: almost like life. She sends Rocky ahead with the wagon, weaving in the road toward home, Bob an impossible engine.

"Dell's coming," she says. She shakes the letter out: it crackles and refolds. "He'll be here tonight or tomorrow. He wants to see the kids. Sure he does."

We walk back. We say nothing.

Her face is nearly not familiar, like the palm of someone else's hand.

Which leads us to the long lunchtime—I eat three sandwiches—and then we carry the boys upstairs for early naps. Bob's resigned; Rocky is angry and wants to dig up Indians. The sky is smoky with early snow, and through Rocky's window I see the black field-hands nod their heads and tighten up. They come from Burlington to work for thirty-five cents a bag. The farmer comes from his truck and lays a row of brown burlap bags beside a quarter-mile furrow the tractor has made. Now the snow comes down, a fine fast grainy fall, and Katherine and I lie down on her very historical double bed and listen to her children bounce around as the tractor changes gears and returns from the river over the field toward the road, pulling earth and potatoes up.

We're dressed. She's under the quilt, waiting. I say, "Kath? You think I ought to go home?"

She doesn't answer.

I'm still breathing heavily from climbing the stairs, and I know she's listening to that, too—to my lungs, and perhaps to my heart in its damp wrappings. "Listen," I tell her, "you should decide about this. It'd be easier, wouldn't it?"

She says, "Easier for Rocky and Bob, I guess. Less embarrassing for me. Weaker."

"No. What weak? It's your *life*."

"By now I should be able to deal with him. And you're a fact now, Harry. I don't have to get married for you to be a fact."

"But you *could.*"

"I don't want to be married anymore. Shut up."

"Katherine—*I* want to be married anymore."

She doesn't answer, the tractor roars, a field-hand's voice comes up. When I look over, her eyes are closed. I think of her driving me to the bus stop, and then the ride to Burlington with travelers and their old suitcases, shopping bags, cigars, then the wait in the terminal, the longer ride to Albany, then Syracuse, in darkness, and the half-lighted Greyhound station, all the people there not knowing me or that I've left a New England farmhouse and a family and people grunting over food dug up from cold soil.

I tell her, "I don't want to go back."

"What?"

"Go back. Leave."

After a while she moves on the bed, says, "Then that's the decision."

She turns over and with one hand unbuttons my shirt, puts her icy hand inside, draws her knees up and becomes a small girl falling into sleep. We lie like that, and I reach to the bedside table for something to read—an old *New Yorker* with a long profile of the Metropolitan Opera's new director, who is recently dead in a car crash.

Think what a check for $100,000 can mean to your loved ones at such a time.

And then four o'clock in the far western corner of the field, the burlap sacks in their rows, the tractor cutting the porridge of snow—it still falls lightly—and the hands, in their thin jackets or only shirts, pulling up potatoes with the curved-metal long-handled forks, making deep noises, talking sometimes. We are near the river, its rich cold smell comes through the dense little forest on its bank, and Rocky, with a shovel impossibly long for him, is digging with total seriousness through snow and hard ground to find an Indian longhouse or a fallen warrior's skull. Bob is on my back in a baby-carrier, solid and happy and still, swathed in woolen cap and long scarf. I pant as I move with him; he listens to my rhythms and pants to my time.

A short coal-gleamy field-worker in an aqua-colored windbreaker stands, stretches his back, blows on his hands. He calls over, "You got yourself a burden, now."

I nod, smile. I have what I want for a minute, and he knows that. I say, "Not as bad as yours."

He shakes his head. He calls, "You want some of these for the missus?"

"Do I look like I need potatoes?"

He laughs and shakes his head. Bob laughs, too.

Rocky comes over with a small lump of limestone. "Harry, is this from the bones of someone?"

I say, "Probably. But put your *mittens* on, will you? Aren't you cold?"

His lecturing face comes on as he ignores mere weather to say, "See this mark over here? This is where the bullet from the settler's gun went in. Isn't it, Harry? Here. You hold this while I go back to find the bullet. It probably fell out when his brains got rotten."

The field-worker drinks from a pint of something dark. The cracks on his hard hands are white. Wind comes across the river to blow him into motion again. The tractor rips slowly past and Bob says, "Choo!"

Then the man who harvests potatoes nearby says, "This is a bad-ass day for living. You give me some other day for that."

Down the row a heavier man who is drunker—he slips whenever he moves from his knees—says, "Pick the day with care, son. They coming bad more often. I noticed that."

The short one says, "Your cold black ass told you that, isn't that right?"

The drunker one says, "My cold black *life,* son."

The snow is thicker—Bob says, "Rice!"—and Katherine's

house moves farther away, diminishes. Rocky pokes with the tall shovel. An old green truck with snow chains in the southeast corner, near the road, is loaded with filled brown sacks. Bob says, "Rice!" and then pants to my rhythms. The tractor starts toward us.

Then, far away, at the distant house, a small red car is in the drive, a man beside it. I see Katherine on the back porch. The man goes up to the steps, stands below her, and they talk. She points toward us in the field. The tractor comes closer, Bob in the backpack stirs to watch. The man raises his hand, drops it, walks past the clothesline in the backyard, then past the swings the wind has set drifting on their chains, then over the chewed land in a fog of blown snow, toward Rocky and Bob and me.

Arms across her chest, Katherine watches.

I consider the field-hands and their long lives and think of *TV Guide.* Rocky digs for dead Indians, Katherine watches from her distance, the tractor comes closer, its steel fork tears up food and huge stones, and think what a check for $100,000 can mean.

But the people in the story include that baby tied to the fat man's back.

Everyone stands still, including Dell at the edge of his former freehold. Then Rocky drags his shovel toward the man who waits, not looking anyplace but down, and I lug Bob back too, walking in the path the shovel makes.

The tractor is past. There has been no accidental death.

And Katherine watches us all come home.

Now there are the usual backstage noises: clatter of stainless steel and crockery, the battle of the kids being fed, the utter politeness of conversation among adults who cannot imagine how to survive the hours flat ahead of them—stony field they have to somehow work. When the children offer a chance, we drop all over them like sudden snow. There is the sound of corks being pulled and the tops of beer cans exploding. Now here are the grown-ups at the kitchen table (it's a litter of chicken death and vessels), and here are the sounds of Bob in his crib too early to sleep and Rocky upstairs playing Indians.

There is one partly nibbled drumstick on my pottery plate and the wreckage of some servings of salad. My wineglass shows the scallops of many pourings. Dell, who has removed his sport coat and tie and rolled up his sleeves, drinks ale from a can—he has stowed a case in the refrigerator. His ironed-in shirt creases are still firm, and in his oxford cloth he looks like Katherine's date, warming up for the evening's abandon. I feel as if I look like me: an ocean of rumples. Katherine drinks more wine. Some of it has run onto her thick tan sweater, and her hair is up, and I consider how important it is that I lick the wine that has gotten through to her front.

Lean pale Dell, with his left eye bloodshot, his large hand wrinkling empty Red Cap cans, his legs jiggling up and down, a smile on his long face—I sneak my looks at him.

He says, "Harry, you didn't eat much." The host.

"Well."

"I *know* you tend to put away more than that."

"Well, I've got big bones."

Katherine, now my mother or my aunt, says. "He ate a lot of salad. Didn't you, Harry?"

"Yes, ma'am. A good deal of salad."

Two wall lamps light the big room and Dell inspects the shadows. He says, "You forget how intimate the kitchen looks."

"*You* forget," Katherine says. And then she says, "I didn't mean to be rotten," and pours more wine for her and me. My stomach cheers for political triumph, since Dell is excluded by his ale. But he pours water from his goblet into mine and hold the glass out for Katherine to fill, and she does. She looks at my plate. I slump in the chair and stretch my legs for better breathing; it doesn't work, and I sit up straight.

"So I'm a success," Dell says. "I'm a dean of students. What do you think of that? I'm into administration and right guidance." He drinks ale. "I will deftly guide them through the thickets of life."

"And along the abyss, don't forget," I say.

"Absolutely. Abyss, and crumbling ledge. *And* gorse and hawthorn and virulent ivies. Never ignore the virulent ivies. You get really fucked over if you fail to keep the virulent ivies in mind. I've always found that to be true—haven't you, Harry?"

"It's a safe rule to live by, Dell."

Katherine pours us more wine, and Dell holds his goblet up for more, too, though he hasn't drunk any.

She says, "So here we are. The extended family." This is supposed to be humorous, so we do our duty, laugh.

Katherine puts her glass down and pushes at the stem with one finger, which suggests that she's about to suggest something. She says, "I wonder why you came here, Dell."

I say, "I think I'll take a walk. I'm taking a walk."

As I get my coat from the wall hook, not looking at Katherine, Dell stands up and takes his long black tweed dean's overcoat down.

Katherine says, "No."

Dell says, "But it's your answer—that's why I came. I wanted to address the gentleman currently in your life."

"And see the children, of course," she says.

He says, "Of course."

She says, "Let's all stay inside."

But he is pushing my arm at the door and we go, not drunk enough yet, but going, and then already down the back steps and into the snow in our street shoes, which fill with slush, walking past the swings and onto the field. There's a shape out there I wonder about, and a bright moon, strong wind.

"Dell, don't you think someone should keep Katherine company?"

He strolls a little ahead of me, says, "Why, someone always does, you see."

Now even though he's a dean, he's a dangerous man. He has beaten Katherine with his hands and once with a rolled-up newspaper they were using to train a dalmation that was later killed by an electrician's truck. Of course, she's beaten him, too—he's a dean. But Dell is drunk in a gaseous loose-jointed way that thin men have which frightens me. And he hates the history of their house. And he has to hate me, too—unless he thrives by dining on pain. He grips my sleeve as we walk toward the river and—the moon turns it on like a lamp now—the stubby chipped station wagon snuggled into hard mud.

Dell says, "I don't think my wife hates me anymore, do you?"

"Me? No. No, I don't think so, Dell."

"Did you ever get divorced, Harry?"

"No, I never got married, actually."

"So you couldn't have gotten divorced, then."

"Right."

"Yeah. You're pretty young, still. So you don't know what me and Katherine are talking about."

"Well . . ."

"Unless you think playing house's the same thing as what Katherine and me're talking about."

"Look, Dell. This is very embarrassing."

"It *is*? Oh, I'm sorry there, Harry. It was not my intention to drive all the way here at risk to life and limb just to throw shadows on your soul."

"Dell, you want us to go back inside and have some more to drink, maybe? I don't know what to *say* to you. Maybe if we all got very drunk, I would find it easier."

"Actually, old Harry, I am fairly well drunk at the present time. And I don't honestly give two pounds of llama shit what makes anything in the whole world easier on you." He lets my sleeve loose so he can indicate the whole world. "You got shadows on your soul because I'm a long-term cuckold on account of you. You put the shadows on your own soul, Harry."

Near the station wagon I stop and he stops, too. Around us the wide white field spins out, and the furrowed potatoes, the unfilled bags, curved forks. I decide not to discuss the logistics and amenities of divorce, or the question of when precisely a woman is

allowed to need the presence of someone without being digested by the major figures of her history. I do consider the gleaming points of potato forks, and Dell's deep craze, and how much, at a time like this, a check for $100,000 can mean. Does homicide count as an accident if you really don't want to die? My chest is shaking at my clothes: breathing is a serious business again.

Dell comes closer, stands before me, takes my glasses off and puts them in his pocket. "Being in the academic trade," he says, "I appreciate what these could mean to you."

I have watched too many TV shows of violence to be unwary. I am on my wet cold toes, moving backward, squinting at her blurry husband. And when he moves in again, I scream a judo-kung-fu-karate noise to paralyze his reflexes; I spin on my left foot and kick backward with my right for the nerve complex just below his sternum. I strike nothing, something collapses in my ankle, I go down. He cries, "You terrific bag of weakness, you don't snort the scraps off my plate!" And his knees or elbows land on my chest, my face opening up beneath his hands. I push up, strike up, swinging wide loose powdery punches, get lucky, and something other than mucus streaks on my hand. He shouts—no words—and I stick up fingers as if I were a maddened typist. He screams, and then his breath is in close, his teeth on my cheekbone: he bites down—and though I roll and kick and punch on his skull, he bites in harder.

I scream in his ear.

He's off. I'm helped to my feet by people I can't see. I stand on one leg and hold to someone's hard shoulder. There's a smell of deep cold and whiskey, sweat. Dell sits before me on the field, blurred face. I see the tailgate of the station wagon open—courtesy light, I remind myself. There are brown unfocused faces in the light and much commentary.

Dell says, "Like it's an academic situation, brother, dig? Much as I appreciate your interest, I don't think you see the subtleties here."

A deep voice near him says, "I don't believe we your brother, *man*."

The potato picker I hold to says, "You own one chewed face, you know that, mister? I don't wonder if you got yourself some rabies."

The one with the deep voice far away says, "Yeah, well that's the trouble with being food, son."

I listen to my body breathe and I whisper, "Are my glasses broken?"

"If not, they the only things that's whole now. So come on to your home."

We slide and lurch to the house I can't see, me thanking and him saying never-you-mind, and then, by the time we reach the drifting swings, I am gasping in the cold air, silent.

In the window above the back porch there's a dim brown light. I say, "Who is that? Upstairs?"

"A small kind of Indian. Red and yellow feathers. Watching you drag home."

The clicking of the storm door, and Katherine's—fury? fear?—and alcohol on the eaten face, an elastic bandage on the ankle, Rocky's wagging headdress, the hobble upstairs, the weight of blankets, Katherine's insistence on silence, sleep, and the sound of Dell's car starting down the drive: they wash into morning, the grey and golden early light in her still house, the curl of her body on the bed.

Rather than consider, I twist down.

Rather than consider that an accident—by civil law, Papal Bull, Torah, or the New York Builders' Code—is what you don't make plans for. Rather than consider that the final sentence of the Sears, Roebuck contract no doubt says, *In the event that the Insured is counting on this Policy for a measure of design in his little story, the Contract is nullified—it becomes just one more Voided Petition to end whatever pickle, puzzle, plot, or unofficial war Insured can't deal with.* Rather than consider, truly, whether I heard Dell whine away. Rather than consider that I first heard Dell and Katherine yowl and sigh, make a long silence, and maybe leathery love, before he rode for home with part of my face in his war bag. Rather than consider shadows on my soul, or the thickets and abysses and the crumbling ledge.

My cheek feels wrong, the ankle complains, but I twist down, slowly diving, and nose beneath the covers for her flesh. I push at the nightgown, kiss her cool thigh and crotch, then stomach, as she stirs. I come up onto her chest and suck a nipple, turn at it.

She slams me, under the covers, and I sit up, the quilt like a shawl all over me.

"Goddamnit! Will you stop biting me!"

I wait. Because here it comes.

She pushes her nightgown down. And then she covers her eyes with her hand, whispers, "I don't want to live with *anyone*, Harry. Not even weekends for a while. All right? I think just *alone* right now. All right?"

I cover her with the blanket and put a pillow over my lap and bellymound and hold it with a hugging arm.

She squeezes her eyes with her fingers.

We wait.

Bob bangs his crib slats to start the day.

It will not be a fertile pursuit. It will finish with a ride to Syracuse, the bullet-whipped fragment of a Mohegan's skull, another truth and trophy wrapped in my clothes. It will finish with an elevated leg, some great living stack of sausages and eggs and chocolate milk, and lean men on the TV screen easily breathing. It will finish with the extra pair of glasses, an old prescription, nearly strong enough, which I've kept in a drawer with my socks for emergencies.

Katherine says, "All right?"

Sure.

Bloodshed

CYNTHIA OZICK

Bleilip took a Greyhound bus out of New York and rode through icy scenes, half-countrified, until he arrived at the town of the hasidim. He intended to walk, but his coat pockets were heavy, so he entered a loitering taxi. Though it was early on a Sunday afternoon, he saw no children at all. Then he remembered that they would be in the yeshivas until the darker slant of the day. Yeshivas, not yeshiva: small as the community was, it had three or four schools, and still others, separate, for the little girls. Toby and Yussel were waiting for him and waved his taxi down the lumpy road above their half-built house—it was a new town, and everything in it was new or promised: pavements, trash cans, septic tanks, newspaper stores. But just because everything was unfinished, you could sniff rawness, the opened earth meaty and scratched up as if by big animal claws, the frozen puddles in the basins of ditches fresh-smelling, mossy.

Toby he regarded as a convert. She was just barely a relative, a third or fourth cousin depending on how you counted, whether from Bleilip's mother or from Bleilip's father who were also cousins to each other.

Toby came from an ordinary family, not especially known for its venturesomeness, but now she looked to Bleilip altogether uncommon, freakish: her bun was a hairpiece pinned on, over it she wore a bandanna (a *tchepitchke*, she called it), her sleeves stopped below her wrists, the dress was outlandishly long. With her large red face above this costume, she almost passed for some sort of peasant. Though still self-reliant, she had become like all their women.

Toby served Bleilip orange juice. Bleilip, his bald head bare, wondered whether they expected him to say the blessing, whether they would thrust a head-covering on him: he was baffled, confused.

But Yussel said, "You live your life and I'll live mine. Do what you like." So Bleilip drank it all down quickly.

Relief made him thirsty, and Bleilip drank more and more from a big can with pictures of sweating oranges on it—some things they bought at a supermarket like all mortals.

"So," Bleilip said to Toby, "how do you like your *shtetl?*"

She laughed and circled a finger around at the new refrigerator, vast-shouldered, gleaming, a presence. "What a village we are! A backwater!"

"State of mind," Bleilip said. "That's what I meant."

"Oh, state of mind. What's that?"

"Everything here feels different," was all Bleilip could say.

"We're in pieces, that's why. When the back rooms are put together, we'll seem more like a regular house," Toby said.

"The carpenter," Yussel said, "works only six months a year—we got started with him a month before he stopped. So we have to wait."

"What does he do the rest of the year?"

"He teaches."

"He teaches?"

"He trades with Shmulka Gershons," Yussel said. "The other half of the year Shmulka Gershons lays pipes. Six months study with the boys, six months on the job. Mr. Horowitz the carpenter also."

Bleilip said uncertainly, meaning to flatter, "It sounds like a wonderful system."

"It's not a *system*," Yussel said.

"Yussel goes everywhere, a commuter," Toby said.

Yussel was a salesman for a paper-box manufacturer. He wore a small trimmed beard, very black, black-rimmed eyeglasses, and a vest over a rounding belly. Bleilip saw that Yussel liked him—he led him away from Toby and showed him the new hot-air furnace in the cellar, the gas-fired hot-water tank, the cinder blocks piled in the yard, the deep cuts above the road where the sewer pipes would go. Yussel pointed over a little wooded crest—the two men could just see a bit of unpainted roof.

"That's our yeshiva, the one our boys go to. It's not the toughest, they're not up to it. They weren't good enough. In the yeshiva in the city, they didn't give the boys enough work. Here," Yussel said proudly, "they go from seven till half past six."

Bleilip believed in instant rapport and yearned for closeness—he wanted to be close, close. But Yussel was impersonal, a guide: he froze Bleilip's vision. They went back into the house by the rear door and passed through the bedrooms, and again it seemed to Bleilip that Yussel was a real-estate agent, a bureaucrat, a tourist office. There were a few shelves of books—holy books, nothing frivolous—but no pictures on the walls, no radio anywhere, no television set. Bleilip had brought with him, half-furtively, a snapshot of Toby taken eight or nine years before: Toby squatting on the grass at Brooklyn College, short curly hair with a barrette glinting in it, high socks and loafers, glimpse of panties, wispy blouse blurred by wind, a book with its title clear to the camera: *Political Science.*

Bleilip offered this to Yussel:

"A classmate," he said.

Yussel looked at the wall. "Why do I need an image? I have my wife right in front of me every morning."

Toby held the wallet, saw, smiled, gave it back.

"Another life," she said.

Bleilip reminded her, "The joke was which would be the bigger breakthrough, the woman or the Jew." To Yussel he explained, "She used to say she would be the first lady Jewish President."

"Another life, other jokes," Toby said.

"And this life? Do you like it so much?"

"Why do you keep asking? Don't you like your own life?"

Bleilip said, "I like my life; I like it. Where I am is in the world." He told her, without understanding why he was saying such a thing, "Here there's nothing to mock at, no jokes."

"You said we're a village," she contradicted.

"That wasn't mockery," Bleilip said.

"It wasn't; you meant it. You think we're fanatics, primitives."

"Leave the man be," Yussel said.

Yussel had a cashier's tone, guide counting up the day's take, and Bleilip was grieved because Yussel was a survivor; everyone in the new town, except one or two oddities like Toby, was a survivor of the death camps or the child of a survivor.

"He's looking for something. He wants to find. He's not the first and he won't be the last," Yussel said. The rigid truth of this—he had thought his purposes darkly hidden—shocked Bleilip. He hated accuracy in a survivor. It was an affront. He wanted some kind of haze, a nostalgia for suffering perhaps. He resented the orange juice can, the appliances, the furnace, the sewer pipes.

"He's been led to expect saints," Yussel said. "Listen, Jules," he said, "I'm not a saint and Toby's not a saint and we don't have miracles and we don't have a rebbe who works miracles."

"You have a rebbe," Bleilip said.

Instantly a wash of blood filled Bleilip's head.

"He can't fly. What we came here for was to live a life of study. Our own way, and not to be interrupted in it."

Bleilip said, "For the man, not the woman. You, not Toby. Toby used to be smart. Achievement goals and so forth."

"Give the mother of four sons a little credit, too. It's not only college girls who build the world," Yussel said in a voice so fair-minded and humorous and obtuse that Bleilip wanted to knock him down—the first lady Jewish President of the United States had succumbed in her junior year to the zealot's private pieties, rites, idiosyncrasies. Toby was less than lucid, she was crazy to follow deviants not in the mainstream even of their own tradition. Bleilip, who had read a little, considered these hasidim actually Christologized: everything had to go through a mediator.

Of their popular romantic literature, Bleilip knew the usual bits and pieces, legends, occult passions, quirks, histories—he had heard, for instance, about the holiday the Lubavitcher hasidim celebrate on the anniversary of their master's release from prison: pretty stories in the telling, even more touching in the reading —poetry. Bleilip, a lawyer though not in practice, an ex-labor consultant, a fund-raiser by profession, a rationalist—if he had known the word *mitnagged,* he would have applied that fierce epithet to himself: purist, skeptic, enemy of fresh revelation, enemy of the hasidim!—Bleilip, repelled by the hasidic sects themselves, was nevertheless lured by their constituents. Refugees, survivors. He supposed they had a certain knowledge the unscathed could not guess at.

He said: "Toby makes her bed, she lies in it. I didn't come expecting women's rights and, God knows, I didn't come expecting saints."

"If not saints, then martyrs," Yussel said.

Bleilip said nothing. This was not the sort of closeness he coveted; he shunned being seen into. His intention was to be a benefactor of the feelings. He glimpsed Yussel's tattoo number (it almost seemed as if Yussel just then lifted his wrist to display it) without the compassion he had schemed for it. Bleilip had come to see a town of dead men. It spoiled his mood that Yussel understood this.

At dusk, the three of them went up to the road to watch the boys slide down the hill from the yeshiva. There was no danger: not a single car, except Bleilip's taxi, had passed through all day. The snow was a week old, it was coming on to March, the air struck like a bell clapper. But Bleilip could smell through the cold something different from the smell of winter. Smoke of woodfire seeped into his throat from somewhere with a deep pineyness that moved him: he had a sense of farness, of clarity, of other lands, displaced seasons, the brooks of a village, a foreign bird piercing.

The yeshiva boys came down on shoe soles, one foot in front of the other, lurching, falling, rolling. A pair of them tobogganed past on a garbage-can lid. The rest jostled, tumbled, squawked, their yarmulkes dropping from their heads into the snow, like gumdrops, coins, black inkwells. Bleilip saw hoops of halos wheeling everywhere, and he saw their ear curls leaping over their cheeks, and all at once he penetrated into what he took to be the truth of this place —the children whirling on the hillside were false children, made of no flesh: it was a crowd of ghosts coming down. A clamor of white smoke beat on the road.

Yussel said, "I'm on my way to *minha,* want to come?"

Bleilip's grandfather, still a child but with an old man's pitted nose, appeared to be flying toward him on the lid. The last light of day split into blue rays all around them; the idea of going for evening prayer seemed natural to him now, but Bleilip, privately elated, self-proud, asked, "Why, do you need someone?"—because he was remembering what he had forgotten he knew. Ten men. He congratulated his memory, also of his grandfather's nose, thin as an arrow—the nose, the face, the body all gone into the earth—and he went on piecing together his grandfather's face, tan teeth that gave out small clicks and radiated stale farina, shapely grey half-moon eyes with fleshy lids, eyebrows sparse as a woman's, a prickly whisk broom of a moustache, whiter than cream.

Bleilip congratulated his luck.

Yussel took Bleilip by the arm: "Pessimist, joker, here we never run short, a *minyan* always without fail. But come, anyhow you'll hear the rebbe. It's our turn for him."

Briefly, behind them, Bleilip saw Toby moving into the dark of the door, trailed by two pairs of boys with golden earlocks: he felt the shock of that sight, as if a beam of divinity had fixed on her head, her house. But in an instant he was again humiliated by the sting of Yussel's eye—"She'll give them supper," Yussel said. "Then they have homework."

"You people make them work," Bleilip said.

"Honey on the page is only for the beginning," Yussel said. "Afterward comes hard learning."

Bleilip accepted a cap for his cold-needled skull, and the two men toiled on the ice upward toward the schoolhouse. When Bleilip reached for a prayer shawl inside a cardboard box, Yussel thumbed a *no* at him, so Bleilip dropped it in again. No one else paid him any attention.

Through the window the sky deepened; the shouts were gone from the hill. Yussel handed Bleilip a *siddur,* but the alphabet was jumpy and strange to him: it needed piecing together, like his grandfather's face. He stood up when the others did. Then he sat down again, fitting his haunches into a boy's chair. It did not seem to him that they sang out with any special fervor, as he had read the hasidim did. But the sounds were loud, cadenced, earnest. The leader, unlike the others a mutterer, was the single one wearing the fringed shawl—he looked in a cave, without mobility of heart, impersonal. Bleilip turned his stare here and there into the tedium—*which was the rebbe?* He went after a politician's face: his analogy was to the mayor of a town. Or to a patriarch's face—the father of a large family.

They finished *minha* and herded themselves into a corner of the room—a long table (three planks nailed together, two sawhorses) covered by a cloth. The cloth was grimy: print lay on it, the backs of old *siddurim*, rubbing, shredding, the backs of the open hands of the men.

Bleilip drew himself in; he found a wooden folding chair and wound his legs into the rungs, away from the men. It stunned him that they were not old but instead mainly in the forties, plump and in their prime. Their cheeks were blooming hillocks above their beards: some wore yarmulkes, some, tall black hats edged with fur, some, ordinary fedoras pushed back, one, a workman's cap. Their mouths especially struck Bleilip as extraordinary—vigorous, tender, blessed. He marveled at their mouths until it came to him that they were speaking another language and that he could follow only a little of it: now and then it was almost as if their words were visibly springing out of their mouths, like flags or streamers. Whenever he understood the words, the flags whipped at him; otherwise, they collapsed and vanished with a sort of hum.

Bleilip himself was a month short of forty-two, but next to these pious men he felt like a boy; even his shoulder blades weakened and thinned. He made himself concentrate: he heard *Azazel*, and he heard *cohen gadol*—they were knitting something up, mixing strands of holy tongue with Yiddish. The noise of Yiddish in his ear enfeebled him still more, like Titus' fly—it was not an everyday language with him, except to make cracks with, jokes, gags. . . .

His dead grandfather hung from the ceiling on a rope. Wrong, mistaken, impossible, uncharacteristic of his grandfather!—who died old and safe in a Bronx bed, mischief-maker, eager aged imp. The imp came to life and swung over Bleilip's black corner. Here ghosts sat as if already in the world to come, explicating Scripture. Or whatever. Who knew? In his grandfather's garble, the hasidim (refugees, dead men) were crying out *Temple*, were crying out *high priest*, and the more Bleilip squeezed his brain toward them, the more he comprehended. Five times on the tenth day of the seventh month, the Day of Atonement, the high priest changes his vestments, five times he lowers his body into the ritual bath. After the first immersion, garments of gold; after the second immersion, white linen—and, wearing the white linen, he confesses his sins and the sins of his household while holding on to the horns of a bullock. Walking eastward, the high priest goes from the west of the altar to the north of the altar, where two goats stand, and there he casts lots for the goats: one for the Lord, one for *Azazel*—and the one for the Lord is given a necklace of red wool and will be slaughtered and its blood caught in a bowl. But first the bullock will be slaughtered and its blood caught in a bowl; and once more the high priest confesses his sins and the sins of his household and now also the sins of the children of Aaron, this holy people. The blood of the bullock is sprinkled eight times, both upward and downward; the blood of the goat is sprinkled eight times. Then the high priest comes to the goat who was not slaughtered, the one for *Azazel*, and now he touches it and confesses the sins of the whole house of Israel and utters the name of God and pronounces the people cleansed of sin. And Bleilip, hearing all this through the web of a language gone stale in his marrow, was scraped to the edge of pity and belief: he pitied the hapless goats, the unlucky bullock, but more than this he pitied the God of Israel, whom he saw as an imp with a pitted nose, specter dangling on a cord from the high beams of the Temple in Jerusalem, winking down at His tiny high priest—now he leaps in and out of a box of water, now he hurries in and out of new clothes like a quick-change vaudevillian, now he sprinkles red drops up and red drops down, and all the while Bleilip, together with the God of the Jews, pities these toy children of Israel in the Temple long ago. Pity upon pity. What God could take the Temple rites seriously? What use does the King of the Universe have for goats? What, leaning on their dirty tablecloth—no vestments, altars, sacrifices—what do these survivors, exemptions, expect of God now?

All at once Bleilip knew which was the rebbe. The man in the work cap with a funny flat nose, black-haired and red-bearded, fist on mouth, elbows sunk into his lap—a self-stabber: in all that recitation, those calls and streamers of discourse, this blunt-nosed man had no word. But now he stood up, scratched his chair backward, and fell into an ordinary voice. Bleilip examined him: he looked fifty, his hands were brutish, two fingers missing, the nails on the others absent. A pair of muscles bunched in his neck like chains. The company did not breathe; they gave the rebbe something more than attentiveness. Bleilip reversed his view and saw that the rebbe was their child: they gazed at him with the possessiveness of faces seized by a crib, and he, too, spoke in that mode, as if addressing parents, old fathers, deferential, awed, guilty. And still he was their child, and still he owed them his guilt.

He said: "And what comes next? Next we read that *cohen gadol* gives the goat fated for *Azazel* to one of the *cohanim*, and the *cohen* takes it out into a place all bare and wild, with a big cliff in the middle of it all, and the *cohen* cuts off a bit of the red wool they had put on it and ties it onto a piece of rock to mark the place, and then he drives the goat over the edge, and it spins down, down, down and is destroyed. But in the Temple the worship may not continue, not until it is known that the goat is already given over to the wilderness. How can they know this miles away in the far city? All along the way, from the wilderness to Jerusalem, poles stand up out of the ground, and on top of every pole a man, and in the hand of every man a great shawl to shake out, so that pole flies out a wing to pole, wing after wing, until it comes to the notice of the *cohen gadol* in the Temple that the goat has been dashed into the ravine. And only then can the *cohen gadol* finish his readings, his invocations, his blessings, his beseechings. In the neighborhood of Sharon often there are earthquakes: the *cohen gadol* says, let their homes not become their graves. And after all this, a procession, no, a parade, a celebration: all the people follow the *cohen gadol* to his own house, he is removed safe out of the Holy of Holies, their sins are atoned for, they are cleansed and healed, and they sing how like a flower he is, a lily, like the moon, the sun, the morning star among clouds, a dish of gold, an olive tree. . . . That, gentlemen, is how it was in the Temple, and how it will be again after the coming of Messiah. We learn it"—the rebbe tapped his book—"in *Mishna Yoma*. But *whose* is the atonement, *whose* is the cleansing? Does the goat for *Azazel* atone, does the *cohen gadol* cleanse and hallow us? No, only the Most High can cleanse, only we ourselves can atone. Rabbi Akiba reminds us: 'Who is it that makes you clean? Our Father in Heaven.' So why, gentlemen, do you suppose the Temple was even then necessary, why the goats, the bullock, the blood? Why is it necessary for all of this to be restored by Messiah? These are questions we must torment ourselves with. Which of us would slaughter an animal, not for sustenance, but for an idea? Which of us would dash an animal to its death? Which of us would not feel himself to be a sinner in doing so? Or feel the shame of Esau? You may say that those were other days, the rituals are obsolete, we are purer now, better, we do not sprinkle blood so readily. But in truth you would not say so, you would not lie. For animals we in our day substitute men. What the word *Azazel* means exactly is not known—we call it *wilderness*, some say it is hell itself, demons live there. But whatever we mean by 'wilderness,' whatever we mean by 'hell,' surely the plainest meaning is *instead of*. Wilderness instead of easeful places, hell and devils instead of plenitude, life, peace. Goat instead of man. Was there no one present in the Temple who, seeing the animals in all their majesty of health, shining hair, glinting hooves, timid nostrils, muscled like ourselves, gifted with tender eyes no different from our own, the whole fine creature trembling—was there no one there, when the knife slit the fur and skin and the blood fled upward, who did not feel the splendor of the living beast? No one who was not in awe of the miracle of life turned to carcass? Who did not think: *How like that goat I am! The goat goes, I stay, the goat instead of me.* No one who did not see in the goat led to *Azazel* his own destiny? Death takes us, too, at random, some at the altar, some over the cliff. . . . Gentlemen, we are this moment, so to speak, in the Temple, the Temple devoid of the Holy of Holies. When the Temple was destroyed, it forsook the world, so the world itself had no recourse but to pretend to be the Temple by mockery. In the absence of Messiah, there can be no *cohen gadol*—we have no authority to bless multitudes, we are not empowered, we cannot appeal, except for ourselves, ourselves alone, in isolation, in futility. Instead, we are like the little goats, we are assigned our lot, we are designated for the altar or for *Azazel*. In either case, we are meant to be cut down. . . . O little fathers, we cannot choose. We are driven. We are not free. We are only *instead of:* we stand *instead of*. Instead of choice, we have the yoke. Instead of looseness, we are pointed the way to go. Instead of freedom, we have the red cord around our throats. We were in villages, they drove us into camps: we were in trains, they drove us into showers of poison. In the absence of Messiah, the secular ones make a nation: enemies bite at it. All that we do without Messiah is in vain. When the Temple forsook the world and the world presumed to mock the Temple, everyone on earth became a goat or a bullock, a he-animal or a she-animal. All our prayers are bleats and neighs on the way to a forsaken altar, a teeming *Azazel*. Little fathers! How is it possible to live? When will Messiah come? You! You! Visitor! You're looking somewhere else! *Who are you not to look*!"

The rebbe pointed a finger without a nail.

"Who are you? Talk and look! Who!"

Bleilip spoke his own name and shook: a schoolboy in a schoolroom.

"I'm here with the deepest respect, Rabbi. I came out of interest for your community."

"We are not South Sea islanders, sir. Our practices are well-known since Sinai. You don't have to turn your glance. We are not something new in the world."

"Excuse me, Rabbi, not new—unfamiliar."

"To you."

"To me," Bleilip admitted.

"Exactly my question! Who are you, what do you represent, what are you to us?"

"A Jew. Like yourselves. One of you."

"Presumption! Atheist, devourer! For us, there is the Most High, joy, life. For us, trust! But you! A moment ago I spoke your own heart for you, *emes*?"

Bleilip knew this word: truth, true. But he was only a visitor and did not want so much: he wanted only what he needed, a certain piece of truth, not too big to swallow. He was afraid of choking on more.

The rebbe said, "You believe the world is in vain, *emes*?"

"I don't follow any of that. I'm not looking for theology—"

"Little fathers," said the rebbe, "everything you heard me say, everything you heard me say in a voice of despair, emanates from the liver of this man. My mouth made itself his parrot. My teeth became his beak. He fills the study house with a black light, as if he keeps a lump of radium inside his belly. He would eat us up. Man he equates with the goats. The Temple, in memory and anticipation, he considers an abattoir. The world he regards as a graveyard. You are shocked, Mr. Bleilip, that I know your kidneys, your heart? Canker! Onset of cholera! You say you don't come for theology, Mr. Bleilip, and yet you have a particular conception of us, *emes*? A certain idea?"

Bleilip wished himself mute. He looked at Yussel, but Yussel had his eyes on his sleeve button.

"Speak in your own language, please"—Bleilip was unable to do anything else—"and I will understand you very well. Your idea about us, please. Stand up!"

Bleilip obeyed. That he obeyed bewildered him. The crescents of faces in profile on either side of him seemed sharp as scythes. His yarmulke fell off his head, but, rising, he failed to notice it—one of the men quickly clapped it back on. The stranger's palm came like a blow.

"Your idea," the rebbe insisted.

"Things I've heard," Bleilip croaked. "That in the *Zohar* it's written how Moses coupled with the *Shekinah* on Mount Sinai. That there are books to cast lots by, to tell fortunes, futures. That some Rabbis achieved levitation, hung in air without end, made

babies come in barren women, healed miraculously. That there was once a Rabbi who snuffed out the sabbath light. Things," Bleilip said. "I suppose legends."

"Did you hope to witness any of these things?"

Bleilip was silent.

"Then let me again ask—do you credit any of these things?"

"Do you?" asked Bleilip.

Yussel intervened. "Forbidden to mock the rebbe!"

But the rebbe replied, "I do not believe in magic. That there are influences I do believe."

Bleilip felt braver. "Influences?"

"Turnings. That a man can be turned from folly, error, wrong choices. From misery, evil, private rage. From a mistaken life."

Now Bleilip viewed the rebbe; he was suspicious of such hands. The hands a horror: deformity, mutilation: caught in what machine?—and above them the worker's cap. But otherwise the man seemed simple, reasoned, balanced, after certain harmonies, sanities, the ordinary article, no mystic, a bit bossy, pedagogue, noisy preacher. Bleilip—himself a man with a profession and no schoolboy, after all—again took heart. A commonplace figure. People did what the rebbe asked, nothing more complicated than this—but he had to ask. Or tell, or direct. A monarch perhaps. A community needs to be governed. A human relationship: of all words, Bleilip, whose vocabulary was habitually sociological, best of all liked "relationship."

He said, "I don't have a mistaken life."

"Empty your pockets."

Bleilip stood without moving.

"Empty your pockets!"

"Rabbi, I'm not an exercise, I'm not a demonstration."

"Despair must be earned."

"I'm not in despair," Bleilip objected.

"To be an atheist is to be in despair."

"I'm not in athiest; I'm a secularist." But even Bleilip did not know what he meant by this.

"Esau! For the third time: *Empty your pockets*!"

Bleilip pulled the black plastic thing out and threw it on the table. Instantly all the men bent away from it.

"A certain rebbe," said the rebbe very quietly, "believed every man should carry two slips of paper in his pockets. In one pocket should be written: 'I am but dust and ashes.' In the other: 'For my sake was the world created.' This canker fills only one pocket, and with ashes." The rebbe picked up Bleilip's five-and-ten gun and said, "Esau! Beast! Lion! To whom did you intend to do harm?"

"Nobody," said Bleilip out of his shame. "It isn't real. I keep it to get used to. The feel of the thing. Listen," he said, "do you think it's easy for me to carry that thing around and keep on thinking about it?"

The rebbe tried the trigger. It gave out a tin click. Then he wrapped it in his handkerchief and put it in his pocket.

"We will now proceed with *ma'ariv*," the rebbe said. "The study hour is finished. Let us not learn more of this matter. This is Jacob's tent."

The men left the study table and took up their old places, reciting. Bleilip, humiliated (the analogy to a teacher confiscating a forbidden toy was too exact), still excited, the tremor in his groin worse, was in awe before this incident. Was it amazing chance that the rebbe had challenged the contents of his pockets, or was he in truth a seer?

At the conclusion of *ma'ariv*, the men dispersed quickly; Bleilip recognized from Yussel's white stare that this was not the usual way. He felt like an animal they were running from. He intended to run himself—all the way to the Greyhound station—but the rebbe came to him.

"You," the rebbe said (*du*, as if to an animal, or to a child, or to God), "the other pocket. The second one. The other side of your coat."

"What?"

"Disgorge."

So Bleilip took it out. And just as the toy gun could instantly be seen to be a toy, all plastic glint, so could this one be seen for what it was: monstrous, clumsy and hard, heavy, with a scarred trigger and a barrel that smelled. Dark, no gleam. An actuality. A thing for use.

Yussel moaned, dipping his head up and down. "In my house! Stood in front of my wife with it! With two!"

"With one," said the rebbe. "One is a toy and one not, so only one need be feared. It is the toy we have to fear: the incapable . . ."

Yussel broke in, "We should call the police, rebbe."

"Because of a toy? How they will laugh."

"But the other! This!"

"Is it capable?" the rebbe asked Bleilip.

"Loaded, you mean? Sure it's loaded," Bleilip said.

"Loaded, You hear him?" Yussel said. "He came as a curiosity-seeker, rebbe, my wife's cousin. I had no suspicion of this."

The rebbe said, "Go home, Yussel. Go home, little father."

"Rebbe, he can shoot. . . ."

"How can he shoot? The instrument is in my hand."

It was. The rebbe held the gun—the real one. Again Bleilip was drawn to those hands. This time the rebbe saw.

"Buchenwald," the rebbe said. "Blocks of ice, a freezing experiment. In my case only to the elbow. But others were immersed wholly and perished. The fingers left are toy fingers. That is why you have been afraid of them and have looked away."

The rebbe said all this very clearly, in a voice without an opinion.

Yussel said, "Don't talk to him, rebbe!"

"Little father, go home," the rebbe said.

"And if he shoots?"

"He will not shoot," the rebbe said.

Alone in the schoolhouse with the rebbe—how dim the bulbs, dangling on cords—Bleilip regretted the dishonor of the guns. The day (now it was night) felt full of miracles and lucky chances. He had gotten to the rebbe. He had never supposed he would get to the rebbe himself—all his hope was only for a glimpse of the effect of the rebbe. Of influences. With these he would have been satisfied.

Bleilip said again, "I don't have a mistaken life."

The rebbe enclosed the second gun in his handkerchief.

"This one has a bad odor," the rebbe said.

"Once I killed a pigeon with it."

"A live bird?"

"You believers," Bleilip threw out, "you'd cut up those goats all over again if you got the Temple back!"

"Sometimes," the rebbe said, "even the rebbe does not believe. My father, when he was the rebbe, also sometimes did not believe. It is characteristic of believers sometimes not to believe. And it is characteristic of unbelievers sometimes to believe. Even you, Mr. Bleilip, even you now and then believe in the Holy One, Blessed Be He? Even you now and then apprehend the Most High?"

"No," Bleilip said; and then: "Yes."

"Then you are as bloody as anyone," the rebbe said (it was his first real opinion), and with his terrible hands put the bulging white handkerchief on the table for Bleilip to take home with him for whatever purpose he thought he needed it.

Collectors

RAYMOND CARVER

I was out of work. But any day I expected to hear from up north. I lay on the sofa and listened to the rain. Now and then I'd lift up and look through the curtain for the mailman.

There was no one on the street, nothing.

I hadn't been down again five minutes when I heard someone walk onto the porch, wait, and then knock. I lay still. I knew it wasn't the mailman. I knew his steps. You can't be too careful if you're out of work and you get notices in the mail or else pushed under your door. They come around wanting to talk, too, especially if you don't have a telephone.

The knock sounded again, louder, a bad sign. I eased up and tried to see onto the porch. But whoever was there was standing against the door, another bad sign. I knew the floor creaked, so there was no chance of slipping into the other room and looking out that window.

Another knock, and I said, Who's there?

This is Aubrey Bell, a man said. Are you Mr. Slater?

What is it you want? I called from the sofa.

I have something for Mrs. Slater. She's won something. Is Mrs. Slater home?

Mrs. Slater doesn't live here, I said.

Well, then, are you Mr. Slater? the man said. Mr. Slater. . . . And the man sneezed.

I got off the sofa. I unlocked the door and opened it a little. He was an old guy, fat and bulky under his raincoat. Water ran off the coat and dripped onto the big suitcase contraption thing he carried.

He grinned and set down the big case. He put out his hand.

Aubrey Bell, he said.

I don't know you, I said.

Mrs. Slater, he began. Mrs. Slater filled out a card. He took cards from an inside pocket and shuffled them a minute. Mrs. Slater, he read. Two fifty-five South Sixth East? Mrs. Slater is a winner.

He took off his hat and nodded solemnly, slapped the hat against his coat as if that were it, everything had been settled, the drive finished, the railhead reached.

He waited.

Mrs. Slater doesn't live here, I said. What'd she win?

I have to show you, he said. May I come in?

I don't know. If it won't take long, I said. I'm pretty busy.

Fine, he said. I'll just slide out of this coat first. And the galoshes. Wouldn't want to track up your carpet. I see you do have a carpet, Mr. . . .

His eyes had lighted and then dimmed at the sight of the carpet. He shuddered. Then he took off his coat. He shook it out and hung it by the collar over the doorknob. That's a good place for it, he said. Damn weather anyway. He bent over and unfastened his galoshes. He set his case inside the room. He stepped out of the galoshes and into the room in a pair of slippers.

I closed the door. He saw me staring at the slippers and said, W. H. Auden wore slippers all through China on his first visit there. Never took them off. Corns.

I shrugged. I took one more look down the street for the mailman and shut the door.

Aubrey Bell stared at the carpet. He pulled at his lips. Then he laughed. He laughed and shook his head.

What's so funny? I said.

Nothing. Lord, he said. He laughed again. I think I'm losing my mind. I think I have a fever. He reached a hand to his forehead. His hair was matted and there was a ring around his scalp where the hat had been.

Do I feel hot to you? he said. I don't know, I think I might have a fever. He was still staring at the carpet. You have any aspirin?

What's the matter with you? I said. I hope you're not getting sick on me. I got things I have to do.

He shook his head. He sat down on the sofa. He stirred at the carpet with his slippered foot.

I went to the kitchen, rinsed a cup, shook two aspirin out of a bottle.

Here, I said. Then I think you ought to leave.

Are you speaking for Mrs. Slater? he hissed. No, no, forget I said that. Forget I said that. He wiped his face. He swallowed the aspirin. His eyes skipped around the bare room. Then he leaned forward with some effort and unsnapped the buckles on his case. The case flopped open, revealing three compartments filled with an array of hoses, brushes, shiny pipes, and some kind of heavy-looking blue thing mounted on little wheels. He stared at these things as if surprised. Quietly, in a churchly voice, he said, Do you know what this is?

I moved closer. I'd say it was a vacuum cleaner. I'm not in the market, I said. No way am I in the market for a vacuum cleaner.

I want to show you something, he said. He took a card out of his jacket pocket. Look at this, he said. He handed me the card. Nobody said you were in the market. But look at the signature. Is that Mrs. Slater's signature or not?

I looked at the card. I held it up to the light. I turned it over, but the other side was blank. So what? I said.

Mrs. Slater's card was pulled at random out of a basket of cards. Hundreds of cards just like this little card. She has won a free vacuuming and carpet shampoo. No strings. I am here even to do your mattress, Mr. . . . You'll be surprised to see what can collect in a mattress over the months, over the years. Every day, every night of our lives, we're leaving little bits of ourselves, flakes of this and that, behind. Where do they go, these bits and pieces of ourselves? Right through the sheets and into the mattress, *that's* where. Pillows, too. It's all the same.

He had been removing lengths of the shiny pipe and joining the parts together. Now he inserted the fitted pipes into the hose. He was on his knees, grunting. He attached some sort of scoop to the hose and lifted out the blue thing with wheels.

He let me examine the filter he intended to use.

Do you have a car? he asked.

No car, I said. I don't have a car. If I had a car I would drive you someplace.

Too bad, he said. This little vacuum comes equipped with a sixty-foot extension cord. If you had a car, you could wheel this little vacuum right up to your car door and vacuum the plush carpeting and the luxurious reclining seats as well. You would be surprised how much of us gets lost, how much of us gathers, in those fine seats over the years.

Mr. Bell, I said, I think you better pack up your things and go. I say this without any malice whatsoever.

But he was looking around the room for a plug-in. He found one at the end of the sofa. The machine rattled as if there were a marble inside, something loose, then settled to a hum.

Rilke lived in one castle after another all of his adult life. Benefactors, he said loudly over the hum of the vacuum. He seldom rode in motorcars, he preferred trains. Then look at Voltaire at Cirey with Madame Châtelet. His death mask. Such serenity. He raised his right hand as if I were about to disagree. No, no, it isn't right, is it? Don't say it. But who knows? With that he turned and began to pull the vacuum into the other room.

There was a bed, a window. The covers were heaped on the floor. One pillow, one sheet over the mattress. He slipped the case from the pillow and then quickly stripped the sheet from the mattress. He

stared at the mattress and gave me a look out of the corner of his eye. I went to the kitchen and got the chair. I sat down in the doorway and watched. First he tested the suction by putting the scoop against the palm of his hand. He bent and turned a dial on the vacuum. You have to turn it up full strength for a job like this one, he said. He checked the suction again, then extended the hose to the head of the bed and began to move the scoop down the mattress. The scoop tugged at the mattress. The vacuum whirred louder. He made three passes over the mattress, then switched off the machine. He pressed a lever and the lid popped open. He took out the filter. This filter is just for demonstration purposes. In normal use, all of this, this *material,* would go into your bag here, he said. He pinched some of the dusty stuff between his fingers. There must have been a cup of it.

He had this look to his face.

It's not my mattress, I said. I leaned forward in the chair and tried to show an interest.

Now the pillow, he said. He put the used filter on the sill and looked out the window for a minute. He turned. I want you to hold on to this end of the pillow, he said.

I got up and took hold of two corners of the pillow. I felt I was holding something by the ears.

Like this? I said.

He nodded. He went into the other room and came back with another filter.

How much do those things cost? I said.

Next to nothing, he said. They're only made out of paper and a little bit of plastic. Couldn't cost much.

He kicked on the vacuum and I held tight as the scoop sank into the pillow and moved down its length—once, twice, three times. He switched off the vacuum, removed the filter, and held it up without a word. He put it on the sill beside the other filter. Then he opened the closet door. He looked inside, but there was only a box of Mouse-Be-Gone.

I heard steps on the porch, the mail slot opened and clinked shut. We looked at each other.

He pulled on the vacuum and I followed him into the other room. We looked at the letter lying facedown on the carpet near the front door.

I started toward the letter, turned, and said, What else? It's getting late. This carpet's not worth fooling with. It's only a twelve-by-fifteen cotton carpet with no-skid backing from Rug City. It's not worth fooling with.

Do you have a full ashtray? he said. Or a potted plant, something like that? A handful of dirt would be fine.

I found the ashtray. He took it, dumped the contents onto the carpet, ground the ashes and cigarettes under his slipper. He got down on his knees again and inserted a new filter. He took off his jacket and threw it onto the sofa. He was sweating under the arms. Fat hung over his belt. He twisted off the scoop and attached another device to the hose. He adjusted his dial. He kicked on the machine and began to move back and forth, back and forth over the worn carpet. Twice I started for the letter. But he seemed to anticipate me, cut me off, so to speak, with his hose and his pipes and his sweeping and his sweeping. . . .

I took the chair back to the kitchen and sat there and watched him work. After a time he shut off the machine, opened the lid, and silently brought me the filter, alive with dust, hair, small grainy things. I looked at the filter, and then I got up and put it in the garbage.

He worked steadily now. No more explanations. He came out to the kitchen with a bottle that held a few ounces of green liquid. He put the bottle under the tap and filled it.

You know I can't pay anything, I said. I couldn't pay you a dollar if my life depended on it. You're going to have to write me off as a dead loss, that's all. You're wasting your time on me, I said.

I wanted it out in the open, no misunderstanding.

He went about his business. He put another attachment on the hose, in some complicated way hooked his bottle to the new attachment. He moved slowly over the carpet, now and then releasing little streams of emerald, moving the brush back and forth over the carpet, working up patches of foam.

I had said all that was on my mind. I sat on the chair in the kitchen, relaxed now, and watched him work. Once in a while I looked out the window at the rain. It had begun to get dark. He switched off the vacuum. He was in a corner near the front door.

You want coffee? I said.

He was breathing hard. He wiped his face.

I put on water and by the time it had boiled and I'd fixed up two cups, he had everything dismantled and back in the case. Then he picked up the letter. He read the name on the letter and looked closely at the return address. He folded the letter in half and put it in his hip pocket. I kept watching him. That's all I did. The coffee began to cool.

It's for a Mr. Slater, he said. I'll see to it. He said, Maybe I will skip the coffee. I better not walk across this carpet. I just shampooed it.

That's true, I said. Then I said, You're sure that's who the letter's for?

He reached to the sofa for his jacket, put it on, and opened the front door. It was still raining. He stepped into his galoshes, fastened them, and then pulled on the raincoat and looked back inside.

You want to see it? he said. You don't believe me?

It just seems strange, I said.

Well, I'd better get under way, he said. But he kept standing there. You want the vacuum or not?

I looked at the big case, closed now and ready to move on.

No, I said, I guess not. I'm going to be leaving here soon. It would just be in the way.

All right, he said, and he shut the door.

Heart of a Champion

T. CORAGHESSAN BOYLE

Here are the corn fields and the wheat fields winking gold and goldbrown and yellowbrown in midday sun. Up the grassy slope we go, to the barn redder than red against sky bluer than blue, across the smooth stretch of the barnyard with its pecking chickens, and then right on up to the screen door at the back of the house. The door swings open, a black hole in the sun, and Timmy emerges with his cornsilk hair. He is dressed in crisp overalls, striped T-shirt, stubby blue Keds. There must be a breeze—and we are not disappointed—his clean fine cup-cut hair waves and settles as he scuffs across the barnyard to the edge of the field. The boy stops there to gaze out over the wheat-manes, eyes unsquinted despite the sun, eyes blue as tinted lenses. Then he brings three fingers to his lips in a near triangle and whistles long and low, sloping up sharp to cut off at the peak. A moment passes: he whistles again. And then we see it—out there at the far corner of the field—the ripple, the dashing furrow, the blur of the streaking dog, white chest, flashing feet.

They are in the woods now. The boy whistling, hands in pockets, kicking along with his short darling strides, the dog beside him wagging the white tip of her tail, an all-clear flag. They pass beneath an arching black-barked oak. It creaks, and suddenly begins to fling itself down on them: immense, brutal: a Panzer strike. The boy's eyes startle and then there's the leap, the smart snout clutching his trousers, the thunder-blast of the trunk, the dust and spinning leaves. "Golly, Lassie, I didn't even see it," says the boy, sitting safe in a mound of moss. The collie looks up at him—the svelte snout, the deep gold logician's eyes—and laps at his face.

Now they are down by the river. The water is brown with angry suppurations, spiked with branches, fence posts, tires, and logs. It rushes like the sides of boxcars, chews deep and insidious at the bank under Timmy's feet. The roar is like a jetport—little wonder the boy cannot hear the dog's warning bark. We watch the crack appear, widen to a ditch, then the halves splitting—snatch of red earth, writhe of worm—the poise and pitch, and Timmy crashing down with it. Just a flash—but already he is way downstream, his head like a plastic jug, dashed and bobbed, spinning toward the nasty mouth of the falls. But there is the dog—fast as a flashcube —bursting along the bank, all white and gold, blended in motion, hair sleeked with the wind of it . . . yet what can she hope to do? The current surges on, lengths ahead, sure bet to win the race to the falls. Timmy sweeps closer, sweeps closer, the falls loud as a hundred timpani now, the war drums of the Sioux, Africa gone bloodlust mad! The dog forges ahead, lashing over the wet earth like a whipcrack, straining every ganglion, until at last she draws abreast of the boy. Then she is in the air, then the foaming yellow water. Her paws churning like pistons, whiskers chuffing with exertion—oh, the roar!—and there, she's got him, her sure jaws champing down on the shirt collar, her eyes fixed on the slip of rock at falls' edge. The black brink of the falls, the white paws digging at the rock—and they are safe. The dog sniffs at the inert little form, nudges the boy's side until she manages to roll him over. She clears his tongue and begins mouth-to-mouth.

Night: the barnyard still, a bulb burning over the screen door. Inside, the family sits at dinner, the table heaped with pork chops, mashed potatoes, applesauce and peas, home-baked bread, a pitcher of immaculate milk. Mom and Dad, good-humored and sympathetic, poised at attention, forks in mid-swoop, while Timmy tells his story.

"So then Lassie grabbed me by the collar and, golly, I guess I blanked out because I don't remember anything more till I woke up on the rock—"

"Well, I'll be!" says Mom.

"You're lucky you've got such a good dog, son," says Dad, gazing down at the collie where she lies serenely, snout over paw, tail wapping the floor. She is combed and washed and fluffed, her lashes mascaraed and curled, chest and paws white as soap. She looks up humbly. But then her ears leap, her neck jerks around —and she's up at the door, head cocked, alert. A high yipping yowl, like a stuttering fire-whistle, shudders through the room. And then another. The dog whines.

"Darn," says Dad. "I thought we were rid of those coyotes. Next thing you know, they'll be after the chickens again."

The moon blanches the yard, leans black shadows on trees, the barn. Upstairs in the house, Timmy lies sleeping in the pale light, his hair gorgeously mussed. His breathing gentle. The collie lies on the throw rug beside the bed, her eyes open. Suddenly, she rises and slips to the window, silent as shadow, and looks down the long elegant snout to the barnyard below, where the coyote slinks from shade to shade, a limp pullet dangling from his jaws. He is stunted, scabious, syphilitic, his forepaw trap-twisted, eyes running. The collie whimpers softly from the window. The coyote stops in mid-trot, frozen in a cold shard of light, ears high on his head—then drops the chicken at his feet, leers up at the window, and begins a crooning, sad-faced song.

The screen door slaps behind Timmy as he bolts from the house, Lassie at his heels. Mom's head pops forth on the rebound. "Timmy!" The boy stops as if jerked by a rope, turns to face her. "You be home before lunch, hear?"

"Sure, Mom," the boy says, already spinning off, the dog at his side.

In the woods, Timmy steps on a rattler and the dog bites its head off. "Gosh," he says. "Good girl, Lassie." Then he stumbles and flips over an embankment, rolls down the brushy incline and over a sudden precipice, whirling out into the breathtaking blue space, a sky diver. He thumps down on a narrow ledge twenty feet below—and immediately scrambles to his feet, peering timorously down the sheer wall to the heap of bleached bones at its base. Small stones break loose, shoot out like asteroids. Dirt-slides begin. But Lassie yarps reassuringly from above, sprints back to the barn for winch and cable, hoists the boy to safety.

On their way back for lunch Timmy leads them through a still and leaf-darkened copse. But notice that birds and crickets have left off their cheeping. How puzzling! Suddenly, around a bend in the path before them, the coyote appears. Nose to the ground, intent. All at once he jerks to a halt, flinches as if struck, hackles rising, tail dipping between his legs. The collie, too, stops short, yards away, her chest proud and shaggy and white. The coyote cowers, bunches like a cat, glares. Timmy's face sags with alarm. The coyote lifts his lip. But the collie prances up and stretches her nose out to him, her eyes liquid. She is balsamed and perfumed; her full chest tapers to sleek haunches and sculpted legs. The coyote is puny, runted, half her size, his coat a discarded doormat. She circles him now, sniffing. She whimpers, he growls, throaty and tough—and stands stiff while she licks at his whiskers, noses his rear, the bald black scrotum. Timmy is horror-struck as the coyote slips behind her, his black lips tight with anticipation.

"What was she doing, Dad?" Timmy asks over his milk, good hot soup, and sandwich.

"The sky was blue today, son," Dad says. "The barn was red."

Late afternoon: the sun mellow, orange. Purpling clots of shadow hang from the branches, ravel out from tree trunks. Bees and wasps and flies saw away at the wet full-bellied air. Timmy and the dog are far out beyond the north pasture, out by the old Indian burial ground, where the boy stoops to search for arrowheads. The collie is pacing the crest above, whimpering voluptuously, pausing from time to time to stare out across the forest, eyes distant and moon-struck. Behind her, storm clouds, dark exploding brains, spread over the horizon.

We observe the wind kicking up: leaves flapping like wash, saplings quivering. It darkens quickly now, clouds scudding low and smoky over treetops, blotting the sun from view. Lassie's white is whiter than ever, highlighted against the heavy horizon, wind-whipped hair foaming around her. Still, she does not look down at the boy as he digs.

The first fat random drops, a flash, the volcanic blast of thunder. Timmy glances over his shoulder at the noise just in time to see the scorched pine plummeting toward the constellated freckles in the center of his forehead. Now the collie turns—too late!—the

swoosh-whack of the tree, the trembling needles. She is there in an instant, tearing at the green welter, struggling through to his side. The boy lies unconscious in the muddying earth, hair cunningly arranged, a thin scratch painted on his cheek. The trunk lies across his back, the tail of a brontosaurus. The rain falls.

Lassie tugs doggedly at a knob in the trunk, her pretty paws slipping in the wet—but it's no use—it would take a block and tackle, a crane, a corps of engineers to shift that stubborn bulk. She falters, licks at the boy's ear, whimpers. See the troubled look in Lassie's eye as she hesitates, uncertain, priorities warring: stand guard—or dash for help? Her decision is sure and swift—eyes firm with purpose, she's off like shrapnel, already up the hill, shooting past dripping trees, over river, cleaving high wet banks of wheat.

A moment later she dashes through the puddled and rain-screened barnyard, barking right on up to the back door, where she pauses to scratch daintily, her voice high-pitched, insistent. Mom swings open the door and Lassie pads in, toenails clacking on the shiny linoleum.

"What is it, girl? What's the matter? Where's Timmy?"

"Yarf! Yarfata-yarf-yarf!"

"Oh, my! Dad! Dad, come quick!"

Dad rushes in, face stolid and reassuring. "What is it, dear? . . . Why, Lassie!"

"Oh, Dad, Timmy's trapped under a pine tree out by the old Indian burial ground—"

"Arpit-arp!"

"—a mile and a half past the north pasture."

Dad is quick, firm, decisive. "Lassie, you get back up there and stand watch over Timmy. Mom and I will go for Doc Walker. Hurry now!"

The dog hesitates at the door: "Rarf-arrar-ra!"

"Right!" says Dad. "Mom, fetch the chain saw."

See the woods again. See the mud-running burial ground, the fallen pine, and there: Timmy! He lies in a puddle, eyes closed, breathing slow. The hiss of rain is nasty as static. See it work: scattering leaves, digging trenches, inciting streams to swallow their banks. It lies deep now in the low areas, and in the mid areas, and in the high areas. Now see the dam, some indeterminate distance off, the yellow water, like urine, churning over its lip, the ugly earthen belly distended, bloated with the pressure. Raindrops pock the surface like a plague.

Now see the pine once more . . . and . . . what is it? There! The coyote! Sniffing, furtive, the malicious eyes, the crouch, the slink. He stiffens when he spots the boy—but then he slouches closer, a rubbery dangle drooling from between his mismeshed teeth. Closer. Right over the prone figure now, stooping, head dipping between shoulders, irises caught in the corners of his eyes: wary, sly, predatory: a vulture slavering over fallen life.

But wait! Here comes Lassie! Sprinting out of the wheat field, bounding rock to rock across the crazed river, her limbs contourless with speed and purpose.

The jolting front seat of the Ford. Dad, Mom, the Doctor, all dressed in slickers and flap-brimmed hats, sitting shoulder to shoulder behind the clapping wipers, their jaws set with determination, eyes aflicker with downright gumption.

The coyote's jaws, serrated grinders, work at the bones of Timmy's hand. The boy's eyelids flutter with the pain, and he lifts his head feebly—but slaps it down again, flat, lifeless, in the mud. Now see Lassie blaze over the hill, show-dog indignation aflame in her eyes. The scrag of a coyote looks up at her, drooling blood, choking down choice bits of flesh. He looks up from eyes that go back thirty million years. Looks up unmoved, uncringing, the ghastly snout and murderous eyes less a physical than a philosophical challenge. See the collie's expression alter in mid-bound—the countenance of offended A.K.C. morality giving way, dissolving. She skids to a halt, drops her tail and approaches him, a buttery gaze in her golden eyes. She licks the blood from his vile lips.

The dam. Impossibly swollen, the rain festering the yellow surface, a hundred new streams rampaging in, the pressure of those millions of gallons hard-punching millions more. There! The first gap, the water flashing out, a boil splattering. The dam shudders, splinters, blasts to pieces like crockery. The roar is devastating.

The two animals start at the terrible rumbling. Still working their gummy jaws, they dash up the far side of the hill. See the white-tipped tail retreating side by side with the hacked and tick-crawling one—both tails like banners as the animals disappear into the trees at the top of the rise. Now look back to the rain, the fallen pine in the crotch of the valley, the spot of the boy's head. Oh, the sound ot it, the wall of water at the far end of the valley, smashing through the little declivity, a God-sized fist prickling with shattered trunks and boulders, grinding along, a planet dislodged. And see Timmy: eyes closed, hair plastered, arm like meat-market leftovers.

But now see Mom and Dad and the Doctor struggling over the rise, the torrent seething closer, booming and howling. Dad launches himself in full charge down the hillside—but the water is already sweeping over the fallen pine, lifting it like paper. There is a confusion, a quick clip of a typhoon at sea—is that a flash of golden hair?—and it is over. The valley fills to the top of the rise, the water ribbed and rushing.

But we have stopped seeing. For we go sweeping up and out of the dismal rain, back to magnificent wheat fields in midday sun. There is a boy cupping his hands to his mouth and he is calling: "Laahh-sie! Laahh-sie!"

Then we see what we must see—way out there at the end of the field—the ripple, the dashing furrow, the blur of the streaking dog, white chest, flashing feet.

Paco and I at Sea

JAMES THOMAS

A short distance down the deck, a young woman stands at the rail. Like me, she watches the changing sky, the orange sun that will soon touch the sea.

Now and then she glances over at me. I know this because now and then I look at her too, and what my study has revealed so far is that she is not beautiful. At the moment the sky is peaceful, yet she wears a yellow slicker and hat, the kind that can be tied under the chin. It does not flatter her, this costume.

I have not noticed her on board before, even though there are few passengers.

Mostly it has been smooth sailing. But this time of year, with the summer well gone, each day brings some change in the temperature, the sky, the wind.

You can read the weather in the faces of the men who work this ship, the *Aurelia*, just as you can with any sailor at sea. If you are up early in the morning to watch and they are at their stations on time, you might worry. If they are quick and nervous to do their jobs, you might worry.

We have had some high seas but none rough. Mostly the skies have been clear. It has been enjoyable, the food excellent, and these days at sea I have gotten more sleep than is my custom—although I am still up every morning before it is light. It has been relaxing, and even if I have not found a place to land, as Paco expects of me, it has been pleasant to put soil and pavement behind.

The sun has set and the woman has disappeared. She passed me in leaving and she smiled. I also smiled. Her eyes proved brown and very large, her complexion dark, and I saw that she was older than I had first thought, perhaps thirty. She looked Jewish. And the quiet message on her face, behind the coded smile, was easy enough to read.

Paco. It is he I must thank for these pleasant days and nights at sea.

I met him in a café in Córdoba where I had gone to hear some popular singer whose name I have now forgotten. I was standing at the bar drinking cheap brandy, unwilling to leave though the singer himself had left.

Paco. There was a man standing next to me.

You are alone? he asked when we found ourselves looking at each other.

I'm expecting friends, I lied. At first I didn't want to speak with him. His suit was too expensive, he was too well groomed, he spoke to me too freely. Such men interest me professionally but bore me with their talk of art and business and women. I prefer to study them at a distance.

On holiday?

No.

What, then?

I travel in my business, I told him.

I see, he said, and the sad concerned look that broke over his face redeemed him. I will buy you a very good drink, then—for the road, as they say.

His concern was that my road went no place in particular, and soon we were sitting at a table and he was talking across to it to me, a father's worry in his voice. I did not mind.

When I was younger I was like you, Paco told me that first night. Constantly on the move. I could never decide on anything, a place to make my home, a woman, what to do with my life. Now I am fifty, and if my father had not died a rich man I would not have my bank balance to give me pleasure. He patted his breast pocket. How old are you?

I told him I was twenty-nine.

Listen, he said, filling our glasses and leaning over the table with his words. To discover you are no longer young, and have nothing, is no good.

We drank until the bar closed, then he gave me a ride to the pensión where I was staying. He told me he was driving to Málaga in a few days and would I like to come. I said I would. It was a magnificent city, he told me. Perhaps I would decide to settle there.

He arranged for me to stay in a hotel run by a friend of his. Like this ship, it was pleasant. And he was right about Málaga. Beautiful beaches and beautiful women, and more than enough tourists with pockets to keep me busy.

I never saw Paco during the day. Like me, he mentioned business but never suggested what it might be. Sometimes he would stop by in the evening and we would go out for a drink. After a month, I told him I was leaving. But you have everything here, he said, so many possibilities. Where could you be happier?

I told him I had made up my mind. That look entered his face, as though it were the loss of someone dear we were talking about. And then he began telling me about the *Aurelia*. It was one of two freighters owned by a friend of his, and had accommodations for thirty passengers. It would dock in Málaga in a week and he could arrange passage for me. The ship, he told me, had no regular schedule, but wandered wherever its cargo took it.

Perfect, he said, for a fellow like you. You will see many places and choose one of them.

Paco went with me to the pier, embraced me and pounded my back. He told me that he himself was leaving Málaga and did not know when he would return.

I wish you luck in your choice, he said to me. The very best of luck. Then he gave me the leather satchel he had carried with him to the pier. Later, on board, I opened it. It contained five bottles of Five Star cognac and a note.

Pobrecito, it said, Your father is long dead and could leave you nothing.

I have since thrown away his note. I have no idea what it meant.

There is no moon tonight—so the sea and sky are made of the same black. The gulls, of course, have our lights to follow.

We cannot be too far from the coast—the birds say that—but I know we are following it rather than approaching it. No one on board expects to see land for more than a day.

It is much colder out here now that the sun has set and the woman has gone in.

In my cabin, preparing for dinner, I think about her. She too is probably getting herself ready—washing her face or brushing her hair, perhaps at this moment veiling her body with a dress. I decide that she is putting on a brown dress, slipping it now over her head, pulling it now off her breasts so that it falls now at her knees. I am particularly interested in her legs.

As for myself, I wear a tie. It is always the same tie and decorates whatever else I am already wearing. Paco gave me a number of fine shirts, made for him by his tailor in Barcelona. But I am very hard on them. I am afraid they will not last me long.

What sort of smell should I expect from her? Perfume seems unlikely, she does not appear sensational enough for that. Nor would I expect her to smell musky, of perspiration, as I surely do. Clean, she will probably smell clean, a slight scent of whatever soap she uses. And her breath, I am certain, will be fresh.

Paco wanted to give me money before I left. For toiletries and the like, as he put it. I said no, you have done enough. I do not care to have you support my private habits, I have some money, I will buy my own toothpaste.

I am especially interested in her legs. Through the port window above my bed, I look out into the night and see her dress falling slowly over her thighs, dropping like a curtain, again and again.

The *Aurelia* is registered Spanish, but it has no real home. During the war, I am told, guns were put on it and it was used by the Italians. But a freighter is only a freighter and the Italians inevitably lost.

It is old. Its engines wheeze and it has been too many times repaired, refurbished, repainted. Its weariness shows. The men who work it seem weary too. They are of uncommon nationalities, many of them, and speak in strange languages. They have only one home and they are floating on it.

I met the captain my first day aboard, a sour-faced man who nonetheless shook my hand warmly. He knew Paco. We spoke of Málaga. I have not seen him since and sometimes wonder if he is still with us.

It is not a small ship. There are five levels below my cabin and two above, not counting the observation decks and pilothouse. It is easy enough to get lost. But most of the *Aurelia*'s space is taken up with the cargo that fills its huge belly. Into the vast holds I have seen crates of oranges lowered, bellowing cattle, drums of olive oil. Out of them have come carpets, leaking bags of grain, wine.

We have already made many stops. From the deck and through my port window I have watched the cities grow, then disappear in our wake. Annaba. Iráklion. Cagliari. Izmir, I have walked through the dusty crowded streets, talked with the people, occasionally ventured into the countryside. But always I have made the ship's call.

In the dining saloon I sit across from a middle-aged couple who must tell me how good it was to visit their son in Marseilles. He is doing so well, an importer of sporting goods. He is about my age, they note, then want to know where I am going. I ask instead if they have yet met the woman seen on deck in a yellow slicker.

No. We haven't.

Waiters fill our glasses with water and set bread on the table. I look around again. Perhaps she does not feel well, she was gripping the deck rail so tightly. Or is it possible I do not recognize her?

I pour myself some wine and offer to do the same for the couple.

Please.

Thank you.

It is nothing.

Now the soup, ladled from a steaming tureen to my bowl. I fear that I am becoming accustomed to this luxury. It is a thick pasta soup, rich with vegetables. I consider its temperature and watch it shift slowly in the bowl.

Excuse me, young man, but is that the woman you mean?

I follow the nod, look toward the doors. Yes, that is her. Except she is not wearing brown at all, but a pair of faded dungarees and a heavy sweater. Her black hair just reaches her shoulders. She sees me looking at her. She smiles.

I know she will take the place beside me. I concentrate on my soup. It is still too hot to eat. When she sits down, I allow the middle-aged couple to greet her first. They launch into talk of their successful son and of beautiful Marseilles—of tennis rackets, the Mediterranean, the coastal village he will soon be moving to. She says she hates tennis, and smiles.

And where are you going? they ask her.

Israel.

It is your homeland?

It will be.

And do you have family there, or friends?

Not really.

We have good friends in both Tel Aviv and Jerusalem. We must give you their addresses.

The mutton is well timed. One waiter asks us in turn what cut of meat we prefer, another spoons small white potatoes onto our plates until signaled to stop. Water glasses are refilled. The woman takes a sip of wine, turns to me.

You don't seem the type to wear a tie, she says.

Why do you say that? I ask.

I don't know.

That is a forward thing to say to someone you don't know.

I'm Elisa. Who are you?

You may call me Paco, I say.

Wine spills over the edge of my untouched glass and I spot it with my napkin. I taste the mutton and ask the woman where she boarded the *Aurelia*.

Brindisi, she says.

What were you doing in Brindisi?

Waiting for the boat.

Her banter excites me but I keep my head down, purposefully pause before continuing the exchange.

And how did you know it was coming?

Was it supposed to be a secret? Her eyes get larger, ask me to laugh.

The waiters seem anxious for us to finish eating. The moment we abandon our silverware our plates are swept away. For dessert, they bring us fruit and cheese. When we have finished with coffee, I ask the woman if she would care for a drink at the bar.

She would.

The night before I boarded the *Aurelia*, Paco and I went out drinking. Málaga was celebrating its patron saint, and the bars, like the streets, were festive and crowded. Paco was in great spirits, and was soon entertaining a group of young women with an endless tale about his father.

He was a saint too, Paco told them, but misguided. One night he came home to my mother with a long sad story, maintaining that he had been robbed of a small fortune in an alleyway. My mother cried for him. I cried for him. But later, when the true report came out in the newspapers, he admitted to us that he had foolishly given the money away. He had met a young aeronaut, an anarchist, who wanted to bomb the National Palace from the balloon my father's money would buy—with a thousand kilos of donkey shit. But the stench at the airfield gave him away.

The young women had laughed and bargained for the right to sit on Paco's lap. One had her hand on my thigh as well. Yet in the end, the night came to nothing.

In the bar, Elisa drinks brandy and ginger and I drink Irish whisky. One can see we have settled with each other, know the course and outcome of the evening, are watching it progress with a certainty that the bartender must also feel. She has mentioned a party, later, that one of the sailors has invited her to.

It is pleasant sitting here on this old leather, poking at ice cubes now and then with my finger, tweaking my anticipation. Our conversation has become comfortable and predictable, need hardly be spoken.

Why Israel? I ask her.

The usual reasons, she says.

There is a smell about her that I did not expect and cannot quite place. Something like the smell of a field after it has been turned.

The bar is nearly empty. It is strictly for the use of passengers —and although drinks are very cheap in these untaxed waters, few others are taking advantage ot it, and sometimes even the bartender leaves. It seems more like a drawing room that it does a bar, with glass-enclosed bookshelves, maps and charts on the walls, a large nautical clock between the liquor cabinets.

You were uneasy when I saw you this afternoon, I say. The way you were holding onto the rail.

Just anxious, I suppose. I want to get started, have something to do. I'm not used to so much empty time.

We'll be in Haifa tomorrow evening.

I know.

It is not yet late, but in a few minutes the bartender will want to close up, turn out the lights. I ask her if she would like one last brandy and ginger. She is drinking them at my suggestion. I have told her that ginger is good for sea stomach and brandy good for the head.

Paco told me this about women: there is no point in looking for perfection because to find it would only make you afraid of losing it.

Once, in Málaga, he came to my hotel saying he would take me to dinner. He was with a woman. She had high cheekbones, fiery eyes, wore diamonds at her neck, and when we left his arm was around her waist. During dinner they spoke like lovers, and she plainly cared for him. We danced and drank late, the three of us having an excellent time but Paco having the best, and I thought yes, Paco, yes.

At my hotel, she waited in the lobby while Paco walked with me to my room, the two of us drunk and holding each other up. She is beautiful, he said, and I agreed. A tiger in bed, he whispered. I made some appropriately jealous sound. She would make a good wife, no? I said yes, I thought she probably would, and offered to make the necessary arrangements for him. Not for me, he said, for you.

He told me this, too: nothing in the world can hurt a man as much as a woman's truthful words.

Paco was full of platitudes, but uttered them like a god.

On our way to the party, we stop by my cabin and I get out the last bottle of Five Star. She is already a little drunk and holding onto me as the ship sways and rocks. She studies the small cluttered room.

It looks like you've been on the *Aurelia* forever.

A while.

What do you do with your time?

Nothing in particular.

Beneath my bed I find two glasses and rinse them out at the sink, dry them with one of Paco's shirts. I suggest a taste of cognac before we go. She watches me pour.

We don't have to go, she says.

I thought you wanted to. It is up to you.

She thinks for a moment. Kisses me on the lips. If you don't mind, then, she says. It might be interesting.

I want to tell her no, not really, I have been to these parties before, it will not be interesting.

But I say nothing. It is her last night at sea.

She has lifted her glass, holds it a little unsteadily in the air between us.

How about a toast? she says.

I propose Israel; she suggests the *Aurelia*.

We are being nice. I raise my glass and we drink.

It has been a long time now since I have been with a woman, and as we begin our descent down the narrow corridors and ladderways, clinging to each other like the drunken sailors we are becoming, I must admit to myself that I am very much looking forward to it. It will make the party bearable, knowing that afterwards we will return to my cabin and the curtain will rise on her legs.

My arm is around her waist, beneath the bulky sweater, my hand on the smooth inward curve of flesh that shifts subtly as we walk. And her arm is around me too, her fingers playing on the silky material of Paco's shirt. I feel her touch completely. It is the sure touch of a woman who knows where she is going even when she is being led.

I know where the sailors' party can be found, though inexactly. The precise place varies from night to night, but always they gather in one of the dormitory cabins at the other end of the ship, deep in the aft, near the boiler and engine rooms.

With our free arms we guard ourselves against the tilting walls, more difficult for me because of the bottle of Five Star I am carrying and must also protect. As we make our unsteady way, we are mostly quiet. Now and then one of us smiles at the other, a confidence or a promise. We are on a course.

Ahead I hear laughter and I know we are getting close. But the laughter has come from behind a closed door and does not repeat itself—so we continue down the corridor and, at its end, take the last steep ladder down. Below us a rat hurries in our direction, then spins around and rushes away. She sees it and points.

There is so much free grain in the holds they cannot be controlled, I explain.

I know them, she says. They don't frighten me.

At the bottom of the ladder we hear phonograph music, loud voices, singing. Several cabin doors are open, moving slowly back and forth on their big hinges.

Will you take care of me, she says in a voice that means she will take care of herself, using the words as an excuse to hold onto me a little tighter, to rest her head against my shoulder.

Of course, I say, and kiss her hair.

I am convinced we are on the edge of a storm.

I know there is no reason for alarm; the *Aurelia* is old but solidly built. It is big. There is no danger of it breaking up.

It is dim in this bottom corridor, only half the hall lamps are lit. We step to the first cabin door and enter. Inside it is not much brighter, but I can easily see that more men than usual have gathered, fifteen, perhaps twenty. Some of them are leaning against the walls, some are sitting or lying on the dozen bunks arranged in stacks of three, others sit at a large wooden table in the middle of the room. The table's surface is cluttered with bottles and cans and glasses, a backgammon board, magazines, playing cards. The phonograph music I don't recognize at all. It is full of high flutes and the soft strings of a dulcimer weaving through the talk, various languages. The room is full of smoke, drifting white smoke that smells of sweet tobacco and hashish, smoke that burns the eyes. And the air is very hot.

A few of the men I recognize, from other parties or from other parts of the ship. One, an old man I have talked with on deck, greets me with a nod and unshaven smile from a lower bunk, and motions for us to come over. But Elisa is already talking with a young sailor at the table, probably the one that invited her, and we sit down across from him. He cannot be more than twenty-five, and from his olive complexion and curly hair, and from the nearly empty bottle of ouzo in front of him, I think he is probably Greek—and probably drunk.

I am Alexis, he says, and squints at us.

Elisa puts her hand on my thigh and squeezes lightly as she repeats her name.

Paco, I say. She smiles at me. The young Greek looks at me suspiciously, although I am sure that my name is the last thing he suspects.

You were alone when I saw you before, he says to her but with his eyes on me. And now you are with this man Paco.

Yes, she says. She smiles generously at the Greek, but below the table she is again squeezing my thigh and this time it is different.

I do not understand, Alexis says.

He does not understand, I think. This sailor does not understand.

What is there to understand? I say aloud, and in the same moment notice the veins standing out on his forehead, the fingers curled tight around his glass.

He is my fiancé, she says.

Fiancé?

We are going to be married. He will be my husband. Her smile is convincing and her hand has relaxed, is again moving on my leg. Alexis' eyes are no longer angry, merely uncertain. But I can see he is not yet defeated. He is Greek. And drunk.

Have a drink, he says, grabbing the bottle by its neck. We will celebrate.

Yes, says Elisa, and accepts a glass of ouzo.

I will stay with my Five Star, I say, and appropriate a small empty jar from among the movie magazines.

We drink without extra words or much ceremony: to marriage, then to women, to children, to our children's children, may they be born in a less troubled world. The sailor's face softens. We drink to the future, to better weather. His eyes become clouded, his voice uneven. The threat subsides. Her hand has risen, is between my legs. I look around the room.

At the other end of the table, a small pipe is being passed back and forth. Near the phonograph two men are trying to dance, their arms square and locked. On a top bunk, in a dark corner, a young sailor and an old sailor caress each other, fall out of view. The old man across the room who recognized me has gone to sleep.

Where will you marry? mumbles Alexis. Jerusalem, she says. She is smiling. And where will you live? Jerusalem also. His eyes shift to me. What will your profession be? Financier, I say. I invest other people's money.

He is suddenly, violently, on his feet. Dance with me, he yells. Has thrown out his arms. Dance with me. He strikes a pose in front of Elisa.

I don't know how, she says.

I will show you, he cries. You must dance with a Greek before you marry. He jerks her up from the table. They move toward the music, the flutes and the dulcimer.

Sometimes I imagine Paco is dead. His note suggested as much. He often spoke of suicide, although never his own, and admired Seneca, who, like him, was born in Córdoba. But I do not understand. If Paco is dead by his own hand, why? He was not a morose man, never admitted to despair, slept well, like myself. He was not the sort to believe all those easy words he spent on me. On the other hand, perhaps I am reading too much into the note. He told me he was leaving Málaga. On the surface the note said only that it was unlikely our paths would cross again. It is easy enough for me to picture him in Barcelona, buying shoes, having his nails done, taking his niece to the cinema. But the thing that is distasteful to me about it all is that Paco may very well have intended for me to wonder. He was shrewd, sentimental. He wished to be remembered.

She is back. The Greek has stopped to talk with a friend. I see him pointing in our direction, laughing.

He's very drunk, she says.

I know.

He said I should make love to a Greek before I marry—so that I will know the right way.

His experience is with whores.

And yours?

The sailor returns to the table, picks up the bottle of ouzo, but it is empty. He lifts the Five Star and tries to pour himself a drink. As much spills to the table as into his glass.

Hey, Paco, she is a good dancer, he says.

Of course, I say.

She will make a good wife, he says.

The ship lunges and he nearly falls. A bottle slides off the table and shatters on the floor. The lights flicker. My old friend groans in his sleep.

Let's sit someplace safer, says Elisa. I look around. One of the bottom bunks is unoccupied. We move to it. The Greek has his head in his hands, does not seem to realize we are gone.

My stomach is a little uneasy, she says.

I offer her a sip of cognac.

It is a bad storm? she asks.

The first one always seems bad, I say.

What I told the sailor could be true.

What do you mean?

You could come with me to Jerusalem.

I am not Jewish.

You've just been away, she says, and touches my cheek.

The Greek has noticed our absence, finds his feet, is looming over us. His eyes are sullen and glazed. Why do you leave me? he wants to know. She is tired, I say, does not feel well. Her head is on my shoulder. Another sailor has put his arm around Alexis, is pulling him away, arguing with him. Their words are loud and rough.

You should get off this ship, Elisa says.

Why? I slip my hand beneath her sweater. Her skin is warm and soft, and it seems to me I have touched her many times.

Get off this ship, she repeats.

I will think about it, I say.

Don't think about it, she says. Her hand is between my legs, gently moving. From the table I see the Greek and his friend leering at us as they argue.

Deliberation is for old men, she says. I touch her breast, then take it in my hand. Her head falls to my chest. My hand follows the slight weight of her flesh as it rises and falls with her breathing.

I think I'm sick, she says.

It will pass, I say. But I realize that her fingers are suddenly still, her breathing shallow.

We will go, I say, but it is too late. As I start to lift her head, her mouth opens, and my shirt, Paco's shirt, is suddenly wet. From the blue silk rises the stench of her vomit.

There is nothing to be done.

I hold her head and look around the room. The Greek and his friend have settled at the far end of the table, have a new bottle between them, have apparently resolved their dispute. The music is gone, the lights dimmer than before.

I stroke her hair, wait for more sickness, but none comes. She is breathing in gulps. I will have to move her soon.

The ship rhythmically lurches, hesitates, and leans back. Empty cans roll back and forth across the floor. The cabin door bangs heavily at its frame.

I sit her up as best I can, rest her in a corner of wall and bed frame. Still her head falls forward.

This ship, she says.

I take off Paco's shirt. I push back her hair and use what is dry to wipe her face, then drop the shirt to the floor. I cannot take off her filthy sweater here.

A fool, she says.

The Five Star is beside me on the bunk. I pick it up and swallow the rest.

Can you walk? I ask.

Jerusalem, she says.

I know the rest. I will take her to her cabin, help her off with her sweater and soiled dungarees. I will finally see her legs. I will put her to bed and then go alone to my cabin. I doubt she will get up until it is time for her to leave the *Aurelia,* and I doubt the storm will delay our arrival.

Her head rolls from side to side with the motion of the ship and I lean forward, to help her up. I take her hands. She lifts her face and looks at me, looks at me as though she in fact sees me.

Paco? she says, Paco?

And I hear the sailor call: Paco!

But no, I pull her to her feet. I do not answer anyone. I am thinking *Dubrovnik, Palermo, Lindos.* I am thinking *Alexandria. Genoa. Corinth.*

The Long-Distance Runner

GRACE PALEY

One day, before or after forty-two, I became a long-distance runner. Though I was stout and in many ways inadequate to this desire, I wanted to go far and fast, not as fast as bicycles and trains, not as far as Taipei, Hingwan, places like that, but round and round the county from the seaside to the bridges, along the old neighborhood streets a couple of times, before old age and urban renewal ended them and me.

I tried the country first, Connecticut, which, being wooded, is always full of buds in spring. All creation is secret, isn't that true? So I trained in the wide-zoned suburban hills where I wasn't known. I ran all spring in and out of dogwood bloom, then laurel.

People sometimes stopped and asked me why I ran, a lady in silk shorts halfway down over her fat thighs. In training, I replied, and rested only to answer if closely questioned. I wore a white sleeveless undershirt as well, with excellent support, not to attract the attention of old men and prudish children.

The summer came, my legs seemed strong. I kissed the kids good-bye. They were quite old by then. It was near the time for parting anyway. I told Mrs. Raftery to look in now and then and give them some of that rotten Celtic supper she makes.

I told them they could take off any time they wanted to. Go lead your private lives, I said. Only leave me out of it.

A word to the wise, said Richard.

You're depressed, Faith, Mrs. Raftery said. Your boyfriend Jack, the one you think's so hotsy-totsy, hasn't called and you're as gloomy as a tick on Sunday.

Cut the folk shit with me, Raftery, I muttered. Her eyes filled with tears because that's who she is: folk shit from bunion to topknot. That's how she got liked by me, loved, invented, and endured.

When I walked out the door they were all reclining before the television set, Richard, Tonto, and Mrs. Raftery, gazing at the news. Which proved with moving pictures that there *had* been a voyage to the moon, and Africa and South America hid in a furious whorl of clouds.

I said, Good-bye. They said, Yeah, okay, sure.

If that's how it is, forget it, I hollered, and took the Independent Subway to Brighton Beach.

At Brighton Beach I stopped at the Salty Breezes Locker Room to change my clothes. Twenty-five years ago my father invested $500 in its future. In fact, he still clears about $3.50 a year, which goes directly (by law) to The Children of Judea to cover their deficit.

No one paid too much attention when I started to run, easy and light on my feet. I ran on the boardwalk first, past my mother's leafleting station—between a soft ice cream stand and a degenerated dune. There she had been assigned by her comrades to halt the tides of cruel American enterprise with simple Socialist sense.

I wanted to stop and admire the long beach. I wanted to stop in order to think admiringly about New York. There aren't many rotting cities so tan and sandy and speckled with citizens at their salty edges. But I had already spent a lot of life lying down or standing and staring. I had decided to run.

After about a mile and a half I left the boardwalk and began to trot into the old neighborhood. I was running well. My breath was long and deep. I was thinking pridefully about my form.

Suddenly I was surrounded by about three hundred blacks.

Who you?

Who that?

Look at her! Just look! When you seen a fatter ass?

Poor thing. She ain't right. Leave her, you boys, you bad boys.

I used to live here, I said.

Oh yes, they said, in the white old days. That time too bad to last.

But we loved it here. We never went to Flatbush Avenue or Times Square. We loved our block.

Tough black titty.

I like your speech, I said. Metaphor and all.

Right on. We get that from talking.

Yes, my people also had a way of speech. And don't forget the Irish. The gift of gab.

Who they? said a small boy.

Cops.

Nowadays, I suggested, there's more than Irish on the police force.

You right, said two ladies. More more, much much more. They's

French Chinamen Russkies Congoleans. Oh missee, you too right.

I lived in that house, I said. That apartment house. All my life. Till I got married.

Now that is nice. Live in one place. My mother live that way in South Carolina. One place. Her daddy farmed, she said. They ate. No matter winter war bad times. Roosevelt. Something! Ain't that wonderful! And it weren't cold! Big trees!

That apartment. I looked up and pointed. There. The third floor.

They all looked up. So what! You blubberous devil! said a dark young man. He wore horn-rimmed glasses and had that intelligent look that City College boys used to have when I was eighteen and first looked at them.

He seemed to lead them in contempt and anger, even the littlest ones who moved toward me with dramatic stealth, singing ''Devil, oh Devil.'' I don't think the little kids had bad feeling because they poked a finger into me, then laughed.

Still, I thought it might be wise to keep my head. So I jumped right in with some facts. I said, How many flowers' names do you know? Wild flowers, I mean. My people only knew two. That's what they say now, anyway. Rich or poor, they only had two flowers' names. Rose and violet.

Daisy, said one boy immediately.

Weed, said another. That is a flower, I thought. But everyone else got the joke.

Saxifrage, lupine, said a lady. Viper's bugloss, said a small Girl Scout in medium green with a dark green sash. She held up a *Handbook of Wild Flowers*.

How many you know, fat mama? a boy asked warmly. He wasn't against my being a mother or fat. I turned my attention to him.

Oh, sonny, I said, I'm way ahead of my people. I know in yellows alone: common cinquefoil, trout lily, yellow adder's-tongue, swamp buttercup and common buttercup, golden sorrel, yellow or hop clover, devil's paintbrush, evening primrose, black-eyed Susan, golden aster, also the yellow pickerelweed growing down by the water if not in the water, and dandelions of course. I've seen all these myself. Seen them.

You could see China from the boardwalk, a boy said. When it's nice.

I know more flowers than countries. Mostly young people these days have traveled in many countries.

Not me. I ain't been nowhere.

Not me either, said about seventeen of the boys.

I'm not allowed, said a little girl. There's drunken junkies.

But I! I! cried out a tall black youth, very handsome and well-dressed, I am an African. My father came from the high stolen plains. *I* have been everywhere. I was in Moscow six months, learning machinery. I was in France, learning French. I was in Italy, observing the peculiar Renaissance and the people's sweetness. I was in England, where I studied the common law and the urban blight. I was at the Conference of Dark Youth in Cuba to understand our passion. I am now here. Here am I to become an engineer and return to my people, around the Cape of Good Hope in a Norwegian sailing vessel. In this way I will learn the fine old art of sailing in case the engines of the new society of my old inland country should fail.

We had an extraordinary amount of silence after that.

Then one old lady in a black dress and high white lace collar said to another old lady dressed exactly the same way, Glad tidings when someone got brains in the head, not fish juice. Amen, said a few.

Whyn't you go up to Mrs. Luddy living in your house, you lady, huh? The Girl Scout asked this.

Why she just groove to see you, said some sarcastic snickerer.

She got palpitations. Her man, he give it to her.

That ain't all, he a natural gift-giver.

I'll take you, said the Girl Scout. My name is Cynthia. I'm in Troop 355, Brooklyn.

I'm not dressed, I said, looking at my lumpy knees.

You shouldn't wear no undershirt like that without no runnin number or no team writ on it. It look like a undershirt.

Cynthia! Don't take her up there, said an important boy. Her head strange. Don't you take her. Hear?

Lawrence, she said softly, you tell me once more what to do, I'll wrap you round that lamppost.

Git! she said, powerfully addressing *me*.

In this way I was led into the hallway of the whole house of my childhood.

The first door I saw was still marked in flaky gold. 1A. That's where the janitor lived, I said. He was a Negro.

How come like that? Cynthia made an astonished face. How come the janitor was a black man?

Oh, Cynthia, I said. Then I turned to the opposite door, first floor front, 1B. I remembered. Now, here, this was Mrs. Goreditsky, very very fat. All her children died at birth. Born, then one, two, three. Dead. Five children, then Mr. Goreditsky said, I'm bad luck on you, Tessie, and he went away. He sent fifteen dollars a week for seven years. Then no one heard.

I know her, poor thing, said Cynthia. The City come for her summer before last. The way they knew, it smelled. They wrapped her up in a canvas. They couldn't get through the front door. It scraped off a piece of her. My uncle Ronald had to help them, but he got disgusted.

Only two years ago. She was still here! Wasn't she scared?

So we all, said Cynthia. White ain't everything.

Who lived up here, she asked, 2B? Right now, my best friend, Nancy Rosalind, lives here. She got two brothers, and her sister married and got a baby. She very light-skinned. Not her mother. We got all colors amongst us.

Your best friend? That's funny. Because it was *my* best friend. Right in that apartment. Joanna Rosen.

What became of her? Cynthia asked. She got a runnin shirt too?

Come on, Cynthia, if you really want to know, I'll tell you. She married this man, Marvin Steirs.

Who's he?

I recollected his achievements. Well, he's the president of a big corporation, JoMar Plastics. This corporation owns a steel company, a radio station, a new Xerox-type machine that lets you do twenty-five different pages at once. This corporation has a foundation, the JoMar Fund for Research in Conservation. Capitalism is like that, I added, in order to be politically useful.

How come you know, you go up their house?

I happened to read all about them on the financial page, just last week. It made me think: a different life. That's all.

Different spokes for different folks, said Cynthia.

I sat down on the cool marble steps and remembered Joanna's cousin Ziggie. He was older than we were. He wrote a poem which told us we were lovely flowers and our legs were petals, which nature would force open no matter how many times we said no.

Then I had several other interior thoughts that I couldn't share with a child, the kind that give your face a blank or melancholy look.

Now you're not interested, said Cynthia. Now you're not gonna say a thing. Who lived here, 2A? Who? Two men lives here now. Women comin and women goin. My mother says, Danger sign: Stay away, my darling, stay away.

I don't remember, Cynthia. I really don't.

You got to. What'd you come for, anyways?

Then I tried. 2A. 2A. Was it the twins? I felt a strong obligation as though remembering was in charge of the *existence* of the past. This is not so.

Cynthia, I said, I don't want to go any farther. I don't even want to remember.

Come on, she said, tugging at my shorts, don't you want to see Mrs. Luddy, the one lives in your old house? That be fun, no?

No. No, I don't want to see Mrs. Luddy.

Now you shouldn't pay no attention to those boys downstairs. She will like you. I mean, she is kind. She don't like most white people, but she might like you.

No, Cynthia, it's not that, but I don't want to see my father and mother's house now.

I didn't know what to say. I said, Because my mother's dead. This was a lie, because my mother lives in her own room with my father in The Children of Judea. With her hand over her socialist heart, she reads the paper every morning after breakfast. Then she says sadly to my father, Every day the same, dying, dying, dying from killing.

Oh oh, the poor thing, Cynthia said, looking into my eyes. Oh, if my mama died, I don't know what I'd do. Even if I was as old as you. I could kill myself. Tears filled her eyes and started down her cheeks. If my mother died, what would I do? She is my protector, she won't let the pushers get me. She hold me tight. She gonna hide me in the cedar box if my uncle Rudford comes try to get me back. She *can't* die, my mother.

Cynthia—honey—she won't die. She's young. I put my arm out to comfort her. You could come live with me, I said. I got two boys, they're nearly grown up. I missed it, not having a girl.

What? What you mean now, live with you and boys. She pulled away and ran for the stairs. Stay way from me, honky lady. I know them white boys. They just gonna try and jostle my black woman-hood. My mother told me about that. Keep you white honky devil boys to your devil self, you just leave me be, you old bitch you. Somebody help me, she started to scream, you hear? Somebody help. She gonna take me away.

She flattened herself to the wall, trembling. I was too frightened by her fear of me to say, Honey, I wouldn't hurt you, it's me. I heard her helpers, the voices of large boys, crying, We coming, we coming, hold your head up, we coming. I ran past her fear to the stairs and up them two at a time. I came to my old own door. I knocked like the landlord, loud and terrible.

Mama not home, a child's voice said. No, no, I said. It's me! A lady! Someone's chasing me, let me in. Mama not home, I ain't allowed to open up for nobody.

It's me! I cried out in terror. Mama! Mama! Let me in!

The door opened. A slim woman whose age I couldn't invent looked at me. She said, Get in and shut that door tight. She took a hard pinching hold on my upper arm. Then she bolted the door herself. Them hustlers after you. They make me pink. Hide this white lady now, Donald. Stick her under your bed, you got a high bed.

Oh, that's okay. I'm fine now, I said. I felt safe and at home.

You in my house, she said. You do as I say. For two cents, I throw you out.

I squatted under a small kid's pissy mattress. Then I heard the knock. It was tentative and respectful. My mama don allow me to open. Donald! someone called. Donald!

Oh no, he said. Can't do it. She gonna wear me out. You know her. She already tore up my ass this morning once. Ain't *gonna* open up.

I lived there for about three weeks with Mrs. Luddy and Donald and three little baby girls nearly the same age. I told her a joke about Irish twins. Ain't Irish, she said.

Nearly every morning the babies woke us up at about six-forty-five. We gave them all a bottle and went back to sleep till eight. I made coffee and she changed diapers. Then it really stank for a while. At this time I usually said, Well, listen, thanks really, but I've got to go, I guess. I guess I'm going. She'd usually say, Well, guess again. *I* guess you ain't. Or if she was feeling disgusted she'd say, Go on now! Get! You wanna go, I guess by now I have snorted enough white stink to choke a horse. Go on!

I'd get to the door and then I'd hear voices. I'm ashamed to say I'd become fearful. Despite my geographical love of mankind, I would be attacked by local fears.

There was a sentimental truth that lay beside all that going and not going. It *was* my house where I'd lived long ago my family life. There was a tile on the bathroom floor that I myself had broken, dropping a hammer on the toe of my brother Charles as he stood dreamily shaving, his prick halfway up his undershorts. Astonishment and knowledge first seized me right there. The kitchen was the same. The table was the enameled table common to our class, easy

to clean, with wooden under-corners for indigent and old cockroaches that couldn't make it to the kitchen sink. (However, it was not the same table, because I have inherited that one, chips and all.)

The living room was something like ours, only we had less plastic. There may have been less plastic in the world at that time. Also, my mother had set beautiful cushions everywhere, on beds and chairs. It was the way she expressed herself, artistically, to embroider at night or take strips of flowered cotton and sew them across ordinary white or blue muslin in the most delicate designs, the way women have always used materials that live and die in hunks and tatters, to say, This is my place.

Mrs. Luddy said, Uh huh!

Of course, I said, men don't have that outlet. That's how come they run around so much.

Till they drunk enough to lay down, she said.

Yes, I said, on a large scale you can see it in the world. First they make something, then they murder it. Then they write a book about how interesting it is.

You got something there, she said. Sometimes she said, Girl, you don't know nothin.

We often sat at the window looking out and down. Little tufts of breeze grew on that windowsill. The blazing afternoon was around the corner and up the block.

You say men, she said. Is that men? she asked. What you call—a man?

Four flights below us, leaning on the stoop, were about a dozen people and around them devastation. Just a minute, I said. I had seen devastation on my way, running, gotten some of the pebbles of it in my running shoe and the dust of it in my eye. I had thought with the indignant courtesy of a citizen, This is a disgrace to the City of New York, which I love and am running through.

But now, from the commanding heights of home, I saw it clearly. The tenement in which Jack, my old and present friend, had come to gloomy manhood had been destroyed, first by fire, then by demolition (which is a swinging ball of steel that cracks bedrooms and kitchens). Because of this work, we could see several blocks wide and a block and a half long. Crazy Eddy's house still stood, famous 1510, gutted, with black window frames, no glass, open laths, the stubbornness of the supporting beams! Some persons or families still lived on the lowest floors. In the yards between, a couple of old sofas lay on their fat faces, their springs sticking up into the air. Just as in wartime, a half dozen ailanthus trees had already found their first quarter inch of earth and begun a living attack on the dead yards. At night, I knew animals roamed the place, squalling and howling, furious New York dogs and street cats and mighty rats. You would think you were in Bear Mountain Park, the terror of venturing forth.

Someone ought to clean that up, I said.

Mrs. Luddy said, Who you got in mind? Mrs. Kennedy?

Donald made a stern face. He said, That just what I gonna do when I get big. Gonna get the sanitary man in and show it to him. You see that, you big guinea you, you clean it up right now! Then he stamped his feet and fierced his eyes.

Mrs. Luddy said, Come here, you little nigger. She kissed the top of his head and gave him a whack on the backside all at one time.

Well, said Donald, encouraged, look out there now, you all! Go on, I say, look! Though we had already seen, to please him we looked. On the stoop men and boys lounged, leaned, hopped about, stood on one leg, then another, took their socks off and scratched their toes, talked, sat on their haunches, heads down, dozing.

Donald said, Look at them. They ain't got self-respect. They got Afros *on* they heads, but they don't know they black *in* they heads.

I thought he ought to learn to be more sympathetic. I said, There are reasons that people are that way.

Yes, ma'am, said Donald.

Anyway, how come you never go down and play with the other kids, how come you're up here so much?

My mama don't like me do that. Some of them is bad. Bad. I might become a dope addict. I got to stay clear.

You just a dope, that's a fact, said Mrs. Luddy.

He ought to be with kids his age more, I think.

He see them in school, miss. Don't trouble your head about it, if you don't mind.

Actually, Mrs. Luddy didn't go down into the street either. Donald did all the shopping. She let the Welfare investigator in; the meterman came into the kitchen to read the meter. I saw him from the back room where I hid. She picked up her check. She cashed it. She returned to wash the babies, change their diapers, wash clothes, iron, feed people, and then in free half hours she sat by that window. She was waiting.

I believed she was watching and waiting for a man. I wanted to discuss this with her, talk lovingly like sisters. But before I could freely say, Forget about that son of a bitch, he's a pig. I did have to offer a few solid facts about myself, my kids, about fathers, husbands, passersby, evening companions, and the life of my father and mother in this room by this exact afternoon window.

I told her, for instance, that in my worst times I had given myself one extremely simple physical pleasure. This was cream cheese for breakfast. In fact, I insisted on it, sometimes depriving the children of very important articles and foods.

Girl, you don't know nothin, she said.

Then for a little while she talked gently as one does to a person who is innocent and insane and incorruptible because of stupidity. She had had two such special pleasures for hard times, she said. The first men, but they turned rotten, white women had ruined the best, give them the idea their dicks made of solid gold. The second pleasure she had tried was wine. She said, I do like wine. You *has* to have something just for yourself by yourself. Then she said, But you can't raise a decent boy when you liquor-dazed every night.

White or black, I said, returning to men, they did think they were bringing a rare gift, whereas it was just sex, which is common like bread, though essential.

Oh, you can do without, she said. There's folks does without.

I told her Donald deserved the best. I loved him. If he had flaws, I hardly noticed them. It's one of my beliefs that children do not have flaws, even the worst do not.

Donald was brilliant, like my boys, except that he had an easier disposition. For this reason, I decided, almost the second moment of my residence in that household, to bring him up to reading level at once. I told him we would work with books and newspapers. He went immediately to his neighborhood library and brought some hard books to amuse me. *Black Folktales* by Julius Lester and *Pushcart War*, which is about another neighborhood but relevant.

Donald always agreed with me when we talked about reading and writing. In fact, when I mentioned poetry, he told me he knew all about it, that David Henderson, a known black poet, had visited his second-grade class. So Donald was, as it turned out, well ahead of my nosy tongue. He was usually very busy shopping or making faces to force the little serious baby girls into laughter. But if the subject came up, he could take *the* poem right out of the air into which language and event had just gone.

An example: That morning, his mother had said, Whew, I just got too much piss and diapers and wash. I wanna just sit down by that window and rest myself. He wrote a poem:

> Just got too much pissy diapers
> and wash and wash.
> Just wanna sit down by that window
> and look out.
> Ain't nothing there.

Donald, I said, you are plain brilliant. I'm never going to forget you. For God's sake, don't you forget me.

You fool with him too much, said Mrs. Luddy. He already don't even remember his grandma, you never gonna meet someone like her, a curse never come past her lips.

I do remember, Mama, I remember. She lying in bed, right there. A man standing in the door. She say, Esdras, I put a curse on you head. You worsen tomorrow. How come she said like that?

Gomorrah, I believe Gomorrah, she said. She know the Bible inside out.

Did she live with you?

No, no, she visiting. She come up to see us all, her children, how we doin. She come up to see sights. Then she lay down and died. She was old.

I was quiet because of the death of mothers. Mrs. Luddy looked at me thoughtfully. Then she said:

My mama had stories to tell, she raised me on. *Her* mama was a little thing, no sense. Stand in the door of the cabin all day, suckin her thumb. It was slave times. One day a young field boy come stormin along. He knock on the door of the first cabin hollerin, Sister, come out, it's freedom. She come out; she say, Yeah? When? He say, Now! It's freedom now! From one cabin he run to the next cabin, cryin out, Sister, it's freedom now!

Oh, I remember that story, said Donald. Freedom now! Freedom now! He jumped up and down.

You don't remember nothin, boy. Go on, get Eloise, she want to get into the good times.

Eloise was two but undersized. We got her like that, said Donald. Mrs. Luddy let me buy her ice cream and green vegetables. She was waiting for kale and chard, but it was too early. The kale liked cold. You not about to be here November, Mrs. Luddy said. No, no. I turned away, lonesomeness touching me, and sang our Eloise song:

> Eloise loves the bees
> The bees they buzz
> Like Eloise does.

Then Eloise crawled all over the splintery floor, buzzing wildly.

Oh, you crazy baby, said Donald, buzz buzz buzz.

Mrs. Luddy sat down by the window.

You all make a lot of noise, she said sadly. You just right on noisy.

The next morning Mrs. Luddy woke me up.

Time to go, she said.

What?

Home.

What? I said.

Well, don't you think you little boys cryin for you? Where's Mama? They standin in the window. Time to go, lady. This ain't Free Vacation Farm. Time we was by ourself a little.

Oh Ma, said Donald, she ain't a lot of trouble.

Go on, get Eloise, she hollerin. And button up your lip.

She didn't offer me coffee. She looked at me strictly all the time. I tried to look strictly back, but I failed because I loved the sight of her.

Donald was teary, but I didn't dare turn my head to him, until the parting minute at the door. Even then, I kissed the top of his head a little too forcefully and said, Well, I'll see you.

On the front stoop there were about half a dozen midmorning family people and kids arguing about who had dumped garbage out of which window. They were very disgusted with one another.

Two young men in handsome dashikis stood in counsel and agreement on the street corner. They divided a comment. How come white womens got rotten teeth? And look so old? A girl near them said, Hush.

I walked past them and didn't begin my run until the road opened somewhere along Ocean Parkway. I was a little stiff because my way of life had used only small movements, an occasional stretch to put a knife or teapot out of reach of the babies. I ran about ten, fifteen blocks. Then my second wind came, which is classical, famous among runners. It's the beginning of flying.

In the three weeks I'd been off the street, jogging had become popular. It seemed that I was only one person doing her thing, which happened, like most American eccentric acts, to be the most ''in'' thing I could have done. In fact, two young men ran alongside of me for nearly a mile. They ran silently beside me and turned off at

Avenue H. A gentleman with a moustache, running poorly in the opposed direction, waving. He called out, "Hi, señora."

Near home I ran through our park, where I had aired my children on weekends and late-summer afternoons. I stopped at the northeast playground, where I met a dozen young mothers intelligently handling their little ones. In order to prepare them, meaning no harm, I said, In fifteen years, you girls will be like me, wrong in everything.

At home it was Saturday morning. Jack had returned, looking as grim as ever, but he'd brought cash and a vacuum cleaner. While the coffee perked, he showed Richard how to use it. They were playing tic-tac-toe on the dusty wall.

Richard said, Well! Look who's here! Hi!

Any news? I asked.

Letter from Daddy, he said. From the lake and water country in Chile. He says it's like Minnesota.

He's never been to Minnesota, I said. Where's Anthony?

Here I am, said Tonto, appearing. But I'm leaving.

Oh yes, I said. Of course. Every Saturday he hurries through breakfast or misses it. He goes to visit his friends in institutions. These are well-known places like Bellevue, Hillside, Rockland State, Central Islip, Manhattan. These visits take him all day and sometimes half the night.

I found some chocolate chip cookies in the pantry. Take them, Tonto, I said. I remember nearly all his friends as little boys and girls always hopping, skipping, jumping, and cookie-eating. He was annoyed. He said, No! Chocolate cookies is what the commissaries are full of. How about money?

Jack dropped the vacuum cleaner. He said, No!

He said, They have parents for that.

I said, Here, five dollars for cigarettes, one dollar each.

Cigarettes! said Jack. Goddamnit! Black lungs and death! Cancer! Emphysema! He stomped out of the kitchen, breathing. He took the bike from the back room and started for Central Park, which has been closed to cars but opened to bicycle riders. When he'd been gone about ten minutes, Anthony said, It's really open only on Sundays.

Why didn't you say so? Why can't you be decent to him? I asked.

It's important to me.

Oh, Faith, he said, patting me on the head because he'd grown so tall, All that air. It's good for his lungs. And his muscles! He'll be back soon.

You should ride too, I said. You don't want to get mushy in your legs. You should go swimming once a week.

I'm too busy, he said. I have to see my friends.

Then Richard, who had been vaccuming under his bed, came into the kitchen. You still here, Tonto?

Going going gone, said Anthony, don't bat your eye.

Now, listen, Richard said, here's a note. It's for Lydia, if you get as far as Rockland. Don't forget it. Don't open it. Don't read it. I know he'll read it.

Anthony smiled and slammed the door.

Did I lose weight? I asked.

Yes, said Richard. You look okay. You never look too bad. But where were you? I got sick of Raftery's boiled potatoes. Where were you, Faith?

Well! I said. Well! I stayed a few weeks in my old apartment, where Grandpa and Grandma and me and Hope and Charlie lived when we were little. I took you there long ago. Not so far from the ocean where Grandma made us very healthy with sun and air.

What are you talking about? said Richard. Cut the baby talk.

Anthony came home earlier than expected because some people were in shock therapy and someone else had run away. He listened to me for a while. Then he said, I don't know what she's talking about either.

Neither did Jack, despite the understanding often produced by love after absence. He said, Tell me again. He was in a good mood. He said, You can even tell it to me twice.

I repeated the story. They all said, What?

Because it isn't usually so simple. Have you known it to happen much nowadays? A woman inside the steamy energy of middle age runs and runs. She finds the houses and streets where her childhood happened. She lives in them. She learns as though she were still a child what in the world is coming next.

Down the Blue Hole

WILLIAM HARRISON

This mystic arcadian village is called Cedar Ridge, Missouri, and, sure, you've heard of it, but you probably never knew that every day we have dozens of séances, prophecies by seers and visionaries, and the assorted practice of witches, astrologers, magicians, and even, perhaps, one ghoul.

This is the little town where I live, though I've thought of moving away because of all the competition. The pressure to exceed one's best effort is so awful here that I've considered moving up to St. Louis and losing myself in the mercenary and non-psychic life.

For instance, the other night I had sixteen snickering tourists at my table, sitting in a circle with their hands extended, palms up, lights out, and the thunder cracked and everybody jumped and screamed, their index fingers pricked so that a single drop of blood blossomed on each one. When I switched on the lights, there they were, astounded—they all admitted it. And I blotted each finger with a Kleenex and put all the bloody tissues into my big glass cookie jar and told them wild stories about how I would mingle their

blood and put them under a spell. They gasped and laughed and loved it. One of them asked how I ever did such a trick. Then they started talking about old Auntie Sybil, one of my competitors, and the whole effect dissolved.

Someone else wanted to know if I served refreshments.

My biggest act is my disappearing act where I just vanish. I go off into the Blue Hole, don't ask me how.

I've done this trick six times now: sit cross-legged under my velvet cloth, concentrate, melt my bones and my whole petty life into nothing, while the audience watches that cloth sag and empty itself. It's a great act because it's no act at all. Off in the limbo of the Blue Hole I'm frightened, naturally, but I come back every time. Once I did this at the annual Rotary Banquet, vanishing under my velvet cloth at the rear of the hall, then coming up underneath the tablecloth beside the main speaker, rattling spoons and spilling ham loaf onto the floor, rising like Vesuvius forty feet from the spot where I disappeared. They were so pleased they gave me an extra $25 and asked me back next year.

This is such a forlorn life for a great talent.

Funk and Wagnalls Encyclopedia describes our part of the state as flat and alluvial. Sort of dull, right: this is an agricultural stop, a market town for cotton and soybeans, a town with only a few important ranchers and a nice high school.

True, Mrs. Marybush, the town matron and benefactor, dresses like one of the key figures from the Tarot deck. Also, we have some housewives who give the evil eye to the butchers and the boys at the checkout counters at Krogers—where one can sometimes detect a slight levitation in the vegetable scale.

How this place happened I don't now. When I came here years ago, there were just a few spiritualists and a couple of horoscope addicts. I was just a country boy from over in Stoddard County, town of Omega—and Cedar Ridge, I felt, had a ready audience for what I already reckoned was my considerable talent. Yet this town has become a kind of curse; tourists pour in all year, strangers all; there are loonies and charlatans everywhere, and the pressure, as I said, on one's craft is enormous.

Tourists are so unappreciative, too. One night I was making excellent contact with the dead at my table, summoning up a clear apparition, and this farmer recognizes the face and drawls, "Uncle Pardue, hey! This here is Bobby Wayne! Where'd you put that gold watch and fob you promised you'd leave me? We can't find that baby nowhere!"

Just as Las Vegas has its slot machines in the supermarkets, so our town exposes its soul in public; we have tea-leaf readers in every dumpy café, newsstands with astrological charts and no news, and one famous washerwoman—Auntie Sybil, yes—who advertises bona fide trances while she does up your clothes. In truth, Auntie Sybil's act is pretty good; she lives in a simple clapboard house on the edge of town, so a customer can drive out there with his bundle of wash and hear all the dire and wonderful predictions for his future while Auntie Sybil works. She's an old bag, about ninety, and very authentic. There with the Borax, her ironing board set up in her steamy kitchen, running your underwear through her old Maytag ringer, she communicates with the cosmos in your behalf. Also, voices from the past come straight out of her throat while she's in a trance—you pay five dollars extra for this. She does a terrific Caesar Augustus and a good Mahatma Gandhi.

My name is Homer Bogardus, though after I left Stoddard County I dropped the first name altogether and my sign out front now reads Mr. Mystic, and, in smaller letters underneath. The Breat Bogardus. This house of turrets, broad eaves and gothic hallways is my castle and dismay—a pox, dammit, on the plumbing.

My memory of my early real world is dim and colorless and, as I say about that, good riddance, Women, money, plumbing, friends: every reality I ever met addled and confounded me. The town of Omega, symbolic in its very name of last things, almost ended me, true enough, and I used to contemplate mutilation and suicide in that cupboard of an upstairs room in Daddy's farmhouse. I might have been an idiot child chained to an iron bedstead and thrown crusts of bread, for it was that bad: I felt my adolescence like a disease, I pined, I bit my knuckles with anguish. One day—this was after hearing about Cedar Ridge and the lure of its underground—I fell into concentration and poured myself a glass of water from the pewter pitcher on the bureau although I sat twenty feet across my room in the window seat where I gazed out over Daddy's fields. I extended my physical powers across space and moved the pitcher and floated a brimming glass of water into my hands. Ninety magic days later, I packed my bag and came in search of destiny.

Life before that, in all its lousy reality, was a wound. A strapping neighbor girl, Helen Rae, invited me into her barn once, then successfully fought me off, breaking my collarbone in the fracas. My best buddy, Elroy, sabotaged my 4-H project for no reason at all. And Daddy died, to spite me for being different, I thought at the time—though in a séance since, he materialized and denied it. And we were hopelessly poor: cardboard innersoles in my dismal brogans.

So I left everything and hitchhiked to Cedar Ridge and the closets of my head.

What's so good about reality, anyway? My bills are still mostly unpaid, my colleagues consider me odd in a town of oddities, my plumbing groans, my love life is asunder. Some days, like today, I dream beyond my powers—what if I *can* do almost anything?—to the Blue Hole, where it might not be so bad to live forever.

"Produce a girl for me, a true love," I beg Auntie Sybil.

We're sitting in her famous kitchen while she makes lye soap. A Hollywood game show screams from her portable.

"You're unlucky in love," she offers.

"Don't give me that old line. I need what I need."

She fixes me with those depthless eyes; all mystery is behind those black slits, all knowledge, the dream of dreams. "All right, for fifty dollars cold cash I'll give it one hell of a try," she says.

"Conjure hard," I plead, peeling off the bills. "And for this price, please, I ought to get some fast action."

"You shouldn't even dally with the flesh, Bogardus," she tells me, putting my money under the radio. "You possess a great talent, enough for anyone to live for. If you had any talent for promotion, you could get on television."

That night a miracle enters my house. Sally Ritchie is a local girl back home from college, a strange, lovely spirit—incidentally, thin of waist and ample of bosom—who has come, she says, in search of my netherworld. Her heart, she adds, has been broken by an athlete.

"Give me some sign," she breathes.

"I certainly will," I tell her, and I show her my collection of oriental bells with no clappers. Then we sit holding hands in my parlor while I make them vibrate and ring.

"My God," Sally Ritchie breathes more heavily. "You are *good*!"

Though I'm trying to be in love and loved again, the town goes on as usual. In the church the minister begins his sermon and then begins to cry, as if possessed, a Black Mass.

Our postman, Mr. Denbo, refuses to deliver any more packages to the Cabal Institute because, he says, there are live things inside.

At the annual cakewalk some hippie warlocks and vampiresses appear, but Mayor Watson strolls across the gymnasium to reason with them.

"We don't want your kind here," he explains.

One of the kids gets sassy and gives the mayor some vulgar lip. "Decay," he says to the mayor. "Palsy. Extreme. Burp. Bloat. Pimple. Gronk. Kidney. Suck. Waddle."

Sally Ritchie contends that she adores me, but clearly she craves only the sensation of my powers; ever since I told her that I'm capable of complete dematerialization, she has pleaded and insisted.

"Love me, not my talent," I ask of her, but she claims this is psychologically impossible. Her college boyfriend, the one who jilted her, played guard on the basketball team, she points out, and she adored his dribble.

She attends my nightly gatherings, applauding each wonder.

Tonight a dozen tourists receive a superior set of hallucinations; my old reptile-and-animal special. Encircling my table, hands touching, they sit and witness the ghostly albino Great Dane, who moves through the room, passes into walls, emerges again. We detect his panting breath as he haunts us. This beast, I explain —and I tell them the absolute truth—has been a resident of this house for years, long before I came here; he is terribly restless. Harmless pet, no problem, I assure everyone, and they tilt first one way and then another—feel the pull of my fingers, Sally?—to get a glimpse of him padding around.

Then the snakes: I move them into the room and have them slither across our shoes beneath the table. Hands tighten. Audible gasps. But this is just the frightening beginning; soon the serpents are coiling up and over us, a net of white underbellies over our arms and shoulders, and only my soothing voice prevents absolute hysteria.

The table is a writhing pit: black and green snakes everywhere. And now a thick furry adder: it rises among them like a sentinel, one large eye in the middle of its head, and I say, "Look at that eye, ladies and gentlemen, each one of you, look into that eye!"

The one-eyed adder stops before each participant and stares him down. Meanwhile, the other serpents curl away and vanish—and then the big one is gone, too, and the evening is a triumph.

"I could do my giant spider now," I tentatively offer.

"Oh, no, no, don't bother," everyone assures me.

"Wonderful," Sally Ritchie breathes. "And it was your eye in there, wasn't it, Mr. Bogardus? It was your eye inside that big snake, right?"

Deep in the Blue Hole.

I am here because Sally Ritchie wants a thrill.

The hole is like a cave, an indigo cavern, a gigantic drain which spirals down into the basements of the earth. Not so awful in here, really, after a time, so I sit here deciding exactly where I should now emerge. Should it be there in the parlor where I disappeared from Sally's side? No, I decide to make Sally suffer. I shall arise in the garden, calling and beckoning her outdoors, so that she will find me bursting through the ground like a weird pod among all the dying autumnal stalks. A splendid gesture, true, so that's exactly how I do it: clods falling off my shoulders as I rise up, a primordial flower sprouting before her very eyes.

It occurs to me as I emerge that I'm trying to earn adoration.

"Forty minutes!" she breathes. "You were gone forty *minutes*! And look at you! Coming up through the *dirt*!"

"A new record," I observe. "Forty minutes in the Blue Hole."

The town ghoul, whose name is Ralph, is generally popular, but I find him morbid. He throws parties after which he tries to get Sally and her girl friends to stay late and go skipping around graveyards, but thank goodness they don't go for that sort of thing. I like Ralph well enough personally, but his art and mine are at odds; he tends to press reality home, while I just want to divert and delight. Oh, I throw a few harmless scares into the tourists, sure, but why face them with war, pestilence, and man's cruel heart?

Ralph, like most people, can be somewhat deciphered by his rooms. I slip away from one of his cocktail parties at the Christmas season and tour his house, finding on the tables of his den and bedrooms stuffed hawks, daggers, a dusty crystal ball, and ashtrays made of old manacles. His bedroom is a grey dim dungeon of a place.

A few days later, still thinking about rooms, I decide to indulge in a little astral flight and visit my Sally's bedroom. She has the upstairs of her parents' big Georgian over on Maple Avenue.

I watch her sleeping, a brown shower of her lovely hair across the pillow.

Soon, I learn she is returning to school.

Do you want subtleties from me? The difference between my astral travels and complete dematerialization? All my mind-over-matter conquests explained? Do you want me to tell you why I'm so frivolous, why I don't use my powers to cure sickness, or, like that flashy French clairvoyant, fight crime and evil? Why should I compound my despair with endless explanation? What do you need except moments of profound awe?

Sally Ritchie writes that she is flunking biology.

It is darkest January and the Ozarks are blanketed in snow; at my window I can hear the world creaking beneath its ice, swaying and moaning in the winter thrall. The plumbing in my house answers its noises.

I read my own palm and what do I see reflected there? A private landscape as bleak as Cedar Ridge: a powerful life that can do all things, but is leaking away.

Accepting Ralph's invitation, I go over and catch the Super Bowl game on his crystal ball—nice reception, few ghosts, no commercials. We sit close at the table in his den, sipping cognacs, and staring into that small glass dream. Ralph, who is becoming morosely drunk, twitches his moustache and leers at me occasionally, but I don't mind.

"Thanks for asking me over," I tell him, and mean it.

In February I consider the Mardi Gras in New Orleans, the Acropolis, Kaanapali Beach in Hawaii, Marbella: all those vacation spots where I could go in an instant, where I could amaze the jet sets, charge supernatural fees, and forget Sally Ritchie and all the wretched consequences of my talents.

Instead, on the icy street outside the drugstore—valentine in hand, yes, ready for mailing—I draw my cape around me and tip my hat to Mrs. Marybush, who, today, is dressed like the Hanged Man. She smiles at my courtesy and informs me that she is sending friends from Kansas City to my table—skeptics, all, who need a good lesson.

"I'm not interested in the conversion of the masses," I snap at poor Mrs. Marybush. "Nor in offering proofs. Nor in metaphysical debate. I'm not going to call the lightning from the skies for another roomful of hicks. In fact, I'm retiring."

"No need to get huffy, Mr. Bogardus," she answers, and turns with her nose high and walks away.

In the spring there are county fairs, two of them, at Cedar Ridge and at Cape Girardeau more than fifty miles away, and I contract to perform my supreme act at them both—simultaneously.

The fair at Cape Girardeau is one of cheap tinsel and wheezing merry-go-rounds, with all the splendor and illusion of a ghetto, yet the fairgrounds border the mighty Mississippi River, swollen with our winter rains, majestic, the elms and poplars on its banks rattling with extraordinary music.

All the people of my life mill around in the sunlit crowd: Daddy, Mr. Denbo, Auntie Sybil, Elroy, Mayor Watson, Helen Rae, Ralph, Mrs. Marybush, Sally Ritchie, and hundreds I haven't told you about.

Odors of mustard and cotton candy assail us. The television crew hurries around and the director, a sallow young man with a gold tooth, regards me with doubt—although the president of the Cedar Ridge Rotary Club has given assurances that this will absolutely come off as guaranteed. I eat a candied apple and gaze into the sky. A chilly day in April.

The cirrus clouds streak overhead, the pulse of the river is in us all, beating in our blood beneath the hurdy-gurdy sounds of the carnival; today I will melt away under my velvet canopy, I will enter the endless cavern of the Blue Hole, and rise again in Cedar Ridge, miles away, while two sets of cameras record the miracle.

A reporter from the *Post-Dispatch* interviews my colleagues, all of whom are here to bask in the fallout of publicity. There is Auntie Sybil, true to her down-home image, peddling a basket of lye soap and preserves among the crowd. That simple country crone. As Mrs. Marybush and the mayor sign up tourists business for the forthcoming séances, Ralph tells a reporter that "Cedar Ridge is the mysterious metaphor of America"—a phrase which the reporter scribbles in a small spiral notebook.

"You'll meet someone else," Sally Ritchie tells me as we lurk beside a sideshow tent. "You have a lot to give."

Faced with Sally's clichés, I'm tempted to ask her to join me, to disappear with me this afternoon under the velvet—she's such a fool for all the hoopla and drum roll.

She wears an oversized letter sweater, oxfords, a ribbon in her hair. "I'll be proud," she goes on, "to say that I once knew you, Mr. Bogardus." She squeezes my hand, the only way she has ever touched me.

As I mount the stage, cameras whirring, the river glistening beyond the trees, a chilly breeze billowing up under my cape, I think of my house. Not too far away, there it stands: all boarded up at last, my sign removed, the furniture draped and covered in each room, chairs turned upside down on the great table where my powers ruled. I can visualize inevitable details: my kitchen faucet still dripping.

Will the Great Dane remain there, I wonder, to haunt the dust of those rooms? Will my absence be interpreted as failure or as just a mighty one-way effort into the unknown? Will this negate all the sad wonders of my life? Or will societies and scholars come to study me, to peruse my insurance policy and read the marginalia in my volumes? Will they seek to retrieve me in future séances? Or ask Sally Ritchie to recollect, to salvage memories and anecdotes?

The Cape Girardeau High School band plays *Columbia, the Gem of the Ocean,* and down I go, I melt, going away, all gone, never to explain myself or my miracles again, not even these words that vanish now—poof!—from this earthbound page.

His Son, in His Arms, in Light, Aloft

HAROLD BRODKEY

My father is chasing me.

My God, I feel it up and down my spine, the thumping of the turf, the approach of his hands, his giant hands, the huge ramming increment of his breath as he draws near; a widening effort. I feel it up and down my spine and in my mouth and belly—Daddy is so swift: who ever heard of such swiftness? Just as in stories. . . .

I can't escape him, can't fend him off, his arms, his rapidity, his will. His interest in me.

I am being lifted into the air—and even as I pant and stare blurredly, limply, mindlessly, a map appears, of the dark ground where I ran: as I hang limply and rise anyway on the fattened bar of my father's arm, I see that there's the grass, there's the path, there's a bed of flowers.

I straighten up. There are the lighted windows of our house, some distance away. My father's face, full of noises, is near: it looms: his hidden face: is that you, old money-maker? My butt is folded on the trapeze of his arm. My father is as big as an automobile.

In the oddly shrewd-hearted torpor of being carried home in the dark, a tourist, in my father's arms, I feel myself attached by my heated-by-running dampness to him: we are attached, there are binding oval stains of warmth.

In most social talk, most politeness, most literature, most religion, it is as if violence didn't exist—except as sin, something far away. This is flattering to women. It is also conducive to grace—because the heaviness of fear, the shadowy henchmen selves that fear attaches to us, that fear sees in others, is banished.

Where am I in the web of jealousy that trembles at every human movement?

What detectives we have to be.

What if I am wrong? What if I remember incorrectly? It does not matter. This is fiction—a game—of pleasures, of truth and error, as at the sensual beginning of a sensual life.

My father, Charley, as I knew him, is invisible in any photograph I have of him. The man I hugged or ran toward or ran from is not in any photograph: a photograph shows someone of whom I think: *Oh, was he like that?*

But in certain memories, *he* appears, a figure, a presence, and I think, *I know him.*

It is embarrassing to me that I am part of what is unsayable in any account of his life.

When Momma's or my sister's excesses, of mood, or of shopping, angered or sickened Daddy, you can smell him then from two feet away: he has a dry, achy little stink of a rapidly fading interest in his life with us. At these times, the women in a spasm of wit turn to me; they comb my hair, clean my face, pat my bottom or my shoulder, and send me off; they bid me to go cheer up Daddy.

Sometimes it takes no more than a tug at his newspaper: the sight of me is enough; or I climb on his lap, mimic his depression; or I stand on his lap, press his head against my chest. . . . His face is immense, porous, complex with stubble, bits of talcum on it, unlikely colors, unlikely features, a bald brow with a curved square of lamplight in it. About his head there is a nimbus of sturdy wickedness, of unlikelihood. If his mood does not change, something tumbles and goes dead in me.

Perhaps it is more a nervous breakdown than heartbreak: I have failed him: his love for me is very limited: I must die now. I go somewhere and shudder and collapse—a corner of the dining room, the back stoop or deck: I lie there, empty, grief-stricken, literally unable to move—I have forgotten my limbs. If a memory of them comes to me, the memory is meaningless. . . .

Momma will then stalk in to wherever Daddy is and say to him, "Charley, you can be mad at me. I'm used to it, but just go take a look and see what you've done to the child. . . ."

My uselessness toward him sickens me. Anyone who fails toward him might as well be struck down, abandoned, eaten.

Perhaps it is an animal state: I have-nothing-left, I-have-no-place-in-this-world.

Well, this is his house. Momma tells me in various ways to love him. Also, he is entrancing—he is so big, so thunderish, so smelly, and has the most extraordinary habits, reading newspapers, for instance, and wiggling his shoe: his shoe is gross: kick someone with that and they'd fall into next week.

Some memories huddle in a grainy light. What it is is a number of similar events bunching themselves, superimposing themselves, to make a false memory, a collage, a mental artifact. Within the boundaries of one such memory, one plunges from year to year, is small and helpless, is a little older: one remembers it all but it is nothing that happened, that clutch of happenings, of associations, those gifts and ghosts of a meaning.

I can, if I concentrate, whiten the light—or yellow-whiten it, actually—and when the graininess goes, it is suddenly one afternoon.

I could not live without the pride and belonging-to-himness of being that man's consolation. He had the disposal of the rights to the out-of-doors—he was the other, the other-not-a-woman: he was my strength, literally, my strength if I should cry out.

Flies and swarms of the danger of being unfathered beset me when I bored my father: it was as if I were covered with flies on the animal plain where some ravening wild dog would leap up, bite and grip my muzzle, and begin to bring about my death.

I had no protection: I was subject now to the appetite of whatever inhabited the dark.

A child collapses in a sudden burst of there-is-nothing-here, and that is added onto nothingness, the nothing of being only a child concentrating on there being nothing there, no hope, no ambition: there is a despair but one without magnificence except in the face of its completeness: *I am a child and am without strength of my own.*

I have—in my grief—somehow managed to get to the back deck: I am sitting in the early evening light; I am oblivious to the light. I did and didn't hear his footsteps, the rumble, the house thunder dimly (behind and beneath me), the thunder of his-coming-to-rescue me. . . . I did and didn't hear him call my name.

I spoke only the gaping emptiness of grief—that tongue—I understood I had no right to the speech of fathers and sons.

My father came out on the porch. I remember how stirred he was, how beside himself that I was so unhappy, that a child, a child he liked, should suffer so. He laid aside his own mood—his disgust with life, with money, with the excesses of the women—and he took on a broad-winged, malely flustering, broad-winged optimism—he was at the center of a great beating (of the heart, a man's heart, of a man's gestures, will, concern), dust clouds rising, a beating determination to persuade me that the nature of life, of *my* life, was other than I'd thought, other than whatever had defeated me—he was about to tell me there was no need to feel defeated, he was about to tell me that I was a good, or even a wonderful, child.

He kneeled—a mountain of shirt-front and trousers; a mountain that poured, clambered down, folded itself, re-formed itself: a disorderly massiveness, near to me, fabric-hung-and-draped: Sinai. He said, "Here, here, what is this—what is a child like you doing being so sad?" And: "Look at me. . . . It's all right. . . . Everything is all right. . . ." The misstatements of consolation are lies about the absolute that require faith—and no memory: the truth of consolation can be investigated if one is a proper child—that is to say, affectionate—only in a non-skeptical way.

"It's not all right!"

"It is—it is." It was and wasn't a lie: it had to do with power—and limitations: my limitations and his power: he could make it all right for me, everything, provided my everything was small enough and within his comprehension.

Sometimes he would say, "Son—" He would say it heavily—"Don't be sad—I don't want you to be sad—I don't like it when you're sad—"

I can't look into his near and, to me, factually incredible face—incredible because so large (as at the beginning of a love affair): I mean as a *face*: it is the focus of so many emotions and wonderments: he could have been a fool or was—it was possibly the face of a fool, someone self-centered, smug, an operator, semi-criminal, an intelligent psychoanalyst; it was certainly a mortal face—but what did the idea or word mean to me then—*mortal*?

There was a face; it was as large as my chest; there were eyes, inhumanly big, humid—what could they mean? How could I read them? How do you read eyes? I did not know about comparisons: how much more affectionate he was than other men, or less, how much better than common experience or how much worse in this area of being fathered my experience was with him: I cannot say even now: it is a statistical matter, after all, a matter of averages: but who at the present date can phrase the proper questions for a poll? And who will understand the hesitations, the blank looks, the odd expressions on the faces of the answerers?

The odds are he was a—median—father. He himself had usually a conviction he did pretty well: sometimes he despaired—of himself: but blamed me: my love: or something: or himself as a father: he wasn't good at managing stages between strong, clear states of feeling. Perhaps no one is.

Anyway, I knew no such terms as *median* then: I did not understand much about those parts of his emotions which extended past the rather clear area where my emotions were so often amazed. I chose, in some ways, to regard him seriously; in other ways, I had no choice— he was what was given to me.

I cannot look at him, as I said: I cannot see anything: if I look at him without seeing him, my blindness insults him: I don't want to hurt him at all: I want nothing: I am lost and have surrendered and am really dead and am waiting without hope.

He knows how to rescue people. Whatever he doesn't know, one of the things he knows in the haste and jumble of his heart, among the blither of tastes in his mouth and opinions and sympathies in his mind and so on, is the making yourself into someone who will help someone who is wounded. The dispersed and unlikely parts of him come together for a while in a clucking and focused arch of abiding concern. Oh how he plows ahead; oh how he believes in rescue! He puts—he *shoves*—he works an arm behind my shoulders, another under my legs: his arms, his powers shove at me, twist, lift and jerk me, until I am cradled in the air, in his arms: "You don't have to be unhappy—you haven't hurt anyone—don't be sad—you're a *nice* boy. . . ."

I can't quite hear him. I can't quite believe him. I can't be *good*—the confidence game is to believe him, is to be a good child who trusts him—we will both smile then, he and I. But if I hear him, I have to believe him still. I am set up that way. He is so big; he is the possessor of so many grandeurs. If I believe him, hope and pleasure will start up again—suddenly—the blankness in me will be relieved, broken by these—meanings—that it seems he and I share in some big, attaching way.

In his pride he does not allow me to suffer: I belong to him.

He is rising, jerkily, to his feet and holding me at the same time. I do not have to stir to save myself—I only have to believe him. He rocks me into a sad-edged relief and an achingly melancholy delight with the peculiar lurch as he stands erect of establishing his balance and rectifying the way he holds me, so he can go on holding me, holding me aloft, against his chest: I am airborne: I liked to have that man hold me—in the air: I knew it was worth a great deal, the embrace, the gift of altitude. I am not exposed on the animal plain. I am not helpless.

The heat his body gives off! It is the heat of a man sweating with regret. His heartbeat, his burning, his physical force: ah, there is a large rent in the nothingness: the mournful apparition of his regret, the proof of his loyalty wake me: I have a twin, a massive twin, mighty company: Daddy's grief is at my grief: my nothingness is echoed in him (if he is going to have to live without me): the rescue was not quite a secular thing. The evening forms itself, a classroom, a brigade of shadows, of phenomena—the tinted air slides; there are shadowy skaters everywhere; shadowy cloaked people step out from behind things which are then hidden behind their cloaks. An alteration in the air proceeds from openings in the ground, from leaks in the sunlight which is being disengaged, like a stubborn hand, or is being stroked shut like my eyelids when I refuse to sleep: the dark rubs and bubbles noiselessly—and seeps—into the landscape. On the rubbed distortion of my inner air, twilight soothes: there are two of us breathing in close proximity here (he is telling me that grownups sometimes have things on their minds, he is saying mysterious things which I don't comprehend); I don't want to look at him; it takes two of my eyes to see one of his—and then I mostly see myself in his eye: he is even more unseeable from here, this holder: my head falls against his neck: "I know what you like—you'd like to go stand on the wall—would you like to see the sunset?" Did I nod? I think I did: I nodded gravely: but perhaps he did not need an answer since he thought he knew me well.

We are moving, this elephant and I, we are lumbering, down some steps, across grassy, uneven ground—the spoiled child in his father's arms—behind our house was a little park—we move across the grass of the little park. There are sun's rays on the dome of the moorish bandstand. The evening is moist, fugitive, momentarily sneaking, half-welcomed in this hour of crime. My father's neck. The stubble. The skin where the stubble stops. Exhaustion has me: I am a creature of failure, a locus of childishness, an empty skull: I am this being-young. We overrun the world, he and I, with his legs, with our eyes, with our alliance. We move on in a ghostly torrent of our being like this.

My father has the smell and feel of wanting to be my father. Guilt and innocence stream and re-stream in him. His face, I see now in memory, held an untiring surprise: as if some grammar of deed and purpose—of comparatively easy tenderness—startled him again and again, startled him continuously for a while. He said, "I guess we'll just have to cheer you up—we'll have to show you life isn't so bad—I guess we weren't any too careful of a little boy's feelings, were we?" I wonder if all comfort is alike.

A man's love is, after all, a fairly spectacular thing.

He said—his voice came from above me—he spoke out into the air, the twilight—"We'll make it all right—just you wait and see. . . ."

He said, "This is what you like," and he placed me on the wall that ran along the edge of the park, the edge of a bluff, a wall too high for me to see over, and which I was forbidden to climb: he placed me on the stubbed stone mountains and grouting of the wall-top. He put his arm around my middle: I leaned against him: and faced outward into the salt of the danger of the height, of the view (we were at least one hundred and fifty feet, we were, therefore, hundreds of feet in the air); I was flicked at by narrow, abrasive bands of wind, evening wind, veined with sunset's sun-crispness, strongly touched with coolness.

The wind would push at my eyelids, my nose, my lips. I heard a buzzing in my ears which signaled how high, how alone we were: this view of a river valley at night and of parts of four counties was audible. I looked into the hollow in front of me, a grand hole, an immense, bellying deep sheet or vast sock. There were numinous fragments in it—birds in what sunlight was left, bits of smoke faintly lit by distant light or mist, hovering inexplicably here and there: rays of yellow light, high up, touching a few high clouds.

It had a floor on which were creeks (and the big river), a little dim, a little glary at this hour, rail lines, roads, highways, houses, silos, bridges, trees, fields, everything more than half-hidden in the enlarging dark: there was the shrinking glitter of far-off noises, bearded and stippled with huge and spreading shadows of my ignorance: it was panorama as a personal privilege. The sun at the end of the large, sunset-swollen sky, was a glowing and urgent orange; around it were the spreading petals of pink and stratospheric gold: on the ground were occasional magenta flarings; oh it makes you stare and gasp; a fine, astral (not a crayon) red rode in a broad, magnificent band across the middlewestern sky: below us, for miles, shadowiness tightened as we watched (it seemed); above us, tinted clouds spread across the vast shadowing sky: there were funereal lights and sinkings everywhere. I stand on the wall and lean against Daddy, only somewhat awed and abstracted: the view does not own me as it usually does: I am party in the hands of the jolting—amusement—the conceit—of having been resurrected —by my father.

I understood that he was proffering me oblivion plus pleasure, the end of a sorrow to be henceforth remembered as Happiness. This was to be my privilege. This amazing man is going to rescue me from any anomaly or barb or sting in my existence: he is going to confer happiness on me: as a matter of fact, he has already begun.

"Just you trust me—you keep right on being cheered up—look at that sunset—that's some sunset, wouldn't you say?—everything is going to be just fine and dandy—you trust me—you'll see—just you wait and see. . . ."

Did he mean to be a swindler? He wasn't clear-minded—he often said, "I mean well." He did not think other people meant well.

I don't feel it would be right to adopt an Oedipal theory to explain what happened between him and me: only a sense of what he was like as a man, what certain moments were like, and what was said.

It is hard in language to get the full, irregular, heavy sound of a man.

He liked to have us "all dressed and nice when I come home from work," have us wait for him in attitudes of serene all-is-well contentment. As elegant as a Spanish prince, I sat on the couch toying with an oversized model truck—what a confusion of social pretensions, technologies, class disorder there was in that. My sister would sit in a chair, knees together, hair brushed: she'd doze off if Daddy was late. Aren't we happy! Actually, we often were.

One day he came in plungingly excited to be home and to have us as an audience rather than outsiders who didn't know their lines and who often laughed at him as part of their struggle to improve their parts in his scenes. We were waiting to have him approve of our tableau—he usually said something about what a nice family we looked like or how well we looked or what a pretty group or some such thing—and we didn't realize he was the tableau tonight. We held our positions, but we stared at him in a kind of mindless what-should-we-do-besides-sit-here-and-be-happy-and-nice? Impatiently he said, "I have a surprise for you, Charlotte—Abe Last has a heart after all." My father said something on that order: or "—a conscience after all"; and then he walked across the carpet, a man somewhat jerky with success—a man redolent of vaudeville, of grotesque and sentimental movies (he loked grotesquerie, prettiness, sentiment). As he walked, he pulled banded packs of currency out of his pockets, two or three in each hand. "There," he said, dropping one, then three in Momma's dressed-up lap. "There," he said, dropping another two: he uttered a "there" for each subsequent pack. "Oh, let me!" my sister cried and ran over to look —and then she grabbed two packs and said, "Oh, Daddy, how much *is* this?"

It was eight or ten thousand dollars, he said. Momma said, "Charley, what if someone sees—we could be robbed—why do you take chances like this?"

Daddy harrumphed and said, "You have no sense of fun—if you ask me, you're afraid to be happy. I'll put it in the bank tomorrow—if I can find an honest banker—here, young lady, put that money down: you don't want to prove your mother right, do you?"

Then he said, "I know one person around here who knows how to enjoy himself—" and he lifted me up, held me in his arms.

He said, "We're going outside, this young man and I."

"What should I do with this money?"

"Put it under your mattress—make a salad out of it: you're always the one who worries about money," he said in a voice solid with authority and masculinity, totally pieced out with various self-satisfactions—as if he had gained a kingdom and the assurance of appearing as glorious in the histories of his time; I put my head back and smiled at the superb animal, at the rosy—and cowardly —panther leaping; and then I glanced over his shoulder and tilted my head and looked sympathetically at Momma.

My sister shouted, "I know how to enjoy myself—I'll come too!"

"Yes, yes," said Daddy, who was never averse to enlarging spheres of happiness and areas of sentiment. He held her hand and held me on his arm.

"Let him walk," my sister said. And: "He's getting bigger—you'll make a sissy out of him, Daddy. . . ."

Daddy said, "Shut up and enjoy the light—it's as beautiful as Paris and in our own backyard."

Out of folly, or a wish to steal his attention, or greed, my sister kept on: she asked if she could get something with some of the money; he dodged her question; and she kept on; and he grew peevish, so peevish he returned to the house and accused Momma of having never taught her daughter not to be greedy—he sprawled, impetuous, displeased, semi-frantic in a chair: "I can't enjoy myself—there is no way a man can live in this house with all of you—I swear to God this will kill me soon. . . ."

Momma said to him, "I can't believe in the things you believe in—I'm not a girl anymore: when I play the fool, it isn't convincing—you get angry with me when I try. You shouldn't get angry with her—you've spoiled her more than I have—and how do you expect her to act when you show her all that money—how do you think money affects people?"

I looked at him to see what the answer was, to see what he would answer. He said, "Charlotte, try being a rose and not a thorn."

At all times, and in all places, there is always the possibility that I will start to speak or will be looking at something and I will feel his face covering mine, as in a kiss and as a mask, turned both ways like that: and I am inside him, his presence, his thoughts, his language: *I am languageless* then for a moment, an automaton of repetition, a bagged piece of an imaginary river of descent.

I can't invent everything for myself: some always has to be what I already know: some of me always has to be him.

When he picked me up, my consciousness fitted itself to that position. I remember it—clearly. He could punish me—and did —by refusing to lift me, by denying me that union with him. Of course, the union was not one-sided: I was his innocence—as long as I was not an accusation, that is. I censored him—in that when he felt himself being, consciously, a father, he held back part of his other life, of his whole self: his shadows, his impressions, his adventures would not readily fit into me—what a gross and absurd rape that would have been.

So he was *careful*—he *walked on eggs*—there was an odd courtesy of his withdrawal behind his secrets, his secret sorrows and horrors, behind the curtain of what-is-suitable-for-a-child.

Sometimes he becomes simply a set of limits, of walls, inside which there is the caroming and echoing of my astounding sensibility amplified by being his son and in his arms and aloft; and he lays his sensibility aside or models his on mine, on my joy, takes his emotional coloring from me, like a mirror or a twin: his incomprehensible life, with its strengths, ordeals, triumphs, crimes, horrors, his sadness and disgust, is enveloped and momentarily assuaged by my direct and indirect childish consolation. My gaze, my enjoying him, my willingness to be him, my joy at it, supported the baroque tower of his necessary but limited and maybe dishonest optimism.

One time he and Momma fought over money and he left: he packed a bag and went. Oh it was sad and heavy at home. I started to be upset, but then I retreated into an impenetrable stupidity: not knowing was better than being despairing. I was put to bed and I did fall asleep: I woke in the middle of the night; he had returned and was sitting on my bed—in the dark—a huge shadow in the shadows. He was stroking my forehead. When he saw my eyes open, he said in a sentimental, heavy voice, "I could never leave *you*—"

He didn't really mean it: I was an excuse: but he did mean it—the meaning and not-meaning were like the rise and fall of a wave in me, in the dark outside of me, between the two of us, between him and me (at other moments he would think of other truths, other than the one of he-couldn't-leave-me sometimes). He bent over sentimentally, painedly, not nicely, and he began to hug me; he put his head down, on my chest; my small heartbeat vanished into the near, sizable, anguished, angular, emotion-swollen one that was his. I kept advancing swiftly into wakefulness, my consciousness came rushing and widening blurredly, embracing the dark, his presence, his embrace. It's Daddy, it's Daddy—it's dark still—wakefulness rushed into the dark grave or grove of his hugely extended presence. His affection. My arms stumbled: there was no adequate embrace in me—I couldn't lift *him*—I had no adequacy yet except that of my charm or what-have-you, except things the grown-ups gave me —not things: traits, qualities. I mean my hugging his head was nothing until he said, "Ah, you love me. . . . You're all right. . . ."

Momma said: "They are as close as two peas in a pod—they are just alike—that child and Charley. That child is God to Charley. . . ."

He didn't always love me.

In the middle of the night that time, he picked me up after a while, he wrapped me in a blanket, held me close, took me downstairs in the dark; we went outside, into the night; it was dark and chilly but there was a moon—I thought he would take me to the wall but he just stood on our back deck. He grew tired of loving me; he grew abstracted and forgot me: the love that had just a moment before been so intently and tightly clasping and nestling went away, and I found myself released, into the cool night air, the floating damp, the silence, with the darkened houses around us.

I saw the silver moon, heard my father's breath, felt the itchiness of the woolen blanket on my hands, noticed its wool smell. I did this alone and I waited. Then, when he didn't come back, I grew sleepy and put my head down against his neck: he was nowhere near me. Alone in his arms, I slept.

Over and over a moment seems to recur, something seems to return in its entirety, a name seems to be accurate: and we say it always happens like this. But we are wrong, of course.

I was a weird choice as someone for him to love.

So different from him in the way I was surprised by things.

I am a child with this mind. I am a child he has often rescued.

Our attachment to each other manifests itself in sudden swoops and grabs and rubs of attention, of being entertained, by each other, at the present moment.

I ask you, how is it possible it's going to last?

Sometimes when we are entertained by each other, we are bold about it, but just as frequently, it seems embarrassing, and we turn our faces aside.

His recollections of horror are more certain than mine. His suspicions are more terrible. There are darknesses in me I'm afraid of, but the ones in him don't frighten me but are like the dark in the yard, a dark a child like me might sneak into (and has)—a dark full of unseen shadowy almost-glowing presences—the fear, the danger—are desirable—difficult—with the call-to-be-brave: the childish bravura of *I must endure this* (knowing I can run away if I choose).

The child touches with his pursed, jutting, ignorant lips the large, handsome, odd, humid face of his father who can run away too. More dangerously.

He gave away a car of his that he was about to trade in on a new one: he gave it to a man in financial trouble; he did it after seeing a movie about crazy people being loving and gentle with each other and everyone else: Momma said to Daddy, "You can't do anything you want—you can't listen to your feelings—you have a family. . . ."

After seeing a movie in which a child cheered up an old man, he took me to visit an old man who probably was a distant relative, and who hated me at sight, my high coloring, the noise I might make, my father's affection for me: "Will he sit still? I can't stand noise. Charley, listen, I'm in bad shape—I think I have cancer and they won't tell me—"

"Nothing can kill a tough old bird like you, Ike. . . ."

The old man wanted all of Charley's attention—and strength —while he talked about how the small threads and thicker ropes that tied him to life were being cruelly tampered with.

Daddy patted me afterward, but oddly he was bored and disappointed in me, as if I'd failed at something.

He could not seem to keep it straight about my value to him or to the world in general; he lived at the center of his own intellectual shortcomings and his moral pride: he needed it to be true, as an essential fact, that goodness—or innocence—was in him or was protected by him, and that, therefore, he was a good *man* and superior to other men, and did not deserve—certain common mas-

culine fates—horrors—tests of his courage—certain pains. It was
necessary to him to have it be true that he knew what real goodness
was and had it in his life.

Perhaps that was because he didn't believe in God, and because
he felt (with a certain self-love) that people, out in the world, didn't
appreciate him and were needlessly difficult—"unloving": he said
it often—and because it was true he was shocked and guilty and
even enraged when he was "forced" into being unloving himself,
or when he caught sight in himself of such a thing as cruelty, or cruel
nosiness, or physical cowardice—God, how he hated being a
coward—or hatred, physical hatred, even for me, if I was coy or
evasive or disinterested or tired of him: it tore him apart
literally—bits of madness, in varying degrees, would grip him
as in a Greek play: I see his mouth, his salmon-colored mouth,
showing various degrees of sarcasm—sarcasm mounting into bitterness and even a ferocity without tears, that always suggested to
me, as a child, that he was near tears but had forgotten in his
ferocity that he was about to cry.

Or he would catch sight of some evidence, momentarily
inescapable—in contradictory or foolish statements of his or in
unkept promises that it was clear he had never meant to keep, had
never made any effort to keep—that he was a fraud; and sometimes
he would laugh because he was a fraud—a good-hearted fraud, he
believed—or he would be sullen or angry, a fraud caught either by
the tricks of language, so that in expressing affection absent-
mindedly he had expressed too much, or caught by greed and
self-concern: he hated the evidence that he was mutable as hell: that
he loved sporadically and egoistically, and often with rage and
vengeance, and that madness I mentioned earlier: he couldn't stand
those things: he usually forgot them; but sometimes when he was
being tender, or noble, or self-sacrificing, he would sigh and be
very sad—maybe because the good stuff was temporary. I don't
know. Or sad that he did it only when he had the time and was in the
mood. Sometimes he forgot such things and was superbly
confident—or was that a bluff?

I don't know. I really can't speak for him.

I look at my hand and then at his; it is not really conceivable to me
that both are hands: mine is a sort of a hand. He tells me over and
over that I must not upset him—he tells me of my power over
him—I don't know how to take such a fact—is it a fact? I stare at
him. I gasp with the ache of life stirring in me—again: again:
again—I ache with tentative and complete and then again tentative
belief.

For a long time piety was anything at all sitting still or moving
slowly and not rushing at me or away from me but letting me look at
it or be near it without there being any issue of safety-about-to-be-
lost.

This world is evasive.

But someone who lets you observe him is not evasive, is not
hurtful, at that moment: it is like in sleep where *the other* waits—the
Master of Dreams—and there are doors, doorways opening into
farther rooms where there is an altered light, and which I enter to
find—what? That someone is gone? That the room is empty? Or
perhaps I find a vista, of rooms, of archways, and a window, and a
peach tree in flower—a tree with peach-colored flowers in the
solitude of night.

I am dying of grief, Daddy. I am waiting here, limp with abandon-
ment, with exhaustion: perhaps I'd better believe in God. . . .

My father's virtues, those I dreamed about, those I saw when I was
awake, those I understood and misunderstood, were, as I felt them,
in dreams or wakefulness, when I was a child, like a broad highway
opening into a small dusty town that was myself; and down that road
came bishops and slogans, Chinese processions, hasidim in a
dance, the nation's honor and glory *in its young people*, baseball
players, singers who sang "with their whole hearts," automobiles
and automobile grilles, and grave or comic bits of instruction. This

man is attached to me and makes me light up with festal affluence
and oddity; he says, "I think you love me."

He was right.

He would move his head—his giant face—and you could observe in
his eyes the small town which was me in its temporary sophistication, a small town giving proof on every side of its arrogance and its
prosperity and its puzzled contentment.

He also instructed me in hatred: he didn't mean to, not openly:
but I saw and picked up the curious buzzing of his puckered
distastes, a nastiness of dismissal that he had: a fetor of let-them-
all-kill-each-other. He hated lots of people, whole races: he hated
ugly women.

He conferred an odd inverted splendor on awfulness—because *he*
knew about it: he went into it every day. He told me not to want that,
not to want to know about that: he told me to go on being just the
way I was—"a nice boy."

When he said something was unbearable, he meant it; he meant
he could not bear it.

In my memories of this time of my life, it seems to be summer all
the time, even when the ground is white: I suppose it seems like
summer because I was never cold.

Ah: I wanted to see. . . .

My father, when he was low (in spirit) would make rounds,
inside his head, checking on his consciousness, to see if it was safe
from inroads by "*the unbearable*": he found an all-is-well in a quiet
emptiness. . . .

In an uninvadedness, he found the weary complacency and self-
importance of All is Well.

(The women liked invasions—up to a point.)

One day he came home, mysterious, exalted, hatted and suited,
roseate, handsome, a little sweaty—it really was summer that day.
He was exalted, as I said, but nervous toward me—anxious with
promises.

And he was, oh, somewhat angry, justified, toward the world,
toward me, not exactly as a threat (in case I didn't respond) but as a
jumble.

He woke me from a nap, an uneasy nap, lifted me out of bed, me,
a child who had not expected to see him that afternoon—I was not
particularly pleased with him, not pleased with him at all, really.

He dressed me himself. At first he kept his hat on. After a while,
he took it off. When I was dressed, he said, "You're pretty sour
today," and he put his hat back on.

He hustled me down the stairs; he held my wrist in his enormous
palm—immediate and gigantic to me and blankly suggestive of a
meaning I could do nothing about except stare at blankly from time
to time in my childish life.

We went outside into the devastating heat and glare, the blather-
ing, humming afternoon light of a midwestern summer day: a
familiar furnace.

We walked along the street, past the large, silent houses, set,
each one, in hard, pure light. You could not look directly at
anything, the glare, the reflections were too strong.

Then he lifted me in his arms—aloft.

He was carrying me to help me because the heat was bad—and
worse near the sidewalk which reflected it upward into my face
—and because my legs were short and I was struggling, because he
was in a hurry and because he liked carrying me, and because I was
sour and blackmailed him with my unhappiness, and he was being
kind with a certain—limited—mixture of exasperation-turning-
into-a-degree-of-mortal-love.

Or it was another time, really early in the morning, when the air was
partly asleep, partly a-dance, but in veils, trembling with heavy
moisture. Here and there, the air broke into a string of beads of
pastel colors, pink, pale green, small rainbows, really small, and
very narrow. Daddy walked rapidly. I bounced in his arms. My

eyesight was unfocused—it bounced too. Things were more than merely present: they pressed against me: they had the aliveness of myth, of the beginning of an adventure when nothing is explained as yet.

All at once we were at the edge of a bankless river of yellow light. To be truthful, it was like a big wooden beam of fresh, unweathered wood: but we entered it: and then it turned into light, cooler light than in the hot humming afternoon but full of bits of heat that stuck to me and then were blown away, a semi-heat, not really friendly, yet reassuring: and very dimly sweaty; and it grew, it spread: this light turned into a knitted cap of light, fuzzy, warm, woven, itchy: it was pulled over my head, my hair, my forehead, my eyes, my nose, my mouth.

So I turned my face away from the sun—I turned it so it was pressed against my father's neck mostly—and then I knew, in a childish way, knew from the heat (of his neck, of his shirt collar), knew by childish deduction, that his face was unprotected from the luminousness all around us: and I looked; and it was so: his face, for the moment unembarrassedly, was caught in that light. In an accidental glory.

I'm Waving Tomorrow

ALMA STONE

Every Saturday the sisters climbed the stairs to the 125th Street station and took the train to Woodlawn Cemetery. Inconveniences were involved, as in everything now. The steps were steep and dirty, the platform noisy and narrow, but the trip got rid of the afternoon, and often there were diverting incidents. For example, a smoker might refuse to leave the prohibited area, commotion and eviction would follow, and passengers could then exchange views on constitutional rights.

Weaving up the aisle, pretending he was out West on a continental limited with a diner up front, instead of on a commuter coach with half the seats facing backward, Mr. Stewart, the conductor in whose car the sisters always rode, would save them forward seats and entertain them with stories. No trip was complete without his favorite. "Every morning the woman stands on the platform and signals to this fellow on the street if he can make the train or not." Then Mr. Stewart would show them: a beckoning finger—yes, but step on it; palm up—relax, not a chance. "I don't think they even speak after they get on the train. Never sit together. Total strangers," Mr. Stewart would always say.

Maureen, the younger, would nod her head, agreeing: this old world wasn't so bad, after all. But an advanced case of hardening of the arteries had given Sister, soured and of a naturally questioning disposition, a low opinion of most people and a deep suspicion of all good deeds. The affair of the signaling stranger was, to her mind, particularly suspect, and with the conductor Sister always debated the story's authenticity.

"Maybe she's got arthritis," Sister said one Saturday. "She has to exercise her hands. Like this."

Held high, with the swollen veins receding, Sister's hands were still young and delicate, and Maureen, saddened, turned away. Maureen meant to tell Sister later: hold your hands up more.

"That show-off should eat health food," said Sister. "Then she wouldn't have to climb so high to make such a weak wave."

"It is a fine, strong wave," said Mr. Stewart.

"She's probably a chain smoker," Sister said. "She's flipping ashes, not waving."

On the morning run, the maids going to Scarsdale and Bronxville liked Mr. Stewart's story very much. It was a very beautiful thing, they would tell him, and, shutting Sister out, Mr. Stewart would face the black women, counting his tickets and keeping it that way. But close to Williamsbridge and Woodlawn, where often there were mysterious potshots and near-misses from both sides of the tracks, the conductor would come back to remind the women to duck, and the sisters would listen for the sound of a bullet hitting glass.

It was a disgrace, people said. They could hardly believe it. But they ducked.

At Woodlawn, the sisters took the long walk up the hill. Both women were plain-looking, of middle height, their once sharp features softened by age. Both had on hats, carried summer purses with gloves inside, and Maureen, on her feet a lot, wore those comfortable sandals old ladies had found out about. Sister, when she had gone to business, had had a certain style, a flair for clothes that made her still want some heel to her shoes. What with her heels and the heavy shopping bag Sister carried, of the two women, she walked the more slowly.

The women entered the cemetery and paused at familiar gravesites, stopping to rest and to note—the Mitchell grass needed cutting, the Roberts mausoleum looked dingy—before they walked on to the Montgomery plot.

The Montgomery plot was in an older section of the cemetery, and though four others of the family were buried here, the sisters would have plenty of ground for themselves, not boxed in as in their apartment in Morningside Heights, with scarcely space to flap around. When food had gotten so high, tomatoes a scandal, greens outrageous, Sister had had the idea to plant Bibb lettuce in the border—a geranium, Bibb lettuce, a geranium, Bibb lettuce. It had caught on nicely, and when the geraniums bloomed, the lettuce made a fresh and lively variant to the borders of ivy and privet in neighboring plots.

Fixtures of the property, two iron benches painted black, were placed opposite each other across the graves. With scrolled backs of twining floral design and seats of intricate tracery, the benches were of almost antique vintage, yet younger than the sisters who rested on them this late June day, enjoying the local lettuce and cucumber sandwiches from home.

"Will you join me in a preprandial libation?" Sister asked Maureen, and got out the Bloody Mary thermos.

"I'd be delighted," said Maureen, rising.

"Don't walk all the way around," said Sister, pouring. "Jump 'em. They'll never know it."

But Maureen walked the distance, got her drink, and went back, the long way, around each grave, to her own bench.

"It's nice to be out in the country," Maureen said.

"Damned valuable real estate," Sister said. But when the blood did not reach her brain, Sister made four quick gestures, each higher than the other, stacking up old ladies with no real estate, and knocked her hat crooked.

Maureen looked away. "Straighten your hat, Sister," she said.

"Quit telling me what to do." Sister put on her glasses and removed her teeth. She never wore the two together.

Maureen shook salt on her lettuce. "If it hadn't been for Papa looking ahead," she said, "we wouldn't even have this property."

"Papa was a gyp and a boss, like you. He got a hot bargain here in the Crash when the Wheelers went broke and had to sell out. Wonder where the Wheeler girls are all piled up?" Sister took an empty mentholatum jar from the shopping bag and placed it on the bench.

"Papa wasn't bossy," said Maureen. "Papa was a Freemason and worked hard for his money. We could have spoken up. Papa was protecting us," she said. "But I still wish we had something to call our own, what they call a spread or something."

"What's the matter with this?" Sister was all clearheaded business again. "You can spread out here all you want to. Laid out straight, you can come down to here, to the end of the bench." Sister made a point with the toe of her shoe. "Six lettuce plants back from the third geranium. Not a leaf farther. Be sure you wear your low-heeled sandals, though. Cremated, of course, you would come only to about here"—again the toe pointed—"and leave the rest for lettuce and organics. People starving all over the world, what selfish use you make of your part of the property is on your own conscience. Just don't trespass on my part. Remember that I am the older, five feet five, wear heels, and am entitled to a larger plot," Sister said as she dipped into the shopping bag and placed a package on the bench—Christmas cards.

"Hold your hands up more, Sister," said Maureen, watching. "Don't let them drag so."

"Shut up." Sister took off her glasses and put in her teeth. She placed the glasses by the Christmas cards, very straight, very even. She dragged her hands deliberately.

"All I mean is it makes them nicer-looking," said Maureen.

"This lettuce is deficient in vitamins," announced Sister. "It needs a new type of fertilizer." She looked at Maureen and moved the Christmas cards close to her end on the bench, and the Bloody Mary thermos to the middle. Between them and the mentholatum jar she put a nail file and a toothbrush. She saw her mistake immediately, and put the thermos at her end, close by, the Christmas cards at the other, the toothbrush and nail file in the middle, glasses to the side, parallel.

"That looks fine, Sister," said Maureen.

Maureen studied her sister, bent sideways now over the iron bench: should she play the greeting cards on the nail file, or should she shuffle again? How about the can-opener, could she finesse it around the breakfast menu from the *Queen Mary*?

"Sister, how would you like to take a nice trip?" Maureen said.

Sister looked up, suspicious at once. "A nice trip where? To the booby patch?"

"Hatch, not patch," Maureen said. "I mean, how would you like to put our savings together and travel a little?"

"You're not getting into my savings," said Sister. "You're not taking my security away from me."

"All right, we'll use mine, then," said Maureen. "I don't care whose we use, just so we go somewhere. It'll be fun, don't you think?"

"Not much," said Sister. "Two old maids traveling together."

"Well, we can try," said Maureen. "Buy us a small car and get in it and just light out. See something different for a change."

"I'm not getting in any car with you driving," said Sister. "I may be nutty, but I'm not crazy," and she jumped the nail file with the can-opener.

"Now listen here," said Maureen, trying to sound all fun. "I used to drive to school when I taught, remember?"

"Anybody can drive to grade school," said Sister.

"I used to drive up here," said Maureen. "Besides, it wouldn't be all that dangerous. Anything you do these days is dangerous. In a car we could travel around and find some better place to live maybe, where we'd have a sense of security. Some place they don't rape and beat up old ladies all the time."

"Rip off your clothes and stick that fenis right in," said Sister.

"Penis," said Maureen.

"Fenis, penis, what's the difference?" said Sister. "They don't even ask your age or what is your favorite position."

"The amenities are not their chief concern," said Maureen.

"Well, she ought to think up something new to pep it up, then," said Sister, and moved the greeting cards again.

"Who ought?" Maureen stared at her.

"The woman on the platform that signals that man. I think she's a fake. It's a cock-and-bull fake, and so is that jerk of a conductor."

"How do you know?"

"Because I tested it."

"When?" said Maureen. "Where was I?"

"Off somewhere trying to boss somebody and take their security," said Sister. "Anyway, not a soul down on the street saw me wave."

"They weren't looking for it," said Maureen.

"That's what I'm saying. How could *he* see it if he wasn't looking?"

"He knew she was going to do it, so he looked," said Maureen.

"How'd he *know* it? Who *told* him? They never spoke, the conductor said."

"So once they spoke. *'I'm waving tomorrow. Look,'* she told him."

"Where was he standing when she waved?"

"He wasn't standing. He was running."

"How could he look if he's running? Running along, looking up, you'd slip in some dog shit."

"True, Sister," Maureen said. "But it wouldn't be the woman's fault. She doesn't even know that man. She does it out of pure kindness, so he won't rush up those steps after a train he can't possibly make. He might get heart failure."

"I bet it's a love signal. Like this." Sister made an obscene gesture. "I'd signal like this some day and he wouldn't know what to do, standing out there in all that dog shit and the train pulling out right in front of him. He'd drop dead."

Using the Jerome Avenue entrance, a funeral procession approached a newly-dug grave.

"Pick up your glasses, Sister, before you break them," Maureen said.

"Stop bossing me." Flaring, Sister took out her teeth. "I'm not one of your schoolchildren—and quit tilting the thermos. I was an important executive. And I always will be. I was head of the house after Papa died. What I said went."

"Sure you're an important executive, Sister. Otherwise you couldn't line those things up on the bench so straight," Maureen said. "If you weren't such an important executive, you'd get some of those things crooked."

"Goddamn right I'm important," said Sister, "and don't you forget it."

The funeral procession passed on the road.

"There go the Wheelers," said Sister, "hunting a place to pile up." As she rose to see better the route of the cortege, she swept the Christmas cards off the bench. Picking them up, she knocked off her teeth.

"You brought too much stuff again," said Maureen. "I told you to leave the Ace bandage home."

"So you can steal it and take my security," said Sister, and moving the nail file back of the toothbrush, trumped them with the Ace bandage. But that was not quite it yet. She bent low, studying the possibilities.

"The bench is too small," said Sister. "I need another bench." She eyed the empty end of Maureen's. Maureen covered it with her purse. A kind of violence was averted when a stray dog ran through the grounds.

"He hides till night, then digs up the graves," said Sister.

"He does not. He is merely trying to survive," said Maureen.

"On dead people," Sister said.

Neither of them saw the guard come up. New to the Montgomerys, he studied Sister's bench. ''No camping on the grounds here. Private property.''

''It is *our* private property,'' said Sister.

''Pack your stuff off the bench, lady. No selling knickknacks on the grounds. No growing lettuce in the border, either. Or is that marijuana?'' Shaken, the man walked toward the gate, in case he needed help.

Sister stored the articles carefully in the shopping bag. Maureen gathered some lettuce for supper. The two women started back to the station. Halfway down the hill, Sister remembered she had left her glasses behind and the women had to go back for them.

Wobbly on the heels now with the extra walk, Sister moved very slowly and they missed their usual train. When the next one came, it was already crowded with Saturday-night people headed for the city, and seats facing forward were taken. All that were left were two seats going backward. Mr. Thompson, the regular conductor on the regular return train, would have saved them forward seats. But the present conductor, a stranger, made no effort to help the sisters. No one in the car offered to change seats with them. Maureen, afraid Sister, unsteady on the high heels, would fall when the train started, quickly slipped into an empty seat by the window to show Sister how safe it was. Sister, leaning forward, looking back nervously, sat by Maureen's side in the aisle seat. It took a few moments for them to settle in. They were nearly to Williamsbridge when Maureen brought it up again.

''So what about our taking a trip? Having a little fun?''

Sister made no answer. She had dropped her glasses and was bent forward, looking for them. It was not easy, riding backwards, to judge where you were, and, waiting for landmarks, twisting sideways, Maureen had not seen the station sign coming up. Mr. Thompson would have warned them.

The hat fell first, then the lettuce and the purse, then Maureen. Sister looked when everybody else did, and saw the bullet hole displayed on Maureen's left ear.

Maureen made the Sunday paper with two columns, though they spelled her name wrong. The police slapped her in the morgue for a few hours, then Sister had her cremated. There was a brief service.

Cremation cut down the funeral costs and, later on, space. The undertaker charged Sister forty-five dollars to dig the hole for the urn. The marker was yet to come and the inscription, MAUREEN, NOT MAURINE, would be an additional cost. It gave Sister a great sense of security to own all the property herself, and she meant to make some improvements, primarily by planting some fuzzy oat cereal that was so good for you and put the blonde color right back in your hair.

With Maureen's bench, Sister could spread out all her things —her old issues of *Retail Trade*, things she had never had room for before. With Maureen gone, Sister could bring her U.N.I.C.E.F. catalog and her 1954 *Women's Rest Tour: Foreign Lodgings*.

We've got two benches now, Sister told her sorority pin, and jumped it with her name tag from the 1956 Merchandising Convention:

Hello, I'm Miss Montgomery. Who are you?

Cartography

JAMES S. REINBOLD

For many years my aunt rented out a modest but well-kept little house on Fiskegard. It was brick, painted pale yellow, had a slightly peaked tile roof, two front windows adorned with flower boxes, and an immaculate lawn.

The interior walls of the house were covered with white paint and the tenant had to be very clever if he wanted to hang pictures or mirrors, for my aunt strictly forbade the marring of the walls. Of course, my aunt screened prospective renters thoroughly. She demanded references, and subjected all persons to rigid interview, wherein she probed habits of cleanliness and sobriety.

My aunt never went out of doors, and it was therefore my task to collect rent and pay periodic visits to the house to make sure it was being kept up to standard and that the occupant was not indulging in any practice of which my aunt disapproved.

Two small children were once covertly added to the population of the house, and on occasion I found hidden candy bars and cigarettes and liquor. All these infringements naturally resulted in immediate termination of lease. There were no exceptions.

I found the routine of collecting rent and inspecting the house rather pleasant. Besides, it excused small absences from my aunt, who wanted me always nearby, owing to her chronic illnesses.

There had been many tenants in the house. Some stayed several years. Some stayed only a month or so. As for Matthew Essen, the cartographer, his stay was neither short nor long.

Matthew Essen was about seventy and bald. In fact, he showed no evidence of whiskers and his eyebrows were very blond, pencil-thin lines no more than an inch in length. He appeared at my aunt's door early in the afternoon wearing an old homburg and an overcoat that obscured his hands and reached down to the tops of his shoes.

''My name is Matthew Essen,'' he said to me. ''I have come regarding the house.''

''Please step in,'' I replied, and led him into the parlor where my aunt and I were having tea.

''Mr. Essen is here about the house,'' I announced.

My aunt smiled, put down her teacup, and pointed to a chair. Essen handed me his coat and hat and sat down. My aunt poured a third cup of tea and Essen accepted it gratefully. I went to the desk to fetch my aunt's glasses and the long list of questions. But for reasons still known only to her, my aunt waived the usual interview, and she and Essen set off into a conversation that had nothing to do with the regulations governing the house, the terms of the lease, the tenant's responsibilities, and my duties and powers. Instead, Essen promptly tumbled into rambling monologues about his niece's son-in-law, a mariner lost off Sable Island; about pygmies, Eskimos and Bedouins; about anticlines and volcanic eruptions. To be sure, all this led me to conclude Essen was senile. Regardless, my aunt was charmed. I have never discovered why. But she never took her eyes off Essen, and the tea in time grew cold.

Here and there in his nonsense Essen revealed certain personal details. He claimed, for example, to have just relinquished his chair at the university after fifty-three years. Now, in retirement, he wanted to live a solitary life, concerning himself with the compilation of a biographical atlas. He did not elaborate, but the apparent magnitude of the task was sufficient to overwhelm my aunt. Essen said he had often passed my aunt's house on Fiskegard on his way to and from appointments, and had always desired to live there. It was the ideal place to complete the atlas, he insisted.

My aunt was flattered, quite beyond all proportion. She put her hands to her cheeks and shook her head.

"To think that my little house," she said.

Essen smiled and then went on to speak about scores of living accommodations from the South Seas to the Arctic and about the respective advantages and disadvantages of them all.

Then, just before three, in the middle of a sentence, his tea untouched, Essen looked at his watch and said he must take his leave. His luggage and some personal items were scheduled to arrive at the house shortly, he said, clearly having presumed success in his mission, and he wanted to supervise the handling and placement of these pieces.

"Of course, Mr. Essen," my aunt said, and extended her hand.

Essen bowed and put his thin lips to her hand. I could see my aunt blush beneath her heavy rouge. Essen smiled mildly, and whispered, "My pleasure."

"There is the matter of the rent," I said, clearing my throat, and rising from my chair.

My aunt frowned at me. But before she could speak, Essen waved his finger in the air.

"Yes, yes," he said enthusiastically. "The rent. We cannot forget the rent."

He reached into his pocket and withdrew a wallet. I informed him of the monthly amount.

"Your son . . ." Essen began.

"Nephew," my aunt corrected, not without irritation directed at me.

"Pardon me. Your nephew is the practical one, I see. A head for business, as they say." Essen turned to me. "Well, here we are, then," he said, counting out the bills. "Two months in advance."

I took the money, recounted it carefully, and loudly, and pocketed the sum. Then I stepped over to the desk and prepared a receipt.

"Very efficient," Essen said.

"Yes, very," my aunt said.

I gave Essen his receipt, along with the key to the house, and was about to set forth the precise conditions of residence when my aunt spoke.

"Show Mr. Essen to the door, Nicholas, and see he is escorted safely to the house."

"That will not be necessary," Essen said. "I prefer to walk alone. Good day."

I gave Essen his coat and hat and accompanied him to the door.

"There are certain terms," I said.

"Of course, of course," Essen said, and he hurried down the walk.

I returned to the parlor rather annoyed with my aunt. She had rented the house without a moment's inquiry and allowed a foolish, ill-dressed, retired teacher—fired for incompetence, for all we knew—to kiss her hand.

My aunt poured herself a cup of cold tea and sipped, ignoring me. I stood in the archway between parlor and foyer examining my tie-pin and cuff-links.

"We attract a refined, intelligent man to live in the house and you insult him about money," my aunt finally said.

I moved into the room and sat down on the couch next to her. I unbuttoned my vest and ate several ladyfingers, avoiding my aunt's gaze and refusing to answer.

"Must you eat every last one?"

"Yes," I replied.

My aunt sighed.

"Will you not apologize for embarrassing me in the presence of Professor Essen?"

"He is no longer a professor and he was scarcely present," I said. "Perhaps he is no professor at all. What proof do we have?"

My aunt produced her handkerchief and dabbed at glistening eyes.

"All right," I said. "I am sorry, deeply sorry."

I was always willing to apologize, for it really made no difference to me one way or the other. I stood up and kissed her lightly on the forehead.

"Now be a good boy, Nicholas, and go upstairs and get my decongestion tablets. My sinuses are thickening."

I returned to the parlor with her medication and a glass of water. When she had swallowed the pills and a bit of water, I removed the plate of ladyfinger crumbs, the tea service, and the water glass. I placed a cushion on the coffee table and lifted my aunt's slippered feet onto it. My aunt smiled and fell into thought.

"You really should lose some weight, Nicholas," my aunt said to me the following morning at the breakfast table. "It is unhealthy."

"And you are too thin," I said, ending the dialogue.

After breakfast, I suggested that she return promptly to bed.

"You look a little tired," I said, not really exaggerating.

"I did not sleep very well," she said.

"All right, then," I said. "Up we go."

I put her to bed and returned to the kitchen, disposing quickly of the breakfast dishes.

My aunt could have rested just as easily on the couch in the parlor, but in her bed upstairs she would drift into sleep. I waited until I was certain this had happened, and then slipped out of the house and made for a nearby café.

My aunt permitted me only a morning cup of coffee with breakfast and an evening cup after dinner, and so I drank the coffee I wanted to drink out of the house. I had acquired a great thirst for coffee, sometimes drinking as many as twenty to thirty cups in a single day.

My passion for coffee had been aroused several years earlier when my aunt was taken to the hospital for the removal of her gallbladder. Complications developed, and she stayed away for nearly three months.

I was at home, by myself. It had begun innocently enough. At first I stretched my morning cup of coffee to two, three, to four, to five. But soon there was no interval between my breakfast and luncheon coffee, my afternoon and my dinner coffee, my dinner and evening coffee. By the end of a month, I was consuming thirty cups a day. It was the first thing I put to my lips in the morning and the last taste in my mouth when I retired.

I had taken into my possession a galvanized, twenty-cup coffee-maker—the kind used at church socials—and was never far distant from it. Now, whenever I left the house for any reason, real or contrived, I always drank my fill of coffee.

When the waiter came back to my table, I ordered my fifth cup and sent him for a packet of cigarettes.

Over my coffee and my cigarettes, I decided that I would not go to the house on Fiskegard and look in on Essen. I finished my coffee and left the café, giving myself enough time to return home and relax briefly before waking my aunt for lunch. I stopped at a pharmacy along the way and bought aspirin and breath mints.

After lunch, my aunt did crossword puzzles, dozed, and drank tea, all from her bed, and I, when I was not running up and down the stairs with this or that, sat in the living room leafing through magazines and newspapers and thinking about Matthew Essen, the cartographer.

At dinner, I announced to my aunt that I thought I would visit the house the following morning, to see that Essen was comfortable and that everything was in order. My aunt applauded this plan. She asked me to convey her best wishes to Professor Essen.

After I had cleared the table and washed the dishes, we moved to the parlor and played cribbage. I put my aunt to bed at eight-thirty, gave her two sleeping tablets and a glass of warm milk, and went downstairs to the study.

My dead uncle's study was a striking room. The large windows on the north wall gave an excellent view of the lawn and the flower garden. But the heavy purple drapes were nearly always drawn now that there was no longer anyone to sit and look out at that landscape.

The three other walls held books, most of which were rare and expensively bound in emerald, burgundy, and black leather. When I would wander into the study as a child, my uncle would lift me up and, carrying me from shelf to shelf, encourage me to touch the bindings. But I had preferred not to touch them.

The desk was an elegant antique, oak and massive. There were several ornately carved pedestals whose marble tops held ferns and a wooden globe five feet in circumference, the tinted continents spinning on a brass axis. I dusted the room haphazardly once every two weeks, whirling the globe as I worked. I never vacuumed. The thick Persian rug absorbed dust indefinitely. Besides, my aunt never set foot in the study.

The desk drawers were still filled with my uncle's effects: letters, bills, receipts, an ivory letter-opener, gold pens, ink and blotters, his meerschaums and tins of specially-blended tobacco. And in the closet, his green smoking jacket still rested from the single hanger.

I was, after all, as much a stranger to my uncle as I was to his study. A few recollections and his effects, preserved in the room as if it were a museum, were all I had, a museum where I was slovenly custodian and unwelcome visitor.

It took me a long time to find what I was looking for. My uncle had his own peculiar way of cataloguing titles. But at last I found the facsimile editions of fifteenth-, sixteenth-, and seventeenth-century maps of Europe and Asia; the modern world atlas; and an interesting surprise—a rare volume containing a collection of Rasmussen's chartings of the Arctic. I also read the encyclopedia's entry on cartography. It was signed ''M.E.'' I studied the maps and charts until my eyelids grew heavy. Then I looked in on my aunt and went to bed.

My aunt elected to stay in bed the following day, complaining of her usual pains and discomforts. I brought her breakfast—prune juice, tea, richly buttered toast—up to her bed, and reported I thought it wise for me to get an early start over to the house on Fiskegard. If I were hungry, I would take a light breakfast at a restaurant. My aunt frowned, told me to wipe the silverware with my handkerchief, but proved too tired or ill to instruct me further.

I stopped at my usual café and ordered coffee. The café was several blocks from the house on Fiskegard. It was a bright, warm morning, an ideal day for a walk and visit, and there was no reason to hurry. I drank my coffees and smoked several cigarettes. Then I set out for the house.

When I arrived at the house, I would knock on the door and inquire if all were well. Essen would ask me in—perhaps there would be something amiss: a dripping faucet, a burned-out light bulb. Once inside, it would all be very simple. I would tell him there were several things that must be checked: the fuse box, the water heater, the furnace.

I could look around.

But somehow, once within view of the house, this plan, so correct the night before, seemed now to betray my true intention. I feared that Essen would see right through me.

And so, as I passed in front of the house, I quickened my step as if I were late for an important engagement. I even consulted my watch to add authenticity to the drama. And not for an instant did I look at the house. All these things I did so that Essen, who would be observing me from the window, who would see me pass, would not suspect anything.

I took a different route back to the café, drank coffee, smoked, and returned home by one o'clock, angry that I had not knocked on Essen's door. The plan was amply satisfactory. Besides, why should Essen be suspicious of me? Was there reason?

A new tenant must expect the landlord to make an initial inspection of the premises.

I popped a mint into my mouth and climbed the stairs to see my aunt. I went over to the bed and kissed her on the forehead. She awoke and smiled at me.

''How are you feeling?'' I asked, sitting down on the edge of the bed and taking her powdered hand.

''A little better, Nicholas,'' she said. ''It seems all I do is sleep.''

''Nonsense,'' I said. ''You sleep no more than anyone your age in your condition.''

''How is Professor Essen?''

''He was not at home when I called. I shall have to call again this afternoon. Or tomorrow,'' I said. ''Would you like lunch?''

''No, Nicholas. I believe I'll just do a crossword and then take a little nap.''

''Rest is the best thing,'' I said, and replaced her hand at her side.

I kissed my aunt on the cheek and closed the door behind me. Downstairs, I went into the study and examined the maps and charts I had taken from the shelves the night before. I also computed distances on the wooden globe. When I was sure my aunt was asleep, I went back to the café, drank coffee, and considered Essen and his maps.

After several cups, I requested a menu from the waiter. I ordered roll-mops and more coffee.

The café was populated by the regular customers, and these I acknowledged when their gaze met mine. While I waited for my food, I glanced at the newspaper but soon lost interest and put it aside. I lit up a cigarette and tried to imagine what Essen was doing that very instant.

I could see the walls of his study papered with maps of all kinds, each decorated with the cartographer's own cryptic markings —circles and arcs, lines connecting points, latitude and longitude notations. The desk was littered with books, calipers, other measuring devices. Essen was seated at the desk, bespectacled, bent over a map. He runs his finger over a section of the map, refers to a book, rechecks the map, and then makes an entry in his notebook. Pushed to the very edge of the cluttered desk is a plate with the remains of a sandwich.

My picture of the cartographer Essen in his study on a sunny afternoon, unmindful of the world outside his window, concerned only with his desk-top continents and oceans, was abruptly shadowed by the waiter placing my order before me. I glanced up to thank him, *and saw Essen*. He was seated alone at a table, drinking beer and reading a newspaper.

It was at great pains to me that I discovered Essen came to the café every day, usually around five o'clock, and drank one bottle of beer and read the newspaper. I would sit in the corner and watch him, stirring my coffee and rolling the ashes of my cigarette around in the ashtray.

Matthew Essen was a man of habit. While there was beer in the bottle, he would keep his glass half-filled: a sip of beer from the glass, a precise refill, and so on. He read the newspaper thoroughly while he drank, folding it this way and that, sometimes in half, sometimes in quarters. He often tore out an item and stuffed it into his bulging wallet. After he finished reading, he would arrange the pages in order once again, fold the newspaper into thirds, and drink the last of the beer. Then he would rise, pile some coins on the table, and put the folded newspaper in his coat pocket.

After weeks of this foolishness, I too rose from the table as Essen left the café and I admit I followed him as he made his way home. I followed him at a distance, twenty yards I would say. But Essen did not turn around. His hands thrust deep into his pockets, he kept his head down, counting the cracks in the sidewalk, I imagine, or measuring the length of his stride.

On we went through the weak yellow twilight. At times Essen's path seemed circuitous, seemed to be away from Fiskegard rather than toward it. But of course he knew what he was about, and at last we arrived at the house.

Essen entered. I paused. The living room light was turned on, and I could see the man moving slowly about. It was nearly dark, but the streetlamps were not yet lit. Then I moved: across the street . . . onto the pavement . . . closer to the house . . . onto the lawn . . . then to the window.

The walls in the living room were whiter than I had ever seen them. They seemed newly painted or freshly scrubbed. There was not a single piece of furniture in the room, not one book, not one map tacked to the wall.

Essen stood in the middle of the room, the hardwood floor under his feet and the white screaming ceiling over his head. He held his hands in front of him and slowly turned in all directions.

I watched at the window. I could have knocked at the door and demanded to be let in. As landlord, I had that right.

Crossed in Love by Her Eyes

JONATHAN BAUMBACH

"I think you ought to know I'm not going to marry you," I hear the baby say through the closed door of my study. "Marie and I are going together."

Who is Marie?

"So you and Marie are going together," she says, a thin note of pain breaking through the coolness of her tone.

"One of these days we might get married," he says.

A few minutes later the baby's mother comes into my study and asks if she might interrupt my unproductive self-absorption for a few minutes.

"I feel rejected," she says, laughing in a way that implies she thinks she ought to be amused but isn't. "Our baby's got another woman."

"It's my opinion it won't last."

"The worst of it is that the woman he's infatuated with—Marie, you may remember her, that streaky stacked blonde that sat for him a couple of times—won't have anything to do with him. Yesterday, when I asked her if she could baby-sit Friday night, the truth came out. She said she's no longer interested in babies, that they have nothing to teach her."

"Did you tell the baby what she said?"

"He's been so miserable as it is, mooning around the house and sighing in his pathetic way, I couldn't make it worse. Will you talk to him, man to man?"

"I'm not very good at that."

She blows me a kiss. "I was only kidding, you know, about the unproductive self-absorption. I think your self-absorption is as productive as anybody's."

Moments after the baby's mother leaves, almost as if it's been rehearsed, the baby takes her place in the room.

"When you're married," he asks after a point, "does that mean you have to sleep in the same bed as the other person?" He asks the question with both hands over his face, one eye peering through the slats of his fingers.

"Only if both people want to," I say.

"Well, both people do want to," he says, "and that's final." He does a parody of his father storming furiously out of a room.

He returns. "What about love?" he asks.

"What about it?"

His thumb, as if it were just passing by, finds its way into the tunnel of his mouth. It is apparent after a while that neither of us, with all goodwill, can think of anything to say. The word *love* has come between us. We study the silence for clues. Before I can put my thoughts into a sentence, he is gone.

Later that day, I get a phone call from a young woman who calls herself Marie.

"Your little son has invited me to share his bed," she says in a voice that strives for outrage.

"I've heard something about that," I say.

"Have you? In the last house I worked, the father used to come into my bed at night, pretending to be the son. As you might imagine, such a deception couldn't go on for long."

I say something to the effect that I can't imagine how such a deception could go on even once, though my remark, like the father she cites, seems to pass unnoticed.

"I'm prepared to give it a trial run, if you want me," she says. "My boyfriend's moved back in with his wife, and I'm at loose ends."

"It's the baby who wants you," I say. I am about to say something about talking it over with my wife, when the woman on the phone overrides me again.

"I get that," she says. "I only hope he's not too demonstrative. I really love babies, I really do, if they don't expect too much from you. I have a lot to give, you know, if not too much is asked."

An appointment is made for an interview.

Two weeks have passed since Marie has become a part of our household. The baby, whom I've hardly seen since the girl has come to live with us, patters glumly into my study and sits down on the floor with his back to me.

"Is something the matter?"

"Nothing's the matter."

"Are you sad because it's Marie's day off?"

He treats the question as if a reply were too self-evident to deserve notice. "Do you know what?" he says. "Marie won't sleep in my bed."

"She won't?" He has caught me, as he often does, in a moment of distraction.

"Maybe she will if I ask her. Will she? Tell her she has to, okay? Tell her if she doesn't . . . if she *doesn't*, she'll have to sleep with the dog and we don't even have a dog. Okay?"

I indicate, which is something we've been through before, that it's not within my power to compel Marie to sleep in his bed.

He is unconvinced. "I am angry at you," he says. "Also disappointed. And I'm not going to tell you the story I was going to tell you unless you say to Marie, 'Marie, you have to sleep with the baby. That's the rule.'"

"I'll tell her that you would like her to," I say. "How's that?"

He shakes his head in an aggrieved manner. "If you wanted her to sleep in *your* bed, I would tell her that she had to."

I lift him in the air and hug him, to which he offers an obligatory complaint. When I put him down, though he insists he is still angry with me and still doesn't like me, he offers me the story of what may have been his last night's dream. What follows is the baby's account.

THE STORY OF MY DREAM

The baby is in the bathroom taking off his overalls when a woman he's never seen before walks in, carrying a baby about his own size.

"Is it my brother?" the baby asks her.

She doesn't say anything, a reproachful quality in her silence, and puts the baby, who may or may not be the baby's brother, in the baby's place on the toilet.

"Isn't he a little prince!" the lady says.

The baby holds his nose politely, doing the best he can to ignore the foul air of the other.

A big dog comes into the bathroom, not the dog the baby doesn't have, but another one, a large white pig-faced dog with flowerlike spots. The dog sniffs the room, then in one large bite eats the other baby, toilet seat and all.

The lady is very sad. The baby tells her not to cry, but she is too busy crying to listen.

"We were going to be married," she says. "Why did that monstrous dog have to eat him?"

The baby sits on the toilet the way the other did, but fails to make the same kind of splash. Nothing he does seems to please the lady, who is moaning and blowing her nose.

In a voice that makes the windows rattle, the baby orders the dog to return the baby he swallowed. At that moment, a lion comes in and eats the dog.

"Take me away, sweet love," says the lady, "before something really bad happens. I like you better than that smelly baby."

She says her name is Marie, though she is a different Marie.

The baby reaches into the lion's mouth and pulls out the dog, then reaches into the dog's mouth to pull out the other baby, who seems a little smaller for having been eaten.

The lady is so overjoyed she announces that both babies can sleep in the same bed with her if they promise not to kick or wet. When they all go into the lady's room, they discover that someone has eaten her bed.

Marie requests a private interview. The request comes in the form of a note delivered to me by the baby.

I tell her as soon as we are alone that I don't like her using the baby as a go-between.

"I make such a mess of things," she says. "I'm terrible. I really am. I really am terrible."

"No, you're not."

"Oh, yes. It was a terrible thing to do. I'm always doing terrible things." She laughs with self-mockery, offering one or two jewel-like tears. "The baby, you know, your baby, like, doesn't dig me anymore. I told him yesterday that in my opinion it would be to his benefit to have more peer-group experiences, and now he won't talk to me and he won't even look at me."

"He doesn't like to be pushed into anything. Which doesn't excuse his being rude. If you like, I'll talk to him about it."

She throws back her head in a melodramatic pose. "You people make me so angry. No offense. But a baby needs some kind of structure from his adult models. You can't just let him do whatever he wants to do. . . . Now I've said too much and you're going to ask me to leave." Her face turns a deep red.

I indicate that we're receptive in this house to differences of opinion.

"He's really a love," she says. "He really is." She gets down on her knees and pleads with me to change my approach.

Her zealousness is hard to resist. "Have you talked to my wife?" I asked.

"I've always had more success with men," she says.

ANOTHER VERSION OF THE SAME STORY

The baby tiptoes into Marie's room while she is sleeping, or, in any event, giving the impression of being asleep, and asks her if she'd like to hear the story of the Sleeping Beauty. She's heard it too many times, she murmurs, for it still to be fresh and exciting for her. Besides, she's still, ummm, asleep.

"This is a different Sleeping Beauty," says the baby. "This Sleeping Beauty is awake."

Awake? The idea seems to interest the baby-sitter for a moment or two before it slips away into the dead spaces of unrequited loss.

"She's not really awake," says the baby, improvising. "I just said that to make the story sound different. Well, I'll tell it to you in a very low voice. Okay?"

The baby-sitter seems to agree to this compromise, though falls asleep in the middle of the story. When she wakes up—it is at the most surprising part of the story—she is in a bad mood and says that the baby has no business being in her bed. "Only people I ask to come into my bed are allowed to be there," she says. "Now go away."

The baby is tenacity itself, refuses dismissal, buries himself under the covers, attempts to charm.

Marie rolls him over the edge of the bed, like a sausage, tumbling him to the floor with a bang.

"I won't tell you any more stories," the baby says, refusing against disposition of habit to let her see the pain she has brought to his life.

When the baby takes himself away, Marie comes after him, saying she's sorry, inviting him back. "I'm always like this in the morning, baby. When I'm fast alseep, I can't bear to be touched. I'll tell *you* a story if you come back."

"Well, I'm not coming back," says the baby.

All day he refuses to look at the baby-sitter and he refuses to talk to her.

The next morning the baby forgets that he is angry with his baby-sitter and he asks her if he can sleep in her bed.

"Why don't you go out and play?" she says, turning her back on him.

The baby will not. The baby will not do anything she asks of him.

Contemplating the nature of things in the bathroom that adjoins my study, I overhear this exchange between the baby and Marie.

"Do you love me?"

"I love you."

"Do you really love me?"

Kissing sounds, or what I imagine to be the sounds of kissing, follow. Moments after that, I hear the door to the baby's room click shut.

Hours pass. Sibilant whispers snake through the house like a gas leak from some undeterminable quarter.

I am, for no reason I can explain to myself, disturbed by the behavior of the baby and the baby-sitter. It is just not polite, I tell myself, for the two of them to stay by themselves all day in a closed room. It is also, I should imagine, not particularly healthy to be locked in that way. After a point, as an act of responsibility, I knock gently on the baby's door. "Is everything all right in there?"

I am answered by giggles, which I find not a little shocking under the circumstances.

I mumble something about it perhaps not being a good idea, not being exactly healthy, spending a lot of time in a closed room, do you think? More giggles. Some boos.

"It happens to be a beautiful day out," I say, and, when I get no further answer, go out for a walk to prove my point.

My wife returns from shopping late in the afternoon, laden with packages. She laments the difficulty of finding anything in the stores she really likes. Everything is not quite right, has been created with someone else in mind.

I make no mention of the baby and Marie.

After my wife shows me the things she's bought, a pair of socks and a tie for me. She asks if anything interesting happened while she was gone.

"Nothing interesting," I say.

She calls the baby, and gets no answer. "Did they go out?" she asks.

"They're in his room."

"*Are* they?"

She is about to raise an eyebrow when Marie and the baby glide into the dining room, holding hands, the baby's face aglow. At the dinner table, they exchange secretive smiles, which do not, of course, escape notice. The baby sings to himself as he eats, his mother observing him with pained concentration.

After dinner, baby and baby-sitter mumble their excuses and disappear upstairs.

"They seem to be hitting it off," I say, to make conversation.

"*Do* they?" my wife says. She presses her face into my shoulder and holds on.

The next day, when the baby comes into the study to borrow my typewriter, I ask him what he does in his room with Marie when they have the door closed.

He shrugs. "Things," he says.

A certain awkwardness appears to have come between us. I inform him, looking out the window as I deliver my speech, that his mother and I would prefer him to keep the door slightly open when he is alone in the room with his sitter.

When he is gone, I regret having yielded to what seems to me unexamined impulse. I call him back. "Just because it disturbs us," I say, "it doesn't mean necessarily that it's wrong."

"If the door is open," he says, "someone might come in and someone might go out. We do Batman, Batwoman, and Batbaby in the room, and if the door is open, the baby could run away."

We punch each other and hug, having come to a better understanding of our respective situations.

"The Sleeping Beauty doesn't marry the prince that kisses her awake," says the baby. "She marries a different prince."

The baby comes into my study—Marie away on an emergency day off, her father sick—to tell me a new story.

In this story, when the Sleeping Beauty is awakened by the prince she is angry at him. *Why won't you let me sleep?* she says. *If I wanted to be kissed, I would have told you I wanted to be kissed.*

You looked so nice sleeping, I couldn't help it, the prince says. *I hate you,* she says. *Ohhhhh!*

The prince, who knows how the story used to end, asks the Sleeping Beauty if she'd like to get married.

Are you kidding, prince? she says. *I'm not going to marry someone who wakes me up when I'm trying to sleep.*

The prince regrets having wasted a kiss in a lost cause. He asks the Sleeping Beauty to marry him one more time in case she didn't mean her first refusal of him. The Sleeping Beauty says if there is one thing she can't stand it is a man who doesn't take her at her word, which is no.

The prince says that though there may be other Sleeping Beauties in his life, he'll always love this one the best. Then he goes away. The Sleeping Beauty is sad when he is gone, but after a while she falls asleep and dreams of a prince who will never wake her up.

He kisses too much," Marie complains to me. "I don't like so much kissing."

"You don't have to go into his room with him and close the door."

A small glint of surprise animates her otherwise impassive face. "If I had known that, I wouldn't be in the present predicament." She stands with her back to me. "I hope you won't hate me when I tell you this. There's another man in my life."

"Another man?"

She nods, lets out an exhausted sigh. "My boyfriend is insanely jealous. About little things. I had to tell him what was going on, and now he wants me to give up the job. He even talks of punching the baby in the nose."

"He sounds unbalanced to me," I say.

"He's a little unsure of himself," she says. "Like, he's had a difficult life. His real mother gave him up and he was brought up by foster parents, both of whom happened to be blind. It gave him a suspicious view of life. He wants to marry me."

"Your boyfriend?"

"The baby. For my boyfriend's sake, I think it would be best if I gave up the job."

For the baby's sake, I press her to reconsider her decision. Couldn't she stay until he got over his crush?

Again we misunderstand each other. She furrows her brow, a pucker of tension in her forehead. "My boyfriend?"

"The baby."

"And what about me, what about *my* feelings? The baby will grow up and find someone else. I'm twenty-two. In eight months, I'll be twenty-three." Tears fall. I put an arm on her shoulder.

There is a knock on the door. We freeze, unable to speak, watching the door slowly open.

"Oh, my God," she whispers. "What should I do?" She panics and rushes to my closet, opening the door and flinging herself in.

"Where's Marie?" the baby asks.

"She's hiding," I say. "See if you can find her."

He punches me in the side, a gesture more of impatience than of anger, the intent symbolic rather than violent. "I don't want to play that game."

I nod my head in the direction of the closet, give Marie away in silence.

"If you see Marie," the baby says in a loud voice, "tell her I'll be in my room with Polly."

The baby-sitter comes out of the closet. "So young and so unfaithful," she says, hurrying out, turning to give me a sharp look as if I were implicated in some deception practiced against her.

Crashing noises assail my concentration. The baby, red-eyed, furious, returns, saying, "I'm going to tell. Marie is throwing things at me."

"He started it," she says, following him in. "He called me a name. You tell him to stop calling me names."

"She tore up a picture I made of Polly and broke the arms off my Spider-Man model."

Their grievances against the other extend and intensify, a competition of complaint painful to witness. I stand between them, a truce-team to defend against further outbreak of violence.

"You ought to punish him," says Marie. "I think at the very least his television privileges ought to be taken away."

"I think *her* television privileges ought to be taken away," says the baby.

"I don't watch television that much," says Marie, looking at me as if I were the one who would deny her. "Still, I don't need to be told things like that. That's no way to treat someone who lives in your house. I'm not going to stay like that."

The baby goes with Marie to her room to help her pack. Forty minutes later she emerges with a valise under each arm, the baby at her side carrying one of her plants.

"I don't want her to go," says the baby after they've kissed good-bye two or three times.

"I don't want to leave my baby," she says. Her momentum apparently a determining factor, she moves irresistibly to the front door. "I'll come back and see you," she says.

"Will you come tomorrow?" the baby asks.

"I'll try," she says in a voice that acknowledges the odds to be prohibitively against succeeding. "I'm going to miss him."

"I don't want her to go," the baby says.

They say good-bye several more times, and when it seems that the procedure might go on indefinitely, Marie rushes out as if weeks late for an appointment she still hopes to keep. The baby waves and calls to her, banging on the window to catch her fleeting attention. We watch Marie walk away with her head bent forward as if she braces against a hurricane. In the distance, she seems almost as small as the baby himself.

"She was waving," the baby says, "but I couldn't see it because she was turned the other way." His thumb eases into his mouth, a ship entering port.

A week without word of her has passed since Marie's departure. The baby keeps an optimistic vigil on a footstool at the window. He pretends he is studying the weather for signs of change. Her name is not mentioned.

Occasionally, he sings the name to himself. *Marie Marie Marie . . . Marie Marie Marie . . . Marie Marie Marie.*

The day the baby stops watching for her at the window, Marie calls. Her voice is so low that I think at first she is calling from some great distance.

"Where are you?" I ask.

"Here," she says.

"Are you in the country?"

"I'm just a few blocks away." Her voice fading out: "Does he remember me?"

"Of course he remembers. Should I put him on?"

"I don't know. My head's so untogether. I'm such a mess. Maybe I'll come over and see him."

"Why don't you come over tonight and have dinner with us. Look, he'd love to talk to you."

"He would? If he does it quickly, maybe it'll be all right. My boyfriend's in the bathroom and he'll be out, unless he gets into what he's doing, in about five minutes."

I call the baby to the phone. "Is it anyone I know?" he asks, wary about taking the receiver, a stranger to its pleasures.

I step outside to give him privacy, and light up a cigar I was saving for a special occasion. Five minutes later, the baby comes out of my study walking backward. "Why did you give me the phone?" he asks.

"Didn't you speak to Marie?"

"I spoke to Marie," he says, "but it was a different Marie, not the Marie that was my baby-sitter."

"It's the same Marie," I say.

"It's not," the baby says.

One day the baby and his grandmother, walking in the park—this reported to me by the baby—see a young woman pushing a stroller who looks like Marie or who is Marie. The baby calls to her.

(What he is about to tell me is true, the baby says, though it may also be a dream.)

The presumed Marie turns her head in the direction of her name, appears to see nothing, or everything, and then goes on, somewhat more quickly than before.

The baby calls Marie's name again and gets no reaction except that a dog, apparently named Marie or something like it, comes running toward him.

The misinformed dog knocks the baby over and licks his nose. When the baby is restored to his feet, the other Marie is in the distance.

The baby continues his pursuit, stopping every once in a while to pick up his fallen grandma or to call out Marie's name. Each time he calls her name, Marie seems to increase her pace as if—is it possible?—she is actually running away from him.

Does she think he is someone else? Who could he be if not himself?

It is only me, he wants to say, but finds himself restrained by doubts.

His pursuit takes the baby through places he has never seen before outside of books and postcards.

After hours of relentless chase—the baby too tired even to call her name—he arrives at the stroller he saw Marie with, now deserted.

There is not another baby in the stroller (as he might have expected) but a large stuffed bear with a note pinned to its chest.

—To my darling darling Baby.
Love, Marie
P.S. As soon as I have the time,
I'll come and visit you.

"That's the end of the story," the baby says.

"Does she come and visit?" I ask.

"Does who come and visit?"

"Marie."

"When I'm older," the baby says.

The Barber

ROBERT NYE

"You'll know that brook of Tennyson's?" said the barber.

"Yes," I said.

"I come from haunts of coot and hern, I make a sudden sally, and sparkle out among the fern, to trickle down the valley," said the barber.

"Bicker," I said.

He was selecting sharper scissors. "I come from haunts of coot and hern," he said, turning back to my image in the mirror, "I make a sudden sally." He started cutting again. "And sparkle out among the fern." He cut quicker. "To trickle down the valley."

I didn't say anything.

"You'll know that brook in Tennyson's famous poem? His famous brook," said the barber.

"Yes," I said.

"Alfred Lord Tennyson," said the barber.

"Yes," I said.

"Well," said the barber, stopping cutting, "when my stepmother's best friend poisoned her third husband with the deadly nightshade, that was where she put him."

"In the brook?" I said.

"Alfred Lord Tennyson's," said the barber.

"I see," I said.

The barber leaned low over the back of the tiltable chair. "That was what she threw him in, that brook, in the famous poem."

I could not think of anything to say, so looked at myself unable to think of anything to say in the mirror. The trouble with wearing spectacles is that you have to remove them when your hair is being cut so that the barber can get at the hair which grows about your ears and then you cannot see what the other barber is doing to the other you in the mirror, especially when there is no sound of scissors. Now, however, the barber straightened up behind me, the scissors snapped again, and we were back in business.

"She turned left, you see," he said explaining. "Her name was Mrs. Fortescue. Daft thing to do." He sniffed as he snipped.

"Marrying Fortescue?" I asked.

"Dead stupid," said the barber. "If she'd turned right, she'd have been able to throw him in the bogs and morasses and nobody would have found him yet, you follow me? But she has to turn left and go and deposit him in Tennyson's brook."

He seemed to be to be spending a disproportionate amount of time on the one side of my head. It was the left side of my head in the mirror, so it would be the right side of my head out here. I should explain that on the right side of my head the hair is longer, growing combed from a parting on the left. But if the barber cut much more at that one side, there would be little or no distinction. I cleared my throat.

"Wasn't deep enough to cover a little bitsy kitten," said the barber, "let alone a brute like Mr. Fortescue."

"I see," I said.

The barber went on cutting at the left side of my head in the mirror. "Lord Tennyson would have gone by then," he said. "Left and gone away to be Poet Laureate by Lavinia Fortescue's day."

I smiled and nodded, then realized that the nod might have meant a jagged cut with the scissors on the better half of my head and also that I could not see my smile properly in the mirror. My eyes were not getting any better with the years. But I could feel the smile because some longish hanks of hair had fallen in the region of the rictus muscles and a smile must be there for these hairs were moving.

"So his brook went running on," I said.

The barber stopped cutting. "Beg pardon?" he said.

"His brook, Tennyson's, it would have been running on, still, even in Lavinia Fortescue's day."

"Men may come and men may go," said the barber, "but I go on forever." He started cutting again, quite fiercely. "Nevertheless, it never was deep enough to cover a kitten," he added.

He went on working at the left-hand side of my head in the mirror. "Do you know the secret of my success?" he asked as I was wondering whether again to clear my throat. "I inhale. I count to ten. I exhale. I inhale again and count to twenty while holding my breath. I exhale to the count of twenty." He stopped cutting. "All these exercises while performing these services," he said. "Speaking as a member of the public, you would never have guessed?"

"I don't think I would," I said.

The scissors began again. "There are certain sentences which also help," said the barber. His breath was warm upon my neck as he formed the words. "Formulae. I look in the mirror as I say them. I smile. I think beauty and power. I remember—let my eyes talk. I think brotherhood. I say to myself: You will dream tonight of Venus with two arms. You will awaken in the morning feeling good." He straightened up and dropped the scissors in a bowl. He reached for some electrical clippers.

"About Lavinia Fortescue," I began.

The electrical clippers bit into my neck. "Lord Byron," said the barber, "Lord George Gordon Byron, with a clubfoot, became an outstanding swimmer, marksman, horseman, lover, and finally a gentleman of letters."

"Which poems do you have in mind?" I said, irritated by the clippers.

"Criticism no longer bothers me," said the barber.

He was not the usual barber. The usual barber was away in hospital. The usual barber was a nice man called Mr. Milton and we usually talked about racehorses and sermons. Also Mr. Milton paid equal attention to both sides of my head in the mirror and never used electrical clippers.

"I want you to appreciate that I have consciously developed my missionary urges," said the barber.

"Like Byron?" I muttered.

The clippers ceased. "I beg sir's pardon?" said the barber.

"I think that's just fine," I said, "that side. But perhaps a little off the other . . ."

The clippers stabbed again in the one spot. "Consider," said the barber, his lips touching my right ear, which would be my left ear in

there where I was looking in the mirror, "consider. You congratulate your dog and his tail waggles. Pat a friend with praise and the thank-you in his eyes is that tell-tale wiggle."

"What happened to Fortescue's corpse?" I demanded.

The barber stopped his electric aid. He returned to the bowl, retrieved the scissors, wiped them on his white coat and went round the back of me again. His foot pressed a pedal on the floor and the tiltable chair went back. "I want you to know thyself," he said, leaning over my upturned face. "Is eating eggs a happy occasion for sir these days? Does he respect the various ministers of state?"

"A haircut," I said. "I only came in . . ."

"Is sir really breathing?" said the barber, starting on my beard. "Is he exhaling and thinking love and remembering about Lord Byron swimming the Hellespont?" The scissors were searching for hairs in my nostrils. "Mohammed used controlled kindness," said the barber.

"Mr. Milton usually . . ." I said.

There was a silence. The barber did my moustache in one cut and went on cutting cutting at my beard. "Sir?" he said.

"Oh, nothing," I said. "Nothing."

The scissors scraped across my throat. "Never never never say that," said the barber. "Not never nothing." He straightened up. I think he was standing to attention behind me although the barber in the mirror was no more than a ghost. "Inhale," he said crisply. "Exhale." He breathed in and out like a soldier. I could feel his breath behind me. I could not see him properly in the mirror.

"Think Mohammedism," he said. "Experience grass."

The chair swung upright again. The barber must have pressed the pedal on the floor while standing to attention. Now he brushed past me and was saying casually over his shoulder as water rushed hotly into the basin, "Incidentally, have you reached maturity yet?"

"I do not require a shampoo," I protested.

"Know how to cry to relieve your tensions?" said the barber.

"Honestly," I said, "honestly."

"Jesus," the barber said sternly, "wept."

I realized that I would have to let him wash my hair. As he pummeled my scalp with liquid soap squeezed from a plastic bottle, I heard him saying, "I like your sincerity, sir; it's refreshingly unusual." He said nothing else until I was upright again, the ordeal of the washing over, a towel about my head.

The barber leaned back on the sink and lit a black cigarette. I think it was black although without your glasses you never can be sure. It smelled black just as the bottle had sounded plastic. Here was a barber smoking on the job. Mr. Milton would not have done that. "You noticed when I said your sincerity was refreshingly unusual and I liked it?" he inquired.

"Yes," I muttered.

"I didn't mean it," said the barber brightly. "But it's part of the technique."

"I see," I said. "Controlled kindness."

I started to unwind the towel. The barber leaned forward easily and slapped it back in place. "I think sir just doesn't sufficiently know himself."

He threw his half-smoked cigarette into the sink, twirled on a tap, and it was ruined in a hiss. He took a hair-dryer from the cupboard. "Voices are like gardens," said the barber, testing the heat against his hand. "When sir gets home, I want him to talk to himself. Describe the inside of your head. Play it straight, no literature. Even though you can't sing, add another note to your monotone."

He swung round and pointed the dryer at me. A blast of scalding hot air hit my head. "A, E, I, O, U," sang the barber. "Tighten your buttocks as if you were holding a silver thimble between them."

I pretended to be able to consult my watch without my glasses. "Heavens," I said, "is that the time? I . . ."

The dryer was cut off. The barber folded the cord. He put his box of tricks away in silence. Then, still with his back to me, while I sat wondering if I could reach for my spectacles and consider in the mirror what he had done to me out here, he said, in a low voice, "Sir is ironical."

"Certainly," I said. I was appalled to see from the mirror that the haircut was perfect and the beard-trim also. "Forgive me," I said, stepping from the chair. "I'm not worth a haircut."

The barber smiled. "Sir is ironical," he said. "Sir is an ironical sir. Seventy-five pence."

I gave him a pound note and pretended not to be waiting for the change. There was none.

"Knight murdered a monk in the old days," said the barber as I took my coat. "King Henry the Eighth is coming down the Thames, so the knight swims out on his horse and asks the king's forgiveness, his royal mercy, as you would say." He watched me as I struggled with the arms. "King Henry sees his knight come swimming up," the barber went on. "Quite impressed, he is, and he says, 'All right, son, I'll let you off this time, don't let it happen again is all I ask, else the monasteries will be dissolving all over, you know the type of thing.' " I had my coat on now. But the barber's hand came out like a snake and snatched my hat from the rack before I could add it to my appearance. He began banging it and dusting it against his thigh. "Knight swims back with his horse

to the Isle of Sheppey," he said, banging. "Coming up out of the Thames, he meets this old witchwoman, you know the type of person, and she says, 'That horse will be the death of you.' So our knight turns round sharpish and shoots his horse, just like that." He gave a final slap with my hat, which turned it inside out, then handed it to me.

"He was superstitious," said the barber, "so he shoots this horse and buries it in the sand then and there on the island shore and goes off laughing, just like you, sir."

I was making for the door, although I was not laughing. "Seven years later," said the barber very softly, and something in his voice made me stop on the step, "seven years later he's coming home along the same shore, drunk, and he sees the horse's head sticking up out of the sand. Not a ghost, its skull, you follow me? 'Ho,' says the knight, 'I saw to you all right, you bugger.' And he gives his horse's skull one hell of a sweet kick."

The barber looked at me. I looked away.

"Bone of the horse's skull penetrates the knight's foot," said the barber. "He dies inside a fortnight of the gangrene."

"Good afternoon," I said.

"Good afternoon," replied the barber.

Behold the Crazy Hours of the Hard-Loving Wife

HILMA WOLITZER

Sundays

Howard is the beauty in this family. Even the mirrors in our apartment are hung at his eye level. I don't mind. What's wrong with a little role reversal, anyway? What's so bad about a male sex object, for a change? That ability to sprout hair like dark fountains, the flat tapering planes of their buttocks and hips, and oh, those *hands*, and erections pointing the way to bed like road-markers.

Besides, I have my own good points, not the least of them my disposition. Sunny, radiant, I wake with the same dumb abundance of hope every day. The bed always seems too small to contain both me and that expansion of joy.

It's only Thursday or Sunday. It's only my own flesh, pale and sleep-creased and smelling like bread near my rooting nose. Nothing special has happened, for which I am grateful. Anything might happen, for which I am expectant and tremblingly ready.

On the other hand, Howard is depressed, hiding in the bed-clothes, moaning in his dream. Even without opening my eyes, I can feel the shape of his mood beside me. Then my eyes do open. Ta da! Another gorgeous day! Just what I expected. The clock hums, electric, containing its impulse to tick, the wallpaper repeats itself around the room, and Howard burrows into his pillow, refusing to come to terms with the dangers of consciousness.

My hand is as warm and as heavy as a baby's head, and I lay it against his neck, palm up. If I let him sleep, he would do it for hours and hours. That's depression.

Years ago, my mother woke me with a song about a bird on a windowsill and about sunshine and flowers and the glorious feeling of being alive that had nothing in the world to do with the sad still

life of a school lunch and the reluctant walk in brown oxfords, one foot and then the other, for six blocks. It had nothing to do with that waxed ballroom of a gymnasium and the terrible voice of the whistle that demanded agility and grace where there were only clumsy confusion and an enormous desire to be the other girl on the other team, the one leaping in memory toward baskets and dangling ropes.

I didn't want to get up, either—at least not until I had grown out of it, grown away from teachers, grown out of that thin body in an undershirt and lisle stockings and garter belt abrasive on white hipbones. I would get up when I was good and ready, when it was all over and I could have large breasts and easy friendships.

Howard blames his depression on real things in his real life because he doesn't believe in the unconscious. At parties where all the believers talk about the interpretation of dreams, about wish-fulfillment and surrogate symbols, Howard covers his mouth with one hand and mutters, "Bullshit!"

Is he depressed because his parents didn't want him to be born, because his mother actually hoisted his father in her arms every morning for a month, hoping to bring on that elusive period? Not a chance!

Is he sad because his sister was smarter in school, or at least more successful, or because she seduced him to the point of action and then squealed? Never!

He is depressed, he says, because it starts to rain when he's at a ball game and the men pulling the tarpaulin over the infield seem to be covering a grave. He is sad, he says, because his boss is a prick and the kid living upstairs roller-skates in the kitchen.

Ah, Howard. My hand is awake now, buzzing with blood, and it kneads the flesh of his neck and then his back, works down through the warm tunnel of bedclothes until it finds his hand and squeezes hard. "It's a gorgeous day, lover! Hey, kiddo, wake up and I'll tell you something."

Howard opens his eyes, but they are glazed and without focus. "Huhhnn?"

"Do you know what?" Searching my head for therapeutic news.

His vision finds the room, the morning light, his whole life. His eyes close again.

"Howard. It's Sunday, the day of rest. The paper is outside, thick and juicy, hot off the press. I'll make waffles and sausages for breakfast. Do you want to go for a drive in the country?"

"Oh, for Christ's sake, will you leave me alone! I want to sleep."

"Sleep? Sweetheart, you'll sleep enough when you're dead."

I see *that* idea roll behind his eyelids. Death. What next?

The children whisper like lovers in the other bedroom.

"Come on sleepyhead, get up. We'll visit model homes. We'll look in the paper for some new ones." I pat him on the buttocks, a loving but fraternal gesture, a manager sending his favorite man into the game.

Why am I so happy? It must be the triumph of the human spirit over genetics and environment. I know the same bad things Howard knows. I have my ups and downs, traumas, ecstasies. Maybe this happiness is only a dirty trick, another of life's big come-ons. I might end up the kind who can't ride on escalators or sit in chairs that don't have arms. Who knows?

But in the meantime I sing as I whip up waffle batter, pour golden juice into golden glasses, while Howard sits in a chair dropping pages of The *Times* like leaves from a deciduous tree.

I sing songs from the Forties, thinking there's nothing in this life like the comfort of your own nostalgia. I sing *Ferry-Boat Serenade*, I sing *Hut-Sut Rallson on the Riller-ah*. The waffles stick to the iron. "Don't sit under the apple tree with anyone else but me," I warn Howard, willing the waffle and coffee smells into the living room, where he sits like an inmate in the wintry garden of a small sanitorium.

"BREAKFAST IS READY!" I have the healthy bellow of a short-order cook.

He shuffles in, still convalescing from his childhood.

The children come in too, his jewels, his treasures. They climb his legs to reach the table, to scratch themselves on his morning beard. Daddy, my daddy, and he runs his hands over them, a blind man trying to memorize their bones. The teakettle sings, the sun crashes in through the window, and my heart will not be swindled.

"What's the matter, Howie? If something is bothering you, *talk* about it."

He smiles, that calculated, ironic smile, and I think that we hardly talk about anything that matters.

I waited all my life to become a woman, damn it, to sit in a kitchen and say grown-up things to the man facing the children, words that would float like vapor over the heads of the children. Don't I remember that language from my own green days, code words in Yiddish and pig latin, and a secret but clearly sexual jargon that made my mother laugh and filled me with a dark and trembling longing and rage?

Ix-nay, the *id*-kay.

Now I want to talk over the heads of *my* children, in the modern language of the cinema. There are thousands of words they wouldn't understand and would never remember, except for the rhythm and the mystery.

Fellatio, Howard. *Vasectomy*.

He rattles the Real Estate section and slowly turns the pages.

"Well, did you find a development for us? Find one with a really inspired name this time."

I try so hard to encourage him. Looking at model homes has become a standard treatment for Howard's depression. For some

reason we believe the long drive out of the city, the ordered march through unlived-in rooms, restores him. Not that *we* want to live in the suburbs. How we laugh and poke one another at the roped-off bedrooms hung in velvet drapery, the plastic chickens roosting in warm refrigerators. The thing is, places like that confirm our belief in our own choices. We're *safe* in the city, in our tower among towers. Flyspecks, so to speak, in the population.

On other days, we've gone to Crestwood Estates, Seaside Manor (miles from any sea), to Tall Oaks and Sweet Pines, to Châteaux Printemps, and Chalets-on-the-Sound.

But the pickings are slim now. All the worthwhile land has been gobbled up by speculators, and those tall oaks and sweet pines fallen to bulldozers. There are hardly any developments left for our sad Sundays. The smart money is in garden apartments and condominiums, cities without skylines. Maybe later, when we are older, we'll visit the Happy Haven and the Golden Years Retreat, to purge whatever comes with mortality and the final vision.

But now Howard is trying. "Here's one," he says. *"Doncastle Greens. Only fifty minutes from the heart of Manhattan. Live like a king on a commoner's budget."*

"Let me see!" I rush to his side, ready for conspiracy. "Hey, listen to this. *Come on down today and choose either a twenty-one-inch color TV or a deluxe dishwasher, as a bonus, absolutely free!* Howie, what do you choose?"

But Howard chooses silence, will not be cajoled so easily, so early in his depression.

I hide the dishes under a veil of suds and we all get dressed. The children are too young to care where we are going, as long as they can ride in the car, the baby steering crazily in her car seat and Jason contemplating the landscape and the faces of other small boys poised at the windows of other cars.

The car radio sputters news and music and frantic advice. It is understood that Howard will drive there and I will drive back.

He sits forward, bent over the wheel, as if visibility is poor and the traffic hazardous. In fact, it's a marvelous, clear day and the traffic is moving without hesitation past all the exits, past the green signs and the abandoned wrecks like modern sculpture at roadside, past dead dogs, their brilliant innards squeezed out onto the divider.

Jason points, always astounded at the first corpse, but we are past it before he can speak. It occurs to me that everywhere here there are families holding dangling leashes and collars, walking through the yards of their neighborhoods, calling, Lucky! Lucky! and then listening for that answering bark that will not come. Poor Lucky, deader than a doornail, flatter than a bath mat.

I watch Howard, that gorgeous nose so often seen in profile, that crisp gangster's hair, and his ear, unspeakably vulnerable, waxen and convoluted.

And then we are there. Doncastle Greens is a new one for us. The builder obviously dreamed of moats and grazing sheep. Model No. I, The Shropshire, recalls at once gloomy castles and thatched cottages, Richard III and Miss Marple. Other cars are already parked under the colored banners when we pull in.

The first step is always the brochure, wonderfully new and smelly with printer's ink. The motif is British, of course, and there are taprooms and libraries as opposed to the dens and funrooms of Crestwood Estates, les salons et les chambres de Châteaux Printemps.

Quelle savvy!

The builder's agent is young and balding, busy sticking little flags into promised lots on a huge map behind his desk. He calls us folks. "Good to see you, folks!" Every once in a while he rubs his hands together as if selling homes makes one cold. During his spiel I try to catch Howard's eye, but Howard pretends to be listening. What an actor!

We move in a slow line through Model I, behind an elderly couple. I know we've seen them before, at Tall Oaks perhaps, but there are no greetings exchanged. They'll never buy, of course, and

I wonder about their motives, which are probably more devious than ours.

Some of the people, I can see, are really buyers. One wife holds her husband's hand as if they are entering consecrated premises.

I poke Howard, just below the heart, a bully's semaphore. I can talk without moving my lips. "White brocade couch on bowlegs," I mutter. "Definitely velvet carpeting." I wait, but Howard is grudging.

"Plastic-covered lampshades," he offers, finally.

I urge him on. "Crossed rifles over the fireplace. Thriving plastic dracaena in the entrance." I snicker, roll my eyes, do a little soft shoe.

But Howard isn't playing. He is leaning against the braided ropes that keep us from muddying the floor to the drawing room, and he looks like a man at the prow of a ship.

"Howard?" Tentative. Nervous.

"You know, kiddo, it's not really that bad," he says.

"Do you mean the *house*?"

Howard doesn't answer. The older man takes a tape measure from his pocket and lays it against the dark molding. Then he writes something into a little black notebook.

The buyers breathe on our necks, staring at their future. "Oh, *Ronnie*," she says, an exhalation like the first chords of a hymn. I would not be surprised if she kneels now or makes some other mysterious or religious gesture.

"One of these days," Howard says, "*pow,* one of us will be knocked on the head in that crazy city. Raped. Strangled."

"Howie. . . ."

"And do we have adequate bookshelves? You know I have no room for my books."

The oak bookshelves before us hold all the volumes, A through Z, of the *American Household Encyclopedia.*

The old man measures the doorframe and writes again in his book. Perhaps he will turn around soon and measure us, recording his findings in a feathery hand.

Jason and another boy discover one another and stare like mirrors. What would happen if we took the wrong one home, bathed him and gave him Frosted Flakes, kissed him and left the night-light on until he forgot everything else and adjusted? The baby draws on her pacifier and dreamily pats my hair.

Everyone else has passed us and Howard is still in the same doorway. I pull on his sleeve. "The baby is getting heavy."

He takes her from me and she nuzzles his cheek with her perfect head.

We proceed slowly to the master bathroom, the one with the dual vanities and a magazine rack embossed with a Colonial eagle.

"Howie, will you look at this. His and *hers.*"

He doesn't answer.

We go into the bedroom itself, where ghosts of dead queens rest on the carved bed. "Mortgages. Cesspools. Community living." I face him across the bed and hiss the words at him, but he does not even wince. He looks sleepy and relaxed. I walk around the bed and put my arm through his. "Maybe we ought to join Marriage Encounter, after all. Maybe we look in the wrong places for our happiness, Howard."

He pats my hand, distracted but solicitous. I walk behind him now, a tourist following a guide. At the olde breakfast nooke, I want to sit him down and explain that I am terrified of change, that the city is my hideout and my freedom, that one of us might take a lover, or worse.

But I am silent in the pantry, in the wine cellar and the vestibule, and we are finished with the tour of the house, evicted before occupation. We stand under the fluttering banners and watch the serious buyers reenter the builder's trailer. Howard shifts the baby from arm to arm as if she interferes with his concentration. Finally, he passes her to me without speaking. He puts his hands into his pockets and he has that dreaming look on his face.

"*I'll* drive back," I say, as if this weren't preordained.

There is more traffic now, and halfway home we slow to observe the remains of an accident. Some car has jumped the guardrail and there is a fine icing of shattered glass on the road.

"Do you *see*?" I say, not sure of my moral.

But Howard is asleep, his head tilted against the headrest. At home, I can see that he's coming out of it. He is interested in dinner, in the children's bath. He stands behind me at the sink and he has an erection.

Later, in bed again, I get on top, for the artificial respiration I must give. His mouth opens to receive my tongue, a communion wafer. I rise above him, astounded at the luminosity of my skin in the half-light.

Howard smiles, handsome, damp with pleasure, yes, with *happiness,* his ghosts mugged and banished from this room.

"Are you happy?" I must know, restorer of faith, giver of life. "Are you happy?"

And even as I wait for his answer, my own ghosts enter, stand solemn at the foot of the bed, thin girls in undershirts, jealous and watchful, whispering in some grown-up language I can never understand.

Nights

What men must learn is that there are some women in this world who are never satisfied, who move through their homes with the restlessness of dayworkers. Even their blood seems restless, rising and falling so that they are alternately pale or flushed, and suffer from giddiness and capricious moods. I am one of these women.

Sometimes Howard will ask, "What's the *matter* with you?" or "What do you want?" But he knows that these are only mind-mutterings. I want nothing. I want everything. I am given to looking through windows like a sentinel, fumbling through the mail as if for secret messages, picking up the telephone with renewed expectancy.

Hello, hello—but it is always someone I know.

Staring out through the bedroom window in the middle of the night, I wish that everyone else in the complex would wake too, that lights would go on with the easy magic of stars in a Disney sky. I look at Howard, who is asleep, and I can see his eyes moving under those thin lids as he follows his dreams. I lean toward him, look more closely, and see his nostrils flare with his breath.

"Howard? Howard, I can't sleep."

He sighs deeply and his hands open at his sides as if in supplication, but he continues to sleep.

In the next room, the children are asleep.

Across the city, my mother and father sleep on high twin beds, like sister and brother. There is always a night-light, as decorous as a firefly, burning in their hallway, so that my father can find his way to the bathroom. There is a picture of me on the dresser in their bedroom, and another of the children. My father sleeps with his socks on, even in summer. My mother keeps a handkerchief tied to the strap of her nightgown.

Do they dream of each other?

Does Howard dream of me?

If I ever sleep, I will have baroque dreams that would have challenged Freud, dreams that could be sold to the movies.

But I cannot sleep.

On other nights Howard pulls himself awake for a moment, glares at the clock, at my bedside light, at the pile of magazines, suitable for an invalid, balanced on my chest. "For God's sake, go to sleep," Howard hisses, as if it were a matter of choice.

Once I complained to my mother about my insomnia. She is old-fashioned and believes in remedies. "Drink milk," she urged. "Do calisthenics. Open the window."

My father, who likes to get a word in edgewise, said, "Protein. Minerals."

We never questioned his meaning.

But I am here alone in this stillness in which I have a dog's sense of hearing, can hear beds creak, distant telephones, letters whispering down mail slots on every floor.

Who writes letters at this hour? Who is calling?

The dead eye of the television set faces me. If I turn it on, I will find old movie stars carrying on business as usual, stranded forever in time with their hairstyles and clothes. There will be a comedy and I will laugh, taking deep breaths. I will grow sleepy, child-sleepy, milk-warm and drifty, with arms heavy and legs that pull me down. Maybe there will be news, even at this hour. Isn't it daytime in China, midnight in California? Surely there will be bad news and the heavy voice of the commentator to intone it. Ladies and gentlemen, here is some bad news that has just come in. . . . Howard will wake, the children will cry out in their sleep, the old lady downstairs will bang on her ceiling with a broom.

I walk to the window again and there *are* other lights on in the complex—two or three.

At parties we go to, everyone complains of being an insomniac. Women insist they haven't slept in years. One man walks the room repeating, "Three hours, *three hours*," to anyone who will listen. He has a built-in alarm that never allows him to sleep a minute longer. That's too bad, say the women who never sleep, but they are insincere. Another man suggests it is guilt that will not let us sleep, but the women unite against him. Guilt? The truly guilty sleep to escape their guilt. Ask the ones with old mothers in nursing homes. Ask the ones whose children wet the beds, the ones whose husbands are listless or worse. Someone changes the subject. We refill glasses.

It is not even too hot to sleep. It is a perfect summer night, with air rushing in through the screens. The sheets aren't sticky and hot.

Howard is sprawled in wonderful sleep.

I sit on the floor and place myself in the half-lotus position and clasp my hands behind my head. I draw my breath in deeply and then slowly let it out, lowering my right elbow to the floor. Then the left elbow. There is a carpet smell as I lower my head. It is not unpleasant. I look under the bed and see one of the children's shoes lying on its side. I crawl there to get it and then I lie on my back, watching the changes in the box spring as Howard shifts his weight. From my position under the bed, I can see under the dresser and the night tables, where there are glints of paper clips and other lost and silvery things. There is a photograph that has fallen from the frame of the large mirror, and I crawl across the floor and reach for it. It is a picture of a group of friends at a party. We are all holding cocktail glasses and cigarettes. The women are sitting upright to make their breasts seem larger, and one of the men has his hand across his wife's behind.

We are all going to grow old. The men will have heart attacks, the women will lose the loyalty of tissue in chins and breasts.

I want to go to the mirror and raise my nightgown and look at myself for reassurance. But I walk into the children's room instead. Jason sleeps well and is a handsome child, and yet I am filled with sorrow at the sight of him. I see that it is all false—the posters of astronauts, the books to teach him of birds and fishes and flowers. The baby is in her crib, legs and arms opened as if sleep were a lover she welcomes. The Japanese mobile trembles a warning, and I tiptoe out and go into the kitchen.

I choose soft, quiet foods that will not disturb the silence: raisins, cheese, marshmallows. I put the last marshmallow on the end of a fork and toast it over the gas range.

I do not believe it, but I tell myself that I will be able to sleep with a full stomach. I take my mother's advice and drink a glass of milk.

If I had a dog, if we were allowed to keep pets in the complex, the dog might be a companion when I cannot sleep. I had a dog when I was a child. When it was a few years old, I realized with horror I had established an irrevocable relationship that could only end in death. From this grew the knowledge that death was true of all relationships—friendships, marriage. I began to treat the dog indifferently, even cruelly sometimes, pushing him away when he jumped up to greet me. But it didn't matter. The dog died and I mourned him, anyway. For a long time I kept his dish and a gnawed rubber bone.

I suppose a dog awakened in the middle of the night would not understand. He would probably want to eat and be taken for a walk. And of course Howard is allergic to animal hair.

We have a bowl of goldfish in the kitchen. There are two, one with beautiful silver overtones to his scales. There is a plant in their bowl and colored pebbles at the bottom. The fish swim as if they had a destination, around and around and around.

I shut the kitchen light and go back into the bedroom. I yawn twice, thinking, well, that's a good sign. Sleep can't be very far away and the main thing is not to panic. I climb into bed and Howard rolls away to his side.

God, it's the silence, the large silence and the small, distant sounds. If I could talk, even shout, I might feel better. "I can't sleep and life stinks on ice," I whisper. Silence. I raise my voice slightly. "I can't sleep and tomorrow, *today*, I won't be able to stand anything." Silence. "Howard, my mother and father didn't want me to marry you. My mother said that you have bedroom eyes. My father said that you were not ambitious."

A song I have not heard in years comes into my head. First I mouth the words. Then I try to whisper the tune. But my voice is throaty and full.

"Shhhh," Howard warns in his sleep.

Oh think, think. Come up with something else. But the song is stuck there. Doo-bee doo dee-dee, a song I never really liked. I try to overwhelm it with something symphonic. So this is what I've come to, I think, and the song leaves my head, a bird from a tree. Instantly other birds flock in: shopping lists, the twenty-twenty line on the eye chart, a chain letter to which I never responded. Do not break the chain or evil will befall your house. Continue it and long life and good health will be yours to enjoy and cherish. In eight weeks you will receive 1120 picture postcards from all over the world.

Will I?

Learned men wear copper bracelets. My mother weeps over broken mirrors. Hearts are broken, bones. They crack in the silence of the night.

Somewhere, in Chicago or St. Louis or Silver Springs, my lover sleeps in a blond Hollywood bed. He talks in his sleep and his wife promptly wakes, thin-lipped, alert. In a careful whisper, she questions him. "Who?" she asks. "When? Where?"

My lover mumbles something she cannot make out.

She plucks gently at the hair on his chest, in shrewd imitation of my style. "Who?" she asks again.

In Howard's dream he is in the war again. His eyes roll frantically and his legs brace against the sheets.

I whisper, "We're pulling out now, men."

His head swivels.

"For Christ's sake, keep down."

His hands grope at his side, sling a rifle.

"Aaaargh," I say. "They got me. Die, you yellow bastards!"

The bed shakes with his terror.

"Shhhhh," I say. "It's only a dream. Only a dream."

But he'll die anyway. In this bed, perhaps.

Howard in a coffin. Howard in the earth. Good-bye, Howard.

He sighs, resigned.

I walk to the foot of the bed and stand in a narrow bar of moonlight. My white nightgown is silver and my arms glow as if they were wet. "Look at this, Howard," and I grasp the hem of my gown and twirl it around my body. Then I lift myself onto the balls of my feet and turn slowly, catching my reflection in the mirror, spectral, lovely.

I dip, arch and move across the floor in a silent, voluptuous ballet. "Hey, get a load of this," and I do something marvelously intricate, unlearned. My feet move like small animals. Wow, I think, and Howard flings himself onto his stomach in despair.

I am breathing hard now and I sit in the rocking chair and think of my lover again. His wife has given up the inquisition, but now she can't sleep, either. She goes to the window in Chicago or Silver Springs and looks bitterly at her property, at her pin oaks and her hemlock, at the children's swings hung in moonlight, at telephone wire stretching into infinity. She pats the curlers on her head and goes into the next room to look at her children.

Across town, my father walks to the bathroom.

"What's the matter?" my mother asks.

"Nothing. What do you think?"

Before he comes back to bed, she is plunged into sleep again.

Howard, Howard, Howard. Prices are going up. The house is on fire. My lover is dying of something awful.

My lover is dying, his wife at his side. She is wearing a hat and a coat with a fox collar. She leans over him. "Who?" she persists, and her fierce breath makes the oxygen tent flutter like Saran Wrap.

"Howard. My lover is dying in St. Louis or Chicago. No one really cares, Howard."

Real tears fill my eyes and then roll down my cheeks.

I climb into bed again. If I had a hobby, something to take my mind away. A dog.

I yawn, lowering myself carefully to the pillow. Ah, almost there, almost there, I tell myself in encouragement. One minute you're awake and the next you're in dreamland.

I shut my eyes.

That's right. Shut your eyes. Here comes Sandman. Here comes dream dust. Here comes.

My eyes are shut tight. My hands are clenched.

I hear something. There is a noise somewhere in the apartment. Maybe I am asleep and only dreaming noise. Maybe I hear the goldfish splashing in their bowl. My eyes open.

What's that? What's that?

Oh, God.

The whole damn world sleeps like a baby—the superintendent of our building, the new people on the tenth floor, old boyfriends and their wives, their mothers and fathers, their babies, their dogs.

Everyone sleeps.

All of the bastards at those parties are liars. They sleep too, secretly, with cunning, maybe with their eyes open, for all I know. They sleep, they give in, they go under—into the blue and perfect wonder of sleep.

I am the only one here. I am the only one left in the dark world, the only one who cares enough to stay awake the long and awful night.

Overtime

Howard's first wife wouldn't let him go. Her hold on him wasn't even sexual—I could have dealt with that. It would have been an all-out war and of course I would have won. There is something final about me, and steadying.

I wondered why he was attracted to her in the first place. It could only have been her pathos. Renee is little, her flesh stingy and pale. She has large light freckles everywhere, as if she can't decide to be one color or the other. Her bones used to stab him during the night and he couldn't sleep. Howard says I am the first woman he can really *sleep* with, in the literal sense of the word. When he loves me, he says that he feels as if he is embracing the universe, that a big woman is essential to his survival. He feeds me tidbits from his plate at dinner, to support my image and keep up my strength.

Renee called up night and day. She left cryptic messages for Howard. She even left messages with Jason, who was only three or four at the time. Jason called her Weeny, insinuating her further into our lives with that nickname. "Weeny needs ten," he would tell me.

We gave Renee plenty of money, although she denied all legal rights to alimony. They were only married seven months and she decided she didn't deserve alimony after such a short relationship, that you can't even collect unemployment insurance unless you've been on the job for a while. But we were always giving her money, anyway—ten here, five there. Ostensibly, they were loans, but Renee was hard-pressed to repay them.

I suggested to Howard that we adopt her, that it would be cheaper, taxwise and all, but Howard seemed to really consider the idea, getting that contemplative look in his eye, chewing his dinner in a slow, even rhythm. I imagined Renee living with us, another bed in the converted dinette where the children sleep.

I knew intuitively when Renee was calling. The telephone had a certain insistence to its ring, as if she were willing me to answer it. She wanted to know if Howard remembered a book she used to have, something she was very sentimental about. Could he possibly have taken it by mistake when they split up? Would I just take a look on the shelf while she held on, it has a blue cover. She called to say that she had swollen glands, that she'd been very tired lately and in fluorescent light she could see right through to her bones.

We sent her ten dollars for the doctor. We sent her five for a new book.

At night, when the children were in bed, talcum-sweet and overkissed, Howard and I staggered into the living room to talk. This was the best time of the day. We couldn't afford real analysis, so we did one another instead. I was quite classical in my approach: I went back to my childhood, digging up traumas, but Howard liked to deal with the recent past. He took his old life out like a stamp collection and we looked at it together. Howard talked about his first marriage as if he had just begun then himself, and as if he expected me to feel some nostalgia and regret for the poverty of their relationship. I did. I saw them in their marriage bed, ill-fitting like two parts of different jigsaw puzzles. I listened to Renee talk him out of sleep, pry him from his dreams with the wrench of her voice. "Is this mole getting darker? Listen, Howard, is this a *lump*?"

She was always a hypochondriac, and Howard began to be one too. By the time I met him, he was dying from a thousand diseases. I laughed at all of them.

"Are you kidding?" I said.

He was petulant, but hopeful. "How do you know? *You're* not a doctor."

But I wouldn't allow him a single internal mystery, and he was cured. The laying on of hands, I called it, covering him with my own healing flesh. "Oh, you don't know!" he cried, burrowing in. But I did, and he was cured of palpitations, bruises, nosebleeds, fears of castration.

But Renee stayed on, a dubious legacy. One morning Jason answered the telephone. "Weeny," he said, narrowing his eyes, waiting for my reaction.

I wouldn't give him the satisfaction. "Oh?" I said it coolly, raising my eyebrows. "What does *she* want?"

She wanted to stay with us for a few days. Some madman was after her. A boy she met at unemployment, a real psycho.

"I'll have to speak to Howard about it," I told her, but that wasn't true.

I watched a kids' television program with Jason. We tried to make a Chinese lantern, following easy directions, but it fell apart. I decided to speak to Jason instead. "Renee wants to stay here for a few days."

He labored over the lantern, his fingers stiff with paste.

"In my bed?"

"Of course not. On the sofa, in the living room. What do you think?"

"I hate this stupid lantern!" he cried, ripping it apart.

The baby was standing in her crib, toes splayed, rattling the bars. "Guess what? Renee is coming," I told her, despising my own precocity.

That night I gave the news to Howard, carefully, as if I believed it might be fatal. He sighed, but I knew he was secretly pleased. He wanted to know how long she would stay, what time she would need the bathroom in the morning, and if I could possibly make some black cherry Jell-O, her favorite.

"Jesus!" I slammed pots and pans around, and Howard shivered with fear and happiness.

After dinner I called Renee and told her yes. "Only for a couple of days," I said severely.

"Oh, you're a pal," she cried.

Later, she exclaimed over the Jell-O and threw Howard a knowing look. Was I a fool? But her bones pushed their knobs through her clothing. Her nostrils were red and crusty from a lingering cold. Under the table I found the sleek truth of my own thigh, and I grew calm again.

Of course the living room was closed to us for our nightly consultation. Renee was there with a stack of magazines, a dish of trembling Jell-O and the radio tuned to some distant and static-shot program.

I drew Howard into the bedroom and shut the door. It was my turn, and I settled into 1939 with a minimum of effort. It was a memorable year, because my parents were discussing a possible divorce on the other side of my bedroom wall. How was that for trauma? I was Gloria Vanderbilt, a subject of custody, an object of sympathy. I imagined myself little again, diminished in the bed-clothes, and I invented their conversation. *What about the kid*? my mother asked. *Oh, you're the one who always wanted a kid*, my father answered.

Next to me, Howard moved restlessly. "It's a good thing Renee and I never had any children," he said.

"That's true," I conceded, and then I tried to continue my story, but Renee coughed in the other room, two throat-clearing blasts that pinned us to the pillows.

"What's *that*?" Howard asked.

"Oh, for heaven's sake! You broke my train of thought again!"

"I only asked."

"Forget the whole thing. It's no use telling you anything, anyway."

"Go ahead," he said, rubbing my back in conciliation. "Come on. Start from, 'Oh, you're the one who always wanted a kid.' "

"Forget it."

"Jesus!" he said, "Just feel this. My pulse is so slow, my blood must be like clay."

In the morning Renee was watching the playground from the shelter of the curtains, like a gangster holed up in a hideout.

"I'm a wreck," she said. "I keep thinking that nut is going to come here."

"Why should he come here? How could he even know where you are?"

She didn't answer. She moved to the sink, where she squeezed fresh orange juice into a glass with her bare hands. I wished Howard could have seen that. The untapped strength of that girl!

Jason was a traitor. He ran kisses up her freckled arms. "Weeny! My Weeny!" They drank the unstrained juice in sips from the same glass.

Later, I went downstairs and called Howard at work from a pay phone. "She has to go."

"I know that. Don't you think I know that?"

"I mean forever."

"Well, what do you want *me* to do?"

"Nominate her for Miss Subways. Get her deported. I don't know. Why don't you find her a husband?"

"Ha-ha. Should I look in the Yellow Pages?"

"Well, *you* married her."

"That's another story," he said, but I refused to listen.

"Ask around," I said, and I hung up.

At home again, I tried my own hand. "Stand up straight. Give them both barrels." But the narrow points of her breasts thrust out like drill bits. "No, no, *relax*." I let her try on some of my clothes, but they enclosed her like tents. Instead, we worked on makeup and

her psychological approach to men. But it all seemed useless. In ten minutes there were smudges under her eyes from the mascara and lipstick on her teeth.

"Relax," I told her. "That's the whole secret," and she collapsed in a slump as if her spinal cord had been severed.

That night Howard came home with a man from his office. I'd never seen him before. He wore dark glasses and he had a bitter smile. He was divorced too, and spoke about getting burned once and never playing with fire again.

"Oh, *terrific*," I said to Howard without moving my lips.

But he shrugged. He had done his share. Now it was up to me. I did the best I could, flaunting my domestic joy at this stranger like a bullfighter's cape. But everything must have seemed bleak to the fellow through those dark glasses. My dinner was loaded with cholesterol killers, the apartment was overheated and confining, someone was deflating the tires on his car parked two blocks away.

Of course Renee didn't help at all. She pretended to be our eldest child, and ate her french fries with her fingers. There was a huge pink stain on the front of her blouse.

"I'll call you," the man said to her when he left, a phrase torn from memory. We were all surprised that he bothered.

"You didn't have to," Renee said to Howard later, as if he had brought her a frivolous but thoughtful gift.

In the bed, Howard and I listened for night sounds from the other room, and we were rewarded. In her sleep, Renee called out and I could feel Howard next to me, poised for flight on the edge of the mattress.

Dear Abby/Ann Landers/Dr. Rose Franzblau, What should I do? Signed, Miserable.

Dear Mrs., Do you keep up with the national scene? Can you discuss things intelligently with your husband; i.e., name all the Cabinet members, the National Book Award nominees, the discoverer of DNA? Have you looked in the mirror lately? Do you make the most of your natural good looks? Go to an art gallery, make an exciting salad for dinner, reline your kitchen shelves with wild floral paper. And good luck!

The days went by somehow and we began to settle in as if things were fine, as if Renee *belonged* on our couch every night, leaving those shallow depressions in the pillows.

My mother called to offer some advice. "Get rid of her," she said.

My father picked up the bedroom extension and listened. I could hear the hiss of his breath.

"Hello, Dad," I said.

"Are you on, Herm?" my mother asked. "Is that you?"

My father cleared his throat right into the mouthpiece. He was going to offer advice as well, and his style was based on Judge Hardy in the old Mickey Rooney movies. Kindly. Dignified. Judiciously stern. All his days he sat for imaginary Bachrach portraits. In the subway, at the movies. "What I would do . . ." he said, and then he paused.

My mother waited. I waited. I tapped my foot on the kitchen tile.

"What should she do?" my mother insisted. "Should she throw her out the window? Should she stuff her in the incinerator?"

"I believe I was speaking," Judge Hardy said.

"Oh, pardon *me*," my mother said. "For living."

"What I would do," he began again, "is seek professional advice."

"Thanks, Dad."

"Yes," he said. "Professional advice." He paced in his chambers.

"It's not normal," my mother said. "It's not nice." Her opinion about other things as well—homosexuality, artificial insemination, and the hybridization of plants.

The next day I lent Renee twenty dollars and looked through the classified ads for a new apartment for her. "Change your luck," I advised, like a dark gypsy.

When the children were napping, the doorbell rang. An eye loomed back at mine, magnified through the peephole.

"Who?"

"Renee there?"

My heart gave tentative leaps, like the first thrusts of life in a pregnancy. I opened the chains and bolts with trembling hands and ran inside. "It's a man," I hissed, rebuttoning Renee's housecoat, combing her hair with my fingers. But it was no use. She still looked terrible, abused and ruined.

The man burst into the room.

"Oh, for God's sake, it's *you!*" Renee said.

"I told you," he said. "When I want something, I go after it."

"Well, just piss off, Raymond."

"It's you and me baby," he said. "All the way."

I watched from the doorway. He was a big ox of a man, the kind who invites you to punch him in the belly and then laughs at your broken hand. There was a cartoon character tattooed on his forearm—Yogi Bear or Smokey.

"Call the police," Renee said wearily.

"The *police?*"

"Why fight nature, Renee?" he asked.

"That's right," I said, with a conspiratorial wink.

"He's a maniac," she explained. "He's the one I *told* you about. From the unemployment."

My hope began to ebb. "Well, you could just give him a *chance.*"

Jason come in from the bedroom then, barefoot, squinting in the assault of new light. "Stop hollering," he said.

"My intentions are honorable," the maniac said, crossing his heart. "Cute kid," he offered, about Jason.

I reached for that slender thread of hope. "Do you like children?" I asked.

He leaned on his wit. "Say, I used to be one myself!" He laughed and laughed, wiping tears from his eyes.

"Renee, Renee," I said. "Introduce me."

"He-has-a-prison-record," she sang in falsetto behind her hand.

They might have been political arrests, for all I knew, or something else that was fashionable. I snapped my fingers. "*Honi soit,*" I said.

"Bad checks," Renee said. She was relentless.

I always try to find the good in people and he had nice eyes, grey with gorgeous yellow flecks. I offered him coffee and he accepted. Renee sat down finally, giving in.

They were married two weeks later. Howard gave the bride away, which may not be traditional, but it meant a lot to me, for the symbolism. I gave them a silver-plated bread tray and sincere wishes for the future. Raymond had a lead on a job in Chicago and they left in a hailstorm of rice for the airport.

"That's that," I said, never believing it for a moment.

Two months later, Raymond showed up at the door at three o'clock in the morning. Things didn't work out, he said, by way of explanation. Renee was staying in Chicago for a while, to seek new horizons, but she had promised to keep in touch.

Raymond's feet hung over the arm of the sofa when I tucked him in. He snored and the sofa springs groaned in rhythm with his dreams.

He looks through the want ads every day. He takes the garbage to the incinerator and he picks up the mail for us in the morning. My little talks with Howard are expanded into small but amiable group sessions now. Raymond's stories are interesting, as I might have suspected, from the tattoo and all. He never even knew his real parents or his true history. We sent him to N.Y.U. for a battery of aptitude tests and it seems that he might do well in social research or merchandising.

As for me, I have good days and bad. At the supermarket, I am dazzled by the bounty. In bed, I am a passenger, still ready for cosmic flight. My daily horoscope predicts smooth sailing ahead.

I worry about Renee, though. Today there was an airmail letter. She is lonely and her body absorbs only the harmful additives in food. After all, Chicago is not her hometown.

Behold the Husband in His Perfect Agony

BARRY HANNAH

Homeless

When I am run-down and flocked around by the world, I go down to Farte Cove off the Yazoo River and take my beer to the end of the pier where the old liars are still snapping and wheezing at one another. The lineup is always different, because they're always dying out or succumbing to constipation, etc., whereupon they go back to the cabins and wait for a good day when they can come out and lie again, leaning on the rail with coats full of bran cookies. The son of the man the cove was named for is often out there. He pronounces his name Far*tay*, with a great French stress on the last syllable. Otherwise you might laugh at his history or ignore it in favor of the name as it's spelled on the sign.

I'm glad it's not my name.

This poor dignified man has had to explain his nobility to the semiliterate of half of America before he could even begin a decent conversation with them. On the other hand, Farte Jr. is a great liar himself. He tells about seeing ghost-people around the lake and tells big loose ones about the size of the fish those ghosts took out of Farte Cove in years past.

Last year I turned thirty-three years old and, raised a Baptist, I had a sense of being Jesus and coming to something decided in my life —because we all know Jesus was crucified at thirty-three. It had all seemed especially important, what you do in this year, and holy with meaning.

On the morning after my birthday party, during which I and my wife almost drowned in vodka cocktails, we both woke up to the making of a truth session about the lovers we'd had before we met each other. I had a mildly exciting and usual history, and she had about the same, which surprised me. For ten years she'd sworn I was the first. I could not believe her history was exactly equal with mine. It hurt me to think that in the era when there were supposed to be virgins she had allowed anyone but *me,* and so on.

I was dazed and exhilarated by this information for several weeks. Finally, it drove me crazy, and I came out to Farte Cove to rest, under the pretense of a fishing week with my chum Wyatt.

I'm still figuring out why I couldn't handle it.

My sense of the past is vivid and slow. I hear every sign and see every shadow. The movement of every limb in every passionate event occupies my mind. I have a prurience on the grand scale. It makes no sense that I should be angry about happenings before she and I ever saw each other. Yet I feel an impotent homicidal urge in the matter of her lovers. She has excused my episodes as the course of things, though she has a vivid memory too. But there is a blurred nostalgia women have that men don't.

You could not believe how handsome and delicate my wife is naked.

I was driven wild by the bodies that had trespassed her twelve and thirteen years ago.

My vacation at Farte Cove wasn't like that easy little bit you get as a rich New Yorker. My finances weren't in great shape; to be true, they were about in ruin, and I left the house knowing my wife would have to answer the phone to hold off, for instance, the phone company itself. Everybody wanted money and I didn't have any.

I was going to take the next week in the house while she went away, watch our three kids and all the rest. When you both teach part-time in the high schools, the income can be slow in summer.

No poor-mouthing here. I don't want anybody's pity. I just want to explain. I've got good hopes of a job over at Alabama next year. Then I'll get myself among higher-paid liars, that's all.

Sidney Farte was out there prevaricating away at the end of the pier when Wyatt and I got there Friday evening. The old faces I recognized, a few new hearkening idlers I didn't.

"Now, Doctor Mooney, he not only saw the ghost of Lily, he says he had intercourse with her. Said it was involuntary. Before he knew what he was doing, he was on her making cadence and all their clothes blown away off in the trees around the shore. She turned into a wax candle right under him."

"Intercourse," said an old-timer, breathing heavy. He sat up on the rail. It was a word of high danger to his old mind. He said it with a long disgust, glad, I guess, he was not involved.

"MacIntire, a presbyterian preacher, I seen him come out here with his son-and-law, anchor near the bridge, and pull up fifty or more white perch big as small pumpkins. You know what they was using for bait?"

"What?" asked another geezer.

"*Nuthin*. Caught on the bare hook. It was Gawd made them fish bite," said Sidney Farte, going at it good.

"Naw. There be a season they bite a bare hook. Gawd didn't have to've done that," said another old guy with a fringe of red hair and a racy Florida shirt.

"Nother night," said Sidney Farte, "I saw the ghost of Yazoo hisself with my paw, who's dead. A Indian king with four deer around him."

The old boys seemed to be used to this one. Nobody said anything. They ignored Sidney.

"Tell you what," said a well-built small old boy. "That was something when we come down here and had to chase that whole high-school party off the end of this pier, them drunken children. They was smokin dope and two-thirds a them nekid swimmin in the water. Good hunnerd of em. From your so-called *good* high school. What you think's happnin at the bad ones?"

I dropped my beer and grew suddenly sick. Wyatt asked me what was wrong. I could see my wife in 1960 in the group of high-schoolers she must have had. My jealousy went out into the stars of the night above me. I could not bear the roving carelessness of teen-agers, their judgeless tangling of wanting and bodies. But I

was the worst back then. In the mad days back then, I dragged the panties off girls I hated and talked badly about them once the sun came up.

"Worst time in my life," said a new, younger man, maybe sixty but with the face of a man who had surrendered, "me and Woody was fishin. Had a lantern. It was about eleven. We was catchin a few fish but rowed on into that little cove over there near town. We heard all these sounds, like they was ghosts. We was scared. We thought it might be the Yazoo hisself. We known of some fellows the Yazoo had killed to death just from fright. It was the, over the sounds of what was normal human, sighin and amoanin. It was big unhuman sounds. We just stood still in the boat. Ain't nuthin else us to do. For thirty minutes."

"An what was it?" said the old geezer, letting himself off the rail.

"We had a big flashlight. There came up this rustlin in the brush and I beamed it over there. The two of em makin the sounds get up with half they clothes on. It was my own daughter Charlotte and an older guy I didn't even know with a moustache. My *own* daughter, and them sounds over the water scarin us like ghosts."

"My Gawd, that's awful," said the old geezer on the rail. "Is that the truth? I wouldn't've told that. That's terrible."

Sidney Farte was really upset.

"This ain't the place!" he said. "Tell your kind of story somewhere else."

The old man who'd told his story was calm and fixed to his place. He'd told the truth. The crowd on the pier was outraged and discomfited. He wasn't one of them. But he stood his place. He had a·distressed pride. You could see he had never recovered from the thing he'd told about.

I told Wyatt to bring the old man back to the cabin. He was out here away from his wife the same as me and Wyatt. Just an older guy with a big hurting bosom. He wore a suit and the only way you'd know he was on vacation was he'd removed his tie. He didn't know where the bait house was. He didn't know what to do on vacation at all. But he got drunk with us and I can tell you he and I went out the next morning with our poles, Wyatt driving the motorboat, fishing for white perch in the cove near the town. And we were kindred.

We were both crucified by the truth.

Home

I threw a party, wore a very sharp suit. My wife had out all sorts of hors d'oeuvres, some ordered from long off—little briny peppery seafoods you wouldn't have thought of as something to eat. We waited for the guests. Some of the food went bad. Hardly anybody came. It was the night of the lunar eclipse, I think. Underwood, the pianist, showed up and maybe twelve other people. Three I never invited were there. We'd planned on sixty-five.

I guess this was the signal we weren't liked anymore in town.

Well, this has happened before.

Several we invited were lushes who normally wouldn't pass up cocktails at the home of Hitler. Also, there were two nymphomaniacs you could trust to come over in their high-fashion halters so as to disappear around one in the morning with some new innocent lecher. We furthermore invited a few good dull souls who got on an occasional list because they were *good* and furnished a balance to the doubtful others. There was a passionate drudge in landscaping horticulture, for example.

But none of them came.

It was a hot evening and my air-conditioner broke down an hour before the party started.

An overall wretched event was in the stars.

Underwood came only for the piano. I own a huge in-tune Yamaha he cannot separate himself from. Late in the evening I like to join him on my electric bass.

Underwood never held much for electric instruments. He's forty-two, a traveler from the old beatnik and Charlie Parker tribe. I believe he thinks electric instruments are cowardly and unmanly. He does not like the basic idea of men joining talents with a wall socket. In the old days it was just hands, head, and lungs, he says. The boys in the Fifties were better all-around men, and the women were proud of being after-set quim.

Underwood liked to play with this particular drummer about his age. But that night the drummer didn't show up, either. This, to my mind, was the most significant absentee at our party. That drummer had always come before. I thought he was addicted to playing with Underwood. So when Underwood had loosened up on a few numbers and the twelve of us had clapped and he came over for a drink, I asked him, "Why isn't Fred Poor here?"

"I don't know. Fred's got a big family now," said Underwood.

"He always came before. Last month. What's wrong with tonight? Something is wrong with tonight," I said.

"The food's good. I can remember twenty friends in the old days around Detroit who'd be grooving up on this table. You'd thank em for taking your food. That's how solid they were," said Underwood, drinking vodka straight off the ice and smelling at one of the fish hors d'oeuvres.

I saw my wife go into the bathroom. I eased back with a greeting to the sweated-up young priest who had the reputation of a terrific sex counselor. He was out there with the great lyrical lie that made everybody feel good. Is that why he showed up and the others not? His message was that modern man had invented psychology, mental illness, the whole arrogant malaise, to replace the soul. Sex he called God's rule to keep us simple and merry, as we were meant to be, lest we forget we are creatures and figure ourselves totally mental. One night I asked him what of Christ and Mary and the cult of celibacy. "Reason is, Mr. Lee, believe or disbelieve and let be," he answered. "I'm only a goddamned priest. I don't have to be smart or be a star in forensics."

He headed out for more bourbon, and I trucked on after my wife.

I whispered in the bathroom keyhole and she let me in. She was rebuckling her sandal with a foot on the commode.

"Why didn't anybody come tonight? What do you think's wrong?" I asked her.

"I only know about why five aren't here. Talked to Jill." She paused. One of Carolyn's habits is making you pose a question.

"Why?" I asked.

"The people Jill knew about said there was something about our life they didn't like. It made them feel edgy and depressed."

"*What*?"

"Jill wouldn't ever say. She left right after she told me."

When I went out, there weren't as many as before. Underwood was playing the piano and the priest was leaning on the table talking to one of the uninvited, a fat off-duty cop from about four houses up the row I'd waved to in the mornings when he was going out in his patrol car. Sitting down fanning herself was a slight old friend of my wife's who had never showed up at our other parties. She was some sort of monument to alert age in the neighborhood—about eighty, open mind, colorful anecdotes, crepey skin, a dress over-formal and thick stockings.

"Hi, Mrs. Craft," I said.

"Isn't this a dreadful party? Poor Carolyn, all this food and drink. Which one's her husband?" the old lady said.

I realized maybe she'd never got a good look at me, or had poor eyes.

"I really don't know which one's her husband. What would you say was wrong with them, the Lees? Why have people stayed away from their party?" I said.

"I saw it happen to another couple once," she said. "Everyone suddenly quit them."

"Whose fault was it?"

"Oh, definitely theirs. Or rather *his*. She was congenial, similar to Carolyn. And everybody wanted a party. Oh, those gay sultry evenings!" She gave a delicate cough. "We invented gin and tonic, you know."

"What was wrong with the husband?" I asked.

"He suddenly changed. He went bad. A handsome devil too. But we couldn't stand him after the change."

"What sort of change?" I offered her the hearts of palm and the herring, which, I smelled, was getting gamy in the heat. She ate for a while. Then she looked ill.

"A change . . . I've got to leave. This heat is destroying me."

She rose and went out the kitchen, opening the door herself and leaving for good.

Then I went back to the bathroom mirror. The same hopeful man with the sardonic grin was there, the same religious eyes and sensual mouth, sweetened up by the sharp suit and soft violet collar. I could see no diminution of my previous good graces. This was Washington and my vocation was interesting and perhaps even important. I generally tolerated everybody—no worms sought vent from my heart that I knew of. My wife and other women had said I had an unsettling charm.

I got out the electric bass and played along with Underwood. But I noticed a baleful look from him, something he'd never revealed before. So I quit and turned off the amplifier. I took a hard drink of Scotch in a cup and opened a closet in my study, got in, shut the door, and sat down on all my old school papers and newspaper notices in the cardboard boxes in the corner.

Here was me and the pitch dark, the odor of old paper and some of my outdoor clothes.

How have I offended? I asked. How do I cause depression and edginess? How have I perhaps changed for the bad, as old Mrs. Craft hinted?

By my cigarette lighter I read a few of the newspaper notices on me and my work. I looked at my tough moral face, the spectacles that put me at a sort of intellectual remove, the sensual mouth to balance it, abetted by the curls of my auburn hair. In fact, no man I knew looked nearly anything like me. My wife told me that when we first met at Vanderbilt my looks pure and simple were what attracted her to me. Yet I was not vain. She was a brown-haired comely girl, in looks like many other brown-haired comely girls, and I loved her for her strong cheerful averageness. Salt of the earth. A few minor talents. Sturdy womb for our two children.

It was not her. It was me!

What have I done? I asked myself.

Then I heard heels on the stairs of my study. A pair was coming down, man and woman. They walked into the study and were silent for a while. Then I heard the sucking and the groans. For three or four minutes they must have kissed. Then:

"It's not any good *here*."

"I know. I feel it. Even sex wouldn't be any good *here*."

"You notice how all this good liquor tastes like iodine?"

They moaned and smacked a few more minutes. Then the man said, "Let's get out of here."

When they went away, I let myself out of the closet. Underwood was standing at my desk. He looked at me crawling out of the closet. I had nothing to say. Neither did he for a while.

Then he said, "I guess I better not come over anymore."

"What's wrong?" I said.

"The crazy . . . or *off* chick that lives upstairs that always comes down and leans on the piano about midnight every night. She's good-looking, but she sets me off, I get the creeps."

"Did she come down again? I guess it's the piano. You ought to be flattered. Most of the time she sits up there in her chair reading.''

''Somebody said it was your sister. I don't know. She *looks* like you. Got the same curly auburn hair. It's like you with tits, if you think about it.''

''Well, of course it is my sister. For a while we had a reason for not telling that around. Trust me.''

''I trust you. But she makes my hair cold.''

''You loved all types back in the time of the beatniks. I always thought of you as a largehearted person.''

''Something goes cold when she talks. I can't get with the thing she's after. For a while I thought she was far-out, some kind of philosopheress. But nothing hangs *in* in what she says.''

''She can have her moments. Don't you think she has a certain charm?''

''No doubt on that, with her lungs dripping over her gown. But when she talks, well. . . .'' He closed his eyes in an unsatisfactory dreaming sort of trance.

''Can't you see it? Can't you see the charm?'' I demanded.

''Whatever, it don't sweeten me,'' he said, setting down his glass.

He went out the study door.

There, leaning on the piano, in her perfect cobalt gown, was Patricia. She was waiting for Underwood. Near her, as I have intimated, I sometimes have no sense of my own petty mobility from one place to another. I appear, I hover, I turn. Her lush curls burned slowly round and round in the fire of the candle on the mantel. A blaze of silver came from her throatpiece, a lash of gemmy light bounced from her earrings.

Not a soul was in the room with her.

''Underwood's left,'' I said.

''Music gone?'' she said, holding out her hand and clutching her fingers.

''It would be cooler upstairs with your little window unit. You could read. What were you reading tonight?''

''*Heidi*. Such a sugar,'' she said.

''Oh, yes. Much sugar. The old uncle.''

''Mountain,'' she said.

By this time only the priest was left. He was having an almost rabidly sympathetic conversation with my wife. The man was flushed-out and well drunk, a ship's captain crying his *full speed ahead* in the stern-house of a boat rotting to pieces.

I looked over the long table of uneaten fish tasties. The heat had worked on them a couple more hours now and had brought them up to a really unacceptable sort of presence.

''Well. Ho ho. Look at all the stuff. All the cost,'' I said.

''Just garbage God knows who, namely me, has to haul off and bury,'' said my wife.

''Ah, no, madam. I'll see to all. Trust me. I'm made for it,'' swore the priest.

With that he began circling the table, grabbing up the fish tasties and cramming them in his pockets, coat and pants, wadding them into his hat. He spun by me with a high tilt of adieu. But then he bumped into Patricia, who had come in, and spilled some of the muck in his hat on the front of her gown. She didn't move. Then she looked downward into her bosom to the grease and fish flesh that smeared her gown.

''Fishies,'' she said.

''What a *blight* I am! On this one, on this innocent belle! Strike me down!''

The priest wanted to touch her and clean her off, but could not. His hands trembled before the oil and flakes of fish on her stomach. He uttered a groan and ran from the house.

After he'd gone, the three of us stood there, offering no movement or special expression.

''You ought to go up and clean yourself,'' Carolyn said to Patricia.

Patricia put her foot on the first stair and looked at me with an appeal. But then she went rapidly up and we could hear her air-conditioner going when she opened her door and then nothing when she closed it.

We straightened up awhile, but not very thoroughly. Then we got in bed.

''You've ruined my life,'' said my wife. ''This party showed it.''

''What's *wrong*? What do you mean?''

''Stop it. What's to pretend? Your twin goddamned sister. Your wonderful spiritual feebleminded sister.''

''Not! Not! It's just not our language she speaks! Don't say that!''

''*You* taught her all the goddamned English she knows. Oh, when you explained, when she first came, that she was just silent, different! We went through all that. Then we've had her out of pity . . .''

''She doesn't need anybody's pity! Shut your mouth!''

There was a long hot silence. Above us we heard rocking sounds.

My wife hissed: ''She's never even cleaned herself up.''

''I'll see.''

''Oh, yes, you'll *see*! Don't bother to wake me when you come back.''

Carolyn had drunk a lot. I went to brush my teeth and when I came back out she was snoring.

I rose on the stairs.

The cool in Patricia's room had surpassed what is comfortable. It was almost frigid, and the unit was still heaving more cold into the room. She sat in the rocking chair reading her book. The soiled gown was still on her. She raised her hand as I passed her to turn down the air-conditioning, and I held her hand, coming back to stare over her shoulder.

There was a picture of Heidi and her goat upside down.

''Let's get you in your little tub,'' I said.

I stripped the gown from her. Then I picked her up and put her in the tub, turning on the water very slow as I lathered her all over.

I gave her a shampoo. Pulling an arm up, I saw what was needed, ran the razor gently over her pits, then saw to the slight stubble on her legs. This is when she always sang. A high but almost inaudible melody of the weirdest and most dreamlike temptation, it would never come from another person in this world.

I began sobbing and she detected it.

''I love you with everything that lives me,'' she said. ''You love me the identical?''

''Everything. Yes.''

''Mickey,'' she said. She clutched one breast and with the other hand she raised the red curls and lips of her virgin sex. ''Are you like me?''

I had looked away and was getting a towel.

''Yes. I'm exactly like you. We're twins. We're just alike,'' I said.

''That's why we can love each other everything,'' she said.

''Exactly. Just the same.''

''Show me you.''

''We can't. I can't because of the rules.''

''Oh, yeah, darling, the rules!''

She'd always shown a peculiar happiness about the rules.

When I got her in bed, I wound up downstairs, no memory of having traveled anywhere.

I was breathless. My heart was big. Sometimes like this I thought it would just burst and spray its nerves into the dark that does not care, into the friends who would not care.

In bed again I found that Carolyn was not asleep at all. She was sitting up.

''Did you finish with her?''

''Yes.''

''Don't tell me what went on. I don't want to know. I love you too much to do anything about it. But look what you've dragged me into.''

"I know."

"You can't sleep with me tonight. Get out of here."

"I know," I said.

I got the flashlight and got in the closet again, pulling the door to. I went through all the newspaper notices and the college term papers and picked up the love letters. They were on lined paper, grammar-school paper. It was the summer after I'd taught her to write.

Mickey I love you. There isn't anything but love of you for me. I see the way you walk and your shoes are nice. I desire to thank you with my tongue and my legs too. The tongue and legs are good places. But the most is under my chest where it beats.

Sincerely yours,
PATRICIA

I held all the others, her letters, as the habdwriting improved, and saw the last ones with their graceful script, even prettier than I could write on a good day. My essence yearned and rose from the closet and my roots tore from me, standing up like a tangled tree in dark heaven. My mother gave Patricia to me before she threw herself into what she called her patriotic suicide—that is, she used Kentucky whiskey and tobacco and overate fried foods in a long faithful ritual before she joined my old man in the soil near Lexington.

I thought heavily and decided I'd go back down South.

I was tired of Washington, D.C.

I was tired of my vocation.

I was tired of me.

Somewhere near the sea we'd go. Carolyn and Patricia both loved the sea. I'd find a town that would appreciate me for my little gifts and we'd move *there*. Have new friends, more privacy. I might turn back into a Democrat.

Changes like that never bothered my heart.

Home Free

We were very fond of Mrs. Neap's place—even though it was near the railroad. It was a rambling inn of the old days, with its five bathrooms and balcony over the dining room. We had been harboring there for a couple of weeks and thought we were getting on well enough. But then she comes downstairs one morning holding a swab, and she tells me, looking at the rest of them asleep on the couches and rug: "This is enough. Get out by this afternoon."

"Last night you said we were your adorable vagabonds."

"In the light of day, you look more like trash. I had too much of that potato liquor you brought," says Mrs. Neap.

I say, "Give us another chance. It might be your hangover talking. Let's have another conference, say two o'clock. Invite down all the tenants. We'll talk it out."

She says, "It's my decision. I own the place. Property is nine-tenths the law," forearm muscles standing out as she kneads the cleaning rag, one of the lenses of her spectacles cracked.

I say, "But we're the tenth that gives existence quality, the quantum of hope and dream, of laughter, of music. Further, please, Miz Neap, we'll clean, keep this place in shape, paint it up."

"Where paint? What paint? It's ten dollars a quart if you can even find it. You can't find more than four quarts in all South and North Carolina."

"We make our own liquor. We can find a way to make paint too. Gardiner there is close to being a bona fide chemist."

She says, "None of you is any good. You never brought any food into the house. Oh, that sack of onions that fell off a truck and a few blackbirds."

I say, "How can you forget the turkey we brought when we came?"

"Sure," says she, "that's what got you in with, the turkey. But what since, besides potato liquor? Then you ate all the magnolias," says she.

"*One* foolish evening. Your other tenants ate some too," say I.

"You broke the handle on the faucet."

"Nobody ever proved it was one of us."

"There was no fleas before you came, no cockroaches."

"Unproven. Besides, seeing as how there's no more turkey . . ."

The house begins the shiver it does when a train is entering the curve. The train is always, beyond other concerns, an amazement. Mrs. Neap and I walk out to the warped porch to watch. The train is coming in, all right, rolling its fifteen miles an hour, and you can see the people, hundreds and hundreds, standing and sitting on the wooden platforms the company built over the cars, those pipes and chicken wire boxing in about ninety "air-riders" per car top.

Even an air-riding ticket is exorbitant, but that fifteen-mile-an-hour breeze must be nice.

The train passes three times a week. This one must've been carrying about five thousand in all if you were to count the between-car riders and the maintenance-ladder riders.

Resettlers.

When the bad times really came, they brought families back together, and mainly everybody started coming South. Everybody would travel back to the most prosperous member of his family, taking his own light fortune along to pool it. It healed a lot of divorces and feuds. The best thing you could have was a relative with land. You showed up at his place offering your prodigal soul and those of your family as guards of the land, pulling out your soft hands to garden-up the land and watch over it.

There are no idle murders to speak of any more. Almost all of them are deliberate and have to do with food, water, seeds, or such as a ticket on the train. For example, if I tried to jump that train Mrs. Neap and I are looking at, a man in street clothes (you'd never know which one but usually a fellow mixing with the air-riders) would shoot me in the head. The worst to come of that would be some mother would see her child see the cloud of blood flying out of my face, and she'd have to cover its mouth before it could yell because you don't want a child making noise in a public area. Be seen and not heard applies to them, and better not even to be seen very much.

The little ones are considered emblems of felony.

When bad times first settled into reality, the radio announcers told us what conversationalists and musicians Americans were proving to be and that our natural fine wit was going to be retreasured. People began working on their communication. Tales were told. Every other guy had a harmonica, a tonette, or at least was honking on two blades of grass. But that was before they started *eating* grass in New York and then buying up the rest of the nation's.

On the National Radio two years ago, we heard the Surgeon General report on the studies done on survivors of lost expeditions, polar and mountaintop sorties. The thing of it was that you could stay alive a phenomenal length of time on almost nothing if you *did* almost nothing, counting talking and singing. Which sent communication and melody back into the crapper.

The Surgeon General said you had to be sure whatever food you were after surpassed in calories the effort getting it would burn up. Don't run after a clump of celery, for example. *Chewing* celery takes more calories than eating it gives you. But cockroaches, moths, and butterflies will come *to* you and can be caught and ingested with a *bonus* of calories and protein. Wash the cockroaches if possible, the Surgeon General said.

We were chewing on our rutabagas and radishes when this came out and we considered it all laughable, radical overscience for the ghettos above the Mason-Dixon.

That was in the days of cheese.

Then, all the blacks started returning to the South, walking. Five thousand of them came through Maryland, *eating* three or four swamps around Chesapeake Bay, stripping every leaf, boiling and salting all the greenery in huge iron caldrons they pulled along on carts.

Those blacks hit Virginia and ate a Senator's cotton plantation. People started shooting at them, and some of the nigs had guns themselves.

It was a bloodbath.

There were rumors that the blacks cooked their own dead, and you could see that's where their strength was coming from.

When the walking poor of Chicago went through the fields of southern Illinois, over to Kansas, down through Missouri, this sort of thing was avoided. All of America knew about the Virginia horror, and steps were apparently taken among leaders to prevent its recurrence. The radio announcers urged all the walkers to spread out, don't go in large groups. The vegetation of America would feed everybody if all the Resettlers would spread out.

This was good advice, unless you spread out on somebody's acres.

The South was filling up with railroad people from the big defunct hives in the North. Theoretically, everybody could have his own hundred-foot-square place. But too many came back to the South. There were five million Resettlers in Atlanta, they say. Atlanta is very sorry that it prospered as a railhead. The mayor, a Puerto Rican, abdicated with his Chinese wife, leaving everything to the wardens and the stateside C.I.A.

Everybody is quiet. No more music or talking or needless exertion.

Crowds everywhere are immense and docile.

We hear it on the radio.

"They all look at this place covetously, those air-riders," says Mrs. Neap. "Poor souls."

You also had the right to kill anybody who jumped *off* the train *into* your yard. An old coroner might come by on his bicycle and stare at the body for a while, letting off a few platitudes about the old days. Like as not, a town officer, usually a nig or Vietnamese, appears and digs a hole three feet deep and prods the body over into it. This is slow going because the man will eat every worm, every grub, every spider and juicy root he upturns with his spade.

Even Mrs. Neap's run-down house probably looks as if it has gunners at it. But it had no protection at all before we got here. I carry a knife.

The direly thin guy six and a half feet tall who melted into the dawn fog with his bow and arrow before anybody got up and returned at evening with almost all of his arrows lost and not a goddamn ounce of meat to show—to be fair, four blackbirds and a rabbit smaller than the hunting arrow—wanted you to think he was Slinking Invisible itself on the borders of our landhold, when the truth was he was miles away missing ten-foot shots on trifling birds and sticking his homemade arrows into high limbs where he couldn't retrieve them.

He calls himself, JIM. I mean loud and significantly, like that.

Says he knows the game world. When we walked up on that big wild turkey just before we found Mrs. Neap's house, I watched that sucker fire off three different arrows at it. The turkey stood there just like the rest of us, unbelieving. At this point I sicced soft-spoken Vince on the turkey. Vince is so patient and soft-spoken, he could talk a snake into leaving his poison behind and pulling up a chair for stud or go-fish, whatever you wanted to play.

Vince talked the turkey right into his arms.

Then came the last arrow from JIM.

It went through Vince's hand and into the heart of the turkey.

We didn't need this. You can't get medical help. There's nothing left but home remedies.

We started despising JIM right then and there.

But Vince's hand healed and is merely unusable instead of gangrenous.

"My God, one of them jumped off," says Mrs. Neap.

I saw. It was an Oriental.

He is wobbling on the gravel in front of the yard. I pull my knife. This close in to a town you have to perform the law.

But one of the wardens in the air-rider cages shoots at him—then the next one, who has a shotgun, blasts the gook.

The guy lies down.

I couldn't tell whether he went to the dirt before or after the gun blast.

Mrs. Neap kneels down with delicate attention to the dead man. With her cracked lens, she seems a benevolent patient scholar.

Mrs. Neap says, "He's a handsome little man. We don't need to call the coroner about him. Look at the muscles. He was well fed. I wonder why he come running toward the house. I guess he wanted to end up here. He chose," says Mrs. Neap.

"I'll get the bike and tell the coroner," I say.

"I said *not* get the coroner. This is my property. Look. His head is across my legal property line," said Mrs. Neap.

Say I, "Let's push him back a few feet. Then he's the City's. There's no reason for you to take the responsibility or cost of burying him."

The old lady is intent. She'd been through the minor Depression in the Thirties. She'd seen some things, I guess.

"Have you never?" says Mrs. Neap.

Her spectacles are flaming with the rising sun.

Say I, "Have I never what?" slipping my knife back into my hip scabbard.

"Eaten it?"

"*It?*"

"Human *being*."

"Human *being*?"

"Neither have I," says Mrs. Neap. "But I'm so starving, and Orientals are so *clean*. I used to know Chinese in the Mississippi delta. They were squeaky-clean and good-smelling. They didn't eat much but vegetables. Help me drag him back," she says.

She didn't need help.

She has the man under the arms and drags him at top speed over the scrub weeds and onto her lawn. Every now and then she gives me a ferocious look. There is a huge broken-down barbecue pit behind the house. I can see that is her destination.

I go up the front steps and wake up our "family." Vince is already awake, his hand hanging red and limp. He has watched the whole process since the gook jumped off the train.

JIM is not there. He is out invisible in the woods, taking dramatic inept shots at mountains.

(To complete his history, when we move on, after the end of this, JIM kills a dog and is dressing him out when a landowner comes up on him and shoots him several times with a .22 automatic. JIM strangles the landowner and the two of them die in an epic of trespass.)

My wife wakes up. Then Gardiner, the chemist who keeps us in booze, wakes up.

Vince has grown even softer since the loss of his right hand. Larry (you don't need to know any more about him) and his girl never wake up.

"Mrs. Neap wants to cook the man," I say.

"What strength. She did a miracle," says soft Vince.

When we get to the rotisserie, Mrs. Neap has the man all cleaned. Her Doberman is eating and chasing the intestines around the backyard.

My family goes into a huddle, pow-wowing over whether to eat the Doberman.

We don't know what she did with the man's head.

By this time she is cutting off steaks and has the fire going good.

Two more tenants come out on the patio, rubbing their eyes, waked up by the smell of that meat broiling on the grill.

Mrs. Neap is slathering on the tomato sauce and pepper.

The rest of the tenants come down.

Meat!

They pick it off the grill and bite away.

Vince has taken the main part of the skeleton back to the garage, faithful to his deep emotion for good taste.

When it is all over, Mrs. Neap appears in the living room, where we are all lying around. Her face is smeary with grease and tomato sauce. She is sponging off her hideous cheeks with a rag even as she speaks.

She says, "I accepted you for a while, you romantic nomads. Oh, you came and sang and improved the conversation. Thanks to JIM for protecting my place and my dried-out garden, wherever he is. But you have to get out by this afternoon. Leave by three o'clock," says she.

"*Why?*" say I.

"Because, for all your music and merriment, you make too many of us. I don't think you'll bring in anything," she says.

"But we *will,*" says soft Vince. "We'll pick big luscious weeds. We'll drag honeysuckles back to the hearth."

She looks around at all of us severely.

She says, "I hate to get this down to tacks, but I heard noises in the house since you're here." This old amazing woman was whispering. "You know what goes in America. You know all the announcements about food value. You, one of you, had *old dangerous relations* with Clarisse, the tenant next to my room. I heard. You may be romantic, but you are trash."

She places herself with her glasses so as to fix herself in the image of an unanswerable beacon.

She says, "We all know the *Survival News.* Once I was a prude and resisted. But if we're going to win through for America, I go along. *Only* oral relations are allowed. We must not waste the food from each other, the rich minerals, the raw protein. We are our own gardens," Mrs. Neap says, trembling over her poetry.

It costs her a lot to be so frank, I can see.

"But you cooked a human being and ate him," say I.

"I couldn't help it," says she. "I remember the cattle steaks of the old days, the juicy pork, the dripping joints of lamb, the venison."

"The *what*?" say we.

"Get out of here. I give you to four o'clock," says she.

So the four of us hit the road that afternoon.

We head to the shady green by the compass in my head.

I am the leader and my wife is on my arm.

There are plenty of leaves.

I think we are getting over into Georgia.

My wife whispers in my ear: "Did you go up there with Clarisse?"

I grab off a plump leaf from a yearling ash. In my time I've eaten poison ivy and oak too. The rash erupts around your scrotum, but it raises your head and gives you hope when the poison's in your brain.

I confess. "Yes."

She whispers on. "I wanted JIM. He tried. But he couldn't find my place. He never could find my place."

"JIM?" say I. "He just can't hit any target, now can he?"

"I saw Clarisse eating her own eyelashes," she whispers—from the weakness, I suppose.

"It's okay," say I, wanting to comfort her with an arm over to her shoulder. But with that arm I am too busy taking up good leaves off a stout little palmetto. And ahead of us is a real find, rims of fungus standing off a grandfather oak.

I've never let the family down. Something in my head tells me where the green places are. What a pleasure to me it is to see soft Vince, with his useless floppy red hand, looking happy as he sucks the delicious fungus off the big oak.

My wife throws herself into the feast. Near the oak are two terrapins. She munches the fungus and holds them up. They are huge turtles, probably mates. They'd been eating the fungus themselves.

"Meat!" says the wife.

"We won't!" say I. "I won't eat a hungry animal. I just want to hold and pet one."

The hunting arrow from JIM gets me right in the navel when I take the cuter of the turtles into my arms.

The wife can't cook.

JIM's feeling too awful to pitch in.

So it'll be up to soft Vince to do me up the best he can with only the one good hand.

Winner in All Things

SAM KOPERWAS

A kid, I was a whiz with the bat. The Mets' first year in the majors with Hobie Landrith as their top draft, I was hitting .850 in the Rugby Little League for Young and Future Athletes, my picture in the *Journal-American,* already drawing intentional walks as a ten-year-old. Only a skinny black kid my age and a Puerto Rican with a moustache were picked with me out of thousands to play in the First Annual New York Mets Player-Family Game at the Polo Grounds. You can see that I was special because my father was not a Met. I got the most votes.

It was a sellout crowd. I had on the Rugby uniform with Eddie's Cleaners on the back. Center field was five hundred feet away. My father was with me in the Met dugout. He pointed to the string that went just behind the bases and marked off the line for junior home runs.

We both looked far beyond that.

The black kid bunted to start the game and he sped around all the bases. Carlton Willey was pitching and all the Mets made a big deal of trying to catch the kid. Roy McMillan dove after him and dropped the ball, stuff like that. The Puerto Rican hit a double over first.

I was last man up with nine runs already in and one of Cliff Cook's sons on second base and a daughter on third. All the Philadelphia Phillies were on the top step of their dugout waiting for us to finish. Harry Chiti was behind the plate and he told me to choke up on the bat. "Get a good grip, kid, let's see you rip one." I just kept looking at the pitcher. Willey was lobbing them in underhand from about thirty feet away. Richie Ashburn's little kid was running around behind me with a plastic bat and everybody was laughing and taking it easy. Willey showed me the ball. He told me it was coming in belt high.

It did.

I swung and hit him in the thigh. The ball shot off his leg toward the Met dugout and there must have been fifty thousand people who dropped their hot dogs. Willey went down like a rock. Both benches went out to see how he was.

I was captain of the punchball team. In gym class they had to put me in as Official Cleanup Hitter for both sides in order to make things even. In one game I pointed four times to the left-field fence. The upper classes were there and the color guard marched across the schoolyard diamond and they all sang the national anthem from the sidelines. Crossing guards held up traffic each of the four times I was up, and I punched all four into the same garden across the street. Everybody in the school knew my name, girls smiled at me in the halls.

In voting, I beat Herbie Harkavey for class president.

> HERBIE HARKAVEY
> RHYMES WITH NAVY
> VOTE FOR ME
> IT WILL BE GRAVY
> HERBIE FOR PREZ!

He had never lost before. We tied in the first voting and Mr. Zucker sent us both from the room. When he called us back, only my name was on the blackboard. We shook hands.

At my desk I heard a sobbing from the girl in front of me. "I voted for you," she whispered. She dropped her pencil and spoke to me from the floor. It's still the sexiest thing I can remember. I was a genius in that class, an ace. Kids would offer me money for answers. Her glasses were high up on her nose and a little crooked, and with the lights right above her she squinted like an outfielder looking into the sun. "I voted for you."

In a touch-football game on the street with other kids and some parents, I ran back an interception and knocked my father down. I ran into him low and he tore his pants at the knees and started to bleed. Then he slapped the football out of my hands and scooped it up. "Recovered fumble!" he screamed. He bent down so that his face was right next to mine. The other kids moved away, backed off toward parked cars, and the other fathers got together in a circle. I swung up and knocked the ball out of his hands. It wobbled at our feet.

"Competitive spirit!" my father shrieked. "This is a son, fire in his blood! Knocks down his own father for a few extra feet, punches footballs out of his old man's hands!" People came to their windows.

With bubble-gum cards I was unbeatable. Kids came to me to win cards for them at a fifty-fifty deal. I never bought a pack in my life with my own money. In flipping, I matched heads or tails by the hundreds. In against-the-wall, I stacked them like a deck from any distance. In tossing for distance, I flung cards more than half a sewer. On the backs I knew every question without rubbing for an answer.

I started young, I admit it, sleeping with my glove; an Ernie Broglio model. A bat that was too big for me hung by a couple of nails over my bed. When winter came I switched between a basketball and a football, sometimes keeping both next to me on the weekends on either side of my pillow, taking one or the other with me to the school-yard depending on which side I woke up on. My father helped me along, tucking me in at night with whatever I had with me. "Sleep well," he said. "Grow tall."

In the morning I got up with him and he drove me to school until I started running to school, and then he drove next to me, calling out important scores and setting a fast pace. "You can be whatever you want," he called through the window. "I know talent. Basketball, track, baseball, bowling, golf, football, anything you want. Arnold Palmer is a millionaire. Mickey Mantle doesn't starve. Don Carter has a very fine house."

When autograph books went around at graduation, I was written in as Best Athlete in everybody's book. I usually signed: "From one big-leaguer to another."

My father bought me a uniform when I began basketball. He took me to the school yard and showed me how to shoot. I started off throwing bounce-passes to him and then passes chest-high. After that he pointed to the basket and told me to shoot.

I did.

The ball went right in. Then I did it again. Then I did it from farther out. I kept on doing it.

"A Sharman!" he shouted to me. "A Cousy!"

I couldn't miss. People stopped their games around me and applauded after each basket. The uniform came right after that, with matching sneakers, a Celtics uniform, green. I kept a basketball next to me at night.

"You're a star," my father said. "Be rich and famous. Be Hank Greenberg and Al Rosen. Be quick, healthy."

In the school-yard he put me on his shoulders so I could dunk a few. I got chosen into three-man games while older guys waited for next. People watched when I shot. I wore my first jock with the green satin shorts.

I had my father read me the sports section and box scores when he came to see me at night with my basketball and my football. I still remember names and numbers, statistics and figures. Norm Cash, .361 in 1961 with forty-one homers. Jake Early, American League All-Star catcher in 1943. Jim Parker and Jim Mutscheller and Long Gone Dupre. The Syracuse Nats.

I worked at being a lefty. I still swing lefty in stickball games, and I never strike out southpaw, I always get a piece of the ball. To strengthen the arm, I used to go bowling lefty. One time I bowled two hundred lefty. Another time I won twenty bucks by hitting seven of ten from the free-throw line with either hand. The first time I ever held a pool cue I dropped six in a row, then three, then six more to clear the table. My first time on a driving range I slammed out shots at the four-hundred-yard markers, each one right down the middle.

I got laid for the first time in the summer. It was in Atlantic City, where I went to work with a guy I played ball with, and he set up the whole thing in the back of the store. I see the guy from time to time, to have a catch or get a stickball game going, and every once in a while we spar a few rounds at the gym or work the bags. He played shortstop and we were the double-play combination. We did tricks in practice and scouts talked to us after games. I had a .360 batting average for three varsity years and his was about .320.

Of the nine gold medals I have in my drawer, three are in baseball. One is for black-ball handball. It was in doubles. I was tops by myself at the school-yard with a pink ball, and in squash I kept the court all day without getting beaten.

The girl was there when I came in. I knew I was going to get laid. She was by the cash register with the shortstop and he introduced us.

"You have nice manners," she said to me. "Let's do something."

She wouldn't lie down in the back of the store. I spread newspapers but she said no. There was a Mets game on the radio and it was near the end of the game. Ralph Kiner was doing the play-by-play and the St. Louis Cards had the bases loaded and were down by a couple of runs. I think Alvin Jackson was pitching for the Mets. She put her tongue in my mouth and hiked her dress up over her hips. The Mets rallied for another few runs and put away the game.

I was on the basketball team as a Frank Ramsey type. I came in as sixth man and bombed from the outside like a secret weapon, my picture in the yearbook with a stick of dynamite next to it. I mixed it up underneath and grabbed my share of rebounds, but the coach wanted me on the outside to break up zones. I had a good shot, a soft touch. I wound up three years on the varsity with a fifty-two percent average from the field. Colleges offered me scholarships. My father sent letters to Big Ten universities, and they were interested.

On weekends, when there was no practice, I took her to the school-yard with me. Her glasses were thick. She had only one pair that she was afraid to wear for sports, so she always shot from directly underneath the basket. Without them she couldn't see a thing. I tried to help her with outside shooting, tried to get her to wear contacts.

I played baseball. I started in center but the coach thought my future was infield. I was tough, hard-nosed, a rock. My pivot at second base was major-league. I led the city in assists for two years. Sometimes I came in for relief. The coach would come to the mound, make a waving motion with his right hand, and then the starting pitcher would leave and I'd come in from either second base or third. My curve was unhittable.

In one game, tied going into the last of the ninth, I stretched a single into a double. I came into second with a Pete Rose/Jackie Robinson headfirst slide and punched the ball out of the guy's glove when I saw that he had me. Then I scored on a single.

I came up to the plate a few times with the bat that used to hang over my bed when I was a kid, and I cracked it at the handle after a game or two. The coach went out and bought me another one, same model. I was picked twice as team captain.

People knew me at the beach. There were football games that I got into there, a regular crowd, kids and some older guys trying to keep in shape. I was fast in that sand, incredibly fast. They played deep zones and double-teamed me on every play, but still I caught touchdown passes whenever I wanted. Nobody could stay with me.

In the water I was a fish, a shark. I could really move, any stroke, you name it. I got my Junior Lifesaver card when I was nine. The swimming coach wanted me for his team. He followed me to classes, talked to the other coaches about borrowing me, offered me dinners. My father wouldn't let me go. "Amateur," he said. "And chlorine is murder for the eyes." After the swimming test, I paired off against the school's best freestyler and beat him across two laps.

In slow-pitch softball games at P.S. 251 she came to watch me, standing along the fence. She had contact lenses, two pair. We were good in the field. I was the favorite, a center-fielder with deep power alleys on either side of me, like in the Polo Grounds. Once I ran with my back to the plate to catch one that people still talk about. I hit the fence in straightaway center just as the softball caught in the webbing and I needed eight stitches. She kept a bandage over my eye in the emergency room. She took out her contacts to cry better.

We got new baseball uniforms and I asked for number twenty-four. I got it even though I was an infielder, and I wore the uniform around campus after practice. I wore it in the cafeteria one time, and a girl sat down next to me. In my car later I got but good. This was not your junior home run. When she put her face in the flannel, all I saw was her hair and the pinstripes.

At graduation my father made a toast to the kid who put Carlton Willey in the hospital. I put the finishing touch to it by taking off her glasses outside and smashing them between us under my shoe. In the street the sound was like applause and she couldn't see a thing and got upset.

"Very symbolic," she said. "I'm blind and have to hold onto you to go anywhere. I just love that."

We went to the park and watched a game of touch football. I had sneakers and waited for somebody to leave. One guy they called Whitey kept picking off passes on defense and knocking guys down. "You're not with the Giants anymore," one of the guys shouted to him, and Whitey came back on the next play to put a wide receiver out of the game. They called me in and asked what I could do. "I can catch okay," I said.

They threw the first pass away from me. She sat under a tree and didn't even see the ball go over her head. I set Whitey up with an inside move on the play and told them in the huddle I could beat him long. I checked the sideline while setting up and I saw her straining to pick me out. I slanted into the middle and gave Whitey a bad fake outside and then a good fake inside that he went for, and then I shot by him. The ball was over my head and I left my feet to take it, stretching for it and pulling it in just before I hit the ground, going over with the football on my fingertips. Whitey came down on my back but I was already in the end zone and then he kicked the ball out of my hands.

"Nobody beats me long," he shouted.

But I did.

I'm happy. I'm in good shape, still fast. I haven't gained or lost a pound since high school. My closet is filled with trophies.

We have a table-hockey set and now she refuses to play with me. I absolutely kill her, pass and score at will, scream out the action in my Mel Allen voice until she rips my players off their swivel stands and flings them at me across the table.

I admit I get carried away at times.

"Ratelle over to Gilbert. Passes *behind the net* to Hadfield who gives to Park. Park stickhandles cleanly, now feeds back to Ratelle. The defense is positively helpless. Ratelle lines up the puck almost with disdain, now moves closer to the net. He *wants this one*. He shoots: SCORES!"

I'm good at the game, very good.

At basketball games she has to ask me what's going on, and I explain it to her.

"Is that Lucas over there? Is that him under the basket?"

"That's DeBusschere," I point out. "Lucas has that bad back of his."

"Is that Luke on the bench? Is that him with the towel?"

I'm not a stranger to big places, I've been in them before.

There was the Polo Grounds. There was the old Madison Square Garden, where my father took me to Boston-New York games. Carl Braun was there, Charley Tyra. Kenny Sears and Willie Naulls dunked a few and hit from outside, seven or eight in a row. We sat court-side, right behind the Boston team, and my father pointed out how the players talked to each other on the court, how they watched while on the bench.

"Professionals act that way," he said. "Money comes to money," he explained. "It's not just dribbling and shooting."

I jog now, but muggers and queers are everywhere, behind trees, behind rocks, even in the cold. It's suicide. A Puerto Rican Hare Krishna and a smaller guy held a knife on me the first time I got stopped. I was down to a four-and-a-half-minute mile. I was running with a stopwatch, a towel wrapped around my neck, when they stepped in front of me and asked for money. The one with the knife frisked my pants and under my arms.

I had a ten-dollar bill in my sock. Thoughts ran through my mind like halfbacks in an open field.

I ran. I faked a move to my sneaker and the Hare Krishna went for it. I pivoted as he bent down and I took off like a coon, darting in and out of trees, bushes, busting through crowds. I didn't stop till I got home, running, taking perfect strides, one right after the other. I ran great.

I still do.

But it wasn't the best I ever ran.

At a city-wide meet I once ran anchor leg for some track club I didn't know. The baseball coach got me into it. They told me to use somebody else's name and they gave me a uniform right before the race, a 440 relay. It wasn't even close. I had the lead starting the last lap and I put on another twenty yards before it was over. That was the best I ever ran.

We play tennis. I lob a few now and then to keep her honest, but she follows the ball like a hawk, and it makes me think that she's wearing contacts again. At home I can't be sure either. There's mail from her broker that she sometimes asks me to read, but usually she just takes it herself and locks the door.

I could be great at tennis. I can hold my own on any court there is. I can ace half my serves. My backhand is a hammer.

I play three-man games and full-court basketball. They keep statistics and I'm the leading scorer, and I'm also the player on top in games won.

Last time out I was unbelievably fantastic. I scored about a dozen baskets in a row, driving to the hoop and gunning from outside. I was unstoppable, I couldn't miss a thing. They took turns trying to stop me but I ate up one defender after another. I stole the ball on defense and pulled down rebounds, I was all over the court. I bulled my way down the lane for reverse lay-ups and bombed like I used to from outside. Nothing missed. I threw up hooks with either hand, popped on jumpers. I hit a corner-shot by banking it off the backboard. I got my arm in the way of a pass near the foul line and the ball went right through the hoop.

The shortstop has a couple of guys to play us touch football at twenty-five dollars a man. They played college ball but it's money in the bank for us, there's no way anybody's going to stay with me. It's that simple. I'll run hook-and-go patterns, outfight anybody for the ball.

I win.

I've got fingers that can palm a basketball, that hit killers in handball, that won me four straight decisions in P.A.L. boxing. I've got legs that set a district record for the broad jump, a pulse rate under fifty so that I can go forever, moves that I haven't even used yet.

I'm set for football and I'm set for anything.

I win in weight-lifting, win in skiing, in Ping-Pong. I don't lose. Never. I win in shuffleboard. I win in polo. I'm the one who moves, who flies. I wrestle alligators, rope steers. I win in logrolling. I win in barrel-jumping.

Put me anywhere.

I'm the one on top.

My Animal

SANFORD CHERNOFF

It's always the same, the same song, same time of morning, seven-fifteen, there it is, Jakie and *Tea for Two*, and the tenants have been complaining again.

"So talk to him," my mother says.

I have to laugh. *Talk to him.*

"He's your friend," she says.

"My friend? He follows me."

"Talk to him," she says.

You don't talk to Jakie.

Cosomoto the kids call him, and once they even tried to get him up to the bells at St. Mark's. Something to do with his genes, I hear, and that right after he was born his mother went to bed and didn't get up for a long time. She is a stringy, slow woman, Jakie's mother, with no sign of tits or a smile as I hand her the rent receipt I say I was sent up to give her. I say it loud, loud enough to be heard inside. I was hoping it would be the old man that came to the door. He might not be home, I'm thinking, when he appears there, behind his wife. He greets me noisily and calls in for Jakie to come see who it is. A second time he calls and when there is still no answer he motions me inside.

I go, though the woman hardly allows me space to get by, and I follow the old man down the dim hall to the room. There's a chair and some shelves, but otherwise it's just a workbench where Jakie, bent over a bit of wood, does not look up at us.

"Absorbed," chortles the old man and goes immediately to a shelf. "I could have sworn they were here," he says, down on one knee and speaking to me as if I know what it is he's looking for. He gets to his feet, stands there with a finger to his mouth, and then hurries from the room. As soon as he leaves, I go over to Jakie and let him know that he is to do no more of his singing out in the courtyard. I let him know I'll bust his ass if he does. I'm still warning when the old man returns.

He has with him the bookends I began the last time I was here. I don't want to see them again.

"I should go," I say.

"You just got here," says the old man.

He has one of the bookends in the vise and is explaining the next step to me.

"I just came up to drop off your receipt," I say.

"My receipt?"

"For the rent," I say.

"Always running," he says.

"Up yours," Jakie says.

I pretend not to hear, not to see Jakie moving. I go on with what I was saying about going, how I'd love to stay if I could. The old man is smiling at me, or Jakie—I can't be sure. He has his pipe lit now, and there is a great cloud collecting around his face. I see only parts of the old man's face, not always the same ones. But he is smiling—I can see that—and nodding now as Jakie holds out the wood he has been working on. It is for me, I realize, that the old man is nodding, and I know he wants me to take the wood. I do. I take the wood and look at it. I don't know what else to do with the thing.

"Certainly is smooth," I finally think to say.

"He's been working on it for days."

"Has he?"

"Hours at a time."

I shake my head.

"Can't get enough of it."

"Certainly is smooth," I say.

All the time we're talking I'm holding the wood out for Jakie to take back. But he won't. He won't come anywhere near the wood. He is now making filthy gestures at me.

"He wants you to have it," interprets the old man, sucking a new light into his pipe.

"I couldn't," I say, with a sad thought now of the time it is and the little light left for stickball. "It wouldn't be right," I say. "He might want to do something with it."

"He is."

I go home with the wood. My father wants to know what I'm doing with it. It's a gift, I tell him. I'm getting too smart for my own good, my mother says and asks if I spoke to Jakie. I say I did and get one of her looks. I get another one from over her coffee cup the next morning, with the first of *Tea for Two*.

"I told you you couldn't talk to him," I say.

"No stickball today," she says.

"I talked to him," I say.

"And that's every day I have to listen to that." She sips her unsweetened coffee.

Jakie has to be stopped, and he is going to be stopped, I promise myself, and plan to get up early and be waiting for him in the courtyard. I oversleep, though—dreaming of Mrs. Capshun again. Mrs. Capshun lives on the second floor and has pointy knockers. Jakie is on his third chorus by the time I make it downstairs.

I tell him. But Jakie pokes a middle finger up through the air between us and goes right on with his song. I take my father's T-shirt from behind my back and shove it into Jakie's mouth. Tying it there is not easy. To steady him, his head, I have to give up one hand and as I do I lose him. He breaks away. Free and singing, Jakie tears around the courtyard with a middle finger up at me and at all those windows where the tenants stand there watching.

No dreams this night. I hardly sleep. I dress in the dark with my eyes shut and wait in the courtyard.

"Sixty percent chance of rain," reports Mr. T. on his way out with his plastic briefcase. In curlers, her slippers crushed flat in back, Mrs. Price rushes by with her garbage—and then one more, two more, with their dogs, before Jakie, the sound of him, his thick shoes on the stairs. He spots me there and goes into his act. At the top of his lungs he sings and gets halfway around the courtyard before I catch him. He struggles, but I have him, *would* have him, if not for Henry, who lives second-floor rear and plays left-field. Henry shows up trying to help and Jakie ends up bleeding. He bleeds all over my hand.

"He bite you?"

"No."

"Lucky," says Henry, raising a middle finger back to Jakie and looking around for something he could throw after him. "They carry things, you know."

"What are you talking about?"

"Diseases."

He is small, Henry, and does whatever he can not to look up at you when he speaks.

"It's a fact," Henry says. "I read where this guy got bit by one. In Ohio, I think it was. Bit this guy and he died."

Mrs. G. comes out into the courtyard and positions her folding chair in line with the sun.

"Didn't last five minutes," Henry says.

"What would you say that leaves me?"

Henry's passed the word at school. I hear he and some others are planning to wait for Jakie after. But that's Japping, I figure. So I also figure I'll just warn Jakie not to leave without me. During Math I ask out and go down to where the special classes are. They are down a long corridor, on the basement floor. I've passed through before. But I'm still not used to it, and I always have the feeling I'm going to see something I won't ever forget.

I go fast. I look out of the sides of my eyes, see as little as I can. But I miss nothing. Not a crazy hair or a funny smell escapes me—the stain there on the seat of the pants of a boy the size of a man, a boy smiling an endless smile over crooked teeth that make little chips on his lips— and then I see a hand flap bonelessly.

"Is that for me, Jakie? Is that hello?" I say.

But Jakie isn't listening. And Jakie isn't talking. I wait. I wait some more. And when I feel stupid enough I go back up to my class.

And no one is waiting in the school yard after. I walk Jakie home anyway. I walk him home all that week, and I even go up with him and work on the bookends for a while. They are coming along, the old man says and says I ought to start thinking about what I would like to carve in them.

A bat and maybe a ball is all I can think of.

One night in the dream of Mrs. Capshun, I see an animal. It is an animal that I have ahold of, at least part of. The leg is thick with hair and pointed at the foot. If not for the snout, the head would be like what you see on a fox. I am trying to sketch it when my father comes in to ask what I am doing up. He takes a look.

"An animal?"

"Yes."

"Looks like a woman here," he says.

"I saw it that way," I say.

"A dream," he says and says not to forget about the toilet in 2A, which needs a split washer that I'm supposed to pick up on my way home from school.

No one will say who threw the chalk, and we are all kept in after. Then I am almost home when I remember the washer and I have to go back to get it. I was going to work on the animal, fill in certain parts, before letting the old man have a look. But, as I later explain to him, there just wasn't time.

"Forget all those parts," he says and suggests getting rid of even more. "Unnecessary," he says, the pencil he's been looking for found and scratching out the tail, leveling an ear.

"There will be nothing left," I say.

"There'll be enough," he says and rubs away the leg of Mrs. Capshun and both of her tits. I half-close my eyes. It is much better this way. But this way I have no idea how much of the thing he has done away with until I get it home.

I am amazed. It doesn't seem like the same animal. It's not my animal at all. I get another piece of cardboard and start over. I redo it. The work takes time. I can see it's really something to think about.

And I do. I think about it all the time. My off-speed pitch is going out on me. I haven't been getting enough practice. According to Henry, it's Jakie's bite taking effect.

"I thought you go in five minutes."

"Not everybody," says Henry, taking my glove up off the grass where I tossed it a minute ago and fitting it to his hand. "With some people it can take as much as a year," he says.

"A year is plenty of time," I say.

"You got to watch your nails," he says. "You got to watch they don't get brittle."

"I will," I say. "I'll watch them. But my big worry is still his singing. His bite will take its course."

"His singing is no problem," says Henry. "I can take care of his singing."

"I don't want him hurt," I say.

"You want him stopped," Henry says, pounding his fist into the pocket of my glove.

It is a long morning, a long silence after a rushed chorus of *Tea for Two*. My mother is pleased, says it is at least something and asks why I'm not eating.

I get a pass the first thing in school. But his class is not in the room. Later in the day in the hall I catch a look at him. He seems all right. But he is not around after, and I don't find him at home, either.

He walks in about twenty minutes later, while the old man is showing me how to use the tool. The old man has a hand over mine, guiding the tool. Seeing Jakie there, the old man gets his hand off mine—to light his pipe. He's fussing with it. He tells me to go on by myself.

I do. I go ahead by myself and after a while I begin to get the hang of it. It is all in the stroke. The old man nods the one time I turn. He is sitting now, blowing out slow clouds all around me.

I put off going home and finally she comes to tell me to go. I don't need her to tell me, I almost tell her. But I can see she isn't listening, is not even looking. Her attention is off somewhere to my side, where Jakie has just let fly. The wood hits the wall behind me—high on that wall and really nowhere near me at all. Then the tools and whatever else he can lay hands on.

It is hard to tell exactly what it is he means to hit.

The old man takes him by the arms. But it does not look to me as if the old man is going to be able to hold him that way for long.

"Go," she says.

She says it in a whisper, so that at first I don't know it's meant for me.

The animal is beginning to get a look. I have been at it all night. I have the cardboard so it leans against the foot of the bed, and I can see there is a look to it.

Any minute she'll call me for breakfast.

I'm halfway down the stairs before I see I'm still in socks. I might have gone back if Henry wasn't there. He is there—with a boy whose name is Arthur, Henry tells me, and tells me I have Arthur to thank.

"For what? What did Arthur do?"

"You don't hear any singing, do you?" Arthur says.

I do not turn from Henry. All Henry says is Arthur has a brother that can do a hundred and twenty-seven sit-ups and asks what happened to my shoes.

"You better get them," says Henry.

"I'm going to wait," I say.

"For what?" Arthur says and moves so that I am faced with him. It is a small face, full of details.

"He isn't coming down," says Henry. I wait anyway. I wait until the last minute—and in school every chance I get I go down to see if he's there. He isn't. But once on my way down that long corridor to where the special classes are I think I see him. But the boy looks nothing like Jakie, I see when I get close enough.

I use up all my passes. After, I go straight to Jakie's. There at the door, I wish I'd gone home first and got the animal. The animal could be my reason if the woman comes. I could tell her the old man asked to see it. But it turns out not to matter. She doesn't come.

No one does. I knock so long, Mrs. Tamper from across looks out and wants to know what I'm doing.

"They don't answer."

"They're out," she says.

I think I hear something and put my ear to the door.

"Just like your father," Mrs. Tamper says. "Can't tell you a thing."

"She never goes out," I say.

"Goddamned toilet is still dripping, you can tell your god-damned father for me," Mrs. Tamper says.

I wait in the courtyard. I wait as long as I can. After dinner I go up again. I go with my animal this time. But no one comes to the door. It worries me, this silence of theirs. It is like my own, and listening for it, for Jakie the next morning, I find myself thinking it is him I hear.

But my mother is pleased with the quiet. She hears nothing and thinks I look tired. She puts her lips to my forehead, squints, and says she doesn't want me going out.

"Oh, I'm going out, all right," I say.

I beg her, swear to her that I won't be long.

She is not listening. I know she hears things—Jakie's singing when it's there. But I know she doesn't hear me.

I go stiff at the sound of anyone coming. The courtyard is getting cold. Windows are starting to go out. Another five minutes I give them. I give them another five minutes for the next forty-five minutes. I can't think of anything but is that them that I hear coming. I keep looking over my shoulder, keep singing.

Tea for Two.

It is Jakie my father believes he heard. But she says if what she heard from Mrs. K. on the third floor is true it couldn't be Jakie. She says what she heard from Mrs. K. on the third floor is that Jakie is not *home* anymore.

"After all these years?" says my father.

"I'm only telling you what Mrs. K. told me," my mother says. "I'm only telling you not *home*."

I dream of my animal, the part of it my dream always comes to. I suck at it and the nipple cracks off in my mouth. I try to get the nipple back where it belongs. But it won't go. There is no place for the nipple to go.

The next day the old man comes by and leaves the bookends on our mat. He's finished them off and carved in them what looks to me like initials. I wish he hadn't. I wish he'd left it the way it was and that is what I tell him. I tell him it isn't I don't appreciate what he's done, but it isn't what I had in mind. I show him the animal, hold the cardboard up so he can get a look at it. But he walks right by me. He walks by me as if I hold nothing there for him to look at. I go after him. I follow him into the apartment. Much is missing about the place. But I can't say exactly what, and I ask the woman what's gone.

She is no help. She says it was never any different. I don't believe that. It's always different. I tighten a bookend in the vise and ask the old man for sandpaper. I have to ask him again and see that he is crying. The woman says I better go.

"All I did was ask for sandpaper," I say.

She says I better leave.

I won't. I won't leave. "I'll find the sandpaper for myself," I say, and stick a finger up at her.

She stares at me. She smiles at me.

"Up yours!" I shout. She turns and goes off to the kitchen. "With no one around us to bother or hound us!" I shout when I hear her run water in there and see he has his pipe lit now and a good cloud is on the way to me as I begin to sand.

Return to Return

BARRY HANNAH

They used to call French Edward the happiest man on the court, and the prettiest. The crowds hated to see him beaten. Women anguished to conceive of his departure from a tournament. Once, when Edward lost a dreadfully long match at Forest Hills, an old man in the audience roared with sobs, then female voices joined his. It was like seeing the death of Mercutio or Hamlet, going down with a resigned smile.

Dr. Levaster drove the Lincoln. It was rusty and the valves stuck.

On the rear floorboard two rainpools sloshed, disturbing the mosquitoes that rode the beer cans. The other day Dr. Levaster became forty. His hair was thin, his eyes swollen beneath the sunglasses, his ears small and red. Yet he was not monstrous. He seemed, though, to have just retreated from conflict. The man with him was two years younger, curly passionate hair, face dashed with sun. His name was French Edward, the tennis pro.

A mosquito flew from one of the beer cans and bit French Edward before it was taken out by the draft. Edward became remarkably angry, slapping his neck, turning around in the seat, rising and peering down on the cans in the back, reaching over and smacking at them. Then he fell over the seat head-down into the puddles and clawed in the water. Dr. Levaster slowed the Lincoln and drove into the grass off the highway.

"Here now, here now! Moan, moan!" Dr. Levaster had given up profanity when he turned forty, formerly having been known as the filthiest-mouthed citizen of Louisiana or Mississippi. He opened the back door and dragged Edward out into the sedge. "You mule." He slapped Edward over-vigorously, continuing beyond the therapeutic moment.

"He got me again . . . I thought. He. Doctor Word," said Edward.

"A bug. Mule, who do you think would be riding in the back of my car? How much do you have left, anything?"

"It's clear. A bug. It felt just like what he was doing."

"He's dead. Drowned."

"They never found him."

"He can't walk on water."

"I did."

"You just think you did." Dr. Levaster looked in the back seat. "One of your rackets is in the water, got wet. The strings are ruined."

"I'm all right," French Edward said.

"You'd better be. I'm not taking you one mile more if we don't get some clarity. Where are we?"

"Outside New York City."

"Where, more exactly?"

"New Jersey. The Garden State."

At his three-room place over the spaghetti store on Eighty-ninth, Baby Levaster, M.D., discovered teenagers living. He knew two of them. They had broken in the door but had otherwise respected his quarters, washed the dishes, swept, even revived his houseplants. They were diligent little street-people. They claimed they knew by intuition he was coming back to the city and wanted to clean up for him. Two of them thought they might have gonorrhea. Dr. Levaster got his bag and jabbed ten million units of penicillin in them. Then French Edward came up the stairs with the baggage and rackets and went to the back.

"Dear God! He's, oh. Oh, he looks like *love*!" said Carina. She wore steep-heeled sandals and clocked about nineteen on the age scale. The others hung back, her friends. Levaster knew her well. She had shared his sheets, and, in nightmares of remorse, he had shared her body, waking with drastic regret, feeling as soiled and soilsome as the city itself.

"Are you still the mind, him the body?" Carina asked.

"Now more than ever. I'd say he now has about an eighth of the head he was given," Levaster said.

"What happened?"

"He drowned. And then he lived," Levaster said.

"Well, he looks happy."

"I am happy," said French Edward, coming back to the room. "Whose thing is this? You children break in Baby's apartment and, not only that, you carry firearms. I don't like any kind of gun. Who are these hoodlums you're talking to, Baby?" Edward was carrying a double-barreled .410 shotgun/pistol; the handle was of cherrywood and silver vines embossed the length of the barrels.

"I'll take that," said Dr. Levaster, since it was his. It was his Central Park nighttime gun. The shells that went with it were loaded with popcorn. He ran the teen-agers out of his apartment, and when he returned, Edward was asleep on the couch, the sweet peace of the athlete beaming through his twisted curls.

"I've never slept like that," Levaster said to Carina, who had remained. "Nor will I ever."

"I saw him on teevee once. It was a match in Boston, I think. I didn't care a rat's prick about tennis. But when I saw him, that face and in his shorts, wow. I told everybody to come here and watch this man."

"He won that one," Dr. Levaster said.

Levaster and Carina took a cab to Central Park. It was raining, which gave a congruous fashion to Levaster's raincoat, wherein, at the left breast-pocket, the shotgun/pistol hung in a cunning leather holster. Levaster swooned in the close nostalgia of the city. Everything was so exquisitely true and forthright. Not only was the vicious city here, but he, a meddlesome worthless loud failure from Vicksburg, was jammed amok in the viciousness himself, a willing lout in a nightmare. He stroked Carina's thigh, rather enjoying her distaste.

They entered the park under a light broken by vandals. She came close to him near the dark hedges. What with the inconsequential introversion of his youth, in which he had not honed any skill but only squatted in derision of everything in Vicksburg, Levaster had missed the Southern hunting experience. This was more sporting, bait for muggers. They might have their own pistols, etc. He signaled Carina to lie on the grass and make with her act.

"Oh, I'm coming, I'm coming! And I'm so rich, rich, rich! Only money could make me come like this!"

The rain had stopped and a moon was pouring through the leaves. Two stout bums, one with a beercan opener in his hand, circled out of the bush and edged in on Carina. The armed bum made a threatening jab. In a small tenor voice, Levaster protested.

"Please! We're only visitors here! Don't take our money! Don't tell my wife!" They came toward Levaster, who was speaking. "Do you fellows know Jesus? The Prince of Peace?" When they were six feet away, he shot them both in the thigh, whimpering, "Glory be! Sorry! Goodness. Oh, wasn't that *loud*!"

After the accosters had stumbled away, astounded at being alive, Levaster sank into the usual fit of contrition. He removed his sunglasses. He seemed wracked by the advantage of new vision. It was the first natural light he had seen since leaving French Edward's house in Covington, across the bridge from New Orleans.

They took a cab back and passed by French Edward, asleep again. He had taken off his trousers and shirt, appeared to have shucked them off in the wild impatience of his sleep, like an infant, and the lithe clusters of his muscles rose and fell with his breathing. Carina sat on the bed with Levaster. He removed his raincoat and everything else. Over his spread-collar shirt was printed a sort of Confederate flag as drawn by a three-year-old with a sludge brush. Levaster wore it to Elaine's to provoke fights but was ignored and never even got to buy a writer or actor a drink. Undressed, it was seen how oversized his head was and how foolishly outsized his sex, hanging large and purple, a slain ogre. Undressed, Levaster seemed more like a mutinous gland than a whole male figure. He jumped up and down on his bed, using it for a trampoline. Carina was appalled.

"I'm the worst, the awfullest!" he said. Carina gathered her bag and edged to the door. She said she was leaving. As he pounced on the bed, he saw her kneeling next to the couch with her hand on Edward's wrist. "Hands off!" Levaster screamed. "No body without the mind! Besides, he's married. A New Orleans woman wears his ring!" Jump, jump. "She makes you look like a chimney sweep. You chimney sweep!" Levaster bounced as Carina left.

He fell on the bed and moiled two minutes before going into black sleep. He dreamed. He dreamed about his own estranged wife, a crazy in Arizona who sent him photographs of herself with her hair cut shorter in every picture. She had a crewcut and was riding a horse out front of a cactus field in the last one. She thought hair interfered with rationality. Now she was happy, having become ugly as a rock. Levaster did not dream about himself and French Edward, although the dream lay on him like the bricks of an hysterical mansion.

In high school, Baby Levaster was the best tennis player. He was small but devious and could run and get the ball like a terrier. Dr. Word coached the college team. Dr. Word was a professor of botany and was suspected as the town queer. Word drew up close to the boys, holding them to show them the full backhand and forehand of tennis, snuggled up to their bodies and worked them like puppets, as large as he was. Rumorers said Dr. Word got a thrill from the rear closeness to his players. But his team won the regional championship.

Dr. Word tried to coach Baby Levaster, but Levaster resisted being touched and handled like a big puppet and had heard Word was a queer. What he had heard was true—until a few months before French Edward came onto the courts.

Dr. Word first saw French Edward in a junior-high football game; the boy moved like a genius, finding all the openings, sprinting away from all the other boys on the field. French was the quarterback. He ran for a touchdown nearly every time the ball was centered to him, whenever the play was busted. The only thing that held him back was passing and handing off. Otherwise, he scored, or almost did. An absurd clutter of bodies would be gnashing behind him on the field. It was then that Dr. Word saw French's mother, Olive, sitting in the bleachers, looking calm, auburn-haired, and handsome. From then on Dr. Word was queer no more. Mrs. Edward was a secretary for the P.E. department, and Dr. Word was bald-headed and virile, suave with the grace of his Ph.D. from Michigan State, obtained years ago but still appropriating him some charm as an exotic scholar. Three weeks of tender words and French's mother was his, in any shadow of Word's choosing.

Curious and flaming like a pubescent, he caressed her on back roads and in the darkened basement of the gym, their trysts protected by his repute as a queer or, at the outside, an oyster. Her husband—a man turned lopsided and cycloptic by sports mania—never discovered them. It was her son, French Edward, who did, walking into his own home and wearing sneakers and thus unheard—and unwitting—to discover them coiled infamously. Mr. Edward was away as an uninvited delegate to a rules-review board meeting of the Southeastern Conference in Mobile. French was not seen. He crawled under the bed of his room and slept so as to gather the episode into a dream that would vanish when he awoke. What he dreamed was exactly what he had just seen, with the addition that he was present in her room, practicing his strokes with ball and racket, using a great mirror as a backboard, while on the bed his mother and this man groaned in approval, a monstrous twin-headed nude spectator.

Because by that time Word had taken French Edward over and made him quite a tennis player. French could beat Baby Levaster and all the college aces. At eighteen, he was a large angel-bodied tyrant of the court, who drove tennis balls through, outside, beyond, and over the reach of any challenger Dr. Word could dig up. The only one who could give French Edward a match was Word himself, who was sixty and could run and knew the few faults French had, such as disbelieving Dr. Word could keep racing after the balls and knocking them back, French then knocking the odd ball ten feet out of court in an expression of sheer wonder. Furthermore, French had a tendency to soft-serve players he disliked, perhaps an unthinking gesture of derision or perhaps a self-inflicted handicap, to punish himself for ill will. For French's love of the game was so intense he did not want it fouled by personal uglinesses. He had never liked Dr. Word, even as he learned from him. He had never liked Word's closeness, nor his manufactured British or Boston accent, nor the zeal of his interest in him, which French supposed surpassed that of mere coaching. For instance, Dr. Word would every now and then give French Edward a *pinch,* a hard, affectionate little nip of the fingers.

And now French Edward was swollen with hatred of the man, the degree of which had no name. It was expelled on the second day of August, hottest day of the year. He called up Word for a match. Not practice, French said. A match. Dr. Word would have played with him in the rain. At the net, he pinched French as they took the balls out of the can. French knocked his hand away and lost games deliberately to keep the match going. Word glowed with a perilous self-congratulation for staying in there; French had fooled Word into thinking he was playing even with him. French pretended to fail in the heat, knocking slow balls from corner to corner, easing over a drop shot to watch the old man ramble up for it. French himself was tiring in the disguise of his ruse when the old devil keeled over, falling out in the alley with his racket clattering away. Dr. Word did not move, though the concrete must have been burning him. French had hoped for a heart attack. Word mumbled that he was cold and couldn't see anything. He asked French to get help.

"No. Buck up. Run it out. Nothing wrong with you," said French.

"Is that you, French, my son?"

"I ain't your son. You might treat my mother like I was, but I ain't. I saw you."

"A doctor. Out of the cold. I need medical help," Dr. Word said.

"I got another idea. Why don't you kick the bucket!"

"Help."

"Go on. Die. It's easy."

When French got home, he discovered his mother escaping the heat in a tub of cold water. Their house was an unprosperous and unlevel connection of boxes. No door of any room shut properly. He heard her sloshing the water on herself. His father was up at Dick Lee's grocery watching the Cardinals on the television. French walked in on her. Her body lay underwater up to her neck.

"Your romance has been terminated," he said.

"French?" She grabbed a towel off the rack and pulled it in the water over her.

"He's blind. He can't even find his way to the house anymore."

"This was a sin, you to look at me!" Mrs. Edward cried.

"Maybe so," French said, "but I've looked before, when you had company."

French left home for Baton Rouge, on the bounty of the scholarship Dr. Word had hustled for him through the athletic department at Louisiana State. French swore never to return. His father was a fool, his mother a lewd traitor, his mentor a snake from the blind side, the river a brown ditch of bile, his town a hill range of ashes and gloomy souvenirs of the Great Moment in Vicksburg. His days at college were numbered. Like that of most natural athletes, half French Edward's mind was taken over by a sort of tidal barbarous desert where men ran and struggled, grappling, hitting, cursing as some fell into the sands of defeat. The only professor he liked was one who spoke of "muscular thought." The professor said he was sick and tired of thought that sat on its ass and vapored around the room for the benefit of limp-wrists and their whiskey.

As for Dr. Word, he stumbled from clinic to clinic, guided by his brother Wilbur, veteran of Korea and colossal military boredoms all over the globe, before resettling in Vicksburg on the avant-garde of ennui.

Baby Levaster saw the pair in Charity Hospital when he was a med student at Tulane. Word's arm was still curled up with stroke and he had only a sort of quarter vision in one eye. His voice was frightful, like that of a man in a cave of wasps. Levaster was stunned by seeing Dr. Word in New Orleans. He hid in a closet, but Word had already recognized him. Brother Wilbur flung the door open, illuminating Levaster demurring under a bale of puke sheets.

"Our boy won the Southern!" shouted Word. "He's the real thing, more than I ever thought!"

"Who are you talking about?" said Baby Levaster. The volume of the man had blown Levaster's eyebrows out of order.

"Well, French! French Edward! He won the Southern tournament in Mobile!"

Levaster looked to Wilbur for some mediator in this loudness. Wilbur cut away to the water fountain. He acted deaf.

"And the Davis Cup!" Word screamed. "He held up America in the Davis Cup! Don't you read the papers? Then he went to Wimbledon!"

"French want to Wimbledon?"

"Yes! Made the quarterfinals!"

A nurse and a man in white came up to crush the noise from Word. Levaster went back into the closet and shut the door. Then he peeped out, seeing Word and his brother small in the corridor, Word limping slightly to the left, proceeding with a roll and capitulation. The stroke had wrecked him from brain to ankles, had fouled the centers that prevent screaming. Levaster heard Word bleating a quarter mile down the corridor.

Baby Levaster read in *The Times-Picayune* that French was resident pro at the Metairie Club, that French was representing the club in a tournament. Levaster hated med school. He hated the sight of pain and blood, and by this time he had become a thin, weak, balding drunkard of a very disagreeable order, even to himself. He dragged himself from one peak of cowardice to the next and began wearing sunglasses, and when he saw French Edward fend off Aussie, Wop, Frog, Brit, and Hun in defending the pride of the Metairie Club, Levaster's body left him and was gathered into the body of French. He had never seen anything so handsome as French Edward. He had never before witnessed a man as happy and winsome in his occupation. Edward moved as if certain animal secrets were known to him. He originated a new, dangerous tennis, taking the ball into his racket with a muscular patience; then one heard the sweet crack, heard the singing ball, and hung cold with a little terror at the speed and the smart violent arc it made into the green. French was by then wearing spectacles. His coiled hair, the color of a kind of charred gold, blazed with sweat. On his lips was the charmed smile of the seraphim. Something of the priest and the brute mingled, perhaps warred, in his expression. Baby Levaster, who had no culture, could not place the line of beauty that French Edward descended from, but finally remembered a photograph of the David statue he'd seen in an old encyclopedia. French Edward looked like that.

When French Edward won, Levaster heard a louder, baleful, unclublike bravo from the gallery. It was Dr. Word. Levaster watched Word fight through the crowd toward French. The man was crazed with partisanship. Levaster, wanting to get close to the person of French himself, three-quarters drunk on gin he'd poured into the iced Cokes from the stand, saw Word reach for French's buttock and give it a pinch. French turned, hate in his eye. He said something quick and corrosive to Word. All the smiles around them turned to straight mouths of concern. Dr. Word looked harmless, a tanned old fellow wearing a beige beret.

"You ought to be dead," said French.

"As graceful, powerful an exhibition of the grandest game as your old coach would ever hope to see! I saw some of the old tricks I taught you! Oh, son, son!" Dr. Word screamed.

Everyone knew he was ill then.

"Go home," said French, looking very soonly sorry as he said it.

"You come home and see us!" Word bellowed, and left.

French's woman, Cecilia Emile, put her head on his chest. She was short, bosomy, and pregnant, a Franco-Italian blessed with a fine large nose, the arrogance of which few men forgot. Next came her hair, a black field of delight. French had found her at L.S.U. They married almost on the spot. Her father was Fat Tim Emile, a low-key monopolist in pinball and wrestling concessions in New Orleans—filthy rich. Levaster did not know this. He stared at the strained hot eyes of French, having surrendered his body to the man, and French saw him.

"Baby Levaster? Is it you? From Vicksburg? You look terrible."

"But you, you . . ." Levaster tripped on a tape and fell into the green clay around Edward's sneakers. ". . . are beauty . . . my youth-memory elegant forever!"

The Edwards took Levaster home to Covington, across the bridge. The Edwards lived in a great glassy house with a pool in back and tall pines hanging over.

French was sad. He said, "She still carries it on with him. They meet out in the Civil War park at night and go to it in those marble houses. One of my old high-school sweethearts saw them and wrote me about it. She wrote it to hurt me, and it did hurt me."

"That old fart Word? Impossible. He's too goddamn loud to carry on any secret rendezvous, for one thing. You could hear the bastard sigh from a half mile off."

"My mother accepts him for what he is."

"That man is destroyed by stroke."

"I know. I gave it to him. She doesn't care. She takes the limping and the bad arm and the hollering. He got under her skin."

"I remember her," Baby Levaster said. "Some handsome woman, auburn hair with a few grey ends. Forgive me, but I had teen-age dreams about her myself. I always thought she was waiting for a romance, living on the hope of something out there, something. . . ."

"Don't leave me, Baby. I need your mind with me. Somebody from the hometown. Somebody who knows."

"I used to whip your little ass at tennis," Levaster said.

"Yes." French smiled. "You barely moved and I was running all over the court. You just stood there and knocked them everywhere like I was hitting into a fan."

They became fast friends. Baby Levaster became an intern. He arrived sober at the funeral of the Edwards' newborn son and saw the tiny black grave its coffin went into behind the Catholic chapel. He looked over to mourners at the fringe. There were Dr. Word and his brother Wilbur under a mimosa, lingering off fifty feet from the rest. Word held his beret to his heart. Levaster was very glad that French never saw Word. They all heard a loud voice, but Word was on the other side of the hill by then, bellowing his sympathetic distress to Wilbur, and the Edwards could not see him.

"Whose voice was that!" asked French.

"Just a voice," said Levaster.

"Whose? Don't I know it? It makes me sick." French turned back to Cecilia, covered with a black veil, her handkerchief pressed to lips. Her child had been born with dysfunction of the involuntary muscles. Her eyes rose toward the hot null blue of the sky. French supported her. His gaze was angrier. It penetrated to the careless heart of nature, right in there to its sullen riot.

On the other side of the cemetery, Dr. Word closed the door of the car. Wilbur drove. Loyal to his brother to the end, almost deaf from the pitch of his voice, Wilbur wheeled the car with veteran patience. Dr. Word wiped his head and held the beret to his chest.

"Ah, Wilbur! They were so unlucky! Nowhere could there be a handsomer couple! They had every right to expect a little Odysseus! Ah, to see doubt and sorrow cloud the faces of those young lovers! Bereft of hope, philosophy!"

Wilbur reached under the seat for the pint of philosophy he had developed since his tour of Korea. It was cognac. The brotherly high music came, tasting of burnt plums, revealing the faces of old officer friends to him.

"James," he said. "I think after this . . . that this is the moment, now, to break it off with Olive—forever. Unless you want to see more doubt and sorrow cloud the face of your young friend."

Word's reply was curiously quiet.

"We cannot do what we cannot do. If she will not end it—and she will not—I cannot. Too deep a sense of joy, Wilbur. The whole quality of my life determined by it."

"Ah, Jimmy," Wilbur said, "you were just too long a queer. The first piece you found had to be permanent. She ain't Cleopatra. If you'd just've started early, nailing the odd twat like the rest of us. . . ."

"I don't want old soldier's reason! No reason! I will not suffer that contamination! Though I love you!"

Dr. Word was hollering again. Wilbur drove them back to Vicksburg.

Cecilia was too frightened to have another child after she lost the first one. Her body would not carry one longer than a month. She was constantly pregnant for a while, and then she stopped conceiving. She began doing watercolors, the faintest violets and greens. French Edward took up the clarinet. Baby Levaster saw it: they were attempting to become art people. Cecilia was pitiful. French went beyond that into dreadfulness; ruesome honks poured from his horn. How wrong and unfortunate that they should have taken their grief into art, thought Levaster. It made them fools who were cut from glory's cloth, who were charmed darlings of the sun.

"What do you think?" asked French, after he'd hacked a little ditty from Mozart into a hundred froggish leavings.

"Yes," Dr. Levaster said. "I think I'll look through some of Cissy's pictures now."

"You didn't like it," French said, downcast, even angry.

"When are you going to get into another tournament? Why sit around here revealing your scabs to me and the neighbors? You need to get out and hit the ball."

French left, walked out, smoldering and spiteful. Baby Levaster remained there. He knocked on Cecilia's door. She was at her spattered art desk working over a watercolor, her bare back to Levaster, her hair lying thick to the small of it, and below, her naked heels. Her efforts were thumbtacked around from ceiling to molding, arresting one with their meek awkward redundancies, things so demure they resisted making an image against the retina. They were not even clouds; rather, the pale ghosts of clouds: the advent of stains, hardly noticeable against paper.

"I can't turn around, but hello," said Cecilia.

"What are all these about?"

"What do you think?"

"I don't know . . . smudges? The vagueness of all things?"

"They aren't things. They're emotions."

"You mean hate, fear, desire, envy?"

"Yes. And triumph and despair." She pointed.

"This is subtle. They look the same," Levaster said.

"I know. I'm a nihilist."

"You aren't any such thing."

"Oh? Why not?"

"Because you've combed your hair. You wanted me to come in here and discover that you're a nihilist," Levaster said.

"Nihilists can comb their hair." She bit her lip, pouting.

"I'd like to see your chest. That's art."

"You toilet. Leave us alone."

"Maybe if you *are* art, Cissy, you shouldn't try to *do* art."

"You want me to be just a decoration?"

"Yes," Levaster said. "A decoration of the air. Decoration is more important than art."

"Is that what you learned in med school? That's dumb." She turned around. "A boob is a boob is a boob."

Dr. Levaster fainted.

At the River Oaks Club in Houston, French played again. The old happiness came back to him, a delight that seemed to feed off his grace. The sunburned Levaster held French's towel for him, resined French's racket handles, and coached him on the weaknesses of the opponents, which is unsportsmanly, untennislike, and all but illegal. A Spaniard Edward was creaming complained, and they threw Levaster off the court and back to the stands. He watched French work the court, roving back and forth, touching the ball with a deft chip, knocking the cooties off it, serving as if firing a curved musket across the net, the Spaniard falling distraught. And throughout, French's smile, widening and widening until it was just this side of loony. Here was a man truly at play, thought Levaster, at one with the pleasant rectangle of the court, at home, in his own field, something *peaceful* in the violent sweep of his racket. A certain slow anomalous serenity invested French Edward's motion. The thought of this parched Levaster.

"Christ, for a drink!" he said out loud.

"Here, son. Cold brandy." The man Levaster sat next to brought out a pint from the ice in a styrofoam box. Levaster chugged it—exquisite!—then almost spat up the boon as he noticed the fellow on the far side of the brandy man. It was Dr. Word. The man beside Levaster was Wilbur. Word's noble cranium glinted under the sun. His voice had modulated.

"Ah, ah, my boy! An arc of genius," Word whispered as they

saw French lay a disguised lob thirty feet from the Spaniard. "He's learned the lob, Wilbur! Our boy has it all now!" Word's voice went on in soft screaming. He seemed to be seeing keenly out of the left eye. The right was covered by eyelid, the muscles there having finally surrendered. So, Levaster thought, this is what the stroke finally left him.

"How's Vicksburg?" Levaster asked Wilbur.

"Nothing explosive, Doctor. Kudzu and the usual erosion."

"What say you try to keep Professor Word away from French until he does his bit in the tournament. A lot depends on his making the finals here."

"I'm afraid the professor's carrying a letter on him from Olive to French. That's why he's not hollering. He's got the letter. It's supposed to say everything."

"But don't let French see him till it's over. And could I hit the brandy again?" Levaster said.

"Of course," said Wilbur. "One man can't drink the amount I brought over. Tennis bores the shit out of me."

In the finals, Edward met Whitney Humble, a tall man from South Africa whose image and manner refuted the usual notion of the tennis star. He was pale, spindly, hairy, with the posture of a derelict. He spat phlegm on the court and picked his nose between serves. Humble appeared to be splitting the contest between one against his opponent and another against the excrescence of his own person. Some in the gallery suspected he served a wet ball. Playing as if with exasperated distaste for the next movement this game had dragged him to, Humble was nevertheless there when the ball came and knocked everything back with either speed or a snarling spin. The voice of Dr. Word came cheering, bellowing for French. Humble identified the bald head in the audience that had hurrahed his error at the net. He served a line drive into the gallery that hit Word square in his good eye.

"Fault!" said the judge. The crowd was horrified.

Humble placed his high-crawling second serve to French.

Levaster saw little of the remaining match. Under the bleachers, where they had dragged Word, Levaster and Wilbur attended to the great black peach that was growing around Word's good eye. With ice and a handkerchief, they abated the swelling, and then all three men returned to their seats. Dr. Word could see out of a black slit of his optic cavity, see French win in a sequel of preposterous dives at the net. Levaster's body fled away from his bones and gathered on the muscles of French Edward. The crowd was screaming over the victory. Nowhere, nowhere, would they ever see again such a clear win of beauty over smut.

Fat Tim, Cecilia's father, would be happy and put five thousand in French's bank if French won this tournament, and Fat Tim would pay Levaster one thousand, as promised, for getting French back on the track of fame. Fat Tim Emile, thumbing those greasy accounts of his concessions, saw French as the family knight, a jouster among grandees, a champion in the whitest sport of all, a game Fat Tim viewed as a species of cunning highbrowism under glass. So he paid French simply for being himself, for wearing white, for symbolizing the pedigree Fat Tim was without, being himself a sweaty dago, a tubby with smudged shirt cuffs and phlebitis. "Get our boy back winning. I want to read his name in the paper," said Fat Tim.

"I will," said Levaster.

So I did, thought Levaster, French won.

Dr. Levaster saw Dr. Word crowding up, getting swarmed out to the side by the little club bitches and fuzzchins with programs for autographing in hand. Word fought back in, however, approaching French from the back. Levaster saw Word pinch French and heard Word bellow something hearty. By the time Levaster reached the court, the altercation had spread through the crowd. A letter lay in the clay dust, and Word, holding up his hand to ameliorate, was backing out of sight, his good eye but a glint in a cracked bruise, the lid falling gruesome.

"Baby! Baby!" called French, the voice baffled. Levaster reached him. "He pinched me!" French screamed. "He got me right there, really hard!"

Levaster picked up the letter and collected the rackets, then led French straight to the car. No shower, no street clothes.

My Dearest French,

This is your mother Olive writing in case you have forgotten what my handwriting looks like. You have lost your baby son and I have thought of you these months. Now I ask you to think of me. I lost my grown son years ago. You know when, and you know the sin which is old history. I do not want to lose you, my darling. You are such a strange handsomely made boy I would forget you were mine until I remembered you fed at my breast and I changed your diapers. When I saw you wearing new glasses at your wedding if I looked funny it was because I wanted to touch your eyes under them they changed you even more. But I knew you didn't want me anywhere near you. Your bride Cissy was charming as well as stunning and I'm deeply glad her father is well-off and you don't have to work for a living if you don't want to. Your father tried to play for a living or get near where there was athletics but it didn't work as smoothly for him. It drove him crazy, to be truthful. He was lost for a week in February until James Word, the bearer of this letter, found him at the college baseball field throwing an old wet football at home plate. He had been sleeping in the dugout and eating nothing but these dextrose and salt tablets. I didn't write you this before because you were being an expectant father and then the loss of your child. Maybe you get all your sports drive from your father. But can you see how awfully difficult it was to live with him? Certain other things have happened before I never told you about. He refereed a high-school football game between Natchez and Vicksburg and when it was tight at the end he threw a block on a Natchez player. We love him, French, but he has been away from us a long time.

So I fell in love with James Word. Don't worry, your father still knows nothing. That is sort of proof where his mind is, in a way. Your father has not even wanted "relations" with me in years. He said he was saving himself up. He was in a poker game with some coaches at the college but they threw him out for cheating. James tried to arrange a tennis doubles game with me and your father against another couple, but your father tried to hit it so hard when it came to him that he knocked them over into the service station and etc. so we had no more balls.

The reason I sent this by James is because I thought if it was right from his hand you would see that it was not jut a nasty slipping-around thing between us but a thing of the heart. His stroke has left him blind in one eye and without sure control of his voice. But he loves you. And he loves me. I believe God is with us too. Please take us all together and let's smile again. I am crying as I write this. But maybe that's not fair to mention that. James has mentioned taking us all, your father included, on a vacation to Padre Island in Texas, him paying all the expenses. Can't you please say yes and make everything happy?

Love,
Mother

"It was his fingers pinching me," whined French. "He pinched me all the time when he was coaching me."

Levaster said, "And if he hadn't coached you, you wouldn't be anything at all, would you? You'd be selling storm-fencing in Vicksburg, wouldn't you? You'd never have pumped that snatch or had the swimming pool."

Back at his clinic, Levaster slept on a plastic couch in the waiting room. The nurse woke him up. He was so lonely and horny that he proposed to her, though he'd never had a clear picture of her face. Months ago he'd called her into his office. He'd had an erection for four days without rest.

"Can you make anything of this, Louise? Get the *Merck Manual.* Severe hardship even to walk." She had been charming. But when he moved to her leg, clasping on it like a spaniel on the hot, she denied him, and he had since considered her a woman of principle.

She accepted his proposal. They married. Her parents, strong Methodists living somewhere out in New Mexico, appeared at the wedding. They stood in a corner, leaning inward like a pair of sculling oars. Levaster's mother came, too, talking about the weather and her new shoes. Someone mistook her for nothing in one of the chairs and sat on her lap. French was best man. Cecilia was there, a dress of lime sherbet and titties, black hair laid back with gemlike roses at the temples. She made Levaster's bride look like something dumped out of a ship, a swathed burial at sea. Cecilia's beauty was unfair to all women. Furthermore, Levaster himself, compared to French (nugget-cheeked in a tux), was no beau of the ball. He was balding, waxen, all sweat, a small man with bad posture to boot.

Levaster expected to lean on the tough inner goodness of his bride, Louise. He wanted his life bathed and rectified. They resumed their life as doctor and nurse at the alley clinic, where Levaster undercharged the bums, winos, hustlers, hookers, artists, and the occasional wayward debutante, becoming something of an expert on pneumonia, herpes, potassium famine and other diseases of the street. He leaned on the tough inner goodness of Louise, leaning and leaning, prone, supine, baby-opossum position. Levaster played tennis, he swam in the Edwards' pool, he stuck to beer and wine. In the last whole surge of his life, he won a set from French at the Metairie Club. This act caused Dr. Levaster a hernia and a frightful depletion of something untold in his cells, the rare *it* of life, the balm that washes and assures the brain happiness is around the corner. Levaster lost this sense for three months. He became a creature of the barbarous moment; he had lost patience. Now he cursed his patients and treated them as malingering clutter. He drank straight from a flask of rye laced with cocaine, swearing to the sick about the abominitions they had wreaked on themselves. At nights Levaster wore an oversized black sombrero and forced Louise into awkward and nameless desecrations. And when they were over, he called her an idiot, a puppet. Then one morning the hopeful clarity of the mind returned to him. He believed again in sun and grass and the affable complicity of the human race. But where was his wife? He wanted to lean on her inner goodness some more. Her plain face, her fine muscular pale legs, where were they? Louise was gone. She had typed a note. "One more week of this and you'd have taken us to the bottom of hell. I used to be a weak but good person. Now I am strong and evil. I hope you're satisfied. Goodbye."

At the clinic, his patients were afraid of him. The freeloaders and gutter cowboys shuddered. What will it be, Doc? "French. It was French Edward who . . . took it away from me. It cost me. I suppose I wanted to defeat beauty, the outrage of the natural, the glibness of the God-favored. All in that one set of tennis. Ladies and gentlemen, the physician has been sick and he apologizes." He coughed, dry in the throat. "It cost me my wife, but I am open for business." They swarmed him with the astounded love of sinners for a fallen angel. Levaster was nursed by whores. A rummy with a crutch fetched him coffee. Something, someone, in a sputum-colored blanket, functioned as receptionist.

At last he was home. He lived in a room of the clinic. On his thirty-fourth birthday, they almost killed him with a party and congratulations. The Edwards came. Early in the morning French found Levaster gasping over his fifth Cuban cigar on the roof of the clinic. The sky over New Orleans was a glorious blank pink.

"We're getting older, Baby."

"You're still all right, French. You had all the moves at Forest Hills. Some bad luck, three bad calls. But still the crowd's darling. You could've beat Jesus at Wimbledon."

"I always liked to play better than to win," said French.

"I always liked to win better than to play," said Levaster.

"But, Baby, I never played. First it was my father, then Word. I don't know what kind of player I would be like if I truly *played* when I play."

"But you smile when you play."

"I love the game, on theory. And I admire myself."

"You fool a lot of people. We thought you were happy."

"I am. I feel like I'm doing something nearly as well as it could ever be done. But it's not play. It's slavery."

"A slave to your talent."

"And to the idea of tennis. But, Baby, when I die I don't want my last thought to be a tennis court. You've got people you've cured of disease to think about. They're down there giving you a party. Here I am, thirty-two."

"I'm thirty-four. So what?"

"I want you to tell me, give me something to think about. You've done it before, but now I want something big." French pointed to the sky.

"I won't do that. Don't you understand that the main reason you're a star is the perfect mental desert you're able to maintain between your ears for hours and hours? You memorize the court and the memory sinks straight to your muscles, because there is nothing else in there to cloud the vision."

"Are you calling me stupid?"

"No. But a wild psychic desert. I'm sure it works for artists as well as jocks."

"You mean," said French, "I can't have a thought?"

"You could have one, but it wouldn't live for very long. Like most athletes, you'll go straight from glory to senility with no interlude of thought. I love you," Levaster said.

French said, "I love you, Baby."

Dr. Levaster could no longer bear the flood of respect and affection spilling from the growing horde at the clinic. *The Times-Picayune* had an article about his work among the down-and-out. It was as if Levaster had to eat a tremendous barge of candy every day. The affection and esteem bore hard on a man convinced he was worthless. He had a hundred thousand in the bank. No longer could he resist. He bought a Lincoln demonstrator, shut the clinic, and drove to New York, carrying the double-barreled .410 shotgun/pistol with cherrywood handle paid to him in lieu of fee. He sifted into Elaine's, drunk, Southern and insulting, but was ignored. By the time Levaster had been directed to a sullen playwright, some target frailer than he, on whom he could pour the black beaker of his hatred of art, the movement of the crowd would change and Levaster would be swept away to a group of new enemies. Idlers, armchairers, martini wags, curators of the great empty museums (themselves), he called them. Not one of them could hold a candle to Willum Faulkner, Levaster shouted, having never read a page of the man. He drove his Lincoln everywhere, reveling in the hate and avarice of the city, disappearing into it with a shout of ecstasy.

Then Dr. Levaster met V. T., the Yugoslav sensation, drinking a beer at Elaine's with a noted sportswriter. Forest Hills was to begin the next day. Levaster approved of V. T. Heroic bitterness informed V. T.'s face and he dressed in bad taste, a suit with padded shoulders, narrow tie, pointy shoes.

"Who did you draw first round?" asked Levaster.

"Freench Edwaird," V. T. said.

"Edward won't get around your serve if you're hitting it," said the sportswriter. V. T.'s serve had been clocked at 170 m.p.h. at Wimbledon.

"Ees always who find the beeg rhythm. You find the beeg rhythm or you play on luck."

"If you beat Edward tomorrow," Levaster said, "I will eat your suit."

But the two men had turned away and never heard.

He took the Lincoln out to the West Side Tennis Club and tore his sweater clambering over a fence. He slept in a blanket he had brought with him, out of the dew, under the bleachers. When morning came, Levaster found the right court. The grass was sparkling. It was a heavy minor classic in the realm of tennis. The crowd loved French Edward and V. T., the both of them. When Edward hit one from behind the back for a winner off an unseen overhead smash from V. T., the crowd screamed. V. T. was in his

rhythm and knocking his serve in at 160 m.p.h. The crowd adored this, too. French, who had always had a big, very adequate serve, took up the velocity of it to match the great bullet of V. T. At the end, they were men fielding nothing but white blurs against each other. Edward won.

For a half-second the crowd was quiet. They had never imagined the ball could be kept in play at such stupendous speed. Then they roared. French Edward leaped over the net. Levaster swooned. His head sailed and joined the head of French Edward, rolled and tossed in the ale-colored curls. Then Levaster saw Dr. Word run out onto the grass, his bellowing lost in the crowd's bellowing. The old man, whose beret had fallen off on the churned service court, put his hand on French's back. Word looked frail, liver spots on his forearms, his scalp speckled and lined. Levaster saw French turn in anger. Then the both of them were overrun by a whirlpool of well-groomed tennis children and mothers and men who rode trains to work, half of their mental life revolving around improvement of the backhand. Levaster wished for his elegant pistol. He left, picking fights with those who looked askance at his blanket.

A few years passed and Levaster was almost forty. He opened the clinic in New Orleans again. Then he closed it and returned to New York. Now Levaster admitted that he languished when French Edward was out of his vision. A hollow inconsequence filled his acts, good or evil, whenever Edward was not near. He flew with Edward to France, to Madrid, to Prague. He lay angry and mordant with hangover on hotel beds as French Edward worked out on the terrible physical schedule Levaster had prescribed—miles of running, sit-ups, swimming, shadowboxing.

Edward was hardly ever beaten in an early round, but he was fading in the third and fourth day of tournaments now. He had become a spoiler against high seeds in early rounds, though never a winner. His style was greatly admired. A Portuguese writer called him "the New Orleans ace who will not surrender his youth." The Prague paper advocated him as "the dangerous happy cavalier"; Madrid said, "He fights windmills, but, viewing his style, we are convinced his contests matter." Yes, thought Levaster, this style must run its full lustrous route. It cannot throw in the towel until there is the last humiliation, something neither one of us can take.

Then it occurred to Levaster. French had never been humiliated in a match. He had lost, but he had never been humiliated. Not in a single match, not a single game. The handsome head had never bowed, the rusting gold of French Edward's curls stayed high in the sun. He remained the sage and brute that he was when he was nineteen. There was still the occasional winner off his racket that could never have been predicted by the scholars of the game. Levaster felt his soul rise in the applause for this. In Mexico City, there was a standing ovation for the most uncanny movement ever seen on the court. El Niño de Merida smacked down an overhead that bounced high and out of play over the backstop. But Edward had climbed the fence to field it, legs and one arm in the wire, racket-hand free for the half second it took to strike the ball back, underhanded. The ball took a boomerang arc to the other side and notched the corner of the ad court. My Christ, thought Levaster, as the Mexicans screamed, he climbed the fence and never lost style.

When they returned from this trip, Levaster read in the paper about an open tournament at Vicksburg. Whitney Humble had already been signed up. The prize money was $2,000, singles winner take all. They called it the Delta Open.

"I know Word has something to do with this. Nobody in Vicksburg ever gave a damn about tennis but him, you Baby, and me," French Edward said.

"You should let the home folks finally see you. Your image would do wonders for the place," said Levaster. "They've read about you. Now they want to see you. Why not? I've been wanting to go back and put a headmarker on my mother's grave, though it would be false to what she was. I've got all this money hanging around. I get sentimental, guilty. Don't you ever?"

"Yes," French Edward said.

They went back to Vicksburg. On the second day of the tournament, they got a call at the Holiday Inn. Fat Tim Emile had died. Nobody had known he was dying but him. He had written a short letter full of pride and appreciation to Cecilia and French, thanking French for his association with the family and for valiant contests in the tennis world. Fat Tim left them two hundred thousand and insisted on nobody giving any ceremony. He wanted his remaining body to go straight to the Tulane med school. "This body," he wrote, "it was fat maybe, but I was proud of it. Those young doctors-to-be, like Baby Levaster, might find something new in me. I was scared all my life and stayed honest. I never hurt another man or woman, that I know of. When I made money, I started eating well. Baby Levaster warned me. I guess I've died of success."

"My poor Cecilia," said French.

"Cissy is fine," said Levaster. "She said for you to finish the tournament."

So he did.

Levaster looked on in a delirium of sober nostalgia. Through the trees, in a slit of the bluffs, he could see the river. French's mother and father sat together and watched their son. Dr. Word, near eighty, was a linesman. They are old people, thought Levaster, looking at the Edwards. And him, Word, he's a goddamned *relic*. A spry relic. Younger brother Wilbur was not there because he was dead.

Whitney Humble and French Edward met in the finals. Humble had aged gruesomely, too, Levaster saw, and knew it was from fighting it out in small tournaments for almost two decades, earning bus fare and tiny fame in newspapers from Alabama to Idaho. But Humble still wanted to play. The color of a dead perch, thinner in the calf, Humble smoked cigarettes between ad games. All his equipment was grey and dirty, even his racket. He could not run much anymore. Some teeth were busted out.

A wild crowd of Vicksburg people, greasers and their pregnant brides from the mobile homes included, met to cheer French. Humble did not have a fan. He was hacking up phlegm and coughing out lengths of it, catching it on his shirt, a tort even those for the underdog could not abide. The greasers felt lifted to some estate of taste by Humble.

It was a long and sparkling match. Humble won.

Humble took the check and the sterling platter, hurled the platter outside the fence and into the trees, then slumped off. The image of tennis was ruined for years in Vicksburg.

Dr. Word and the Edwards meet French on the court. Levaster sees Word lift an old crabby arm to French's shoulder, sees French wince. Mr. Edward says he has to hurry to his job. He wears a comical uniform and cap. His job is checking vegetable produce at the bridge-house of the river so that boll weevils will not enter Mississippi from Louisiana. Levaster looks into the eyes of Mrs. Edward. Yes, he decides, she still loves Word; her eyes touch him like fingers, and perhaps he still cuts it, and perhaps they rendezvous out in the Civil War cemetery so he won't have far to fall when he explodes with fornication, the old infantryman of lust.

"Mother," says French, "let's all meet at the bridge house."

Levaster sees the desperate light in French's eye.

"Don't you, don't you!" says Levaster afterward, driving the Lincoln.

"I've got to. It'll clear the trash. I can't live if Word's still in it."

"He's nothing but bones," says Levaster. "He's done for."

"She still loves him," says French.

They all gather at the bridge-house, and French tells his father that his wife has been cheating on him for twenty years, and brings up his hands, and begins crying, and points to Word. Mr. Edward looks at Word, then back to his son. He is terribly concerned. He asks Word to leave the little hut for a second, apologizing to Word. He asks Olive to come stand by him and puts his arm over his wife's shoulders.

"Son," he whispers, "Jimmy Word, friend to us and steady as a brick to us, is a homosexual. Look out there, what you've done to him. He's running."

Then they are all strung out on the walkway of the bridge, Levaster marveling at how swift old Word is, for Word is out there nearing the middle of the bridge, Mrs. Edward next, fifty yards behind, French passing his mother, gaining on Word. Levaster is running, too. He, too, passes Olive, who has given out and is leaning on the rail. Levaster sees Word mount the rail and balance on it like a gymnast. He puts on a burst of speed and catches up with French, who has stopped running and is walking toward Word cautiously, his hand on the rail.

"Just close your eyes, son. I'll be gone." Word says, looking negligible as a spirit in his smart tennis jacket and beret. He trembles on the rail. Below Word is the sheen of the river, the evening sun lying over it down there, low reds flashing on the brown water.

That's a hundred feet down there, Levaster thinks. When he looks up, French has gotten up on the rail and is balancing himself, moving step by step toward Word.

"Don't," say Levaster and Word together.

French, the natural, is walking on the rail with the ease of an avenue hustler. He has found his purchase: this sport is nothing.

"Son! No closer!" bawls Word.

"I'm not your son. I'm bringing you back, old bastard."

They meet. French seems to be trying to pick up Word in an infant position, arm under legs. Word's beret falls off and floats, puffed out, into the deep hole over the river. French has him, has him wrestled into the shape of a fetus. Then Word gives a kick, and Olive screams, and the two men fall backward into the red air and down. Levaster watches them coil together in the drop.

There is a great deal of time until they hit. At the end, Edward flings the old suicide off and hits the river in a nice straight-legged jump. Word hits the river flat as a board. Levaster thinks he hears the sound of Word's back breaking.

The river is shallow here, with strong devious currents. Nothing comes up. By the time the patrol gets out, there is no hope. Then Levaster, standing in a boat, spots French, sitting under a willow a half-mile downriver from the bridge. French has drowned and broken one leg, but has crawled out of the river by instinct. His brain is already choked.

French Edward stares at the rescue boat as if it is a turtle with vermin gesturing toward him, Levaster and Olive making their cries of discovery.

Carina, Levaster's teen-ager, woke him up. She handed him a cold beer and a Dexedrine. At first Levaster did not understand. Then he knew that the sun had come up again, seeing the grainy abominable light on the alley through the window. This was New York. Who was the child? Why was he naked on the sheets?

Ah, Carina.

"Will you marry me, Carina?" Levaster said.

"Before I saw your friend, I might have," she said.

French Edward came into the room, fully dressed, hair wet from a shower.

"Where do I run, Baby?" he said.

Levaster told him to run around the block fifty times.

"He does everything you tell him," said Carina.

"Of course he does. Fry me some eggs, you dumb twat."

As the eggs and bacon were sizzling, Levaster came into the kitchen in his Taiwan bathrobe, the huge black sombrero on his head. He had oiled and loaded the .410 shotgun/pistol.

"Put two more eggs on for French. He's really hungry after he runs."

Carina broke two more eggs.

"He's so magnificent," she said. "How much of his brain does he really have left?"

"Enough," Levaster said.

Levaster drove them to New Hampshire, to Bretton Woods. He saw Laver and Ashe approach French Edward in the lobby of the inn. They wanted to shake hands with French, but he did not recognize them. French stood there with hands down, looking ahead into the wall.

The next day Levaster took French out to the court for his first match. He put the Japanese Huta into his hand. It was a funny manganese and fiberglass racket with a split throat. The Huta firm had paid French ten thousand to use it on the circuit just before he drowned in the river. French had never hit with it before.

Levaster struck a hard blow against the heart. French started and gave a sudden happy regard to the court.

"I'm here," said French.

"You're damned right. Don't let us down."

Edward played better than he had in years. He was going against an Indian twenty years his junior. The boy had a serve and a wicked deceptive blast off his backhand. The crowd loved the Indian. The boy was polite and beautiful. But then French Edward had him at match-point on his serve.

Edward threw the ball up.

"Hit it, *hit*. My life, hit it," whispered Levaster.

Showdown at Great Hole

DON DE LILLO

Little Billy Twillig stepped aboard a Sony 747 bound for a distant land. He was fourteen years old, smaller than most people that age—examined at close range, he might be said to feature an uncanny sense of concentration, a fixed intensity that countervailed his noncommittal brown eyes and generally listless manner.

The sound of the miniaturized propulsion system grew louder and soon the plane was in the air. Its angle of ascent was severe enough to frighten the boy, who had never been on an airplane before. With Sweden at war, he had received his Nobel Prize in a brief ceremony on the lawn in Pennyfellow, Connecticut, traveling to and from that locale in the back seat of his father's little Ford.

It was the first Nobel Prize ever given in mathematics. The work that led to the award was understood by only three or four people, all mathematicians, of course, and it was at their confidential urging that the Nobel committee, traditionally at a total loss in this field, finally settled on Twillig, William Denis Jr., premature every inch of him, a snug fit in a quart mug.

In the wall ahead was a darkened arch, through which the linear glide moved. Billy stepped off the glide just as it whispered through. Beyond was a door with a black arrow painted on it. The arrow pointed down. He opened the door and went down a flight of old stone steps. He came to the bottom of the vertical shaft and there found a large jagged hole in one wall and next to the hole a man with a plastic torch in his hand, flames two feet high.

"I'm Evinrude," the man said. "You're late."

"Is this the ceremony?"

"They're working out size places and they want the smallest last. That's the only thing that saved you."

The torch the man held was very large and Billy hoped they wouldn't give him one to carry, particularly if the ceremony were to be a long one.

"What happens next?" he said.

"I ask you why you're late."

"Nobody could tell me where the Great Hall was. Nobody could tell me how to get here."

"You gave them the wrong name," Evinrude said. "It's not the Great Hall. It's the Great *Hole*."

"But this is the ceremony for Ratner, right?"

"Just to make it official, I have to ask you if you're a laureate."

"Yes."

"In what field?"

"Mathematics."

"Because only laureates are allowed beyond this point," Evinrude said.

"Zorgs. I won for zorgs," Billy said.

"What's that?"

"A class of numbers."

"Out of curiosity, would I know what you were talking about if you described them further?"

"No," Billy said. "And what's this about size places?"

"It's to get a dramatic effect with the torches."

"We all hold torches?"

"The laureates," Evinrude said. "All the laureates get a torch and go to their size places and then light the torch and hold it."

"Why are they having the ceremony down here?"

"Ratner's people."

"What kind of people?"

"The doctor, the nurse, the organist, the fella from the bearded sect. They insisted on having the ceremony in the Great Hole because there's a sense of past in the Great Hole and because that's to be considered, awareness of past, respect for heritage. The laureates agreed. Those that were consulted."

"I wasn't consulted."

"You were very, very late. Maybe that's why you weren't consulted. Ratner's people weren't late. They came thousands of miles, but they got here on time."

"They weren't told Great Hall instead of Great Hole."

"Time to go in," Evinrude said. "Step lively, keep it moving, spread it out."

Evinrude dipped the torch and Billy stepped through the hole and walked down a flight of crooked stairs into a small dusty room with nothing in it but a bronze door and a stone bench. He sat on the bench and looked at the door. The door opened, admitting a man wearing a mink fedora and a long black coat. His beard, white and untrimmed, reached to his chest, ends wiry, toughened by decades of misery and grit. The man's coat extended almost to his shoes. He approached the bench and Billy moved over to give him room to sit, but the man stopped short of the bench, put his hands behind his back and leaned forward slightly, head inclined, lips beginning to move a few seconds before he actually said anything.

"The old gentleman wants you to present the roses."

"I thought you were the old gentleman," Billy said.

"I'm Pitkin, who advises on the writings. I'm looking at the person he picked by hand to present him the roses face-to-face. He's one sweetheart of a human being. I advise him on the mystical writings. But if they forced it out of me with hot tongs, I'd tell them I learn more from Shazar Ratner than I could ever teach him if I live to be—go ahead, name me a figure.''

"A hundred."

"Name me higher."

"A hundred and fifty."

"Stop there," Pitkin said. "Many years ago he came back to his roots. Eastern Parkway. Strictness like you wouldn't believe. But the old gentleman, he was tickled to get back."

"What kind of strictness?"

"The codes, the rules, the laws, the customs, the tablecloth, the silverware, the dishes. He's a living doll," Pitkin said. "After you present the roses, he has a word or two he wants to whisper up to you. You're the youngest. He figures you'll be worth telling. The others, he wouldn't give you two cents for the whole bunch. Science? He turned his back on science. Science made him a household word, a name in the sky, but he grew world-weary of it. He returned to the wellspring to drink. They assigned me then and there. I know the writings. Many years ago, I committed the writings to memory. They don't know this, the other elders, because we're not supposed to memorize. It's considered cheating when you memorize. When you memorize, you lose the inner meaning. But how else could a dumbbell like me become an elder? Name me a way and I'll do it. If I'm lying, may both your eyes drip vengeful pus.''

"Why *my* eyes?" Billy said.

"Because that's the oath," Pitkin said. "I didn't word the oath. Go ask who worded it why *your* eyes. So show a little mercy to someone whose whole life has been awe, fear, and kilt."

"Awe, fear, and *guilt*," Billy said.

"A corrector I got in front of me. I need this from a peewee quiz kid? One thing I want to tell you even if it breaks my heart giving advice to a speller. A little advice free of charge straight from the mystical writings. You ready for this? Quiz kid, corrector, you want to be instructed from the writings or you want to go through life waving your shvontzie like a monkey?"

"I'm listening."

"Learn some awe and fear."

"Is that it?"

"White monkey, speller, keep your business out of other people's noses. What did I say you should learn?"

"Some awe and fear," Billy said.

The bronze door opened and a doctor and nurse entered. The doctor held a huge syringe and the nurse was wheeling a device that consisted of a gallon bottle of colorless fluid and a thin black hose that extended from the bottle through a Pyrex vessel and into a small clear cylindrical container. Paying no attention to the old man and boy, the doctor began to fill the syringe with fluid processed through the hose, vessel, and tube.

"Some doctor," Pitkin whispered. "Only the worst cases he takes. He makes so much money, you couldn't count that high. A house with grounds. Two big doors, front and back. A toaster that does four slices. His yacht, he named it *Transurethral Prostatectomy*. Uses a colored nurse. See her? Wtih the tube in her hand? Colored. Walk in any hospital right off the street and that's what you see. Uniforms, shoes, folded hats. Like anybody. Only colored. A total specialist, Dr. Bonwit. The old gentleman swears by him. Only because of Bonwit he could come for the torches all this way. With Bonwit alone he's willing to travel. Round-trip we're paying. Ratner, Bonwit, Pitkin, the organ player, the colored nurse. We took up collections in the neighborhood. This is the respect people have for the name Ratner both before and after he turned his back."

" It's a back problem?"

"Turned his back on *science*."

"What's wrong with him to make him have to travel with a doctor?"

"Not just a doctor, please. A specialist. Never, please, say *doctor* to the doctor's face. You don't know this? What am I looking at here? How many kinds of genius did they tell me to watch out for? Pisher, where should you keep your business out of?"

"Other people's noses," Billy said.

"A little awe and fear never hurt anybody," Pitkin said.

"But what's the old gentleman suffering from?"

"Look it up," Pitkin said. "Turn to any page in the medical book and there he is. Swollen tooth sockets. Brown eye. Urinary leakage. Hardening of the ducts. Hormone discolor. Blocked extremities. Seepage from the gums. The wind is bad. The lungs on the verge. Bonwit gives the lungs two weeks."

"They must love him at Blue Cross."

"How are you behaving that I said you shouldn't behave like?"

"A white monkey," Billy said.

"What am I looking at here?"

"A pisher," Billy said.

"The old gentleman's whole body is moist. The doctor, you should see him, night and day he works to keep it dry." Pitkin's lips continued to move and Billy wondered exactly how old this man Ratner must be if his adviser on the writings thought it suitable to refer to him as "the old gentleman"—an adviser with white hair growing out of his face and with lips that started moving before he spoke and did not stop until well after he was finished.

Syringe filled, Dr. Bonwit walked out and the nurse followed, wheeling the elaborate device.

"Is that for the old gentleman?"

"They're injecting his face. Nonclotting silicone," Pitkin said. "He doesn't like to see them fill up the needle, so they sneak around the nearest corner and do it there. Needles, who can look? His face collapsed coming over the ocean last night. Poof, a shot, it fills right out. If I'm lying, may you inherit a hotel with ten thousand rooms and be found dead in every one."

"These oaths are pretty dangerous to people just standing around listening," Billy said.

"I didn't word them. They were worded five thousand years ago. You want to change the wording, go complain. Tell them Pitkin sent you. It's time to present the roses," Pitkin said.

Pitkin and Billy went through the bronze door and down several flights of stairs even older than the stairs he'd descended earlier. Billy heard organ music below, a reverberating cavern-size snore, and he followed Pitkin through a slit in the wall and out into the Great Hole, a vast underground chamber, fluorescent lights suspended from clothing racks. The organ, set on an outcropping of rock in a far corner, was playing the kind of intermission music featured at hockey games.

"The old gent may or may not make it," Dr. Bonwit said to Pitkin. "One advantage is the air down here, crystal clear, a beautiful purifying agent for the biomembrane. Now here's how we'll work it," Bonwit said to Billy as Pitkin shuffled off. "The laureates are in the antecave off the Great Hole and they're being instructed in torch manipulation. You don't join them until they file in and Sandow gives a hand signal. Sandow's the man at the organ. After he gives the hand signal, the biomembrane is wheeled in by Pitkin and the nurse, me leading the way. Then Sandow makes the opening remarks and the pigeons are released."

"When do I present the roses?" Billy said.

"After the pigeons," Bonwit said.

"What's this biomembrane that's being wheeled in?"

"It's what keeps Ratner alive. Ultrasterile biomedical membrane environment, a total life-support system. The old gentleman never leaves. This is the only non-hostile environment we could work out for him, considering his state of deterioration. If he begins to fail, the shield is raised and I crawl in and operate. The biomembrane is a self-sterilizing operating theater in miniature and it adapts to a postoperative therapy center, he should live so long, as the saying goes."

"Is Sandow a laureate?"

"Sandow is an organist," Dr. Bonwit said. "Unless they give a

Nobel Prize for pedaling, he didn't win. But it adds to the mood, an organ. 'LaMar T. Sandow at the keyboard.' Besides, he's the old gent's lifelong friend. You want a friend to see you honored. I'm all for an organ at a function like this.''

Pitkin returned, bent and shuffling, a bouquet of white roses in his arms.

''The colored nurse told me to tell you the face filled out.''

''Good,'' Bonwit said.

Sandow broke off the intermission music and began playing a triumphal march. Multicolored neon, flashing intermittently, pulsed through the clear tubing that extended above the organ. Pitkin handed Billy the flowers. The laureates started filing in—in size places.

The small parade came to a halt.

Billy, with the flowers, took his place at the front of the line. A massive transparent tank came into view, a cylinder on wheels, a blunt-nosed torpedo set lengthwise on a metal undercasing to which were fixed four scooter-size tires.

Dr. Bonwit walked ahead of the biomembrane, kicking small stones out of the way, and behind were Pitkin and the nurse, pushing. Everywhere on the tank were complex monitoring devices and all sorts of gauges, tubes, and switches. Billy stood on his toes to get a look at Ratner, but the angle wasn't favorable just then. What he could see clearly were the sponsor decals—

MAINLINE FILTRONIC
Tank & Filter Maintenance

STERILMASTER PEERLESS AIR-CURTAINING
The breath you take is the life we save

BIZENE POLYTHENE COATING
U.D.G.A. inspected and approved

WALKER-ATKINSON METALLIZED
UNDERSURFACES
From the folks at Uniplex Syntel

EVALITE CHROME PANELING
The glamour name in surgical supplies

DREAMAWAY
Bed linen, mattress and frame
A division of OmCo Research
''Building a model world''

All was quiet except for an underground stream nearby and the last sobbing echo of the triumphal march, reaching them from a distant surface of the cavern. Then Sandow spoke: ''I'd like to open my remarks by reaffirming my friendship with the old gentleman despite going our separate ways more than twenty-five years ago due to clashing ideologies, which explains my presence here, symbolic of a coming together, a let's-join-hands-type thing, to light our torches in tribute to this gentle soul of science, who, when we were young men, he and I, espoused all there was to espouse in those benighted days of the principles of scientific humanism, including, as I recall, individual freedom, democracy for all peoples, a ban on nationalism and war, no waiting for a theistic deity to do what we ourselves could do as enlightened men and women joined in our humanistic convictions, the right to get divorced, but who, as I understand it, has now returned to the ideas and things from which so many of us were so eager to flee, proving, I suppose, that there's a certain longevity to benightedness, and I won't take up the time here providing you with a list of this great ex-scientist's current convictions beyond mentioning the secret power of the alphabet, the unnameable name, the literal contraction of the superdivinity, fear of sperm demons—so, to enlarge on an earlier statement, this is not only a coming-together but a going away in a way, for having come to science and humanism, so has he gone, and in lieu of an eternal flame, which I had hoped to borrow for the occasion, we are here to light our torches to Shazar Lazarus Ratner, reasoning what better

way to honor this man, this scientific giant, than to have the Nobelists light their torches from an eternal flame, which I wanted to get flown in from one of the nations in or near the cradle of civilization, simply borrowing the flame and returning it after the ceremony and they could bill us at their convenience, but I was wary of pressure groups and I foresaw the remark from someone in such a group saying 'cradle of *whose* civilization?' for there is always this prejudice against Western civilization having its own cradle and calling it *the* cradle when other peoples have their own ideas of where the cradle is and even whether or not there *is* a cradle, and, summing up therefore, I thank you for your time and attention.''

Apparently reacting to a prearranged phrase, one of the laureates stepped out of the line and approached a crate.

''The pigeons!'' Sandow said. ''Let us release the pigeons! The releasing of the pigeons, ladies and gentlemen!''

The laureate raised the top of the box and about fifty pigeons came shaking out, like a series of knots unraveling from a rope.

''The presenting of the roses!'' Sandow declared. ''The boy steps up to the great medico-engineering feat and symbolically presents the roses!''

Billy strode to the tank and was lifted in the air by Dr. Bonwit and held standing on the curved surface of the transparent shield. Below, he saw the small figure of Ratner, pillowed in deep white. The doctor stood on one side of the tank, the nurse on the other, and together they supported Billy as he displayed the flowers for the benefit of the old gentleman.

''Ratner sees the roses!'' Sandow called. ''The old gentleman acknowledges the floral bouquet!''

The doctor and nurse lowered Billy to a straddling position on the tank. Bonwit turned a dial, activating a chambered device set into the shield over Ratner's face. Static came from the interior of the biomembrane, the sound of Ratner breathing through the bacteria-filtered talk chamber.

''The boy prepares to listen to the circulated words!'' Sandow announced.

Bonwit took the flowers and inserted them into a sort of scabbard at the side of the biomembrane. Ratner looked into Billy's face. Billy leaned forward, trying to indicate his eagerness to hear the old gentleman's remarks, a black beret and a long fringed prayer shawl covering Ratner from shoulders to feet.

''The old man speaks to the boy!'' Sandow declared. ''Sunk in misery and disease, Ratner speaks actual words to the little fellow on the tank!''

Slowly the withered lips parted—and the old man spoke.

''The universe, what is it?''

''I don't know.''

''It began with a point. The point expanded so that darkness took up the left, light the right. This was the beginning of distinctions. But before expansion, there was contraction. There had to be room for the universe to fit. So the *En-Sof* contracted. This made room. The creator, also known as G-dash-d, then made the point of pure energy that became the universe. In science this is what they call the big bang. Except for my money it's not a case of big bang versus steady state. It's a case of big bang versus little bang. I vote for little. Matter was so dense it could barely explode. The explosion barely got out. This was the beginning if you're speaking as a scientist. The fireball got bigger, the temperature fell, the galaxies began to form. But it almost never made it. There was such density. Matter was packed in like sardines. When it finally exploded, you almost couldn't hear it. This is science. As a scientist, my preference is definitely little bang. As a whole man, I believe in the contraction of the *En-Sof* to make room for the point.''

Billy raised his head and looked toward the laureates standing in line with their unlighted torches.

''He votes for little bang,'' Billy said. ''The noise was muffled.''

Then he crouched over the biomembrane as Ratner prepared to speak once again.

''The *En-Sof* is the unknowable. The hidden. The that-which-is-not-here. The neither-cause-nor-effect. The G-dash-d beyond G-dash-d. The limitless. The not-only-unutterable-but-by-definition-inconceivable. Yet it emanates. It reveals itself through its attributes, the *sefiroth*. G-dash-d is the first of the ten *sefirothic* emanations of the *EnSof*. Without the *En-Sof*'s withdrawal or contraction, there could be no point, no cosmic beginning, no universe, no G-dash-d. I learned this growing up as a boy in Brooklyn. Not long after, I looked through my first telescope. But I failed to understand at that time.''

Ratner paused to regain his strength, and Billy glanced toward the others and made another capsule report as he assumed they wished him to do, their having traveled from every part of the world to be here for the ceremony.

''No universe without contraction. Grew up in Brooklyn, a boy, nonbelieving.''

He turned his attention to Ratner once more.

''We come from the stars,'' Ratner said. ''Our chemicals, our atoms, these were first made in the centers of old stars that exploded and spread their remains across the sky, eventually to come together as the sun we know and the planet we inhabit. I started out with binoculars, viewing the sky. It seemed remarkable to a boy like me, underfed and pale, with a small mental vista, that there was something bigger than Brooklyn. In those days of no television, the stars could be awesome to a boy, the way they swarmed, thin as I was, growing up, with binoculars. Later I got a telescope, my first, bought from a junk dealer, and, with a tripod, borrowed, I stuck it out the window, top floor, and gazed for hours. Star fields, clusters, the moon. I read books, I learned, I gazed. Knowledge made me punch my fists against the walls in awe and shame. Our atoms were formed in the dense interiors of supergiant stars billions of years ago. Stars millions of times more luminous than our sun. They broke down and decayed and began to cool. Atoms from these stars are in our bones and nervous systems. We're stellar cinders, you and me. We come from the beginning or near the beginning. In our brain is the echo of the little bang. This is science, poeticized here and there, and this you can compare with the cabalistic belief that every person has a sun inside him, a radiant burst of energy. Try to reach a mystical state without radiant energy and see what happens.''

''Secondhand telescope,'' Billy said to the others. ''Gazed at the stars and learned we're made of them. Pale and thin for his age.''

''When I go into mystical states,'' Ratner said, ''I pass beyond the opposites of the world and experience only the union of these opposites in a radiant burst of energy. I call it a burst. What else can I call it? You shouldn't think it's really a burst. Everything in the universe works on the theory of opposites. To see what it looks like outside the universe, you have to go into a trance or two. According to Pitkin, G-dash-d could live anywhere. He doesn't need the universe. He could set up headquarters east or west of the universe and not miss a thing. But this is Pitkin. The mystical writings. The mystical oral traditions. The mystical interpretations, oral and written. These exist beneath the main body of thought and thinking. You don't go into a trance reading the everyday writings. The hidden texts, try *them*. The untranslated manuscript. The oral word.''

Billy looked at the laureates, then shrugged.

''Written, oral,'' Ratner said. ''Black, white. Male, female. Let's hear you name some more.''

''Day, night,'' Billy said.

''Very good.''

''Plus, minus.''

''Even better,'' Ratner said. ''Remember, all things are present in all other things. Each in its opposite.''

Billy turned and shrugged once more.

''I gazed constantly, learning, a young man, top floor still, gaining weight. Finally I realized a portable telescope no longer suited my needs and aspirations. I married a woman whose father had a house with a backyard. I thought here I could build what I truly needed, a ten-inch reflector with rotating dome. So with his permission and blessing we moved into his house. In Pittsburgh,'' Ratner said. ''There we lived and built. Halvah helped me, my wife, grinding the mirror, assembling the mount, measuring and cutting wood, sending away for instructions, pasting and hammering. I started to accumulate academic degrees, to go beyond amateur ranking. All that reading, it was paying off. I continued to gaze. It was awful, Pittsburgh, in those days. Smoke, soot, particles of every description. There was a steel mill two blocks away. I had to gaze between shifts. Many times Helvah's father tried to read to me from the writings. I paid no attention, acquiring my degrees, corresponding with leading minds in the sciences and technologies. He would hum as he read, a sound of piety, fear, and shame. Smoke came pouring over the backyard. Thick black ash fell all over the dome. I had to stand on a chair and sweep off the top with a broom. I gazed whenever possible, I ate the cooking, I corresponded with the leading minds. Sometimes I punched the wall, plentifully replete as I was with a knowledge of the physical world. My father-in-law hummed, Fish, my father-in-law. I asked Halvah what kind of writings these were that her father never ceased to read from. I said, Halvah, what writings are these? I inquired of her what manner of writings her father so incessantly read. The mystical writings, she said. I resilvered the telescope's mirror, these being the days before widespread aluminum. He tried to give me instructions, Fish, in the secrecy of things, the hiddenness, the buried nature. Did I listen or did I sit in my dome, rotating, gazing, an occasional belch from the food?''

Billy reported to the others. ''Telescope in a dome in the backyard. Marriage to the man's daughter owning the house. Science pays off. He gazes between shifts.''

''You know what you remind me of?'' Ratner said.

''What?''

''Somebody who's giving only one side of the story,'' the old man said. ''Don't think I can't hear that you're reporting only science, leaving out the mystical content, which they could use a little exposure to, those laureates with their half a million Swedish kronor. It was less in my day. And don't think I didn't notice all that shrugging when I was saying black-white, male-female, a little bit of everything present in its opposite. Because I noticed.''

''Some things are hard to summarize,'' Billy said.

''Give the whole picture,'' Ratner said. ''If you want to repeat, repeat both sides.''

''From now on you'll see improvement.''

''How many *sefirothic* emanations did the *En-Sof* emanate?''

''Ten.''

''In words, what can we say about the *En-Sof*?''

''I don't know.''

''Something or nothing?''

''Nothing,'' Billy said.

''There is always something secret to be discovered,'' Ratner said. ''A hidden essence. A truth beneath the truth. What is the true name of G-dash-d? How many levels of unspeakability must we penetrate before we arrive at the true name, the name of names? Once we arrive at the true name, how many pronunciations must we utter before we come to the secret, the hidden, the true pronunciation? On what allotted day of the year, and by which of the holiest of scholars, will the secret pronunciation of the name of names be permitted to be passed on to the worthiest of the initiates? And how passed on? Over water, in darkness, naked, by whispers? I sat in my dome, rotating, knowing nothing of this. Nor of the need to exercise the greatest caution in all aspects of this matter. Substitution, abbreviation, blank spaces, utter silence. The alphabet, the integers. Triangles, circles, squares. Indirection, numerology, acronyms, sighs. Go into your own bottom parts.'' Ratner said. ''Here you find the contradictions joined and harmonized. This is a good place to look for the secrets you didn't even know existed. If you think I'm lying, knock on top of the tank. Progressing as a man, winning prizes in the sciences, sharing the marriage bed with my Halvah. But the way Fish hummed as he read, it began to get to me. What is there in these writings, I asked myself, that this man should hum? A noise of shame, fear and humiliation, my Halvah's father's humming. I refitted the tracks under the dome so it could rotate more smoothly. I learned physics to go with astrophysics. Radio astronomy to match my astronomy. I punched the walls with knowledge. Halvah gave birth, a baby, born screaming. The only non-mystical state where the oposites are joined is infancy. So perfect they often die, babies, without cause. What's your opinion?''

"I was an incubator baby."

"Then you know what it's like, living in a tank. Climb in for a minute," Ratner said. "Come, lift the shield. I want to whisper in your ear."

Pretending he hadn't heard these last words, Billy looked away to make his report.

"The mystical humming of his father-in-law. A child is born. Punching the walls. The dome rotates with added smoothness."

Billy turned once again to the figure in the biomembrane.

"Don't look down your nose at esoterica," Ratner said. "If you know the right combination of letters, you can make anything. This is the secret power of the alphabet. Meaningless sounds, abstract symbols, they have the power of creation. This is why the various parts of the mystical writings are not in proper order. Knowing the order, you could make your own world from just reading the writings. Everything is built from the twenty-two letter elements. The alphabet itself is both male and female. Creation depends on an anagram."

It's hard to picture," Billy said. "Do you have numbers?"

"Is Mickey a mouse?" Ratner said. "Of course we have numbers. The emanations of the *En-Sof* are numbers. The ten *sefiroth* are numerical operations that determine the course of the universe. Constant and variable. The *sefiroth* are both. I could go into *sefirothic* geometry, but you don't have the awe for that, being mathematical. *Sefiroth* comes from the infinitive *to count*. The power of counting, of finger numbers, of one to ten. We also have *gematria*, which you probably heard about, assigning numerical value to each letter of the alphabet. I won't even tell you about the hidden relationships between words that we discover in his way. It would be too much of a feast to set before someone who isn't ready for it, a lifelong eater of peanuts, by which I refer to myself as viewed in the face of Fish's revelations, gazing, a man, backyard, night upon night, galaxies and nebulas, my head filled with N.G.C. numbers. The steel mill went on strike. I gazed like a madman. You couldn't get me out of the dome with threats to my child. I decided to study the sun. Adjustments, new equipment, unsilvered mirror, precautions. The sun is a frightening thing to view through a telescope, solar wedge or no solar wedge. I thought ahead to the helium flash. The final expansion. Having come from the stars, we are returned. The sun within us, the source of all mystical bursts, is perfectly counterbalanced by the physical sun that presses outward, swallowing up the orbits of the nearest planets."

Beneath the beret, Ratner's face sagged a bit.

"Picture this," he said. "From that great unstable period, the sun collapses drastically. It becomes the same size as the former earth. Now we're right inside it, mongrelized with three other planets compacted down to a whiff of gas. The sun proceeds to cool, white dwarf, red dwarf, black dwarf, a dead star, dark black. No energy, no light, no heat, no twinkle. The end."

"Can I get off now?" Billy said.

"We come from supergiant solar bodies, great, hot, ionized objects, and we end in the center of a dead black sphere. We're part star, you and me. Our beginning and end are made in the stars. Light, dark. High, low. Big, little. Go ahead, take it from there."

"East, west," Billy said.

"Up," Ratner said.

"Down."

"In."

"Out."

"Give me a few, to test my fading powers."

"Love," Billy said.

"Hate," Ratner said.

"Innocence."

"Kilt."

"Very good." Billy said after a thoughtful pause.

"The old man lay back, panting gently. A few minutes passed. Finally he stirred himself.

"Gazing, gazing, I studied eclipsing stars, flare stars, variables of every kind, reading star catalogs in my spare time, memorizing star tables, taking the cooking into the dome with me, a real fanatic. Also, I feared the sight of Fish, always with the writings in his hand. He took books and folios into the toilet with him and stayed for hours. We could hear the humming from his bedroom half the night. He pushed his armchair into a corner and sat with his back to the room. This kind of transcendence I feared, a scientist, still young, pledged to the observable, welcomed into organizations, reaching a peak of knowledge, Pittsburgh, the backyard, my own dome, handmade, that rotated. The night sky was sensational. I made charts and calculations, identifying nova-like variables, Cepheids, cool and hot stars, egg-shaped doubles. The child developed putative diarrhea, terrible, a living diaper. Did I realize I was being punished for knowledge without piety or did I sit in the observatory, scanning, light from the universe entering my eye?"

"Looks like trouble's coming," Billy said to those assembled in the Great Hole. "He fears this person Fish who's always in the toilet reading. The kid is sick. A question is asked about piety and sitting."

"Come in and browse," Ratner said. "I know a few words I want to whisper in your ear. Come, pay a visit. Bonwit does it all the time, the doctor, holding his breath. Come, let me whisper."

"I can hear you from right here."

"Pay a dying man a visit," Ratner said.

"I'll catch something. The shield might jam behind me and then where am I? I can hold my breath just so long."

"Browse awhile."

"Put yourself in my place," the boy said. "What if the shield jams while I'm in there and then you die? What happens then? I'm probably taking a chance just sitting up here. All they told me was the flowers. Present the flowers."

"So this Fish," Ratner said. "This in-law Fish of mine. My Halvah's father. He begins to get to me with a remark passed at dinner about the hidden source of the mystical writings, doctrines and traditions. A secret beginning in the Orient. All this esoterica. Born in the East. Moving as if by stealth to other parts of the world. Always this obscurity. This secret element. I'll tell you an intersting piece of news. If you think I'm making it up, tap once on the shield. A dying man has no shadow. First heard from Fish. The person about to die lacks all shadow. Knock once if I'm lying."

"I don't understand the question," Billy said.

"You know what you remind me of?"

"What?"

"A golem," Ratner said.

"What's that?"

"An artificial person."

"No such thing," the boy said.

"Light from the universe entered my eye," Ratner said. "I am in the dome, gazing, an ordinary night, through the eyepiece, open clusters, rich fields, my name being mentioned in the journals, this and that prize coming my way, a signer of petitions, the arts, the sciences, the humanisms, our child still in diapers, a tragedy, making watery excess thirty times a day, my Halvah up to her wrists in baby-do. Suddenly what do I see? A thing beyond naming. Not a thing at all. A state. I am falling into a state. Radiance everywhere. An experience. I am having an experience."

Breaking the long silence that followed, Billy spoke to the others.

"An ordinary night in the dome, getting famous, he starts to see something. The in-law Fish is winning."

"There's nothing more I can say," Ratner said. "I lived my life. Good, evil. Aphelion, perihelion. Hungry, full. Since then I have often fallen into states, passing beyond the opposites of the world. What use was a telescope after this? I had the states. Every experience was a new experience. It's something you don't get used to. Fish instructed me. In time I went back to my original roots, Eastern Parkway. We prospered as a family, learning fear, shame, piety, awe, my mind no longer filled to satiation with knowledge of the physical universe. Being pious, I felt no need to punch the wall. They kept in touch with me, the leading minds, still an award or two, invitations every week. Only one I accepted, to visit Palomar, the two-hundred-inch reflector. I sat in the observer's cage right inside the telescope. Just the cage was bigger than my whole dome. I looked at some galaxies in detail. Nice, I liked it. When I climbed out, they told me they had a special honor. A star. They gave a star my name.''

"Falling into states," Billy said to the others. "Back to Brooklyn, the walls no longer punched. He visits Palomar. A star is named.''

"Lift the shield and climb in," Ratner said. "I know some words to whisper. Come, take time. Make the sacrifice. A dying man needs visits. Be a sport for once in your life.''

"Infectious danger," Billy said.

"Hold your breath and lift the shield. Take time. It's a worthwhile whisper or I wouldn't ask.''

"I'm scared, in plain English.''

"We're all scared," Ratner said. "Who isn't scared? You, me, the laureates. Terror is everywhere. This I learned from the writings. Fish, humming, gave me his folios to take back to Brooklyn. Pitkin advises every day on the terror around us. Nothing in the writings is easy. If I give the impression I abandoned science for the easy life, knock once.''

The old gentleman's face appeared to be collapsing. Clear matter was being discharged from his pores as the face began to settle. This degenerative action was such that the beret slid forward and to one side, coming to rest over Ratner's eyes.

"What is this but a place?" Ratner said. "Nothing more than a space. We're both here in this place, occupying space. Everywhere is a place. All places share this quality. Is there any real difference between going to a gorgeous mountain resort with beautiful high thin waterfalls so delicate and ribbonlike that they don't even splash when they hit bottom—waterfalls that *plash*? Is this so different from sitting in a kitchen with bumpy linoleum and grease on the wall behind the stove across the street from a gravel pit? What are we talking about? Two places, that's all. There's nowhere you can go that isn't a place. So what's such a difference? If you can understand this idea, you'll never be unhappy. Think of the word *place*. A sun deck with views of gorgeous mountains. A tiny dark kitchen. These share the most important of all things anything can share. They are places. The word *place* applies in both cases. In this sense, how do we distinguish between them? How do we say one is better or worse than the other? They are equal in the most absolute of ways. Grasp this truth, sonny, and you'll never be sad.''

Billy felt himself lifted. It was Dr. Bonwit, removing him from the biomembrane and setting him on the floor. Observing size places, Billy returned to the front of the line. Pitkin approached the tank, put his ear to the chambered slot and then departed. As Bonwit and the nurse busied themselves at the cart that held the silicone preparation, Sandow rose from the organ bench.

"Let us light the torches!" he declared. "The lighting of the ceremonial torches! The torch-lighting commences, ladies and gentlemen!''

Holding a lighted candle, Pitkin stood waiting. As Sandow called their names, the laureates proceeded in alphabetical order to touch the wicks of their torches to Pitkin's candle flame. Then each returned to the line. Sandow took his place at the keyboard and began playing a profound lament, the neon pulsing through the clear pipes in slow motion. Dr. Bonwit put on a surgical mask, raised the shield, climbed into the tank, and administered the facial injection. Then he and the nurse wheeled the biomembrane out, its sponsor decals gleaming. They were followed first by Pitkin and then, as the music reached a triumphantly despondent coda, by the laureates in single file, their lighted torches casting tremors on the walls of the Great Hole.

Billy Twillig went last, not a mark on him.

Growing Old

JONATHAN BAUMBACH

It has been two months since the baby told anyone a new story, a period not sufficiently long to presage a trend. Talk of his retirement, of course, seems premature. He has taken to forming words on paper, a barely intelligible scrawl that he conceives to represent a variety of narratives. Today he is sick and running a fever of 102.6, consigned against his will to bed.

I hear him get up and pad to the bathroom, complain of discomfort, and return to bed. "I'm getting old," he groans. I set aside my work and go up to his room for a visit.

"There are these balls going around in my head," he says, as if in answer to some question I had asked. "They fall into holes, which makes me sad.''

I ask why that should make him sad.

"Too many things are in my mind," he says vaguely. His fever smiles on dry lips. "Tomorrow I'm going to write a story about getting old.''

I don't have to wait until the next day for the baby's story. An hour later, he is ready, he says, for me to write the story down exactly as he tells it. He would write it himself, he says, if his arm wasn't sick. The story is about an old man with glasses and a white beard who isn't Santa Claus.

"Are you writing this down?'' he asks.

I take my pen out of my jacket and write the following, as instructed, on a clean page of the baby's notebook.

THE VERY OLD MAN
Once upon a time there was a very old man. The end.

When I remark on the brevity of the story, the baby offers as explanation an extremely limited knowledge of his subject.

"That's not really the end," he adds. "It's just the end of the chapter. The next chapter is about an old man who's not as old as the first old man.''

THE OLD MAN THAT'S NOT SO OLD
There was an old man with white beard and glasses. He wasn't as

old as the other old man, who was very old. He was just old. I think he was dead. One day a lady came to visit the old man. "Hello," said the lady. "Hello," said the old man. "What's new?" said the lady. "Not me," said the old man.

The baby turns on his side and goes to sleep.

Later in the day, I return to see how he is. "I'm better," he says, his face flushed, his sunken eyes webbed with lines. "Only my mind feels worse."

I ask him if his mother has given him his medicine, and he says he can't remember. "Did you come to write down the rest of that story I was telling you to write?"

"When you feel better," I say, "you'll tell me the rest of the story."

"There's something I want to tell you," he says, "but my mouth is tired."

"Would you like me to tell you a story?"

"I don't like stories anymore," he says. "Do you know why I don't like stories? Because they're real. They sound like they're not real, but they are."

"I would have thought," I tell him, "that it would be the other way around. That stories deceive one into imagining them real."

He thinks about it or seems to be thinking about it, his forehead wrinkled, eyes dull with paradox and fever. "Stories *are* real," he says. "I'll tell you why. If people write them, they have to be real. People are real, aren't they?"

The fever hangs on. The baby's illness is unresponsive to the antibiotic the pediatrician has prescribed for him. "What I recommend," says the doctor on the phone, "is that you let me have a look at him. I have hours after one on Tuesday and Thursday."

Report of the baby's visit is in another story, a synopsis of which is included here.

The doctor's waiting room tends to be crowded no matter what time you come. The baby, who thinks of himself as no longer a baby, sits in a businesslike, dignified way, his thumb thoughtfully inhaled.

An hour passes (two hours in the full story), and the baby has hardly moved in his chair, oblivious to the feckless world at his feet.

Finally, the nurse ushers us into an examination room—there are four other such rooms, all of them apparently occupied. My instructions are to undress the baby to prepare him for his examination.

The baby is unusually silent, indicating with a gesture that he would prefer to remove his clothing himself, which he does in a listless though efficient manner. He sits naked on the doctor's table, shivering slightly, browsing through a picture book of monsters exemplifying family life. He has read it a number of times before and seems now to be turning pages for something to do. "Are you cold?" I ask him. He denies it. I am putting my jacket over the baby's lap when the doctor makes a dramatic appearance. "What have we here?" the doctor says.

Tall, with big hips, perpetually teetering like an inflated toy, the doctor is a man of almost no personality, who manages, through what seems to be a carefully rehearsed routine, to disarm his patient's fears. "The bird is pecking in your ear," says the doctor, looking in the baby's ear with the funnel-like flashlight requisite to that chore.

"That's no bird," says the baby.

After the doctor examines the baby's ears, nose, and left eye, he rushes out as if he has just remembered a prior engagement. He indicates that the baby is to be kept warm until his return.

"My neck hurts," says the baby.

"Is it your throat?"

He opens his mouth as if to look. "I don't want it to hurt," he says.

The doctor steps in, saying, "What have we here?" then shakes his head and backs out. "Wrong room," he says.

I follow him into the hall in the hope of convincing the doctor to complete the baby's examination, but he has already gone into one of the other little rooms.

"Maybe he doesn't like me," says the baby.

His remark seems to hasten the doctor's return. "What have we here?" says the doctor again. As he examines the baby, the doctor becomes increasingly grim under the anxious overlay of charm. Is it merely manner or is the baby sicker than we thought?

"What next?" asks the baby from time to time, holding himself together, anticipating the worst.

"You will have to have a little shot," says the doctor, turning the baby over to keep the needle out of view. "I'm not going to lie to you. It will hurt a little, like a pinch."

"I know what it hurts like," says the baby, with a slight show of pique.

"Do you know what?" the baby says the next day.

"No, what?" I answer. It is an old routine we do. He is in my study, his fever mostly gone, pacing the floor. "During the night, when I was sleeping, do you know what happened? What happened was I died."

I try to disabuse him of the notion, but he is insistent on the validity of what he assumes to be his experience.

"I *did*," he says. "When I woke up, I was older."

How can I put it to him? "When you die," I say, "as far as anyone knows, you don't wake up."

"Well . . ." he says, "sometimes you do and sometimes you don't. Do you want to know what happened to me when I died?"

"Okay, what happened to you?"

His face, defleshed by illness, takes on a wizened aspect. "I'm thinking about it," he says. He rests his face, slightly squashed, against that flat of his hand. "Maybe what happened was my dream died." He raises his head. "Did you write that down?" he says.

"It's a matter of record," I say.

The baby goes out without announcing his destination and returns with his pants open, offering a glimpse of where he has been. He makes an unsuccessful, melodramatic effort at snapping the pants shut, then comes to me to do it for him. "You belly's too big," I say.

"If I didn't have a belly," he says, "I wouldn't have any place to hang my legs."

He opens his notebook to a clean page and poises his Magic Marker like a gunfighter at the ready. "I'm not a baby in this story," he says, making a few fastidious, indecipherable marks on the sheet of paper in front of him. "I'm a spy with a secret identity. Do you want to know who my secret identity is?"

The baby's story is interrupted—his secret identity temporarily preserved—by an unexpected visit from his friend Adam, who seems to come and go as he pleases, a slightly older child, obscurely supervised.

They exchange traditional greetings.

"Hello, dummy," says Adam.

"Hello, dummy," says the baby.

I stop listening for a while, absorbed alternately by flashes of anxiety and rage and an unaccountable pain in my right side. Age troubles me. Failed commitments, an insufficiency of feeling.

Mixed in among my own memos, there is a note in a familiar hand. I WANT ANOTHER BABY, it says. Perhaps I have written it myself and have forgotten, attributing it to another as a self-deception.

When Adam leaves, the baby is in an angry mood. "I don't like Adam," he says. I nod. "I don't want him to go home. I'm going to be like Adam when I get bigger. Adam says I can't because my hair is the wrong color."

"Did he say that? Well, I guess you'll have to settle on being yourself."

The baby makes an impatient face, an indication that the obvious is old news.

"What are you doing?" says the baby, coming in on us silently.

"Your father and I were kissing," says his mother, which, if not literally true, has a certain symbolic validity.

His mother's answer seems to satisfy him, for he lets the subject drop, or seems to, sitting primly on the edge of our bed with his back to us. I make mention that we intend to sleep a little longer and that we'd like him to play by himself for a while until we're ready to get up.

"Okay," he says, though he makes no effort to move. After a moment, he swings around and rolls on top of us, a knee digging into my back. He puts an arm around each of our necks. "It's all right. You can go back to kissing," he says.

"You're hurting me," says his mother to one of us. We kiss, the baby's face wedged between ours. .

"That's funny," he says.

"What's funny?" says his mother.

"Kissing," the baby says. "When I was a baby, you didn't used to kiss like that." On the wings of this remark, he evacuates the bed.

"You two are the best father and mother," he whispers.

He leaves us without further elaboration, creaking up the stairs to his own place of operation. We listen in silence until he completes his ascent.

We are both, for reasons not wholly clear, smiling broadly.

"What are you so happy about?" I ask, a mock accusation, as if neither of us has that right.

"What about you? You're the one that's really grinning."

We have been married too long to let the word *love* slip between us, a word with a history of effacing what it affects to represent.

As my wife will allow no outsider to speak for her, there can be no report of her feelings until her own account is published. As for myself, I am experiencing a sense of extreme precariousness, my life in danger, the cost of my restoration still to be paid.

"I miss not having a baby around the house," she says.

With no major warning, a masked and caped figure opens the door with a clamor and presents himself, feet apart, in the center of the room. "I'm not the one you think I am," he announces. "I'm not the boy you usually see in this room."

"You know you're supposed to knock when the door is closed," I say.

He scratches his head. "The person that lives here knows that, but I never heard it before. How could I hear it?"

"You're hearing it now," I say.

"I'll tell you why I don't have to knock," he says, thrusting his sword into an imaginary assailant. "I don't have to knock because this is a story I'm making up."

He rushes out, not bothering to close the door, closing it with a bang as an afterthought, some dim injunction interrupting the flow of his escape. Return, one suspects, is imminent.

"You'll have to hurry," I'm told.

There's always something in this life to move you on more quickly than you mean to go.

Secret grey hairs appear. Like the baby, I am no longer who I was. Who will he be, I wonder, when he returns?

In the meanwhile, we conduct our business as if we had an existence independent of his story.

Biographies

JONATHAN BAUMBACH is co-director of one of the more notable writers' cooperatives, the Fiction Collective, and is the author of four novels: *A Man to Conjure With, What Comes Next, Reruns,* and *Babble.*

T. CORAGHESSAN BOYLE studied at the Iowa Workshop and is now an editor with *The Iowa Review.* His fiction has been seen in *Paris Review, TriQuarterly,* and *North American Review.*

HAROLD BRODKEY was for many years silent subsequent to the publication of his collection *Early Love and Other Sorrows,* a silence since broken by the appearance of elements from his novel-in-progress *A Party for Animals,* this in *The New Yorker, The American Poetry Review,* and *American Review,* as well as in *Esquire. The New Yorker* excerpt, "A Story in an Almost Classical Mode," was the 1975 co-winner in William Abrahams's *Prize Stories: The O. Henry Awards* (Doubleday), and the *Esquire* excerpt, presented herein, won first place in the 1976 edition of the Abrahams anthology, a rare concatenation of honors.

FREDERICK BUSCH teaches literature at Colgate, and has published short stories with *American Review, New Directions,* and *Harper's.* His novels are *I Wanted a Year without Fall* and *Manual Labor,* his collections *Breathing Trouble* and *Domestic Particulars.* Busch's critical study of the work of John Hawkes *(Hawkes: A Guide to His Fictions)* was brought out by Syracuse University Press in 1973.

RAYMOND CARVER has published three books of poems, and this year brought out his collected stories *Will You Please Be Quiet, Please?* with McGraw-Hill. He has lectured in writing at the Iowa Workshop and at the University of California at Berkeley and Santa Cruz.

JOHN CHEEVER continues to prove the critical opinion that places him among the considerable literary artists of our time. In favor of remarking a widely known list of distinguished books, the editor chooses to cite a new short story, "The Folding-Chair Set" *(The New Yorker,* October 13, 1975), an unusual achievement in the possibility of knowing.

SANFORD CHERNOFF drives a mail truck and writes short fiction, some samples of which have been displayed in *Partisan Review, Antaeus,* and *Epoch.*

TOM COLE very seldom publishes fiction, his central concern having shifted to the making of movies. He lives in Boston with his film-maker wife.

DON DE LILLO recently published a novel, *Ratner's Star,* with Knopf. His three earlier novels are *Americana, End Zone,* and *Great Jones Street,* and he has had short fiction in *The New Yorker, Kenyon Review, Epoch,* and *The Atlantic.* He now lives in Canada.

RICK DE MARINIS has had work in *The Atlantic* and *Iowa Review.* Simon and Schuster this year published his first novel, *A Lovely Monster,* and a second novel, *Scimitar,* is forthcoming. He has for some while taught writing at the University of Montana and at San Diego State University.

BRUCE JAY FRIEDMAN is currently visiting professor in English at York College. His novels are *Stern, A Mother's Kisses, The Dick,* and *About Harry Towns;* his story collections *Far from the City of Class* and *Black Angels;* his plays *Scuba Duba, Steambath,* and *Turtlenecks.* He is at work on *Detroit Abe,* a novel, and is fond of being addressed by the nickname "Buddy," but nobody calls him that.

GAIL GODWIN is the author of three novels—*The Perfectionists, Glass People,* and *The Odd Woman.* She held a Guggenheim fellowship in 1975, and in 1976 Knopf brought out her collected stories under the title *Dream Children.*

BARRY HANNAH teaches in the writing program at the University of Alabama. He published the novels *Geronimo Rex* and *The Night-watchmen* with Viking, and has a third and distinctively conceived novel, *The Tennis Handsome,* still in pursuit of print.

WILLIAM HARRISON heads the writing program at the University of Arkansas, and has just completed *Pack of Dogs,* a novel whose beginnings reside in the story "The Warrior," an entry in the preceding *Esquire* fiction anthology, *The Secret Life of Our Times.*

SAM KOPERWAS has appeared in *Fiction,* and has published a first novel, *Westchester Bull.*

WILLIAM KOTZWINKLE is known for his books *Elephant Bangs Train, Hermes 3000, Night Book, The Fan Man,* and the recently published *Dr. Rat.* But it is his *Redbook* short story "Swimmer in a Secret Sea," (first reprinted in *Prize Stories: The O. Henry Awards* and now available as a paperback from Avon) that the editor wishes to direct attention to.

MILAN KUNDERA is a Czech now teaching in France. Knopf has done the American editions of his novels *The Joke, Life Is Elsewhere,* and *The Farewell Party,* and his collected stories *Laughable Loves,* which was among the first entries in the Penguin reprint series presenting the work of Eastern European writers, an undertaking under the general editorship of Philip Roth.

JOHN L'HEUREUX teaches at Stanford and serves as a contributing editor of *The Atlantic.* Four books of poetry, an autobiography, a collection of stories, and three novels are now followed by a fourth novel, *Jessica Fayer,* published this year by Macmillan.

ROBERT NYE is principally a poet and critic. He is fiction reviewer for *The Guardian* and poetry reviewer for *The Times,* and of course lives in England to be close to his sources of income.

CYNTHIA OZICK has lately established herself as a uniquely pitched voice in the general call made by those addressing themselves to readers of fiction that matters. On the strength of her novel, *Trust,* and her collection, *The Pagan Rabbi,* she has placed herself at the forefront of serious critical attention. In 1976 Knopf published *Bloodshed,* three novellas and a short story, which story appears herein along with the novella *Usurpation: Other People's Stories.* This latter was the 1975 co-winner of the first-place citation in William Abrahams's *Prize Stories: The O. Henry Awards.*

GRACE PALEY published a collection of ten stories, *The Little Disturbances of Man,* whose widening audience has secured her place in the national literature. Her second collection, *Enormous Changes at the Very Last Minute,* was brought out two years ago by Farrar, Straus, and Giroux.

JAMES PURDY has brought out many books, among which, the editor purposely notes, are *Color of Darkness* and *Children Is All,* two collections of stories. But he remains best known for his novella *63: Dream Palace,* the novels *Malcolm* and *The Nephew,* and a more recent novella, *I Am Elijah Thrush.* He continues to live in Brooklyn.

JAMES S. REINBOLD has had five stories in *Esquire* over the last six years, a near-record number that represents the bulk of his publishing history. He lives in Cranston, Rhode Island.

MICHAEL ROGERS first published fiction in *Esquire* when he was nineteen. He regularly writes journalism for *Rolling Stone,* and in 1975 his piece on a total eclipse of the sun earned him the American Association for the Advancement of Science Award. Knopf brought out his first novel, *Mindfogger,* and will presently publish his book reporting on the crucial activity in the study of molecular genetics.

ALMA STONE was born in Jasper, Texas, a goodsome number of years ago, and has for some while been a librarian at Sarah Lawrence. Her short fiction has appeared in *The Yale Review, The Antioch Review,* and *The American Literary Anthology,* and her longer works are *The Banishment* and *The Harvard Tree,* novels, and *The Bible Salesman,* a collection.

JAMES THOMAS now teaches at Utah and is co-editor of the *Itinerary* anthology series published by Bowling Green State University Press.

JOY WILLIAMS published *State of Grace* with Doubleday in 1974, and has since been named a Guggenheim fellow. She has completed work on a second novel, *The Changeling.*

ROBLEY WILSON, JR., edits *North American Review* and has had fiction in *Carleton Miscellany.*

HILMA WOLITZER has appeared with short fiction in *American Review.* Her 1974 novel *Ending* has been adapted to film, and will be seen under the direction of Bob Fosse. She has for some years been associated with Anatole Broyard's writing seminar.

PATRICIA ZELVER has had short fiction in *The Atlantic* and *The Virginia Quarterly,* and has published two novels, *The Honey Bunch* and *The Happy Family.*

GORDON LISH was editor in chief of Behavioral Research Laboratories and special-projects editor of Educational Development Corporation before joining *Esquire.* His books include *English Grammar, The Gabbernot, New Sounds in American Fiction,* and *The Secret Life of Our Times,* and he designed the vocational guidance instruments *Why Work?* and *A Man's Work.* He was the editorial director of the literary magazines *The Chrysalis Review* and *Genesis West,* and conducts a fiction-writing workshop at Yale. In 1976 he began producing a series of books for McGraw-Hill.